GUARDIANS OF THE TALL STONES

Kyra shivered slightly as she looked at the Stones on the hill. They had always seemed holy before, protective, the priest's concern and none of hers. But now it came in to her mind that somehow her destiny was crossing theirs and her life was going to change. She stopped walking and stared at them. They grew longer and longer, dark shapes reaching great distances into the universe, the light behind them growing in intensity of pale yellows and greens to an incredible white. It seemed to her that she was staring into the heart of Light and it was blinding her.

She dropped her face into her hands and squeezed her eyes shut to avoid the hurting of the light, but she could feel it still.

The Light and the Circle were both within her in some way, and yet, at the same time, outside her, encompassing everything that existed.

She encompassed everything that existed.

She was the circle encompassing everything that existed.

Nothing existed that was not within herself.

Also in Arrow by Moyra Caldecott
THE TOWER AND THE EMERALD

GUARDIANS OF THE TALL STONES

Moyra Caldecott

ARROW BOOKS

Arrow Books Limited
62–65 Chandos Place, London WC2N 4NW

An imprint of Century Hutchinson Ltd

London Melbourne Sydney Auckland
Johannesburg and agencies throughout
the world

The Tall Stones first published in Great Britain
by Rex Collings Ltd 1977; Corgi edition 1979
The Temple of the Sun first published in Great Britain
by Rex Collings Ltd 1977; Corgi edition 1979
Shadow on the Stones first published in Great Britain
by Rex Collings Ltd 1978; Corgi edition 1979
First published in Great Britain in one volume 1986

Printed and bound in Great Britain by
Cox & Wyman Ltd, Reading

ISBN 0 09 942810 5

01684263

For my family
past, present and future
with my love

Book 1
THE TALL STONES

Contents

The Discovery

Karne and Kyra lay on their bellies in the long grass within sight of the tall Stones of the Sacred Circle, but well hidden from view themselves. They were about to commit an act of blasphemy. They were about to spy upon a priest.

Behind them, some distance to the east, was the straight silver line of the sea from which liquid strangeness the Sun came each day to watch over them.

The Sun!

It was said that men of power had built a Temple to the Sun in the South that contained within its circumference the answer to all the secrets of the Universe. It was to this Temple Karne longed to go; it was these secrets he longed to learn.

But first there were matters in his own village that needed explanation.

The priest of their community knew many things. He stood alone within the Circle of Stones and learnt answers to questions that most ordinary people never dared to ask. Karne dared to ask, but Karne was a boy among other boys supposed to work the fields and not question the ancient mysteries. He did not know why he felt compelled to question. The other villagers seemed content enough to follow the daily routine and accept whatever the priest told them, but Karne always found himself discontented, wanting to know more.

The rituals satisfied the others. They chanted the words, beat the drums, lit the fires, did everything the priest commanded and found that that was enough for them. But to Karne there was an invisible part to the ritual which he knew was the most important part of all, understood only by the priest.

1

Why?

Why were these things kept from him? His mind felt capable of grasping much more than he was given.

'These things are no concern of ordinary people,' his father told him. 'Maal is special. He was chosen in the ancient days and born to bear the burden of knowledge for our people. It is not an easy way. He has nothing of the love and companionship we ordinary people have among ourselves. He lives alone and carries all our lives upon his back. See sometimes how he bends with the weight of it all.'

Karne thought about the priest. He was old, bent and shrivelled like a withered fruit. Surely Death itself walked not far behind his back. But—and now another picture of the priest came to the boy's mind—on holy days when he walked the processional way towards the Standing Stones upon the hill his back straightened and he carried himself tall and steady, like a young man. He entered the Sacred Circle and he was transformed. Karne had seen him, his eyes burning with a sudden fire as though he saw things they could not see that made him young again.

Karne was silent, thinking on these matters, but on another day Karne asked his father, 'What if Maal dies? There is no in our village or in the land as far as any of us has ever travelled who is trained to be a priest. What will become of us without a holy man who knows the mysteries?'

'These matters are not for us to think about,' his father replied. 'It will be taken care of.'

And he would say no more.

'It will be taken care of!'

How that sentence irritated Karne.

How?

How would it be taken care of?

By whom?

When?

In what manner?

Karne felt his head would burst if he did not get some answers.

Maal lived alone and, as he aged, hardly ever spoke except

2

on holy days. When it was the turn of Karne's family to provide food for the priest, Karne volunteered to take it to him, hoping to have an opportunity of conversation. But the old man was not at home and Karne was forced to leave the food and go back to his chores before Maal returned.

But one day when Karne had forced himself between the adults crowding beside the processional way to see Maal pass during one of the rituals, he fancied he caught Maal's eye looking into his. He had a strange feeling that the eyes of the priest could see right into his head, see what he was thinking. He fancied the priest's lips moved slightly in a smile, but it was all so fleeting and so quickly past that Karne could not be sure he had not imagined it. All he knew was that he was trembling and his head felt as though it were buzzing.

It was just after this that he first noticed there was something unusual about his sister Kyra.

Up to that time he had been aware of her as one of his family, two years younger than himself, female and therefore of not much interest to him. His brothers were more fun to be with, companions on hunting expeditions, helping him by taking his place when he wanted to escape some planting or some ploughing, coming with him when he explored beyond the village to the far hills or the forests, even helping him with the building of a boat of wood and hide which he was planning to take down to the sea one day in an attempt to find the fabled Temple of the Sun. He did not believe it was as impossible as the Elders said it was and he had managed to persuade at least two of his younger brothers to be companions in the adventure.

It was on one of the days when he was working on the boat by himself that the thing happened with Kyra. She came looking for him with some bread she had baked and, while he finished what he was doing, she sat on a log and watched him, breaking off pieces of the bread bit by bit and popping them into her own mouth.

He had told everyone he was making the boat to go fishing.

Only Ji and Okan knew what it was really for and he had forced them to draw blood and swear they would tell no one. He did not want his handiwork broken up by some irate Elder on the grounds that it was against the will of the Holy Ones that he should go looking for the Temple.

Karne pulled one of the hide thongs tight with all his strength, binding it again and again round one of the ribs. He tried to hurry, smelling the delicious hot bread and feeling annoyed with Kyra for breaking off so many pieces.

'The journey to the Temple of the Sun requires more than just a boat, you know,' she said suddenly.

'What do you mean?'

He finished the last knot hastily and shot out his hand for the last piece of bread before it vanished down his little sister's throat.

'It is a journey on many levels,' she said calmly.

He stared at her astonished. Her face had a strange expression.

'You know I am right,' she continued patiently, 'there is no need for you to pretend.'

He swallowed a lump of bread unchewed and it stuck in his throat. He choked and thought bitterly about his two younger brothers. But even as he thought up suitable punishments for their betrayal of his confidence, he knew there was something more to Kyra's knowledge than it was possible for the boys to have given her.

She was staring at him calmly and for a second he had the same peculiar feeling that he had had when he had met the eyes of the priest.

Kyra could see into his head!

She also knew things that he did not know.

He was horrified and dismissed the idea immediately.

'Get going!' He was angry with her. 'What do you think you are doing interrupting me like this? I am busy! And besides,' he added with extreme irritation, 'you have eaten all my bread!'

He picked up a stick and pretended he was going to throw it at her. She laughed and jumped lightly to the ground. As he

4

watched her running and leaping across the field she looked just like an ordinary little girl again and he was sure he had imagined that she could see into his thoughts.

He returned to his work disturbed and disgruntled.

Somehow it no longer went so well. He lost confidence that the boat was ever going to be able to sail acrosss the sea. The hides, however taut and oiled, would not withstand the buffeting of the really big waves. He had seen sea-going boats, in fact had modelled this one upon them (though his was smaller) and he knew this one was not good enough.

Perhaps that is what Kyra had meant.

No, it was not what Kyra had meant.

'The journey to the Temple of the Sun requires more than just a boat', she had said, and she had said it with authority as though she had secret knowledge.

'Nonsense,' he said loudly, packed up his belongings, pulled his boat under the awning of leaves and branches he had built for it and left, marching and striding back to his home as though he were being watched by someone he was trying to impress.

Some days passed without much of note happening. It rained a great deal. He saw Kyra but she seemed such an unexceptionable little girl that he thought more and more he had been mistaken about her.

And then on the next ritual day something happened to renew his suspicion that his sister was not quite as she seemed.

The people gathered as usual along the processional way on the night of the full moon to watch the priest tread his slow measured way to the Stone Circle at the top of the hill. They bowed their heads as usual as he passed, whispering softly the names of the gods so that their voices sounded like wind through the leaves and the air vibrated gently to a kind of rhythm. This was not to be the Spring ritual when they brought the branches of blossom, nor the Winter ritual of fire, it was the Moon ritual when the priest stayed alone with the spirit of the full Moon and listened to the messages of Night.

5

For the Rising the people stayed with him, the vibrations of their voices important for his work.

'Why is it so important?' Karne thought defiantly. 'What are these sounds that they matter so much?'

He knew they were the names of gods, but there were many gods and these were only a few of their names.

'What would happen if I whispered different names?'

'Do not,' Kyra whispered in answer to his thought, 'it would be dangerous for him.'

He spun round and stared at the dark shape of her face. The moon had not yet risen and it was too dark to see clearly, but he had the feeling her eyes were upon him and that she could 'see into his head'. A chill ripple passed under his skin, but he said nothing. He made sure he whispered the correct words.

At moon rise the momentum of the vibrations changed and finally stopped. With the first glint of brilliant light the whispering became chanting which grew louder and louder, faster and faster, until the time when the enormous disc of blazing light was in full view, its lower rim resting on the horizon. At this point the priest raised his arms in a sudden splendid movement, and with that the immense vibrating sound of the chanting cut, stopped, utterly ceased. In dead silence the visible counterpart of the invisible Moon Spirit lifted clear of the horizon and sailed majestically into the realm of the stars.

The villagers watched with an awe that never grew less no matter how often they took part in this ceremony.

After a timeless moment of watching, of worshipping, the priest moved again, his arms lowered to shoulder height, cutting the air sideways with a sharp movement. The villagers turned to go, leaving their priest to communicate with the spirits and the gods.

In the morning, when they gathered again at the coming of first light, Karne noticed that the priest who normally walked lightly as though he felt no strain stumbled slightly on the path, and as he did so looked up swiftly to see if anyone had noticed. No one, except for Karne and Kyra, had, and the priest's eyes found them out immediately. His sharp eyes

6

penetrated Karne's mind briefly and blazingly, daring him to repeat what he had seen, and then turned to Kyra's, where his gaze stayed, and Karne could sense a shaft of consciousness leap between them like lightning in a stormy sky.

But even as he registered it, it was over, and the old priest was gone, surrounded by the Elders.

This time Karne was determined to find out what was happening with Kyra.

'I did *not* imagine it,' he told himself and followed her closely. But she was walking with her mother, their arms linked, and there was no way he could talk to her alone.

It was not till late that afternoon that he managed to corner her.

'I must talk to you,' he said urgently, knowing that it was only a matter of moments before their baby sister would tire of playing in the mud puddle and demand Kyra's attention again.

She knew at once what he meant and nodded.

'Where?' he asked tersely.

She thought about it seriously for a moment.

'Near the boat?'

She knew this was a relatively secret place and a place he went to often to get away from people. Ji and Okan were far away this afternoon helping their father in the forest, so they would be no bother.

'Good,' he said. 'When?'

She shrugged and looked at the baby covered in mud from head to foot. It grinned up at her with its little toothless gums black with the mud it had been stuffing into its mouth.

They could not help laughing.

'You had better get it cleaned up,' Karne said. 'I will be at the boat. Come when you can.'

He was glad he did not have the task of cleaning the baby and he wondered how much mud it had swallowed and whether it would be sick as it had been the last time. Poor Kyra.

Poor Kyra?

The priest had looked at her in a way he had never seen him look at anyone else.

The priest had smiled at *her*.

Why?

He had looked at Kyra as though he knew her in some way.

Something was beginning to happen out of the ordinary, and Karne was finding it very intriguing and exciting.

He waited impatiently for Kyra to come to him. If she did not hurry they would have no time to talk, it would be time for the sun to set and the setting sun meant family prayers and then the evening meal. By rights he should be helping now with the animals, but with any luck the rest of the family would manage and he would get away with a mild reprimand from his father. For all his questioning he would not like to miss the evening prayers. The dark was not a thing to face unprepared.

Kyra came at last.

He pounced on her.

'What is going on?' he demanded.

She hesitated a moment.

'I do not really know,' she said slowly, her face thoughtful, 'but it seems to me . . . sometimes . . . I know things . . . I mean I *feel* as though I know things . . . I cannot possibly know . . . like . . . like people's thoughts . . . before they say something . . .'

'I knew it,' shouted Karne triumphantly. 'You can see into my head!'

'I cannot!' Kyra answered indignantly and vehemently.

'Well, sometimes you look as though you can!'

Kyra's expression was distraught.

'I do not mean to,' she said miserably. 'It just happens.'

Karne was very excited and was walking up and down restlessly.

'It is great! It is the most wonderful thing! Why on earth are you looking so miserable?' He was talking faster and faster as he walked about. 'There is no end to the things we can do with a talent like that . . .'

8

'We?'

Kyra looked astonished, but Karne took no notice of her.

'The priest Maal can do that. I know he can. He looked into my head in just the same way as you did the other day. We will be able to find out all kinds of things this way. We may even be able to find out what *he* is thinking . . .'

'Karne!' Kyra began to be really alarmed. 'What are you saying! You will be stricken by the gods for such blasphemy! A priest's thoughts are sacred. All his ways and his knowledge are secret. They *must* be secret . . .'

'Why must they be?' Karne challenged, his eyes blazing at the thought of all the power they could have if Kyra really could see into people's thoughts.

'It has always been so, since the ancient days!' she cried.

'Well, these are not the ancient days! And why do I feel in myself such urgency, such desperation to know the things it is forbidden to know if the time has not come to know them?'

Kyra looked at him with wide eyes. He seemed inspired. Possessed?

'Karne,' she whispered, afraid for him. 'It *cannot* be! Calm yourself! Besides . . .'

She hesitated.

'Besides what?' He found himself shouting.

'Besides . . . I do not have this great power you seem to think I have . . . only sometimes . . . occasionally I get glimpses . . . only bits and pieces . . . nothing one could rely on. And besides . . .' she said again.

'Besides what?' He shouted again, his voice amazingly loud and unlike his own.

'Besides . . . even if I had the powers you think I have I would not use them the way you want me to use them. Only the priest can know the High Secrets. It is not fit for us to know them.'

'Why not fit?' He challenged her angrily, but she held her ground bravely.

'Well, not safe then.'

'How not safe?'

'We cannot know the whole, and to know only the parts can be misleading.'

9

He thought about this for a while, somewhat sullenly. He sat on the grass with his head in his hands, thinking deeply.

'You see,' she said at last in a very small voice, 'I cannot see what you are thinking now. I can never *make* it happen. It just seems to happen . . . by itself . . . sometimes . . .'

He still said nothing.

She strained to catch his thoughts, 'to see into his head', but she could not.

She felt miserable and wished that she had never told him. She wished that it had never happened to her in the first place. Before this day she had found it disturbing, but not frightening. Now she was wondering if it was an evil. She had never seen Karne in such a mood.

But his mood was changing even as she was thinking this.

'Kyra,' he said, raising his head from his hands and looking at her more calmly, but with something in his eyes that had not been there before. 'I am sorry. I did not mean to frighten you.'

She noticed that there was a hint of respect in his voice, and affection.

She looked at him uncertainly.

'This matter is important. We must think about it. The gods must have given you this gift . . . surely to some purpose?'

She still looked doubtful and unhappy.

'Think!'

She shook her head sadly.

He could see there was no point in pushing her further at the moment. Her pace was not his pace. He would have to be patient with her, but he would not let the matter rest for ever.

They walked home together, and yet not together, two very small separate figures in a huge landscape, the gigantic red Sun god that ruled over their lives sliding past them into the dark regions of the west, the tall Stones on the hill growing taller as they grew darker and sharper in outline against the brilliant luminosity of the sky.

Kyra shivered slightly as she looked at them. They had always seemed holy before, protective, the priest's concern and none of hers. But now it came in to her mind that somehow her destiny was crossing theirs and her life as a little girl minding babies and grinding meal for the family was going to change. She stopped walking and stared at them. They grew longer and longer, dark shapes reaching great distances into the universe, the light behind them growing in intensity of pale yellows and greens to an incredible white. It seemed to her that she was staring into the heart of Light and it was blinding her.

She dropped her face into her hands and squeezed her eyes shut to avoid the hurting of the light, but she could feel it still.

The Light and the Circle were both within her in some way, and yet, at the same time, outside her, encompassing everything that existed.

She encompassed everything that existed!

She was the circle encompassing everything that existed.

Nothing existed that was not within herself.

Karne was shaking her.

'Kyra! Kyra!' he was calling, his face a study of anxiety. 'What is the matter? Kyra!'

The vision disappeared and she was left a shaken and shuddering little girl in the growing dark, her brother's rough hands upon her shoulders, his worried face, very much outside her own, staring at her in consternation.

Still shivering, she looked around her. The light was gone and the sky was dimming rapidly. The Stones on the hill looked very ordinary and were almost fading from sight. A last straggling string of birds was trailing off to the forest in the south, some of them calling mournfully. Friendly smoke from home fires was rising beyond the barley field.

'Oh Karne,' she cried, tears streaming from her eyes, but laughing at the same time with the sheer pleasure of the ordinariness of everything. 'That beautiful, beautiful smell of wood smoke!'

Karne dropped his hands from her shoulders and took her

11

hand. They ran towards their home together, looking at nothing but the ground beneath their feet.

The Mind of Maal

They did not refer to this again for some time, but both thought a great deal about it. They had touched on something they had not understood, about themselves and about the world they lived in. Although there was no outward sign in their daily lives that anything had changed, they both knew there was no going back to where they had been before.

One day the Elders called a meeting of the community.

There was some murmuring and grumbling from many of the villagers. It was not convenient to leave the work they were doing at this point, but a command from the Elders could not be disobeyed.

As Karne hurried from the fields in answer to the call he found Kyra carrying their baby sister on her hip. He walked beside her.

'Do you know why there is to be a meeting?' he asked.

She shook her head.

At that moment they were joined by others asking the same question.

The village gatherings were always held beside an enormous flat stone that formed a kind of natural platform. It was heavily striated from north to south, scratched and gouged in the ancient days by some force the villagers did not dare to contemplate.

While the people were arriving the Elders walked with measured, dignified steps around the outside circumference of the Sacred Circle on the hill and when everyone was present and the expectant chattering had died down, they took their places on the platform, each one standing in a position echoing the position of one of the major Stones in the Sacred Circle. They formed a kind of living Circle, their chief spokesman nearest to the people.

The Sacred Circle of Standing Stones was never entered by the ordinary members of the community. The seven Elders were permitted under special conditions at special times, but otherwise no one dared to go within range of its powerful influence except the priest who had been trained for many years to work safely with its secret energies.

There was something very awesome about the Stones. They had been chosen in the ancient days in ways the villagers did not understand, for purposes they did not understand. They were content to leave them well alone.

Karne was beside Kyra and they put the baby on the grass to play. He noticed that as the Chief Elder, Thorn, began to speak Kyra stiffened slightly and began concentrating on his words in a way that gave Karne the impression that she was hearing more than he was saying. He was so interested in her reactions he missed the whole first part of the message. When he became aware at last of what the man was saying it was something about change . . . and adjusting their lives . . .

His attention was rivetted at once. Was something actually going to *change* in their settled ways at last?

'What . . . what is going to change?' he whispered urgently to Kyra.

She raised her hand to stop the interruption of her concentration and he fell silent immediately. This was not the gesture of his little sister, but of some stranger with authority.

'. . . he has been chosen by the gods and will serve us with the dedication that the Lord Maal has shown throughout his time with us. Nothing will be disturbed. It is the natural time for change.'

For the first time Karne noticed that the priest was not present in his usual place.

Was he dead?

As the Elder stopped speaking a kind of movement went through the crowd of listeners that Karne had seen in a barley field on a windy day. The hillside did not seem to be covered

14

with individuals but with a kind of composite being that reacted, sighed and moved as one. Only Karne, seeing it, felt himself separate and apart.

He turned to Kyra. She too stood alone.

'Is the Lord Maal dead?' he asked.

She shook her head.

'No, but he is about to die,' she said calmly.

'Is he ill?'

Karne remembered seeing the old priest stumble.

She shook her head again, but said nothing. There was a line between her eyes and he could see that she was deep in thought. He tried to keep from asking her questions, but he found he could not hold the silence between them for more than a few moments.

'Who will be the new priest?'

Kyra had picked the baby up and turned to go. She did not reply.

Karne followed her insisting on an answer.

'A new priest is coming to take Maal's place?'

'That is what he said,' she replied, but there was something in the flatness of her voice that made him know that there was more to the story.

'What do you mean "*said*"? Do you think he will come?'

Kyra walked on thoughtfully for a while.

'Kyra?'

'I do not *know*,' she said impatiently at last. 'He said there would be a new priest coming from the Temple of the Sun, but . . . I do not know . . . I sensed something else . . . something wrong . . .'

'What do you mean?'

'I cannot be sure . . . but Thorn seemed not to be speaking the truth . . . and it is a strange thing . . .' Here Kyra seemed to be staring at something Karne could not see. 'I do not *see* a new priest coming to us . . .'

'Perhaps Maal will not die?'

'Maal will die . . .'

'Perhaps he will die before the new priest has arrived and there will be a period when there is no priest.'

'The gods would surely not allow that,' Kyra said firmly, but she sounded more like her ordinary self when she said it.

Karne had taken to distinguishing two people in Kyra, the child sister and the stranger who could 'see into heads'. The stranger had been there a moment before, but already the child was taking over. There was no point in questioning her any longer. He moved off and went back to his duties with much to think about.

The priest in the community was the guardian of the Mysteries, the messenger of the gods. He communicated with a network of priests across the world and spirits across the universe, so that their community could develop in harmony and peace as part of a greater whole.

Maal had served them well for many years, attending to their sick, presiding at birth and death, guiding them on Good and Evil, on rain and drought. They were sorry his time had come to move on to other duties in the hierarchy of the spirit world, but they accepted it.

It was the way.

While the rest of the village was anticipating the arrival of the new priest with pleasurable excitement Karne was worried and intrigued by what his sister had experienced.

It was to find out what was behind that experience that he and his sister came to be lying on their bellies in the long grass within sight of the Circle of Sacred Stones, unseen but seeing, as the priest Maal came alone and without the ceremonial crowds, to commune with whoever he communed with, within the Circle.

As they watched he seemed not to be aware of their presence. His face was thoughtful and withdrawn as he walked evenly and calmly between the entrance Stones.

They had never been so near the sacred place before and Karne could hear his heart beating loudly. At first he thought it was the earth pounding with a kind of deep rhythm, but

16

then he realized it was coming from inside himself. He wondered if Kyra's heart was doing the same, but she looked calm enough. Her head was raised slightly and her expression was one of concentration and intensity.

The priest walked to each Stone in turn, touching it with his forehead and pausing as though he were sensing something from the Stone through his forehead, and came to stand at last before the huge recumbent one in the southwest quadrant that was a different shape to the others and was flanked by the tallest pair of Standing Stones. He stood for a long time in front of it, his head slightly bowed, thinking . . . or was it listening? Then he put his back to it, lay against it, with his arms spread out on either side, the tips of his long and sensitive fingers stretched towards the two uprights on either side. He tipped his head back to lie upon the stone with a sigh and the two watchers noticed the sun was at its highest point of the day and blazed down upon his face.

They dared to creep a shade nearer the Circle the better to observe his face and were startled to see a strange pallor upon it, the muscles relaxed in a way that made them think of dead people they had seen.

'He is dead!' Karne whispered in horror. 'He has come here to die!'

But Kyra held up her hand and her inner senses were alert. She shook her head almost imperceptibly and with the gesture of her hand prevented Karne making any further movement or sound. Her face was strained and she was leaning forward as though she were trying to catch some minute breath of sound too small for normal ears to catch. He recognized the stranger in her and waited patiently, watching her more than the priest now, admiring the concentration of her attention, the stillness of her body. She scarcely seemed to be breathing.

As the time went on every muscle in his body ached and itched to move. He dared not and yet he could not stop himself. He sensed there was almost a thread as fine as a spider's web from the girl to the priest and any movement on his part would snap it. But he could bear it no longer. They seemed to have been there for hours and as far as he could see

17

nothing was happening. He moved at last and as he had feared his movement cracked the girl's delicate and subtle concentration.

An expression of loss, followed by irritation and almost dislike, flitted across her face as she turned to him. She seemed at first bewildered as though she had forgotten where she was and looked as though she were about to say something. He seized her shoulder and pulled her lower in the grass, at the same time indicating with a jerk of his head the danger of their situation so close to the Sacred Circle, spying on the priest.

Her face registered recognition, quickly followed by panic. He flung his arm around her comfortingly and they lay flat in the grass. They could hear the priest moving in the Circle now, but were too frightened to raise their heads. Karne could feel his sister's body trembling under his arm. He suddenly wished they were far away and had not done this blasphemous thing. It seemed to him the footsteps were coming nearer and nearer and he braced himself for some terrible blast of wrath.

But nothing happened.

Maal walked calmly out of the Circle between the two entrance Stones and steadily and quietly down the path as though he knew nothing of their presence.

'He knows,' whispered Kyra, tears streaming down her cheeks. 'He knows!' She was very much the little girl again.

'Nonsense!' he said, feeling bolder now that the priest had moved off. 'He would have said something to us. Come on, let us leave this place!'

He was longing to ask her what had been happening when she had been concentrating so intensely. He was sure something had been going on that was beyond his senses, but the place had become oppressive for him now and he wanted to get as far away as he could from it.

She felt the same and before the priest was safely out of sight the two were scrambling down the hill and running and tripping and sliding down into the valley where Karne kept his boat.

Once there they flung themselves panting down on the grass and tried to collect their thoughts. After giving her what he considered enough time to recover Karne asked her what had happened in the Circle. She was a long time answering and then spoke slowly as though she were trying to find words for an experience that did not really have words to express it.

'Strange,' she said, 'very strange. He seemed to . . . I mean . . . he seemed to . . . go away . . .'

Karne was staring at her intently, anxious not to miss a word.

'What do you mean? As though he were dead?'

'No. Not like that. As though he had gone away . . . somewhere else. At first when I was trying to reach his thoughts I could not get anything . . . but it was different to the other times when I try to see people's thoughts and I cannot. Those times I cannot because there are too many thoughts crowding . . . making too much "noise" somehow . . . This time there was nothing there . . . a sort of absolute blank . . . a sort of silence . . . as though there *were* no thoughts to see.'

'He looked dead.'

'At first I thought he was dead . . . as you did . . . but I knew he was not. I could not make out what was happening . . . and then it seemed to me I was inside his head looking out.'

Karne sat bolt upright at this.

'What did you see?'

She was silent, struggling to find the right words.

'I did not see what I expected to see,' she began slowly.

'What did you expect to see, for the gods' sake!' cried Karne impatiently. She was so *slow!*

'The Sacred Circle, the sun, the hills and fields all around us here . . .' She swept her arms in an arc to indicate everywhere in every direction they could see.

'What did you see then? Darkness?' Karne prompted.

'Sort of. At first.'

'And then?'

'And then . . . I saw other people . . . very dimly . . . I could not make out their faces . . . standing round him in a circle all touching hands . . . in a circle . . .'

19

'And? . . .'

'And beyond them, Standing Stones . . .'

'Ours?'

'No. Much bigger . . . different ones . . . the circle seemed to be enormous . . . and beyond the Stones there seemed to be a kind of hill . . . I suppose a bank that went right round behind the Stones . . . you could not see over it . . . there was no landscape beyond . . .' Her voice trailed away.

'What else?' he cried impatiently.

'I am sorry,' she said miserably, putting her head in her hands, 'I am trying . . . but it was all so . . . so . . . strange . . . and already I cannot believe I really saw it . . .'

'You *did*. You did see it! Try and remember.'

She shook her head.

'That was all.'

'Were they saying anything . . . the other people . . .?'

'No . . . I do not think so . . .'

'What were they . . . priests? . . . Elders? . . . ordinary people?'

'Priests I think . . . I am not sure . . . but they were *inside* the Stone Circle and they were trying to communicate with Maal . . .'

'Communicate? You said they were not saying anything!'

'They were thinking . . . they were all thinking the same thing . . . that was why they were holding hands in a circle. They were really *trying* . . .'

'What were they thinking?'

'I do not know.'

Karne gave an exclamation of disgust.

'*Think!*'

'I am! I am!' she cried, 'but it is so hard. My head is hurting!' She rocked backwards and forwards holding her head in her hands.

Karne pulled himself together.

'All right. I am sorry. Let us see now what we have. Maal enters the Sacred Circle, *our* Sacred Circle, goes round touching the Stones with his forehead . . . goes into a kind

20

of . . . a kind of death . . . or . . . sleep . . . and in that sleep he travels somewhere else to another, larger Sacred Circle . . . leaving his body behind here. You somehow get into his head and go with him. Other priests "think" in a circle round him . . . but you do not know what they are thinking. Is that right so far?'

'Yes.'

'What happened then?'

'I do not know. I was suddenly in my own body again and you seized me and pushed me down in the grass.'

Karne was silently cursing himself for having moved when he did. It was his fault she had jerked back. He sat, thinking hard, his hand automatically stroking Kyra's hair. He could see from her eyes that she had a very bad headache. She had become very important to him and must be looked after. The germ of an idea began to grow in his mind but he had sense enough to see that Kyra had had enough strain and worry for the day and would not take kindly to his latest scheme, which was even more dangerous and daring than the last. How he wished he did not have to work through Kyra all the time. If only he had these powers himself! He wondered if she could teach him, but he knew she did not really know how they worked, nor even how to control them herself, although it seemed to him they were certainly growing. What she had done this day was so much more complicated than what she had ever been capable of before.

'Kyra,' he said gently, 'how do you do it?'

She looked at him questioningly.

'I mean . . . can you explain . . . what do you *do* to get into someone's head?'

'Nothing,' she said sadly. 'It just happens.'

'But surely you notice something? . . .'

'No,' she said firmly, 'it just happens.'

And she would say no more. He decided to leave it for the day and led her home. Their mother watched them coming slowly along the path and was ready with a sharp and voluble stream of abuse for their laziness in leaving her to do all their chores for a whole afternoon. They would not be drawn on where they had been and eventually she gave up trying to find out and settled for doubling their evening duties as punishment.

Karne, seeing that Kyra was near to dropping with fatigue, took over some of her tasks and let her crawl into her warm straw bed early.

Although he was tired too when he came to lie down he could not sleep for a long time. There was much to think about. A shaft of moonlight came through the doorway and fell upon Kyra as she lay sleeping, one pale arm outside the fur rug, lying beside her on the stamped clay floor, her face hollowed with shadow but curiously beautiful and peaceful.

'She is growing up,' he thought. 'It will not be long before she will be given in marriage.' And he began to feel the urgency of what he wanted to do with her pressing upon him. But he knew that if he rushed her too much, worked her too hard, he could get nothing from her. It was like watching a plant grow, nothing would hurry it beyond its natural pace, though watering and care would help a little.

The Experiment

The next day Kyra would not talk of the matters of the previous afternoon. She avoided him and worked very hard and very close to her mother. He decided not to push her but to work on the background to his new plan by himself. When Ji and Okan called him to work on the boat he said he had more important things to attend to and that they could have the boat for fishing sometimes if they were prepared to spend time on it by themselves. They were overjoyed and rushed off to it at once.

He sought out one of the Elders of the Community, Faro, and set about questioning him as much as he dared. He wanted to know all there was to know about the Sacred Circle and the priest, and how often the priest visited the Circle. He really wanted to know when it would be safe for him and Kyra at the Circle. He also wanted to know if Faro could throw any light on the mystery Kyra had sensed surrounding the arrival of the new priest.

No one knew when he would arrive, Faro told him, but he was expected soon. They all hoped Maal would not die before the new priest appeared.

'He does not seem ill,' Karne said as casually as he could.

'That is because he is a brave man and knows how to hide it,' Faro said. 'Thorn says he is very ill and very near to death.'

'How does the new priest know when it is the time to come?'

'The gods tell him.'

'Where does he come from?'

'From the Temple of the Sun in the South.'

'What is this Temple of the Sun? Is it for men or for gods?'

'It is for both. It is a place so holy that families of importance come from all over the world to worship and to

23

bury their dead within sight of its Sacred Circle. But it is used for training as well and initiates from this land and from beyond the seas come to learn the mysteries from its powerful priesthood.'

'It sounds a place of great wonder. How I would love to go there!'

'No one of our community has ever been there except the Lord Maal,' Faro said. 'He was trained there. He has told me of it.'

'What did he tell you? What is it like?' Karne's voice was eager.

'There are many temples to our gods in our land but none so grand as The Temple of the Sun upon that southern plain. It is not just one Circle, but several. One is so filled with magic that it controls the sun and moon.'

'How can that be? The Sun and Moon are gods! No man, however holy, can command obedience from them!'

Karne's face registered his amazement and old Faro was delighted at the attention he was getting.

'Ah, but in this holy place, the Stones are taller than you have ever seen and there is a god-like priest who commands the moon to disappear, even when it is full in the sky, blazing in all its glory, he commands it and it *disappears*!'

By the end of this sentence Faro's voice had risen from the low, hushed note of awe to a crescendo of triumph. He was enjoying impressing Karne.

The boy was truly shaken. These were wonders indeed.

'And from this place our new priest will come?' he asked, impressed.

'Not the very same. There is another Great Circle, part of the same Temple, but a day's hard walking from it. A Circle so great that we cannot conceive of it. I believe it has a wall of earth surrounding it that took a thousand men a thousand days to build.'

'A wall of earth surrounding it?' Karne almost shouted, remembering Kyra's description of her experience in Maal's sleep-mind. 'And many Standing Stones, much bigger than the ones we have?'

24

'Yes,' Faro said, surprised.

'And many priests, not only one like ours?'

'Yes, many priests and many acolytes, initiates and students of all degrees.'

Karne was sure this was the place. He was wildly excited and had great difficulty in stopping himself dancing about and hugging the bony old man.

'Has Maal ever been back there,' he said, trying to restrain himself, 'I mean . . . since he left as a young priest to come here?'

'It is a journey of many, many moons. Seasons of planting and of reaping would go by and still one would not arrive there.'

'I know. I know it is a long way. But has he ever said he has been back there?'

'He has not left this village since he arrived here when I was young,' Faro said with conviction.

Karne tried another tack.

'From whom does he receive his messages?' he asked, trying to sound casual.

'From the gods, of course,' old Faro said impatiently, as though any fool would know that.

Karne thought about it for a while and was shrewd enough to know that he would not find out anything more from Faro. Faro, although a long-established Elder, did not know all there was to know.

Karne decided to speak directly to Maal.

During the next few days Karne watched for an opportunity to speak with the old priest every moment of his waking time. He volunteered to dig a certain field strip that had not been dug for years and consequently was particularly difficult, because it overlooked Maal's house. He broke many a sturdy digging stick and antler pick and worked until his back was aching. His father was amazed, but said nothing.

'Perhaps my prayers have been answered,' he thought, 'and Karne will settle to being a good farmer yet.'

The boy's determined effort gave him some rewards. He learnt something of the priest's movements. Sunrise, sunset

25

and midday seemed particularly holy times. Maal was often at the Sacred Circle then. He had heard from Faro, and indeed he knew from his own experience, certain rituals had to happen at night, but the times of these he could not figure out without the star knowledge possessed by the priest. He decided against the night for his plan. The priest's movements were too unpredictable then and the darkness, faced alone, too full of danger. There were nights when even the moon did not shine and on those nights the wolves and the spirits of darkness prowled freely.

On the third day of work on the field there was a time when Karne might have approached Maal directly. He could see the old man standing between the wooden entrance columns of his house, looking over the land to the far line of the sea. Karne fancied that he looked once or twice in his direction, and he could feel the old priest's gaze almost like a touch upon his skin, almost like an invitation.

The second time this happened Karne put his digging stick down and prepared to run the distance between them, his heart pounding strangely, because what he was about to do was contrary to rule and custom in their community. But even as he took the first step the priest took a step back into the shadows, and Karne was unnerved. It would mean he would have to approach in full view of the old man, but Maal himself would not be visible to him. Karne hesitated, but he still might have dared to go ahead had he not seen Thorn approaching the house from the direction of the village. It must have been the sight of him that made Maal retreat so suddenly into the shadows.

Karne abandoned his plan, picked up his stick again and dug so viciously with it that he snapped it in half. He flung the pieces down with irritation, turned on his heel and strode back to his father's house.

'Kyra!' he said in a commanding tone that surprised even himself. 'Come!'

He led her away from the place where she was scouring some

earthenware bowls with sand and ash.

'What is it?'

She had to run to keep up with his striding pace.

'There is something I want you to do for me,' he said with such determination that there seemed to be no question but that she would obey him.

'Not spying on the priest again!' she cried.

'No, not spying on the priest again.'

She was relieved, but not for long.

'Karne, where are we going?' She realized suddenly they were making for the Sacred Circle again and approaching it from the side away from the village so that they could not be seen. 'We are not going to the Sacred Circle?'

'Yes, we are. And this time you are going inside!'

Kyra stopped immediately, horrified.

'Karne!' she gasped. 'You *cannot* mean it!'

'Yes, I do.'

She turned to run, but he was too quick and too strong for her. He held her arm so tightly that she cried out with the pain.

'Karne, you are hurting me!'

He released his grip slightly, but did not let her go.

'Now listen, I have worked it all out. There will be nothing to fear.'

'Then why do you not do it yourself?'

'Because I do not have the powers you have.'

'I have no powers!' she cried miserably.

'You have. We both know you have. Think for a moment and stop crying like a baby. Would the gods have given you these powers, almost those of a priest, if they did not intend you to use them for their benefit?'

She was silent, knowing unhappily that he was somehow going to trap her into doing something she *knew* she should not do. He had always had this power over her. She loved him and she hated him at the same time and somehow he *always* won.

'You said yourself when you were listening to the Message about the new priest that you felt there was something wrong.

27

No new priest is coming. The Elders believe he is coming. The community believe that he is coming. Maal even believes that he is coming. But you know he is not. This is important. You must find out what is going on. You are needed. You are our only hope of finding the truth.'

'But I may have been wrong!'

'I hope you were. But we must make *sure*.'

'But Maal's powers are great. He would not be misled or mistaken.'

'How do we know that? He is an old sick man. We saw how his flesh hung loosely upon his bones, how pale his face, how he stumbled after the long night of Messages. His powers may not be as strong as they used to be. He may need our help.'

'This is blasphemy!'

'No. Believe me, we do it for the gods' sake, for Maal's sake. I have seen him look at you. He *needs* you.'

Kyra was silent. It was true he had looked at her in a way that was no ordinary way of looking. It was true that he was old and probably ill, otherwise there surely would be no talk of a new priest for their village. It was also true that she had the strangest feeling that she could not *see* a new priest coming. But how could she know if this was imagination or not? When she was having these strange 'feelings' she was sure she was not imagining them, but once they were past she was not so sure.

Karne could see that she was hesitating, and he released her arm very gently. She rubbed it absent-mindedly where his grip had reddened her skin, but her attention was far away.

'But it is forbidden to enter the Circle if one is not an initiate of the priesthood or an Elder,' she said at last, but her voice had no more serious protest in it.

Karne smiled, relieved, knowing that he had almost won.

'No one has forbidden us. It is just an old custom. I admit it would be wrong to go to a sacred place to play or fool about, but to find the truth to help one's people . . . that must surely be allowed!'

Kyra allowed herself to be led to the very rim of the Circle — and there she stopped.

'No,' she said, 'I cannot.'

'You saw what Maal did that day. Do the same . . . see if it works. *Try*.'

She seemed to be pulled from every direction now. She was standing close to the tall Stones and she could almost believe she felt them pulling her towards them. She was in many ways as curious as Karne to explore her capacities and find out more about the Mysteries, but she had a stronger respect for law and custom than her brother and feared the consequences of meddling with forbidden things.

His voice was soothing and his arguments convincing.

'Would it really harm,' she thought, 'to try?'

Still hesitating, she put her hand upon the nearest Stone, tentatively, compelled by curiosity. The Stone itself was taller than the tallest man she had ever seen. As her hand touched it her eyes were drawn to study it. The surface seemed cold and hard at first, like ordinary stone, and then began strangely to 'hum' through her fingers, as though it were forming a deep relationship with her which she would find hard to break. It had seemed grey from a distance, but when she looked at it closely it was a mass of crystals pressing together, black, white, silver and grey, their myriad surfaces glinting light in different intensities, from different angles, and through them all, running from earth to sky, from sky to earth, long intricate passages of crystal, ribs and paths and channels of crystal of dazzling whiteness. Her finger traced one of the lines upwards and she had the strangest feeling for a moment as though she herself was within the stone and somehow flowing upwards.

She withdrew her hand hastily and took a step back. Karne was close behind her and very gently, but very firmly, propelled her forward. Her shoulder rubbed against the Stone as she passed into the Circle and she noticed that her flesh tingled slightly. She fancied for a moment that the Stone could feel her presence as clearly as she could feel the presence of the Stone. But she did not think about this for long because she became aware that she, Kyra, was within the Sacred Circle and committed now beyond recall.

She was trembling and her heart was pounding with the enormity of the sacrilege she was committing, but somehow she was held within the Circle and could not have left even if she had tried.

Karne was outside, watching her anxiously, afraid now too that he had gone too far, but she was not aware of him. It seemed to her she was alone in all the world and no one could help her.

And then she remembered dimly Maal's movements on the day they had watched him and slowly, tentatively, she went to the first Stone and placed her forehead close against it as she had seen him do. She closed her eyes and waited, not knowing what to expect. She had chosen to start with the one she had already touched. Somehow she felt there was already a rapport there between them that would be less frightening than with the others. At first her own body was reacting so violently with fear she could feel nothing but the racing of her blood and the pounding of her heart. But gradually the Stone seemed to take over and she quietened down, restful peace began to seep through her and as she went from Stone to Stone repeating the ritual, she grew calmer and calmer, till when she reached the final Stone she was in such a state of peace she had no recollection of her former doubts and fears and leaned as she had seen her master do as though it were the most natural thing in the world and she had done it often. She lay, relaxed and still, her arms stretched to their limits, but not straining. At first she felt nothing but peace and well-being, almost as though she were falling asleep on a grassy bank in the sunshine.

Karne watching had noticed the change in her and was frozen to the spot with interest. From being a frightened little girl, his sister had become a dignified and elegant woman, treading the ritual round of Stones like an initiate. He could see the calm confidence with which she laid herself in the last posture and was full of hope that the experiment would succeed. He noticed how still she became, how pale, but he reminded himself of the priest and refused to worry about her condition.

He sat on the grass outside the Circle and waited patiently for her to 'return'. He enjoyed the sun, the song of birds, the sea glinting and winking far away to the east. From time to time he looked back at his sister. She had not moved. The same still pallor was upon her. He longed to know what was 'happening', but there was no way he could until she told him.

Suddenly he was shocked to see her jerk 'awake' with tremendous force, her face distorted with fear. She half tumbled, half scrambled off the leaning Stone and almost fell out of the Sacred Circle into his arms. She was sobbing and clinging to him, at the same time beating him with her fists. He did not know whether to hold her off at arm's length, or hold her tight and comfort her.

'Why did you not *help* me!' she screamed. 'You just *left* me there!'

'What? What!' He tried to ward off her blows. 'How could I help?'

She sobbed and sobbed and he could get no sense out of her. But she stopped hitting him and he drew her down beside him on the grass and held her in his arms and tried to calm her.

'I want to go away from this place,' she said, the little girl again. He decided not to say anything, but to help her to her feet and lead her away. When they were well away from the Circle and out of sight of it they sat down side by side and he tried to make her tell him what had happened.

'You just seemed to lie there. You looked peaceful enough. I did not know you were in any kind of trouble.'

'It was horrible,' she said, shuddering. 'I thought I was dying.'

'But Maal looked as though he was dying, but he was not,' Karne said. 'Did you not think of that?'

'I could not think of *anything*! It was so horrible!'

'What happened? Tell me about it.'

'At first it felt all right,' she said, sniffing slightly, 'as though I was just falling asleep. But I did not fall asleep. I sort of *died*!'

'How do you mean?'

'Well, one moment I was lying there just the same as usual and the next moment my *body* was lying there but somehow *I* was not in it.'

31

He raised his eyebrows.

'Were you in the place you saw when you were with Maal?'

'*No*. I was still here, in this Circle! I could see you as clearly as anything looking at the sea and some birds and not paying any attention to me, and I could see my body as clear as I could see you . . . only I was looking at it from *outside* and it looked dead. I tried to move my legs and arms but nothing would move. I tried to scream out to you but no sound would come. I even tried to open my eyes thinking that would make me wake up. But my eyelids would not move! And anyway I was not asleep. I really was awake, but I was not *in* my body.'

'Are you sure you did not go anywhere else?' Karne asked, visibly disappointed.

'No!' she screamed. 'You do not care about me at all! You just want your stupid questions answered. If I could not have returned to my body I would have *died*!'

'How did you get back?' Karne asked with interest.

'I do not know. I just tried and tried to get back in and suddenly there was a snap and I was *in* and everything was normal again except that I am never, *never* going to try that again!'

'I am sure it is a beginning,' Karne said thoughtfully. 'I mean . . . we could not expect you to do too much the first time . . .'

'It is not a *beginning*,' she said vehemently, 'it is an *end*!' And with that she stood up and marched off.

Karne remained sitting for a long time thinking about it all.

The Midsummer Festival

Not long after this the Chief Elder, Thorn, ordered the construction of Maal's burial mound. Maal asked for it to be sited on the line of earth power that ran invisible but straight as a spear throw from the Sacred Circle, along the processional route, through Maal's house, beyond and through an older burial mound, to the horizon where a notch had been cut in the skyline to lead the eye to sunset on Midsummer's Day.

Karne was among those deputed to gather stones of the right shape and size to line the tomb and the path leading to it. The actual construction was left to men who had the skill of building, the boys gathered the stones and piled them near the site. They worked in pairs and chatted cheerfully as they worked, not really thinking much about the purpose of their work.

Midsummer's Day was near approaching and there was much talk of the ceremonies and festivities that accompanied it. Dawn was always something special. Everyone brought flowers to the Circle and Maal prayed and made obeisance to the Sun. There was singing and music and the whole day was holiday and pleasure. A great deal of barley ale was drunk, and there was dancing from the oldest to the youngest. By the evening they were all greatly tired and when the sun came to set directly into the notch on the hill it was a very solemn moment. The evening ceremony was a quiet one, and afterwards they wandered contentedly home to rest.

This year there was the added poignancy that it was Maal's

last midsummer ceremony. Kyra went far into the forests in the south the afternoon before to gather some special white lilies she had set her heart upon. The forests were always considered dangerous places by the villagers because of the wild boars and other beasts and they did not venture there alone if they could help it. But Kyra was determined and she slipped away without anyone seeing her.

From the bright hillsides near her home it was as though she had entered a cave of dark and sinister green. It was much denser than the light woods she had known before and she could not help a moment of hesitation and fear. But the lilies hunters had once brought to the village from deep within the forest called to her and she plunged into the shadows trying to shut her mind to the dangers. Sometimes she heard the leaves rustling and twigs crackling as though creatures were lurking and moving in the undergrowth. She kept her attention sharp and moved quickly, making sure to note unusual things so that she would be able to find her way out again. After a long time searching she decided, tired, discouraged, filthy and scratched, to abandon the search. Hearing the whisper of water running she pulled aside some heavy and dangerously thorned branches to find a tiny stream picking its way carefully over moss covered stones to fall and disappear into a cleft in the rock. Drinking thankfully from it she could hear that it continued underground and longed to follow the intricate passage of its course, wondering what secret and beautiful delights of crystal and moss frond she would uncover. As she lifted her head from the water she met face to face the delicate, glowing whiteness of the very lilies she had been seeking. Breathlessly she stared at them, half afraid they were a vision and would disappear. But a very practical bee appeared and busied itself with one of them and that gave her courage to believe in their reality. She picked some, careful to leave enough behind for them to fruit and seed and reproduce themselves. The ends of the stems of those she had picked she wrapped in damp mossy earth to keep them fresh, and then she set off to find her way out of the forest again.

When she returned home just before nightfall, exhausted

and very much muddied and scratched by thorns, but clutching triumphantly in her hands the lilies of her choice, her family realized where she had been and she was treated to a severe lecture on the dangers of the forest. But when she had finished her harangue, her mother hugged her close, greatly relieved that she was safe, and bathed her scratches herself as though she was a little child again, muttering many a tender phrase and name.

Karne brought rushes from the marsh in full flower and as tall as himself. Most of the rest of the family just picked the wild flowers from the hills and fields around. Even the baby had a little crown of daisies tied to its bald head. Karne could see it with its chubby hand trying to pull it off as they walked together as a family in the dim light just before dawn towards the Standing Stones.

Maal was there already. It is probable that he had been there all night. He was standing now in the dead centre of the Circle facing east, his arms raised, his full ceremonial robes giving him a stature he did not normally possess.

One by one they arranged their offerings of flowers around the outside of the Sacred Circle. Kyra climbed to her special Stone, the one she had first touched, the one with the ribs of crystal pointing to the sky, bowed slightly and put her lilies at the foot of it. As she raised her eyes she met those of the priest looking directly into hers. She stood very still, feeling his mind closing in on hers. He was trying to tell her something, but the 'noise' of all the other minds around was getting in the way. He was appealing to her, asking for her help, searching her for some way out, as though he were caught in some kind of trap.

She stood amazed. This could not be! She must be misinterpreting. She strained to catch something more specific but she could not. As more and more the general hubbub of the minds around intervened and pulled them apart she thought she caught the word 'Thorn' several times and then something that sounded like 'take care', and strangely she had a mental image of the sunset through the notch in the hills, but this time there seemed to be something in it . . . something dark. She could not make it out.

35

Someone pulled her back. She was too close to the Sacred Circle. It was against the custom for ordinary people to go so near to the Tall Stones.

'I see you put your lilies next to your Stone,' Karne whispered to her as she joined him. Her face was troubled and she did not reply.

'What is the matter?'

She shook her head.

'It will not be long now,' her mother said and they all began to turn towards the East. By the time the first running point of blazing gold appeared above the distant liquid line, the whole community was aware of it. A kind of gasp that seemed to come from one throat, but came from all in unison, greeted the god of Fire and Life. Maal lifted up his voice and the most beautiful hymn in the world, the hymn affirming life and the renewal of life forever, burst and rose upon the clean, clear air of the land. The gasp the people had given was the first note of the hymn and the last note was the people's too. Their voices rose above the priest's and seemed to fill the land from horizon to horizon. Tears came to Kyra's eyes. It was the most moving ceremony of the year and somehow this year it meant more to her than it ever had before. Somehow she was part of life's mysteries, life's renewal, life's magic. Life would never again be for her a humdrum and meaningless daily routine of waking, chores, eating and sleeping. There was something more to it. Something she did not yet fully understand but which she knew would unfold to her as she grew, revealing with every unfolding something new and magnificent.

When the hymn was over and the sun fully risen one might say the secular festivities began. The women had prepared a special festival breakfast, the communal eating of which took up most of the morning. Karne's task was to help move the smooth, hot cooking stones from the fire into the hollowed log filled with water in which a special broth was boiling and back again to the fire when they had started to cool. He liked the way the water bubbled and boiled around the hot stones. But it was a tiring task and he was not sorry when he was relieved by his brothers.

After the meal there were the competitions, the log chopping, the pole climbing, the spear throwing, the steer catching, the dancing, the singing, the reciting of heroic poems handed down from their forefathers and extended by themselves.

The priest was not part of all this and Kyra did not see him again until he arrived for the sunset ceremony when everyone was more or less over-fed and worn out.

Karne was drunk on rough ale and impossible to talk to. He kept following one of the girls around, the one called Mia, the village flirt. She giggled at everything he said and Kyra felt sick that her brother looked at her with such eyes when there were girls like Fern present, tall and beautiful, thoughtful and dignified.

At the end of the afternoon the Elders gathered first and stood in front of their particular Stones very impressively. The tardy and somewhat dishevelled villagers gradually gathered themselves together for the last big event of the day, the sunset.

Maal approached with dignity.

The sky had become somewhat overcast without anyone paying it much attention. Now, however, there was some speculation that they would not be able to see the sunset in the special place because of the ominous black clouds that were gathering in the West. In fact the approaching storm lent drama and splendour to the scene. The clouds were broken enough for the dazzling light of the dying sun to illumine them in strange and royal ways. Purple and crimson were the predominant colours, where gold and silver and mother-of-pearl had been the gentler colours of the dawn.

Where the sky was not black and sullen with the weight of brooding storm, it was rent with blazing flame and flagged in purple and red. Directly above the notch on the hill there were no clouds at all, but a weird and sickly green.

The villagers grew very quiet as they turned to look at the West. While the morning sun had lifted up their hearts to joy and hope, the evening one was causing depression and despair. Kyra could not see Maal's face, but she was thinking of the experience of the morning and was watching for the sunset with some anxiety. The warning she had felt she sensed from Maal had something to do with the sunset. Perhaps it was the storm. Perhaps the storm would do great damage to their crops and houses. A rumble of distant thunder disturbed the air that had become so thick and silent. The sun sank blood red into the hole in the hill. Maal's voice, deeper than usual, droned the incantations of the evening, and for a moment as the great orb touched the hill they saw silhouetted against its fiery furnace a small but distinct black figure.

Kyra remembered the vision of the morning in a flash. Strange. Strange. A man standing in the sun!

How she longed to talk to Karne. This once when she would have liked to discuss matters with him he was incapable of it. She looked for him despairingly and he was standing as she had thought he would be with his arm round Mia, who was simpering and not even looking at the sunset.

How could it be!

She looked back to the hill but the figure had gone. The sun itself was sinking fast.

After it was over everyone started talking at once. It seemed most people had seen the figure, but some refused to believe that it had been there. Others believed, took it as an omen, and were afraid.

Thorn, the Chief Elder, lifted his impressive arms for silence and when he had obtained it, spoke in a loud and awesome voice.

'The man you saw walking in the furnace of the sun is the priest for whom you wait.'

A stunned silence followed his words.

Kyra looked beyond Thorn at Maal. He seemed to have shrunk in size. Thorn had spoken in his place, with his authority. No one seemed to notice it but Kyra. She remembered the half-formed warnings of the morning . . . 'take care' . . . and 'Thorn' . . . and the vision of the black mark in the setting sun.

There were things she needed to understand.

The Arrival of Wardyke

The coming of the new priest brought a great deal of excitement to the small community.

Midsummer's night had been, as the sunset foreshadowed, a night of violence and storm. After the dramatic disclosure by Thorn that it was indeed their new priest who stood upon the hill, a deputation of villagers was sent to welcome him and guide him safely through the night to his new home. The father of Karne and Kyra was one of those chosen and the two young people stood beside their mother watching the flickering torches as the small group set off into the rapidly spreading darkness. As they reached certain high points on the track they lit beacons and the Sacred Circle itself was ringed with flame till it looked to Kyra like the flickering spectre of the Sun god itself.

Usually when darkness came to the land and the sea the people were safely in their homes, but this night, wild as it was, saw the whole community still upon the hills. At first the numerous fires upon the earth made up for the lack of stars and moon but as the wind rose that was the harbinger of the storm the flames were whipped every way, pulled and torn by the demons of the night, till some of them could hold their own no more and were extinguished. The villagers were afraid, but hesitated to leave.

Maal stood still within the Circle as though in trance. They could see his figure with its giant shadow intermittently as either the flames or the growing frequency of the lightning illuminated it.

Thorn and the other Elders stood at the entrance to the Circle and exhorted them to put more wood upon the fires.

Karne, sober now, worked energetically, Kyra at his side.

The women and smaller children were sent back to the huts and Kyra could see them as a sudden sheet of lightning lit the valley, scattering like leaves before the wind, wailing a high-pitched wail of fear.

She herself was very much afraid, but was determined not to give way to it. As long as Maal is there, she thought, he is in control. Concentrated in his body, through the Circle, through the inexplicable forces she had sensed in the Standing Stones, was a power that held chaos at bay. Around them, moving darkness was ripping at the trees, tearing the very roots from the soil, shaking and pulling and whirling, trying to reduce their ordered community to a scattering of useless fragments. But the centre held, the Circle held. *Somehow* they were held together. They were stronger than the demons of the air.

Was the power, the magic, that held them still working against the forces of disorder and disintegration, in the Stones themselves, in the shape of the Circle itself (the divine and perfect shape), or was it in the man within the Circle holding them together with the powers within himself, the powers of which she had only recently become aware?

She found herself smiling, in spite of the situation, thinking that she was becoming as curious about things, as questioning about the hidden mysteries, as Karne himself. Her brother would be proud of her.

Even as she thought of him he looked up from his work at her.

'Come on,' he said, 'stop standing about and give me a hand with this log!'

She bent to the work willingly. Moving logs was certainly easier than trying to answer questions.

They expected rain any moment, but strangely rain did not come. The main weight of the storm seemed to fall elsewhere and the wind, the weird flashing of lightning over the hills and the growling of the thunder in the neighbouring valleys showed that the night demons were satisfied with the role of warning and frightening for the moment.

As the storm moved off to the south, their fires grew

stronger and the Stone Circle stood up clear against the immense blackness of the sky. Their hearts began to lift and there was talk amongst them about the coming changes. All were curious about the new priest. Maal had been with them so long it was almost impossible to imagine how it would be with a different priest.

'Of course the rituals will be the same,' someone said.

'Will there be new Elders chosen?'

Kyra pricked up her ears at this. She had never realized it before this day, but she had never really liked Thorn. It would be no bad thing if new Elders were chosen.

'No,' someone replied. 'Elders are chosen for life.' Kyra's heart sank. 'Only death or disgrace releases them from their duties.'

'Besides, who would we choose? Those already chosen are the best men we have.'

'Ay,' murmured someone else, 'Thorn knows the ways of this village better than the priest does.'

'That is blasphemy,' came a voice from the shadows.

'It may be blasphemy,' one of Kyra's uncles said with a laugh, 'but it also happens to be true!'

'Ay!'

There seemed to be general agreement on this.

Kyra thought about what she had heard and she thought about Thorn. As long as she could remember he had ruled the village. Everything that had been done had been on his command. It is true he always spoke as though he was only delivering a message from Maal, but what proof had they that Maal's messages were being delivered honestly? She was shocked at herself for daring to think such a thought and looked round hastily, worried that someone might have caught it from her mind. But she need not have worried. Her kind of talent was very rare indeed.

What did she know of Maal? He was an old man, very much revered and honoured. So much so that no one dared speak to him, except Thorn and the Elders. She had seen him walking about the place from time to time. When he passed, the villagers bowed and kept silent. No one spoke to him. As far as she knew there was no law that said they could not speak to him, it was just a matter of respect and diffidence. Even when he came to their homes when there was illness, Thorn came with him and Thorn did most of the talking. But it was Maal who put his long gentle fingers on the ailing person and it was Maal who did the healing.

Kyra had seen such a healing once. A friend of her mother's was in great pain. Her husband brought Maal to her and the priest stood quietly by her for a while and then placed his hands upon her, bowed his head and closed his eyes.

The woman looked up for the first time as though she were aware of someone else in the world. She looked into his eyes and Kyra would never forget the dawning trust and peace that spread over her face. After he left she stood up and went about her chores.

Kyra remembered thinking that of all the powers in the world, the power of healing was the one she wanted most.

It was almost sunrise before the new priest arrived. Kyra and Karne were with the group of villagers still tending the fires and so were present when he and the deputation that had been sent to meet him arrived. From time to time they had taken it in turn to doze off so they were not too weary. Kyra was still asleep, curled up in a small hollow of grass, Karne's fur jerkin tucked round her, when the shout went up that greeted his arrival. She leapt up immediately, somewhat dazed, momentarily having forgotten where she was and what was going on. She was in time to see the new priest, immensely tall and broad, striding up the processional way alone, long cloak flowing, head held high, eyes blazingly fixed upon Maal still standing in the dead centre of their Sacred Circle. Above and behind him, as though his presence had disturbed them and his power was calling them from the secret places of the earth, an immense flock of crows was beating across the sky. Kyra looked up in alarm and in the half light of dawn, the crows,

42

the flowing cloak, the hugeness of the man, all served to make her shiver. Karne put his arm around her.

'Cold, little sister?' he whispered gently. But even he could sense something did not *feel* right and he was cold too. They stood very close together trying to take warmth from one another.

'Is he not *huge*?' Kyra whispered.

'More like a warrior than a priest,' Karne replied.

The man had reached the Circle and Maal stood like a Standing Stone himself challenging him with his eyes. The man paused as though for a moment he had encountered an invisible barrier. Kyra and Karne hardly breathed, they were watching with such fascination. They no longer dared even to whisper. Karne increased the pressure of his arm on his sister's waist and she nodded. Yes, she *had* noticed. Yes, she *was* trying to find out what was going on.

Thorn now stepped forward beside the man and together they stood confronting Maal.

Kyra put her hands to her head, pain searing through it.

'No!' she cried within herself, 'no, I cannot!'

Maal was calling her to stand beside him, to add her strength to his. But she was afraid. Afraid she was not really hearing the call but imagining it, afraid of what she could sense but could not understand, afraid of getting involved in something beyond her capacities. Even afraid she might make a fool of herself.

'What is it?' Karne's brotherly voice broke through the roaring of her inner voices. He shook her slightly.

'Kyra! Are you all right?'

Her face was filled with fear and pain. Her arms were over her head as though she was fending off something.

'Oh Karne,' the tension broke with tears and she clung to him. 'Oh Karne . . . I cannot . . . he cannot expect me to . . . he cannot . . . I would not know what to do . . . I am not ready . . .'

'What is it? Tell me!'

He tried to lift her face and look into her eyes but they were obscured by tears and she could say nothing but 'I cannot' and try to hide her face. He held her close, bewildered, but knowing that she needed comfort. He turned his head to see if anything in the scene before them would give him a clue to her behaviour. Much had changed since he had last looked.

'Kyra,' he gasped, 'look!'

The new priest was within the Circle now, in the centre, facing East, his arms raised to the ocean where the sun would soon be rising. Thorn and the Elders with heads bowed were in their ritual places by the Stones. Maal had disappeared.

'Kyra!'

Kyra looked and saw.

She spun round and looked back along the processional way, tears forgotten now. The figure of Maal, ignored by all his community, small, steps somewhat unsteady, was making its way towards the pile of stones that had been gathered for his burial mound.

She began to run.

When she reached him he was sitting on one of the larger stones, contemplating the pile, looking no longer like a priest, mighty in magic and mystery, but like a very tired, old man who had decided to give up trying.

Out of breath she arrived and stood a little distance from him, watching. He did not seem to notice her but went on staring at the pile of rocks, his head turned from her. They stayed so, in that configuration, for some time.

Then he said, very distinctly and calmly, without turning his head, without apparently having seen her approach, 'Come, my child,' and he indicated another stone beside the one that he was on. 'Sit awhile.'

She approached like a shy fawn, step by step, watching him, ready to take off at any sign of anything untoward. He did not turn his head towards her until she was seated near him and then he looked at her with great gentleness and tenderness. As her eyes met his she opened her mouth and tried to say all the things that were hurting in her heart. The regrets, the fears, the apologies.

He held up his hand and stopped her before one word could leave her lips.

'I know, my child,' he said quietly, 'you were not ready. I should not have asked you.'

So she had not imagined his voice calling to her!

She dropped her head and sat very quietly, gradually becoming more relaxed and peaceful in his presence.

It seemed to her now, as the first rays of the sun crept across the landscape and rested upon his white hair, that she had known him always. This was no strange god-like creature, remote from her everyday life, this was someone she *knew*.

She looked up with the realization and met his eyes again.

They were as old as the hills . . .

But so were hers!

The Questioning

The new priest took over vigorously and from the time of his arrival not much was seen of Maal in public places.

The younger man strode about in the village and in the fields beyond, surveying the narrow strips of cultivated grain the villagers worked, the cattle they owned, the wood and straw houses they had constructed. He was interested in finding out all he could about their ways. And wherever he went Thorn followed him, explaining things.

Wardyke (for that was his name) nodded imperiously at the people he passed but did not speak to them. Wherever he went, whomever he met bowed the head and knee to him and did not dare to look into his eyes. It was well known that if you looked directly into the eyes of a priest-magician he could see your inmost thoughts and had power over you.

The villagers were delighted with the novelty of change and there was talk of little else in the evenings when the families gathered from their work to enjoy the evening meal. Karne and Kyra's family were no exception.

'He will be a good priest,' Karne's father said.

'We had need of a change,' Karne's eldest brother Thon spoke boldly, aware that he was offering a tacit criticism of Maal and that this normally would be construed as blasphemy. He was aware also that the tide had imperceptibly turned against Maal and he would not now be called to account for it.

Kyra spoke up suddenly.

'Why?'

Everyone looked at her.

'I mean . . . why do we have need of a change? Maal has always served us well.'

46

'He is very old, dear,' her mother said soothingly, sensing a quarrel building up.

'It is not just his age,' Thon said, 'he was incompetent as well.'

'I do not agree,' said Kyra fiercely.

'What about the drought last year? We lost most of our grain.'

'And the storm this Spring,' her father interjected.

'He did his best! The gods do not *always* give what the priest asks. We do not know the ways of the gods. There may have been a reason why the harvest should fail last year.'

'What reason?' Thon jeered.

'Perhaps . . .' Kyra thought desperately for a possible reason, but it was Karne who unexpectedly gave her one. He had been listening very carefully to the talk while he was eating.

'If the grain had not failed,' he said thoughtfully, 'we would never have learned that those plants in Fern's garden were so good to eat.'

'And if we had not had that storm in the Spring,' Kyra cried triumphantly, 'we would not have had those giant trees blown down in the forest to use for building.'

'Nor the animals to eat that were driven out of the forest by the storm practically on to our spears,' Karne added.

'Nor the houses blown down . . .' Thon said sourly.

'Well, the houses that we rebuilt are much better than the old ones . . .' Kyra was still defiant.

'Nor the water-logged earth that spoiled our first planting . . .' Thon persisted.

'We planted again . . . There was no real harm done . . . and besides, Bera and Finn would not have fallen in love and married if they had not been trapped together for so long during the storm . . .'

'But that is not the *point*,' Karne's father intervened here. 'The point is that a competent priest would not have *let* those things happen!'

'Maal is a competent priest,' Kyra insisted. 'There are just some things that have to happen, priest or no priest. There are

47

reasons for everything. It is just that we cannot always *see* them.'

'But the priest should see them and it is his task to explain things he cannot avert!' Thon said.

'No, I do not agree with that,' Karne's mother interrupted.

'What do you not agree with?' Her husband looked at her sharply.

'I think the priest should see the reasons even if we cannot, but I do not think he has any duty to explain them to us.'

'I wish there was more explanation of things,' Karne said regretfully. 'There are so many things I want to understand.'

'It is not your *place* to understand,' his father said. 'Your place is to work for your family and worship the gods. It is enough that Maal, and now Wardyke, understand things. I must say I feel Wardyke will be good for the village.'

'Maal used to come amongst us more,' Karne's mother said musingly. 'I remember when my children were born he came to bless them and talked quite a bit to me.'

'What did he say?' Karne asked eagerly.

'Oh, I cannot remember . . . it is such a long time ago. He hardly said a word the last time he came.'

'Please try and remember,' begged Kyra.

'Something about new life being precious, coming from the past, going to the future . . . everything linked in some way . . . tied . . . so everything . . . even my scrawny little baby howling its head off . . . is of vital importance to the Whole. I did not listen much, I must admit, I was feeling so embarrassed that he was in our humble house and everything was in such a mess.'

'Oh mother!' cried Kyra impatiently.

'Did he say much when I was born?' Karne asked.

His mother thought for a while.

'He stood looking at you for a long time and then made the blessing sign. Then he said, "This child has the strength to be a leader among men. Pray that before he leads he may be well led." '

'And I? What did he say when I was born?' Kyra asked anxiously.

'I remember when you were born,' Thon said. 'I was hungry and I thought Maal would never leave.'

'Yes, that is when he did most of the talking about everything being important and everything being dynamically (you see I remembered that word!), dynamically part of everything else. He went on and on . . .'

'What did I do?' Kyra was passionately interested in every detail.

'You just howled and howled as though this was the most miserable experience of your life. You were such a sickly, mewling creature I was not at all sure you were going to live. Maal said you were. And you did!'

'You see he is not so incompetent after all!' Kyra said, pleased.

'Oh, in those days,' her father said, 'we had no complaints. But lately he seems to have withdrawn himself more and more from the people. He stays in his house most of the time or walks in the hills by himself.'

'He performs all the rituals well,' Kyra said quickly in Maal's defence.

'True. But he used to do more.'

'He used to speak comfort to us on days that were not ritual days,' her mother said. 'But now he never seems to know when we need him.'

'He came when Nidav was killed by the boar.'

'Big things he still knows about. But before he used to know about the little things as well. He just seemed to know and care . . . about everything.'

'Well,' said Kyra defiantly, 'I will be interested to see if Wardyke knows and cares about the little things!'

'Why are you so against the new priest?' Kyra's mother asked worriedly.

'I am not against him. It is just that I like Maal. There is something about him I trust.'

'But surely you trust Wardyke? He was chosen by the gods and specially trained for our community.'

'Yes, that may be true . . .' Kyra's voice carried no conviction.

49

'Enough of this talk!' The head of the household remembered his position. 'Next we will be criticizing the gods!'

Kyra's mother threw up her hands in horror at such a thought.

'Then we are surely finished!' she said.

The next day Kyra took Karne aside and told him all that had transpired between Maal and herself on Midsummer's Day and the following dawn.

'What happened then?' he asked with curiosity. She had stopped talking when she had told him how she had felt Maal and she were as old as each other and that she had known him before.

'I do not know,' she said sadly.

'What do you mean?'

'I just sat there . . . feeling those things . . . and I could not think of any words to say them in . . . and he just sat there not speaking . . . so after a time . . .'

'Yes?'

'I just walked away.'

Karne looked annoyed and disappointed.

'You would!' he said bitterly.

'Do not be angry, Karne,' she said miserably. 'I have no one but you to tell these things to . . . no one but you to help me . . . and besides . . .' and here her voice took an upward turn with a hint of resentment in it, 'besides . . . it was you who got me involved in the first place!'

'Nonsense!' He denied it vigorously as he felt a twinge of guilt. 'You were involved by just being *born* . . .'

She sighed deeply.

There was silence between them for a while as they both tried to work the situation through in their own way.

Kyra was thinking how much she would like to speak to Maal and ask him outright the answers to all the questions that were now bothering her as much as Karne.

'I think our next move,' Karne spoke slowly and with deliberation, 'is to try and see Maal privately, without Thorn around, and talk to him, ask him outright the things we want to know.'

'Oh Karne, do you think we can?' Kyra was relieved he was making the decisions.

'Yes, that is what we will do,' Karne continued his line of thought, almost as though Kyra was not there. 'I should have done this years ago . . . it was just that he seemed so difficult to approach . . .'

'I know. I think mother is right. He has withdrawn himself the last few years more than I remember when I was small.'

'I tried to talk to him a little while ago . . . the time when Thorn announced that a new priest would be arriving and you said you felt that there was something wrong . . .'

'What happened?'

'I was just about to go to his house . . .'

'Karne!' Kyra was shaken at the daring of this.

'. . . When I saw Thorn on the path.'

'And then?'

'And then . . . nothing. I thought I had better leave.'

'I wonder about Thorn . . . there is something about him . . .' Kyra's voice was puzzled.

'He seems to have organized everything . . . the new priest . . . everything . . .'

'And he talks about Maal's death as though it is pre-arranged!'

'I noticed that,' Karne said thoughtfully.

'And Wardyke frightens me,' Kyra said with a shiver, her mind running on.

'I think,' Karne said slowly, 'I would have accepted Wardyke quite happily if it had not been for the strange things you have been feeling. He seems right enough as a priest. I mean, he looks as I imagine a priest to look. I cannot sense anything wrong with him. Everyone else seems to like him.'

'There is *something*, Karne, I am sure of it,' Kyra said worriedly. 'Or rather, sometimes I am sure of it. At other times, I do not know. Oh Karne . . . I am so confused!'

Karne put his arm around her shoulders.

'All right, little sister, calm down. We will go and see Maal

51

about it.'

'Now?'

She looked up, alarmed.

'Why not? While we are in the mood.'

'I do not think we should . . .' She had lost all her conviction and courage.

'I think we should,' said Karne firmly.

'But what are we going to do?'

Kyra ran along beside her striding brother, still flustered with anxiety about the whole project.

'We cannot just go in to his house and demand to speak with him!'

'Luckily that will not be necessary,' Karne said.

She looked questioning.

'I saw him set off for the hills when we left home. If we hurry we may be able to come upon him as though by accident.'

Kyra was relieved. This was certainly easier than braving the mysteries of the dark interior of his house, but she had her doubts that they would come upon him 'by accident'.

The day was hot and pleasant, the birds busy about their songs, the villagers peacefully pursuing their age-old customs in the valley, content that they were well protected from all harmful spirits by the ministrations of their new and magnificently tall guardian-priest.

The hills to the north of their village were rocky and wild, but there was quite a walk before one even reached them. Karne began to wish that they had brought some refreshment with them. He stopped when he found a little brackish stream running through the heather and had a drink, and then he plunged his whole head into it to cool himself and shook the water from his hair like a dog. After her drink Kyra sat on the bank with her sandalled feet dangling in the water, her eyes on the hills, thinking . . .

Once they started climbing they were soon above the spring line and there was no more water to be found, but the views around them were almost as refreshing as drink to Kyra.

Karne was just about to say that they must be prepared for a long hard day as they had no way of knowing exactly where the old priest had gone to find his solitude, when he noticed that Kyra was walking purposefully. as though she knew exactly where she was going. Having faith in her strange powers, although not understanding them, he fell back so that he was walking behind her, following her lead.

At first she cut straight across the rough heather and their legs were sorely torn by the tough little branches. At one time she even disappeared to her shoulders in a sudden hole, the heather having hidden it from her sight, but Karne, after laughing at her discomfiture, soon had her out and on her way again. After that experience she went slower and picked her way more carefully, but she showed no sign of being uncertain of the direction to take.

She found a track and followed its meanderings for a long way. In the distance, further to the north, a lake was gleaming like a jewelled clasp in the folds of a soft blue cloak.

About noon they found Maal sitting on a granite boulder gazing into the distance. He turned to them as they arrived but showed no surprise that they should be there.

The two young people flung themselves down at his feet, exhausted and somewhat out of breath. No words were spoken, but even Karne could feel they were not unwelcome.

The silence went on for so long that Karne began to wonder if the other two were communicating in some way without words. He looked hard at both of them, but he could not notice anything. They were both sitting, relaxed and peaceful, gazing at the beauty of the ever receding lines of hills and valleys that stretched away through every shade of blue to the northern horizon.

He decided it was up to him to take the initiative.

He stood up.

'We have come,' he said firmly, 'to ask you many questions.'

Maal looked at him with his piercing eyes, but they were not unfriendly. Karne remembered how he had been warned when he was a small boy never to look directly into a priest's eyes. He was half afraid, but his own determination to find out all that he wanted to know sustained him in his purpose.

'What is it that you wish to know?' Maal asked quietly.

Karne hesitated. Where to begin? There was so much he wanted to know.

'To phrase the right questions is as difficult as to provide the right answers.' Maal smiled quietly as he spoke.

He was right. Karne had never realized it before. Somehow he had never had difficulty asking questions in the past, but that might have been because they were not so important or, if they were, that there was not much chance of their being answered.

He knew now the old priest would answer his questions and the answers might change the course of his life. He must be careful what he asked.

In that moment, as he stood upon the hill, with the rocks and the wild plants around him, the lake now a shining eye staring blankly at the sky, he knew the answer to at least one of his questions. He knew why it was that the community was content to let the priest carry the burden of knowledge, the Mystery of Mysteries, by himself. They were afraid that, if they knew what he knew, more would be required of them than was required by the comfortable round of daily chores, the friendly chat, the warming hearth fire. They were deliberately preventing their own development, afraid of what the next step would demand of them. By facing the priest, asking to enter his Secret Knowledge, he, Karne, was taking a step from which there would be no going back. The way to deeper and deeper understanding was through deeper and deeper commitment.

As these thoughts came crowding upon him he felt shaken and breathless, almost as though they had entered his mind by physical force. He took a deep breath and looked first at Kyra and then at Maal.

They were both sitting quietly looking at him, and it was as though they were together and he was a stranger.

'What shall I do?' he asked helplessly, as though he had spoken his other thoughts aloud and they knew what they were.

54

'It has to be your decision,' Maal said.

Karne turned away from them and strode about on the rough hill top, trying to sort out in his mind this new development. All the time he was doing this they sat very still. It was almost as though they were part of the hill, the rock, the growing things, the air. And he, the intruder, was stirring things up, bringing change and discord.

At last he stopped and faced Maal, his decision made. He wanted to know. No matter what happened.

And as he made this decision all the sense of being torn apart by discord ceased. He joined them in their calm acceptance of what must be.

Maal lifted his hand and made a gesture for Karne to sit. Karne sat.

'Your first question?' Maal asked with a smile.

'Who is Wardkyke,' Karne said immediately, 'and why are we afraid of him?'

'Two questions,' Maal said mildly.

'They *are* connected,' Kyra spoke up for Karne.

Maal smiled again, sadly this time.

'Yes, they are connected,' he said, and was silent so long Karne was beginning to think he would not answer. Kyra and he looked at each other, uncertain what to do, wondering if they should repeat the question. But they need not have worried. The old priest was preparing to speak at last.

'I do not know who Wardyke is, but I know he is not the priest who was chosen and trained for you.'

Kyra took a sharp breath at this. This confirmed her impressions.

'You mean he is not from the Temple of the Sun?'

'He has been there. He knows much of the mysteries that are taught there, but he does not carry with him the final mark of the priest.'

'What is that?' Kyra asked quickly.

Maal looked at her closely.

'You will know that mark one day.'

'Why not today?' Karne's curiosity had made him bold, but Maal was not to be drawn on matters he had decided were not yet for them to know.

'Did you know that a new priest was coming before Thorn announced it?' Kyra asked.

'Yes, I have known for some time. It is the way.'

'Is it because you are getting old?' Kyra tried to soften the harshness of the question by the gentleness of her voice and expression.

Maal bowed his head in affirmation.

'Thorn says you are ill?'

'I am tired and I must move on. There is other work that I must do.'

'Another community?' Karne asked.

'No.'

'I thought you said . . .'

'I did not.'

'But . . . but surely that is what you meant?'

'You cannot know what I meant until you know a great deal more than you do now.' Maal's voice was sharp. Karne was momentarily silenced.

Kyra spoke up.

'Please,' she said, 'I know we should not be questioning you like this. But you *did* call for my help . . . and I need to know . . .'

Maal's face softened. He looked affectionately at her.

'You are right, my child. I owe you much and will owe you more before the sun is back to its full height. But I cannot tell you now everything I have taken many years to learn.'

'Tell us at least more about Wardyke and how we can help.'

Maal was silent again at this, thinking hard.

'I think,' he said at last, 'the way you can help me most is for Kyra to go once more into the Sacred Circle . . .'

At this Kyra flushed slightly. So he *had* known of their trespass!

'. . . and,' he continued, 'take a message for me to the Lords of the Sun.'

'But how . . .?' Kyra was bewildered and frightened. 'How can I?'

'And who are the Lords of the Sun?' Karne asked

56

breathlessly.

'Across the world, in places beyond even your imaginings . . .'

'Beyond the sea?' Karne interrupted.

'Yes, even beyond the sea and beyond the lands on the other side of the sea . . . there are people believing as we do in the Sacred Mysteries, and amongst them some have been chosen as Lords of the Sun. Their training is long and arduous, but they have great powers and can see much that is closed to even the most highly trained priest.'

'But surely,' Karne said, noticing Kyra's terrified face. '*You* should be in touch with them. How can Kyra possibly . . .?'

'Wardyke knows this is what I want to do. He will not let me near the Sacred Circle.'

Maal spoke with conviction.

It was true. They had noticed and remarked that Maal had not been near the Sacred Circle since Wardyke had arrived.

'But . . . it is not guarded. Perhaps you could get in some time when Wardyke is not there.'

Maal smiled and shook his head.

'It is not so easy, my children. Wardyke is a powerful magician and has cast an invisible ring of force around the Stones so that they will not admit me.'

Kyra gasped.

'But what about me?'

'Wardyke does not realize you could be a threat to him. There is no ring of force cast to keep *you* out.'

Kyra looked miserable. It became clearer and clearer that somehow a great deal was expected of her and she did not feel at all confident that she could fulfill Maal's expectations.

'But . . .' Karne realized her predicament. 'Even if she does manage to pass unnoticed into the Circle . . .'

'As she did before,' Maal said with a sudden twinkling smile.

'As she did before,' Karne admitted. '. . . But last time she tried to travel in the mind as you had done she could not manage it and nearly died.'

Maal nodded.

'I know,' he said. 'I would not ask if there were another

57

way.'

'Besides,' said Karne with sudden inspiration, 'if Wardyke is a magician, so are you! It is part of being a priest.'

'Yes!' cried Kyra joyfully, thinking she saw a way out.

Maal shook his head sadly.

'I have been neglecting the magic aspects of my priesthood for many years now, and could not compete with Wardyke.'

'But why?' Kyra cried accusingly.

'Because, my child, I found something more important.'

What could be more important than magic! Karne would have given his right arm to be able to practise magic effectively.

'I used to think, as you do, that the practise of magic was of great importance and gave me great power. One day I tried to use my magic on a traveller from a far-off land, he was a merchant bringing flints from the south, a simple man I thought. We met on these very hills and fell into conversation. He challenged me as priest to perform magic for him. Being foolish I chose to accept the challenge and said I could ring him with an invisible wall of force through which he could not step. It was very similar magic to the one Wardyke now has wrought on me. I know I should not have used my priesthood knowledge for an idle trick, but he was mocking our religion and the ancient mysteries and I wanted to prove him wrong. I performed the rites perfectly and confidently expected him to be trapped within the ring. But he was not. He walked out of it with a smile and said, and this I will never forget, "Your magic is worked around my body. You forget I am spirit and am everywhere".

'I sat till it was dark upon these hills and thought about it.

'He was right, and what he had said I had always known.

'Indeed, this I had been taught in the Temple of the Sun, but somehow it had become overlaid by all the ritual and the magic tricks so that they had become the most important part of my religion to me. It was as though I had been given a great and precious Truth wrapped in layers of dry straw, and I had come to believe the straw was the Truth.

'Much of what he had said in criticism of our religion began to make sense to me. I resolved to throw away the straw and find the inner gift of Truth.

'But in doing this I made yet another mistake.

'I was so continually searching into the depths of my own Being to find "the spirit that is everywhere", that is more powerful than magic, and that nothing can cage if it has the will to be free, that I sought solitude, I resented the intrusion of people, of duties, of anything that distracted me from my purpose. Before, I had neglected the inner life by concentrating on the outer; now I neglected the outer by concentrating too much on the inner. To me the whole of material existence became unimportant. Only spirit mattered.

'But this is not as it should be. Spirit and matter are part of the same Whole: different manifestations of the same God. The same Source. Each develops because of the other, not in spite of the other. We are not material form for no reason, as we are not spirit for no reason. We must use both. We must learn from both.

'I see this now, but it is too late.'

'What do you mean—too late?' Kyra said. She had strained to understand what he had been saying. It was not easy, but she thought she grasped some of it. The rest she stored in her mind to think about later.

'I have had my chance as your priest and I have failed.'

They both opened their mouths to protest but he raised his hand to silence them. It was strange to think a priest could make mistakes like any common man.

'If I had my time again, knowing what I know now, I would be a better priest to your community. No. Say nothing. Time, an ambitious Elder and an unscrupulous impostor-priest have forced me to see where I was wrong. I left a gap which Wardyke could fill. I should have taught this community to rely on the living truth and the individual power of their own Eternal Selves so that *no one* could come and take them over as Wardyke has done.

'But my time in this life is used up. I can pursue the matter further only in another life.'

'You mean you are going to die?' Kyra asked in a hushed

voice.

'You may call it dying if you wish.'

There was silence between them for a while.

'And you cannot use magic any more?'

'I cannot and I will not.'

'But if it would help . . .?'

'It would only help the immediate future—if at all. We must not defeat Wardyke with magic, it is too temporary a measure. We must defeat him by growing in ourselves till we are greater in inner strength than he. Till his magic circles will have no effect upon us, as they did not upon that flint merchant.'

'But it has taken you *years* and you still have not managed it!' Kyra said wonderingly. 'What chance have we?'

'Every chance. You have not made the mistakes I have made. You come fresh and strong to the task. I will help you and necessity will give you wings.'

'But if we cannot . . .'

'You forget we plan to call upon the Lords of the Sun.'

Karne decided that it was time for practicalities.

'What is the first move we should make?' he asked.

'I may be able to pass within the Circle without his seeing me,' Kyra remembered her terrifying tasks, 'but how do I reach the Lords of the Sun?'

'I will have to teach you many things. It will not be easy, and it will not be safe, particularly for someone who has had no training in the Temple of the Sun.'

Kyra looked even more miserable, and even Karne was beginning to think the whole thing was becoming too difficult.

'Would it not be possible . . .' Kyra started tentatively and then stopped.

'Would what not be possible, my child?'

'I mean . . . how do we know Wardyke is really bad? Does it matter very much that he has not the final mark of the priest upon him?'

'The final mark is put upon a priest when he has passed the

60

most stringent moral tests. Without that mark it is possible the priest has all the powers of priesthood, but there is no guarantee he will use them for the good of the people.

'If Wardyke has been refused the final mark, that means the High Priest of the Temple of the Sun thought he was capable of the misuse of his powers, and that means that your people are in danger.'

'The very fact that he put up that ring of force to keep you out of the Circle is a bad sign,' Karne said.

'Certainly it is. I think we should start Kyra's training as soon as possible. She has much to learn.'

She looked so wretched and so small, he put his hand on her shoulder and through his fingers she felt the warm flowing of his own confidence in her, his love and need of her.

She bowed her head. So be it.

At least she would try.

The Training of Kyra

As the weeks went by Karne and Kyra became more and more deeply involved in the new knowledge they were gaining from the priest. Maal arranged to meet them secretly at certain times in the hills, where they had met before, but one day he suggested they meet at the home of a friend of his, remote from the village and yet not as remote as the hills. Karne and Kyra had been finding it difficult to slip away unnoticed for quite the length of time required for visiting the northern hills. They were surprised when he mentioned a friend and thought perhaps he meant another priest or maybe even one of the Elders who was not totally loyal to Wardyke and Thorn. But they discovered it was Fern, a girl they had known slightly for years, a year older than Karne, living some way from the village in a beautiful leafy glade. On ceremonial days she came quietly to the village but on the whole she kept herself separate from the community. The richness of the plant growth around her homestead was well known and in times of drought the villagers had fed on food grown by her.

It was her father who had introduced the seed that gave the community the best wheat crop they had ever had and now it had become common practice to grow it year after year. Travellers from other communities had been astonished at the prolific yield and had bartered various goods for some of the seed.

Fern's parents were dead now and she lived alone, still keeping the land lush and green around her.

Some of the villagers worried about her.

'It is not good for a young girl to be always so alone,' Karne's mother often said.

And some thought her strange.

'She talks to the spirits,' Thon said. 'Thera saw her the other day talking to that tree next to old Faro's strip.'

'There is no harm in talking to the spirits,' Kyra said. 'We do it every time we pray.'

'But such talking, such prayer, is at the right time and the right place. We use the words of our fathers, at the times our fathers have chosen . . . the priest is our channel.'

Karne said nothing but he thought a great deal. It seemed to him in the last year he had become increasingly impatient with the round of prayers they had to chant each day. No matter how he concentrated on the ritual he could feel nothing flowing back from it. He had no sense of the spirits he was talking to hearing him in any way or even being aware that he was there and trying to communicate. He had not dared admit even to himself that at times he wondered if the spirit world existed at all. He thought about Fern and wondered if she had found a way to communicate that was better than the one that they were using.

Maal first took them to Fern on a day when rain had fallen, but the sun had followed soon afterwards. Everything was fresh and smelling good. In Fern's garden raindrops were trapped on leaves and shone with sudden splendour as they passed. Kyra found herself gazing at one caught and poised on the tip of a tall grass spear, its weight slightly pulling the leaf towards the earth. She felt herself being absorbed into its luminosity and somehow becoming a form of light which shone upon the whole Universe . . .

'Kyra,' Karne shattered the precious experience and brought her back to the limitations of being contained within a human frame, 'did you ever see such flowers?'

Kyra looked and marvelled. Every flower she had ever seen growing in the fields or in the forests was growing in Fern's garden, but somehow larger, richer, more magnificent. And flowers she had never seen were there in great profusion too. The colours, from the deepest crimson to the palest cream and white, midnight blue and mountain shadow purple, wove together in an intricate and dazzling pattern of delight, all set in rich and varied green.

Fern led them to a grassy bank and a fallen log and they sat surrounded by the garden. It was so beautiful and peaceful it was a while before they could bring themselves to talk and in the silence Kyra could almost fancy she heard the secret, intricate processes of growth going on all around them, roots pushing strongly but infinitely slowly through the rich black earth, branches lengthening, leaves unfurling, buds opening. Bushes of every kind of green surrounded them, some laden with berries. Fern saw Karne looking at them and asked if he were hungry.

His expression was answer enough.

Fern smiled and then to Karne's amazement stood very still in front of the bush with the most berries, not moving and not touching them. She seemed to be in a kind of silent communication with the plant world. After a moment or two she opened her eyes and picked the berries gently.

Karne's eyes met Kyra's.

When they had eaten their fill and all their mouths were stained with purple, they settled down to talk.

'How is it that your plants grow so well?' Kyra asked. 'I have never seen such profusion of growth.'

No one Kyra had ever met cultivated plants for beauty or for pleasure alone. The villagers grew crops in the strips that were allotted to them outside the village, but never had she seen a dwelling house surrounded by flowers.

Fern was shy and seemed uncertain what to answer.

'Fern has special powers, Kyra,' Maal spoke for her, 'not unlike yours. She is in tune with the earth, senses its inner needs and works with the flow of life within it.'

'You seemed to be talking to that bush . . . I mean . . . in your head . . .'

'I was asking for the berries,' Fern said simply.

Maal noticed Karne's expression.

'All life is animated by spirit,' he said. 'We should treat all things with respect. Our relationship with the plant world should be a relationship between two life forms, each respecting the other, different as they may be.'

Karne looked at the bush. He remembered with shame how often he had walked through a field with a stick, absent-mindedly knocking off the heads of flowers and grasses.

'The earth has forces flowing through it, lines of power through which renewal and regeneration come,' Fern said gently. 'I work with these, and the feelings of need I get from the plants themselves.'

'My brother says you talked to that old tree next to Faro's plot. It used to look as though it were dying, but now I see it has new leaves.'

'I know,' Fern flushed slightly, 'I did not mean to talk aloud. The words themselves mean nothing to the plants. It is the *feeling* inside one, whether one is genuinely concerned for its welfare or not, that matters. It is a kind of communion through loving. Sometimes I use words just to help myself concentrate. But the plant cannot hear them, of course —unless perhaps it responds to the tone of them . . .'

'You mean whether your voice sounds angry or loving?'

'Yes. I suppose that could have an effect. Perhaps the resonance . . . But it is really the feeling that matters.'

Karne was still curious about the renewal of Faro's tree.

'But how did you make Faro's tree grow again?'

'It was not "Faro's tree",' Fern said firmly. 'No man can own a tree. A tree is a free spirit, like man.'

'Sorry. But anyway . . . how did you make the tree grow again?'

'I did not make it grow,' Fern said patiently. 'It grew, like man, when the life force, the spirit flow if you like, was not impeded any more by fear and anger.'

'The tree "feared"!' Karne was bewildered.

'You could say that. Faro had cut many of its roots and branches, brutally and without warning, to extend his growing strip. If a tree has to be cut there are ways of doing it, with preparation and with the flow of nature, that does not harm the living creature or make it angry or afraid.'

'Where does this flow come from?' Kyra asked with interest.

Maal held up his arms and looked around him. He

indicated everywhere, everything.

Kyra remembered the feeling of wholeness, of identity with the Universe she had experienced recently.

'In a sense,' Maal said, 'it does not come from anywhere or go anywhere. It is a flow that is within us and within everything else which makes us all part of the same Whole. The flow is within the Whole and so consequently within us.'

'As though we are all in a closed circle with the flow going round and round within the circle?' Karne asked.

'Something like that.'

'Is that why our temple is a circle? A sort of symbol of the Great Circle in which everything is contained?'

'Something like that,' Maal said again. 'Our little stone Circle concentrates power by trapping a bit of it within itself and then as it follows round and round within the circle it gains strength . . .'

'But that in a sense is impeding its free flow through everything and you said that was bad.'

'Ah,' Maal sighed. 'It is all so complex and we have so little time. But I will try and explain. To capture the force within the Circle and to use it for your own purposes should not be done lightly. That is why only the priest is allowed within the Circle. Only he has the training and the strength to use the power the Circle has generated creatively. An unwary and untrained person might be destroyed by the concentration of power.'

Kyra looked horrified. She had not forgotten she was expected to go within the Circle and use its powers.

Fern saw her expression and put her arm around her and kissed her gently on the forehead. She had been informed by Maal of the situation as it stood and was prepared to help them in any way she could. She was sensitive to the earth and all its life forms but she could not leave her body and travel in the spirit, which is what Kyra must do to reach the Lords of the Sun.

There was silence for a moment as they all looked at Kyra and thought about her ordeal.

'Come,' Maal said, taking her hand, 'we will go away from

Karne and Fern and practice what you must do.'

He led her deeper into the leafy wood and found a small
clearing ringed with fronds of fern and feathery white flowers.
The rocks lying scattered around were beautiful with lichen
and moss. Sunlight flickered and scittered through the leaves
of the trees high above them, their trunks tall and straight,
forming a circle of living columns around them, a wooden
circle of power.

Kyra lay down in the centre, her head to the east, her body
aligned along the path of the sun. She looked straight up to
the roof of interlocking branches above her and noticed the
intricate patterning of leaves, subtly changing moment by
moment as light breeze stirred among them but did not
penetrate to where she lay in stillness on the earth. Maal sat
beside her and waited for the frightened hammering of her
heart to quieten down. She would not be able to travel far
without the concentration of power from the Sacred Stones,
but at least she could learn something of the technique.

He had questioned her again and again about every detail
of her last experience and he was convinced that the most
cogent reason for her failure was that she was afraid. He
talked to her now quietly, gently calming her fears, trying to
get her to relax, limb by limb. At last he could sense every bit
of her body was lying limp.

'Feel as though your body is heavy . . . sinking into the
earth . . . sinking into the earth . . .' His voice was soft,
repetitive, hynotic.

'Sinking . . .'

He let her lie feeling this for a while. Then he as quietly fed
her other suggestions.

'Now feel as though your body is expanding . . . feel it
stretching . . . your legs are growing longer . . . your
arms . . . you are swelling . . . growing . . . becoming
lighter and lighter . . . you are filling with air . . . you are
floating . . . floating . . .'

She had her eyes shut and she could feel everything he

67

suggested she should feel. His voice came as though in a dream from a long, long way away.

The solidity of her body was no longer there. She could make it become whatever she chose. But somehow she was still 'inside' it. She was not travelling.

'You are separate from your body . . .' Maal's voice droned on and on. 'Separate . . . You, Kyra, are not your body . . . your body is nothing but a dress you can put on or take off . . . put on or take off . . . a dress you can put on or take off . . .'

She could feel herself slipping, floating, separating . . .

Strange, now she was with the leaves, the brilliance of their flickering was hurting her. Far below her she could see two figures, an old man and a young girl. They looked familiar, but she was too comfortable, too relaxed to bother to work it out. She just kept drifting . . .

She could see so much more now, the rich profusion of Fern's garden, Fern and Karne sitting very close side by side on the log, deep in conversation. She could see beyond them, beyond Fern's little house, to the path that led to the village. Momentarily she seemed to drift off to sleep and lose her bearings and when she became conscious again she was not in the clearing with Maal, but beside the heap of stones that had been gathered for Maal's burial mound. She looked around her in some confusion, wondering how she came to be there, and then she noticed that she was not alone. Wardyke and Thorn were standing quite near, talking.

'He cannot have it here,' Wardyke was saying. 'We will put it over beside the clump of trees.' He pointed.

'But . . .' thought Kyra, 'but . . .' She knew there was something wrong with this but she could not think clearly enough to decide what it was. She still felt half dazed and could not understand how she came to be there.

'Do you still want a mound built?' Thorn was asking.

'Oh, yes,' said Wardyke, 'we will give him a mound but it will not do him any good over there.'

That was it! She knew what was wrong.

Before she could stop herself she cried out.

'But that is not where he wants it. It is not on the alignment!'

Her voice seemed loud to her and she was not standing far from the two men, but neither of them seemed to hear her. Wardyke half turned his head and listened as though something had disturbed him, but Thorn was looking right at her and yet did not see her.

He did not see her!

As she realized this a shock wave of fear passed through her. She felt a terrible jerking and heard a snapping sound and suddenly she was back in the clearing with Maal, shaking with fear, very much the ordinary little Kyra. As she came back she had cried out and Karne and Fern came running to see what the matter was. Maal had his arm around her and she was crying.

'I had such a horrible dream,' she sobbed, 'I heard Wardyke and Thorn plotting to move your burial mound away from the place you have chosen and then when I called out to them they did not hear me or see me!'

Maal looked very interested.

'Where did they say they were going to put it?'

'By that clump of trees to the left, right across the field, nowhere near the alignment you wanted with the midsummer sunset mark and the Sacred Circle.'

'Never mind your dream,' Karne said impatiently, 'what about the travelling? Did you do any?'

'I do not know,' she said miserably. 'I think I went to sleep.'

'I think not,' Maal said quietly.

'You mean . . .?' Kyra opened her eyes wide.

'I mean . . . I think you made your first journey. Now tell me everything you felt and saw.'

They returned to the log as Kyra was anxious to get away from the clearing where she had had such a strange experience. Under Maal's skilful questioning she told them every detail. They were all very excited and even Kyra could not help feeling a kind of nervous elation and pride at her achievement.

'You see,' Maal said, patting her on the head, 'it was not so bad after all.'

'I cannot believe it really happened!'

'Will you believe it if Thorn and Wardyke really do move the grave to the very place you described?' Karne asked.

'Of course. But surely it will not be so?'

'We shall see,' Maal said thoughtfully.

'But if it is so,' Fern said, 'that will be bad for you surely?'

'In one way, yes. In another way, no. It will mean we are making progress with Kyra and we are that much nearer to being able to contact the Lords of the Sun.'

'Why is it so important where you have your burial mound?' Karne asked. 'What did they mean by it not "doing you any good" beside the trees?'

'It is all connected with the channels through which the earth powers flow,' Fern said. 'Where Maal chooses to place himself at the moment of death is very important.'

'I want my dying to be a conscious and deliberate act,' Maal said.

Karne and Kyra looked horrified. Fern seemed to understand.

'I have chosen this way,' Maal said calmly.

'I do not understand!' Kyra cried. 'Are you going to kill yourself?'

'Not quite. When I know I am about to die I am going to compose myself for death, use it as I have been trained to do, to influence the direction of my journey through the spirit worlds, maybe even the time and place of my rebirth on this earth.'

Karne and Kyra were looking astonished. They had been told in ritual words many times that this life was only one of many, but until this moment neither of them had really thought about it.

'You mean . . .?'

'So you see it is important that he should meet his death while he is on the line of maximum life force,' Fern interrupted eagerly, 'so that he can have all the help he can in the difficult task of transference from one level to another.'

'Wardyke knows this,' Maal said, and there was a trace of

bitterness in his voice, 'and that is why he wants to move me *off* the line of maximum power.'

Kyra gasped:

'We must not let him do it! We must stop him!' Karne cried angrily.

Maal raised his hand.

'Not so hasty, my friend. You are dealing with a very powerful magician.'

Karne was silenced for a moment and then muttered 'There must be a way!'

'There will be a way,' said Maal confidently, 'but we will not find it when our minds are all muddied and disturbed by anger.'

'If we sit still and let our minds flow naturally,' Fern said, 'the solution to the problem will probably just float up from deep inside ourselves. I have noticed that. There seems to be another "Me" somewhere deeply inside that I hardly ever notice, but when I do it seems to make more sense of things than the outside "me". I think it is this one that communicates with the plant world.'

'Well, I am no good at sitting still,' Karne said impatiently. 'Things come to *me* when I am active!'

'That may be your way,' Maal said, 'but it is not ours. Bear with us while we try to find our hidden Selves. You yourself might be surprised if you were to join with us in this.'

Silence fell between them and almost immediately the other three began to look remote and calm. Karne could *not* still his mind. The more he tried the more his angry thoughts churned and turned within him.

At last he could bear it no longer and burst out with the suggestion that the only way out of the situation was to kill Wardyke.

Kyra was horrified.

'If you killed Wardyke you would be just as bad as he is,' she said indignantly.

'One must try to re-route . . . not to destroy,' Maal said patiently.

'But killing him would be re-routing him!' Karne called out

71

triumphantly. 'I would re-route him straight out of this life in to the next!'

Maal could not help laughing, but Kyra and Fern were even more indignant. The old priest would have preferred to change the subject, but he had to say something more to soothe the girls and prevent Karne rushing off and carrying out his hot-headed threat.

'We are all part of the same pattern', he said. 'We are dependent on each other in subtle and complicated ways and no man dare decide the fate of any other man. The mysteries of life and death are beyond our understanding and are meddled with only at our peril. By our interference we may bring about greater harm than that which we had hoped to cure. There will be ways of stopping Wardyke that do not run this risk.'

'I wish we could think of something,' Kyra said sadly.

'We will,' said Maal with conviction.

It was time for them to separate.

Maal went first as it was important that no one saw them together.

As they watched his slightly stooping figure disappear around the curve of the hill, Kyra said,

'We are not even sure if any of this is going to happen. I may have dreamed the whole thing.'

'I am certain it is going to happen,' said Karne. 'Of that I have no doubt!'

Kyra sighed.

Her brother had always had more faith in her powers than she had herself.

The Retreat

During the next few days nothing was said in the village about the changed site of Maal's tomb and even Karne was beginning to think Kyra's experience might have been a dream.

They saw Wardyke once or twice but Maal had warned them to avoid him if possible and certainly not to meet his eyes. Their plan would only work if Wardyke's suspicions were not in any way aroused. Karne helped in the fields as usual and also spent some time gathering stones for Maal's burial chamber.

It was on the fifth day after Kyra's experience that Faro came to the place where they were piling the rocks and asked the boys to move them towards the clump of trees. He pointed out exactly where he wanted them.

'Why is that?' Karne asked, trying to keep his voice as unemotional as possible.

'I do not know,' Faro said, 'Thorn told me to tell you. It must be a better place for some reason.'

Karne could not wait to tell Kyra.

The other boys grumbled bitterly at the extra work involved, but Karne worked silently and as he worked he began to think of a plan. Fern's wood was on the line of alignment from the Sacred Circle to the midsummer sunset notch. What if they dug another burial place in the woods behind her house, keeping it hidden and secret, and Maal buried himself in that instead of the official one?

He rushed home and dragged Kyra out to their meeting place near the boat. As they walked he poured out his scheme.

At first she was confused, but when she caught the gist of what he was saying her feelings were mixed. She was pleased

73

that she had proof that she had started to 'travel', but she was also afraid of the implications. How soon would Maal consider she was ready to enter the Circle? Surely it would be a long time before she was prepared enough for that. She had no real control yet over where she went or what she did. She remembered with a shudder that awful jerk with which she had returned to her body.

'What do you think of it?' Karne asked her eagerly.

'I am frightened, Karne. What if I cannot get back?'

'What on earth are you talking about?' He was genuinely surprised. He thought she had been listening to every word of his excellent plan.

'From the Lords of the Sun.'

'Oh, *them*!' he said impatiently. 'That is another problem. What do you think of my idea about the burial mound?'

He had to explain the whole thing again. She thought it was a good idea, but raised a few useful objections. The burial of a priest was always a ceremonial affair and the whole community would be there to see him go. There was no way Wardyke would let them use their own tomb.

'Of course not! He must not even know about it!'

'How are you going to manage it then?'

'I am not sure. There are things I need to know from Maal.'

'What things?'

'How long does he stay alive after the tomb is closed? If he can stay alive long enough for the crowds to leave and for us to dig him up again, it will be quite a simple matter to transfer him from the one tomb to the other. He need not start his special life transference process until we get him safely into his proper place on the alignment of power.'

Kyra thought of something else to worry about.

'I hope he does not die before we have another priest in Wardyke's place!'

'I think that is why he is driving you so hard with the training. He knows he cannot leave until he has seen that we are safe.'

Kyra realized it was selfish of her to put up so much resistance to the training.

'We will see him tomorrow,' she said decisively. 'You can take the message to Maal now and I will go home and keep mother from sending someone out to find us.'

Maal liked Karne's scheme and when they were once again with Fern they spent a great deal of time searching out the right place in the woods to dig the new burial chamber. He thought there would just be time enough for the move from the one tomb to the other to take place if everything went smoothly and quickly. As a priest of the Sun he was trained to control all his bodily functions himself, including breathing and blood circulation. He could so control his body that he could lie in trance without access to air or food for a long time, apparently dead.

'Almost like a seed that lies in the ground over winter and then springs back to life when the warm weather comes?' Fern asked.

'Something like that,' Maal said. 'But I could not compete with the seed.'

'What time of day will they have the burial,' Karne wanted to know.

'At sunset, so the darkness that follows swiftly upon it will be a convenience to us,' Maal answered. 'You must have the route well marked out so that you do not stumble or get lost. It would attract too much attention to carry torches.'

'Try to have the ceremony on a moonlit night and we will place white marker stones to show us the way.'

'You may not be the only ones to follow them to their source!'

'But we need something!'

'Rely on your own natural skills. Train your eyes. Familiarize your memory with the shapes of trees and rocks.'

'We must go over the route several times at night,' Karne said thoughtfully.

Kyra was worrying again.

'It is not going to be easy to slip away from home at night.'

'No part of it will be easy, I am afraid,' said Maal and this

75

reminded him that the most important and most difficult part of all was the part Kyra had to play.

'Come, child, we must have another lesson,' and he led her away.

While they were busy Karne and Fern took two sticks of equal length as sighting rods and set about trying to work out an accurate alignment from the Circle to the notch. It was not as easy as they had first thought, because the trees often obscured their view, but they solved the problem at last by Karne climbing the tallest tree and Fern climbing the hill outside the wood.

Karne came down from the tree just as Fern arrived back from her work on the hill, and by swinging quickly from branch to branch he managed to land on her with a wild and frightening cry. They fell in a heap together on the mossy, spongy ground, she laughing at the fright she had suffered and he laughing at the pleasure of having frightened her. After a while they stopped laughing and lay quietly side by side, her hair spread out around her on the dark fallen leaves, like fire. They could feel the wood watching them, caring for them, being gentle with them.

'You know,' he said at last, sitting up, 'it is a strange thing but there is almost a pathway, a gap in this wood opening up along the line of alignment.'

She looked where he pointed and it was true. The trees seemed to form a natural avenue, interlocked above, but at trunk level clearly grouped to suggest a kind of living tunnel leading the eye through the wood to the Stone Circle on the hill to the east, and to the notch on the hill in the west.

'We need not have gone to all that trouble,' Karne said, 'the line was there all along.'

Fern smiled. She had enjoyed the afternoon and was not sorry they had worked it out for themselves. Karne caught the expression and smiled broadly. Yes, he had enjoyed it too.

But while they were having a happy time poor Kyra was in trouble again. She had managed to 'travel' after a few false starts, but this time she found herself in a strange and horrifying situation. She was aware of her body lying on a beautiful golden couch but she was surrounded by a group of terrifying and hideous figures. Each had the body of a man clad only in a loin cloth that shone like metal, and each had the head of an animal, grinning and jeering and leering at her. She tried to get up but found she could not move her body. She tried to scream, but no sound would come from her throat. She realized she was outside her body again and had no control over it. She screamed and screamed, struggled and fought. She could *feel* herself doing all this, but she could see her body still lying there soundless and inert as though it were dead.

The creatures began tugging at her body. She could see them doing it, but could not feel their touch. They raised her into a sitting position and pointed at something on the ground that they obviously wanted her to see. They were laughing in a ghastly way that sounded more animal than human, laughing and pointing and poking at her, anxious for her to see what they had for her. She got the impression it was some kind of present. She could see, though not with her own eyes, what appeared to be a rug. As she looked at it one of the creatures pulled at it so that it moved and what was on it became sickeningly clear to her.

The rug itself seemed not to be of skin like the ones she was accustomed to, but of woven cloth, coloured and patterned in a way she would not have thought possible. Rich crimsons and blues and golds, amazing patterning of animals and birds. But upon all this beauty lay the hideous, rotting carcase of her friend Maal.

As she recognized him she screamed and the creatures jumped about with delight.

'Oh God! Oh God!' she cried with all the force and concentration of her Inner Being, 'God of Life and Light, save me!'

She could feel the words bursting in her head and even as

77

she finished them there was a kind of explosion of light and the same snapping sound she had heard before.

She was back with the living Maal in the clearing in Fern's wood, the creatures of evil nowhere in sight.

She was ashen and shaking and it was a long time before Maal could get a clear picture out of her as to what had happened. When he had heard the tale his face was very grave.

'What does it mean?' she cried. 'Oh Maal, what does it mean!'

He was silent, his expression sombre.

'Tell me,' she insisted, frightened by the gloominess of his expression and his refusal to answer.

He shook his head.

She jumped up and seized him by his thin shoulders and shook him fiercely.

'I *must* know,' she shouted, 'tell me!'

He just kept shaking his head. Tears of frustration poured down her cheeks and she did not stop shaking his shoulders for an instant.

'Kyra!' shouted Karne and Fern, arriving to find what to them had been an idyllic, peaceful afternoon shattered by the fury and despair they saw before them.

Karne took hold of his hysterical sister and pulled her away from the old man. Fern put her arms about Maal and tried to comfort him, amazed that Kyra should have attacked him so.

When at last Kyra was silent, sitting pale and tear-stained within the circle of her brother's arms, and Maal had walked away from them into the wood to think a while and returned looking calmer and more composed, Karne and Fern were told briefly what had occurred. They were both shaken and puzzled by the experience. Although Kyra would dearly have liked to ask yet again the meaning of it all, Maal offered no explanation, and she was too weary to insist on one.

'I have decided,' Maal said calmly. 'The work is too dangerous for Kyra. We must abandon it.'

'But,' said Karne, '. . . Wardyke?'

'I know. But a priest would train for years before he would take the risks I am asking Kyra to take. We cannot do it in the time available. We must try and think of another way.'

'Who were those creatures?' Fern asked anxiously.

Kyra sat still and quiet, showing no interest or emotion now, too worn out to care if he answered Fern's question or not.

He paused a long time, but the expression on his face showed them that he was trying to answer.

'What I have been doing with you is wrong,' he said slowly at last.

Karne opened his mouth to deny it, but Maal stopped him with a gesture.

'Yes, wrong. The world you lived in before, the world the villagers see all around them is a comfortable world. It is not the only world they live in, but it is the only world they think they live in. It fits them like their own clothes and they are happy with it. Only certain of their faculties are developed so they see only certain things about the world. Because they are not aware of anything further they are quite content that what they have is everything there is to have.

'But there *is* more to reality than meets the eye of the average person.

'There are ways of growing naturally like Fern here, or being trained like me, so that one becomes aware of some of the other levels to reality. The more one grows, the more one learns, the more complex and wonderful the world becomes, deeper and deeper levels, higher and higher levels open up to one!

'You have started this growth with me. You will never be content again as the villagers are, with an inadequate sense of reality.

'But there is a pace to learning, to growing, to unfolding. Fern can tell you that, from watching her plants grow and flower and fruit and fall. All should be done gradually. As one is ready so one moves. That way whatever one grows to be aware of, one is ready for. I have been pushing Kyra too far too fast. She has come upon things she is *not* ready for. They will destroy her mind.'

The three young people were silent.

Karne and Fern were thinking deeply upon what Maal had said.

Kyra was asleep, her head fallen upon her brother's shoulder. As he looked down upon her face he was moved almost to tears himself at the paleness of it, the weariness and despair of it.

The Training changes direction

During the next few days Kyra moved about as though she were ill. She was extremely tired all the time, and very pale. Her mother fussed and kept her close about the house. Karne watched with some anxiety but could do nothing for her. She did not seem to want to talk and indeed, even if he had wanted to call her away to their talking place at the boat, there were two reasons, apart from Kyra's own reluctance, to prevent it: his mother's vigilance over his sister and the presence of his two brothers, Ji and Okan, almost constantly at the boat.

Karne watched them go off one day eagerly discussing the day's work plan and realized he was feeling like a grown man watching two children going off to play. The boat had been so important to him at one time, but that enthusiasm seemed a hundred moons ago now, when he was a child. He smiled to think that he had once thought he could only find the answers to all his questions about life and death and the gods by sailing away across the sea. He knew now that the answers to life's mysteries lay wherever one happened to be. It was only a matter of the acuteness of one's vision whether one could see them or not.

Although he was forced reluctantly to agree with Maal that they should not push Kyra any further than she was able to go, he was determined to continue learning from Maal himself.

Fern too had much to teach although he learnt from her more by watching and being with her than by discussing things with her. She was not so good at putting things into words as Maal, but the way she lived her life was a lesson in itself.

Sometimes he went to see her when the others were not there and always found her quietly, gently, going about her daily work tending the plants. She seemed to sense everything they

81

needed and would never allow herself to be too tired or too harrassed to give it to them. She paced herself steadily through the day. Karne noticed that with admiration. There were never moments in her orderly life, as there were in his, of rush and bother as too much to be done became bunched up into too little time. He noticed that when she was tired or overworked and beginning to get tense, she would stop what she was doing immediately and sit cross legged and still, her head tipped slightly back and her eyes closed. When he found her like that the first time, there was such a stillness about her he thought she had somehow fallen asleep sitting up. But she was not asleep and after only a few moments of this kind of intense rest, this sinking into the still point at the centre of her nature, she was refreshed and would rise up gracefully to start work again.

'Are you not lonely always by yourself?' he asked her one day as they sat together.

'I am never by myself,' she said, smiling, 'and I am certainly never lonely.'

He believed her. Around her her trees and bushes and plants were sweetly growing, long tendrils of creeper reached down from the trees to stroke her as she passed. He could *feel* the love and peace all around, the feeling of companionship. She sat in the centre of a green world and light both radiated from her and to her. In some ways she looked as though she herself was of the plant world. The stillness with which she sat, the quiet gleam of her red-gold hair, her eyes the colour of dark wood flecked strangely with the gold of sunlight, her skin nut brown and her body slim, supple and lithe like a young sapling. Living alone she worked hard, doing all the chores normally shared out among a family. She needed no wood for cooking, as she ate only plant material and that fresh and uncooked, but for the winter she had to gather wood and break it into reasonably sized pieces for her small hearth. She took only branches that were already dead, and chopped them with a fine flint axe her father had left her. All summer she worked on the wood little by little, so that when the cold winds came howling down from the north she was well prepared.

When her house needed mending she mended it. When the earth needed digging she dug it.

Karne sometimes felt she had the strength of a boy and yet the beauty of a woman's shape. He felt totally at peace with her as though her thoughts flowed in unison with his. He never sensed as he did with other people that he was cut off, isolated within his own skin, unable to communicate.

As time passed Kyra gradually became less pale. She seemed to have decided to regard the whole experience as a bad dream, but nevertheless she was determined not to put herself in the position of having another such a one. It was a great relief to her that she was no longer expected to 'travel', and Karne found her almost irritating in the way she put the whole thing from her mind and in some way returned to childhood. She played with the younger children noisily and enthusiastically, avoiding him and refusing to visit Maal and Fern. Indeed she was so unlike herself he began to wonder if her mind had been affected already, as Maal said it might be if they contined with their experiments.

Chafing at the inactivity and lack of progress he decided as they could no longer rely on her for any help and they must be sure at least that Maal's secret chamber was ready for him when he needed it, Fern and he must proceed with the work on it by themselves. They started digging on a day after rain when the earth was fairly soft.

'We will have to gather stones to line the chamber and keep them hidden somehow,' Karne said.

Luckily the woods were very deep and lush with undergrowth and it would not be difficult to keep things hidden.

Fern wove a kind of raft of vines and branches which could be lowered over the hole they were making so that it would totally disappear from view when they were not actually working on it. Not many people came to the woods as a rule, but one could not be certain they would not. Children sometimes came to gather berries for themselves and their families a little later in the year. The wild berries were still unripe although those in Fern's garden were already edible.

'Maal seems to be avoiding us,' Karne remarked one day. 'Have you noticed?'

'I am worried about him,' Fern said. 'He seems very low in spirit.'

'He even looks older. I hope he will not need this chamber until we are ready.'

'How is the work on the other tomb? You never mention it.'

'The stones are all collected and the digging has started, but I am not involved in that. I did enough collecting the rocks. Half of them had to be brought from the hills. It was no easy task!'

'But should you not still be working there?' Fern asked.

'Why? I have enough to do here and in the fields.'

'But,' said Fern a trifle anxiously, 'surely it is essential one of us should know exactly how it is constructed? Remember we have to fetch Maal out of there, probably in the dark.'

'I had not thought of that,' Karne was silent. He had stopped work and was frowning as he thought about the problem.

'In fact, not only that, but I should find a way to make it easier for us to open it. We will never be able to move the great stone that seals the entrance. We will have to work in from the side or back somehow.'

'Could you make a tunnel?'

Karne strode about restlessly. A tunnel would be the answer, but he was appalled at the amount of work involved, and all of it in secret. As it was he was beginning to ache with tiredness and in the morning when light came he could scarcely bring himself to rise and start the day.

'I cannot do it by myself,' he said despairingly.

'I will help you,' Fern said, 'we will work at night. I am sure Kyra will help as well.'

'Kyra!' he said bitterly.

He had told Fern about the way Kyra was behaving.

'You must not judge her too harshly, she is very young and has been under great strain.'

'She is fourteen. That is not so young. She behaves like a

small child.'

'She is trying to protect herself. She is frightened.'

'How will behaving like a child protect her?'

'People do not ask children to face danger and responsibility. If she can convince us she is too young to do the things we want her to, she will not have to do them. I think she is trying to convince herself as well, which is not easy.'

'Why would she do that?'

'So that she will not feel guilty.'

Karne sighed. Fern was right, of course. But nevertheless it was most irritating that Kyra was the only one of them who could be asked to 'travel' and she was too afraid to do it.

'If it were I,' he thought with fierce pride, 'I would do it without a second thought! I would give anything to have a chance at it!'

Kyra agreed to help with the tunnel and indeed seemed to have recovered enough of her old spirit for her mother to leave her alone again. She would still not think about spirit travelling, but with Maal's tomb she was prepared to help. The one in the woods was almost ready and Fern insisted she could finish it off herself. Maal had instructed them in its construction and it was of a much humbler size than the official one. Because of Fern's knowledge of earth currents and channels they dug *with* the grain of the earth, and the digging was easy. It was almost as though the earth was helping them. Worms loosened the next layer of soil for them overnight and it was ready to dig in the morning.

But on the open hillside beside the clump of trees Maal's official tomb was not so easy to construct. It was on no natural channel of energy and the soil seemed heavy and lifeless to dig. Many men and boys were engaged all day in digging with antler picks and hollowed hardwood shovelling logs. The boys carried the soil away in leather buckets, putting it aside to be replaced as the mound over the stone chamber when the priest was laid to rest.

Thorn came occasionally to check on progress and once

Wardyke came and told them angrily to work harder. It was as though he was impatient to see it finished.

Very early in the morning before anyone else was stirring Karne, Kyra and Fern would creep out of their homes and meet at the tomb. They were digging a tunnel and it was hard and painful work. They were lucky in that the clump of trees beside the mound hid the entrance.

Time went by. Maal returned to them and lifted their spirits when they were ready to collapse, answering their questions and teaching them many things. No more was said of 'travelling' but much was said of growing in strength within themselves so that they would be strong enough to overthrow Wardyke by themselves if it became necessary.

One day Karne had yet another good idea.

'If you had help,' he said to Maal, 'would you be able to break through the barrier at the Circle?'

Maal thought about it.

'Maybe,' he said.

'Well then,' cried Karne triumphantly, 'all we have to do is give you some help to get through the barrier and *you* will be able to travel to the Lords of the Sun!'

Maal looked doubtful still, but Karne, Kyra and Fern looked jubilant. It certainly seemed to be solution to the problem.

But how best to give the help?

Kyra thought of something.

'You know that day,' she said, 'the day Wardyke arrived and I thought I heard you calling me to help but I did not know what to do?'

'Yes,' Maal said.

'I had the feeling Wardyke was trying to drive you from the Circle but that he was not succeeding when he was by himself. It was only when Thorn joined him that he began to gain control.'

'That is so. That is why I was calling to you. If you had joined your powers to mine, we might have been able to

86

withstand them at that point.'

Karne was fascinated.

'But could you do it now,' he said, 'I mean, the two of you together?'

'It is possible,' Maal said slowly.

'That would be a way!' Fern cried.

'But you would do the travelling!' said Kyra anxiously, half questioning, half stating fact.

'Yes, I would do the travelling.'

'But together you could probably pass through the barrier. Particularly as it is not designed for Kyra at all,' Karne insisted.

Maal began to look really interested.

'This may be possible,' he said with growing confidence.

Karne smiled with relief.

'That is decided then!' he said firmly. 'When do we start?'

Maal laughed.

'Impatient as ever, Karne! It is not as easy as you think. Kyra and I have much work to do together before we can attempt it. We may get only one chance to reach the Circle and cannot afford to bungle it.'

Kyra began to look anxious.

'I will not have to go within the Circle?' she asked, still worried.

'I will try to avoid it,' Maal said soothingly.

'I am *not* going within the Circle!' Kyra was alarmed now and made this announcement with great force.

'Of course you will not,' Karne said hastily. 'Maal will do all the work. You will just have to help him through the barrier.' And then to Maal he said, 'You do *believe* you can do it together, do you not?'

'Our two wills together will make it possible,' Maal said with great conviction.

Kyra looked somewhat pacified.

'All right,' she muttered, 'as long as I do not have to do the "travelling" or go within the Circle.'

'That is understood,' Karne said firmly.

The First Challenge

While Maal was training Kyra to project her will and mind to join with his, and Karne and Fern were working secretly upon the tunnel, new settlers began to come to their valley.

At first one or two families arrived, were greeted with great warmth by the community and soon made to feel at home, but within weeks others came and what had once been a very close-knit and related group of homesteads became an untidy and sprawling collection of disparate elements. The strangers were everywhere, taking over land that since the ancient times had been common grazing land. They put up their homes which were no more than badly built shacks wherever they wished with no regard to the harmonious flow of village life.

The original villagers began to grumble.

'They seem to have no sense of the flow of the earth spirit,' Fern said. 'All the other sites for homes were chosen carefully by Maal or my father, so that they fitted into the rhythm of the land. But these people just put their houses anywhere, making everything ugly and disorderly. It is no wonder they look so restless and dissatisfied!'

The original villagers at last bestirred themselves to have a meeting at the Meeting Stone. It was a mystery to them why so many settlers had come at one time. Over the years families had arrived from other communities and settled in, but never more than one at a time.

These people seemed to move in hordes, and be rough and noisy. They carried themselves with such arrogance and confidence that the milder mannered villagers found it impossible to stand up to them. They arrived and moved in as

though they had a right, and each villager in his turn re-
frained from saying anything because he thought it was his
own ignorance that made him unaware of the reasons for their
arrival. It seemed to have been arranged in some way. But no
one could make out how, or by whom.

At the meeting some of the Elders were present but
Wardyke and Thorn had been away for three days and no one
knew where they were or when they would return. It was a
measure of the desperation of the villagers that they had dared
to call a meeting without the sanction of their two formidable
leaders.

Faro was in charge and he was particularly angry as the
Strangers had put up their untidy shacks close to his home and
were encroaching on the land he had always thought was his.
No one actually *owned* land in the community, they all knew
the earth belonged to the gods and the earth spirits, but
certain parts of it were by long-standing custom used by
certain families. When a family cared properly for the land no
one questioned their right to use it, but if a family, as had
happened from time to time in the past, misused or neglected
the land, it was taken by common consent from them and
given to the community until such time as the offending family
proved itself worthy again to be trusted with the care of it.

The Strangers were certainly misusing the land. Their
rubbish was never returned to the earth to fertilize the new
crops as Fern's father had taught them, but left lying about in
untidy, smelly heaps. They killed animals wantonly, ate only a
little of each, and threw away the rest, again to rot within sight
of the dwellings. The winter was not far off and the meat
should have been cured and hung for the long cold months
ahead when no grain grew in the frosty earth and most of the
animals had moved south or gone to sleep. The Strangers
seemed to be making no provision for the winter. This made
the villagers uneasy. Where were they going to get their food
in winter? Where their wood and furs? The villagers feared the
Strangers were not above taking what they needed from their
more circumspect neighbours, by force if necessary.

Some villagers had even seen the Strangers killing birds and everyone knew that birds who flew so close to the sun and the moon were sacred, friends of the spirit-gods and not to be harmed in any way.

It was time indeed to meet and talk about what could be done.

Many of them felt they should have waited till the return of Thorn and Wardyke, but many others were too impatient to wait. A new family of settlers had moved in that very day and were chopping down trees most wastefully at the edge of the south pasture.

'Strangers have always been welcomed in our community and before this time we have never regretted our hospitality,' Karne's father said.

'They do not follow the ancient laws.' Someone else spoke. 'Not one has called a meeting of the Elders to ask permission to live within our community. They have taken land no one has agreed that they should have.'

'They do not seem to have a leader. There is no one among them elected to speak for them.'

'Thorn has been seen talking to them,' a nervous little man spoke up. He had been one of those opposed to the calling of the meeting without Thorn's approval.

'But that is not the way,' Karne's father said. 'A full meeting of the Elders should settle land rights. Not just the word of one Elder.'

'Or a priest,' someone else muttered bitterly.

It seemed to Karne not all the villagers were as pleased with Wardyke as they had at first been. It might be time for Maal's return.

'Should we not call for Maal's help here,' he said suddenly and with boldness. It was not usual for the young to talk at meetings and Karne had never spoken before. Heads turned to look at him in surprise, but no objection to his speaking was raised. He was tall, nearly sixteen, and without their noticing had become a man. It was more what he had said that called for objection.

There were murmurs.

'Maal? What could that old man do!'

'He has not been near the Sacred Circle or the people since Wardyke came!'

'He waits only to die.'

There was a faction who was still blinded by Wardyke, it seemed.

Karne flushed with anger at these remarks and prepared to answer them but, seeing the situation and knowing his son well, Karne's father spoke quickly .

'Maal's advice as one who has lived long in our village and served us well . . .' and here he looked fiercely at the maker of the last remark, 'should certainly be sought. But he is no longer priest here and his word is no longer our law,' and here he looked hard at his son.

'I mean only his advice, father,' Karne said mildly, realizing in time the wisdom of tact. 'He has had much experience and has travelled further than any of us. Perhaps he could tell us where these people come from.'

'Send for him.' The man who had muttered earlier against Wardyke's sole word being law spoke up now.

Karne was off before anyone could offer an objection, and Maal was fetched. In hurrying him back to the meeting, Karne noticed impatiently that Maal was slow and feeble in his movements.

'Hurry,' he cried. 'Wardyke is not there. You may have a chance to influence the people.'

'I am not as young as you, boy,' Maal complained, out of breath.

'Could you not go a little faster,' Karne pleaded.

'I am going as fast as I can,' puffed Maal. 'I am sorely in need of a new body.'

Karne tried to swallow his impatience. Maal's mind was so vigorous and young, he always forgot it was housed in such a decrepit body. Karne had noticed that since Kyra's last experience with spirit-travelling, Maal had grown feebler. He remembered her description of Maal's rotting corpse and wondered fleetingly again if it was prophetic.

When they arrived back at the meeting everything had changed. Wardyke and Thorn were back and were enraged to find the villagers had taken the initiative in anything without their permission.

Wardyke was standing on the flat rock that served them as a platform and his eyes were blazing with anger. The villagers were terrified. Even those who had murmured against the control of Thorn and Wardyke were cowed.

Seeing the situation instantly, Maal pushed Karne aside.

'Go, boy, do not be seen with me,' he whispered with the sudden strength of command in his voice.

Karne obeyed and ducked into the crowd, appearing again within sight of Wardyke and Thorn, but far from Maal.

Wardyke's voice was like thunder as he berated them for 'forming this unruly mob to cause trouble and disorder in the community'.

'Who called this meeting?' he roared.

There was silence. No one dared answer.

'Who called it, I say!' he roared again, and his eyes lashed at them with fire. Not one person dared raise his head and look him in the eye. He lifted his arm, his hand bony and immense, pointing to the sky, his black cloak falling from it in magnificent folds. He seemed about to cast a spell upon them when a voice spoke up and he turned his attention to it.

It was Maal and he was standing straight, an old man sustained by determination and desperation.

'The people of this village called it,' he said boldly, looking Wardyke straight in the face.

'Oh you gods! I wish Kyra were here now!' Karne could have wept that she was not. Maal was alone, and Wardyke was roused against him.

All eyes were on Maal now and there were many who were grateful to him, and were amazed and impressed with his dignity and courage.

'You!' screamed Wardyke, and Karne knew he was no longer in control of himself, he was so angry. The boy feared for Maal's life but did not know what to do.

'Yes, I.'

Maal strode with amazing strength towards the centre of the crowd. The people fell back till Maal was facing Wardyke directly. Wardyke was still upon the rock and so towered above Maal, but Maal's eyes were blazing and he did not for a moment relax the beam of his concentration on the younger man.

'These people did not meet here to cause trouble but to prevent it. Since the ancient days strangers have been welcomed in our community. They bring new life and new skills. Where our ways are different from theirs we learn from them and they from us. But there are some who have come in to our village who bring nothing but disruption and dismay. They desecrate the earth spirit, taking what is not any man's to take. You as priest should have been working amongst them, guiding them and teaching them our ways, easing the difference between us. But time has passed and nothing has been done . . .'

'Enough!' bellowed Wardyke, and if his voice had been loud before, it was now more like a clap of thunder than a human voice.

'These are *my* people! I will not have them criticized!'

'Your people? Does Wardyke own *people* now?'

And Maal's lips had a curl to them that Wardyke could not miss. He seemed to rise upon the air with rage. His long and deadly finger pointed straight at Maal.

'Die, old man!' he screamed.

There was a gasp from every throat. Every eye was upon the doomed old man. Karne expected a flash of lightning to come from the sky and devastate the land. Every muscle in his body was tensed against it.

Maal stumbled and almost fell. Karne could see him crumpling as though he were a pile of dust and then . . . and then . . . to another gasp from the community, he stood up straight again as though he had received new strength from somewhere, and, slowly and with great dignity, he turned and walked away.

Stupefied the villagers stared.

Maal had not died. Maal was walking away.

Karne broke from the circle and ran as hard as he had ever run, over the fields to Fern's wood. Kyra had gone to see Fern that afternoon and neither of them had been at the meeting. He *must* know if what he suspected had indeed happened.

He found the two girls in the house. Kyra was lying down looking very pale and Fern was stroking her head.

'What is the matter?' he cried out, bursting in upon them, sweating from the run.

Fern looked at him in surprise.

Kyra opened her eyes and sat up reaching out her arms for him.

'Oh Karne, I do not know, but it seemed to me Maal was in trouble and needed me. I tried to reach him as he taught me to . . . and I felt the most terrible pain shooting through my head as though . . . as though I had been hit by a battle axe . . .'

'Or a lightning bolt?' Karne asked.

'Yes, something like that. It was horrible.'

'She kept screaming and holding her head,' Fern said, 'and then she became all calm and pale. I brought her in here because she said the light hurt her eyes.'

'Poor Kyra,' Karne said gently, stroking her. 'But you have saved Maal's life.'

'What?'

The girls were eager to hear what had been going on and listened in tense silence while he told the whole story.

Kyra was awed and frightened by her own part in the drama. She knew her powers were important, had indeed proved themselves without any doubt, but she was still uneasy about them.

'I do not know what I do or how I do it,' she said miserably. 'If only I knew what I was doing and could control it!'

'It will come,' Fern said gently.

'Even without knowing what you are doing, you manage all right!' Karne said admiringly.

Kyra gave a deep sigh and looked doubtful.

When Karne and Kyra returned to the village early that evening there was no outward sign that anything was wrong. The tangy smell of the blue smoke of the cooking fires permeated the air. The boys were bringing the animals back to the stockades and they could hear their constant whistling as they walked behind them. Karne ran on ahead of Kyra knowing that his father's herd was his responsibility this particular evening. He was late bringing it in and his father was not pleased, but after the evening meal the family settled down and there was a chance to talk.

'What did Wardyke mean,' Karne asked his father, 'when he said "these are my people"?'

'It turns out,' his mother interrupted indignantly, 'all these people come from the community where Wardyke used to be priest, and he invited them here!'

'But surely,' Kyra said, 'priests train for one particular community and stay with it for life?'

'I know,' her mother said and her children could tell that the events of the day had left her agitated and anxious, 'but Wardyke announced it as though it was perfectly normal. I suppose we are old fashioned and isolated here and do not know what is going on in the rest of the country.'

'He says,' Karne's father spoke now and there was an edge of harshness in his voice, 'he wants us to be "great", to expand and multiply and take over more land from our neighbours.'

'*I* think it will be good for us,' Thon said, 'we have been too small and set in our ways for too long. I for one will be glad to have more land, more people around to talk to, a few changes about the place.'

'But the land we have supports us well. We have everything we need, food, shelter, warmth in winter . . .'

'A healthy and a loving family around us,' Karne's mother interrupted.

'If we had more land we would have more problems. More work to be done, excess food to be stored . . .'

'We could barter for more things.'

'What things? We have everything we need.'

'You have no imagination!' Thon cried impatiently. 'No

ambition! I am sure there are a lot of things we could do with if we only set our minds to it.'

'If we have to "set our minds" to look for them, they cannot be very necessary or urgent.'

'And surely,' Kyra said, remembering something she had heard from Maal, 'the good life is based on proportion and balance. We have a good balance of work to what we need at the moment. If we either had to work harder, or we invented more "needs", the balance would be destroyed.'

'She is right,' her mother said, 'more possessions only bring more harassment.'

'We could do with a bigger house,' Thon muttered.

'What is wrong with this house?' Kyra's mother looked around proudly at her neatly built and beautifully maintained home. No space wasted, and no space too crowded. These little round houses built sturdily of tree trunks filled in with a mixture of firmly packed twigs and clay, the roof thatched with marsh reeds and covered with hides lashed firmly down against the wind, had been built this way for generations and she could see no reason for change. The family slept together and kept each other warm and safe. The circle that surrounded them was the circle of the Sun, the Moon, the Sacred Stones. It gave them security and peace. They had no need of change.

But Thon could not see it. Since Wardyke's arrival he had felt restless. A different kind of restlessness to Karne's. Karne wanted to *know*. Thon wanted to possess. In a sense the houses of the two priests summed up the difference in the two attitudes.

When Wardyke had first come to the village he had stayed in the guest house the villagers always kept empty but clean for the use of travelling strangers. It was a modest circular construction similar to the others in the village. But within days of his arrival he had set the community to doing two things: constructing Maal's tomb and building his own house.

It was accepted that he would not take over Maal's house as it was the custom to burn the previous home of a person who had died. The people felt very strongly that the home of a person was in a sense like a further skin that enclosed him, that was personal to him and should die with him. After years of living in a house it became impregnated with the occupant's personal feelings and if someone else were to come and live in it, he would be troubled with the memories and concerns of his predecessor.

The villagers did not have any excess possessions. Those they had were in constant use and in a sense extensions of themselves, usually made lovingly by themselves or by their relations. A man's axe, a woman's bone needle, were steeped in personal history by the time they came to die and these things were not taken from them but left for their own use in the next life in a place where they would expect to find them, the chamber of the burial. Sometimes pottery vessels that had belonged to them but were not of prime importance to them were smashed against the burial mound or, in some communities, against the Standing Stones of the Sacred Circle itself.

As each child grew up and took a mate they would leave the family home and build one of their own which they would inhabit until their death. If parents died leaving children, the house would still be burnt and the children would go to live with relatives. It was accepted. It was natural.

Wardyke made it known that he did not want a house like the villagers, or like Maal's. He frequently came to the site and drew pictures in the dust of what he wanted. But first he chose the trees with care from the great southern forest. Some of the men were uneasy about penetrating so deeply into the forest. It was heavy work breaking through the undergrowth and chopping down the giant trees Wardyke chose, and there was a danger of wild boars and wolves as well.

Wardyke's timber was hard won and two men suffered for the rest of their lives because of it. One lad of seventeen had his leg crushed by a falling tree and for the rest of his life dragged himself around in pain. Another man lost an eye to a sharp and deadly branch. After these accidents some of the men murmured that the timber was cursed in some way, the spirits of the forest did not want Wardyke to have it for his house. On hearing this Wardyke called all the community together at the edge of the forest and held a ceremony to cleanse it of any evil curse that might have been lurking there. He chose his time well and as he intoned the age-old words of exorcism clouds as black as night gathered above the tall trees, wind groaned in the high branches and the people shuddered with sudden cold. His long black robes spread out around him in the wind like the wings of a bird of prey and his eyes were the colour of lightning.

'I command,' he bellowed into the gathering rage of the storm, 'the thwarting spirits of the dark! Begone and leave the forest to my pleasure!'

As he finished the storm broke and the people were drenched in hard and hammering rain. The wind tore at the trees and they could hear within the forest the ripping, cracking roar of a giant tree uprooted and flung upon the ground.

Terrified they fled, their last sight the figure of Wardyke like the pointing figure of the storm aimed at the forest.

In the calm morning that followed this upheaval, many trees were found to be upon the ground. Wardyke claimed that they were his, given to him by the repentant forest.

His house was to be circular as the others were, but many times the size. Concentric rings of tall and beautifully smoothed tree trunks held the roof of wood and thatch aloft. In the very centre the house was unroofed so that light could penetrate, and Wardyke could walk if he so wished in sunlight within his own house. Channels were dug to lead rain water out if it should fall to excess and hangings of hide between the inner columns kept inclement weather from the inner chambers.

'What does he need so many chambers for?' Karne's father asked. 'He lives alone.'

'The meetings of the Elders are held in there now,' Karne said, 'in secret, where the people cannot argue with what is said.'

Karne's father shook his head sadly.

'I do not care for such changes. The old way was the best.'

This time Karne was inclined to agree with him.

Maal's home on the other hand was small and compact. Ky.
stood within it for the first time the day after the confrontation
at the Meeting Stone. Maal had not been seen since the
moment of his dramatic stand against the magician and she
was anxious about his health.

He did not respond when she stood at the entrance and
called to him, and after a few moments of hesitation she
stepped into the shadows of the interior. In contrast to the
brilliant sunlight without, the inside of the house was very
dark indeed. She paused a few moments and gradually the
darkness appeared to lift and she could see quite clearly. As
with their own homes there were columns of wood holding up
the roof, but unlike their own, these were carved with amazing
designs, mostly circles within circles within circles, a great
many of which seemed to be built round the spindly figures of
men, as though (but she was not sure of this) they were
standing with their arms raised holding a series of arcs above
their heads, the arcs almost completing themselves as circles
behind and around them. Some designs looked more like
trees, each branch of which supported one of these concentric
multiple circles. Amazed, she gazed from one to the other and
had almost forgotten the purpose of her visit, when she
suddenly became aware of Maal sitting in the dead centre of
the room observing her.

'My lord Maal!' she cried with a mixture of confusion and
relief. 'I was worried about you. Are you all right?'

'Yes,' he said quietly, 'thanks to you.'

She flushed slightly.

'Was it really me?' she murmured, hanging her head in
embarrassment. 'I cannot believe it!'

'Yes, it really was you,' and he raised himself to stand beside
her, taking her arm lightly.

Not knowing what to say next her heart was so full, she
looked around her at the surroundings and gestured at what
she saw.

99

'It is all so beautiful,' she said with awe. 'I have never seen anything like it.'

Maal smiled and there was some secret knowledge in his smile.

'I will show you greater wonders than these, my child.'

At a loss to know quite what he meant Kyra returned to the carvings.

'Did you carve them yourself?'

'Yes.'

'All of them?'

'Yes.'

'What do they mean?'

'They mean a great deal and one day you will understand them all.'

'I would like to understand them now if it is possible,' she said as humbly as she could.

'Ah,' he smiled, 'you remind me of Karne now, wanting to understand everything, immediately. Have you not learned that understanding is a slow growth and comes only in stages and when you are ready?'

'I know . . . but . . . there is so little time . . .' She meant until Maal was to die but she was sorry she had said this as soon as the words left her mouth. She could not help feeling, and Karne agreed with her, that Wardyke would not rest now until he had destroyed Maal. It was endangering his own position to allow someone to escape whom he had cursed.

Maal knew what she meant and looked thoughtful.

'You are right. There is no time to waste. Come, sit with me and I will teach you things you need to know.'

'About the carvings?'

'The meaning of the carvings is only a small part of a greater whole, some of which you already know.'

'Are the different circles the different levels of reality one can discover around one . . . gradually as one's understanding and awareness develops?'

Maal smiled.

'You see, you do not need me to explain things to you.'

'But . . .'

But he held up his hand and she knew she had to stop talking.

'As you said . . . there is not much time. Today we must try something that I would not have chosen to try till much later in your apprenticeship.'

Kyra looked anxious. Maal noticed.

She w~~ dangerous so much as . . . difficult,' he said re-~~if you do not succeed no harm will come to you.

'What must ~~work together will be that much easier.'

'First, sit.'

She sat.

'Now relax and go quiet within y~~ as I have taught you.'

At first she had found this very difficult to do. Her mind seemed to be continually chattering on and on, going over things repeatedly, worrying at new things, even remaking old memories with slight alterations. She had caught herself at this several times and had been quite shocked at herself. Somehow by the time she had 'remade' a memory in words in her head her own part in it always looked better than it had at the time of the actual happening. Maal had been trying to teach her to control her mind so that it did not run on and on like this. At first he had taught her to blot out the incessant gabble by replacing it with one image or word that was so insistently and repeatedly thought of by her there was no room for any other. Once she had mastered this, it was her task to do away with the blocking word itself and keep her mind poised and still ready for messages from her deeper self, her Real Self, which was in touch with the other levels of Reality.

Another trick he had suggested to her to help her achieve this was to choose a word and use it as a kind of magic flower from which a thousand petals of meaning and association could be plucked.

'This way,' he said, 'you think of the word and what it suggests to you, and then you think of the word again and what else it suggests to you. You repeat this again and again, coming back each time to the original word, until you find somehow the word is associated with everything. Everything is associated with everything else. We are parts of a Whole and nothing is separate. As this conviction grows on you you will feel yourself more and more receptive to the Whole. Your separate identity will lose its hold, your protective wa... wordage will be down, and influences from... beyond yourself will be able to penetrate.'

It was this method she chose to use t...

And the word she chose was 'St...

Stone . . . .one . . . cliffs . . . stone . . . rocks in rivers . . . mountain water working at the rocks of stone . . . water br... g rocks of stone into sand . . . stone sand . . . ...one earth . . . roots in earth sand . . . roots in stone earth . . . roots drawing nourishment from stone earth . . . water containing grains of stone . . . earth . . . crushed stone . . . nourishing plants . . : plants containing stone . . . crushed stone . . . nourishing her and animals . . . stone . . . animals with crushed stone from the plants nourishing her . . . she, part stone . . . part earth . . . part universe . . .

She could feel her identity growing and growing until it encompassed everything . . . she was part of the universe and the universe was part of her . . . and as she became aware of this she also became aware that she was no longer Kyra in Maal's house, she was Maal but Maal was a younger man and he was standing in the thick dust of a parched country.

She looked at her feet and they were Maal's feet clad in unfamiliar sandals made of hide thongs. She noticed they were not covered in dust although they should have been. It puzzled her that they were not covered in dust. It puzzled her that she should think that they should be.

Behind her stretched a steep road curving down a rocky hill into a dry valley. The sun was blazing on everything, brighter than she had ever known it, bleaching the colour out of the landscape. Beside her was a gigantic wall built of huge stones placed one upon the other, one beside the other, each one a slightly different shape and size and yet all fitted neatly and intricately together with great skill so that there were no spaces at all between them.

Before her was a gateway so large one would think it was made for giants and above it two great beasts facing each other were carved out of solid rock. She gasped, straining to lean far enough back to see the height of it all. But even as she was doing this she could feel herself impelled forward to enter the gate. Guards were posted, wearing strange clothes and carrying tall and deadly looking spears, but they seemed not to notice her. She found herself walking past them and facing a kind of citadel or palace built of stone.

The road from the valley continued through the gate and spiralled up the hill, the huge walls curving with the curve of the road. She walked on unnoticed by the people who were going about their daily business. To the right and to the left she saw more of the pale dust-coloured stone. She could not believe men could do such wonderful things with stone and wondered that her own people did not build temples and palaces in this way.

The hill was steep but the high walls gave shade. She walked where she fancied, exploring doorways and courtyards, confident that she could not be seen. As she climbed higher the view of the distant landscape she occasionally caught was breathtaking. She could see a line of ocean so deep in the colour blue that if it had not sparkled so, she would have thought it was a field of flowers. The palace-citadel was built on a high and isolated hill. To the left there were rocky mountains, the colour of ripe wheat, devoid of grass or heather. But in every other direction for a long way there was nothing but arid plains, until on the far horizon a line of hills ran down to meet the unbelievable blue of the sea.

'Greetings,' a voice said suddenly beside her — or was it in her own head the word formed?

She spun round. She was in a vast courtyard paved with cool stone dazzling white and so smooth that a moment before she had stooped down to stroke it but strangely had felt no sensation in her hand. She saw now that she was not alone. An old man clad in a robe of a deep violet colour was looking directly at her.

'Greetings,' she said tentatively, for the first time in this strange place at a loss to know what to do next.

The man smiled and approached.

'You have come a long way and you are welcome,' he said kindly.

'Thank you,' she said, but it was Maal's voice she heard saying it. She still could not make out if they were speaking aloud or merely 'thinking' the words.

'Could you,' . . . she began and hesitated, but his expression seemed so friendly she decided to take the plunge.

'Could you tell me where I am?'

He smiled.

'You are in the Palace of the King,' he said proudly.

'Oh,' she said, and the flatness of her voice indicated that this meant nothing to her.

'Come,' he said, and he gestured for her to follow.

He took her across the white sunlit courtyard into the dark interior of a chamber and there he fetched an object and held it up to the sunlight that came shafting through the entrance. He held it with both hands above his head as though it were some kind of sacred object. She looked up and her eyes were dazzled as the sunshine glanced off and spun from a cup of gold of such beauty that she could scarcely breathe as she gazed upon it. As her eyes grew more accustomed to staring into the concentrated light of its surface she noted that there was a design beaten upon it, a design of bulls. Two bulls charging each other. So powerful was the impression of vigorous life within their rippling golden muscles, she almost stepped back as though they could harm her. Her sense of scale, of what was moving and what was not, of what was within her and what was without, had long since disappeared. If she had ever thought to put a limit to what is real and what is not she would have abandoned the attempt now.

She knew this was all happening to her. She had a strong

sense that it was real . . . and yet . . . and yet . . . it was like nothing she had ever experienced before. The cup was real. She was sure she could reach up and touch it, and yet at the same time . . . as she gazed at it it was no longer a cup but an experience of sun, of gold, of fear and thundering hooves and tossing horns . . . an experience of overwhelming power and light.

She met the eyes of the old man and in them she saw herself reflected.

But it was not an image of herself. It was Maal, and Maal as a young man as she had never seen him.

She shut her eyes and for the first time she felt afraid of the strangeness of it all.

'Kyra,' a voice said gently.

She opened her eyes and Maal, the old man, was outside her, looking deep into her eyes with affectionate concern. Around him the dark carved wood of the columns of his house enclosed them in familiar comfort. She dropped her head upon her chest wearily.

She was tired . . . so tired . . .

'Sleep,' he said gently, helping her to lie down. 'You will feel better after sleep.'

'So tired . . .' she murmured to herself.

She wanted to think about the experiences she had just been through but she was too tired.

'Another time . . .' she whispered as she drifted off into a blessed dreamless sleep.

When she awoke Maal was still with her. She sat up and looked round her hastily, worried that she might have slipped unwittingly into yet another strange place.

'It is all right,' he said, 'you are here in your own village where you feel most at home.'

She remembered the experience in the strange palace.

'Tell me,' he said quietly.

'Do you not know,' she asked, 'you were there.'

'Tell me,' he repeated gently.

She told him everything.

'What was it?' she asked when she had finished. 'Why did I seem to be you?'

'You were not travelling in the way you did before when you saw Wardyke and Thorn. In a sense you were not travelling at all. You were identifying with me and experiencing my memories.'

'You mean all that happened to you once when you were a young man and you were remembering it in this room now, and I somehow was inside your mind remembering it as though it had happened to me?'

'Something like that,' Maal said smiling.

Kyra was silent for a while thinking about the complexities of it.

'Did it *really* happen to you?'

'Yes.'

'I mean, did you *really* go there . . . to that *very* place?'

'Yes.'

'Why was it that only that one man could see me . . . I mean, you?'

Maal looked as though he did not know where to begin to explain it to her.

'You see . . .' he began hesitatingly, but she interrupted. She felt she must get it straight.

'You were *really* there?' she insisted.

Maal laughed and threw up his hands.

'"Real"? "Really"? what do the words mean?'

'You know what *I* mean by them,' cried Kyra.

'What do you mean by them?' he said with a touch of gentle irony in his voice.

'I mean . . . quite simply . . . that you were there as I am here now.'

'And how are you here now?' he asked quietly.

She was stunned.

'I am *here*!' she shouted indignantly.

He just looked at her and for a terrible moment she was not

106

sure if she *was* there now or not. After all, the experience in the palace had felt just as real.

But he saw her distress and decided she had had enough insecurity for one day.

'I will explain,' he said soothingly, 'as best I can. I was not "really" there in the sense I think you mean. My body that you can touch in this room at this moment was not there. But the inner me, the spirit Me, was really there.'

'You mean you "travelled" in the way I did when I saw Wardyke and Thorn that day?'

'Yes.'

'And the other people could not see you because you were in your spirit body, but the one old man could because he was a trained priest?'

'Yes.'

'That was a real golden cup he held up for me to see?' she said wonderingly, her voice filled with awe.

'Yes.'

'Somewhere in the world at this very moment that gold cup still exists?'

'Very probably.'

'Oh Maal!' she cried, 'I wish I could see it again. I wish I could hold it in my hand.'

'Maybe you will one day. I know there is a long journey in your life.'

'You mean a real journey . . . I mean in my body . . . not just spirit travelling?'

He smiled at the epithet 'just'. How she had already come to take one of the greatest wonders of the universe for granted. 'But then,' he thought, 'so do we all,' and he fingered the green and delicate shell of a sea urchin that he wore on a thong around his neck.

She flushed slightly, realizing what she had said.

'Yes,' he said smiling, 'a "real" journey.'

'Where to?'

'That I do not yet know.'

'When will you know?'

'*You* will know when it is time.'

'How will I know?'

'There will be an omen, a sign.'

'How will I recognize it?'

'You will recognize it,' he said with confidence.

She did not look so sure.

He wondered if he should tell her more about the nature of omens.

He wondered if he should tell her that omens are around us all the time. Everything is an omen if we choose to make it so. What makes an omen work is something in ourselves. We sense something from deep within us, on a level in which we are not used to being conscious, and we choose something from the 'outside' world to project it on, to make it understandable for us. For instance, she would sense a need to take a journey, a readiness, a ripeness . . . and because she was not used to recognizing such deep instinctual drives she would see a giant bird flying or a wind blowing a tree in a particular way and she would believe it was an omen telling her to go. She would think the message was coming from outside herself.

If she saw the same bird flying, the same tree bending, when she was not ready to go, she would not see them as omens at all. It was another case of what was reality. The omens were real, but not in the sense the people believed them to be.

He looked at her and decided she was not ready to recognize omens as part of herself. She had too much that was new already to cope with. It would be more comfortable for her to believe as most people believed, that omens were messages from the gods telling one what to do. Making decisions for oneself was always difficult and it was a sign of maturity when one could take responsibility for decisions. Kyra was maturing rapidly, but she was still a long way from this point.

'Will it tell me where to go?' she asked anxiously.

'Yes,' he said comfortingly, 'it will tell you everything.'

'But . . .'

'No,' he said firmly, 'I have answered enough questions for one day. You will know everything you need to know when it is time to know it. Go home now, child. Relax. Everything is working out well.'

'I did everything right today?' she asked, anxious for confirmation.

'You did.' He patted her gently on the shoulder. 'But now it is time to be Kyra again, the daughter in a family.'

She slipped out of the priest's house and ran home, over-joyed to be greeted by the noisy barking of Faro's dog and the crying of her baby sister wanting to be fed.

The Visit

While Kyra was having these experiences with Maal, and Karne was at work on Maal's tomb, Fern was disturbed in her green world by an unexpected and unwelcome visit from Wardyke. She was digging a small patch of earth not far from the clearing Maal and Kyra were wont to use for Kyra's 'travelling' lessons and she was singing as she worked. The sun was warm on her back and a friendy robin was perched on a clod of earth nearby, glad to see her disturbing the earth worms. Every time she stopped digging for a moment to rest he would swoop in, tug out a worm and fly off to deliver it to his hungry family. Other birds were singing in the trees and the scent of summer honeysuckle was heavy in the air.

She first sensed something was wrong when she paused in her own song and noticed that the birds had gone quiet. The robin who should have been back from his mission to his family had not returned and there was a distinct feeling of waiting and tension in the air. She straightened up her back and kept quiet, trying to work out what could be wrong. She noticed she was no longer in sunlight and yet sunlight was everywhere else. The shadow of a man had fallen over her and she could feel the chill of it on her bare arms. She spun round to find Wardyke standing a few paces from her, his arms folded and his face brooding as he stared at her. As far as she could remember he had never been there before although she had heard that he had visited every one else within the first few weeks of his arrival in their community. She had been glad she lived so far away from the village, so hidden by the shoulder of a hill and the cloak of the wood. She had seen him when she went to the village and had taken the measure of him very quickly. What she had learned of him from Maal had not surprised her but had only confirmed what she already suspected.

She stood now as straight as she could, looking him in the eye boldly, unlike the other villagers, feeling around her the plant and bird world as poised on anxiety as she was. His eyes were black and fathomless, his granite face in shadow. She could not tell what he was thinking, but she could feel malevolence in the air.

'You are welcome, Lord Priest,' she said at last with quiet dignity. No one would have been able to tell her inner disquiet from the steadiness of her voice. 'Did you wish to talk with me or is it refreshment you seek on such a warm afternoon? You have strayed far from the village.'

He continued to gaze in silence for a moment and then seemed to relax slightly under the influence of her calm voice.

'Refreshment would be good,' he said, 'I hear the waters of your spring are sweeter than those from any other in the district.'

She bowed slightly. The water was good and fresh to drink at all times and on certain days of the year she knew it had healing properties. She herself drank from it daily and was never ill.

'If you will follow me I will show you where it is, my lord,' she said politely and led him to the spring. It was quite a way into the wood and she hated bringing him among her much loved trees. Somehow his presence felt wrong and she could sense the growing things resented it too. The spring from which a small and lively stream sprang started as a filagree fall of water over moss and stone in an alcove deep with fern. Even when she was not thirsty she spent many an hour in this shady place listening to the silver voice of the water over the rocks, and tracing with her eyes the satisfying and exquisite robes of moss and fern and lichen that clothed everything in the area.

In leading him to the water she was leading him away from the tomb they had built for Maal. It was finished and ready now and skilfully hidden, but Wardyke was no ordinary man and she did not want to risk his finding it. The spring would distract his attention and take him further away.

He stooped to drink at once, using the small hollowed stone

111

cup that had always been beside the spring since the days of her grandfather.

She stood very straight and stiff beside him as he drank, wondering if he was sensitive to the influences and vibrations that came from people and things. If he was, he must surely be aware that there was not a living thing around him that was not fearing and resenting him.

If he was aware he showed no sign.

When he had drunk, he smiled. His eyes stayed shadowy but the rest of his face smiled at her.

'What I have heard is truly an understatement. It is the sweetest water I have ever tasted.'

She bowed gravely again in acknowledgement, and then turned to lead the man away.

'No, stay,' he said, raising his hand. 'This is a most peaceful and delightful place. I would rest awhile here. The sun is hot on the long walk from the village.'

She stood still, her head slightly bowed for a moment, and then moved as though to leave him.

'No,' he said again, 'stay.'

She stopped, but did not look at him. Her whole being was crying out with dismay that this alien, malevolent creature was sharing her peaceful grove.

'Sharing? No,' she thought, 'he is here and I am here, but we are sharing nothing.'

In a sense, so different were the waves of feeling that came to each from the surroundings, they might well have been in totally different parts of the world. If each were to describe the place, an impartial judge might not recognize that it was the same scene being described.

'Are you not lonely, girl, living so far from the village?'

'No, my lord,' she said in a low voice, thinking of the time Karne had asked her the same thing.

'Do you have many visitors?'

'No, my lord,' she repeated.

'But you have one, many times,' he said slyly, pacing about on the soft mossy ground restlessly, looking at her closely.

'My lord?' She looked up enquiringly and with some alarm.

112

'I have been told that the old priest has been seen coming here often.'

So that was it! That was why he had come. She was even more afraid now and the fear from the living things around her seemed to increase as well.

'You do not answer? You know you cannot lie to me.'

'I did not know, my lord,' she said at last as calmly as she could, 'that there was any reason a priest could not visit one of his community.'

'Maal is no longer priest here,' Wardyke said with sudden harshness, standing still.

'But he has been our priest for many years. He helped my mother when I was born. Has he done something, my lord,' she asked with exaggerated innocence, 'that is against the laws of the gods and so is banished from our company?'

Wardyke drew in his breath sharply and resumed his pacing.

'He has no longer the role of a priest. He should not practise still as one.'

'He does not, my lord. He visits only as an old man, a friend.'

'What do you speak of when he visits?' His voice was sharp and he was standing before her in an attitude of interrogation.

'Why, many things.'

'What things?'

'Mostly about plants, my lord. My garden is well known in the village and my lord Maal is interested in the methods I use.'

Wardyke studied her face, but could not see further than the smooth sun-ripened skin, the long lashes and brown, deep eyes, flecked with yellow. He noticed that she was very beautiful, young and firm and lithe, standing like a young doe ready to take off at the slightest scent of danger.

The harshness of his expressions faded and he walked round her, studying her with a new expression she liked even less. It was as though he had entirely forgotten what they had been saying.

'My lord!' She spoke with alarm.

He smiled, but continued to circle her, looking at every part of her. In spite of her dress of soft brown bark cloth she felt naked. She drew herself back, muscles tense, ready to dart away as soon as she could seize an opportunity. She had seen this look in men's eyes from time to time, indeed had encouraged it in Karne's . . . but this time . . .? This time it was not welcome.

'How old are you, girl?' he asked, still prowling, still stalking his prey.

'Seventeen,' she replied but so low she had to repeat it as he thrust his face close to hers the better to hear what she said.

'Seventeen?' he said thoughtfully. 'Why is it you are not wed?'

'I have not wished to be, my lord.'

'Everyone should be wed, girl.'

She was silent, her heart beating very loud.

'Only priests should not be wed.'

'Why is that so, my lord?' Her voice was trembling slightly. She was not thinking of what she was saying. She was thinking only of how she could escape. She knew there was no one who could come to her rescue. The only possibility was that Karne might come visiting, but although she longed for this with the frightened part of her heart, she knew she would rather he did not. It would mean nothing but trouble for him and would probably mean they would never be able to be free of Wardyke. Maal would die and the Lords of the Sun would never know of their trouble.

'Priests must be free to serve the gods,' Wardyke murmured, but it was obvious he too was not thinking about what he was saying. 'Women are a distraction . . . they weaken one's resolution . . .'

'Then they are best left alone,' Fern said, summoning up the courage to speak loudly, hoping that the sound of her voice would snap the web that he was weaving around them. But it was too late. Her voice broke the web, but it was the web that was holding him back. He suddenly seized her, flung her on the ground and, roughly and with great harshness, forced himself upon her.

114

When he was done he looked so dishevelled, off guard and tired, that it was easy to forget he was a priest-magician.

She pulled herself away from him easily now and rose swiftly to her feet. Her eyes were blazing.

'Wardyke,' she said bitterly and there was no trace of fear in the way she said it, 'you will be cursed for this day's work. When you taste water it will be bitter. When you taste sleep it will be full of dread!'

She turned and walked away with great dignity.

If she had paused to look back at him she would have seen him still half lying, half crouching where she had left him, his face dark and twisted, his eyes like charcoal.

The Night of the Rising Star

Maal arranged with Kyra in the days that followed that they would make their bid to contact the Lords of the Sun on the Night of the Rising Star. He claimed that during this night the powers of the Circle were at their greatest. At the rising of the star called Magus from the sea horizon, directly over the Stone of the Star, their particular Circle was in closer contact than at any other time with the forces of the unseen world. At a certain point in the night when the whole star pattern had wheeled silently over their dark fields and hills to lie in a particular configuration, Maal would best be able to manipulate his powers in conjunction with the powers of the spirit world and travel greater distances and with greater surety than at any other time.

'Is it a better time than even the Night of the Full Moon?' Kyra asked with interest.

'It is better,' Maal said. 'Different forces are at work. Deeper forces, more secret and hidden. The Moon's influence is strong but it is more on the surface of things. Have you noticed how the sea answers to the Moon's call, the animals grow restless? Even people who are not particularly sensitive can feel the influence of the Moon.'

'But if this Night is so important,' Karne said, 'Wardyke himself will surely be in the Sacred Circle?'

'That is so,' Maal said calmly.

Kyra was surprised that he seemed to be showing so little concern for this problem.

'The whole village will be there for the ceremony of the Rising Star!' she cried.

'Not all night,' Maal said.

'But surely for the important time, the actual rising?'

116

'The rising of the Magus star is but a signal. In itself it is nothing. The priest will be alone when the moment of the right configuration comes,' Maal explained.

'But how are we going to manage if Wardyke is there?' pleaded Kyra, her forehead creased with worry.

Even Karne was beginning to feel the whole thing was impossible. But Maal was smiling a little secret smile.

'What is it,' Karne demanded, 'you are keeping something from us?'

'Yes, I am afraid so,' said Maal cheerfully.

'That is not fair!' cried Kyra indignantly.

Maal laughed and then, seeing that she was genuinely upset, and knowing that he indeed was being unfair, he added, '. . . but Wardyke has the wrong configuration.'

Kyra gasped.

'What do you mean?' Karne demanded.

'It is the duty of the departing priest,' Maal explained carefully, 'of every Sacred Circle to pass on the secret of the configuration of the Night of the Rising Star to his successor. It is a secret knowledge kept very close within the priesthood of a particular community, as it is the key to great powers and, in the wrong hands, the key to great dangers.'

'How do you mean?' Kyra said in alarm.

He put his hand soothingly on her arm.

'You know, my child, I have explained many times, nothing is good or evil in itself. It is the way it is used that makes it good or evil. Wardyke and I have great powers that we have worked long years to obtain. They are the same powers. It is to what use we put them that decides whether they are good or evil. It is in *us*, in the inner drive we call the *will*, in the key to action we call *motive*.

'The powers of the spirit world could be called upon and, if the motive and the will of he who calls is strong enough for evil, the spirit action will be evil.'

'You mean *you* could call up evil spirits to help you?' Kyra asked, not quite understanding. 'Even if you are good?'

'*I* am not Good, nor Evil. I am Maal.'

'But could you call up evil spirits?' Kyra insisted.

'It is not as simple as that. Spirits are not necessarily good or evil either!'

'It is so complicated,' complained Kyra.

'That is why the ordinary person is usually content to pursue his own life, accepting a few simple precepts to follow and leaving the complexities for the priest or the Elders to bother about.'

'I think that is wrong,' Karne said firmly.

Maal looked at him with interest.

'I think we should think about these things. There should not be one life for the priest and another for the ordinary person. I feel the urge to know as strongly as any priest. I want to understand! I want to make choices and know what the possibilities are! I want to know myself so that I do not deceive myself by thinking I am doing a good deed when the motive for doing it makes it bad. I want to be responsible for myself! Even if I make mistakes, I would rather do that than be a kind of straw doll played with by someone else . . . even if the someone else is a spirit!' he added defiantly, looking upwards at the bland blue sky.

Maal smiled and Kyra could see that he was pleased with what Karne said.

'I think,' she said, 'I agree, even though it seems so difficult at times. I would not like to go back to the time when I did not think about these things. It was so boring.'

'You will not go back,' Maal said to her, 'nor,' he added, turning to Karne, 'will you ever be the slightest bit like a straw doll!'

'If I were a priest,' Kyra said, her eyes blazing with inspiration, 'I would set about changing the old ways. Teach people the things you have been teaching us, let them expand and grow and flower!'

Maal smiled, partly in sympathy with her enthusiasm and agreement with her ideas, and partly also with amusement that she did not realize how difficult this would be to carry out. But he said nothing to discourage her. If what she spoke of could be brought about, it would be a great achievement.

'And what,' he asked gently, 'would you teach them about

118

good and evil?'

'I would teach them . . .' she started, and then hesitated.

'Why do you hesitate?'

'I do not know if I want to "teach",' she said, frowning, 'it sounds a bit like the old ways where people were told what to think.'

'If by "teaching" you mean "telling" then you are right not to teach,' Maal agreed.

'I want them to think for themselves. Perhaps I should guide them a bit at first . . . point out things for them to watch out for . . . things I had noticed when I was struggling at first . . .'

'What would be the first thing that you would want to point out?'

'That everything is not always as it seems when you first look at it. That everything that happens has its roots in something else and the unseen roots are usually more important than that which you can actually see.'

Karne and Kyra were thoughtful for a while.

'It is not easy to understand things . . .' Kyra said at last.

'It is not only the understanding that I find so difficult,' Karne said ruefully, 'it is the explaining.'

Maal smiled.

'As long as you try to understand,' he said, 'try to explain, even if it is only to yourself. Always keep your mind open and ready for exploration, ready to consider any new ideas, any new explanations. The very act of trying helps you to grow. You will surprise yourself one day with how much your understanding has grown while you had thought you were making no progress.'

At this point they had to break off as they heard someone coming. As Karne and Kyra slipped away. Kyra said, 'He never did tell us what he meant by Wardyke having the wrong configuration.'

'It is obvious,' Karne said impatiently. 'It was his duty to pass on the configuration to Wardyke and because he had his suspicions that Wardyke was not our rightful priest he took the precaution of giving him a false one, still keeping the real one a secret.'

'So when our real priest comes . . . after we have consulted with the Lords of the Sun . . . he will be given the real one and then Maal can concentrate on dying.'

'And this will mean that Wardyke will be in the Circle on the Night of the Rising Star but will have left it when the time comes for the real configuration of power. You and Maal can then slip in and . . .'

'Oh no!' Kyra stopped short and her voice was indignant. 'Not *in*! You *promised* I would not have to go in the Circle . . .'

'A slip of the tongue, little sister,' laughed Karne. 'I meant, of course, Maal could slip into the Circle with your help.'

'From outside,' she insisted.

'From outside,' he agreed.

Fern had not been with them during this discussion so at the first opportunity Karne went to visit her. Some days had passed since he had seen her last and, impatient to make up for this, he ran most of the way to her house. He slowed down just before he reached the curve in the path from which her garden suddenly became visible, and because of this he came upon her quite silently as she was stooping over a flower. He stopped and watched her for a moment, thinking how graceful she looked, feeling a sort of warm glow of pleasure welling up from inside himself as though the sunshine was coming from within his very inmost being this lovely golden day.

But the peacefulness of the scene did not last for long. Fern must have sensed his presence because she suddenly straightened up and spun round, her face momentarily quite distorted with fear and dislike. He was startled. He had never seen such emotions on Fern's face before. She had always seemed so calm and poised on an inner centre of happiness.

'Fern!' he gasped, 'What is the matter?'

As she recognized him she instantly turned her face away, her expression no longer the same, but still compounded of something Karne did not understand. She usually lit up with

120

pleasure when she saw him. What had gone wrong?

'Fern?'

She turned back to him now, and this time she was composed.

'Why, Karne,' she said, 'I am sorry. You startled me.'

He was still puzzled. He had never known her to be startled like this before.

'What is it?'

'Nothing.'

He was close to her and trying to look into her eyes, but hers would not meet his. For the first time since he had known her there was the shadow of something held back between them.

'There *is* something.'

'No.'

He took her hands, but she still would not meet his eyes.

She tried to smile at him, to reassure him, but her smile was not very convincing. She pulled her hands away and drew back.

'Come, Karne,' she said brightly, 'I want to show you something.'

'You do not look well,' he still persisted while he was following her down the little winding path that ran deeper into her garden, brushing aside trailing fronds of bracken as he walked. He had noticed that she was paler than usual, the healthy bloom of her cheek considerably reduced. There was also something about the garden, he could not make up his mind what it was but it somehow did not look as flourishing and vigorous as it normally did.

She noticed the frown in his blue eyes and took his arm. Her composure had returned. She smiled and kissed him lightly on his brown cheek and ran her fingers through his long, light hair.

'Come on,' she said laughing, 'are you going to be as gloomy as this all morning?'

He looked at her bright face and there were no longer shadows there. He began to feel he had imagined what he had seen a few moments before. He shrugged and smiled.

'That is better,' she said, 'and now I can show you something special.'

121

She drew him to a place where that morning she had found a new flower growing, one she had never seen before. A tiny, spiky, defiant one, half hidden in the grass, but growing as though it meant to stay. She cupped her hands around it and their heads were very close together as they admired it.

'It looks as though it was trying to be a star,' she laughed, 'but it was too small so it had to settle for being a flower instead.'

'I wonder where it came from?'

She shrugged and indicated the arching sky.

'The birds sometimes bring me presents. They fly to lands of which not even Maal has heard.'

Karne laughed.

'That is hard to imagine. Maal has heard of everything.'

'Not everything,' she said suddenly, sadly, and again he fancied that he saw the shadow of secretiveness cross her face.

'In fact, I have brought a message from Maal,' he said, and stood up.

She joined him and they walked awhile in the garden, Karne telling her about the night of the Rising Star and the timing of the attempt to reach the Lords of the Sun. She was greatly interested and added up in her mind the number of days left. Not many. She was glad.

As they walked she was tempted several times to tell Karne about Wardyke but she knew that if she did the boy would go crazy with rage and probably rush off to attack the man. Karne would not stand a chance against the giant magician, and she could not bear him to be hurt or killed.

None of them knew quite what to expect from the Lords of the Sun, but Karne, Kyra and Fern certainly expected the situation to be resolved immediately. If pressed, they might have admitted to expecting a sudden thunderbolt to remove Wardyke dramatically from office.

Maal knew it would not be quite like that, but he said nothing of what he expected.

During the next few days Kyra spent a great deal of time with

Maal, learning everything she could, and so it was that neither of them noticed the many changes that were taking place in their community.

Wardyke had doubled the workers on Maal's tomb and it was very near completion. There was talk that the building of it was to be finished by the Night of the Rising Star and that it would be during that night, or very near to it, that Maal would be interred. Maal was not informed of this and was surprised when Karne, out of breath from running, told him of it.

Kyra was horrified.

'But how will we contact the Lords of the Sun if Maal is not with us?'

Maal looked grave and shook his head.

'Surely Wardyke has no right to set a time for your death?' Karne asked.

'No right at all,' Maal said sadly and was silent, thinking hard.

At last he spoke.

'Was this an official announcement at the Meeting Stone?' he asked Karne.

'Oh no,' Karne said, 'it was just talk, just rumour. It may not happen at all, but I thought you ought to know that people were talking about it.'

'What people?'

'Mostly Wardyke's Strangers. They have been working on the tomb with me and they are full of confidence that they know what is in his mind. There is something about a prophetic dream of Thorn's too.'

'If it is only rumour I do not think we should concern ourselves too much.'

'Maybe not . . .' Karne sounded doubtful, 'but when I hear them talk like that it makes me angry!'

Maal smiled at last, the gravity lifting like a cloud from his kind face.

'You must learn to control that anger, lad, it will be the undoing of us yet!'

'Everything grows worse and worse . . . and I am doing nothing,' Karne protested. 'You and Kyra work every day, but all I do is wait! Even Fern,' he grumbled, 'seems to have secrets these days!'

Maal looked surprised. He had been so busy with Kyra he had not seen Fern for quite a time.

'What secrets?'

'How would I know,' Karne replied irritably, shrugging his shoulders. '*I* cannot see into people's minds!'

Maal was thoughtful.

'I have neglected her,' he said regretfully. There was so little time and so much to be done.

Kyra was about to say something, but Maal raised his hand to keep her quiet. There was much he needed to think about. His expression became more and more withdrawn.

'Come,' Kyra whispered to Karne, and took his hand. Quietly they started to move away.

When they were out of earshot, Kyra said, 'I thought we ought to leave him. He looked as though he wanted to think things through by himself.'

Karne nodded. He had sensed it too.

'Perhaps you could go and see Fern,' he said. 'You and Maal have been so busy in that house of his . . .' His voice almost carried a touch of resentment.

'I know,' Kyra said, 'but you have no idea how complicated everything is and how delicate the balance is between success and failure. Sometimes,' she added miserably, 'I get so desperate. I cannot believe I will do everything right, and if I do the slightest thing wrong we are finished!' She gave a deep sigh. 'And now . . . what will happen if Wardyke puts Maal away before we can reach the Lords of the Sun?'

Karne shook his head, momentarily as despairing as Kyra. And then he pulled himself together.

'Somehow,' he said, 'we have to prevent that.'

'But how?'

Karne shook his head.

'Somehow,' he repeated, frowning with determination.

The following day Kyra slipped away to see Fern before she

124

went to Maal.

She found her sitting by the spring, her knees drawn up and her head resting upon them, her whole posture one of despondency.

'Fern,' cried Kyra with concern and knelt down beside her, her arm around her shoulders.

'Oh, Kyra,' Fern said with relief and turned to bury her head upon her friend's shoulder.

'You are crying?' Kyra was amazed, feeling the warmth of the tears. Fern, who was always so calm and strong, was crying!

She did not ask what the matter was but held her and rocked slightly backwards and forwards as a mother does with a weeping child. Her cheek was upon Fern's bright hair and occasionally she kissed the top of her head.

Gradually as they sat together Kyra began to feel that strange feeling of knowing something she had no ordinary way of knowing.

'It is Wardyke!' she said suddenly with conviction. 'Wardyke has been here?'

Fern nodded miserably.

The two girls were silent, sitting side by side. Kyra's arms had fallen from Fern's shoulders and they both gazed into the moving water of the busy little spring.

Kyra did not put it into words, but she knew exactly what had happened to Fern. She was surprised how calmly she was reacting. Although the knowledge had startled her at first, it seemed that almost immediately she had accepted it as something that had happened and in no way could be changed. There was no point in being shocked or moaning about it in any way. The situation existed and they must somehow cope with it.

'I have not told Karne,' Fern said quietly. She was calm now too.

'I think you were right,' Kyra agreed. Karne's reaction would have been violent and angry. She remembered Maal suggesting that it was just this quality in Karne that would be their undoing.

'He suspects something is wrong.'

125

'I know,' said Fern miserably. 'I hate keeping anything from him, but this . . .'

'Yes, this . . . must be kept. At least till we have reached safety on the other side of the Night of the Rising Star.'

Fern nodded sadly.

After a while the two girls parted, Fern to work on her garden with greater composure now that she had shared her burden, and Kyra to visit Maal. She felt as though she had imperceptibly aged since the day before. Some days were like that. One seemed to take a leap into further knowledge and understanding as though a lot more time had passed than could be measured by the passage of the sun across the sky.

In fact in this summer as a whole time seemed to have speeded up. She looked back on the long slow days of quiet routine she used to have with nostalgia. Everything had been so much easier then!

Maal had obviously been thinking a great deal about the problems facing them since they last met, and seemed to have worked out certain things in his mind. He seemed less disturbed.

He listened to Kyra's news about Fern quietly, his only reaction being a deepening line between his brows and a conviction that what he had decided to do was right.

'I am going to break a very ancient and very strict law,' he said to Kyra, his face grave and tired.

Kyra looked alarmed.

'Is that wise?' she asked.

'I have no choice,' he said heavily.

'I thought you said we always had choice?'

'I did,' he said wearily, 'and in a sense now, literally, of course I have choice. What I mean is . . . I have chosen this way because I think it is the only way in which we can be sure to stop Wardyke in the time we have available.'

He paused.

'What is it? What law are you going to break?'

'The law that says the departing priest should tell no one the sacred configuration of Stars but the priest who takes his place.'

'Who are you going to tell?' Kyra was intrigued.

'You,' he said simply.

Kyra gasped.

'No!'

'You need to know,' he said quietly and gently now, knowing that she would need persuasion.

'You mean? . . .'

'I mean that if anything happens to me . . .'

'But I cannot . . .' Her face was a study in alarm and dismay.

'You can,' he said firmly.

'But . . .'

'Listen my child . . . listen to me . . .' He put his hand upon her arm. She was beginning to protest again, but was silenced by the soothing power of his touch. When he could see that she was calmer and prepared to listen he began to speak again.

'You mention choice. I have said we always have choice. Our ability to choose, to make decisions, is crucial to our development in all the different levels of existence through which we are journeying. When we reach the Source of Light and Consciousness, we will no longer see bits and pieces among which we have to choose, but will see the Whole as a magnificent pattern in which everything fits together in harmony. We will see it and we will Be it simultaneously. The agony of choice will at last be over.'

Kyra sighed. It was a grand idea, but she was a long, long way from that kind of realization at this moment.

'I know . . .' he said softly, sympathetically, and sat quietly a few moments for her to absorb what he had said.

'But these choices we have to make,' he continued at last, 'are not always made with the surface and most obvious level of our Selves. The Kyra whom the villagers can see when she walks among them wants to make one decision, one choice, but the Kyra whom they cannot see, the one that is in touch with the deeper levels of Reality, knows the decision has to fall another way.'

127

She knew he was right, but she tried still to fight against it.

'But I know on every possible level I cannot do what you ask of me!'

'That is not true,' he said simply, and she was silent.

'If it were true,' he continued, trying to give her more help, 'you would not come to me for lessons . . . you would not ask the questions you have been asking, develop the powers you have been developing. Over this summer you have been gradually getting ready for this moment . . . I had hoped you would have had longer . . . but no moment ever seems perfect to us . . . we can see so little of the Whole.'

'But what if I am not ready . . .?'

'We will not know that until you have tried . . . but I would say the moment of crisis will make you ready.'

Kyra buried her face in her hands. It seemed to her that inside her head was a great space full of darkness that was whirling and roaring.

'I cannot . . .' she cried, turning her head from side to side as though she was trying to escape some physical attack.

Maal put both hands upon her head.

'You can,' he said. 'You must!'

He held her head still, putting more and more pressure upon it until she cried out in pain. Then he withdrew his hands and they sat together in silence for a while.

Kyra at last lifted her face and it was pale and drawn, but resigned.

'What must I do?' she said quietly.

Maal moved away from her and fetched something from a shelf in one of the darkest places in his house. She watched him with interest as he returned to her holding something carefully in both hands. He motioned her to sit relaxed and he sat opposite her, putting what he carried between them. It was a small parcel wrapped in bark cloth. She looked at it with curiosity and stretched out a hand to take it.

'No,' Maal said, putting his own hand over it to protect it from her. 'Do not touch.'

She could sense that a change had come over him. He was no longer the friendly, fatherly figure with whom she could talk so easily. He had become Lord Maal, the priest, and sat straight and tall, his face masked so that she could not read his eyes.

She was a little afraid and sat straight herself, feeling the solemnity of the moment most intensely.

When he saw that she had grasped the situation, he began to unwrap the parcel very carefully, using ritualistic movements, his lips murmuring something inaudible to her as he proceeded. Her heart began to beat faster and as he reached the last layer of bark cloth she was leaning forward breathlessly to see what lay between them.

It was a sphere of yellowish-grey stone, small but exquisitely carved, the patterning following the curvature of the surface in intricate spirals.

She stared at it fascinated.

Maal folded his hands. She noticed he had touched only the wrappings, the sphere itself he left strictly alone.

She looked up at him, her eyes questioning but not daring to say anything to break the impressive silence surrounding the stone sphere.

'Move your head from side to side,' Maal said, speaking his priest's voice, 'but keep your eyes on the sphere.'

Kyra was puzzled but did as she was told. As she moved the light that fell on the stone from the doorway struck it from different angles. With sudden splendour the sphere seemed to send up shafts of green-blue light. Kyra gasped and retreated.

The stone lay still and dark again.

Maal drew her forward with a gesture and again as she moved the stone seemed to come alive with an inner luminosity. Each surface that had been carved reflected light in a different way. Reflected? No. Kyra was sure the light came from within the stone.

'How can that be?' she whispered to herself.

'Take the sphere,' Maal said in a deep, quiet voice. 'Hold it between your hands.'

She hesitated.

'Hold it,' he commanded.

Tentatively and hesitatingly she put her two trembling hands forward and cupped them around the magical stone. The light within it seemed to go out and it felt like ordinary cold stone.

'Close your eyes.' Maal spoke still with firm authority.

She closed her eyes.

'Feel the pattern of the stone with your fingers.'

Delicately she moved her finger tips over the cold surface. She felt the pattern.

'No. Do not open your eyes.'

She was in a very dark darkness. It seemed darker within her head than it normally did when she closed her eyes. No images whatever came to her, not even those peculiar little wisps of shape that usually seemed to float upon the inside of her eyelids.

She could feel the icy ball of stone within the cup of her hands. Her fingers began to trace the spiral round and round the surface.

It seemed to have no end. Her finger tracing . . . the groove . . . the spiral . . . the sphere.

The spiral never left the sphere and yet never ended . . . as though the sphere and the spiral were eternal . . . She began to drift . . . to feel only the spiral groove going round and round the sphere until at last she lost consciousness of even her own finger in contact with it and was aware only of herself the spiral . . . herself the spiral . . .

In this state she was no longer aware of the darkness as darkness, but as the night sky, immensely vast and filled with countless stars. When she had looked at the sky at night on other occasions she had seen the myriad sparks of light dotted about apparently at random. Now she was aware of it as an intricate but definite pattern.

She *saw* it as a pattern, each star linked with each other star in a relationship that was unmistakable. It was as though fine gold lines, as fine as spider's web, were drawn between each spot of light to make an exquisite network, complex and yet ultimately simple.

But even as she grasped this the vision was altering slightly.

130

The web was not flat but had depth as well. The stars she had thought were all the same distance from her appeared now to vary, some nearer, some further away. The golden threads linked them not only sideways, but backwards and forwards as well.

She felt herself moving nearer to them, somehow being among them so that the network of fine gold lines was around her in every direction . . . stars were around her in every direction.

As the sensation of movement grew she realized that it was not only herself that was moving. The stars, the golden lines, the darkness itself . . . everything was moving and everything was changing in relationship to everything else in subtle ways at every moment, and yet the overall web of relationship was still there . . . the threads never broke . . . only adjusted, stretched and altered.

And still as she moved the vision developed further.

It seemed to her the points of light that were the stars were not only moving, but were growing. Or was it that she was approaching them?

They were no longer points of shapeless fire, but huge spheres rolling through the darkness, immense balls of concentrated power.

As they rolled the sound of them roared in her head until sound and vision so overwhelmed her that she found herself screaming, a small insignificant creature, back on Maal's floor, trying to hold the full fearful magnificence of the Universe at bay.

She dropped the small sphere of stone and saw Maal move swiftly to catch it.

She flung herself down and beat her fists upon the hard floor.

'It is too much!' she cried despairingly. 'I cannot bear it alone!'

Maal had quietly and quickly wrapped the small sphere in its coverings of bark cloth and had put it safely aside. He could now turn his attention to the hysterical girl.

'You will not be alone,' he said, 'Kyra! Kyra! No one is alone.'

She sobbed.

'Was it not beautiful?' he said quietly when he could see that she had cried enough.

She nodded miserably.

'Are you not excited to be part of such a beauty?'

Tearfully she nodded again.

'Well then, accept it. Enjoy it.'

She sat and thought about what she had just seen. Already the splendour was passed and she only had a shadowy memory of the experience, but even that was more beautiful and exciting than anything she had ever known before.

Enjoy it? Why not? She could no longer fight against it. As Maal had said, deep inside her the forces that were at work in her had already made a choice. She was only hurting herself by fighting against them all the time.

He saw the change in her and was glad.

'You may tell me the configuration now,' she said calmly. 'I am ready.'

He smiled gently. The priest was gone. The man was back.

'You know it already,' he said smiling at her.

She looked surprised, a line forming between her eyes.

'Was I supposed to get it from . . . ?' and she pointed at the stone sphere.

'You did,' he said simply.

She shook her head slowly, trying to remember.

'I think I did not.'

'Do not worry about it,' Maal said, 'you know it at the level that matters.'

'But I can hardly remember . . . I remember a pattern . . . but I cannot remember exactly . . .'

'It will come to you when you need it,' Maal said confidently.

She looked doubtful, but if he said so, perhaps it would be so.

'Promise me,' he said seriously, 'if it becomes impossible for me to go into the Circle on the night of the Rising Star, you will.'

She sat very still, her heart beating painfully. How could she promise that!

132

'Promise!' he repeated, and he spoke with urgency and authority.

'I promise,' she found herself saying in a very small, thin voice.

'Louder!' he commanded.

'I promise,' she said, this time with a conviction that amazed her.

He relaxed.

'Good,' he said, 'now we can begin the lesson.'

The Burials and the Promise

It was three days later that Karne and Kyra woke to a feeling of oppressive malevolence in the air. The sky was obscured by heavy cloud which hung, grey and discouraging, neither falling as rain nor blowing away. Kyra particularly felt uneasy. She wondered what would happen if the sky was cloudy for the Night of the Rising Star. What use would knowing or not knowing the correct configuration be if none of them could even see the stars? It crossed her mind that perhaps there would be ways of sensing it that she did not yet know about, but this line of thought was cut short by her brother Ji tugging at her arm and wanting her to follow him.

'What is it?' she said impatiently and irritably.

'We have finished the boat,' Ji said excitedly. 'Come and see!'

'Not now, Ji,' she said, 'I am busy.'

'You do not look busy,' he said, disappointed.

'One does not necessarily have to *look* busy to *be* busy,' she said grandly, and turned away. He stood contemplating her back forlornly.

'You never pay any attention to the family these days, Kyra,' her mother said, witnessing the incident. 'What is the matter?'

'Nothing.' She wished they would leave her alone. She had things on her mind.

'I think there is something the matter,' her mother persisted.

But luckily for Kyra Karne arrived at this moment and Ji pounced on him. Their noisy exchange of friendly blows diverted their mother's attention from Kyra and she could slip away.

She was sorry she had been so short tempered with Ji and when he appeared again, somewhat dishevelled from the roll about with Karne, she asked to see the boat. Joyfully he led her to the secret place they knew so well, pulled back the cover of leaves and sticks, and revealed a tidy, well-constructed little boat, that looked as though it could withstand the onslaught of the waves quite well.

'It is good!' she cried in surprise. 'I did not know that you and Okan were so skilful!'

'I did most of the work,' Ji said proudly.

She ruffled his hair and laughed.

'You had better not let Okan hear you say that.'

'I want to be a fisherman,' Ji said, 'we are going to try it out quite soon, will you come?'

'Oh, well . . .' she hesitated. 'I do not think I have time, but I am sure Karne . . .'

'Karne is always too busy these days,' Ji said sadly.

'I am sure Karne will . . . even if he is busy. After all, it is his boat.'

'Will you ask him?'

'Ask him yourself.'

'He always listens to you.'

Kyra laughed.

'Not always.'

'He does not seem to care about the boat now.'

'Of course he does! It is just that he has other things he has to do now.'

'What things?'

'Just . . . things.'

'You and Karne are always going off by yourselves. He never takes us anywhere any more.' Ji's voice sounded quite miserable.

Kyra put her arm around him, full of sympathy.

'Oh Ji,' she said, 'I am sorry.'

She left Ji lovingly covering up his prized possession, and went in search of Karne.

She found him looking for her. His face was worried and

135

gloomy.

'What is wrong?'

'I do not know,' but he looked very anxious. 'There is something about to happen. I can feel it. Maal's tomb was finished yesterday and all the Strangers are talking as though the burial is to be soon. I saw Wardyke going to Maal's house a little while ago. I have been looking for you everywhere! Where have you been?'

'I have been to see the boat. It is finished,' Kyra said.

Normally Karne would have been interested in this piece of news, but today he was preoccupied.

'You must come with me,' he said, turning towards Maal's house. 'We must see what is going on.'

'But,' said Kyra, 'it is important Wardyke does not notice our interest in Maal!'

'I know. That is why I want you to come. We will hide somewhere nearby and perhaps you can listen in to their minds or something.'

'I cannot do it just like that!' complained Kyra.

'Oh,' he said impatiently, 'there is no time to fuss about what you can do and what you cannot. Just *do* it!'

She started a resentful reply and then thought better of it. It was important that she did what she could to protect Maal, more important than whether she was irritated with Karne's attitude or not.

She followed him and they tucked themselves behind some bushes.

'Is Wardyke still inside?' she whispered.

He shrugged and shook his head.

'I have been away looking for you for ages. Can you not tell if he is inside or not?'

She stayed very still and concentrated, but nothing would come to her. She was still aware of the pricking of the grass against her leg, the sound of Karne breathing and moving from time to time beside her. She was still aware of herself crouching uncomfortably behind the bushes trying to get in touch with Maal. If she had learnt nothing else that summer she had learnt that her powers could not work until she had completely forgotten herself and somehow merged absolutely with something or someone else.

'It is no good,' she whispered at last. 'I am trying too hard. It will not come.'

Karne gave an expression of disgust.

'I cannot help it,' she complained bitterly.

'Try!'

'I *am* trying! That is the trouble. I need more time to relax first.'

'We have no time!'

'I know! I know.'

She looked ready to cry.

'Oh no!' he muttered, thumping his forehead with the palm of his hand in frustration.

At that moment a sound from the village called their attention away from themselves and Maal's house. It was the sound of the horn that was blown when a special meeting or ceremony was to take place. The sound of its weird hollow call went out across the valleys and the hills, disturbing even the animals in the forests and putting a flock of jet black birds to flight from the grain fields. They wheeled above the village, their wings adding a strange resonance to the sound of the horn, their dark, shadowy bodies in flight adding a touch of the ominous to the already oppressive air.

Some of the villagers had started wending their way to the Meeting Stone, while others were preparing to leave their fields and their work.

Karne and Kyra were in a quandary.

'What shall we do?' Kyra asked anxiously.

Karne hesitated.

'I think we ought to see if Maal is all right before we go,' he said at last.

'Wardyke will be at the Meeting Stone. He has forbidden us to have a meeting without his presence. But I wish we knew if he was there already.'

'There is nothing else to be done,' said Karne, with sudden determination. 'I will have to go to Maal's house.'

'Why you? Perhaps I should go,' Kyra said.

'No. You are the only one who can work with Maal to contact the Lords of the Sun. It is even more important that you escape suspicion than that I do.'

This was true. She nodded, but she wished that neither of them had to go.

'Wait here and keep watch for me,' Karne whispered and before Kyra could say anything more he was gone. He walked swiftly and boldly up to Maal's house as though it was the most natural thing in the world for him to be doing.

Kyra saw him pause at the door to call out and then she saw him go inside. She did not have long to wait before he came running out. He seemed shocked and distressed and came leaping over the uneven ground almost as though he were flying. He flung himself down beside her, out of breath.

'What is it?'

'Maal is gone,' he gasped, 'and all his things are smashed about and strewn everywhere. It looks as though there has been a struggle in there. It also looks as though whoever did it was looking for something among Maal's possessions.'

'O Karne!' She was horrified. 'That poor old man!'

Shock on Karne's face was giving way to anger. He stood up and his face was black with rage.

'Karne!' she cried. She leapt up and seized his arm. 'We must not do anything wrong now.'

'I will tell you what I will do to Wardyke!' he snarled, shaking himself free.

'You must not, Karne! We dare not! We have a real responsibility now and Maal is relying on us.'

Karne stood still, his face still thunderous.

'Karne!' she pleaded.

He looked at her with smouldering frustration.

'All right,' he said. 'I will hold back for now . . . but just wait . . .'

She had realized very quickly that for once she had to be in charge of the situation. An image of Maal's special stone sphere came most clearly and insistently to her. She knew he would not want that to be in the hands of Wardyke. Perhaps that was what he had been looking for.

138

She thought swiftly.

'You go to the Meeting, Karne,' she said decisively, 'keep control of yourself and do nothing to arouse suspicion. It is very important. Promise.'

'I promise,' he said unwillingly.

'See what is happening. I will go to Maal's house to see if I can rescue any of his most precious possessions. I will take them to Fern for safe keeping. She can bury them in the wood somewhere until we can give them back to Maal.'

She was not prepared to admit even to herself that she might not see Maal alive again.

Karne nodded affirmation and was off to the village immediately.

No one saw Kyra slip into the old priest's house and she was not disturbed in her search. Karne was right. The place was a mess. His handsome drinking vessels and water jars were smashed to pieces on the floor. What clothes and rugs he had were ripped and flung around. The collection of delicate sea urchin shells he kept in orderly rows ranging from the smallest to the largest were powdered on the shelf on which they had stood as though a hard fist had smashed down upon them.

Her heart beating loudly, she felt in the dark corner from where she had seen Maal take the stone sphere and, miraculously, it was still there. She held it close to her heart in its bark wrappings, thankful she could rescue at least one of Maal's precious possessions.

She looked around, tears beginning to come to her eyes at the devastation of the room in which she had spent so many interesting hours. She would have stood there indefinitely if she had not suddenly 'felt' the approach of someone.

She rushed to the door and looked out. Thorn was approaching. She had not heard him for he was too far away. She had 'felt' his approach.

A lump of fear began to rise in her throat. She stood poised, uncertain what to do. Thorn was approaching rapidly, a burning branch in his hand. She looked round frantically for somewhere to hide, but the burning branch suggested he might be intending to burn the house and if she were inside she would certainly be burnt with it. She had seen this kind of house burn before. Wood and straw, twigs and furs, turn to flame fast.

Another thought came to her distraught mind. If he was burning the house, Maal must be dead!

Before the full implications of this could take effect, however, she saw Thorn pause on the path and turn to look back at the village. He was straining his neck to see the Meeting Stone as though he were looking for a signal.

Like a shadow Kyra slipped out of the house and ran for cover, clutching the small stone sphere close to her, some of the bark cloth wrappings working loose as she ran. Her fear sharpened her instincts and she found a route to Fern's house that was quicker and safer than any that she had ever taken before.

Meanwhile, at the Meeting Stone, nearly all the community were gathered. Karne was hovering on the outskirts, occasionally looking anxiously in the direction of Maal's house. Strangely the Elders were not on the platform in their usual formation but scattered amongst the villagers looking as puzzled and as ill at ease as their fellow men. Only Wardyke was on the platform and he was in his most magnificent cloak with a tall headdress of hard dark leather and tall black feathers to add even greater height to his stature. He was standing still as rock with his arms folded on his chest, only his smouldering eyes moving continually, scanning the faces of the cowed people below him.

Karne had the presence of mind to slip behind a taller man so that he would not be subjected to the deadly scrutiny. He knew Wardyke would not miss the hostility in his own eyes if he were to look into them. The others were trying to avoid his eyes as well, but somehow the beam of his attention forced their eyes up to meet his no matter how hard they tried to avoid it.

If he saw the slightest flicker of anything but fear and awe in their expression, he concentrated longer upon them until at last they were forced to surrender their independence and cringe like the rest. Karne escaped only because he was aware in time of what was going on and kept well out of sight.

When everyone was gathered Wardyke lifted his left arm to point at the grey and lowering sky above Maal's house. It must have been a signal because almost immediately a low and sombre drumming started, and a column of smoke rose from the direction of the old priest's house. The villagers gasped, but had no time to talk to their neighbours about what was happening. The drumming was growing louder and as all heads turned from the smoke to the direction of the sound, six men, Wardyke's men, were seen approaching carrying a bier of branches on which the body of their old priest was lying.

A murmur of dismay started, but swiftly ceased as Wardyke's burning eye fell upon them. Behind them walked six drummers. Again, Wardyke's men.

Karne could have burst with the feelings that were racing through him, but he managed to keep control of himself. He had no doubt Wardyke had killed Maal and with the one act had frustrated their chances of reaching the Lords of the Sun and so rescuing the hapless villagers from his clutches, and at the same time frustrated Maal in his plan to influence his passage at the moment of death. All that they had been working for during the past few months was now wiped out. He thought of the sweat and the backache moving all those rocks, digging that tunnel. He thought of Kyra's troubles, trying to link her mind with Maal's.

It was strange she had felt nothing when Maal was killed. He had called to her when he was in trouble before. Why not this time?

The bier came nearer and nearer. The drumming grew louder and louder until he could feel the vibrations of it coming as it were from the thump, thump, thump of his own heart.

Maal was carried amongst the crowd of villagers, who drew back in respect as he passed. Karne could see him quite clearly for a few moments. His face was composed and white. The face of death. His body lying straight, hands folded on his breast. There was nothing to show that he had died violently.

For a moment a thought went spinning through Karne's heart. What if Maal was not dead after all? What if he had managed to cheat and was doing what priests were quite capable of doing, feigning death?

With the coming of this thought everything became possible again. They would keep to the original plan! If Maal was truly dead it would not hurt to move him. If he was not, his passage through the many different planes of spirit could be made easier.

But against this hope he thought of the signs of violence he had seen in Maal's house and he knew that if Maal was to feign death he would have needed a long time to compose himself. It could not be done under conditions of harassment and stress.

Karne wondered about Kyra. There was no doubt that Maal's house was being burnt to the ground. Thorn must have set the torch because Thorn joined the Meeting from the direction of Maal's house almost immediately after they had seen the smoke. He hoped Kyra was safely away with Fern. How he longed to be with them, but he dare not leave. He was in danger both of missing something that they needed to know, and of drawing attention to himself.

After the bier had been carried right round the community it was lifted on to the platform to lie at Wardyke's feet. Thorn made a move to step up and join him but, surprisingly, Wardyke gestured him down. Karne saw the look of puzzled fear that suddenly passed through Thorn's eyes. Karne felt a sense of satisfaction at that. It looked as though Wardyke had used Thorn to come to full power, but now no longer needed him.

Seven men from Wardyke's old community stepped up at this point and took their places behind Wardyke in the positions of the Sacred Stones, in the positions of the Elders of the Village.

A gasp went round the confused villagers and a few men

stepped forward as though they were going to protest, but immediately there was a move from behind them and they realized they were entirely ringed by Wardyke's people, armed with axes and spears.

Without their realizing it the friendly, peaceful villagers had been taken over completely by a hostile group.

The rest of the Meeting passed like a nightmare. Wardyke spoke the words of burial over Maal and the villagers listened to the age-old terms of respect and comfort, realizing for the first time that they meant nothing in themselves. Only the feeling that was in the heart of he who spoke to them meant anything. And in Wardyke's heart was malevolence and greed.

After the words of burial he made a brief announcement that he had appointed seven new Elders for the Community, silenced any protest with a look of such ferocity that no one even dared to think dissent, and then gestured for the funeral procession to lead off to Maal's tomb.

The six men carrying the bier went first. The drummers next. The villagers followed them in a straggling untidy line and Wardyke's Strangers came behind as though to make sure no one strayed.

Wardyke himself came last of all and they had to wait for him at the tomb, listening to the sullen and disturbing pulse of the drums and their own thoughts struggling to find a way out of the situation.

Karne could see Maal from where he stood and he had to admit to himself that he looked very dead. His thoughts went round and round, trying to decide whether to risk transferring Maal's body to the other tomb and wondering if Wardyke would post a guard overnight. It was fortunate that they were having the burial ceremony so late in the afternoon for there would not be time to cover the burial chamber properly and complete the mound. The rest of the work would probably be done over the next few days, the whole community working in shifts.

There were no prayers said aloud while the villagers waited for Wardyke, only the insistent low throb of the drum, but Karne for one (and he did not think he was alone), was praying

143

privately and silently. He had never wanted anything as much in his life as he wanted Maal to be alive at this moment. There were many of the villagers, even among those who had welcomed Wardyke and slighted Maal, who were now praying for Maal's spirit, for his help in the dark days to come.

Just before Wardyke's arrival Fern and Kyra joined the crowd unnoticed. Karne's first knowledge of their presence was when he felt a touch on his arm and Kyra's hand slipped into his. She stood close to him, her eyes dark with sorrow, seeking comfort in him. He kissed her forehead, thankful that she had come to no harm in the fire. On his other side he felt another touch. He looked around and Fern was beside him, her bare arm against his. His whole body responded to it in spite of his sorrow. Her face was as grave and as pale as Kyra's.

They had found a hiding place for the stone sphere and had hurried back to the village in time to see the funeral procession winding along the path to the tomb Wardyke had chosen for Maal. They had paused to weep and to compose themselves. Now they were with Karne and the combined strength of their love for Maal and for each other was helping to sustain them.

Wardyke's arrival was announced with an impressive roll on the drums. The day, which had been dark from dawn, was growing darker every moment. The magician strode between the silent rows of mourners and took his place at the entrance to the tomb, facing the crowd, the dark cavity they had dug for Maal behind him so that he seemed to have two cloaks, one of black fur and one of icy shadow.

A chill passed through the watching villagers. Kyra could feel it creeping along her flesh and she shuddered slightly, pressing closer to her brother. He put his right arm around her and made to put his left around Fern, but she had withdrawn from him since Wardyke's arrival and was standing stiffly away from him. She shook her head sharply at his overture and insisted on standing clear. He looked at her closely, hurt and puzzled. Every muscle in her body was tense and taut. Kyra could see at once what was happening and drew Karne's attention back to Wardyke.

The drums rolled again and then cut dead. The silence was palpable. Wardyke used it to full effect and then, sensing the tension was at breaking point, broke it himself with a high pitched and dreadful wailing sound that reminded the villagers of nights of fear in the forests surrounded by wolves.

Transfixed, they stared at their priest who at this moment seemed half-animal, half-god. He lifted his great arms slowly as he wailed until they were high above his head at the peak of the sound, and there he held them till the sound of the howl that came from him had penetrated the marrow of their bones.

No one could have moved. They were locked rigid in a kind of terrified fascination.

Kyra was paralysed like the rest, but what she saw was not quite what they saw.

In an arc behind Wardyke, but crowding him closely, were standing shadowy figures, and she knew with a deadly certainty that she had seen them before. Their bodies were those of men, brown and strong, clad only in metallic loin cloths. Their heads were the heads of animals and their eyes were the eyes of demons. At their feet (at Wardyke's feet), the body of Maal was lying and as she looked in horror at it it began to change from the calm, pale priest, lying as though asleep upon the bier, to an ugly, rotting corpse.

Inside her head she screamed.

'No!'

No sound came from her. No movement of her body betrayed her, but she knew at this moment a force was working from her to blast the evil influence of their power away from Maal.

Her eyes if anyone had looked were blazing with a kind of vivid light. Her love for Maal, her longing to protect him, gave her the strength. Her training gave her the skill.

Even as her will cried yet again 'No!', the figures behind Wardyke seemed to cringe and waver, their eyes, no longer triumphant, seeking their enemy.

Standing among the crowd of villagers no ordinary mortal

could have noticed Kyra was different from the others, but these creatures' eyes ranged everywhere and it was not long before they found the source of their discomfiture. As Kyra held with great strain the concentrated power of her will to protect Maal, the cringing creatures recognized her with demonic malevolence. She summoned up one last and desperate effort and in that moment the air around Wardyke seemed to vibrate in a way Kyra had seen it sometimes on a very hot day, and with the vibration the image of the creatures dissolved and disappeared.

Wardyke was alone again at the entrance to the tomb and, as Kyra's eyes fell upon him, she thought that he too had momentarily lost strength. His arms were lowered and the once livid blaze of his eyes was dimmed. She fancied he too was looking around, seeking an answer to something that puzzled him.

Aching with exhaustion from her experience she could face no more and took a step back so that she was hidden from his sight. Karne looked down at her questioningly. She looked ill. He held her tightly thinking that she might faint. She rested her head against him and shut her eyes. Oh, if only she could sleep!

It was fortunate for her and Karne that they were not the only ones to move at this time or they would certainly have been picked out by Wardyke. Kyra's power had temporarily broken the spell with which he held them, and everyone was shifting and murmuring uneasily in their places.

Suddenly realizing this, Wardyke postponed his search and set about regaining the attention he had lost. He nodded sharply at his drummers and within seconds the pounding of their insistent beat had wound the villagers to a fever pitch of anxiety again. From there he took them through a range of emotions ending with passive acceptance of whatever he wished.

Kyra was not listening, but Karne, who was, was impressed with the way he handled the crowd. He watched it all as though he were somehow outside the whole scene and when he realized this, and that he was not a slave to Wardyke's power

146

as the rest appeared to be, he was surprised. He looked at Kyra resting against his shoulder also unmoved by Wardyke's will and Fern beside him still standing straight and independent, but he could feel the strength in her that was separate from the crowd.

'Why are we three the only ones not to fall under Wardyke's spell?' he thought. 'Not all these villagers are fools.'

His eye fell upon Maal, lying quietly almost forgotten on his bier. Wardyke was using the funeral for his own ends, for power weaving and establishing control. The ordinary human emotions of a burial had been forgotten. Karne studied Maal's face, sadness returning to him. It was still calm, composed, pale as stone. There was no way of telling how he had died, or indeed if he was dead at all.

The key to their power to withstand Wardyke lay partly with Maal, partly with themselves. Maal had helped them develop certain tendencies already within themselves. He, Karne, had asked questions the other villagers never asked before Maal knew him, Kyra had seen into people's heads before she had become Maal's pupil. Fern had talked with trees. Each of them were what they were, but Maal had helped them to grow. He had not tried to change them into something they were not or could not be, but had helped them develop along the lines they were already going. The rest, and here Karne looked around him at family and friends, were content to stay as they were, content to use over and over again the things they already knew, too afraid to take in new knowledge, new skills, in case their comfortable routine would be disturbed, their comfortable view of existence have to be revised. That way they were easy prey for people like Wardyke. They followed him blindly, until too late they realized he was leading them away from the very comfortable and familiar world they were trying to preserve.

Maal was right, Karne thought, the most important thing in life is to grow inwardly, to move always towards greater awareness, greater understanding, of all the different levels in which things are existing and happening simultaneously.

The villagers shut off whole areas of thought as taboo,

limiting themselves, stunting themselves.

Karne remembered Kyra's description of her vision of the stars and the incredible web of constantly changing relationship between them and yet the overall pattern of relationship staying the same. Everything is moving, he thought, changing, ceasing to exist one moment and coming into existence in a different form the next. If one did not accept this but tried to keep everything rigid, damage would certainly be done. One must move with the movement, flow with the flow, become new with each renewal . . . judge each person and each incident on its own merits, from its own unique standpoint . . . and yet see it in relationship to the whole.

Wardyke was evil because he was reducing the individuality of people and welding them into a single tool for his own use. This was very different from Maal who believed in the delicate balance of individual to whole, increasing each person's individuality while at the same time making them aware of their responsibility to the whole.

After Wardyke's peroration Maal's body was carried into the dark cavity of the tomb and the first stones were put in place to seal it overnight.

Darkness was moving in upon them now and the rest of the work was left until the morning.

As they turned to go the dank clouds that had hung above them all day began to leak and before they reached the village it had grown to a steady downpour. Wet, bedraggled and discouraged villagers tramped sadly back to their homes. Karne could hear a group of Strangers laughing as they passed on their way. They at least seemed pleased with the turn events had taken.

Fern was invited by Kyra's mother to spend the night with them and she accepted gratefully. She helped prepare the meal and fitted so well into their family circle that Karne found his mother looking at him and then saying loudly to Fern, 'You know, you really ought not to stay so much alone in that valley of yours. You are always welcome here!'

Fern smiled and Karne looked embarrassed. He was longing to find out why she had withdrawn herself so sharply from him at the funeral but he knew that they had much to arrange about the transference of Maal, and his personal affairs would have to wait.

It was Kyra's weariness that gave them the opportunity for action earlier than expected. She was obviously so exhausted that her mother suggested they all retired to sleep earlier than usual. The day had been an unusually heavy one and no one was in a talking mood.

One by one the fires flickered out all around the village.

Karne lay a long time conscious of Fern not far from him, silent in the dark. Kyra was fast asleep and he was in a quandary as to what he should do about her. They needed her help. Two of them could scarcely handle the task that lay ahead and yet he realized that Kyra must have been through some particularly harassing experience at the tomb to make her so unnaturally and excessively tired. He did not know how much he dared push her beyond her normal strength. To add to this the rain was pouring down outside heavily and steadily as though it would rain forever. The whole project, which had seemed so feasible when he had first thought of it, began to look impossible. He again wondered if the point of it was now lost. Maal was dead, killed by Wardyke. There was no way they could bring him back to life. He knew Maal had wanted to be buried on a particular line of invisible force within the earth and that he had wanted to be in conscious control of his death because he knew that the way he reacted to it, his self-control and his acceptance of his place in the design of the universe, would influence, as all that he had ever done would influence, the progress of his life beyond death. Each life is part of a long and varied process of learning, each thread of will and motive, love and hate, good and evil, has to be gradually refined until the Being is at his full potential which, Maal had told Karne, was far beyond our present imaginings.

Maal knew he had learnt a great deal from his mistakes in this life, but there was still a great deal he knew he had to

149

change within himself before he was ready even to take a lowly part in the next level of spiritual existence whose Beings no longer needed to be reborn on earth in bodies, although they still worked with Earth Beings through the medium of spirit on the inner levels of the Self. With their help and his own effort he hoped to make a leap in progress, but there was a long way to go to reach the ultimate. Beyond the spiritual Beings who were helpers to mankind were other levels of Beings, each level with its own purpose to fulfil, its own work to do.

Having seen a vision of how things were, he was anxious to make what progress he could at the swiftest pace he could master.

Had Wardyke succeeded in slowing down this pace?

Maal had tried to describe Existence to them once but Karne's mind could not grasp the idea of everything being at once infinitely diverse and yet ultimately simple. Many, and yet One.

'It is as though millions of different entities, some so small that they cannot be seen, some so huge the earth would be small beside them, were each occupied with its own individual unfoldment, and yet everything it did at every moment of its existence affected something else, which in its turn was subtly altered because of this to affect something else, and this process was not only happening once to one Entity, but all the time to every Entity.'

Here Maal paused looking at his three pupils, their faces a study in concentration and, in Karne's case, bewilderment.

'This you will say,' smiling at Karne, 'would make for complexity and confusion?'

Karne nodded dumbly.

'It does not,' Maal said quietly. 'Look around. Be silent, "feel" the Universe. It is working with great efficiency. Out of all the disparate elements working at their own Being, the whole is held together harmoniously as a single unit.'

'So what we do at any given time does not really matter . . . everything will even up in the end and it will all go on working harmoniously?' Karne said.

'Yes, and no,' Maal answered. 'Although the Universe as a

whole, as a unit, *will* go on working harmoniously in spite of us, our own individual existence is affected vitally by what we are and how we react to what happens to us.

'Good may come out of evil, and evil may come out of good, in a way we cannot understand yet because we can see no further than the immediate and limited part of the whole in which we are at present, but what we do, what choices we make at any given time, affects us, our surroundings and our development crucially.'

Karne lying in his fur rug on the night of Maal's funeral knew that he had a choice to make. His body cried out to stay warm and snug, protected from the cold needles of the rain and the exhausting and difficult, not to say, dangerous, task that he knew he ought to be preparing for at that very moment. But he knew deep inside himself that he had committed himself to this action and could not shirk it. He did not understand the full implications of it, but Maal had wished it and he must honour that wish.

Even as Karne decided he must pull himself together Kyra suddenly awoke and sat upright. Fern must have been awake all the time because she arose immediately to join them. They crept out from amongst the sleeping family like shadows, the snoring of the father effectively covering any sound they might make.

Once outside they found the rain was petering out and the clouds were breaking up. Mercifully some rays of moonlight were beginning to penetrate the dark valley. Stumbling through the wet grass and clinging mud, Karne holding Fern's hand, they hurried, bare-footed and shivering, towards the dark bulk of the clump of trees beside Maal's tomb. Once clear of the houses they ventured to whisper to each other.

'I thought you were unwakable,' Karne whispered to Kyra.

'It was a dream,' she said.

'What?'

'That woke me.'

She slipped and nearly fell. Karne and Fern steadied her and they hurried on.

151

'Tell us about the dream,' Fern said when they had reached an easier, grassier place for walking.

'It was nothing much,' Kyra said. 'I seemed to be in a thick fog . . . moving but not seeing anything . . . and then I heard Maal calling me.'

'Did you see him?'

'No. I just heard his voice and he sounded muffled and strange at first and I went on drifting in the fog not taking any notice. I still felt tired although I was asleep. And then suddenly he sounded quite sharp and commanding. You know how he does sometimes? And it was then that I snapped awake.'

'Do you think,' Fern's voice sounded eager, 'it might be that he is still alive?'

'Maybe . . . ,' Karne said, and their hearts lifted. They were more determined than ever to move Maal from the wrong tomb.

Karne did not know about the other two, but he had decided, if Maal was still alive, to persuade him to live on hidden in the woods near Fern at least until they had contacted the Lords of the Sun.

The night was a long, hard one. The tunnel they had dug was difficult to locate in the dark. Once found, the crudity with which it was constructed hampered them in every way. Bits of it had fallen in and had to be scooped out. They had sensibly left dry wood and straw and digging implements within the first few yards of it and they soon had a torch burning to give them light as they worked.

They worked in the tunnel by turns, one keeping watch at the entrance all the time. During Kyra's watch she was frightened almost into hysterics by the sudden screech of a night bird which took noisy flight just above her head. Fern had to spend valuable time comforting her before she was prepared to stay alone again. She was constantly looking over her shoulder for the half animal, half man, demon figures she had seen there earlier. She could feel the presence of something hostile but she could see nothing.

She was glad when it was her turn to go inside, crawling in the earth like a worm, to be beside strong, dependable Karne who was always so unaware of mysterious presences that being near to him she could feel that they did not exist at all.

At last they broke through to the burial chamber itself and stood side by side looking at Maal by the flickering light of the torch. There was no sign of breath or pulse. Kyra clung to Karne's arm.

'He is dead,' she whispered miserably.

Karne was silent. It certainly seemed like it.

'Go and fetch Fern,' he said at last, 'she is stronger than you are. We will take him to the wood as we planned. He would want that.'

Kyra nodded and crawled back along the tunnel. Fern took her place in the chamber and she and Karne dragged the stretcher-like bier behind them to the entrance. It was heavy work and breathing was not easy in the dark and confined space. Panting and sweating, their bodies aching from the strain, they finally emerged from the earth. Kyra started the work of filling up the tunnel while they recovered.

The moon was fully out now but low in the sky, touching everything with an eerie beauty. Karne and Fern sat back to back, leaning on each other, too exhausted to talk, almost too exhausted to think. Each glad of each other's company but making no sign of it.

At last Karne was recovered enough for action.

'It will not be long before the moon sets, we must be in your woods by then or we will never find the way.'

Fern nodded wearily.

As he removed his supporting back from hers and stood up, he turned and put his hands upon her shoulders, leant down and kissed the top of her head. This time she did not withdraw herself. He could just see the little wan smile at the corner of her lips as she turned her face up to his. Fleetingly he brushed his lips across hers and then turned to call Kyra. She crept out of the tunnel almost immediately but they could see she was agitated.

'I am not nearly finished,' she complained, out of breath.

'Never mind. We have no time to finish now. We will cover it up again and come back tomorrow.'

They dragged the heavy cover of leaves and branches and grass over the entrance and set off with Maal as best they could. The load was heavy, the ground uneven, the light inadequate, but somehow familiarity with the route and sheer determination sustained them. The last thing they saw as they entered the dark but friendly woods surrounding Fern's garden was the magnificent sight of a giant moon, the colour of blood, slowly sinking below the horizon. They put their load down for a few minutes and stared transfixed. When it was gone they resumed their journey. At Fern's house they dared to light a torch again and so found their way to the secret burial chamber with greater ease. Their main difficulties were now over. Within minutes Maal was safely laid to rest in the place he had chosen and the three stood beside him, the light of the torch revealing their muddy, haggard and dishevelled appearance beside his calm, composed and peaceful one.

What to do now?

They looked at each other. It would soon be dawn and they should be back with their family, but they were loth to leave Maal.

'Should we say some prayers?' Fern asked tentatively.

Karne nodded.

'That is a good idea.'

But they hesitated. What prayers, and who should say them?

Fern and Karne looked at Kyra.

She caught their look and seemed alarmed.

'But I do not know the words of the burial ceremony,' she said.

'That does not matter,' Fern said. 'Say what you feel.'

'Pray for him, Kyra — any way you know.' Karne said.

Kyra sat on her heels beside Maal. For a while she looked silently and with deep love at his gentle, strong face, then she shut her eyes and lowered her head. The two beside her could hear no words, but fancied they could feel the warmth of her

154

love for Maal and the concentration with which she was thinking about him.

Inside her head no words were forming. The shutting of her eyes plunged her in a featureless, wordless darkness. She waited, quietly breathing, letting the darkness happen to her. Gradually, gradually she began to distinguish darker shapes within the darkness. She thought at first they were the figures of men, but later she realized they were the shapes of gigantic Standing Stones, different from their own in that they were taller, closer together, and joined at the top from one to the other by slabs of stone, curved to follow the shape of the circle.

She seemed to be in the centre of the Circle, looking out, and there were other Stones around her within the Circle. She could barely make out the shapes and sizes in the dark. There were no stars. No moon. She was not even sure that it was night. The darkness with its darker shapes was not like anything she had encountered before in her ordinary life. She let the experience happen and waited for whatever would come next. As nothing changed, her mind began to drift back to Maal and as the thought of him came to her an image of him appeared as a slightly lighter area in the darkness of the mysterious Stone Circle.

'Maal!'

It seemed to her she cried out and moved towards him, but something prevented her from going too near. The image of him grew slowly lighter and lighter until she could see him as though through a light mist. She could see that he was holding something in his hands and that he was trying to attract her attention to it, although he was not moving in any way. Her eyes kept going to the object in his hands, but the image was too blurred for her to make out what it was. She could see his eyes beginning to despair, his image beginning to fade. She was conscious that she had let him down by not recognizing what he was trying to show her. She began to feel anxiety.

'Maal!' she cried, 'Come back! Give me another chance.'

But the image had disappeared and all the dark shadows of the Standing Stones had gone with it. She was left with the featureless darkness she had experienced first.

She opened her eyes and found Karne and Fern looking anxiously at her.

'What is the matter?'

'What happened?'

She looked from one to the other and then to Maal, her face pained and bewildered.

'He was trying to tell me something . . . trying to show me something . . . and I could not make out what it was . . .'

She was trembling. Fern put her hand on her arm.

'I think he may be still alive,' she said. 'I *feel* it.'

'So do I,' Kyra said tearfully, 'but I do not know what to do to help him and I can feel he needs my help.'

Karne bent over Maal and listened to his chest. There was no sound. He hoped the girls were right, but he could feel no life in the old man.

'There is something he needs . . . the thing he was trying to show me!'

'Try and go back into the trance you were in,' Karne suggested. 'Perhaps this time . . .'

Kyra tried to compose herself, but she could not. She stayed where she was.

'It is nearly dawn,' Karne said urgently. 'We have not much time.'

'I know,' Kyra said miserably, 'if only . . .'

'Perhaps it is that little stone sphere of his,' Fern said suddenly.

Kyra gasped.

'Of course!'

The two girls clutched hands excitedly.

'Well,' cried Karne impatiently, 'where is it?'

'I will go and fetch it,' Fern called, already on her way.

'I am sure it was that,' Kyra said happily to Karne. 'Now that I think of it I cannot imagine why I did not think of it before.'

'Try and make contact with him again. Now that we have come so far we do not want him to slip away thinking that the whole thing is hopeless.'

Kyra knelt beside Maal and tried to make contact with him

as he had taught her, but she found that she could not.

She opened her eyes again and looked at Karne.

'It is no good,' she said. 'I cannot.'

Karne looked worried.

'I wish Fern would hurry,' Kyra said anxiously.

'I am sure she is,' Karne spoke in her defence quickly. 'I do not know why you did not put the stone in here. It seems the obvious place.'

'We did not think of it,' Kyra said gloomily. 'We did not really think Maal was dead. It all happened so quickly.'

Fern arrived back at this point with the little parcel of bark cloth in her hand.

'It is getting light outside,' she said, out of breath, 'the birds are making a tremendous noise.'

'Here,' Karne took the parcel from her and handed it to Kyra. 'Do whatever you think Maal wants you to do with it, but hurry. We will be in trouble if people start looking for us and it reaches Wardyke's ears that we are missing.'

Kyra took the parcel and knelt down beside Maal. She tried to compose herself again. After a moment or two she looked around at Karne.

'Be quiet,' she said sternly.

He looked indignant.

'I did not say anything.'

'You are worrying and disturbing the air,' she said, fixing him with an accusing eye.

He flung up his hands in disgust and muttered something under his breath.

'You see!' she said triumphantly.

'Just get *on* with it,' he snapped impatiently.

Fern put her hand on his arm and drew him back a little way.

'Perhaps we should leave her,' she said quietly. 'I too am agitated and probably making it impossible to concentrate.'

He nodded and they slipped out of the stale-smelling burial chamber into the glory of the dawn light in the wood flickering with green leaves and bird song. He took a long deep breath.

'I could do with some of your spring water,' he said, and she led him there.

157

After they had drunk, they washed themselves and then wandered through the wood tasting the freshness of the air and the closeness of each other. The sorrowful and harassing experiences of the past night and day began to fade slightly, and only the aching of their limbs reminded them of the darker side of the reason for their being together at this early hour.

Inside the chamber Kyra unwrapped the little parcel as carefully as she had seen Maal do it, and when she reached the little sphere she placed it gently on Maal's chest, folding his hands over it to keep it in place.

Then she sat beside him very quietly, trying to offer herself to him to be used in any way he wished. She tried to imagine how it felt for him to be dead. This was not difficult as she had the experience in the Sacred Circle to remember. She began to feel it was herself lying on the bier unable to move her limbs, but this time she was not afraid. She lay there as still as stone, at first feeling nothing, and then gradually beginning to feel the weight of the little stone sphere on her chest. After the weight of it, the sensation associated with it was one of tingling. Then of warmth. The sphere seemed to be generating flow and warmth in her chest which was gradually spreading to the rest of her.

She fancied she heard (or was it 'felt') a deep, low drum beat (or was it a heart beat?). She opened her eyes in surprise and found she was not on the bier at all but was crouching beside Maal looking at him. She stared fascinated at his chest and could have sworn she saw the little sphere rise and fall, rise and fall, with the rhythm of what *must* be breathing.

She wanted to call the others, but did not dare break into the sequence of slow awakening. She did not want to do anything that would set back the process in any way.

There was no doubt in her mind now that Maal was not dead, and her heart was filled with joy.

She watched and waited. The process was painfully slow.

She took his finger and used it to trace the spiral pattern of

158

the stone sphere as he had taught her to do. She thought this might help, and indeed it seemed to, as his eyelids started to flicker as though he were dreaming. She was just wondering if she dare call his name aloud when Fern and Karne broke into the chamber, fresh and bright from their walk in the woods.

They were amazed to see the breathing, but she held up her hand to keep them quiet. The three of them watched over him now, each one in their own way calling his name inside their heads, *willing* him to wake up and be with them again.

'Maal!' Kyra dared to whisper the word, and as no ill effect seemed to follow, she said it again and again, louder and louder until it became a kind of chant which they all joined in. The flickering of his lids became more agitated, his breathing more definite, colour began to creep back to his cheeks, his fingers gripped the sphere of spirals without Kyra's help.

At last he opened his eyes and looked at them.

'Maal!' they cried joyfully.

Wardyke had not won after all!

Their first overwhelming excitement soon gave way to a more sober appraisal of the situation.

Maal was very weak, so weak he could not sit up and could barely talk. He had been through a great deal and although he was certainly alive now, it was obvious to them he was only just so. Karne began to realize he probably would not be well enough to go to the Sacred Circle on the Night of the Rising Star and undertake the difficulties of the journey to meet the Lords of the Sun.

'What can we do?' Kyra pleaded. 'Tell us . . . how can we help you to get better.'

Maal turned his head a fraction to look at her, his eyes full of love.

He was trying to speak but his voice was so weak she had to lean very close to his mouth to hear what he was saying.

'There is no way I will get better with this old body,' he whispered.

'Do not say that!' cried Kyra.

159

He shook his head very slightly and a smile flickered at the corners of his lips.

'One must accept it, my child. It is so.'

'I do not *want* to accept it,' she said with unusual fierceness. 'I cannot live without you. I *need* you.'

'You will have to live without me,' he said gently but firmly, 'but not forever. I promise you . . .' and here his voice faded to nothing and he closed his eyes as though he were slipping away again.

'Maal,' she cried desperately, seizing him by the shoulders and trying to force him back to life by the sheer passion of her desire.

'What do you promise?' she almost shouted into his face.

His old, tired eyes flickered open again.

'I promise you . . .' he whispered and his voice was like a breeze rustling in dry grass '. . . that I will join you again some time, some place . . .'

Tears streamed down her face. She tried to stop herself sobbing so that she would not miss a word that he was saying.

'. . . we have been together before . . . and we will be together again . . . many times . . .'

'How will I know you?'

'You will know . . . you will know.'

'But how?'

'You will know when the time comes. Now you must leave me . . . I must prepare for the transfer of my spirit . . . it is not an easy matter . . .'

'But what about the Lords of the Sun?'

Karne thrust his question forward anxiously.

The old man turned his tired eyes to the boy.

'Kyra must do it herself.'

Kyra drew in her breath sharply.

'And you,' he said to Karne, 'and you . . . ,' he turned to Fern, 'must help her and protect her in every way you can. You must do it,' he said directly to Kyra and his eyes were anxious. 'It is very important. You have promised.'

'And *you* have promised!' Kyra sobbed, 'You have promised to come back to me.'

He nodded almost imperceptibly and then his eyes closed.

They could not rouse him again.

Fern and Karne held back the weeping Kyra, afraid she might harm him, she was so desperately trying to wake him again.

'He is so old,' Fern said gently to Kyra, 'and he has been through so much. Let him go his way in peace now.'

Kyra drew back and tried to control herself. She did not want in any way to harm Maal, but she felt very much alone and vulnerable without him.

'Come,' Fern said, taking her arm. 'You have done everything you can for him.'

'I will leave the sphere with him. It might help him in some way,' Kyra said, looking her last at the frail discarded shell of her friend, his thin hands locked around the spiral stone.

'Yes, do that,' Fern said, and gave her a gentle tug.

The two girls went out first into the sunlight. Karne stayed behind to have one last look around to see that everything was safe and ready for the long centuries ahead. They had built this little chamber well, half dug into the earth and lined with stone. During the day the girls would cover it with soil and then Fern would transfer growing plants to it so that soon it would look like nothing but a natural mound of trees, ferns and bushes, and would be unnoticeable.

He beat out the torch and followed the girls.

In the early morning sunlight they worked together to put the largest stones they had found to seal up the entrance.

It was arranged that Karne would run home and make up some story to cover their absence. Fern and Kyra would meanwhile have a few hours' sleep and then do their best to disguise the tomb.

When Karne could find an opportunity he would fill in the tunnel to Maal's official tomb. As no one suspected it was there he was not anticipating any trouble.

Kyra awoke from her sleep at noon to find Fern already at work on the mound.

'You look better,' Fern said with a smile as she saw Kyra approaching. She did indeed. Fern would almost have said she looked happy as well as rested.

Kyra smiled cheerfully.

'Yes,' she said, 'I had a good dream.'

'About Maal?'

'Yes.'

'Is he all right?'

'I am sure he is.'

'What did you dream?'

'I cannot remember exactly . . . but I know it was all good. Instead of the fog I had in the dream I had about him before . . . there was a great deal of light and beautiful luminous things . . . even the people were tall and shining . . .'

'Did you see him choosing a new life?'

'No. I do not think it happens quite like that.'

'I cannot imagine how it happens.'

'Nor can I,' Kyra said thoughtfully, 'but all the darkness and fog was gone. Of that I am sure. Everything was light and beautiful. But it was as though I was looking at it reflected in something . . . I think it was a pool because something dropped and the whole image shimmered and broke up . . . sort of shattered into millions of sparkles of light . . . and then I woke up.'

'Perhaps being still in a body you could not look directly at the scene, but only at a reflection of it. The direct brightness of it might be too much for you.'

'Something like that,' Kyra said, and then they both laughed at one of Maal's much used phrases.

'Come on,' said Fern then, 'we have a lot to do.'

They worked hard together and the mound was finished and covered with growing plants before the sun set over the hills.

Kyra washed herself in Fern's little stream and walked home, her limbs weary, the shades of the night gathering around her.

The Triumph of Wardyke

When Kyra woke to the dawn of the next day she knew that she would not sleep again until she had spoken with the Lords of the Sun. All day she thought about it as she went about her work and the more she thought about it the more anxious she became.

She had not been given specific instructions about what to do. Maal had said enigmatically that she would 'know' when the time came, but even that was referring to working together. It was he who was supposed to find the Lords. Her task was to have been to help him through Wardyke's invisible barrier and boost his failing strength with what embryo power she had. Even the secret knowledge she was supposed to have about the correct configuration of the stars was a mystery to her. She could remember the beauty and the splendour of the vision, but no specific configuration. The impression she had gained in that moment of illumination was that there was no set and rigid pattern, but that everything was moving and changing all the time. The driving force of the Universe worked through a process of minute, delicate and orderly adjustments between each specific thing, great and small.

In the afternoon her family task was to grind the grain to make flour. She knelt beside the grinding stone, crushing the grains of wheat into the hollow of it with a sea-rounded pebble. As she worked she tried to bring together in her mind all the teachings of Maal, to see if from their accumulated bulk she could pluck what she needed for the night. She had learnt a great deal, but Maal had warned her that knowledge never really took root until one had occasion to use it.

As she worked and pondered, her baby sister sat in the dirt beside her and played with the pebbles she was not using. One by one they were picked up in the chubby little hands and chewed and slobbered over. Those that were too big to lift the baby leant down and gnawed at with toothless gums as Kyra had seen a dog gnaw at a bone.

Sometimes Kyra would have to break off what she was doing to thrust her finger into the baby's mouth to remove one of the smaller pebbles she was in danger of swallowing. It seemed to her no matter how hard she concentrated on the work of grinding, her mind was working busily on several other levels at the same time. One on the difficult task of creating order and system out of the bits and pieces of knowledge she had gained from Maal, another looking after the baby and noticing when it did anything that was potentially harmful to it, yet another noticing the village life around her, Faro and her father talking in lowered voices, women bringing washing back from the stream, children playing a game of hopping and jumping. It seemed a long time since she had played such a game and she felt the urge to drop everything she was doing and go and join them.

And through it all, separate from all these different threads of consciousness, she was aware of herself being aware of them.

'And Maal says we only notice a few of the threads with our ordinary minds, there are many others within me at this very moment.'

She knew she wanted more than anything else to train herself to be aware on all these different levels, of all these different states.

'How rich it would make life,' she thought. 'How much richer than it already is.'

She stopped her work for a moment and bent down to pick up the baby. She held it high above her head and noticed with a smile that it was beginning to be really heavy. The little creature laughed delightedly as she dropped it to chest level and gave it a hug. It clung with its legs and arms around her, nuzzling its dirty little face against her neck, loving her.

She was just about to put it down again and resume her work with the grain, when she heard a shout and turned to see what was happening.

Her brother Thon was running, waving his arms and shouting. He seemed agitated and shocked. Villagers were looking up at him and some left what they were doing to follow him. He stopped when he reached Faro and her father and waving his arms and gesticulating he began to tell them something. A little group of villagers began to gather round the three men.

Kyra, still holding the baby, ran to join them. She could not make out quite what was happening because everyone was talking at once, but she gathered it was really horrifying.

'What is it?' she cried, nudging people, trying to get nearer the centre of the group so that she could hear what Thon was saying.

At last one of the women, unable to make herself heard against the strident voices of the men, and anxious to communicate her horror with someone, turned to Kyra and told her the whole story.

Thon had found the body of Mia, battered to death amongst the trees just beyond the north pasture.

'We are going to fetch her now,' the woman added and moved off with the others, led by Thon.

Kyra rushed back to her home and deposited the baby unceremoniously with her busy mother.

Breathlessly she ran to catch the others. Mia was a pretty girl, much sought after by the village boys, a little dull Kyra had always thought, but nevertheless she was fond of her.

What a terrible thing!

What was happening to their village?

There had been anger and hatred between people from time to time but no one in her memory, or indeed in the memory of her father and grandfather, had killed another except by accident. Now Maal was dead and probably Wardyke had killed him. Was he responsible for Mia's death as well?

A group of people had already gathered round the body of

the girl when they arrived. Standing in a circle round her, silently staring. Kyra pushed forward to see, gasped and withdrew immediately. Whoever had done that to her was evil beyond anything Kyra had come across before. She stood back, her heart beating. The girl's clothes were ripped and soaked in blood. Where the bones were broken Kyra could see white splinters sticking out of the flesh.

She must find Karne. She was afraid for Fern, for herself, for all of them. The feelings she had had that Wardyke was evil and inspired evil in others were being confirmed with dreadful speed. The urgency of her mission to the Lords of the Sun was becoming greater at every moment.

Karne met her on the path leading back to the village from Maal's tomb.

'What is wrong?' he called as soon as he saw her face.

Words tumbled from her. His face went black with anger. She could see the muscles tensing along his arms and shoulders.

'No, Karne!' she cried in alarm.

'We *cannot* let this happen!' he shouted and left her, running like a deer across the rough terrain towards the village. When she arrived panting and out of breath, he had already joined a group of men all of whom were angry and ready for action. She heard his claim that Wardyke had killed Maal, and Wardyke must surely have killed the girl.

'Wardyke is no true priest. He is an impostor!'

'Karne! Karne!' she cried, trying to stop him. This was not the way. This way they would not stand a chance. This way Maal had warned them not to try.

But her voice was thin and womanish and did not carry across the storm of their anger.

As one unit they turned and strode towards Wardyke's house, seizing wood and stones as they went, determined to put an end to what they were beginning to feel more and more as a tyranny. The mood was ugly and there was the scent of more blood in the air.

166

Kyra ran behind, desperately trying to think of a way to stop the inevitable catastrophe.

As the angry marchers neared Wardyke's magnificent house they were joined by others, until almost the whole village was marching. As they marched they chanted, an impromptu chant of hate.

'War-dyke! War-dyke! War-dyke!'

Kyra's blood ran cold to hear her peaceful, friendly villagers so twisted and locked upon a knot of rage and blind hate. She knew there was no way they were going to win against Wardyke in this battle. In a sense they were becoming just what he wanted them to become, a senseless mob pulled by primitive feelings that he could manipulate as he wished, their god-given gift of reason and intelligence overthrown and helpless.

As they mounted the last ridge before his house they were brought to a sudden halt. He was standing before them, gigantic and imposing. He held up his hand and for a moment they were cowed, then one of their number, it might even have been Karne but Kyra could not be sure, shouted belligerently,

'Who killed Mia?'

The others took up the cry.

'Who killed Mia?'

'Who killed Maal?'

The shouting and the noise was deafening, some of the younger boys clattering sticks together to make a kind of terrifying drumming sound. But although they shouted and they were still angry they did not move forward. Wardyke's hand was up and it was as though there was an invisible barrier keeping them back.

He waited as though he were carved of rock. Only his eyes had life in them and they were like black fire, their flames licking the earth in front of the marchers, daring them to take a step forward.

Suddenly another noise joined the one the marchers were making and a quick imperceptible movement of Wardyke's hand and head subtly directed the marchers' attention to it.

To the left of them was another mob, mostly consisting of

Wardyke's Strangers, and they too were shouting and angry and they were dragging the figure of a man in their midst.

Wardyke took advantage of the momentary pause of surprise amongst the hostile villagers to say in a voice of thunder, the deadly dagger of his bony finger pointing directly at the captive man,

'He is your enemy. He killed Mia!'

A sort of composite scream went up from the mob and within a second they had transferred all their hate from Wardyke to the captive.

Horrified Kyra saw them turn upon him and join with the Strangers in beating him with sticks and stones, until he was lying bleeding and broken in a heap on the ground.

Only then did the people pause and think about what they had done.

They did not even know who it was they had destroyed. If questioned they might have said they thought it was one of the Strangers because he was among the Strangers, but they had not used their minds. They had moved like one body of concentrated venom on the point of Wardyke's finger.

Kyra, trembling, looked for Karne. She found him back from the mob, alone on the path. He had realized what was happening in time and had not joined the mob in stoning the man, but his face was a study of stunned horror. He had played his part in rousing the rebellion. His words against Wardyke had seemed justified at the time. But now, when he could see where it had led, he knew Maal had been right to warn them against this course of action. They were deeper in the mesh of Wardyke's evil than they had ever been.

Someone cried out. The broken body of the man was lifted and recognized. It was one of *them*, one of the villagers, not a man at all, but a boy of sixteen, simple-minded but gentle. The villagers knew with a terrible certainty that he could not have killed Mia.

There was silence now as they realized what they had done. The Strangers had cunningly disappeared, leaving the stunned villagers to survey their handiwork.

Wardyke had disappeared as well.

They were alone on the hill with their pain and their guilt.

A woman started sobbing and this was the only sound as they picked up the mangled heap of bones and carried it home.

That night the bodies of the two young people, Mia and the boy, were laid side by side to await burial. The villagers lit fires around them and kept vigil all night.

Never had they needed guidance and help so much but there was no one to whom they could turn.

As the stars wheeled quietly across the sky many of them turned inwards for help, trying to think it all out for themselves, questioning themselves . . . looking at the bodies, the dark earth, the fires around them and the stars in the sky . . . puzzling about the relationship of each to each and the meaning of the whole.

The Lords of the Sun

Wardyke was within the Sacred Circle when the bright and wandering star the villagers called Magus rose above the Stone of the Star. He stood in the centre and spoke the incantations to the gods that were expected of him. Around the Circle, making another circle, the seven new Elders walked with slow and measured tread, keeping a constant circular current going. Beyond them Wardyke's Strangers stood, and beyond them again some of the villagers who were not at that time keeping watch by the burial fires waited forlornly, still numbed by the events of the past few days.

Karne, Kyra and Fern were among these but well to the back, in the shadow, keeping carefully out of sight.

Kyra was very tense. Her fingers gripped those of her brother with an almost crippling force. Once or twice he tried to loosen her grip, but it was no use. She needed him and she was not letting go.

They could see Wardyke clearly as torches were placed between each Standing Stone. The combination of flickering fire and darkness and the fact that the Circle was higher than the watching villagers made him and his Elders seem like giants.

As the star rose it was the custom to sing and some with stringed instruments and reed flutes would play sweet music. But this night the watching crowd remained silent and the star rose only to the sound of Wardyke's voice. He lifted his arms and called on the gods to give him strength to carry out his work among the people of the Magus. He spoke of his prowess as a priest and how he had gathered together people of many communities to form a larger community which he would lead to be the greatest people on the earth.

'They will glorify the names of the gods and carry your power wherever they go.

'They will spread over the face of the earth making one people, led by one priest, Wardyke your servant. Wardyke your right hand.

'They will trample on your enemies and slay your foes.

'Your names will be revered and feared as they were in the ancient times.'

His voice rose in a kind of ecstasy. It magnified against the rocks and reverberated among the people.

Fern drew closer to Karne and slipped her arm through his. Kyra bit her lip until it bled.

But suddenly the gods answered in a way no one had ever seen them answer before on the Night of the Rising Star.

The hand of Darkness seized a group of stars and flung them to the earth. With a sharp intake of breath the villagers saw the burning embers fall from the heavens in a shower of swift and vivid light. As suddenly as it happened, it was over.

Wardyke was temporarily silenced, shocked by the un-expectedness of the meteor shower, but before the villagers had recovered their breath he was in charge of himself again.

He bowed his head, and this was the only time since he came to the village anyone had seen him bow, and said in a deep and apparently humble voice,

'We thank you, gods, for this sign of your favour. With this burning seal of light you have sealed forever with your approval the appointment of Wardyke as your natural spokesman upon the earth.'

Bewildered, the villagers looked at each other. They had put a different interpretation on the sign of the falling stars. But who could say which was the one the gods intended?

Not long after this Wardyke dismissed them all and they silently dispersed, the villagers to watch beside their friends over the bodies of the two young people, some of the Strangers to their homes, and some to prowl the night watching that the villagers gave no more trouble to their lord and master, Wardyke.

Fern, Karne and Kyra remained behind some bushes, well hidden, watching Wardyke. The torches were burning low and they could not see as clearly as they had done, but they could still follow his movements. He walked the Circle as Maal had done the first time they watched him, touching his forehead to each stone. He then leaned against the leaning stone, extending his immensely long arms on either side to touch the two uprights, shut his eyes and went into the kind of trance state that they had become familiar with since knowing Maal.

Kyra put her head in her hands and cringed as though she could feel great pain. Fern and Karne looked at each other worriedly over her head, but did not interfere. Kyra's role was not an easy one but it was necessary. They were finished with games and childhood now. On her shoulders rested the lives of many people.

Wardyke remained still for a long time and then suddenly strode out of the Circle. As he passed the brightest remaining torch they could see his expression quite clearly. It was angry and disappointed. He strode down the path and out of sight, the very sound of his footsteps giving away the impatience he was feeling.

When they were quite sure he was out of earshot Karne and Fern asked Kyra what had happened.

They were amazed to find her smiling triumphantly.

'I tried to play a trick on him,' she said joyfully, 'and it worked!'

'What did you do?' Karne asked, surprised at her daring.

'I thought the deaths of Maal and Mia and the boy, over and over again as vividly as I could manage. I was determined he should suffer at least a little for what he has done.'

Karne was impressed.

'Do you think he saw the images you were trying to project upon him?'

'I am sure he did. You saw how he looked when he left the Circle. I do not think he managed to do any spirit travelling at

172

all. Whenever he turned to try and leave the Circle an image of one of the people he has just murdered came before him, blocking his way.'

'You took a terrible risk,' Fern said anxiously. 'What if he had suspected that it was your doing?'

'I had to be very careful not to project anything I did not want him to know.'

'Do you think he has any idea how it happened?'

'I do not think so. He has never really noticed me and I am sure he has no idea anyone in the village has any special powers now that Maal is dead.'

Kyra could not help feeling pleased with herself. Karne was delighted as well, but Fern was still uneasy. She knew Wardyke was no fool. He had spirit-travelled many times and would know this failure had some special explanation. With his skill it would not take him long to track down the reason.

'I am afraid for you, Kyra,' she said.

Kyra wondered if she had been wrong to do what she had done.

'Perhaps it was a mistake, perhaps it was not,' Karne said. 'At any rate it is done, and it is now time for you to go into the Circle and find the Lords of the Sun.'

Kyra swallowed hard. So it had come at last!

He took her hand and led her to the Circle, but before she went inside he put out the remaining torches one by one so that no one would see her. At first the darkness was so intense that they found it difficult to move about, but as their eyes grew accustomed to it the Stones loomed darkly against a less dark sky and they could orientate themselves.

Karne kissed Kyra on the cheek and hugged her close.

'Little sister, do not be afraid. We will be right here. If it looks as though things are going wrong we will rush in, Sacred Circle or no Sacred Circle, and rescue you.'

'Promise?' she said in a very small voice.

'I promise.'

Fern kissed her too and held her very close.

'If there were another way . . .' Kyra said in a low voice.

'If there were another way,' Karne said softly, 'Maal would

have told us about it. He believed you could do it. For his sake, at least try.'

Kyra nodded dumbly and broke away from their comforting and loving arms. She knew the urgency. She knew the necessity . . . it was just that she felt so very small and the Sacred Stones that loomed out of the darkness seemed so very large.

She passed through into the Circle itself and stood for a moment or two looking upwards at the sky. As she did so the giant Stones themselves seemed small and insignificant against the vast and arching dome of infinity above.

It seemed to her all scale and measure had altered instantly as she entered the Circle. She now was the pin-point centre of the Universe, the millions upon millions of stars that rode the darkness above her were turning on the centre point of *her* Being. The earth itself beneath her feet no longer felt like grass and sand, but like a huge ball of living rock which turned slowly and inexorably with the stars. She rode the earth like a ship that sailed the sky. But even as she felt all this, the scale and image changed again. From being the minute point on which vastness turned, she was vastness itself and all that was happening was happening within herself. All these stars moving were moving within her, the earth turning was turning within her. As she had looked up and out, she now looked in, and saw the same vision.

Somewhere in her mind she remembered she had something important to do and as much as she would have liked to stay and enjoy the constantly changing visionary experience, she knew she must fulfill her purpose there or many people would be lost.

It seemed to her she heard Karne's voice in her head reminding her.

Slowly she moved, trying to think what she must do first.

She remembered the configuration. She must be sure that was right if she was to travel as far as was needed to find the Lords of the Sun.

She noticed with one part of her mind that she was not so much afraid as she had expected to be. She felt she was

174

moving in some strange dream. The reality around her was very different to the one to which she was accustomed as Karne's sister.

She looked up at the sky again, trying not to let the filigree of gold seduce her from her task. She tried to see the pattern in the stars she had seen when she had held Maal's stone sphere.

At first she saw nothing but brilliant and random lights. Then she thought to focus on the star Magus which was directly above the Stone of the Star at this time. As it became for her the brightest and most central point in the sky, the rest of the stars seemed to fall into place around it in a specific way. The configuration! It must be! It looked so right!

She felt strange as though there were currents of power running through her, circling round her. Slowly, as though already in a trance, she walked from stone to stone, touching each as she had done before with her forehead. This time with each touch she seemed to be becoming more and more in tune with the vibrations of power that were all around her, so that by the end she no longer felt them as vibrations outside herself but as part of her own inner rhythm.

When she came to close her eyes upon the final stone she was completely at one with the forces in the Sacred Circle and she slipped out of her body with no trouble at all.

Karne and Fern fancied they heard a faint humming coming from the Stones but could not be sure. They crouched in the darkness just outside, their arms around each other to keep fear at bay, watching Kyra's every move within the Circle. At first they were worried that she was taking too long and Karne wished impatiently that she would stop staring at the sky, but now that she had started the process of 'travelling' he was content to wait as long as it would take.

How he longed to be with her! How he longed to see what she was seeing.

She found herself standing in the yellow dust of a road, a high wall built of stone of the same colour on her right, stretching a long way past her in both directions. She stepped back somewhat to get a better view of the height of the wall and saw upon it for the first time a disc of dazzling gold. It was pure and plain, no carvings, no attachments. The polished gold of the Sun. Against its surface the real sun, high in the sky, was reflected, the beam of its brilliant light touching the disc and bouncing back along a straight line to fall upon a building many measures away. Within the courtyard of the building a tower, on which another such disc was placed carefully at an angle, reflected the light yet again and beamed it further across the landscape where it was picked up and reflected on. Kyra could see that where she was standing must have been the highest point because she could see for a long way in every direction. Below her a landscape of great subtlety and harmony unfolded, low and gently rising hills were separated by water courses threading their way, beaded with willow trees. Buildings with strangely peaked roofs were upon the surface of the land so naturally placed that they looked as though they had grown from the earth. It seemed to her the whole was held together within the golden network of the sun's light reflected from disc to disc.

She looked for an entrance to the wall beside her, remembering the citadel she had visited as the young Maal, although she realized instinctively that this was not in the same country. As there seemed to be no entrance she turned her attention to the building nearest to her in the valley and decided to walk towards it. There was something compelling about the ray of light that beamed from the disc directly above her head to the disc on the tower of the building. She followed it and found there was a path leading directly to it.

As she approached she realized it was much larger than she had thought. The plan as seen from above was a series of squares and circles within each other.

The outer wall surrounded a square. Within that great square smaller squares of even shape and size surrounded a central courtyard. The squares themselves consisted of rooms built round small courtyards. The great central courtyard and each smaller one had the same design. Although they were constructed as squares, within them circular fountains and flowers of every kind of beauty were planted in circular beds so that, looking from above, there were circles within all the squares. The central tower itself was square, but the disc of the sun that was placed upon it was circular. Kyra remembered something Maal had told her that she had not quite grasped before.

'The circle is the symbol of the spirit. It contains within itself its own completeness which has no end. The square is the symbol of the earth, of body, of material things, made up of angles and relationships. The circle within the square is spirit manifest in body.'

'This must be some kind of temple,' Kyra thought. 'Perhaps here I will find the Lords of the Sun.'

She found to her surprise that one moment she was looking down upon the temple, contemplating the harmony and the symbolism of its overall design, and the next she was standing in the central courtyard, the water of a ring of fountains softly singing to her, the scent of a thousand varied flowers soothing her, the sun disc on the tower above her giving her the feeling that the people who had built the tower were accustomed to using knowledge gained from nature in an orderly and significant way.

'If only Fern could see this garden,' she thought. It did not have the wild profusion of Fern's garden. It was much more formal and controlled. Beds of contrasting colours were placed to form a pattern within the whole, where Fern had flowers of every colour growing together instinctively forming a beautiful relationship. Kyra was impressed with the formal elegance of the design and moved by the feeling of peace and security it engendered, but if she were asked she would have to say she preferred the feeling she had in Fern's garden which was one of overwhelming joy and pleasure at the sheer fact of living and growing.

Someone had joined her in the courtyard. She spun round to see a man watching her. He was small and wizened with age, his skin folded in hundreds of wrinkles, his eyes, which were a strange and slanting shape, like black beads.

She found herself bowing to him with respect. He acknowledged the obeisance with a slight inclination of his own head. He did not seem particularly surprised to see her, though he was curious.

He walked towards her and then circled round her looking her over very carefully. She was suddenly aware that she must look as strange to him as he to her, a fourteen-year-old girl, slim, wiry, fair hair in a loose plait down her back, brown, rough woollen dress tied at the waist with a leather thong, sandals of leather with thongs crisscrossed over bare legs. He was clad in a soft flowing garment, of a cloth so fine and shining she could not imagine how it could be woven. It hid his whole body so that when he walked he seemed to glide. Traced on his cloak was the shape of an animal in coloured threads, a kind of serpent, with legs and jaws breathing fire.

She stared fascinated and as she stared she began to understand things. She understood somehow that this was a 'dragon', a symbol to these people of the unseen forces of the Universe that move throughout the sky and the earth revitalizing it with spirit. She understood somehow this idea was similar to that spoken of by Maal and Fern, the lines of power and force that flow through the earth and can be tapped and used by all living things.

These people seemed as a whole to take much more interest in this idea than her own did. She understood the man before her had a special kind of knowledge, a knowledge of these lines of power, and his task was to plot them for the people so that they could use them, build upon them, design their lives around them. She realized suddenly that the beauty and the harmony with which the man-made constructions she had seen from the top of the hill fitted so perfectly into the landscape was probably due to the skill of this man in plotting the flow currents of the dragon spirit. She realized also that the system of alignments in straight lines from one Sacred point to another used by her own people was crude compared to the subtle following of curving and constantly changing flow paths that these people had mastered. She wished Maal was still alive and she could discuss it with him.

She looked with even greater respect than she had at first at the small figure before her.

He was shorter than she was, yet had such presence she would not have dared cross him in any way.

She found herself asking him if he were one of the Lords of the Sun. This she did in her mind, forming images, not in words of her own race.

He in his turn spoke no words, but lifted his delicate hand and indicated that she should follow him.

She left the bright and beautiful garden, the colourful butterflies, the bees and singing water, and entered the chill darkness of an enormous chamber. At first the contrast from the sunlight shining on so many light surfaces to the shadows of the room made it impossible for her to see anything at all but when her eyes grew accustomed to the change she could see a man of great bulk sitting cross-legged in front of a small brazier gazing into the embers with great concentration. The little man she was with indicated she should draw nearer. The huge man did not look up even though her sandal scuffed against something and made a noise.

'Perhaps he cannot see me,' she thought.

But even as she thought it she knew the answer was that he was very well aware of her presence, but was not yet prepared to break off what he was doing. He went on staring into the small fire so long she became restless and began to look around.

Several large bronze vessels caught her eye, one in particular lit clearly by the light coming through the door from the courtyard. It was huge and cast with great skill, and designs that reminded her of the fiery serpent on the cloak of her new friend, but somehow more formalized, covered the surface, which was broken up into three main sections. The base on which the heavy vessel stood itself was decorated most beautifully, and the centre section, which was the largest and seemed to be a container casket of some sort, was decorated among other things with two piercing eyeballs.

'To keep off evil spirits,' Kyra thought.

The lid was heavy and dependable, but also beautiful. She

had never seen such bronze work in her whole life. What kind of people could these be to have such knowledge, such temples, such gardens, such fine and shining cloth, such skill with metal and enough gold to decorate the landscape with discs to represent the sun.

She felt eyes upon her and turned to see that both men were looking at her. When they were sure they had her attention they pulled something out of the fire with little bronze tongs. She stepped forward to see more clearly and found that they had what looked like pieces of bone on a dish of bronze in front of them. The bone was crisscrossed with delicate little cracks probably from the heat of the fire. Both men concentrated on them, bending low and ignoring her again. She wandered about the room, noticing the door into another smaller courtyard and finding it an exquisite miniature of the central one, but without the tower. All the flowers in this one were scarlet and their rich colour fairly took her breath away. She found more bronze vessels of many different sizes and shapes. One small jug in the shape of an owl she longed to take home with her to show to Fern and Karne.

The men were looking at her again so she returned to her place before the brazier, looking at them with a question in her mind. Neither spoke, but the huge man pointed with his fat finger to the little pieces of bone. He wanted her to look closely at them. She did so, puzzling what it was she was supposed to see. As she puzzled thoughts came into her head that were not her own. This was a kind of divination, she realized. They were asking the gods, who in some way were connected with their ancestors, to tell them if she was to be trusted or if she was an evil spirit.

At this she felt quite indignant. She? An evil spirit!

Her indignation cost her her concentration and the channel of their communication was temporarily lost. She intercepted an impatient look passing between the two men. She tried to be calm and concentrate again.

'What do your ancestors say?' she found herself asking aloud.

They frowned at her and she realized she had made a

180

mistake to talk aloud. She tried to think the question.

The men seemed to understand. The fat one raised his great bulk from the floor and stood beside his colleague, and both looked at her with their strange slanting eyes, but no feeling of fear came to her. The look was kindly and welcoming. The ancestors must have given a favourable answer.

She was just beginning to frame another question of her own when she realized she was no longer in the room. The whole scene, room, courtyard, temple, landscape, yellow road and wall of yellow stone, was gone.

She was in darkness and she was alone.

She was trembling uncontrollably as a kind of current thrust its path through her. She tried to keep from being afraid, knowing that fear was her worst enemy.

She tried to think the words 'Lords of the Sun' over and over again with all her concentration. Maal had told her to do this if she were in difficulties. It would help them to home in on her, he had said. She was not sure that this is what she wanted, but she was enough in control to know that it was not what she wanted that mattered now.

As she waited in the darkness beating out the words 'Lords of the Sun' over and over again, it seemed to her that the sound of the words became louder and louder until she fancied they were not in her head at all but were coming from outside, and although she could still distinguish them they were part of a greater gabble of words, most of which she did not understand. She felt she was no longer alone but in a crowd, a noisy, ebullient crowd shouting frantically for the victory of someone.

She heard the thundering noise of hooves coming towards her and she opened her eyes in terror. She was horrified to see an enormous and muscular bull approaching in a cloud of red dust, every ligament straining, steam coming from his nostrils, his eyes wild and bloodshot. She screamed and leapt back, but she need not have worried. He turned before he reached her and pounded off across a huge enclosure.

There were people all around her, people everywhere, dressed as she had never seen people dressed before. In amazement she saw women with breasts bare, flounced and flaring skirts of varied colours, bright ribbons in black hair coiled and towered upon the tops of their heads. Young men with brief skirts but otherwise bare and gleaming bodies, hair in strange curls, eyes accentuated with black paint. Old men in tunics. She stared and stared, knocked and pushed from side to side every now and again by excited people who were trying to see the sport of the bulls.

Behind one of the barricades was a raised dais and upon it such grand people sat that she was sure they must be Royalty. She had heard of Kings and Queens, Princes and Princesses, Chiefs and Chieftainesses, but never had she seen anything like them before. Round the Queen's neck was jewellery of such splendour, gold and amber, combined in strings so many and so thick they appeared almost solid, amber hanging from her ears and gold snakes coiling around her arms. She was the most beautiful woman Kyra had ever seen. The king beside her, although dark and magnificent, was outshone in every way. Behind them a palace of translucent stone rose, tier upon tier against the panorama of a distant mountain range.

Someone brushed past Kyra and caused her to turn. It was a young girl not much older than Fern, almost naked, so beautiful in a healthy animal way that Kyra drew in her breath with awe. The girl looked at her and Kyra realized she was the only one in the whole throng who could see her.

Amazed she stared into the girl's dark eyes. She too had paint around her lids to accentuate the almond shape. Her hair was bound tight with gold ribbon so that not a thread of it dared stray.

She seemed as surprised to see Kyra as Kyra was to see her.

'You want me?'

Kyra thought she heard the words but knew now they were only in her head.

'I do not know,' Kyra replied carefully. 'I am looking for the Lords of the Sun.'

Acknowledgement and recognition flickered in the almond

eyes but before she could phrase a reply a shout of such a pitch went up from the crowd all concentration was shattered and impossible. The girl moved like a young doe and leapt with the economy of an arrow to stand poised and beautiful upon the barrier wall that divided the crowd from the bull.

Kyra rushed forward and before she knew what she was doing thrust her hand out to seize the girl and pull her back to safety, but before she could do this the crowd roared again, this time with adulation, and Kyra realized the girl was the subject of their attention.

She stood magnificently poised for an instant. Her arms were raised to accept the greetings of the crowd and then she leapt and was down on the red dust with the bull.

Horrified, Kyra stared.

Like whipcord the body of the girl twisted and leapt in the most amazing way. She was dancing to the bull, challenging it with the flickering fire of her movements. For a moment he stood bemused and then could stand no more.

He charged.

Kyra's heart nearly burst with anxiety for the girl.

But as he was upon her she seized his horns and with a graceful arcing flip she somersaulted across his back and was gone, dainty as a bird, across the other side.

The crowd went mad. Kyra thought her head would explode with the sound. Dust and noise and violence was everywhere.

Kyra shut her eyes and put her hands to her ears.

But as suddenly as it had come, it cut out.

'Oh no!' she cried, disappointed, and opened her eyes again. But it was too late. She was back in the ante-chamber of darkness waiting for the next part of her journey.

She was growing used to the strangeness of the things that were happening to her by now, but could not help being a little anxious that she did not seem to be getting any nearer to the Lords of the Sun.

She started her silent but urgent chant again and this time when she opened her eyes she was in a colonnade of stone columns so huge that it seemed they would reach to the sky. She bent her head back and looked up the length of them. They were carved and spread at the top like trees and the sky was roofed out. Between them she could see further columns and beyond them dim chambers.

It seemed to her she was walking along the outer colonnade of a temple and from her left bright and burning light shafted in to fall between the columns in stripes on the stone flags of the floor. Dimness and coolness were to her right. Beyond her at the head of the colonnade more sunlight streamed in white heat on endless plains of white sand. This must be the desert country over the sea in the far south that Maal had told her about.

Having felt the force of the sun falling through the columns she decided to turn inwards and seek the cool depths of the Temple, but as she passed close to one of the columns she noticed that its surface was not smooth. It was marked its whole length with strange little markings and figures. As she gazed at it she was startled to come across several small representations of the figures of the half-human, half-animal demons she had seen before. She drew back in horror. Was this a temple to *them*?

She was just thinking she had better try and get away when a young man emerged from the darkness within the Temple and beckoned her.

She stared at him nervously, but was relieved to see he did not have the head of an animal. He was tall and well featured, shoulders broad, nose aquiline. The upper half of his body was bare except for a necklet of marvellous workmanship. His hair was thick and must have been mixed with something to make it stand so stiffly around his face. A band the same deep blue colour as his necklet, similarly decorated with a central eagle figure, was bound around his forehead. His feet were clad in gold sandals, the lower half of his body in folds of soft white cloth, bound with a girdle of gold.

She was attracted to him immediately and felt no more dread. She followed him first through colonnades of columns, then through dim chambers and even dimmer passages. At last he brought her to a halt within an inner chamber lit by torches. She stared around her and felt her old uneasiness come back as the same half-human, half-animal figures were depicted large upon the walls.

Ahead of her on a great plinth of black stone, a stone eagle stared back at her, a sun disc carved upon its forehead.

He noticed her fear and touched her arm comfortingly.

She looked at him and then looked questioningly at the dread figures around the walls. It was true she could not feel the malevolence from them she had felt before, but she could not forget the horror with which she had encountered them on other occasions.

He put his finger on her lips and another on her forehead.

His thoughts came clearly to her.

'These are our gods,' he said.

'Your gods!'

He could feel the revulsion in her.

'Why do you fear them so?' he asked.

She thought about the other two occasions and he seemed to receive the image of it.

Gently he shook his head.

'I was wrong,' he said, 'these are not our gods. They are the images of our gods.'

'How does that explain it?' she thought, still suspicious of the place.

He smiled.

'There is one God, and beneath him hierarchies of spirits we call gods, but God and spirit are impossible for human minds to understand. We are too undeveloped, too primitive,' he added.

She hoped he did not add that last epithet after looking at her. She was beginning to feel more and more like a primitive country girl of no account faced with so much grandeur and skill. He caught her thought and smiled again. She noticed that there was no condescension in his look. He liked her and respected her in spite of her crude clothes and untrained mind.

185

'Having no words and images that are adequate to describe their intuitive feelings about God and the spirit world, people choose images from their own earthly experiences and use them somehow to "parcel up" the feelings that they have.'

She looked puzzled.

'Some people choose the Sun and call it God, some the Moon, some the king, some an animal or a bird. They know deep down when they begin that what they have chosen is only a symbol, a representation of what they really mean. But there are times when they forget that this is how it is and you will find people worshipping the image and not what it is supposed to represent.

'My people carve a statue of a man with a jackal's head and it is supposed to represent the spirit who guides the dead into the spirit world.

'To some who are far along the path to enlightenment the figure in stone is no more than a sign post that points in the direction where the truth about death and the crossing from the material to the spirit world may be found. It is the sign at the entrance to a whole group of understandings. It is no more than that. They look beyond the image to the Reality.

'But to someone not so far developed, incapable of grasping subtle and abstract concepts, it is accepted as the Reality itself. The worshipper stops short at the image, sees no further, may even see himself reflected back from it. The statue, the image itself, is believed to be a god.

'The jackal's head was chosen originally maybe because jackals are creatures of the night who seek out the dead. The human body was given to the jackal to add, symbolically, the human dimension. In one hand he carried a divine sceptre, denoting divine power, in the other the ankh, the symbol of life.

'It is clear that Death and Life are contained in this one image, with the power that transforms the one into the other.

'But when the symbol becomes downgraded into an image of a god that is taken literally, all kinds of misinterpretations of the symbolism can occur.

'A holy image that set out to bring comfort is turned into its

186

opposite and brings fear. The jackal head can suggest devouring nocturnal beasts preying on the dead.'

'I understand,' cried Kyra, 'that makes sense.'

'So you see the images of the gods can bring comfort and fear depending on the interpretation of the people who worship them, the same god-image can be good or evil depending on the worshipper, can bring death or life.'

Kyra frowned, trying to grasp it all.

'Demon or kindly spirit, beast or human. Both interpretations are possible from the one image. It is we who draw the one, or the other, from deep within ourselves. That is how it is possible for men to kill and commit atrocities in the name of their god. They have forgotten the god behind the word and use the word with all its powerful connotations to excuse whatever it is they wish to do.

'The priest who sees the jackal-god as a powerful weapon to inspire fear and keep his people cowed has brought this from within himself.

'The priest who sees the jackal-god as a powerful but kindly guide and guardian brings this also from within himself.

'There are no gods of stone or fire or flesh, but there are unimaginable spirit influences from the Source of All that we clothe for convenience in words, in images, in stone and paint.

'Those figures you saw as demons were figments of your own mind.'

'But they were *there* — as surely as you are now.'

The young man looked at her kindly.

'Evil influences you feared were there. *You* gave them the clothing of our gods.'

'But I had never seen or heard of your gods before!'

He looked thoughtful at that.

'It is possible someone near you knew of our gods and used them in thought form to frighten you.'

She thought about it and told him about Wardyke and Maal.

The young priest walked with her back through the Temple, passing sights of great strangeness. There was hardly a section of wall that was not covered with their weird signs and paintings. He listened quietly to all that she had to say and when they reached a quiet shady garden with a lily pond he motioned her to sit on a warm slab of stone.

'I think this Wardyke,' he said at last, 'has had dealings with some of our people.'

His face was grave and sad.

'There is much that is wrong with our priesthood,' he said. 'Many have lost the insight and use the image-gods to extract blind obedience and riches from their people. Fear is a weapon they are very skilled at using.'

Kyra knew she had found someone at last that she could ask about the Lords of the Sun.

He listened and nodded.

'You have not been wasting your time . . . each journey you have made has been an invitation to one of the Lords of the Sun.'

'Who are they, these Lords?'

'I am one,' he said, and she started back in amazement.

'Probably you met several others. They are not pure spirits, but people who are trained amongst the priesthood in the special tasks of communication over great distances, over the whole world.'

She was shy of him now. She had thought he was some kind of trainee priest, much nearer her own level.

'Do not be afraid of me,' he said quietly. 'You have come a long way to find me and I will help you.'

'What must I do?' she asked humbly.

'That I cannot tell you now. No, do not look so disappointed. You have found me and I will not desert you. But what Maal wanted you to do was to call a meeting of the Lords of the Sun in your country. That you must do and we will all be there. Together we will help you. Together our powers are greater.'

'But how do I call a meeting?' she asked despairingly.

He looked at her with great affection. She seemed so small

and vulnerable, far too young to have the burdens of her community upon her shoulders.

'*Will* it,' he said simply.

She looked puzzled.

'Shut your eyes,' he said patiently.

She shut her eyes.

'Now *will* that the Lords of the Sun will come together to help your community.'

She squeezed her eyes tight shut and wished, as she had never wished for anything in her life, that her travels and her troubles would be over and that the Lords of the Sun would come together to help her and her people.

The good-looking priest was gone. The huge temple of red sand stone columns was gone, the little garden surrounded by a wall painted with a scene of wild ducks and reeds was gone.

She was alone again and she was afraid.

This time it *must* work. She could not go on much longer.

'Please!' she whispered, tears pricking at the back of her eyes. 'Please!'

Music made her open her eyes and the scene before her staggered her imagination.

She knew that she was back in her own country, but a long way from her home. She was in the giant Sacred Circle that she had visited once before as a passenger in the mind of Maal.

It was early dawn. First light was creeping over the sky, some stars still shining in the rich blue air. A light and gossamer mist was drifting close to the ground, so that everything, even the gigantic blocks of Stone that stood around the circumference in their hundreds, seemed to be floating and moving.

As she had noticed before a high ridge of earth and grass surrounded the whole and blocked out the rest of the world. She had never seen outside this Circle and could not imagine how the community who used such a great place would live.

Within the great Circle of Standing Stones she was aware of circles within circles of people moving rhythmically to the music of drum and flute, stepping sideways slowly and with elegance, their arms raised so that the tips of their fingers brushed their neighbours' as they moved. On a certain beat they dipped their heads and bent their knee in a way that gave the whole ring movement a sinuous serpentine character. As each concentric circle was moving around the Stone Circle in a direction opposite to the one within and without itself, the currents and eddies of invisible force generated were complex indeed.

Kyra quite forgot she was supposed to be playing a part in the ceremony and stared blatantly at everything she could see.

She noticed that the people in the rings were placed alternately man and woman, boy and girl. The force they seemed to be trying to create this day was to come from the tension between, in a sense the friction between, differing elements. She knew that a mysterious energy was released when man and woman came together. She had felt the spark of it when she had been near the young desert priest. The priests of this community appeared to be using this force to build up energy for the use of the Lords of the Sun.

Curious about the people themselves who lived and worked in the presence of such a temple, Kyra began to look at individuals. There were people there she recognized as country villagers like herself, in roughly woven woollen garments, their bodies liberally browned by the sun and muscles well developed from work in fields. There were people she knew were metal workers, stone masons, flint miners, merchants. Others were stranger to her. Tall people. Elegant people. Dressed in flowing cloth, finely woven, the very way they held their heads different from the farmers and the villagers. The women of this type wore jewellery, some of which reminded her of her 'travels'. She saw necklaces of black jet, collars of sun metal, earrings and bracelets. The men wore studded belts and bands of leather on their heads and arms.

And then there were the Strangers from other countries, darker people, lighter people, dressed in different ways but all part of the ring moving with the same rhythmic movement.

Undeniable forces and vibrations were set up, currents and

eddies of power. She could feel it. She could almost see it. The pulsing of the music added to the intensity of the feeling. The mist that moved with its own serpentine life about their feet added to the impression of detachment from the earth. Everything was charged and potent. She was on a level of reality that she had not known before. Her heart began beating loudly. She had finally reached the conjunction of the Lords of the Sun.

The figures of the concentrically moving circles began to dim for her and she became aware with greater clarity of the smaller Stone Circle within the greater, in which she herself was standing.

She was in the centre and around her in a ring but standing as still as the Tall Stones themselves were figures she could only think were the Lords of the Sun. They were impressive figures dressed strangely in the styles of their countries, each different from the other, and all different from the circling figures around them. The stillness of her Circle was astonishing in comparison to the movement surrounding them. It was as though they were enclosed in a capsule of great peace, the still point at the centre of ceaseless motion.

She felt the movement was generating power for them in some way, but leaving them undisturbed.

Within her circle there seemed to be no one in charge, no priest conducting the meeting. With a sudden tremor she realized that she was expected to speak, she had called them together and they were waiting for her to tell them what to do.

She looked around in despair. So many strangers! And then her heart leapt. She saw first the girl athlete from the Palace of the Bulls, this time dressed like her countrywomen in long, flounced skirt and sleeved bodice open over the breasts, and then her young priest from the desert temple of the sandstone columns. Her face flooded with the warmth of a smile and she took a step forward. But the young priest shook his head slightly and she knew she had to stand in the centre and make a 'speech'.

She glanced up at the sky and she remembered that with the dawn her body would not be safe in the Sacred Circle of her community. She remembered also these Lords had work of their own to do and she must not waste their time.

She drew herself up to her full height and prepared to 'think' the whole story of Wardyke coming to their village and what had happened since.

When she had done she stayed quietly, trying to keep her mind a blank, ready for their thoughts. The drumming and the movements of the people around them had become like a low vibrational hum and was no disturbance at all.

Slowly thoughts that were not hers began to come to her. She was not sure if they came from individuals, and if they did, from which ones. It seemed more likely that it was their composite thinking that was reaching her.

'. . . It is true Wardyke has not received the final seal of the priesthood and so has no right to practice as a priest. . .'

She found herself wondering why they had not prevented him doing so.

'. . . You are reminded that we are human and know only what is communicated to us. Before you had told us the story we had not known what was going on . . .'

She felt ashamed that she had questioned, and doubted in this way and determined not to interrupt with her own thoughts again. She shut her eyes the better to concentrate.

'. . . He must be stopped, but Maal was right to say that you must not do it with force . . .'

She smiled with pleasure at the warmth of their approval for Maal.

'. . . It is the evil in Wardyke that must be destroyed, not Wardyke himself . . .

'To kill him would be to surrender onself to the same evil that ruled his life . . .'

Kyra agreed. But how?

'. . . Confidence and belief are the strongest forces in a man's nature . . .

'. . . It is here that you must mount your attack . . .'

In answer to Kyra's unspoken question the Lords of the Sun patiently explained.

'. . . The key to Wardyke's power in your community lies in

192

confidence and belief. He believes that he has the right and the power to do what he is doing, and you believe that too. This gives him his strength . . .

'. . . No magician . . . (and here Kyra remembered Maal had said this too) . . . has power over you if you do not *believe* that he has . . .'

She understood this, but did not know if she would have the strength, faced by Wardyke, to doubt his powers. When Maal talked, when the Lords of the Sun explained, it all seemed quite simple. But meeting the burning eye of Wardyke was another matter. Then she *could not* doubt.

'. . . We know it is not easy, but it must be done. You must return to your people and speak to them, make them understand that Wardyke has no power of himself. It is their *belief* that he has power that gives it to him. Without their belief he is helpless. You must render him helpless and thereby harmless.

'. . . That way your community will be free without becoming the slaves of evil themselves . . .'

Kyra's eyes were open now and she was looking worried. She knew they were right but how she wished, how she had hoped, that they could do something sudden and dramatic to remove Wardyke from their midst. She knew it would be a long hard struggle to persuade the villagers to change their beliefs like this. In fact she did not think she could do it.

'. . . You *can* do it . . . You can! You have powers within yourself that you are only just beginning to tap, and we will give you help . . .'

Kyra looked up hopefully at that.

'. . . Before the Spring a new priest will arrive to work in your community. He will have the final seal and he will be a good man . . .

'. . . When he comes, you will leave, your work there done . . .'

She looked startled. Leave her home?

'. . . You will travel south through many trials and dangers and you will come, in the flesh, to this place and you will train to be a priest yourself . . .'

193

She gasped.

'Me?'

'. . . Yes, you. You have been chosen. . .

'. . . But there is much still for you to do.

'When you return to your home this dawn you will go to the place where Maal is ·buried and you will find a small stone upon his burial mound. Yes, you will know which one it is when you see it. You will take it and keep it close with you until Wardyke is overthrown. Maal's help will be in that stone.

'. . . Our help will be in the sky. Look at the sky and you will see a sign that is confirmation of our help . . .'

'Now?'

'. . . No, not now. You will know when to look . . .'

'This is like Maal's advice,' Kyra thought with a certain discontent, 'always telling me I will mysteriously "know" something and then leaving me by myself!'

But she was comforted that she would have definite help.

'. . . You have already proved to yourself that you are capable of projecting images into Wardyke's mind. Work on this. Encourage your friends to help you. There is strength in communion of thought. Choose a time for as many as possible of you to project the same image into Wardyke's mind. Never let him forget his crimes. Haunt him night and day. You will find that particularly when he is asleep it will be easy to influence the images of his dreams. His surface mind will be off guard and there will be no interruptions from superficial distractions . . .

'. . . We will join with you in this work . . .

'. . . Finally eroded by guilt and undermined in confidence, he will be helpless and will have to look for a new way to live his life . . .

'. . . Believe it, child, for it is true . . .'

Kyra looked around the Circle. The thoughts of these great people were locked in her heart and she would draw upon them in the difficult days to come.

One by one she looked at them. Each the possessor of

194

knowledge and skills far beyond the ordinary man, each from a country far distant from her own. She recognized the large man from the Temple of the Squares and Circles and beside him stood a woman of dark skin and hair of black silk streaked with silver flowing to the silver sandals on her feet. Beyond her a man clad in a magnificent cape of multicoloured feathers stood beside an old man dressed in rags, so thin and wasted that he seemed more of a skeleton than a living man, his hair wild and straggling, leaning on a gnarled and knobbled stick to keep himself upright, but his eyes full of light and fire.

Then she saw her beautiful athlete and could not help wondering at her youth. The girl met her eyes and smiled.

'Age has nothing to do with it,' she said in Kyra's head. 'We are all thousands of years old and yet still in our infancy.'

Beyond her was a priest standing straight and tall, dressed simply in woven wool except for one magnificent pendant of green jade that he wore on a thong about his neck. She knew instinctively he was a countryman of hers. He was the high priest of this Great Circle. The host of this extraordinary gathering. She looked closer at his face and was impressed with its calm strength. In these people she had confidence. If they said she could bend metal with a mere touch, she would believe it and she would do it. If they said she could be a priest, she would believe it and she would do it.

The task she had to do within her own community no longer seemed impossible. She would not be alone. She would have their strengthening thoughts with her in everything she did.

She began to think about her own powers and her own relationship to those around her.

'I cannot be too helpless,' she thought, 'otherwise I would not be here now. Otherwise I would not be chosen to be trained as a priest!'

And with that she had a surge of self-confidence that would see her through many a difficulty.

Pleased to feel the strengthening confidence that was coursing through her, the Lords of the Sun prepared to leave.

Kyra became aware of it when she suddenly noticed that the undercurrent of rhythmic sound from outside their small circle had risen to a crescendo and was beginning to deafen her.

Startled she looked around and noticed that the Lords who had looked so solid a moment before were beginning to dissolve in the air, whose visible vibrations were increasing every second.

'Oh no!' she cried, loth to let them go.

She turned to the young desert priest and had such an overwhelming feeling of yearning for him to stay with her that it was almost a pain.

As though her desire for him was holding him back in some way he was the last to go. She was sure his eyes were seeking hers as longingly as hers were seeking his. For a moment they seemed to melt together and Kyra had the strangest feeling that she was within his arms, although she knew she was not and could see him separate from herself across the Circle.

She opened her mouth to cry out in real words and at that second he and all about her disappeared.

Shaken and trembling she found herself on a slab of cold stone, early sunlight streaming everywhere, and the anxious faces of Karne and Fern looking down at her.

'Kyra!' Karne was calling urgently. 'We *must* go! Someone will find us here.'

'Are you all right?' Fern put her arm around her gently and helped her upright.

Kyra looked dazed.

She could not answer. Everything was shaking and whirling around her. She felt as though she were going to faint.

'Kyra!' Fern cried, and Karne caught her as she fell.

'Oh you gods protect her!' he muttered fervently.

'We must take her out of here,' Fern whispered anxiously. 'Perhaps when she is out of this Circle she will be better.'

Together they lifted her and carried her out and down the hill and as far as they could go from the Standing Stones.

In the valley the tired villagers were preparing for the funeral of the two young people. The fires of vigil that had burnt all night were nothing more than smouldering embers.

196

The Forest is Punished

As autumn gradually came to the community Karne and Kyra
worked hard to change the villagers' attitude to Wardyke. As
they had expected, it was not easy.

They explained much of what had happened to them to
people they felt were ready for it, starting with their family.

Their father listened to everything they had to say with
great attention and asked few, but pertinent, questions. Their
mother was immediately horrified at the risks Kyra had been
taking and the blasphemy of her entering the forbidden
Sacred Circle. She was so occupied with fussing about these
things that she did not seem to grasp the real implication of
what they told her.

Thon was angry almost immediately and wanted action,
arguing that the Lords of the Sun were soft and that there was
only one way to deal with Wardyke, with force. He had had his
eye on Mia for a wife and could think of nothing but revenge.

Patiently Kyra explained the reasons the Lords of the Sun
had advised against this. Patiently she went over the whole
ground again. But Thon was not convinced. The only reason
he had not already killed Wardyke was that he had not had
the opportunity. The other villagers refused to rise again after
what had happened, and alone he stood no chance against
Wardyke. There always seemed to be some of his most
unpleasant Strangers with him as bodyguard and Thon had
noticed they were now carrying weapons, short bronze daggers
tucked into the top binding of their sandal leggings and stone
axes in their belts.

Kyra pointed out that Wardyke could not be such a
powerful magician if he needed armed men to defend him.
This made the people think and one by one they joined her in

197

her efforts to discomfit him by projecting disturbing images into his mind. This was not easy, as they were not used to sustaining one image for a long time, nor to disciplining their minds so rigidly. Most of them found as they lay in their warm rugs at the appointed hour of the night that they started with great enthusiasm to project the image of Mia's death and the boy being stoned, and then one by one they drifted off the point, some to sleep and some to think of other things.

Many times Kyra felt close to despair. Weeks passed and though they tried projection every night Wardyke showed no signs of being disturbed. He strode about surrounded by his lackeys, more confident than ever.

He had set the villagers to work making battle axes from the hard granite of their local hills. Day after day they sat chipping and hammering and banging away, making weapons of war that they did not want.

He spoke to them of enemies about to invade, and remembering the fall of stars they obeyed his every command. Most of them were too afraid openly to oppose a man whom the gods had apparently set their seal of approval upon.

He told them flint was coming in great quantities from the south and that they would be able to make arrow and spear heads with it. Swords and daggers were on their way as well.

One evening, at her lowest ebb, Kyra sat upon the hillside feeling very much alone. There seemed no way she could carry out the instructions of the Lords. She, Karne and Fern were consistent and dedicated to the plan, but the others listened, agreed and seemed to want to help, but as soon as the slightest difficulty got in their way they gave up.

It seemed to her they had forgotten about Mia and the boy, were in fact deliberately trying to forget. It was so much easier to drift with each day, occasionally grumbling, but on the whole obeying Wardyke. If only she could show them some sign of success their resolution might be strengthened and they might be prepared to take more chances and make more effort.

She thought longingly about the Lords of the Sun. If only they were here to help! Perhaps she could summon them with her will as she had done before.

She shut her eyes to the pale gold of the evening sky, the red gold of the autumn woods, and thought about the Lords of the Sun. At first she could not get beyond the young desert priest, but her longing to see him was not entirely connected with the problem in hand and she forced her mind to visualize the others, one by one, and to call upon them with all her might for help.

She heard no voices, thought no thoughts that were not her own, and at last, defeated and depressed, she opened her eyes.

Before her in the sky, veil upon veil of shining light fell from the uttermost height of the heavens almost to the earth, in folds finer than the finest drapery she had ever imagined. Stunned, she gazed as it changed through every possible shade and finally faded.

'Look in the sky and you will see a sign that is confirmation of our help,' they had said, and now as she called to them for help the sky was transformed beyond belief.

That night every person in the community, including Wardyke's Strangers, had dreams that kept them tossing and turning, groaning and sighing. Mia's death and the stoning of the boy was played out in every detail, grotesque and horrible, within the minds of every sleeping person. If they awoke they would fall asleep soon afterwards and within seconds the ghastly scene would be enacted yet again in the arena of their minds.

Wardyke woke in sudden terror in his own house and cried out, fighting off imaginary stones and sticks as they came flailing at him. Around him, eyes wild with hate and accusation were closing in on him, and for a moment such fear took him over that he was powerless to withstand them.

He woke, sweating and trembling, and rose, lit torches and strode about his rooms the rest of the night. In the morning he looked haggard and tired, and Kyra was not slow to point this out to the villagers.

That day when Wardyke walked amongst the community there were many who dared look him boldly in the eye and there were many who looked and felt as though they had a secret knowledge that gave them strength against him.

For the first time he was uneasy. Something was going on over which he had no control. He tried questioning some of the villagers, but they pretended not to know what he was talking about. They became instantly humble, but in such a way that he was not sure it was real.

He alerted the Strangers to look out for any kind of disaffection and report it to him. If the villagers were beginning to turn against him, there must be a ring-leader. And that man he *must* have before it was too late.

In the afternoon he went again to Fern's house and surprised her sweeping the fallen leaves away from the entrance to her small home. She jumped slightly when he appeared and then gripped the branch she was using until her knuckles showed white. Her eyes were blazing and defiant.

He approached her, his own eyes like whirlpools of darkness.

'No!' she cried.

'I need you,' he said, and his voice was filled with a strange kind of pain.

'No!' she cried again and lifted the branch to strike him if he took a step nearer her.

His mouth twisted slightly, and with a swift movement he knocked the branch out of her hand with one of his giant hands and struck her across the face with the other.

'I *need* you!' he repeated, his voice strained and menacing.

She reeled back with the force of the blow, but when she had regained her balance her expression was as defiant as ever. Indeed slightly mocking now, as though she despised him for having resorted to petty violence.

An ugly red flush began to creep across his face.

His hands began to rise and with a leap of fear in her heart she remembered Mia.

'Help me!' she cried deep inside her to all the forces of nature that she loved so much.

As though in answer to her prayer a sudden violent wind sprang up and Wardyke, who was standing near the door post of her house which was covered with creeper, was lashed in the face by its long and thorny tendrils.

With a scream he sprang back, covering his eyes as the thorns ripped and scratched at them. Leaves swirled everywhere and dust choked him.

'I cannot see! I cannot see!' he screamed, staggering and almost falling.

She stood looking at him, the wind swirling her long red hair like flame around her. Her eyes blazed with triumph as she remembered she was not alone.

'Go, Wardyke!' she cried with tremendous and surprising authority. 'And never come to this wood again!'

A whirlwind pushed and buffeted him, he choked and spluttered with the dust, staggered and almost fell. He could feel blood on his hands and on his face. His eyes were stinging and painful, his chest aching with the effort of coughing.

He turned and half ran along the path, a fallen branch that he could have sworn had not been there when he arrived tripped him up and he crashed to the ground like a felled tree.

As suddenly as it had started, the wind ceased. There was absolute silence as Wardyke picked himself up. He looked around at the bushes and the trees of the wood and he could *feel* the animosity. but he could see nothing.

He looked back at Fern and she had a strange grandeur. This was her kingdom, and he was banished.

He left, mopping the blood from his cheeks and thinking bitterly of the experience. He was shaken, but by no means defeated. He would be back.

That night Fern woke to a feeling of great unease. She sat up and looked around her, every sense alert, like a small animal. Something was wrong. Something did not feel right. As she listened she seemed to hear thousands of minute voices raised in pain and fear, clamouring for her help. Appalled, she leapt up and left the house, still not knowing what the trouble was. As she stood in the entrance an overwhelming smell of wood smoke met her nostrils, and her ears were filled with the cruel crackle of flames in dry twigs.

Fire! Her wood was on fire!

She could see it now, leaping scarlet from branch to branch, tearing at the dry leaves, devouring the delicate fronds of bracken.

'Wardyke!' she cried. Wardyke's revenge. She might have known he would not give in so easily.

Torn with pain to see her beautiful and living wood so tortured and destroyed, she could not see what she could do to rescue it. There was no way. The wind that had helped her before was now helping Wardyke. The flames were driven before it to wilder and wilder excesses and if she were not careful the fire would have her too. Weeping with pity for the trees she ran as fast as she could. Other creatures joined her and the ground was full of leaping frogs, deer, squirrels and hares. The luckier birds were screeching in the sky.

She called and called for help, but who was there to hear her?

Meanwhile in the village Kyra was having an uneasy dream in which the villagers had all been put in a deep pit by Wardyke and set on fire. She woke as the flame licked her own flesh and she could feel the pain. Once awake she lay puzzled. The feeling of fire on her arm had been so vivid and yet here she was, perfectly safe, in her sleeping rug. She was just turning over to sleep again when Karne tapped her on the shoulder.

'What is it?' she whispered.

'I am not sure. But I feel something is happening that should be stopped.'

She sat up.

'Wardyke?'

'It must be. I am going outside to prowl around a bit to see if I can discover anything.'

'I will come too,' Kyra said, wide awake.

She pulled on her dress and her warm cape and slipped out into the night after her brother. The village was dead quiet and dark. Nothing was stirring but themselves.

'What is that?'

Karne pointed in the direction of Fern's home. There was a faint glow.

They both stared at it for a moment puzzled, and then the same conclusion hit them simultaneously.

'Fire!' gasped Karne and was off like a startled wild animal towards the red and ugly stain, Kyra close behind him.

If only Fern were unharmed!

The woods were dry at this time of year and would burn easily, and there was a wind blowing.

'Oh no!' thought Kyra, 'all those beautiful trees and plants!'

But her main concern was Fern.

Karne covered the ground as though he had wings. He had reached the outskirts of Fern's valley before Kyra was within sight of it. He saw at once the smouldering devastation, the blackened husks of trees and beyond them the fire still raging, still tearing at the living wood. Scarcely noticing the pain in his feet he ran across the still smoking earth towards Fern's house, to stand appalled in sight of the pile of embers that marked the place where it had stood.

He knew now how a wolf must feel when it lifts its anguished head and howls in the deep hollow of the night. His heart was howling too.

He heard Kyra shouting, and looked back. She was on the rise just where the fire had begun. She was shouting and pointing but he could not hear what she was saying. He followed the line of her hand. She kept pointing and shouting, more and more desperate as he did not understand. At last she started to run in the direction she had been pointing, her feet less tough than his hurting against the hot earth.

'Go back!' he shouted, and ran towards her.

Within earshot at last he heard her cry, 'Fern! Fern!' and look beyond at the woods still burning.

He did not stay to question further but ran towards the place.

On the way he came upon the stream and followed its merciful length for as long as he could. Before he left it he plunged himself into the water and made himself as wet as he could.

Through the flames and smoke suddenly he could see Fern. She was beating at the fire with branches, weeping and choking at the same time.

'Fern!' he shouted and without another thought plunged straight through a barrier of flame.

Startled, she saw him emerge from the fire as though he were the manifestation of some demon. She shrieked and fainted, the whole experience too fraught to bear another second.

Before she touched the ground she was in his arms and he was back through the wall of fire, smothering the sparks on her with his damp clothes. Staggering under her weight, he managed to get back to the stream and out on to the bare hillside where the stubble was almost burnt out.

Kyra was waiting for him and wept with joy to see them both safe, and from there they limped home on feet that were burnt and painful.

Kyra woke their sleeping family and within minutes they were being looked after. Karne's horrified mother rushed to put soothing animal fat upon the burns on her son's feet, and on Fern's arms and back. Kyra herself secretly rubbed some on her own soles. She was not blistered like Karne and Fern and did not want a fuss made of her, but her feet were tender and sore.

The dawn found Karne, Kyra and Fern fast asleep. The mother insisted the family should be quiet and leave them to rest as long as they could, so one by one they crept out and went about the day's business.

Most of the villagers went to see the fire, which by now was almost burnt out. They looked with sorrow at the blackened scar that had once been a lovely, leafy forest.

Wardyke came to survey the scene. Of course there was no proof that he had caused it, but more than one villager noted an expression of satisfaction on his face.

The Second Challenge

After the fire Fern stayed on with Karne and Kyra's family, but she did not recover as quickly as they expected. Karne's burns healed fast and although he probably would always have scars on his feet to remind him of that terrible night, he was soon back to normal. Fern's wounds took longer to heal and even when the skin was whole, she was so listless and pale that Kyra's mother insisted she rested most of the day. Fern, who was usually so full of energy that she rarely did nothing, sat now day after day beside the hearth or in the sun beside the wood pile, content to be inactive.

Everyone was anxious about her, but no one knew what to do. Karne particularly hovered over her and worried.

'What is the matter with her,' he asked Kyra desperately. 'The burns healed ages ago. She cannot still be in pain.'

'It is something inside,' Kyra said thoughtfully. 'Perhaps she is mourning for her woods and her garden. They were like people to her.'

Karne nodded and took Fern a present of some particularly beautiful autumn leaves and berries he found on the hill.

Fern accepted them in silence and lowered her head so that he would not see the tears that gathered in her eyes. But she was not quick enough. He stooped down and kissed the top of her head. With the touch of his lips she broke down completely and sobbed and sobbed. He gathered her to him and held her, not knowing what to say or do. But she did not need words or deeds. She needed him.

At last she had cried herself out and was still.

He sat down beside her and held her hand, she leant her head against his shoulder and, saying nothing to each other, they sat for a long time.

After that she began to take a small interest in things again and started to busy herself helping Kyra's family.

'In the spring the plants will all grow again,' Kyra said to her one day. 'You will see, your garden and your wood will be beautiful once more.

Fern nodded, but her smile was still sad.

'Shall we help you build your house again?' Kyra's little brothers Ji and Okan asked. They loved making things. They used the boat sometimes for fishing, but somehow it was not quite so much fun as the actual building of it had been, and it was such a long walk to the sea, carrying the boat the whole way, that they tended not to do it as often as they had planned.

Fern looked as though she were thinking about their proposal, and at last she made a decision.

'That is very kind of you. But we have to get the wood from somewhere else. All my wood is burnt.'

'Wood is no problem,' said Okan joyfully.

'We know where we can get plenty!' said Ji.

'And we can made a sled to haul it on.'

'I do not want living trees chopped down heartlessly,' Fern said warningly.

'Oh no,' they said. 'These were blown down in a storm. They have been lying all summer waiting to be used.'

Fern smiled.

'I will show you how I want my house and when you are ready where there is more wood that itself is ready to be used,' she said.

'Can we start making the sled now?'

'Of course.'

They rushed off excitedly, delighted to have something else to make.

Kyra smiled at Fern.

'That is better,' she said gently, 'you are beginning to come alive again.'

'I am sorry I gave up like that . . . it was just that . . .' · She hesitated.

'What is the matter?'

Kyra could see there was something still worrying Fern.

'Are you afraid to go back? Would you rather stay with us?'

Fern shook her head, but still could not bring herself to speak.

'Stay with us!' Kyra pleaded, suddenly sure this was the root of the difficulty. 'We would all love to have you — particularly Karne!' she added with a mischievous smile.

At this Fern looked more miserable than ever.

'It *is* Karne!' Kyra cried in amazement.

'No,' said Fern quickly.

'What then?'

'Oh, Kyra,' said Fern in despair, 'I am with child.'

Kyra looked stunned.

'Karne?'

'No. Wardyke.'

'Oh no!' Kyra was horrified. She took both of Fern's hands in hers and held them very tightly.

The relief of having told someone sympathetic was wonderful for Fern. She told Kyra everything, the visit she had had from Wardyke on the afternoon before the fire and the horror with which she had realized that he had burnt her precious trees in revenge for her rejection of him.

'I hate him, Kyra,' she cried. 'I cannot help it. I hate him and I fear him!'

Kyra did not know what to say. They both knew hatred and fear were self-destructive emotions and caused nothing but more evil to come from any situation, but she could not blame Fern for hating and fearing Wardyke.

'And what are we to do about Karne?' Kyra said thoughtfully.

Both she and Fern were loth to let him know the situation, and yet they also knew they should not keep it from him much longer.

Dumbly Fern shook her head. Hopelessly she shrugged her shoulders.

It was some days later that events forced an answer to this question.

Karne came briskly to Fern as she was helping Kyra shake out the sleeping rugs. It was a clear and shining day and before the long wet winter set upon them Kyra's mother liked to clear out all the dust and dirt of summer.

'Come,' he said commandingly to her, his face the face of someone who has a happy secret he is longing to share, but is determined to make the most of it before he does.

She looked a question.

'I want to show you something special.'

She shook her head.

'I cannot. Kyra and I must do these rugs.'

'They can be done another time!'

'Oh no, they cannot!'

He was tugging at her now and she was laughingly resisting.

'Oh, go on Fern,' Kyra said, 'find out what it is. I can do these by myself.'

'Of course you cannot! It is heavy work for one,' Fern said indignantly, still holding back.

'Well, Karne will help us and it will be done more quickly.'

'Oh, will he!' mocked Karne.

'I am not coming with you until it is done,' warned Fern.

He shrugged.

'Women!' he exclaimed, but he was not unwilling to help them. He could spin out the delight of anticipation that much longer.

The work went faster with his help, but not fast enough for the two girls, who were by now much intrigued by Karne's secret.

At last they were through and Karne took Fern's hand. Kyra watched with tenderness and affection as the two people closest to her walked away.

But there was still the shadow of Wardyke lying between them.

Karne took Fern a long way from the village. Somewhat in the direction of her former home, but carefully choosing the route

208

so that the gloomy sight of the burnt wood did not intrude upon their mood.

He led her north, around the far side of her wood, but out of sight of it.

'What is it?' she kept asking.

But he would not tell her.

'You will see.'

At last he paused on the ridge of a small hill and looked ahead of him in a way that made Fern realize that they had arrived. She looked to see what it could be.

What she saw was a beautiful little glen, trees of pure gold beside a stream, bracken- and heather-covered hills dipping down to join it, huge grey rocks covered with an exquisite patterning of lichen in orange and grey-green making a natural and almost circular sun trap just above the tree line.

'There,' said Karne in triumph, pointing to the flat grassy patch of earth surrounded by the rocks, 'is the natural place for our home!'

She gasped, her face a study of conflicting emotions.

It was truly beautiful. It was truly home!

But . . .

Karne was not looking at her. He saw only the future.

'We can use the rocks as part of the house,' he said, 'we can build on to them in some way. The garden can spill out through the gaps and run down to the stream. These are still your woods but on the other side . . . the fire did not come this far . . .'

'Karne . . .' she said at last, and there was something in her voice that made him look at her in surprise.

She was not smiling with joy and excitement as he had expected her to be. Her face was pale and drawn, her eyes dark. A sudden chill came to his heart. Surely she would not refuse to live here with him and be his wife. Surely there could be no doubt . . .

'Fern?'

She held up her hand as though to keep him from touching her. She shook her head sadly.

'Oh, Karne, you should have spoken to me before you

209

started to think such things.'

'But we love each other!' he cried.

She shook her head miserably.

'We *love* each other!' he repeated with force, seizing her arms and looking desperately into her eyes.

Her eyes were full of pain, but they did not deny what he was saying.

'It is not as simple as that,' she said.

'It *is* as simple as that,' he insisted.

'Let me go, Karne, there are things you do not know . . .'

'What things?' he demanded angrily, still not releasing her.

'Let me go.'

He dropped his hands from her arms, but his eyes were burning into hers.

She was silent for a long time, her heartbeat almost stifling her, but she could not hold back forever.

'I carry Wardyke's child,' she said at last, simply and flatly. Unable to say more.

He recoiled.

She dropped her eyes and could not look at him. She did not dare imagine what was going through his mind. She could feel his presence on the hill, feel the natural things around poised and waiting, the very air strained and tense.

And then the tension snapped. He moved.

She looked up but he was already gone.

She longed to explain, to tell him that she loved him, but the feelings that were conflicting in her heart were too strong and too complex.

She could not even call his name aloud, although in her heart it was called a hundred times.

She watched him as he strode away, and he did not look back.

Hours later Fern returned to the village.

Kyra met her with a bright and eager face and a question on her lips, but when she saw Fern's face the light went out of her own.

'You told him?' she said.

Fern nodded and walked past her to the house.

Kyra did not ask any more questions.

Fern spoke quietly but firmly to Kyra's mother, thanking her for the refuge in her home but saying that she must now return to her own.

'But you *have* no home!' Kyra's mother cried.

'I must be with my garden. I have been too long away. I am ashamed I left it when it needed me most. I should have been working there all this time trying to comfort it and to help it grow again.'

Kyra stopped her mother's protests.

'Let her go, mother. It is important for her.'

The woman responded to the sudden authority in her daughter's voice and let Fern go, but she insisted on giving her many things to help her start her life again.

When the kindly villagers who had helped Fern carry all their gifts back to the remnants of her home had left, the evening star was already out.

Fern sat in the midst of the ruined wood and tried to communicate with it. They needed each other. Both in pain and darkness. She laid her suffering close to the charred branches and asked for help as she now offered it. Small voices came to her. Sad voices, lonely. Tears fell from her eyes.

'I am sorry,' she whispered.

And then she heard the voice of her little stream calling softly, and went to it. On the banks some tiny shoots of green were beginning to push up defiantly through the blackened earth. They had not even waited for the Spring.

She dried her eyes.

In the morning she would start work on the garden again.

For two nights Karne did not return home.

Kyra began to worry about him and on the second day she set off to visit Fern hoping to find out if she could what had happened to him. Her mother was convinced he was visiting Fern but Kyra was not so sure.

She came upon her friend trimming back the dead wood of

211

the berry bushes they had enjoyed so much in the summer. She had worked hard since she had returned and the concentration on the needs of her plants had helped her to forget her own longings and uncertainties.

She was overjoyed to see Kyra and fairly flung herself at her, but her pleasure was soon snuffed out when she heard that Karne had not been seen since he had left her.

She recalled the whole scene for Kyra and they agreed that from the direction in which he had been seen striding off he had probably gone to the hills where Maal used to go to think.

There was a line of anxiety between Kyra's eyes. It had been a cold night with frost upon the ground and Karne had not been dressed particularly warmly.

Fern thought of this too and her heart's pain returned.

'Will you come with me?'

Fern nodded.

The two girls packed away Fern's gardening tools and set off to look for Karne.

They searched the hills until they were exhausted but could find no sign of him. They called and called, but no sound other than the cry of birds disturbed from their nesting places returned to them. Hill beyond hill stretched into the blue, enigmatically holding to themselves any secret that they might have.

'These hills *feel* empty,' Fern said sadly at last, and Kyra had to agree with her.

They plodded back to the village, too tired and dispirited to think where else to look. The evening mists were already beginning to gather in the marshy places of the valley, and the sun although still far from setting was staining the sky red and turning the hills from blue to purple. They could see the little group of houses, each with its plume of smoke, settled comfortably and pleasantly at the foot of the hill of Sacred Stones. Cattle and sheep were coming in from the pastures. Everything seemed to be drawing inwards to a centre, except for the birds who were flying outwards towards the forests and the hills that lay distantly encircling the little community.

One lone sea bird flew above their heads, crying forlornly

for all the world like a child in pain, winging inland as though it had lost its way. But when the sound of it had died down the two girls realized that what sounded like an echo of its lonely cry was something else, a thin and haunting thread of sound coming from the village itself . . . the horn that called the villagers together at the Meeting Rock.

Kyra and Fern looked at each other and then started to run. It was downhill all the way and they were not far behind the last of the villagers to reach the place.

Expecting to see Wardyke upon the platform rock everyone was astonished to see Karne, holding the horn to his lips defiantly and blowing again and again, the sound resonating through bodies and minds to generate a kind of wild feeling of apprehension and excitement.

As he blew the last note Wardyke came striding towards the platform, his face dark and angry.

The villagers drew back to let him pass.

Karne stood straight and proud, watching him come. A thrill of admiration passed through the villagers. For the first time they had hope that someone was going to be strong enough to stand up to Wardyke.

Wardyke reached the platform but before he took the steps up to it Karne raised his hand imperiously.

'No, Wardyke,' he said, and the villagers noted that he gave him no titles of respect. 'This meeting is of the people. You are not welcome here.'

Wardyke's face was a study. He could not believe this slim, fair lad was daring to speak to him like this.

''Boy,' he spoke with clipped and disciplined bitterness. 'Step down or it will be the worse for you.'

'No, Wardyke,' Karne held his ground. '*You* step down!'

The people gasped.

A few of Wardyke's Strangers moved forward threateningly, but something in the situation, perhaps the very confidence with which Karne held himself, confused them and they were not quite sure what to do.

The villagers pressed closer to watch what was happening and the Strangers could feel the growing strength within them.

If Wardyke did not strike soon it might be too late. Everything hung on the knife-edge of tension between Karne and Wardyke.

The air was fraught, silent, the villagers scarcely breathing as they watched to see what would happen.

Kyra and Fern at the back of the crowd clutched each other for comfort.

Wardyke took another step forward.

Karne, eyes blazing with a light of anger and determination that no one had ever seen in them before, took a step forward and made one of Wardyke's own gestures towards him, thrusting his pointing finger dramatically at him.

'You *will not* step upon this stone! You are *not fit* to be our priest!'

His voice and his sense of command were impressive. He seemed to be a man much taller than his normal self.

By keeping Wardyke from reaching the platform he was insuring that he was above him and therefore appeared taller. If Wardyke, who was much greater in bulk and height, and who cunningly wore robes and headdresses to accentuate this advantage, once stepped on to the rock Karne would lose visual precedence immediately.

Wardyke tried to take another step, but strangely the passion in Karne was so strong, fed by the resentment and hatred of the villagers supporting him, that he found himself hesitating. This hesitation was his undoing. Kyra helped her brother in every way she knew, clutching the white crystal stone she had found on Maal's tomb. She used the powers she had to project into Wardyke's consciousness the image of the boy being stoned, but altered it so that Wardyke would feel he was the boy and everything that had happened to the boy seemed to be happening to him. As the image came pressing in on him, as Karne's accusing finger powerfully drove into his mind, he tried to fight with all his skill to regain control.

Kyra's head seemed to be cracking with the pain of concentration. Karne's will was stretched beyond anything he had ever thought he was capable of. As he outstared Wardyke his vision seemed to split and shatter into flying angular shapes of black and scarlet. He could scarcely see the man before him, but he drove his will to concentrate and overthrow straight to the central point of the flying, splintering images. The three began to tremble with the strain, but not one of them would falter. There was no movement, no sound from the waiting crowd. Even Wardyke's Strangers were waiting for the outcome and did not think to touch their weapons.

Wardyke had been called and on the outcome of this encounter his future and the future of the community hung.

Suddenly Fern moved. She ran lightly and swiftly to the platform and leapt upon it. She joined her strength to Karne's and in that moment, unnerved by seeing the hate and disdain in the eyes of the woman he desired, feeling the pain in the burning of her trees, Wardyke momentarily faltered and in that moment Kyra managed to break through his defences.

The crowd saw him suddenly stumble, his eyes showing fear. He raised his arms to protect his face as though something was attacking him, and in that moment they realized they had won. It was possible to outface Wardyke, the magician.

With a roar they moved forward and Wardyke was lost.

Some of the villagers seized the Strangers and fights broke out among them, but the majority moved in on Wardyke. They might have torn him apart had not Karne, who was completely in command, managed to stop them in time.

'Hold him,' he cried, 'but harm him not. There are things we have to do, but killing is not one of them!'

Kyra moved back out of the seething crowd and sat down on the grass, holding her head in her hands. The pain in it was almost blinding her but at least she could relax now. Nothing more was expected of her for a while.

Karne was issuing orders as though he had done it all his life. His face was flushed with excitement and his eyes were very bright. It was not an easy victory he had just won and he was conscious of it, but he was also aware of the necessity to follow it up with action that would not allow Wardyke to regain his power. He had thought the whole thing through by himself in the hills and knew every move he should make.

When Wardyke and his Strangers were unarmed and held,

215

some admittedly with bloody noses and black eyes, but none killed, he ordered an election of new Elders to be held there and then, without the long ceremonies of the past, but at least with the justice of fair choice open to the villagers.

Names were put forward and the villagers stamped their feet to indicate approval. The seven who roused the most passionate stamping would be elected, among them some of the original village Elders, and some new ones to replace people like Thorn. Karne's father was one of the new ones chosen. Karne himself could not be elected as he was not a family man. Thorn's name was put forward by one voice, but the silence with which it was greeted gave clear indication of what the villagers thought of him.

When they reached the last name to be called, Karne held up his hand for silence and suggested that one of the Strangers should be proposed. A murmur of dissent went through the community.

'These people are living among us whether we like it or not. Most of them have behaved badly but some have not. I do not see that those who wish to live the way we live and work with our community should be penalized because of the viciousness of the others. Choose one among them and let your feelings be known.'

There was silence for a few moments as everyone looked around and thought about it. At first they could see nothing but evil in the Strangers and then one or two of them remembered things about some of their new neighbours that were not so bad.

Ji tugged at his father's arm and when he leant down to hear what he had to say, the boy whispered the name of one of the Strangers. He had become friendly with the family and a boy of his own age had often come fishing with him and was helping him to make the sled to haul Fern's wood.

Karne's father proposed the father of this boy. There was silence for a moment and then gradually the stamping began, led by Karne. The man was brought forward looking awkward and embarrassed and installed as the seventh Elder. It was in his favour that he had not been noticeably one of Wardyke's men. His wife burst into tears of joy and one of the villagers' wives put her arm around her.

Kyra noted this and was pleased.

Fern meanwhile had left the platform almost as soon as she had played her part. She knew she must not distract Karne from his work. Everything depended on swiftness of action while the wave of self-confidence still lasted. Karne had become like a kind of god to them and could do no wrong.

She joined Kyra and the two watched with amazement and admiration how Karne handled the crowd, keeping its baser passions in check, drawing from it commitment to worthwhile action.

The Elders chosen with extraordinary efficiency were installed upon the platform almost immediately, in the positions corresponding to the Standing Stones. Faro, being the eldest, and the one who had served longest as an Elder under Maal, naturally became the leader. But Fern and Kyra noticed how he turned to Karne for guidance on what was to be done next.

'Wardyke has usurped the place of our true priest,' the boy said, 'and we will have to make our own decisions until the gods send us a new one. The first decision to be made is what to do with Wardyke.'

With this Karne left the platform and took his place among the villagers. As he moved among the people many turned to him and smiled with gratitude and admiration. But he had only one thought in mind now. He had done half of what he had decided to do, the other half remained.

Torches were being lit and placed round the platform Stone as the darkness gathered close around them. Karne could barely make out faces in the dim light, but he had noted where Fern and Kyra were and was quick to seek out the place.

Wood was fetched and an enormous fire was lit to give warmth and light to what was now to be the trial of Wardyke. The villagers who were not taking part directly huddled round it for warmth. The Elders knew whatever decision was made must be made swiftly before Wardyke had a chance to gather his strength again.

He was bound with leather ropes and pushed forward to face the Elders on the platform. With stooping shoulders, his back half bent by the position of the ropes, his arms unable to make those deadly gestures they feared so much, he was reduced in every way. Even his eyes, usually his deadliest weapon, were veiled with fear. He was not used to failing, and failure came hard to him.

His crimes were listed and considered and while this was happening his one-time supporters crept away one by one, many of them to flee the valley without waiting to pack their belongings.

Some who could have left stayed and added their voices to the accusations against their one-time Lord.

Karne found Fern, firelight flickering on her long copper hair, her tired but lovely face. He emerged from the crowd and stood before her, his own face in shadow. She could not see his eyes but she knew they were upon her and she felt them almost like a touch upon her body.

She stood silently for a while. Strangely all the sounds of the crowd disappeared, as though they were in a pocket of reality that had no sound, no movement. She was aware of nothing, no one but Karne, and he of her.

At last he stepped forward and before she knew it had happened she was close in his arms and his lips were on her face and neck. She shut her eyes and the overwhelming feeling that she had longed for, of him enfolding her and loving her, was hers.

Kyra moved away quickly to leave them alone together, her heart full with love for them both and pleasure at their pleasure.

Wardyke's trial was not protracted. After the list of accusations, suggestions for punishment were put forward. Kyra joining the crowd was in time to hear that banishment was the most favoured, to be preceded by a ceremony at the Sacred Circle to call down the help of the gods to keep him from practising his evil ways again.

He was then stripped of his magnificent robes and made to walk naked and ridiculous, shivering in the night air, to his grand house, which was then set on fire, together with all the trappings of his power. As the flames roared upwards and lit the determined faces of the people gathered around, there could be no doubt in Wardyke's mind that he was finished as a magician-priest.

The fire lasted a long time and the night turned into a kind of weird celebration. Drums were brought, and other musical instruments. People danced and sang, lit fitfully by the red glow from Wardyke's house. He was clad in the oldest rags they could find and tied to a stake to watch the festivities. He had to endure many indignities. People spat in his face, people jeered at him.

Kyra watched him for a long time, wondering at all that had happened.

The pivot on which the whole thing had turned was, as the Lords of the Sun had said it would be, confidence.

Karne standing so tall and proud upon the platform, sustained by the pain of his love for Fern, had *believed* that he could overthrow the magician. And in that moment Wardyke doubted, and he was finished.

Too weary at last to endure any more, Kyra crept back to her home and to her warm, soft, sleeping rug. She had seen no sign of Fern and Karne, but as she slipped into a deep and blessed sleep she knew they were all right.

The Invisible Binding

The next dawn found Wardyke alone and shivering, still tied to the stake, beside the cold embers of his home. The villagers had all gone to get what rest they could before the excitement of the ceremony at the Sacred Circle and only a stray dog was abroad, sniffing and lifting its leg against the blackened stumps of the great columns that had once held up the grandest house that had ever been in this village.

Wardyke was tired, stiff, dirty and cold. No one was guarding him and yet not one of the Strangers had come to set him free. He saw some of them leaving with all their animals and their belongings in the early dawn, without so much as a backward glance. Bitterly his hungry eyes roamed the valley, trying to summon up some of his old will-power, his old command. But it is not easy to be commanding when you are cold and hungry, aching in every limb, and tied in a crouching position to a stake.

As the first rays of the sun began to melt the frost up-on the grass the village began to stir again. Not one person seemed to notice him, seemed to remember him. They went about their business as though he were invisible. He could smell warm food cooking, hear cheerful voices talking, and tears of longing began to come to his eyes. He began to think about banishment and the fact that he would be travelling in winter, with conditions at their worst and food difficult to come by. He had never been a hunter. Everything had always been provided for him and to fend for himself in the hostile forests or the mountains, where certainly he would be driven by the malicious villagers, would be almost impossible.

'I will die,' he thought gloomily, and the thought of death made him afraid. When he was riding high he had not thought of the consequences of his actions. Everything had seemed justified to magnify his power. But now that he was low, he began to realize that what he had done had no justification and would have to be faced.

At his lowest ebb he turned his face to the east and thought about the gods he had so mocked. He remembered the falling stars and knew now they had a different interpretation. He remembered how even in the Circle at the height of his power he had been unable to 'travel'. Not believing in the gods he had used them to fool his gullible people. Now he was not sure they did not mock him.

It could not have been that boy alone who overthrew the mighty Wardyke.

At this moment he heard his name called and looked round. A village girl holding a bowl of hot food was beside him. His eyes were those of a hungry dog. She fed him carefully and gently with her fingers. He gulped and swallowed thankfully, feeling warmth creeping into his cramped and icy limbs as he did so.

'What is your name, girl?' he asked when he was finished. He could remember seeing her in the village from time to time.

'Kyra,' she said quietly, standing up, the bowl now empty.

'Thank you, Kyra,' he said from his heart. 'I will not forget your kindness.'

She smiled and bowed slightly.

'I think there are many things you will not forget,' she said quietly and walked away.

Was she woman or child? He could not tell.

The ceremony was held at noon. No one knew quite what to do as this situation had never arisen before, but on Karne's advice it was agreed that Kyra should enter the Circle and pray for help to the gods. It was hoped that the gods would give some sign that they had heard and that Wardyke would effectively have all his powers as a magician-priest somehow removed from him, like sand upon the beach that had pictures

221

drawn upon it in the morning and by the afternoon had been washed clean and bare by the tide.

It was also agreed that until their new priest arrived Kyra would act as best she could, as it was unthinkable to them to live without the constant two-way flow of communication with the gods. She would not be able to handle all the winter ceremonial but at least they would not be completely alone through the long and dangerous months.

Just before noon the villagers began to gather round the Sacred Circle. There was a feeling of excited apprehension among them. They had heard of Kyra's adventures within the Circle, but were still not sure the gods would allow an untrained villager to meddle in their affairs. She had been safe before, would she be safe again?

When the sun was almost at its zenith for that time of year Kyra entered the Circle. She had no priest's clothes to wear, no magnificent regalia, but she walked with such dignity and poise it was as though she were fittingly clad. Her hair had been combed a hundred times by her mother and stood out about her shoulders like a fine golden cloak. She had tied the white crystal from Maal's tomb with a thin hide thong so that it could hang around her neck as she had seen the priest's jade in the Temple of the Sun. Before she appeared in public she held it against her forehead and said a silent and passionate prayer to Maal for help. After that she felt much calmer and as she walked she felt its comforting weight against her heart reminding her of the promise of Maal and of the Lords of the Sun.

Strangely she felt no fear as she entered the Circle this time. It was as though she had a right and it was as though she knew what to do.

The crowd was very quiet, holding their breath, as she took the step through the entrance Stones, but when nothing untoward happened to her they drew breath again and bowed their heads briefly in acknowledgement that she was speaking for them to the gods.

She walked with measured tread around the Circle bowing slightly to each Stone and each time calling on the unseen

Spirits of the spirit world and the one great God who ruled over them to give her people council and help in this difficult time.

Since she had spoken with the young priest in the desert temple she had tried not to think of the gods in any kind of Form, and now standing within the Sacred Circle she saw them as influences used by the One who wore the whole magnificence of Existence as we wear our bodies, a cloak that gives appearance to our invisible Reality.

She knew that if All that existed in Material Reality were to be discarded as we discard our bodies in death, there would still be the One, Nameless, Formless, Power Source which could create another material universe in any form It willed, however many times It willed.

And if It willed to stay without a manifest form then It could and would.

She knew there was no necessity to Existence as we know it. But because it Is at this moment and we Are at this moment, we should accept it and enjoy its multifarious forms, not wasting a second of it, learning what we can from it while it lasts.

Knowing what consciousness means to us, that marvellous faculty imagination makes the leap to help us understand the Consciousness of God. But this leap is not easily made and happens only in splendid moments of illumination, hardly at all at the beginning of our journey, increasing as we grow in capacity to understand, and finally becoming a permanent state when we return to our Source, capable at last of taking our part in His kind of Consciousness, His kind of Will, Motive, Choice and Imagination.

At this point we add to Him as He has been adding to us and we play our part in the great cycle of Being and non-Being that turns forever.

Standing transfixed in the middle of the Sacred Circle Kyra saw these things with great clarity. But even as she grasped them they began to slip from her and she slithered back into her imperfect body.

'No,' she whispered, 'please do not go,' and lifted her arms to plead with them to return.

223

But as she lifted her arms the watching crowd who were unaware of her inner experience took the movement as a sign for the ceremony to commence.

Wardyke was brought to the entrance of the Circle by the Elders and propelled by a deft push to fall at her feet.

Dazed she looked down and saw the man who had been so powerful and grand, clad in rags, bound with hide ropes, dirty and dishevelled, at her feet. Tears came to her eyes and she stooped down and raised him up. To their astonishment the crowd saw Kyra undo his bindings and brush the dust from his face and body.

Then she took his hands and stood looking deeply into his eyes.

Wardyke had been amazed to see the girl within the Circle and as he was pushed and chivvied along the path to her he had begun to hope that he could get back his lost control. Now as she lifted him up and released his bonds he was sure he could. Something of his old fire came back to his eyes and he looked boldly into hers, expecting hers to waver and fall before long.

But strangely the deep blue pools of her eyes seemed to draw his strength from him. He found too late he could not withdraw his gaze and she was compelling him in some way to follow her.

He seemed to be getting deeper and deeper into something he could not understand. But she drew him on. Visions of the sea came to him and he was sinking within it, seeing in great detail all its strange and varied denizens, its intricate and secret life. He swam among great beasts in the deeps and floated in the flickering light of sun on crystal sand in the shallows, seeing minute fish exquisitely shimmering with luminous blue and silver, creatures so small he knew he was seeing in a way no human eye had ever seen before. He knew in some magical way he was seeing within the creatures the curious and beautiful constructions of their inmost parts.

From this vision of the infinitely minute, his awareness seemed to expand and he was floating in the sky surveying mountains and plains, till they in their turn grew smaller and he was yet higher, amongst worlds and suns and stars . . . the infinitely huge was not beyond his vision . . . and all that he had seen was moving in constantly changing relationships, in patterns of perfect proportion and harmony.

When he had grasped this, Kyra and her spirit helpers allowed him to return. Dumb with awe at what he had seen he felt like an infant who was seeing the world for the first time and did not know what to make of it.

Kyra released his hands, released his gaze, and slowly and with measured steps began to circle round him . . . round and round and round . . . holding in her hand an invisible thread . . .

When she was done she looked at him and said,

'You are bound now with bindings that you cannot see. They will prevent you practising as magician-priest, but as you learn the meaning of the vision that you have just seen and begin to treat the Universe and its Creator with respect . . . the bindings will gradually disappear.

'When you are ready, you will be free.'

He bowed his head, feeling very weak and very humble.

She pointed to the path leading away from the Circle.

In a daze he walked out of the Circle and on to the path.

No man touched him. In silence the villagers watched him go.

Kyra lowered her head once more to the Tall Stones that represented the different states of the unseen world, and she in her turn trod the path into the valley.

It was not until she was out of sight that the villagers shivered slightly and moved. They, although they had not understood all that had happened, had felt the presence of the spirit realm and knew that something very significant had taken place.

But enough was enough. With movement came release and within seconds they were all chattering and comparing notes, children were dashing about, mothers were hurrying home to prepare a meal and all was noisy but comfortable confusion.

The Wedding and the Call

Wardyke was given warm clothes, good food and weapons for hunting and defence, and sent on his way. The last of his supporters left with him. Those Strangers who remained asked to be members of the village and showed every sign of wanting to settle down and be integrated with the community. The community accepted them.

A pleasant time of peace returned to the valley and as though to put the seal of the gods upon it the weather stayed bright and mild much later into the winter than anyone could remember it doing before.

The whole community helped Fern and Karne erect their little house on the new site among the rocks and within days it was ready for occupation. The day after its completion was declared the wedding day, and the whole village looked forward to a real festival. There would be no priest for the blessing, but every one was content that Kyra should say a few words. For the rest the wedding ceremony in the village community had never been very elaborate. It was enough that the community accepted a young couple setting up home, and celebrated with feasting and dancing the day they took up residence together.

Each family contributed food and ale and the cooking fires were laid in a great circle in the flat area near the Meeting Stone.

From a very early hour the village was alive with activity. The children were everywhere, running messages, carrying things, decorating a special place for Fern and Karne to stand during the blessing with arching boughs of gold and scarlet berries. Ji and Okan and their new friend had scoured far and wide to find leaves still upon the trees and in fact the best

226

branch was from Fern's new glen which was sheltered and warm compared to the rest of the valley. They had been taught by Fern to treat the trees with respect and took only branches that the tree no longer needed, cut them swiftly and cleanly with their father's sharpest flint axe, warning the tree well in advance so that it could prepare itself.

The day of the wedding was still and golden and the wedding arch was beautiful. As the final touches were put to it by a triumphant Ji the village children cheered and danced around it chanting little jingles of love for Fern and Karne.

Karne was busy accepting presents of cows and sheep and goats from warm-hearted neighbours. He and some of the older lads set about building make-shift pens for them on the outskirts of the festivity area. Fern and Kyra lent a hand for a while until they were called home by Kyra's mother. As she turned to go Fern gave one big shaggy cow with soft dozey eyes a big hug.

'Welcome to the family,' she said and kissed it on its hairy nose.

Kyra laughed.

'My favourite is that pure white goat,' she said, 'I know she is going to bear many kids.'

Fern ran her hand across its soft and silky back.

'You are pretty enough to be married today,' she laughed, and then called on one of the little girls to decorate the goat's horns with little streamers of wool and feathery grasses.

Kyra's mother was fussing over what Fern should wear. Fern could not see the problem but Karne's mother insisted that it should be something special.

'You must wear the dress that I was married in,' she said and brought out a dress the colour of Spring.

Fern gasped.

'It was specially woven for my wedding,' Kyra's mother said proudly. 'I think every woman in the village had a hand in it somehow.' Her eyes looked misty as she gazed at it.

Fern and Kyra fingered the cloth gingerly. It was the softest, finest weaving Fern certainly had ever seen, and only on her 'travels' had Kyra seen better.

'The colour!' Fern exclaimed in amazement.

'I know,' Kyra's mother's face glowed with pride at this. 'A travelling merchant sold it to us for a great deal of my father's best wool. He would not tell us how it was made so no one else in the whole village has a similar dress.'

'You must wear it, Fern,' Kyra cried. 'It is the colour of new leaves and would be perfect for you!'

Fern stroked it lovingly.

'Could I really?', she said, smiling at Kyra's mother.

'Of course you must! Try it on now.'

Kyra helped her take off her old dress, the two girls bubbling with excitement over the new. As Fern raised her arms above her head and Kyra pulled her dress over her shoulders, Kyra's mother caught her breath. The girl's slim figure was definitely showing signs of thickening around the stomach.

'Fern,' she said sharply, 'you are not with child?'

Fern lowered her arms and stook naked, looking at her with a shadow of anxiety across her face.

Kyra held her breath.

After a pause Fern said quietly and soberly, 'Yes, I am.'

The mother stared at her for a moment as though she was not quite sure how she was going to take the news, and then her face broke up into smiles.

At that moment Karne came in.

'You never told me Fern was with child!' his mother cried joyfully.

He looked at Fern standing forlornly in the middle of the room, clutching her dress, Kyra beside her with her face all worried.

His hesitation was barely noticeable and then he was across the room in two strides, his arm around his love, his lips warmly brushing the top of her hair.

'Yes,' he said to his mother, 'we were keeping it a surprise.'

Kyra saw Fern's face lift to his and the relief in it was

228

beautiful to see.

He laughed and looked at her all over.

'You will be a bit cold getting married like that!' he teased.

'Oh, get away with you,' his mother chided, 'Go on—get out! We have things to do even if you have not!'

She gave him a slap as though he were a small boy again and he laughingly left, giving a quick backward glance of amusement and love at his bride.

Kyra suddenly hugged Fern. They were both aware that in that moment when Karne had not denied the child was his the whole course of their life together had been made that much easier.

Unaware of the drama that had just been played out under her very nose, Karne's mother continued her fussing and bustling, dressing the girl in the new dress, chattering with joy about the prospect of the new baby, chivvying Kyra to make alterations on the dress before the ceremony while she rushed off to supervise the food.

A deputation of little girls from the village arrived with an exquisite crown of woven grasses, jewelled with green, orange and yellow berries, for Fern to wear. One of their number gave it to her shyly. It was obvious she was expected by the others to make a speech, but the words would not come. Fern stooped and kissed her and the child ran away happily with her friends.

Then Kyra gave Fern her present, a necklace of sea shells so long that it could be wound several times around her neck and still hang low across her breast. Kyra had gathered the shells from time to time since she had been a very small child. Her collection of sea shells was very precious to her and she had kept it all these years in a secret place. Now the whole collection was in the necklace, apart from the few she broke in threading them, and she gave the gift with great love to her new sister.

Fern gasped and gazed with wonder at the delicate and exquisite shapes and colours of the shells.

'Oh Kyra,' she whispered and could say no more.

At last it was time for the festivities to begin. Fern was led through the village by a gay band of dancers and flute players to Karne who was waiting impatiently under the arch.

She caused a gasp of admiration as she appeared and Karne himself was stunned by her appearance.

Always a beautiful girl, now in the long flowing softness of the green dress, her hair red-gold and shining in the sun, the little crown proudly worn upon her head, she looked like some princess of the nature spirit world. He wondered if he dared take her in his arms as he saw her walking so gracefully among the admiring crowd, but when she reached him her eyes were shining so much with love for him he did not hesitate. A cheer of pleasure went up from all his friends and neighbours as he welcomed her into his embrace.

Kyra then moved forward and spoke simply and with dignity the words of blessing she had heard Maal use at weddings in the past.

After that the feasting and the merriment began. Kyra could not remember when she had known such a day of happiness.

The villagers were celebrating victory and release from the dark spell of Wardyke as much as the joyful union of two of their favourite people. Music was played the whole day long. Dancing and kissing and eating seemed endless. The children were never still.

At the high point of the afternoon grain was thrown into the air in great sweeping arcs, and all the birds from miles around came swooping down to enjoy it. The air was filled with the sounds of their flight, their cries of joy were added to the music and singing.

Seven times the grain was thrown. Seven times the wheeling, swooping flight of birds descended. On the seventh and final time a black bird dropped its feather as a gift at Fern's feet and Karne picked it up for her. As the sunlight caught it, every colour in the rainbow flashed from its jet surface. He kissed it before he placed it in her hair.

Kyra wandered off by herself during the afternoon and sat beside the deserted ring of Ancient Stones. She could hear the noise of the party clearly enough, but it was not obtrusive. The Circle itself was absolutely silent.

She thought back along the summer and all that had happened to her and could not believe that she was the same person who had lain with Karne that day so long ago to spy upon the old man, Maal.

She fingered the white crystal that hung about her neck and thought about Maal, his kindness, his wisdom, his death. She wondered where he was now and when she would see him again. She had kept her promise to him and had no doubt that he would keep his to her even if it meant only in another life.

She thought about the Lords of the Sun and her heart longed to see the young priest from the desert Temple once again. She was tempted to enter the Circle and attempt to call him to her.

One part of her mind gave her arguments for trying it, the other told her the Sacred Circle was not to be used for personal matters.

She buried her face in her hands and tried to stop the conflict, but the discipline of mind she had managed to achieve with such effort lately seemed now of no avail. The tempter won and with beating heart she slipped into the Circle. Trembling with anxiety she made the rounds from Stone to Stone, trying to calm herself, but with every step becoming more agitated.

So determined was she to see if she could do it, she ignored all the warning signs within herself, and put herself against the Leaning Stone in the position she had learnt.

Nothing happened.

She remained exactly as she was.

Heart beating, conscious of herself.

There was no separation. No vision. No travelling.

Disappointed, she opened her eyes and stood up.

The Circle felt dead in a way she had never experienced before.

She left, ashamed.

That night when Karne and Fern were happily in their new home, and all the village was sleeping peacefully, worn out by the day's activities, Kyra lay awake. She knew she had done wrong to go into the Circle for no good reason but her own selfish desires. She wondered if she would be punished by her powers being taken from her. It was certain there was nothing in her feelings or in the atmosphere of the Circle that afternoon to suggest that she had any powers at all.

She thought about the prophecy that she would travel south to the Temple of the Sun and be trained as a priest. She and Karne had talked about it a great deal and planned the journey between them. He and Fern were to go with her, first in the boat Ji and Okan had helped build on the great sea and then by river as far as they could, travelling overland when they had to, avoiding the forests as much as possible, resting at villages. The new priest who was travelling this route at this very time would give them advice.

Fern's baby would be born on the journey and live its first years within the influence of the Temple of the Sun.

Karne would have his greatest ambition satisfied. She knew that for as long as she could remember Karne had longed to see this famous Temple. He had even built the boat they were to use for the first stage of the journey for this very purpose.

She thought about that day so long ago when she had said to him, 'The journey to the Temple of the Sun requires more than a boat . . . it is a journey on many levels . . .'

She knew now the journey had started on that day.

But had she forfeited all this now?

Tears came to her eyes and she felt very much alone and miserable. She had tried so hard to be worthy of Maal's trust and now she had let him down. It must have been because she saw Karne and Fern so much in love, that she began dreaming of the only man she had ever seen who roused her in the way Karne seemed to rouse Fern.

'It is ridiculous!' she told herself crossly. 'If I cannot manage self-control, how can I expect it of other people? I would be no good as a priest anyway!'

She sobbed herself to sleep like a child, and as the moon

232

rode above the village strangely vivid dreams began to come to her.

She saw herself in the Great Circle of the South, one among many initiates, bowing to the high priest with the kind face and the jade stone about his neck. He touched her head and pressed his thumb hard upon her forehead.

'You who now have my mark upon you will follow me and learn what I have to teach,' he said in a flat ritualistic voice.

She saw him pass down the line of initiates pausing only at one or two, making the same sign to them and speaking the same words.

Her heart lifted. She had been chosen.

When he had passed out of sight the line of initiates broke up and went towards different parts of the Great Circle, where they gathered in groups around the particular priest-teacher who had been assigned to them.

As she passed one group she found her eyes drawn to it. She could not see the priest in charge, as he was hidden by his students, but the students were different from the others she had noticed. With a sudden jerk her heart registered that the clothing of these students was similar to that she had seen in the wall pictures in the desert Temple of Red Sandstone, and as she discovered this the group moved and the priest who was in charge of them stood clearly in her sight.

It was the young and handsome Lord of the Sun.

As she recognized him, he saw her.

Their eyes met.

But in that instant, before she could be sure what expression was in his eyes, she jerked awake and lay in her own house in the far cold north, wrapped in sleeping rugs and trembling from head to foot.

For the rest of the night she tossed and turned, unable to be sure whether it had been a vision or an ordinary dream.

The dawn found her pale and dark eyed. At first light she crept out, too restless to spend another moment trying to sleep. At the door she paused and then returned to her sleeping place to fetch Maal's stone. She had grown used to wearing it at all times, and particularly when she was unhappy and uncertain of herself.

As she came out into the cold light of the early morning she glanced down at it before she put it round her neck.

And then she paused and stared.

The stone that had been white as frost before was now unmistakably green as jade.

Trembling, she turned it every way in the light, afraid to accept too soon its miraculous transformation.

Jade!

'You who now have my mark upon you will follow me and learn what I have to teach.'

It had not been a dream.

Book 2

THE TEMPLE OF THE SUN

Contents

The Warning and the Journey

The High Priest, the Lord Guiron, was in the Great Circle of the Temple of the Sun by himself, the dawn rituals over, the other priests and initiates departed. He too should have left and be attending to the business of the Temple.

Something held him back.

Something made him break his routine and pace the Tall Stones around the circumference, not as a priest drawing energy from them, not as a suppliant speaking with spirits, not as Lord of the Sun in robes of splendour with the power to roam the world at will, but as an old man suddenly lonely and afraid.

It was as though the people leaving the Circle after the Ceremony this particular morning drained him of his significance. He had not felt this way before, or not for many years. He had been in the Circle alone many times, as High Priest it was his Right, but it had always sustained him in his confidence and strength.

Now he felt like a peasant who had wandered unwittingly into a Sacred Circle and was overwhelmed by his own smallness and in awe of the Giant Forces surrounding him.

He, Guiron, Lord High Priest, was afraid.

Afraid in his own Temple?

Afraid of what?

He did not know.

The shoulders he usually carried so straight and proud were bent.

'What is it?' he kept asking himself.

But for all his knowledge of the Mysteries, and for all the control of Mind and Body he had learned through the long years of priesthood, this time he was an ordinary man faced with an uneasiness to which he could not put a name, which he

1

could not define.

He thought of entering one of the two Inner Circles within the Great Circle which were reserved for very special occasions. Perhaps their extra strength would give him back his stature as a Priest.

But as he approached the Northern one, it was as though he were held back.

'Not now,' a voice that was not his own voice spoke within his head. 'Not now.'

Feeling himself an exile he stumbled slightly and returned to the Outer Circle. Beyond the immense Standing Stones that carried the flow of Spirit power from earth to sky, from sky to earth, the high ridge, walled with rough chalk blocks, rose above him, cutting him off from the rest of his fellow men. It was designed to isolate the Temple for its work, to concentrate its energies and keep intruders out, and he now felt as much a prisoner as a small beetle would that had fallen on its back within a steep-sided hole.

There were things in his past that he did not wish to think about. He pushed them back into the darkness. Long years of service as Priest of Light had surely undone whatever harm he might have done once long ago!

But from the crevices of darkness in his mind unease was stirring and this time he could not put it down.

With no one to observe him he allowed himself the luxury of tears and put his head against a Tall Stone to the East of the Circle, a Stone for which he had always felt a particular affinity. He put his arms around it as though it were a man and could give him comfort.

'Lord,' he whispered, 'Lord of Light. Help me.'

He tried to clear his head of the irrational and disorderly murmurings of his mind.

Where was his training now?

Slowly order came.

Slowly the clamour of his fear died down.

He tried to visualize, to call before him a picture of what it was that threatened him.

He could feel a low drumming or throbbing in his head.

2

Whether it was from within himself or from within the rock he pressed himself so closely against, he could not tell.

He listened to it and it seemed to him at last that it was the sound of the ocean, beating relentlessly against the shore, the ocean rising and falling, swelling and subsiding, and upon its vastness there was a small seed, a fragile boat tossed among the waves, that bore within it something that threatened change to him and the Great Temple that lay around him.

The image was not clear.

The menace was not strong.

It was a hint, a stirring, a whisper . . . but it was there.

He strained for a clearer vision.

It would not come.

But pain entered his body from the North, so it was from the North that he expected the threat to come.

He pulled back from the Stone with a sudden movement and with a surge of great determination he pulled himself to his full height as a Priest, his eyes sparked with his old fire of office and, turning his face to the North, he spoke these words aloud and with great authority.

'You who come from the North to bring disruption and change to this man and this place, turn back. Turn back! There is no welcome for you here!'

He tried with all the force of will and thought at his command to reject the unknown intruders and turn them from their course.

His Will was strong, the beam of his Thought powerful, but the deep and featureless blue of the sky into which he thrust his desperate barb gave no sign that it had reached its mark.

'So be it,' he thought, and turned to leave the Circle. 'I have tried, and I will try again!'

In the North Kyra stood upon the cliff she had just climbed and stared at the sea that lay impassively silver, ominously vast.

They had sailed in their frail homemade boat since the first stirrings of Spring and the journey that lay behind them, which had seemed so long and painful, was nothing to the journey that lay ahead of them.

She could see her brother Karne, tall and fair and bronzed, out beyond the rock line of the shore fishing for their lunch. Fern, his wife, who was heavy with child, was gathering driftwood on the pebbled beach for their cooking fire. When Kyra was with them the community of their love gave them each strength and comfort, but from the height of the cliff top they seemed very small and vulnerable against the immense panorama that stretched as far as she could see and then . . . beyond . . .

The joy of purpose that had sustained her in their travels since they first set out suddenly deserted her, and she looked at the huge landscape of impenetrable forest behind her and the seascape that lay forever and forever below her and a sharp cold feeling of fear stabbed her heart.

'How is it possible,' she thought in panic, 'how *dare* we venture into this vastness and hope to find our way!'

Appalled at the foolhardiness of their journey, the immense scope of it, and the inadequacy of their preparation for it, she decided they must turn back at once to their comfortable little village where everything was known and loved, understanding and achievement easier.

'Karne!' She called. 'Fern!'

She must tell them at once before it was too late and they were lost forever!

But no matter how loud she shouted the thin whistle of her voice was blown backwards on to the land and dispersed among the tough coastal grasses and flowers that lived on the thin crust of earth above the unfathomable dark rock.

'Karne!' She called again. 'Fern!'

But there was no way they could hear her.

She started to scramble down the cliff, loose pieces of rock and earth scattering under her feet and hands. Sea birds shrieking with indignation flew up from hidden ledges and her heart began pumping with an urgent and powerful fear.

She must be careful.

On the way up, so intent on the moment by moment

4

examination of the beauty of the rocks and the lichens nearest to her, she had not noticed how sheer the cliff was. Now, looking down, she was shocked at the danger of the descent.

Karne and Fern looked up on hearing the pebbles rolling down the cliff and saw Kyra coming down too fast for safety.

They both gasped and called out.

Fern ran immediately over the sharp and uneven rocks, the child lying within her body making her progress clumsy and painful. Karne, thinking that Kyra was being pursued, ran back to the boat to fetch his sling catapult and stood high upon a rock where he could see further up the cliff, the stone in his sling held back, the leather thong taut, ready for action.

But it soon became clear Kyra was alone. Whatever was driving her to such careless speed was not visible to their eyes.

She slid the final slope in a flurry of stones and landed in a heap at Fern's feet, considerably bruised and shaken, her skin grazed in many places, but otherwise unharmed.

Karne was angry.

He raged for several moments at her recklessness.

'I am sorry,' she brought out breathlessly, and repeated it when his words continued the bruising she had just suffered from the cliff, as Fern helped her dust herself off and wash the open places clean with sea water.

'What were you trying to do?' Karne demanded at last indignantly.

'I tried to call you from the cliff top,' she said miserably, smarting as the salty water touched the open grazes.

'We did not hear you,' Fern said gently.

'Of course we did not!' Karne exclaimed, looking at the height of the cliff. 'How could we *possibly* have heard you?'

'I know. It was foolish. It just seemed so urgent . . .'

She hesitated. Things were not so clear at the bottom of the cliff as they had been at the top.

'What was so urgent?' Karne asked sternly.

'I thought . . . we ought . . . to turn back,' Kyra said in a low voice, aware that this would not be received well by Karne.

They stared at her.

'Turn back! Why?' Karne demanded.

5

'It just seemed . . .' Kyra's voice was losing conviction every moment, 'at the top of the cliff looking at how huge the ocean is and thinking about the journey . . . it just . . . all seemed . . . impossible!'

'But the Lords of the Sun *told* you to make the journey!' Fern cried.

She herself would not have been sorry to turn back, but she knew Kyra had been commanded to attend The Temple of the Sun to study for the priesthood. Without Karne's help and protection she could not make the journey, and without Karne, she, Fern, was not prepared to live. So their journey had become her journey.

Kyra was silent.

Karne was silent too. His anger was gone. He knew his sister well and the burdens she had to bear, the fears she faced from time to time.

'It will not be an easy journey,' he said, quietly now, 'but it *is* necessary.'

'Karne . . . ' Kyra said in a very small voice.

'Yes,' he said gently.

'Sometimes I think I am not fit . . . It seems to me I may have misunderstood. It is very *possible* that I misunderstood,' she pleaded.

'I do not think so, my sister,' Karne said soberly.

'Think back on all that has happened,' Fern said. 'You *know* you have been chosen! You *know* you have special powers not many people have! Powers that could and should be trained for use within the priesthood.'

'But,' Kyra said sadly, 'there are so many ordinary things I want to do. Surely if I were fit to be a priest I would have my mind on higher matters all the time?'

'You are not a priest yet,' Fern reminded her. 'There will be years of training.'

'But I do not *want* to reach the point where ordinary things do not matter to me any more!'

'And I do not think you ever will reach that point,' Karne

said seriously. 'You are training to be a priest, not a god. Maal still enjoyed ordinary things. Maal even made mistakes. Remember?'

Maal was their friend and teacher, the old priest of their community whom they had loved and trusted, and who had been cruelly ousted and then destroyed by the false but powerful priest-magician Wardyke.

'Maal always said the Universe is made up of ordinary things,' Fern said. 'It is in our Seeing of them, our appreciation of them, that they become extra-ordinary, that they take on splendour and magic. So you will not have to give up ordinary things. They will just become for you less "ordinary". You will have *more* Reality, not less!'

Kyra was somewhat comforted, but the sight of all that endless ocean, that endless land, that she had seen from the top of the cliff came back to her. She felt again that sudden cold twinge of fear.

'How will we ever find our way?' she said, tears coming to her eyes. 'Oh, Karne, everything is so huge, and we are so small!'

He put his hands on her shoulders and the warmth of the contact made her feel less small, less alone.

'There is no point in thinking about it like that,' he said briskly after a pause, 'there is a fire to be made, fish to be roasted. I, for one, am starving!'

Kyra could not help smiling.

It was so like him to busy himself with practicalities and take one step at a time! And yet he had vision too and knew when two steps were necessary.

She looked at him with great love and trust, and then turned to help Fern with the fire.

After the meal, while the other two made the boat ready for sailing, Kyra clambered over the rocks to the furthest and largest one standing almost like an island in the sea.

She needed to think.

She remembered Maal with aching heart and all that he

had taught her before his death.

She called on him for help. She called on The Lords of the Sun, on the spirits who lived in the realms that led to the one God who was Nameless but the Source of All.

'Tell me what I must do!' she cried aloud in pain, her voice becoming part of the water crashing onto the rock, part of the rock, part of the light splintering off its surface and the dark germinating in its depths.

Fern and Karne on the beach packing away the things in the boat simultaneously felt they heard a sound and looked up to see Kyra poised triumphantly on her rock, raised as tall as she could be, pointing with dramatic excitement to the swelling sea.

As the eyes followed her finger they saw, rising from the sea in dark and rhythmic folds, the bodies of innumerable dolphins, plunging, rising, plunging, rising, travelling the ocean with their slow and ancient dance, and all of them moving South. Moving South!

Kyra had her answer.

They launched their little boat of wood and hide and followed the course they had planned to the South, keeping land always in sight to the West of them.

It was during Fern's watch one night that, for the first time, they lost all contact with the land and with their course.

She sat huddled in her fur cape hour after hour while the other two uncomfortably and fitfully snatched some restless sleep. Karne had shown her the star she was to keep always behind them in the North and the others she was to watch progressing across the sky, the dim, dark hump of the land always to the West.

For the first hour of her watch her eyes grew weary with the number of times she checked their direction against those frail points of light.

But during the second hour the moon rose and she was overwhelmed by the splendour of its rising.

Without her realizing it and perhaps because the wind had

8

subtly altered its direction, their little craft began to move along the spectacular silver path towards the moon. The dark and brooding ocean became transformed into a sparkling, shimmering mist of silver. 'Moon Metal' her people often called what we now call silver, and the sea shone now with moon metal.

Darkly the deeps may have been waiting beneath the shining ripples of the surface, but Fern was no longer conscious of them. She no longer noticed the passage of the night, the progress of the stars, the disappearance of the land shadow to the West. She saw only the moon and felt the urge to reach towards it.

As the moon rose higher in the sky Fern urged the little craft faster along the metal path, taking out the paddle and scooping the silver water back to add speed to its progress.

Her first exultant urge to speed turned to despair as the great disk lifted higher and higher, further and further from her reach.

She stood at last, arms uplifted, calling to the moon with a strange and unnatural call.

Kyra jerked awake with the sound, seeing the girl transformed.

'Fern!' she cried in alarm.

Fern did not hear her, but stretched her arms to their limits . . .

The moonlight caught her eyes and to Kyra they seemed to be made of moon metal.

She seized her and shook her. The boat rocked dangerously and Fern's eyes became pools of dark.

'Come back!' Kyra cried. 'Fern, you are possessed!'

Karne grumblingly awoke now and stared bewildered at the scene.

He saw his sister Kyra shaking Fern violently, felt the boat rocking.

In an instant he was up and in control. He pushed Fern and Kyra down with oaths of command, seized the paddle and righted the spinning and jerking of the boat.

Fern crouched with her head against Kyra's breast sobbing

and shivering. Kyra enclosed her with her arms and comforted her with soft sounds.

'What is this?' Karne shouted. 'What have you done?'

Kyra looked above Fern's head and could see no land to the West and the stars they had set their course by were not where they should have been.

They were caught in a sickly white light in the middle of darkness, far from home, far from anywhere they knew, and creeping over the face of the moon was the dark hand of a cloud.

Within a short while the stars had gone out one by one, the whole sky was overcast and they were in absolute darkness.

They sat huddled together, the cold they felt as much from within as from without.

Karne and Kyra had quietened Fern's sobs and had silently agreed to say no more about the incident. What was done was done, and now they must think what to do next.

'There is nothing we can do, but wait for morning and the light,' Karne said.

He held Fern close to him, knowing that what she had done she had not done deliberately to bring them into danger, but that something from deep within those mysterious levels we all have within ourselves had stirred and an urge to reach and follow something she herself could not control or understand had taken over.

In the darkness, drifting with the deep sea currents, the three young people and the unborn child waited.

They saw no sun in the morning, but they knew it had risen because the black pit of darkness in which they had been marooned gave way to a dull and sombre grey, neither sky nor sea distinguished in any way.

Gloomily the three made breakfast of wheat biscuits and water from the goatskin bag. Up to now they had fed off the land each day and had not needed to draw on their emergency

10

store of food.

Karne stared around him at their featureless world.

They had pulled down the rough sail in an attempt not to travel any further off their course, and lowered strings of fibrous rope over the side to watch which way they drifted, hoping their rudimentary knowledge of currents and tides, gleaned from fisherman friends, would help them decide which way land lay.

It was Fern who noticed the first sea bird and after that they concentrated on the sky and noted with desperate attention which way the birds flew. But this at first was not much help as the birds seemed to come and go from many directions.

Kyra buried her face in her hands and tried to 'feel' the presence of the land. Karne kept quiet, knowing this was a power Kyra sometimes had which she was hoping would grow with training as a priest.

Fern joined her in her concentration, thinking of the forests and the growing plants with whom she had lived in close harmony all her life. She needed them now and called on them for help.

At first no help came.

The sound of the slap, slapping of the water against the side of the boat was all they were conscious of, that and the coldness of the air that enclosed them.

Karne watched the ropes, counted sea gulls and noted the direction of the drift of flotsam.

Gradually through the darkness in her head Fern began to feel little stirrings, hear little sounds like leaves rustling, small animals moving through undergrowth. . . .

She opened her eyes with excitement and found Karne pointing in the same direction, and Kyra looking decisively along the line of both their pointing fingers.

Laughing, they all talked at once.

'I am sure it is that way — I heard forest sounds,' Fern cried.

'And I saw a gull carrying nesting materials in its mouth travelling that way. It must have been returning to the cliffs!'

11

'And I,' Kyra said dreamily, 'felt the presence of a Sacred Circle and someone in it calling to us.'

They looked at each other joyfully and set about turning the boat around to head in the direction they had all agreed was the right one.

While Fern was following the moon they must have drifted a long way off course and it took them the best part of a day to reach again the comfort of the land.

Great was their delight to see at last a darker smear of grey upon the Western horizon, and even greater was their pleasure to distinguish the tall stones of a Sacred Circle crowning the highest point above the sea as they drew nearer.

They were still a long way from their destination, the Great Temple of the Sun where the Lord Guiron waited so uneasily for them, but as they pulled into the rocky cove at the base of the cliff that housed the Stone Circle Fern was singing and Kyra's eyes were shining. People who used the Tall Stones of a Sacred Circle to communicate with the spirit realms must be of their own kind, and it would be good to be among such people again. Karne, who felt the responsibility of carrying Kyra and Fern safely over so great a distance and through so many dangers, was particularly relieved to break the journey for a while and seek the advice of people who would certainly know these waters and this coast better than he did.

He leapt into the shallow water and hauled the light craft as high out of the sea as he could, the girls joining him with enthusiasm.

It was almost dark but they could still see fairly well, and when they finally drew breath from all the effort of attending to their boat they found that they were not alone.

Standing on some rocks a short way from them and holding in their hands what looked like clubs stood several men, rough and uncouth, clad in furs and not in woven cloth.

Kyra, Karne and Fern froze, unsure of their next move.

The men stared at them and they stared at the men.

The first movement came from Kyra who took a step or two

towards them in spite of Karne's warning touch upon her arm. She stood vulnerable, her hands empty and open in front of her, as though showing them that they had nothing to fear from the people from the sea.

At the same time she tried to project friendly thoughts towards them, knowing that all people respond, whether they know it or not, to the thought flow from others.

Her overtures must have succeeded because they approached and there was no menace in the way they came. Their faces were smiling and friendly, though dirty, and as they drew nearer Karne could see that the sticks they carried were not clubs, but bundles of rushes, probably dipped in fat, to use as torches against the dark of the night that was fast closing in around them.

The men spoke their language but with a more gutteral sound. From what they said it became clear that the travellers were expected. Their priest had sensed their presence at sea during the dawn watch in the Sacred Circle and sent greetings and offers of hospitality to the strangers.

Karne accepted with gratitude on their behalf.

While the leader of the group and Karne exchanged these words, two of the men busied themselves making fire with a bow-like tool. It spun fast on a piece of kindling wood until it smouldered and set light to the rushes which became their torches for the climb up the rocky cliff path.

At the top of the cliff the whole village seemed to have gathered to greet the strangers, but the one who stood out among the others was the priest, the only one clad in woven cloth and wearing leather on his feet. He was shorter than his charges but of enormous bulk, the folds of his garments falling over a great belly. He raised his two plump hands to them in salute while the villagers crowding behind him waited eagerly but silently to join their greeting to his.

'Welcome, my friends. It is not often I have the pleasure of sharing my hearth with one of the brotherhood,' and he looked straight at Karne who stood tall above the girls and slightly ahead of them.

Karne was puzzled by this, but said nothing more than

polite greetings in reply.

'Come!' the priest said imperiously but kindly, indicating that Karne should follow him.

Instantly the rest of the villagers closed in on Kyra and Fern and, chattering excitedly, led them off away from Karne, to the group of wooden huts surrounding a small circle of open fires.

'You will eat with us,' some said.

'Our house is your house,' others cried, and Kyra and Fern could see that they were to be quite smothered with hospitality.

Although the people were very different from their own the whole atmosphere was so friendly and festive they did not think to feel alarm.

Both girls were glad they would have the comfort of sleeping in a warm house for a change, but both wondered somewhat anxiously what had become of Karne. There was no sign of him or the priest.

When Kyra could at last make herself heard above the hubbub of questions and friendly offers of food she ventured to ask where her brother might be.

'He is with the Lord Yealdon, of course,' she was told as though her question had been a foolish one. 'He will eat well and sleep soft. You have no cause to be concerned. It is a great day for the Lord when he has someone of equal stature to talk the Mysteries with!'

Again Kyra felt a small twinge of puzzlement, but she was hungry and tired and cramped from the long hours on the boat and soon dismissed thoughts about her brother and the priest to enjoy the good roast deer and pungent root ale. The firelight flickered from every side, dim figures wove in and out through it and when the light caught their faces she saw nothing but friendliness and pleasure.

After the eating and the drinking, when Fern and Kyra were feeling decidedly dizzy from the ale, the villagers performed a dance for them, singing a strange song very different from any

14

the girls had ever heard before. It seemed to be a hunting song accompanied by a ritual dance. Half the dancers had antlers fixed to their heads on strange masks and tails of fur hanging between their legs, while the other half had spears which they pretended to throw from time to time.

The dance started slow, the hunters close to the ground stalking their prey, the 'animals' feeding peacefully and unaware of danger. Almost without Kyra and Fern noticing it the tempo of the slow drumming music and muted song changed, becoming faster and faster, louder and louder. The chase was on! The 'animals' leapt and twisted trying to escape. The 'hunters' circled and pursued, drawing their trap tighter and closer.

Kyra and Fern found themselves caught by the savage rhythm of the beat, so unlike the music of their own peaceful farming community, and began stamping their feet in time to the dance. The impact of so many stamping feet raised the dust and the air seemed to vibrate with frenzy. Dust and sparks and smoke mingled with the dancers, the heady smell of ale and of roasting meat, the loud and louder chanting of so many throats, began to work on Fern and Kyra so that they found themselves leaping up and joining in, a surge of primitive ecstasy burning them up like the stubble in a field of straw on fire on a windy day.

Kyra could feel the sweat pouring from her, but she could not stop dancing. It was as though she was *being* danced, rather than herself dancing. The drumming of her feet had become her own heartbeat.

On and on the sound went, the movement went faster and faster until at last a composite scream broke from the throats of all the dancers . . .

'Kill!'

Ice cold the word like a flung dagger stopped all movement, all frenzy, instantly. Kyra was dimly aware in the immediate and deathly silence of the humming whine of dozens of spears travelling through the air.

'Oh you gods,' she cried within herself, 'they have not killed them!'

She tried to pull herself together enough to see what had happened, but the dancing and the ale and the unaccustomed emotions of the whole evening had told on her and she could feel herself slipping into unconsciousness. Her last thought as the weirdly falling dust disappeared from her sight was for Fern. Fern who carried a child within her body and must surely be feeling even worse than herself.

Karne seated on a thick rich bearskin rug within the priest's comfortable house, which was some way from the feasting and the fires, could hear the sound of singing and the loud thud of stamping feet, but it was very much a background noise and he did not take much notice of it.

He was amazed at what he saw. The dwellings of the villagers he had noticed in the firelight seemed no more than temporary shelters against the weather. In his own village the houses were built with pride and care, circular and of wood and rushes, bound over with hides to keep the weather out. They were built to last a man's lifetime. He wondered if these people were nomadic. He had heard of such people, wanderers who had not learned the way to use the land skilfully so that it yielded year after year the crops needed for sustenance. People who used the land once and then moved on. Hunting people. Restless people.

But the priest's house was sumptuous with the most magnificent furs Karne had ever seen hung from every beam and spread across the floor. He was given a sweet wine made of honey to drink, and bowls of rich and tender meat, spiced with nuts and herbs he had not tasted before, to eat. Several young girls slipped in from time to time silently and discreetly to replenish their goblets and their bowls.

At first he was delighted with it all, but gradually as more and more wine was pressed upon him and his refusals were ignored, he began to have misgivings. The friendly face of the priest seemed to him too friendly. He smiled too much and his plump hands that had been raised in greeting with such dignity began to look greasy and unclean as he fingered the food.

16

Karne wondered at the great disparity between the style of living of the priest and his people. He seemed an alien among them. In Karne's own community the priest Maal, who had been with them for many years, had held a position of great respect and, although master of Mysteries that the ordinary people never questioned, had a relationship with them that was friendly and loving.

Karne noticed that the fat priest had many large rings upon each finger, some in silver and some in gold, but one in particular he noticed and disliked. It was of a greyish metal that he had not seen before and was shaped like an eye. As the priest's hands moved the eye seemed to glint and gleam and never take its attention off Karne. He tried to shake himself free of the feeling, telling himself that it could not possibly be an eye that could see, but was a blind piece of metal fashioned by a man, but, whether it was the wine or whether it was the monotonous and softly droning voice of the priest, Karne felt himself slipping further and further away from the reality he knew how to control.

'It is not often we welcome such a distinguished traveller as yourself,' the man said at last, smiling.

Karne through his confusion knew enough to try to protest that some mistake was being made, but his voice seemed to come out thin and dim and carry no conviction. The priest ignored it.

'You are too modest,' he said, still smiling, indicating to the girl with his much beringed hand that Karne's cup needed refilling.

'No . . .' said Karne feebly.

'I insist,' the priest said, smiling.

He paused a while, and Karne struggled to work out what was happening, but his mind was too confused by the influence of the wine.

'I must hold on,' he told himself desperately, 'something is not right!'

But the man's charming voice was speaking again, soothingly, softly.

'I have been cut off here among these barbarians for longer

17

than I care to remember!'

He said the word 'barbarian' with great venom and bitterness. Karne wondered what the girl who stood behind him to serve the wine was thinking. These were her people and although she was poorly clad and possibly not as advanced in knowledge and skill as the girls in his own village were, she was by no means deserving of such scorn.

He had thought it was a priest's duty to educate and guide his people, not to keep them in a state of savagery and then despise them for it.

'We could exchange knowledge and ideas,' the fat priest continued smoothly. 'It is many years since I learnt the Mysteries, and you are young. There must be many new things taught in the Temple Schools these days that would add to an old man's strength. You could teach me these things, while I,' and here he leaned very close to Karne and his rheumy eyes seemed to leer into the boy's, 'could teach you things I have learnt over the years of practice as a magician-priest that no school ever taught or ever would. I have powers that would startle *you*, young priest!'

'I assure you . . .' Karne began feebly, really worried now, realizing the misunderstanding had been allowed to go too far.

'No, do not protest,' the old man's voice was suddenly sharp. 'I assure *you* I need to know what they are teaching these days and if . . .' and here he paused and his face was harsh and cold, 'if you refuse my offer of a peaceful trade . . . I have ways of taking what I want . . .'

There was a cruel and relentless edge beneath the smoothness of his voice now and he raised his right hand slightly, turning the deadly eye of his ring towards Karne so that just briefly, as though it was a taste of things to come, the firelight in the brazier glinted off its metallic surface and pierced his eyes with light so icily inhuman, that for a moment he was blinded.

Karne was afraid now, deadly afraid. He had tried to tell the man he was not a priest, but to no avail.

He struggled to gather together his bemused wits and think of ways to outwit his formidable foe. Before he had noticed

18

the extent of the man's unpleasantness he had thought to tell him that he himself was not a priest, but that his sister Kyra, although not yet a priest, was at least a candidate on her way to training.

Now he realized he must protect Kyra and somehow deal with this man himself. His heart felt heavy. Not only was his own mind befogged by the wine, but his adversary was obviously a trained and unscrupulous magician.

Karne tried to remind himself that it was he, Karne, who had finally outfaced Wardyke, the false priest who had destroyed their friend Maal and taken over their village, but it had not been an easy victory and he had had the help of Kyra, Fern and the Lords of the Sun behind him.

As his thoughts raced to find a way out, his senses brought him something else to worry about. Kyra and Fern were with the villagers and the dance and music he had been vaguely conscious of as part of a festival occasion, he noticed now had the same cruel undertones as the voice of the priest before him. It would not take much for Kyra and Fern to become prisoners of these people.

'Speak,' the fat priest said now, smiling again, knowing that he had made his point and could afford to hide the barb of his threat once more under his ingratiating manner.

Karne could see a bowl of water to the left of the tent.

He rose and boldly took it in his hands.

The man watched warily, the hand with the ring tensed for action.

But Karne showed no sign of threatening him. Standing as tall and commandingly as he could, he lifted the bowl of water high over his own head and then tipped its icy contents over himself.

The man was puzzled, but said nothing. He continued to watch him like an animal watching its prey.

The shock of the cold water had done what Karne hoped it would do, clear his mind, freshen his body and sharpen his wits.

'You know as well as I,' the young man said now as sternly as he could, 'our brotherhood is sworn to secrecy.'

19

'But not among ourselves,' the man was quick to reply, leaning forward eagerly, knowing that the vows had been instituted to prevent the quite considerable power of the Mysteries from falling into the hands of those not ready to see their full implications and use them wisely.

Karne looked at him coldly, standing tall above the bulky but seated figure.

'What is it you wish to know?' he said at last.

The man leant forward, his eyes for the moment failing to hide his real feelings. It was clear to Karne his host needed some specific piece of knowledge very badly, and would kill to get it. His face was twisted with a mixture of greed and anxiety.

'Of late it has become difficult for me to . . . contact . . . certain . . . people . . .'

He was trying to choose his words carefully, but every moment Karne was more certain that the man was now the suppliant and he the one in the position of power.

As Karne grew bolder, the fat priest Yealdon grew less sure of himself. Karne remembered what he had learnt — the crux of all power is belief and confidence.

'What people?' he said sternly.

'The Lords of the Sun,' Yealdon muttered the words so low it was as though he hoped Karne would not hear them.

Karne's heart leapt. This was good news.

One of the skills a priest was trained to have, vital to his work, was the ability either himself to 'spirit-travel' across the world to seek the help and communion of other priests, or in times of stress to call upon the Great Lords of the Sun, who were the highest in the hierachy of priests and who moved most freely about the world in spirit form, most knowledgeable in the Secret Mysteries.

Karne felt almost sorry for the man. A priest who could not communicate with other priests and The Lords of the Sun was cut off in his own isolated village, among people with whom he could not exchange thoughts and ideas, particularly as in this case he had taken no trouble in the past to educate them to any kind of companionable level.

Karne's own people were simple enough farmers but they were not ignorant savages. The rapport between the old priest Maal and his people had been good, and he had kept the vital elements of priestly wisdom continually renewed and refreshed by contact with his peers across the world. When they were in difficulties and Wardyke had usurped his place and ruined their ancient way of life, Kyra, a mere child, but with training from Maal and a natural aptitude for priestly powers, had called upon The Lords of the Sun for help, and they had generously given it.

'And what . . .' Karne said boldly, 'will you trade for my help in contacting the Lords of the Sun?'

Yealdon almost crawled forward. He began to look more and more like a toad. The boy could feel the balance of power in his own favour. The man was crawling to *him*. He needed to know what he thought the boy knew, more than anything else in the world.

'I can make an enemy die,' Yealdon said eagerly, 'by nothing more than the use of this ring!' And he took the one that had so disturbed Karne off his finger and held it triumphantly aloft.

It glittered balefully in the firelight.

Karne swallowed imperceptibly. He had not conquered his fear of this man completely, though so far he had it well hidden.

'You mean you will trade your ring for the knowledge I can give you?'

Yealdon smiled and his eyes were evil. He cradled the ring within his hands, holding it close to himself as though it were the most precious thing in the world.

'I will trade anything you ask,' he purred, still cradling the ring.

'I ask the ring!' Karne spoke loud and clear.

There was a deathly silence between them for what seemed to Karne like a very long time.

'Certainly,' Yealdon said at last, but Karne knew it was a lie. 'First the knowledge, and then the ring.'

'No,' Karne said, his heart beating loud against his ribs.

21

'First the ring, and *then* the knowledge!'

'But how do I know that you will not cheat me?' Yealdon almost spat out the words.

'How do I know that you will not cheat *me*?' Karne replied. Deadlock.

The two eyed each other warily.

'You may take my knowledge and then kill me with the ring, thus keeping both!' Karne said.

'You may take my ring and kill me, and so save yourself the trouble of giving me the knowledge,' Yealdon countered.

'Why should I do that? Would a priest of the Brotherhood do that?' Karne asked.

'Would a priest of the Brotherhood do what you suggested I would do?' Yealdon snarled.

Again the two watched each other silently.

Apart from the heaviness of the old man's breathing it was uncannily quiet. The serving girls had left them alone.

Karne became aware that even the sound of stamping and singing had ceased from the direction of the huts.

How he longed for Kyra's strength to help him at this moment.

He had no plan. He knew only he must keep the balance of power as it was now, and stall for time until he could think of a way of dealing with the situation. He had no secret knowledge to give the man, nor if he had would he have given it.

Karne realized that his own belief that the ring could kill was adding to its power. If only he could doubt enough that it could harm him, he would be safe from it. But the glint of the dull and unusual metal, the acrid smell of some strangely potent herb that was burning in the brazier, the heavy, staring eyes of the man before him, all helped to dull his mind, and primitive fear was gradually undermining his control.

To break the influence of the priest, surrounded by his tricks of power, Karne forced himself to move with a last and desperate effort of will.

'I will give you the knowledge you ask for, and I take your word as sworn upon the Tall Stones of The Temple of the Sun that you will use no treachery.' Karne spoke at last. 'Now, follow me.'

'Where are you going?' Yealdon spoke sharply and uneasily.

'To the Sacred Circle,' Karne said as calmly as he could. 'You must know that knowledge of this kind can only be passed within the Sacred Circle!'

Yealdon was not pleased. He had hoped to find out what he needed without leaving the protective ambience of his house. But he took a rush light from its holder and by its low and flickering flame the two found their way to the top of the cliff where the Tall Stones rose darkly against the grey surge of the sea. The sky was still overcast but the clouds had thinned considerably in places and a faint and eerie light emanated from the moon behind them, not enough to make the silver path upon the water that had so bemused Fern, but enough to make the land and the Stones of the Circle darker than the sky or sea.

The village lay silently behind them, the fires reduced to embers and no sound coming from the dark huts. Karne wondered if Fern and Kyra were safely asleep. He knew they were extremely tired.

How he longed to be far away and safely sleeping too!

As they approached the Circle Karne was faced with another problem.

In his community it was an ancient law that no one but the priest or at special times designated by the same law, village Elders, could enter the Circle. It was full of power that ordinary men were not trained to handle or withstand. Kyra had been afraid but she had so far progressed in her apprenticeship that she could enter safely and use its ancient forces.

Karne had no right to tamper with the mysterious forces in the Circle.

He was afraid.

But what was he to do?

In despair he called to Kyra for her help, and in that moment of desperation believed implicitly that she would come.

'Why do you wait?' Yealdon cried impatiently. 'The night will not last forever!'

Of that at least Karne was glad.

'I must first consult with The Lords of the Sun,' Karne said, trying to hide the tremor in his voice. 'They may not wish you to have this Secret Knowledge. There may be a reason they have withdrawn themselves from you.'

Karne caught the glint of the deadly ring as Yealdon raised it warningly.

'And if I die,' Karne said loudly and clearly, though in his heart he was feeling very far from bold, 'my Knowledge dies with me!'

He called again for Kyra deep inside himself. Why did she not hear? She had the power to enter men's minds and see their thoughts. Why did she not now see his?

'Push me no further, boy!' Yealdon said with anger in his voice. 'I have waited a long time for this Knowledge, and I can wait a while longer.'

He too was trying to control his face and voice. He did not wish Karne to sense his eagerness and impatience. He did not want to wait longer! How many winters and summers must pass before the sea threw up another priest upon his shore. Maybe never, and he had grown too fat and lazy, used to comfort and routine, to endanger his life by travelling on the sea or through the dark and savage forests that ringed his hunting village to a depth no man had ever measured. For some while now he had not been able either to leave the place in the flesh or in the mind, nor could he reach out to other priests in the world on any spiritual level. He had absolute power in his own small community, but in a sense he was a prisoner there. This was the first contact he had had for a long, long time with anyone outside his village. It was a kind of miracle. He might never get another chance.

Kyra came out of her faint (or was it sleep?) in the dark interior of a foul smelling hut. She could see nothing, but heard snoring and heavy breathing all around her. Her first

24

thought was for Fern and she whispered her name, but received nothing back but further grunts and snores. She tried to still her fears and concentrate as Maal had taught her to, to sense with her inner senses where Fern might be.

She sensed nothing from Fern, but kept half seeing at the corner of her eye in the dark an image of Karne. When she turned to look directly at him he was gone and it was only the dark blankness of the hut she could see.

It seemed as though he were trying to tell her something.

But what?

Fern?

She must find Fern.

She sensed danger but whether it was to Karne or to Fern she could not make out.

She was sure neither of them were in the same hut as herself.

She must crawl out of it somehow.

She must have air.

She almost choked on the staleness of the smell.

It seemed to her as her senses gradually became used to her surroundings and the dark that the hut contained far more people in a more confined space than ever would have been allowed in her home village. The roof was low and as far as she could make out the only opening was a small hole to one side, through which she would have to crawl. No one could go in or out of this noisome hut except on hands and knees.

The task of reaching the hole (she refused to call it 'doorway') was not an easy one. She was surrounded by gross and noisy sleepers and she dared not wake them.

Tiny movement by tiny movement she prepared to make the journey, pausing every moment to check that the general level of the sleeping noises had not dropped in any way. Luckily for her the excitement of the night and the potency of the root ale had made the rude sleepers sleep heavily and deep.

Her head was aching and her thinking was not as clear as she would have liked, but at least she was conscious and was making progress to the hole.

At one point while she was climbing over a man's body, his arm came up to hold her down to him, his lips muttering something to her. Her heart almost stopped beating and she lay against him as still as stone, feeling the dead weight of his muscular arm upon her. But after a while by the limpness of his limbs she realized he was still asleep and she carefully released herself from his embrace and continued creeping to the hole.

At last outside!

She took great gulps of air.

And as her head cleared she heard within it quite distinctly Karne's cry for help.

At the same time she saw Fern sitting on her haunches before the last remnants of a fire, rocking backwards and forewards on her heels, rubbing her arms and trying to warm and comfort herself.

'Oh, Kyra,' she sobbed when her friend put her arm around her shoulders. 'I have been so frightened and alone. I thought you were dead when they carried you off, and I cannot find Karne anywhere.'

'Did they kill anyone?' Kyra asked anxiously.

'I do not think so. It was a mock hunt. The ones with antler-masks fell flat when the spears flew, but I saw them get up afterwards. I have been so frightened! These people are not like our people. I insisted on staying out here by the fire. They wanted me to sleep with them in those horrible huts, but I would not. They could not understand it and were really rough with me.'

'Are you hurt?' Kyra asked quickly.

'Only a bit bruised, I think. I finally made them understand and they left me alone. I think they were too tired to keep it up for too long. Oh, Kyra, I am so thankful you are all right! But Karne! Where is Karne?' Her voice was desperate.

'He is in danger, I fear. I can sense a call from him. Come, we must go to him.'

'Where?'

'Be quiet a moment. I must "feel" the direction of the call.'

She stood still, concentrating, and felt the flow of Karne's anxiety coming to her from the Sacred Circle on the cliff top.

Compared to the inside of the hut, the night was relatively

light. She and Fern stumbled many times, but nevertheless made their way swiftly to the source of his danger.

Within the Circle they could make out the figures of two men. One slender and tall, one bulky and gross. Her brother and the priest.

Kyra sensed great evil and danger surrounding her brother and stood in the shadows unseen by the men trying to locate the centre of the menace. She held Fern, who wanted immediately to run to Karne, and indicated to her to keep silence and be still. Fern obeyed, though it was painful for her to do so.

Kyra felt the priest was greedy and unclean, but somehow weak. She did not sense the strength in him that Wardyke had had.

No, the menace was not coming entirely from the priest.

What then?

Something the priest wielded?

A dagger perhaps.

She had seen cruel daggers forged of bronze and sharpened to a deadly cutting edge.

No.

Something else. .

She heard Karne's voice raised unnaturally high and saw his hands rise up above his head.

'Lords of the Sun!' he was declaiming.

What was he doing, she thought with horror! He knew he had no right to be within the Circle and certainly no power to raise the Lords of the Sun.

Had her brother gone mad, and was this the menace that she sensed? Karne had always longed to have the powers she had!

She drew nearer, trembling with anxiety.

'Continue!' she heard the fat priest's voice commanding Karne.

'You, Lords of the Sun,' Karne repeated and hesitated again.

Yealdon moved closer to him and lifted his right hand with something that glinted in it, but which Kyra could not make

27

out from this distance.

'You, Lords of the Sun and Spirits of the many worlds that lie within our world! . . . Come to the aid of one who wishes to preserve your ancient laws against the one who would betray them!'

His voice was loud and ringing.

Kyra caught the message, and in that instant saw with great clarity what the priest held over Karne to make him do what he was doing.

She shut her eyes and formed a mental picture of the ring he held towards her brother. She felt the malevolence of its power and she visualized it shattering in a thousand pieces. At the same time she joined her voice to Karne's, leaping into the Circle and repeating loud and clear the prayer he had just prayed.

Yealdon screamed as the ring he held above his head seemed to burn his fingers. He dropped it, shrieking with the pain, and as it hit the stony ground it shattered and splintered into a thousand fragments, some of them striking his cheeks and causing them to bleed. Tearing at his own face as though it were on fire Yealdon further ripped his own flesh, convinced the ring had turned against its Master.

Quickly Karne seized the hands of Kyra and Fern and they ran fast and low for the path that led down to the bay where their boat was moored. The first glimmerings of the dawn light helped them and they were away, bruised and shaken from the scramble down the cliff path, before the villagers awoke amazed to find their priest crawling on his hands and knees within their Sacred Circle, muttering and sobbing and sifting through the earth to find thin splinters of metal, his face a mess of tears and blood.

He looked up to find them staring at him and for an instant fear of *them* showed in his eyes.

In that instant he was finished as the tyrant he had been.

Where the splinters of the ring had struck his face, sores festered and never healed.

Illusions

When the time came to leave the ocean and turn their little craft into the wide and muddy estuary of the river that cut deep into the land, the three tired and discouraged travellers felt a surge of new hope and energy.

It marked the end of the first phase of their journey.

Fern was particularly glad. She sat in the front of the boat as they rode in with the tide, her long red-gold hair blowing back with the wind and her voice raised in song. Although they would still travel for many days on water, the land with all its rich profusion of growing things would be near. She could talk with the trees, 'feel' the surge of living sap in growing plants, take guidance and comfort from her familiar green world. The ocean was so cold, so unfamiliar and so vast. She knew the same force that gave life to the land was no less present in the ocean, but somehow she could never feel it there. She who had never been lonely in her life although she had lived most of it alone, tasted loneliness for the first time on the great and surging deeps. She would have clung to Karne but he was always busy keeping them afloat and moving in the right direction. Lines of concentration from staring into distances were becoming a common feature between his eyes. She turned to Kyra, but Kyra too seemed occupied in ways within herself that Fern could not share.

The land was Fern's medium, the forests and the thickets her domain. She would be happy there.

The meeting of the river waters and the sea was not easy to navigate. Several times their little boat nearly capsized in the turbulence and Karne and Kyra were kept very busy and nearly lost their nerve and balance.

But once through this obstacle, the tide and a following breeze carried them easily to where the estuary narrowed and became a river.

Ayrlon, the new priest of their home community, had said that for many days they could travel inland on this waterway. It led West and gently South. But when they found the course turning sharply North as it did at one point, they must leave it and travel overland for a while until they found another South-flowing river. There were many such and he gave them advice on how to choose the best. Luckily their boat was very light and could be carried between them when they had to cross the land, and it would always be useful as shelter in the night.

'Always keep a fire going,' Ayrlon had advised. 'The forests are full of animals, some of whom may not be friendly. Fire frightens them and keeps them at a safe distance. Where there are caves use them, but look first that they are not inhabited by man or beast. Make your fire in the mouth of the cave. Many bears, wild cats and wolves seek shelter there from time to time.

'Where you find villages rest with them awhile. Do not push yourselves too far too fast. You will find many dangers and difficulties on the way and if you are tired you are that much less able to deal with them.

'Give my greetings wherever you find people of our faith. I made many friends on my journey North and it is possible you will meet with them and they will give you kinder hospitality for my sake.'

Kyra, Karne and Fern had listened to everything he had said.

It had been a good day for their village when he arrived. The snow was still on the ground but the earliest shoots of Spring were beginning to show through it. He came quietly, with none of the dramatic showmanship Wardyke had used that fatal Midsummer's Day the year before.

The people took Ayrlon to their hearts within a few hours of his arrival. He was a quiet man, small in build. He listened more than he spoke, but those who told him of their troubles knew he understood and walked away comforted, though more often than not he had said nothing.

Kyra tested her feelings for him by a long night vigil of prayer and meditation near Maal's grave, and in the morning knew for sure her first feelings had been true. He was to be trusted with her village, and their customary ways of peace would be safe in his hands.

When she left she looked back with pain to leave her much loved home, but with calm in her heart knowing that everything was now as it should be.

The first night up the river they camped on high ground on the Southern bank in a dull and drizzling rain.

Fern rushed about, ignoring the wet, joyfully gathering special roots and shoots to eat. Karne and Kyra could hear her talking excitedly wherever she went as though she were greeting long lost friends.

They busied themselves by setting up the boat as tent and trying, at first unsuccessfully, to find a place where it was possible to make a fire. They had just succeeded in encouraging a rather damp and smoking version to ignite when Fern returned, still happy, but dripping wet, her hair clinging in long wet strands to her shoulders and back, water trickling off the end of her nose.

The next day they paddled upriver still in rain and camped damply upon the bank again.

The third day was better. The sun came out and their spirits were so uplifted that they made much greater progress and found, when it was time to camp, a small community of people living on rising land a short way from the water's edge.

After the initial suspicions were allayed the villagers made them welcome and they enjoyed a real feast of river trout and heard many tall stories of river demons and monstrous forest ogres.

Karne went fishing with the men the following morning and learnt to glide so silently in the water that the fish were not alarmed at his presence and he was able, after many attempts to dart his hand out and seize a fat fish before the creature knew that it was in danger.

He shouted and danced with joy at his first success so much they all had to move to another reach of water to continue their fishing, every fish within a great range having been frightened away by his exuberance.

Kyra and Fern took some of the women into the forest and spoke to them of the gentle tree spirits and the living force that flowed through everything and had its source in that which was limited by no Name, but had power and energy to drive life's multifarious forms within a great and ever harmonious pattern.

The river women listened attentively, but the girls could see they could not understand what was being said.

'No matter,' Kyra said to Fern, 'it is like planting a seed. The ideas we give them now may lie dormant in their minds for many years, but one day the warmth of some experience will stimulate them into growth.'

'But what about the ogres?' a woman asked fearfully, looking around.

'*You* give them their ugly shapes, their terrifying attributes and then cower in the night from them.'

'But we *feel* them around us in the dark!' the woman said.

'What you feel are the urges in your own minds to evil, and you give them shape and form with your imagination. You put them outside yourself so that you need not feel guilty about them, so that you need not fear *yourselves*!'

The woman looked at her with eyes that comprehended nothing of what she was saying.

'Have you not felt hate for someone and wished him harm?'

'Yes,' the woman admitted reluctantly.

'Then you have felt guilty to feel such hate, to wish such harm, so you have pretended to yourself that it is not *you* hating, not *you* wishing harm, but some other creature, some monster, some ogre. And you vividly imagine it destroying what you want destroyed. But gradually this image becomes so real to you you begin to believe it exists apart from you. You tell others and they join their fears, their hates, their guilts to it as well. And so it grows and grows in your minds until you have all forgotten how it first began!'

'But children have gone into the forest and been eaten by the ogres!' Some of the other women joined in now.

'The children may have been killed by wild boars or wandered so far they have not been able to find their way back,' Fern said. 'There may be a thousand natural dangers in the forest which could be overcome if you could control your fear of them.'

'Fear can kill,' Kyra warned. 'It is very powerful. If a child is fed on stories of monsters and ogres and it goes into the darkness of the forest, the cracking of a twig trampled by a small deer, the whirring of a bird's wings, could so destroy the balance of its mind that it might run and stumble deeper into the forest, terrified, no longer taking care, a prey to any natural danger.'

The women looked doubtful, but as though they wanted to believe.

'If you like,' Kyra said after a pause to think, noticing that they were not ready to understand such teaching yet. 'Fern and I will go into the forest and pray to the Spirits of Light we know and they will drive whatever it is you fear away from this place forever!'

'The forest is not safe!' the women cried.

'Kyra has magic powers,' Fern said, realizing what Kyra was trying to do. 'She has started training as a priest.'

The women were still puzzled. They lived cut off from the rest of the world and had no Sacred Circle and no priest.

'I have magic powers greater than the ogres that you fear,' Kyra said with confidence, 'and I will destroy these monstrous ogres once and for all if you will do exactly what I say.'

They did not fully understand even yet, but knew enough to realize that these strangers were very different from themselves. The one called Kyra spoke with such authority and conviction they were prepared to believe she was some kind of magician.

The women began to draw back from them a little after this and their friendliness was now tempered with caution.

33

'While we are in the forest asking the help of our Spirit Gods make me a model of the ogre that you think lives in the forest. Fashion it of river clay and bring it to me at the river bank when it is ready,' Kyra commanded.

'There are several types of ogre,' someone said.

'Then make them all for me . . . in clay . . . as nearly as you can to how they look.'

Fern looked at Kyra, but said nothing.

For the rest of the day the women worked busily at the models.

The men returned from fishing and were told the story. Some argued. Some helped. But by mid-afternoon they were all taking part in the activity even if it was only to offer advice about the look of some particular eye or nose.

Karne took Kyra aside.

'What on earth . . .?' he said.

She put her finger to her lips.

'It may help to dispel their fears. Why not this way, if they are not ready for the truth as we know it?'

He shrugged and smiled and left her to it, setting about the task himself of gutting the fish they had caught and roasting them on the fire.

Kyra chose sunset for the staging of her exorcism.

She, Fern and Karne built a small circle of river boulders on the narrow sandy beach just below the bank, scooped out the sand from within it, allowing the water to seep up from below.

When the models were prepared and, the sun a red and gigantic sphere sinking into the tree tops to the West, the villagers gathered to watch with some apprehension as Kyra lowered the hideous clay figures into the little pool of water she had prepared.

She walked round and round the circle many times chanting improvised prayers of exorcism, Karne and Fern meanwhile scooping more and more river water over the models.

Gradually the clay softened, the hideous features disintegrated and, as the sun finally set with a shaft of brilliant light catching the ripples in the river close beside them, the last ogre dissolved and was no more than muddy water.

34

As this happened Karne, Kyra and Fern raised their arms and sang a song from their own village, a moving, rising hymn of praise to Light and Life and the Spirit Guardians of the World.

So sweetly did the sound of their voices mingle with the birds homing to their nests, so uncannily did the last shaft of light from the sun fall now upon the little circle of stones and dye the muddy pool of water the colour of blood that the villagers gave a great gasp of relief and *believed* their ogres were finally dead.

That night the villagers sang and danced to the strangers, and this time there was no menace or cruelty in the dance as there had been in the hunting dance of their last host village, where, although no one was actually killed, the lust for killing was in the air.

This dance was only of joy, and the air was filled with feelings of release..

A day or two later the three were sorry to move on. They had made friends. The villagers believed that their monsters had been destroyed and they had been taught to pray to the friendly spirits of the River and the Forest and the Sun for help and comfort in everything they did.

Karne had learnt to fish in a new and exciting way.

Fern had found plants she had not encountered before.

And Kyra had been taught to weave baskets of river reeds far superior to any she had ever seen before.

They parted with warm feelings, villagers and travellers each having benefitted in some way from their time together

Overland travel was not easy. The boat became ever more cumbersome and heavy to carry and, after several rivers had degenerated into rocky rapids before they had a chance to make for shore, it became virtually useless as a boat. They decided at last to abandon it and make their way as far as possible by land, crossing rivers when they found them by inflating their water carrying skins to use as floats and then refilling them with fresh water on the far side.

Kyra was particularly sorry to see the boat go.

The last day before it finally sprang a leak too serious for them to mend had been in many ways idyllic.

For most of the day they had drifted and paddled gently down a very quiet and narrow river, the mossy banks close beside them, honeycombed with the holes of little furry river creatures who came frequently out to swim or bask on floating logs, totally unafraid of the unfamiliar creatures drifting past them.

Karne hummed quietly as he occasionally pulled the paddle through the water to keep it on course and Kyra lay back upon their sleeping rugs and other travelling things, gazing at the sliding slopes of interlocking branches and light new leaves above them.

They were in a kind of green tunnel. The reflections of the trees below them and the trees above, leaning sometimes down to water level, caused reflection and reality to join on an interface that was neither reflection nor reality, but a kind of otherness into which Kyra's thoughts slipped and received a new and deeply stirring peace.

Light played its part, sparkling between the leaves and flickering in the green world reflected in the water and in Kyra's eyes. She hardly dared breathe for fear of dispelling the delicacy of the beauty that moved her spirit through so many levels of awareness.

Karne and Fern were forced to bend their heads to avoid the branches of white hawthorn blossom and their hidden protective thorns.

They were happy too, but in a different way from Kyra.

Fern leant her body against Karne and they felt totally together, absorbed within each other, the green sunlight clothing them in one garment.

Kyra did not notice when the boat stopped and Karne tied it to the brown and knobbled root of a tree. She lay still, gazing upwards in her own secret world, while he and Fern left to find a private place of their own among the tendrils, flowers and grasses.

The day had to end.

But not one of them would ever let it fade in the slightest detail from their memories.

It was one of those precious days, seemingly out of time.

The next day was rougher. Rapids battered at their boat, and muscles grew tired with hauling it in and out of the river, climbing banks, cutting through undergrowth. The whole character of the land had changed remarkably with the change in the rock formations.

From the slow and gentle progress through a wide and meandering valley, hills began to close in upon the river and chasms of rock, with small trees and bushes clutching a precarious living in shallow crevices in their sides, took the place of the mossy peaceful banks they had loved so much.

By midday they agreed the boat's usefulness was finished. From Ayrlon's description they had about exhausted the navigable rivers leading South. They decided to leave the boat, strapping everything they could carry about themselves, and set off to climb the steep side of the chasm wall, hoping to have a better view of the land still to travel from the top.

Fern found the climb with the added weight of her unborn child more than she could bear at times, and Karne, noticing this, suggested they make camp for the night on a broad shelf of rocks and grass, little more than half way up. There was a good overhang of rock to shelter them and plenty of dry wood for a fire, their goatskins were full of fresh water, and they had a plentiful supply of fresh hare meat caught by Karne earlier in the day with his catapult.

While Fern rested and Karne attended the cooking fire, Kyra wandered off to explore. She felt restless and did not want to settle yet to the chores of making camp.

The rocks of these mountains were different from the ones she knew nearer home. She fingered them and brooded, wondering what it was she felt in them that seemed to lead her on and stir some feeling in her that she could not explain.

She kept moving further and further from the camp site, led on by a kind or urge, almost a kind of hunger. Tender and beautiful ferns grew from the cracks in the rocks, lichens of greater variety than she had ever seen clung to the long exposed surfaces of stone and the older branches of the trees. Hanging festoons of filigree lichen, reminding her of pale silver-green hair, hung from the twigs high above her.

But it was the rock cliff that was speaking to her.

It was something inside the rock cliff that was calling her name.

Puzzled, she wandered on and on, looking without realizing it, for an entrance into the cliff. The sun had disappeared behind the hill on the opposite side of the chasm before she found it. The shadow was cold, but it was still light. No doubt on plains beyond the hill the sun was still shining. She knew it was not yet time for night and looking upwards she could still see the sun shining on the topmost branches of the trees at the top of the cliff face under which she was standing.

The entrance was half closed over with tangled briars, but she felt the darkness and the emptiness behind them and knew that there was a deep cave there.

She thought about it for a while. Should she return to the others and tell them? Perhaps they were meant to use it for their camp.

She felt strongly, but in an undefined way, that she was *meant* to find this cave.

But it would take her a long time to return to the others and by the time they had carried all their belongings back to the cave night would be upon them.

She decided to have a quick look inside the mountain herself, and then return to the others.

She peered inside and was surprised to see how deeply the cave had eaten into the rock. It was larger and darker than any cave she had ever encountered before, but still she felt the need to explore it.

She ignored the little chill of fear that rippled under her

skin and looked around for a suitable branch to serve as a
torch. Having found one she worked to set it alight and finally
she was ready to bend the briar bushes back and enter, in some
trepidation, but nevertheless impelled by a force she could not
control.

The flame of her torch took her through the fairly capacious
entrance hall of the cave, the only thing here to startle her
being a sudden flight of bats that fell from the roof and swirled
like dark and solid smoke about her head. She could not
prevent herself screaming and throwing herself at once upon
the dry and sandy floor. Luckily, although she dropped her
torch in her panic, it did not go out and after the bats had
swarmed once or twice in wide arcs and had settled back to
their places, and she had given herself a stern reprimand for
having given way to such a foolish fear, she was ready to
continue.

After a while the cave wall showed two separate crevices,
wide enough for a human to pass through. She hesitated,
knowing that it was foolish to go further but still unable to
resist the urge to do so.

She chose the right hand crack and proceeded down a fairly
adequate passage way. She became more and more convinced
it was leading her to some special place, and so eager was she
to find out if she were right and so easy was the passage to
follow that she did not notice that it branched frequently in
many directions and she had long since turned off from the
main one leading back to the entrance cave. The passage she
was following was becoming narrower and narrower, lower
and lower, sloping always downwards deeper into the
mountain.

The torch light flickered on the walls beside her and
suddenly she became aware that it was not bare, smooth rock
she was seeing, but that the light and shadow of the guttering
flame was throwing up in relief what seemed at first to her to
be the most amazing man-made carvings. The walls were full
of the shapes of creatures, many of which she recognized from
the sea, but some she had never seen or dreamt of before.

She stopped and touched them, staring with astonishment.

One came away in her hand and she stood transfixed with the perfection of a sea urchin, each detail of tiny radiating spots where the living spines had been joined to the shell perfectly preserved. But in stone! Cold hard stone.

What skill the carver must have had to bring such detail to his carving!

She gasped again .

The wall was full of them, not only upon the surface, but where she broke them off there were others in the rock behind. Shells she remembered from the beaches.

But all in stone.

Icily the realization came to her that these were no man-made carvings.

Living things had turned to stone.

She shuddered and touched her own cold flesh.

Would she too turn to stone in this weird place?

Was it some baleful influence, some dark force, that had led her there, not the Spirits of Light she was wont to follow?

Fear gripped her now and she began to shiver uncontrollably. As she did so the torch in her hand shook and the creatures in the walls seemed to mock her with a strange dead dance.

She turned and ran, horribly aware that she had come a long way and her torch would not last much longer. The sea urchin was still clutched in her hand. She moved to throw it away, but something made her keep it and she put in in the carrying pouch at her waist. If she ever saw them again she would show it to Karne and Fern.

She ran and ran, grazing her arms against the narrow jagged walls, scarcely thinking which way to turn as each new gallery of darkness opened its entrance to her blind and hurrying form.

At the peak of her panic she turned the corner in a passage that she now realized she had never been down before and stood staggered and breathless at what she saw.

Before her, illuminated fitfully by the still burning stump of the torch into her hand, was a gigantic cavern, the far recesses of which disappeared into darkness, but where the light touched Kyra could see that from the magnificently high ceiling to the floor it was hung with spectacular columns of crystal.

Forgetting her fear Kyra stood stunned. Tumbling in folds like a water fall turned to ice, great curtains of dazzling white fell around her, gigantic statues of translucent stone arose on every side, icicles of stone hung from the domed roof to join flowers of stone upon the floor.

This was what she had come for!

Her heart rose and it seemed to her a crescendo of splendour, almost like a song of triumph but using no earthly means of sound, soared around her, through her and above her.

She was in ecstasy with the beauty and the greatness of it.

She moved forward, walking in wonder, through the exquisite filaments of crystal.

She could hear water dripping and in the centre the cavern floor was lower than the rest and filled with a milky liquid.

Staring into it, her light picking out the reflections in it, she was suddenly jerked into fear again as her torch, burnt now to its very end, scorched her hand and dropped into the water.

As suddenly as the darkness had revealed this splendid, dazzling sight to her, as suddenly it snuffed it out and she was in utter blackness.

Fear welled back and she turned her head every way trying to see something, anything, any variation in the dead blackness of the hole in which she was trapped, that would give her some idea of what direction she should take to find her way out.

But there was no variation.

She stood very still, listening to her heart beating fast and the drip, drip of the water from the roof. She wondered if there was any way she could make fire, but she had no wood with her and everything in the cavern was wet, the walls, the floor, the rocks, the hanging veils of crystal.

Her own skin felt damp and clammy.

'I must think,' she told herself.

But all she could think about was that she was deep inside

the earth, deeper than in any tomb.

'I must move about. I must feel for the entrance,' she told herself, knowing that if she stood still and thought about her situation any longer the fear that was already clouding her mind would take possession of her completely.

Cautiously she moved.

She established the pool of water was ahead of her by finding her feet and ankles suddenly immersed in icy liquid.

'Good,' she said to herself, 'that means the entrance is behind me.'

She turned carefully around. She had never noticed before how difficult it is to be sure how far you have turned, when there is absolutely nothing to which you can relate.

But she had to make a decision.

Carefully she eased herself forward, hands held out in front of her, knowing there were many hanging columns in the way. Where was their brilliant, luminous, crystalline splendour now, she thought bitterly. All their magnificence came from the little flame she had carried in her hand. Darkly they waited now as no doubt they had waited in the same darkness while the sun a million times a million times shone upon the fortunate creatures of the earth's surface.

How she longed for light!

Gradually she progressed across the cave, bumping herself against rock, feeling her way, slipping and sliding, but at last coming into contact with what she was sure was the wall of the cavern.

She sat awhile to rest, her heart thumping and her breath coming fast. She told herself there was nothing to worry about, she had found the wall and it was just a matter of time as she worked her way round it until she found the entrance. She refused to think about the confusion of passages beyond.

After a while, too cold to be still for long, she started to feel for the entrance. The cold, damp hardness scraped her fingers, but she found no hole. She moved and moved, always in the same direction, always her hand upon the wall. Time passed that there was no measure for. Only her weariness and despair told her that she had been going a long, long time.

At last she paused. She *must* have been around the full extent of the cavern. She must have been!

She tried again.

Again.

The fear was becoming uncontrollable. She could feel cold sweat upon her forehead.

If only she could see!

She stared and stared into the dark and for a moment fancied that she saw a lighter dimness to one side.

Her heart leaping she moved swiftly towards it, but she missed her footing, slipped and twisted her ankle. Now tears of pain were in her eyes and she was trembling and shivering with cold, pain and fear.

The lighter patch she had thought she had seen was now upon the other side of her. She turned her head and felt there was another lighter patch where she had looked before. It seemed to her the cavern was no longer so dark.

It also seemed to her that she was no longer alone.

'Who is there?' she called, her voice rasping with fear.

The sound echoed eerily around the cavern and came back to her as a hiss.

Trembling, still she tried to see, to listen for someone other than herself, and then she felt presences and could see dim figures.

She called to them and raised herself in spite of the pain of her ankle, and they drew nearer.

But as she saw them more clearly she screamed aloud. Sickly vapours they were, in monstrous shapes.

'No!' she screamed. 'No! No! Not you!'

She pressed her hands to her eyes to shut them out. She tried to run and fell again.

Weeping and bleeding and frantic with pain and fear she felt it was the end of everything for her!

And then . . .

And then somewhere in her mind a thin thread of memory came to her.

'These are not *real*,' she told herself. 'It is my fear that calls them into being!'

43

She remembered the clay ogres and the water, and felt ashamed that she could presume to teach others about the images of Fear and yet fall prey to them herself so easily.

She forced herself to open her eyes.

But they were still there.

The Fear was still in her.

No matter how she reasoned with herself she could not drive them from her presence.

She remembered Maal and prayed for his help. He had told her many times of all the Spirit helpers in the endless realms of different Realities. They too had no form but that which thought gave them. Humans invented forms for them, just as she had invented forms for her fears and for the evil influences she could feel around her.

She shut her eyes again and forced herself with all the inner strength she had to visualize forms of Light and Love and Kindness, Spirits that would help and protect her.

When she opened her eyes again the crystal rocks seemed to glow with inner light.

She forced her mind to obey her will.

She drew herself up to stand as straight as she could.

Her ankle hurt but she ignored it.

She told herself again and again she was not afraid.

She was protected by hierarchies of helpers who came when they were needed.

Her fears had created the others. Her confidence would destroy them.

'I will think only of love and those I love,' she told herself, and thought of Maal, of Karne and Fern, but mostly of . . . someone else.

Another figure appeared to her now and the shadowy ones she had hated seemed to draw back and begin to fade.

Standing before her was the one she had called most urgently, one of the powerful Lords of the Sun, the young priest from the desert Temple of the South, from across the sea. The young priest she had met in 'spirit-travel' when she was seeking help against Wardyke.

He held out his hands to her but did not approach, and

44

although she gazed at him with such joy she thought her heart would burst, she did not dare make a move towards him.

'You have passed the first test,' he said quietly.

She looked her question.

'The illusions of Fear are powerful, but you have recognized them for what they are.'

She noticed there was no sign of the demons now, only the beautiful young man shining with the same strange light as the crystal columns.

'Can you do the same for the illusions of love?'

She stared at him.

She longed for him.

She began to reach out her hands, to move forward.

He stood still, appearing very real, watching her with great kindness, but with a question in his eyes.

She paused.

'The illusions of love?' she asked herself, and then, 'What am I doing!' she thought. 'As a priest people will come to *me* for help and I must not fail them.

'You are here and not here,' she said aloud, steadily, looking directly at him, 'as I am. What we appear to be and what we are, are very different.'

'This shell I use, called "Kyra", I can throw away this moment and will suffer no loss. I am more than Kyra. I am God's creation, and God "creates" by "becoming". Nothing can be separate from Him. All of Him, all the time, is in everything He has "become", is in me now, and I would feel the joy and power of it if my mind would only stop holding back the realization that it is so.

'The Real Me is Forever and Everywhere. I am One with All that Is.'

She was in the dark.

She was not afraid.

When Karne and Fern found her the next afternoon she was sitting cross legged on the floor of the cavern, her face composed and calm, and she looked up at them as they stood,

45

their faces grey with anxiety lit by the torches they carried, as though it had only been a few moments that she had been waiting for them, instead of a whole night and the best part of a day.

The Birth of Isar

About the time the moon reached full for the third time since they left their home village, Fern began to feel the child in her body was ready to be born. She who had always been so lithe and agile was beginning of late to be clumsy, to feel her body cumbersome and heavy, and many times she accepted the helping hand of Karne over rocks and ridges where before she would have scorned to be so dependent.

At night she could feel it moving inside her restlessly and she lay under the stars staring all night into the immensity of the sky and wondering about the child that was to be born.

It was not Karne's child, but Wardyke's, the result of rape and fear. Karne and she had discussed it many times since he had recovered from the initial pain and shock of the knowledge and they were agreed that the child who would be born was an individual in its own right and must not suffer in any way for something which was not its fault, the manner of its conception. Fern had carried it and nourished it. Karne would father it and protect it. Wardyke was long gone, punished and banished for all the things that he had done, and he had no more part in this new life.

Fern believed passionately that everything that lived was its own Self and belonged to no one but to the Great Source of Life Itself, and that was not 'belonging' in 'the slave to Master' sense, but in 'the lover to lover' sense. The loving and the wanting to belong and to be part of the whole harmony of Existence was the only binding force. It was your choice if you chose to be part of it and to flow peacefully with it. Just as it was your choice if you chose to reject it and to drift into disharmony and chaos, suffering pain as you beat your head against the constricting walls which were of your own construction.

47

Fern, who had once said so ringingly, 'No man can own a tree!' knew more than anyone that no one could own a child. Children were born through the medium of male and female flesh, but this was just a kind of door through which they stepped into the world from regions where they had lived millennia before..

The role of parents was to cherish and nourish the infant in its bodily form, teach it how to use the new and unfamiliar tool of flesh it had been given, until they sensed that it was ready to recognize the obligations and powers of its nature and walk freely as it was meant to do.

One morning after such a night of staring at the stars Fern told her husband and Kyra her friend, calmly, that the baby's birth was very near.

They had made camp in what had once been a clearing in the woods. From the charred marks on boulders and the remnants of animal bones upon the ground, it would seem it had once been inhabited and then deserted. Nature had started to reclaim it and young slender saplings of birch, hazel and alder were growing from the undergrowth of bracken, bramble and flowering plants. It was a beautiful place, full of bird song and early sunshine.

Kyra and Karne looked at each other. They had planned to rest at the next community they found while Fern had her baby among friendly and helpful people, a priest at hand knowledgeable in the ways of healing in case anything should go wrong.

But Fern insisted that she could go no further and that indeed she could wish for no better place for the birth of her child.

She looked up at the shimmering leaves and the slender silvered trunks of the young trees.

'These are my friends,' she said. 'I would rather be among them than among strange people.'

'We need water,' Karne said, beginning to feel anxious and bustle about, putting more wood on the fire.

Kyra stood still and seemed to be listening, though not necessarily with her ears.

'There *is* water,' she said. 'I will fetch it for you.'

She took all the skin bags they had and set off to the East.

'Watch where you go!' called Karne sharply, remembering the terrible long night and day Fern and he had spent worrying about her the last time she had wandered off to explore. They had only realized she was not coming back when it was too dark to risk looking for her. They had passed a sleepless night and a worrying morning before they located the entrance to the cave. The bending back of the bushes and the remnants of the fire she had kindled to light her torch had shown them where she was. When Karne had seen the ramifications of the passages within the cave he had insisted on returning to camp to bring all the ropes and fibres he could find so that they could tie some to the entrance and always have a thread to follow back.

It was in this way that they had tracked her through the labyrinth and found her at last.

This time Kyra was not away long and returned with plenty of fresh water to warm at the fire to wash the little creature when it finally emerged.

They made Fern as comfortable as possible and sat close to her while she worked to bring her baby into the light. Karne cradled her head and shoulders in his arms when the effort seemed too great, and Kyra waited to receive the child into the world, her heart beating with a strange excitement.

What an awsome mystery this was, the clothing of the immortal in the mortal, the Spirit from regions far beyond our knowledge, opening its physical eyes in our world, our reality.

She was always amazed how suddenly the last phases of the immensely long process passed. One moment Fern was lying in Karne's arms as she had always known her. The next moment her face distorted with effort into a stranger's face, and then there was the slithering arrival of a whole new Being upon the soft grass.

Swiftly Kyra did her part as she had seen others do in her home village when children were born, and soon the strange

49

new person who was to be from then on an integral part of their lives was washed and wrapped in soft woollen cloths and held close to the breast of a mother whose face was transformed with joy and love.

Karne leant close, thinking more of Fern than the child, but happy too.

There was no look of Wardyke in the tiny creature, but much of Fern. Upon his head, standing up on end like fur upon a squirrel's tail, was a shock of Fern's red-gold hair.

Kyra found herself crying with delight, and kept touching the tiny, perfect hands.

'Look at the nails!' she said. 'How can *anything* be so small and yet so beautifully just as it should be!'

This set them all to laughing and the rest of the morning passed joyfully in tending their new charge and wondering at the magnificence of its construction.

When Fern and the baby at last were sleeping in the warm sunlight, Karne and Kyra sat a little apart talking softly.

They both felt tired, but unable to relax. They talked of many things but mostly of the thought that had struck both of them as they watched the little creature feeling blindly for the source of milk and nourishment in its mother's breast, wonder at the sheer miracle of consciousness, the primitive form the baby now showed which in a few short summers would become as complex and as sophisticated as their own.

'This experience more than anything I have ever had,' Karne said, 'has convinced me that we do not just begin in flesh and end in dust. Nothing could learn as much on so many levels as this child will need to learn to reach the kind of consciousness that we now have, unless it brought with it some skills and aptitudes, some form of memory or consciousness, which would give it readiness to accept all that this world can teach, interpreting it upon its ancient knowledge.'

Kyra smiled.

She knew that many times in the past Karne had doubted much of what she and Fern and Maal believed. It was good to see that he had now found a way of understanding and accepting.

Later they talked of Wardyke and wondered if he had left his trace upon the child as Fern had left the colour of her hair.

Karne's face grew grave when they were discussing this. He would say nothing to Fern and he wished it had not even arisen in his mind, but he could not stop a faint trace of misgiving.

'I would feel happier, Kyra,' he said at last in a low voice, 'if you would try to reach within the child and set my mind at ease upon this point. Pray for it, weave protection about it. Give it strength to withstand any influences that would be harmful to it or to Fern.'

He did not mention himself. She knew his concern was only for his wife.

'I will try', she said, 'but you know my powers are very uncertain, they sometimes work and they sometimes do not. I can promise nothing.'

'Try,' Karne said firmly.

Kyra carefully took the baby from its mother. Fern stirred slightly and murmured Karne's name, but did not wake. Karne sat beside her while Kyra took the baby to the other side of the clearing, sat upon a boulder and rocked it gently in her arms. When she was sure the disturbance of the move had not woken it she kept it still, cradled in her arms, and lowered her own head to rest her forehead on its forehead. Karne could see her going very still, as she had many times before when she was sensing things beyond the capacity of his own senses.

He watched with great attention but could not see her face nor anything that would indicate to him what she was thinking as she held the child.

At first she was distracted by the sweet snuffling noises the baby made as it slept, the way its mouth and cheek muscles moved as though it were dreaming of sucking, and she had to fight her loving sentimentality and force herself to ignore the baby shell and look for the real self within.

The immediacy of the soft, warm forehead upon hers began to fade and gradually images began to come to her, images of distance and feelings of wandering in strange places. Nothing

51

definite at first. Nothing that she could recognize.

The feeling that she had most persistently was of another world, of skies that were not blue but like burnished copper, of people who protected themselves from light instead of seeking it. Of strange plant forms that grew in darkness and withered with the touch of the fiery light that radiated from more than one giant sun.

She felt a fear of light. She found herself longing for the cold dark cave she had been trapped in recently. Strangely she could see in the dark. Or could she? Was she looking at objects outside herself or were they all projections from her own mind, as in dreams upon this earth?

'Strange to be afraid of light,' she muttered to herself. 'Light goes always with the highest forms of Understanding and Awareness . . . the light of the Spirit Realms . . . the light of God.

'Are these people evil then, that they seek the Dark?'

She searched herself, the child, for more information, but felt no trace of evil.

'Light is a construct too, a Symbol,' she thought she heard the words within her head. 'Light and Dark have no relevance to what Eternally Is. You have made an idol of Light, as others have made idols of wood and stone. You can see in darkness *and* in light.

'You do not See.

'The Seeing is You.'

She was puzzled by this, but stored it in her memory to ponder upon at another time.

'Is this child in my arms from this strange world of burning suns?' Kyra asked the voice that seemed to be speaking these words within her head.

'The child is called Isar and lives now upon your earth. Ask no more of him than that.'

'I must ask one more question,' Kyra cried. 'Please, I need to know. Will he have Wardyke's lust for power and cruel needs?'

'The child is called Isar and lives now upon your earth. Ask no more of him than that.'

'But . . .'

But she knew there would be no more answers.

She opened her eyes and looked at the child within her arms. His eyes were open now, but instead of the wandering bluish blindness so familiar in newborn babies' eyes, she knew he was looking directly at her, and *seeing* her.

She stood up and held him out to Karne.

'His name is Isar,' she said quietly, humbly. 'I know no more than that.'

And Isar he was called.

When Fern felt rested and strong enough to continue on the journey Kyra wove a little carrying basket for Isar and Karne strapped it on to Fern's back.

When they had left the waterways they had thought that they would have great trouble making progress towards the South across the land, most of which was deeply forested. But they soon found the network of trackways that Ayrlon had described to them. The whole country seemed to be criss-crossed with narrow tracks that led straight from Sacred Circle to Sacred Circle. Where the tracks had become overgrown and difficult to follow there was always something they could use to sight their course upon, a Tall Stone standing singly, directing the eye to a notch on a far hill and indicating the direction of the track, or through a burial mound raised above the landscape, or even through a series of shining ponds leading the traveller onwards with little flashes of light. Sometimes there were marking stones or, on hill tops, cairns built up high that could be seen for great distances.

Strangely when they were on the track, however indistinct it might be, Kyra could 'feel' a kind of power flowing through it that led her on. On several occasions when markers had disappeared and Karne had insisted the right direction lay one way Kyra would argue and claim that she could 'feel' it was in another direction altogether.

After the second time Kyra had been proved correct Karne gave up and left the orientation entirely to her, no matter how illogical it seemed at times. It was as though she were following definite but invisible lines of energy that ran through the earth, which at some points had been marked visibly by the inhabitants of the area, but which at other points had not.

Where they came upon well-worn, well-marked tracks they knew they could not be far from human habitation and they rarely failed to find welcome waiting for them in villages. Many times they were sorry to move on and leave new found friends behind.

Where they found a Sacred Circle Kyra would question the priests about The Temple of the Sun, and the picture she built up of it intrigued her more and more. There seemed to be a great deal of inconsistency in the descriptions and she formed the impression that it was something different for each priest who had studied there.

She wondered what it would be for her.

Not all the Stone Circles they encountered gave rest and peace to their weary limbs and spirits.

One day in a mounting storm they hurried to follow Kyra's instincts that told them a Stone Circle was not far away. The branches of the trees above them were groaning and creaking ominously in the rising wind and they hoped to reach its shelter before the storm broke. Clouds like the black wings of night were closing in on them.

Isar upon his mother's back howled and sobbed. Fern took her husband's hand and they walked faster than they had ever walked, in silence and growing fear. The storm had some strange quality about it, some malevolence that seemed supernatural.

Kyra was troubled. She 'felt' the Stone Circle not far away and yet she also 'felt' a kind of warning.

'Perhaps we should stay her,' she said, 'and see the storm out before we go any further.'

'No,' Karne said, 'at the Circle there will be houses. We must be under cover when this breaks.'

It seemed sensible and in the wild cry of the wind there was such menace they could think of nothing else but getting to the village as quickly as possible.

They hurried on.

As the rain broke from a black sky ripped asunder by a tremendous dagger of lightning they saw the Stone Circle before them, livid in the eerie light of the storm.

But nowhere in sight were the houses that they had expected and longed for.

Karne ran forward, the rain already soaking him through and tearing at his flesh.

Nowhere were there houses.

The Circle was deserted, overgrown with brambles and stinging nettles.

It seemed a long time since anyone had used this desolate place for worship.

Fern crouched against the dead trunk of the only tree in the area and tried to protect her baby from the icy stinging rain and the constant frightening flashes of lightning.

Kyra stood in the middle of the Circle soaking with the water that poured over her and tried to 'sense' where the nearest shelter would be.

Nothing came to her but a feeling of great evil. This was a cursed place.

'We must leave at once!' she tried to cry out, but for some reason she seemed trapped where she was and her voice would not carry through the storm to the others who were crouched together, outside the Circle.

Her limbs were becoming cold as stone and impossible to move. Terror was in her heart. She remembered the feelings she had first experienced when she had tried to 'spirit travel' for the first time and had thought she was dying, but this was somehow different. Different and more horrible.

Meanwhile Karne and Fern had been startled by the visitation of an old and hideous crone who appeared apparently from nowhere and suddenly beside them.

When Karne had pulled himself together from the shock he spoke to her as boldly and as calmly as he could.

'We are travellers, weary and far from home. Is there a

village or shelter nearby we may use while the storm lasts?'

The woman laughed harshly.

'There is no shelter here,' she said.

'Nearby perhaps?'

'Nowhere! No shelter anywhere!' she almost screamed.

Fern was trembling uncontrollably with fear and cold, but Karne managed to keep himself enough under control to say sternly,

'Old woman, you must live somewhere! Will you not give hospitality to strangers?'

The old creature shrieked with laughter and as suddenly as she had appeared she vanished.

Karne put his arms round his terrified wife and child and tried to think what to do next. He looked for Kyra and saw her in the Circle, crouching in an unnatural position as though she were being twisted and knotted by an invisible force.

Not pausing to think but that he loved her and she was in trouble he rushed into the Circle and seized her stiff and icy form and dragged it back to where Fern and Isar were weeping against the dead wood of the old tree trunk.

He rubbed his sister's icy arms and slapped her stony face.

'Help me!' he cried to Fern, and they rummaged in their bags and found what furs they had and wrapped Kyra in them, all the while calling her name and beating and rubbing her, trying to get the blood flowing again.

'She is dead!' sobbed Fern.

'No, she is not, but she will be if we do not get her warm!'

They clung together, their own bodies trying to warm each other and her.

Mercifully the rain and storm began to pass and when Kyra finally opened her eyes there were already breaks appearing in the windy clouds.

But Kyra's eyes were bloodshot and feverish. Her lips, blue with cold, uttered strange sounds as though she were talking another language.

They had brought her back to consciousness, but she was in some kind of dreadful fever and incapable of speaking to them in any way they could understand.

Fern and Karne looked at each other in despair.

'It is this place,' Fern said, shuddering. 'It is full of evil. See, no trees grow, no birds fly about or sing! We must get her away from here.'

Exhausted as they were, Fern gathered up all she could carry and Karne lifted his sister in his arms. They had no idea in which direction to walk, but they knew they had to walk.

Stumbling with pain and weariness, at last, at nightfall, they saw the fires of habitations, and the people of the village took them in.

Karne told them their story, while Fern and Isar and Kyra were put to bed in a warm house and covered with dry fur rugs.

Once rested and refreshed Karne and Fern were told the story of the derelict Circle they had so unluckily stumbled across in the storm.

'It is said that in the ancient days a witch lived in that place, an old crone, hideous and disgusting, who had the power to make herself into a beautiful young girl for brief spells of time.

'All the communities had refused to take her in and she lived alone, riding the wind it is said and causing storms to devastate the crops of all the villages that had refused her hospitality.

'One day a handsome young man and his friends were walking in that place and found her in her temporary guise as a beautiful young girl, and the young man fell in love with her. He spoke of taking her to live with him and told her how much he loved her and how he would never leave her.

' "Not even when I am old?" she asked.

' "Never!" he said, gazing at her beauty.

'At that moment the spell she had put upon herself wore off and she returned to her hideous, ancient self.

'He drew back in horror, and he and all his friends turned to run.

'But she stood upon a boulder and screamed at him,

' "You promised never to leave me, and you never will!"

'And with that she cast a spell that to this day no one knows how to break.

'The young man and his friends were turned to stone and anyone who crosses her path within that circle turns to stone as well!'

Karne and Fern were horrified.

They remembered the unnatural, twisted stiffness of Kyra, the terrible coldness of her flesh . . .

Had they saved her just in time from that dreadful curse?

Kyra was very ill for a long time, and even the priest who had some knowledge of healing was doubtful of her chances of survival, but she did not die, nor did she turn to stone.

One day her fever seemed to have gone and they told her the story.

She lay for a long time with her face turned to the wall, tears dripping down her cheeks, too weak to say anything.

But that night her fever rose again and in her delirium they heard her call again and again for Maal, complaining that he had promised to return to her and be with her.

In the early hours of the morning, Fern, keeping vigil by her side, thought she heard Maal's voice speaking from Kyra's mouth, saying quite distinctly that he *would* return, but that he had not promised it would be in *this* lifetime.

When Kyra recovered enough to be aware of what was being said to her Fern told her of this.

Kyra could remember nothing, but tears gathered in her eyes as she listened to Fern's words.

'I want him in this lifetime! I need him *now*!' she said, her face pale and desperate.

Fern stroked her head.

'You think you need him. But no one knows what he truly needs. Maal will come to you when you really need him.'

Kyra wept.

She felt so weak, so tired. It was all too much to bear.

After a while she drifted off to sleep and in her sleep she dreamed fitfully about the cave she had been trapped in and the strange stone shells and sea creatures she had found so deeply in the earth.

When she awoke she felt in her carrying pouch for the perfect stone sea urchin she had brought from the cave.

She turned it over and over in her hand. She knew there was something she was ready to learn and it was somehow connected with this stone shell.

Was it that the Universe was full of forces that we did not understand and that they were available to us if we made ourselves available to them?

Words that Maal had said about Good and Evil came to her now. To him Good and Evil lay in the motive, the will, behind an action, not in the action itself. A force that could be used for Evil, could just as easily be used for Good.

The stone shell lay in the palm of her hand. Why or how it had been turned to stone she did not know, but she felt no trace of evil in it, no menace, only significantly that it was part of the natural processes of the Universe.

'I will keep this with me always,' she said to herself. 'It will be to me like Maal's stone sphere with the spiral markings. It will be my talisman, my centre of strength. I survived the test within the cave,' and she knew this had been a severe and important test, 'and I survived the cursed circle. I will take it as a sign. A power has been brought to my notice and I will use its positive energy and not its negative. For me it will bring life, not death; spirit, not stone.'

Having decided this she held it in both hands and tried to *will* herself to feel better.

'My talisman will cure me,' she said firmly. 'The mysterious force or energy that transformed it from living shell to stone, I now reverse!'

She concentrated her whole being on what she was trying to do.

She felt the cold stone warming in her hands and began to tremble, wondering briefly if she was mistaken in trying to use it in this way.

The trembling grew more violent.

Karne and Fern returned from being with the villagers to find

59

her seated on her rug clutching her hands together, and shuddering from head to foot as though she were in the grip of some supernatural force.

'Kyra!' they cried, 'Kyra!'

But she could not stop shaking.

Thinking that it was coldness that made her shiver so they pulled all the rugs that they could find over her.

'No,' she said at last, pushing them aside. 'No, I am not cold.'

Gradually the shaking stopped.

She sat quite still and carefully released her hands. The knuckles had gone quite white with the tension of her fingers gripping the stone talisman.

She looked at it for a few moments and then looked up at them with a beautiful smile.

'It worked!' she said.

'What do you mean?'

'This is my token of power. It will work for me whenever I truly need it. I was meant to find it and I was meant to suffer in the finding.'

'Are you sure it is not an evil power like the witch who turned those men to stone?' Fern asked anxiously. She was ill at ease that something that had once lived and moved in the ocean should now be stone and buried deep in the earth.

'It will be what I make of it,' Kyra said. 'Its powers can be used for good or evil.'

'Do you mean you will be able to turn living things to stone!' Fern cried in horror.

Kyra looked at her.

'Did you learn nothing from Maal?' she asked. 'If he would not call Spirit power to do evil work for him, I would not call this strange power to do evil work for me.'

The answer did not really satisfy Fern, and she was never really at ease with Kyra's talisman at any time, but she dropped the subject now and turned to tend to Isar who was ready for his milk.

Kyra insisted on standing up in spite of their protests and claimed that she was completely cured and felt strong enough to walk.

Karne tried to persuade her to spend at least a few more days at the village, but when he saw that she looked perfectly healthy, he decided to delay their journey no longer and they set off the following morning.

The last stages were relatively easy. It was late summer and the weather was warm and pleasant, fruits, nuts and berries were ripe for picking, and a track along a ridge was so well trodden and wide that it seemed designed for pilgrims to The Temple of the Sun.

They found themselves singing as they walked and were often joined by other travellers for days at a time. The ridge way was mostly clear above the forest level and the view on either side of mildly rolling countryside, frequently cleared for terracing and planting, comforting. Unfortunately it was also above the spring line and Karne had to make frequent descents to find water when they made camp for the night.

Villages were more frequent than they had been and seemed to grow larger and larger. When they remarked on this to the people in one of the villages, they laughed and suggested they should wait until they saw the size of the community that served The Temple of the Sun before they were impressed.

'In these parts we call it Haylken, the valley of priests and kings.'

'Kings?' Kyra asked.

'It used to be a place of kings in the ancient days,' they were told, 'but now there are only Spear-lords who walk in procession with the priests with gold upon their heads, their women decked in amber and in jet.'

'They might as well be kings compared to us,' the wife of their informant said. 'We farming people all bow to them, and what they demand of us we give them. When they ask our labour no one dares deny it.'

'In the valley nearer the Temple each village is ruled by a Spear-lord. But here we are still free.'

'One came to our village once,' a boy said eagerly, 'and

carried on his wrist a hawk with yellow eyes who did his bidding and tore at flesh whenever he commanded it!'

'Birds are sacred and should not be used thus,' Kyra said.

'If you had been here I wonder if you would have spoken so boldly on the subject then,' the boy's mother said.

Kyra was silent.

She remembered the time when she had 'travelled in the mind' to The Temple of the Sun to meet the great Lords who gave help in the matter of Wardyke. She had seen many such tall, grand people as the villagers described, but no hawks to tear at flesh.

'Haylken,' Karne said musingly, ' "the valley of priests and kings". It has an exciting ring to it!'

His eyes shone.

For a long time he had chaffed at the constrictions of his own village and longed to travel to the centre of the world. The Temple of the Sun was this for all their countrymen and now that they were nearing it he found that it was not only a place of priests and learning that Kyra would enjoy, but of splendour and adventure that would have challenges for him.

Fern was not so pleased. She loved the country life and would have preferred to settle in a forest glade somewhere nearby and leave Kyra to her studies in this strange, alarming place. But she knew Karne would not be content with this, so she and Isar must follow and see what comfort they could find in this valley of priests and kings.

'There must be trees there and growing things,' she thought. 'We will make a garden and draw it about us like a veil, and live our lives as quietly there as though we were in the heart of a wood.'

Karne was as anxious now as Kyra to finish their journey. Even he, with all his restless energy, had had enough of travelling and of discomfort and danger.

'First you will see the Field of the Grey Gods,' and old man told them. 'Then on every side the smooth round humps of the burial mounds.'

'The Grey Gods?' Kyra enquired.

'Yes. The Grey Gods in anger among themselves shattered the mountains in the ancient days and scattered their debris over all the area. It is said the stones have magic properties and none but priests dare approach them. The gods in olden times helped the priests to take some of the tallest stones to build their Sacred Circles, but no man alive today can tell when that occurred.'

Kyra was intrigued. She longed to learn about the powers of stone. Would she be allowed to approach the Field of the Grey Gods when she was a priest and learn from their secret energies?

'Come,' she said to Karne and Fern, 'let us be on our way.'

They left with many offerings of food from their friends and many warnings not to be tempted to enter the Field of the Grey Gods no matter what happened.

'Not even animals go in there,' called one voice after them.

'And do not forget to bow the knee to the burial mounds,' another called. 'Much evil comes from lack of respect to the dead.'

Fern shivered slightly and wished she were back in her own village, her own wood.

Karne gazed about him impatiently as though he half hoped something would pounce and need to be fought off.

Kyra fingered the stone sea urchin in her hip pouch and said a little prayer for help and protection from the Spirit Realms.

'We will be all right,' she said at last. 'We have come so far and through so many dangers, and it *is* the wish of The Lords of the Sun that we should come to this place. We will have protection.'

'And anyway,' Fern said hastily, 'there is no reason for us to go anywhere near the Field of the Grey Gods *or* the burial mounds. We will stay on the track and make our way straight to The Temple.'

'I wonder if they know you are coming,' Karne said to Kyra. 'I mean . . . did The Lords of the Sun . . . ?'

'Of course. Remember the vision I had the night Maal's white stone turned to the green jade of the High Priest?' And she fingered the jade pendant that hung about her neck on a leather thong.

She heard the High Priest's voice as she had heard it in her vision. 'You who now have my mark upon you will follow me and learn what I have to teach.'

She had no real doubt that she was expected, but what exactly would happen when she arrived and how she would know where to go worried her somewhat.

They stopped talking and proceeded in silence, each with their separate and different thoughts.

By evening they had seen nothing of the Field and the mounds and settled with some disappointment to another night of camping.

Isar was restless in the night and cried a great deal. Whether he sensed his mother's anxiety or whether there was something else that bothered him in the night so close to the Field of the Grey Gods they could not tell, but when the morning finally came none of them had had much sleep.

They broke camp earlier than usual and when the sun had barely started its journey across the sky they suddenly came upon the field of grey rock they had been told about.

They stood amazed.

It did indeed look as though an angry god had scattered broken rock in every direction, and it was almost as though plant life as well as animal life did not dare venture among the magic stones. The grass was poor and a few brambles and briars grew, but the trees stopped neatly at the edge of the Field as though a giant knife had cut a swathe and forbidden them to advance further.

For a great distance the rock seemed to have been dropped in chunks from above, instead of pushing up from within the earth as it normally does.

They stopped and stared for a long time, and then continued on their way, looking always over their shoulders to see if the rocks were still there.

Isar wept inconsolably.

Kyra would dearly have loved to venture off the path and try her secret senses against them. Surely at last she would be able to tell what it was that made priests choose one stone rather than another for their Sacred Circles.

'I will just . . . ' she began, unable to restrain herself any longer.

'Oh, no, you will not!' Karne said sharply, seizing her arm just in time.

'I would not go far . . . just let me test that stone there . . . it is hardly in the field at all!'

'Do not let her, Karne,' Fern said anxiously. 'We have been warned and Isar can "feel" something here. I know he can. Listen how he cries!'

'We have only been warned by simple superstitious people who understand nothing, and Isar is just hungry and tired of travelling. If I can stand within a Sacred Circle and not be harmed, surely one stone . . . ?'

'No!' Karne snapped.

'Why not?' Kyra challenged. 'Surely you do not believe the story that they told!'

'What I believe or do not believe has nothing to do with it! We are near the end of our journey and I do not want any more delays!'

Karne could be very authoritative when he chose. 'There will be time enough for you to test yourself against those rocks . . . '

'With priests to guide and help you,' Fern added.

Kyra sighed deeply.

It would be good to reach their destination at last.

She allowed herself to be persuaded and they continued on their way.

They saw many burial mounds as they had been told and bent the knee to every one of them.

And then they gasped, for what they saw they were not prepared for, in spite of all that they had been told.

Below them on a plain and on gently rolling hills that stretched as far as they could see, there was a sight that took their breath away.

A giant circle of raised earth, overgrown with grass, and within it the hugest Standing Stones they had ever imagined, and running towards it and then out on the other side, like the curving body of a snake, an avenue of Standing Stones that seemed to run forever.

The Temple itself stood in some isolation, but beyond it in every direction stretched clusters of habitations to the horizon.

How many people lived around and served this Temple? The number was unbelievable! Kyra began to feel very insignificant and very much afraid. Fern sensed it and held her hand. She was horrified herself to think of so many people living so close together. The forests and wild places seemed mostly to have been pushed aside, and little plumes of smoke from cooking fires seemed more common than the trees.

They stood upon the ridge way looking down upon the scene for a long time, trying to make some sense of it.

They noticed that the houses nearest the Temple were the largest. Some were circular as those in their own home village were, but many were long and straight as though they housed a great many people under one roof.

Fern looked beyond at the spreading landscape wondering where her own small hearth would be. She noticed that what had at first appeared to her to be an unruly mass of houses formed a kind of pattern. The habitations were in groups with fields and trees dividing them from their neighbouring group and each one seemed to be centred on a home much larger than the others. The plain was dotted with small villages, not one vast shapeless mass of people as it had at first appeared. The travellers were not used to seeing two villages nearer than a few days' travelling and this is what had confused them at first.

Fern was a little less upset.

'What is that strange hill?' Kyra pointed beyond the Temple, to the South West, where a tall unnatural-looking hill rose suddenly from a flat field.

'It looks manmade, but there are no Sacred Stones upon it!'

'It must be some kind of burial mound,' Karne said.

'But who would be so great as to command such burial splendour?' Kyra asked, awed.

Indeed it was a gigantic mound, steep sided and different in character from all the other mounds they had seen. It had a kind of sombre majesty, a brooding watchfulness.

'We will find out nothing by standing here,' Karne said decisively. 'Before the night we must find a place to settle.'

They started moving again, Kyra and Fern growing more and more ill at ease as they approached the Temple. It was so huge!

'We will leave the ridge path here,' Karne said. 'This track leads down towards the Temple.'

'I do not think we should go directly to the Temple!' Kyra said nervously.

'Why not? It is to reach The Temple we have travelled all this way!' Karne said impatiently.

'Perhaps . . . we should make some enquiries first among the villagers.'

'You have not come as a villager. You have come to be trained as a priest!' Kyra could sense a note of determined pride in Karne's voice. She remembered those early days when there was no doubt he felt possessive of her powers. He had encouraged her to use them and driven her well beyond her own wishes in the matter.

Her nervousness was making her fall back into her old submissiveness to him, but she was older now and grown greatly in inner strength, and managed with an effort to assert herself at last.

'We will wait here,' she said suddenly, with great determination, 'at the crossing of the paths, and I will go into the Silence and look for guidance.'

Karne looked as though he were going to protest.

'Sit!' she said with a sternness that surprised even herself.

Karne sat.

Fern sat close beside him and was glad of the time to rest and suckle Isar. She was not looking forward to meeting so many strangers.

The Arrival

Kyra sat apart from her companions and composed herself. She knew that the most crucial part of the process that Maal had taught her was to forget herself as 'Kyra' completely, and 'open' herself to the influences from deep within herself and from the Universe, the influences that were always present but not always noticed. As the trick to use upon her unruly 'surface' mind, she chose this time the flight of a black bird she had noticed in the sky, circling round and round, round and round, in a perfect and harmonious arc. She followed it with her eyes for some time, and then closed them, following it still, but now as a projection of her mind. Round and round the black bird went until she was aware of nothing else. Faint sounds that had been rising from the valley, the rustle of grass as Karne moved about impatiently, the chattering of nearby sparrows faded. She heard nothing, felt nothing, thought nothing, saw nothing but in the inner recesses of her mind the circling of the black bird. For all she knew it might have long since ceased to circle in the sky that Karne and Fern could see.

It existed now only within herself.

Gradually she let the image go, the black bird fade, until nothing was in her mind but a kind of readiness, an emptiness that was waiting to be filled.

Maal had warned her that at this time she must be particularly careful not to have any preconceptions. She must wait in readiness, expecting Nothing. She was not waiting for something she already knew, but for something . . . she knew not what.

So she sat. Very still.

And after a while it seemed to her she was not sitting on the grass any more, but was drifting upwards, as gently as a gliding bird on a current of air. She could see everything below her in perfect clarity and detail. She seemed to imprint the pattern of it on her consciousness and knew she would never forget a single detail of it.

Then she felt herself turning as the black bird had turned, arcing slowly and with dignity at first and then gradually going faster and faster until the whole scene was spinning and blurring. She could see the landscape now as nothing but a series of whirling circles.

The air above them seemed to whirl and spin in the same way and she found herself caught in a downward whirlwind spiral to land in the greatest circle of them all.

As she touched earth all movement ceased and she was alone in stillness surrounded by giant Standing Stones and giant ramparts of earth.

She thought she had her eyes open and was truly standing there, but to Fern and Karne upon the ridge way she was still sitting cross legged at the crossing of the two paths, in silence, with her eyes closed.

She looked around her and could see no one. The black bird she had watched was perched on one of the tallest Stones nearest her, watching *her*.

She felt strangely ill at ease under its scrutiny.

Was it a spirit?

Would it understand if she were to speak with it?

She bowed to it at last.

The bird stared at her unblinking.

'My Lord,' she said politely to it, 'if you have been sent to guide me . . . please guide me!'

She heard a chuckle from behind her and blushed to find she was no longer alone.

A girl a bit younger than herself and slightly deformed was watching her with great amusement.

'Do you always talk to rooks?' she asked, smiling broadly.

Kyra was embarrassed.

'No . . .' she stammered, 'but I thought . . .'

The girl laughed out loud.

'We have all kinds of people here, but none who talk to rooks! Is he your god?'

'No, of course not . . .' Kyra said indignantly.

'Then why . . .?'

'I thought he might be a messenger,' she muttered defensively, still feeling foolish. The girl seemed more than ordinarily mocking and unsympathetic.

'Oh, well,' the girl said shrugging, 'anything is possible! But to me he is just an old rook looking for a worm.'

And as she said it he dived and seized something in the grass, tugged fiercely for a few moments and then flew off with his long and wriggling victim in his beak.

'You see!' the girl said triumphantly.

'I know it must have looked foolish . . .' Kyra said, trying to be friendly, though she felt irritated by the child. 'But I *am* looking for someone to show me the way. Perhaps you . . .'

'Where to?' the girl asked sharply.

Kyra hesitated.

Where to begin?

'I am a new student,' she said at last, 'and I do not know where I have to go to be accepted.'

The girl stared.

'I mean . . . I have just arrived from the far North. My brother, his wife and baby and myself have been travelling since early Spring to reach this place. And now I do not know exactly where to go or what to do.'

'What are you doing in the middle of The Temple?'

'I . . . am not sure . . . I suppose I was lost . . . '

'No one is allowed in here except the priests and those that they have chosen.'

'What are *you* doing here?' Kyra asked quickly.

The child certainly looked neither like a priest nor a student.

'Oh, I am useful about the place,' she said airily. 'I go where I please.'

Kyra decided not to follow this up until she had settled some more important questions for herself.

'Could you tell me where to go?' she asked as politely as she could.

'I suppose to the house of the High Priest would be the best place,' she said, looking at Kyra's jade pendant. 'It seems you are one of his.'

This at least was something!

'Where will I find this house?'

'I will take you there.' She turned jauntily and immediately began to hop and skip away from Kyra. Kyra had to run to keep up with her, but strangely felt no breathlessness or strain no matter how fast she ran.

They passed through the Circle of Tall Stones and found a narrow entrance gap in the high earthen bank. Kyra noticed that the bank looked higher than it had appeared from a distance as there was a deep ditch around the inside. Where it was broken for exit and entrance, a wooden bridge was across the hollow. It seemed of flimsy build and possibly would be taken away on certain occasions.

Kyra stared around her at the magnificence of the carved and decorated wooden houses the girl led her among. She saw many of the spiral and concentric circle motifs she had noticed on the wooden columns of Maal's house and on many rock faces during the journey. She began to feel more at home and less afraid as she remembered that Maal had been here and learned his skills in this place. She would learn the Mysteries too and be a priest among priests, not a frightened girl among strangers.

The girl led her to the largest circular house of all and stopped.

Kyra stared at the tall columns flanking the entrance, the beautifully high, thatched roof, the strangely shaped river worn boulders arranged in a double row leading to the entrance. She noticed that they were of different stone to the Tall Stones of the Temple, and fancied she saw in them the tracing of shells and sea creatures similar to the ones she had found in the passages leading to the giant cavern.

'Is this the house of the High Priest?' she asked, her voice low with awe and respect.

When the girl did not answer, Kyra turned around and found that she was no longer there. As silently as she had appeared, so silently had she vanished. Kyra heard a sound above her and looked up. On the highest point of the High Priest's house the rook she had seen earlier was sitting, and he was watching her.

'Oh no!' she thought, and in that instant found herself back upon the path beside Karne and Fern and baby Isar, their dusty travelling packs beside them and her own worn sandals upon her feet.

'At last!' Karne cried in relief. 'I thought you were going to sit there forever.'

'Have I been here all the time?' Kyra asked, amazed.

'Of course. Where did you think you had been?' Karne answered irritably; and then, remembering Kyra's peculiarities which in his impatience he had overlooked, he added more kindly, 'Have you been "spirit-travelling"?'

'I suppose,' she said, still confused.

'Where did you go?' Fern asked eagerly.

'I think I know where we must go now,' Kyra said standing up and stretching her stiff limbs. She looked around to see if she could locate the rook, and was half relieved to find that she could not.

She did not know what to make of him. Bird or spirit? Which?

'That is a relief,' Karne said, at once picking up their packs.

'The path you suggested *is* the right one,' Kyra said to her brother. 'I know now where the High Priest's house is, and we must go there . . . I think! . . . ' she added under her breath. Once her visionary experiences were over she was never sure she had actually had them. At the time they always seemed so real. But as soon as they were over, she wondered . . .

But Karne had no doubts.

They made their way quite quickly down the hill and towards the grand houses nearest to The Temple.

'Which one?' Karne asked as they drew nearer.

'It was one of the round ones . . . ' Kyra's voice sounded a trifle uncertain.

'Which round one?' Karne persisted.

'Do not push her so hard, Karne,' Fern suggested gently. 'She will find it if she is left in peace.'

Fern had always noticed her own and Kyra's instincts worked better in quietness and without harassment.

Kyra eventually found the house and stood hesitating on the path between the river-worn rocks. She looked up at the topmost point of the thatch and again was relieved to find there was no sign of the rook. She glanced around her, half expecting to see the strange girl who had brought her here the first time, but she too was nowhere in sight.

When her eyes returned to the entrance of the house she was startled to find the High Priest standing quietly observing her.

She had seen him before in 'spirit-travelling', but to Karne and Fern he was a stranger, and they held back in some confusion.

He was immensely impressive, tall and regal, clad in long and flowing robes with a huge and elaborately carved jade circle upon his breast.

His eyes in his bearded face looked deeply into their own, one by one.

It was as though they were frozen to the spot unable to move until he had explored their minds more thoroughly than they themselves had ever done.

They had the uneasy feeling that there was *nothing* they could keep hidden from him.

After what seemed a long and gruelling experience, he moved forward a step and smiled. They were instantly released from whatever it was that had kept them so rigidly in his power.

He held out his hands to Kyra in greeting and smiled at her.

'I believe you have something for me,' he said.

She was horrified. Of course, she should have brought a gift!

He was holding out his hands still as though he was sure she had one.

But what did she have that she could possibly give him?

And then, as though in a dream, she found her hand going to her hip pouch and drawing out her stone of power, her **precious sea urchin.**

She found herself holding it out to him, offering it to him.

He smiled and accepted it with a slight bow of the head.

'I have been waiting for this,' he said in his deep, gentle voice.

Kyra tried to suppress the signs of her disappointment. She did not want to part with it. It was her own, and within it she felt were concentrated great energies and powers that only she could use. Through suffering she had learned the secret and earned the right.

As though she had said these things aloud the High Priest smiled at her and said quietly,

'You are not ready for such a thing, my child. When you have learned how to use it properly and control it, you will receive it back.'

She felt ashamed of her ungenerous thoughts, but she was not sure she liked the ease with which the tall priest seemed to see into her head.

Karne and Fern were looking quite terrified.

The High Priest now took another step forward and held out his hands for Isar.

Fern drew back instantly, her eyes suddenly sparkling like an animal protecting its young.

No one was going to take her baby from her!

Karne too suddenly recovered his courage and took a defensive step forward to protect the child.

'Nay,' the priest said kindly, 'I will not take the child from you or harm a hair upon his head. I wish only to give him my blessing. He is a stranger in this world and needs more protection than you can give him.'

Karne and Fern looked less worried, but still did not offer the child.

Kyra felt only goodness and kindliness emanating from the man.

'It will be all right,' she said reassuringly. 'I am sure he will not harm the baby.'

Karne stepped aside, but still kept a wary eye upon the priest.

Fern found herself holding her baby out to him as Kyra had

found herself offering him her most precious possession.

The priest took the babe in his enormous hands and held him aloft.

Isar stared unafraid into his eyes.

Something passed between them, but not even Kyra could interpret what it was.

At last the old man handed the child back to its mother, and there was a strange look upon his face.

'What is it?' cried Fern. 'What did you see?'

The priest said nothing.

'Tell me!' shrieked Fern with unaccustomed passion.

Again the priest was silent.

'Please!' Kyra pleaded with every level of her being.

The man spoke at last, but slowly, as though he were choosing his words very carefully.

'This child and I have been destined for a long time to meet.'

'Is it good . . . the destiny I mean . . . or is it bad?'

Fern's face was anxious and strained.

The priest's face was thoughtful, removed.

'Please!' pleaded Kyra yet again.

'It is good for one of us, and bad for one . . . but I cannot yet see . . . for which one good or which one bad.'

Fern was crying and holding Isar close.

Karne put his arm around her.

'We will keep him away from you,' he said. 'You need not see each other ever again. It is Kyra who has come to work with you, not us.'

The priest smiled a shade mockingly.

'You underestimate the powers of destiny,' he said. 'There is no way you can prevent the crossing of our paths. They have already crossed.'

'But,' Kyra said, 'have we no control over what happens to us? Is everything laid down?'

'Our meeting was laid down as the result of our own actions. That is why I can see it in his eyes. But what we will make of the meeting, that is up to us.'

'And that is why you cannot see which one will suffer, which one benefit?'

The High Priest looked at Kyra with approval.

'I see you will fit well in to our ways of thought.'

And then he looked at the tired and dusty travellers on his path with the kindliness of a host, all shadows gone.

'You need somewhere to rest and refresh yourselves. I will call someone to take care of you.

'In the morning, at sunrise,' and here he looked at Kyra only, 'you will come to this house again. And you,' he said to the others, 'will be shown where you may build your house and live in peace within the community.'

'Will Kyra not live with us?' Fern asked anxiously.

'No, she must live in the College with the other students. From tomorrow her way and yours must part.'

'Will we not see her again?' cried Karne now in dismay.

'You will see her, of course, but not all the time.'

The three were silent. Sad. Astonished at how fast their lives were changing. The journey had seemed so long it had lulled them in to thinking that things would always be the same.

They had never really thought about how it would be at the end of the journey.

As they stood, the long shadows brought by the setting sun creeping around them, a black bird swooped past them and landed with a whir of wings upon one of the river sculpted stones just behind them.

Kyra spun around and standing on the path beaming at her was the peculiar little girl she had met before.

There was no sign of the black bird after all. It must have flown away.

'This is Panora,' the priest said calmly. 'She will show you to the guest house for the night.'

Isar who had been so calm when the stranger priest had taken him from his mother seemed very restless in the night again. The guest house was comfortable and warm and Panora appeared from time to time with bowls of delicious food and helped them light the little lamps of earthenware filled with oil that they had never seen before. She even helped set up a little hammock for Isar which could be rocked to comfort him to sleep.

'He does not like it here,' Fern said. 'I can feel it.'

'As soon as it is morning we will look for a place for our home as far from the Temple as it is possible to be without being too far from Kyra,' Karne promised.

'Will you help us, Panora?' Fern asked the spritely girl. She liked her and allowed her to jog Isar up and down upon her knee.

Kyra still felt ill at ease with her. She could not decide what it was, but she thought it must have had something to do with the way she disappeared and reappeared so suddenly.

'I am here to help,' Panora said cheerfully, 'and I will sing Isar to sleep if you like.'

'If only you could!' Fern cried. 'But it seems to me we are in for a bad night.'

'Not necessarily,' Panora said cheerfully, and started to sing. It was a weird little song like nothing any of them had ever heard before.

'It is not even our language,' thought Kyra, but that was her last thought until the morning. The song did its work not only on the restless baby but on the others too, and within moments they were all fast asleep.

Panora stood a moment looking at them all with amused eyes, and then flicked her fingers. Instantly the little lamps went out and the travellers were alone in the guest house in the dark, peacefully and dreamlessly asleep.

Kyra woke as a beam of sunlight shafted through the door.

She was alert at once, remembering that she should have been at the High Priest's house at sunrise.

Shouting, she poked and nudged Karne awake.

'I am late!' she cried 'I must go!'

She left him waking slowly as though from a deep and drunken stupor.

She ran as hard as she could in the direction she

77

remembered. There was pale sunlight everywhere and people were going about their early morning business as though everything were in order.

Breathlessly she arrived at the High Priest's house to find no one there but Panora sitting on a rock and drawing pictures in the dust with a long stick.

'Hello,' she said cheekily.

'I am late,' almost sobbed Kyra. 'What can I do now?'

Panora's eyes twinkled as she squinted into the sunlight above Kyra's head.

'Follow that rook!' she suggested, and laughed hilariously.

Kyra was on her way before she realized how ridiculous it was, but she was so confused by the strange girl, who by now she was quite convinced was no ordinary girl, that she followed the bird who she was also convinced was no ordinary bird.

She found herself, hot and breathless, in time to join a procession led by the High Priest over the little bridge into the Temple.

She was not dressed as the others were dressed and felt conspicuous and awkward.

The High Priest walked first, clad in very regal robes, and behind him many people of different ages, the younger ones at the back of the line, but all clad in neat tunics, well-tied sandals, with different coloured cords about their waists.

'The cords must be some kind of indication of the progress of their studies,' she decided, and looked around anxiously to see if there were any there like her without cords at all.

No. It seemed she was the only complete beginner.

She saw many of the others looking at her curiously, but no one spoke. She was ashamed that she had left in such haste she had not been able to comb or plait her hair and it stood around her shoulders now in a blonde and tangled mass.

Once within the Circle the little procession made a slow progress around the circumference of the outer ring of Stones.

This was followed by a hymn to the Sun not unlike the one Maal had often spoken at the dawn. She began to feel less lost and strange. Ritual words were comforting, specially ones that linked people from so many different places.

She began to join in the responses to the hymn and found herself chanting quite a few that she did not know she knew. The voices of the others seemed to draw the right words from her until she was not sure if the sound she thought she heard from the voices outside herself was not actually her own voice from within. In some way she had become part of a composite Being and the strength of all the people in the group was in that Being.

At the end of the hymn the High Priest raised his arms and they were all silent. She knew she had to bend her head and shut her eyes. She did this and remained a long time in darkness and in silence.

In this state she knew that her first studies would be of dreams. How she knew this she could not say. But the knowledge came to her with the force of a command.

Simultaneously they all opened their eyes though no spoken word of command was given. She found herself following a particular group of students, knowing that they were the ones to be studying dreams.

She sat with them, crosslegged on the grass, at the feet of a teacher who asked each one in turn to relate the dream of the night before. Afraid that she would be asked to describe hers she racked her brain to remember what it had been. But her memory was blank. Since the beginning of that eerie song from Panora until she woke in the morning, everything in her mind had totally disappeared.

She gave up and listened attentively to the other students.

Each told what he had dreamed, the teacher interrupting occasionally to question and draw something out that the narrator had apparently been trying to hide. He seemed greatly skilled at knowing when the truth was being spoken and when it was not.

When the dream was exposed enough to satisfy the teacher, he began to ask questions of the class and draw out of them what they had understood by it.

Kyra was amazed by some of the suggestions and felt unwilling to expose some of her most secret fantasies to the scrutiny of these apparently ruthless critics.

After a dream had been analysed by the class and Kyra was sure there could not be a single thing left in it unaccounted for, the teacher would step in and reveal yet layer upon layer of significance hitherto hidden in the symbolism.

She was staggered at how complex a reflection of every level of consciousness in a person a dream reveals.

She was glad that for this day at least there was no time left when it came to her turn, and the class was dismissed before she had to speak.

The teacher indicated that Kyra and a boy called Vann were to remain behind. He smiled kindly at the two of them, more kindly than he had during the lesson. Kyra had begun to think she was afraid of him, his tongue had been so sharp, so ruthless in its quest for honesty.

'The two of you are new,' he said now, and Kyra looked with relief at the boy and he at her.

'What is your name, girl?'

'Kyra,' Kyra said, relieved to find that not everyone in this formidable place could see directly into her head.

'And where do you come from?'

'From the far North,' Kyra said.

'Vann is from the West country. From the mountains.'

She smiled at him. He was not good looking, but had a pleasant face. Although he looked older than her, he was smaller in build.

'He has been here a day longer than you and will show you where you will live and where you will find food. You will both wear an orange cord until you have passed the tests I set for you. Meanwhile you will work hard and obey me in everything.'

'Yes, my lord,' she said humbly.

'Now go. You must be hungry.'

She was.

The First Training and the Test of Dreams

While Kyra was settling in to her new life in the College of Mysteries, Panora was helping Karne and Fern find a suitable place for their new home.

Isar and Panora seemed to have a bond between them from the first and the girl became more and more a part of their lives, carrying the baby upon her hip while they walked from village to village looking for the one where Fern felt most at home. Karne agreed for Isar's sake that they should go as far from The Temple as they could and at last settled for a village that lay beside the banks of a stream, particularly rich in leafy shade and moss. The people seemed friendly and pleasant and not unlike the country people they were accustomed to in the North.

'The first thing to be done,' Panora said, 'is to visit with the Spear-lord and ask his permission to join his community.'

They had heard of the Spear-lords before they had reached the Temple, and Fern looked alarmed.

'In our village we have the priest and seven chosen Elders to look after us,' she said. 'We know nothing of Spear-lords!'

'Here it is different. The Inner Council of The Temple is the ultimate authority in the land, but in each village a Spear-lord rules his own people. They serve him and do his bidding in all things and in return he gives them protection and tenure of some of his land.'

'How did this come about?' Karne asked with interest.

'In a time the oldest people now living heard their grandparents talk about, a tall warrior people came to this land from over the sea. They were so strange and grand, carried such weapons and wore such clothes, the local people offered no resistence but welcomed them as lords. Many of them became priests in The Temple and took powerful

81

positions on the Council. In time the custom we now have came about. It seemed to happen, naturally, without violence. No one even questions it these days.'

'Are they still warriors?' Karne asked.

'We have had no wars here for many generations. But I have seen them fight amongst themselves with long daggers and axes, sometimes in anger, but more often for the sport of it. Some of their weapons are very beautiful. I have seen a dagger held to its haft with pins of gold intricately worked in a magnificent design.'

Karne's eyes shone. How dearly he would love to have such a dagger.

'Is this way of the Spear-lords a good way?' Fern asked.

'If the Spear-lord is a good man, it *is* a good way. If he is not . . .' Panora shrugged and did not finish her sentence.

'And what of the Spear-lord who rules this village?' Fern asked anxiously.

'Look around,' Panora said, '"feel".'

Fern looked around.

'I feel peace here.'

'And in the eyes of the people who live here?'

'I see peace.'

'Then he is good,' she said shortly. 'You would feel it if he were not.'

She led them through the village to the Great House standing clear of the other houses, half way up a gradually sloping hill. Fern was happy when she noticed there were healthy looking plants and trees clustered about it.

The Spear-lord, Olan, was not at home, but his wife and daughter gave the strangers a warm welcome, a drink of milk and a sweet-tasting honey cake to eat.

It was clear they knew Panora well and Fern noticed with surprise with what respect these grand and elegant people treated the ugly, unkempt little girl. They listened to her request with favourable smiles and for a moment Fern fancied she had seen them bend the knee in a slight bow to her when she first entered their house. But she dismissed the idea from her head as soon as it entered. It could not be! To her Panora was just a friendly village girl who had adopted them because she was lonely and because she enjoyed organizing things and showing people round.

Olan's wife and daughter were very beautiful and calm people, dressed in fine woven garments, both with earrings and bracelets of gold. The inside of their house had low couches spread with rugs of fur from animals they had never seen.

Fingering an unusual spotted fur Karne asked if the animal had been hunted locally.

The woman smiled.

'No,' she said, 'these have come from over the sea. My husband has visitors from many lands. We often exchange gifts of local artefacts for things we do not find here.'

She held up a cup to the light that came streaming through a slit in the wooden wall, and it glowed translucently with a kind of amber light.

In answer to Fern's unspoken enquiry she said, 'Yes, it is amber.'

Fern was overwhelmed by the beauty and the richness of everything she could see, and by the grace and warmth of the two women.

It was arranged that Panora and Olan's daughter should go with them to choose land for their home. It was made clear that Olan's permission had still to be granted but, as Olan's wife said, looking significantly at Panora, 'if it is the wish of the High Priest, the Lord Guiron, there should be no difficulty in obtaining it.'

Again Fern felt there was something being communicated between Panora and the woman that they could not intercept.

And so it was that before the autumn turned all the leaves to the colour of fire Karne, Fern and Isar had set up house. Fern had even succeeded in starting the rudiments of a garden by taking plants already rooted and growing from the woods and fields and, with great tenderness and care, transplanting them to enclose her little home.

'It will be better in the Spring,' she told Isar. 'The seeds I have planted will grow then. You will see. You will live in a garden full of love and loveliness and no harmful thing will come near you!'

She held him very close and kissed the top of his head. He was most precious to her. Most precious! She could not bear to think of the strange shadows that hovered over him.

Panora came on most days to help them or to play with Isar. She brought them many tales of what was happening in the other villages or at The Temple and so, although they hardly left their own small place, they were not out of touch with the rest of the area.

Karne grew to like and admire his Spear-lord Olan very much. He worked on Olan's land for part of each day, but most of his time was spent on the strips of land he had been given for his own. The community cattle, sheep and goats were kept together and the villagers took it in turn to tend them, to lead them to pasture in the morning and back to the communal compound at night. Each villager had his mark upon some of the beasts. Not all belonged to the Spear-lord.

Karne made sure both his land and the land of Olan under his charge was well dug and turned over before the frosts came to harden it. That first autumn Karne and Fern had never worked so hard in their lives, but they were together, and they were happy.

The Southern soil showed white when it was turned over and the strip fields waiting through the long winter for the early Spring sowing made the landscape seem unusual to Karne. From the rugged North with its hard rock and dark earth, the soft, pale shading of the fields made them look ghostly and unreal.

Olan laughed when Karne told him this.

'It is real enough in the Spring when the wheat is growing boldly. You will see how real it is!'

Fern delighted in the colours of the autumn trees, the gold and bronze of leaves and black of branch against the chalky earth.

She began to feel less homesick for the North.

Meanwhile in The Temple College Kyra's life was very different.

Although her main work at first was concerned with the significance of dreams she soon found that all the branches of learning in the Great College were inter-related and from dawn to dusk under the guidance of different priests, they studied not only dreams, but group and private meditation, healing, divination, prophecy, and, together with these more spiritual disciplines, disciplines of the body, control of muscles, of breathing, of every part of the body including its use together with creative imagination to design and make physical objects of satisfaction and beauty.

Under the guidance of Maal she thought she had learned a great deal about 'going into the Silence' within herself. In that Silence she could be away from the distractions of the outer world and aware of the subtle and numerous realms of consciousness within her which linked her with the Whole of which she was an organic part. In The Temple College she found that what she had learned from Maal was only the beginning. She learned greater control of herself, so that when she chose to 'go into the Silence' she went smoothly and efficiently instead of plunging in clumsily and almost accidentally.

She learned that what she did in the 'Silence' was not only of benefit to herself, but like a stone in a pool of water, the influence of it spread out in ever widening circles around her.

Not only in the 'Silence', but all the time, whether she knew it or not, she was influencing with the flow of her thought people outside herself and they were influencing her.

Thought became more than just the rambling monologue she was accustomed to hearing within her head.

It became a Force that she respected, a force that perhaps had shaped the Universe in the first place, but certainly shaped the day-to-day existence of all around her.

Each person creates his own world by his own thinking. It is given shape by how he sees it, and how he sees it depends on how he is, inside, from the first moment when he begins to notice the Universe around him, through his struggles to understand it, using all the tools at his disposal, his body, mind and spirit, until at last he stands fully Aware and Conscious of All the implications and subtleties of the Whole.

'In the study of this force we call "Thought",' the teacher said, 'we use many methods. Before we can use its power to influence the world around us we must learn its power to influence us. We will not have the final mark of the priest upon us until we have learned not only what "Thought" is and how to use it, but Who We truly Are and how we stand in relationship to the Universe as a Whole. Once we understand this we will use "Thought" as a tool and not as a weapon, and it will be safe for us to be released upon the outside world as priests.'

They were taught that the Thought that came from their 'surface' minds was the least significant, least reliable of all the forms of 'Thought' available to them.

In the silence of meditation, consciously and with strong self control, they explored the realms of understanding most close to the all enveloping Being of the Universe, but in their study of dreams they became familiar, through painstaking interpretation of image and symbol, with the deeper layers of their own personal being.

With the dusk their studies were not done. Sleeping became a kind of work as well. For it was sleep that gave them the material for their explorations of the inner levels of their consciousness.

When the priest-teacher thought it advisable they worked within the Sacred Circle, using its ancient forces to strengthen their own powers of understanding, but all the preliminary discussions were held outside the Circle.

In the Winter hide tents were erected for their shelter in the worst of the weather, but Kyra noticed one particular group never used the tents and in the fiercest, coldest conditions sat cross legged and flimsily dressed at the feet of their Master.

'Why is that?' she asked, and was told that this was yet another branch of training that must eventually be undergone, training to control one's body in such a way that heat or cold, pain or pleasure, could have no effect upon it.

Kyra remembered how Maal had controlled his own dying, lying buried in the earth for a long while apparently dead, and yet not dead.

'They can even walk through fire and are not burned,' Kyra's informant told her.

'You mean they just do not *feel* the burning?'

'No, their flesh does not even *show* the burning!'

She was amazed once more at the incredible power of 'Thought'.

Each day was so full of interest she scarcely felt the passing of time and woke one morning after a dream of Karne and Fern to realise that she had not seen them for a long time.

She determined to ask for time off from her studies to visit them.

That morning she told her teacher of her dream and how it showed quite clearly that she was missing them.

He smiled.

'I see you are an expert already,' he said, and his voice was slightly mocking.

She decided not to rise to this and asked instead, politely, if she might have the day off work to visit them.

He did not give her a straight answer to this, but turned to the whole class and said,

'This day there is a special ceremony, the inauguration of a new priest. We are expected to attend. We will take positions on the West of the avenue, half way between the Sanctuary and the Sacred Circle. When the procession has passed us we will enter the avenue and follow it as far as the earth ring. It is our privilege to stand upon the ridge and watch the ceremony from there.'

'Do the ordinary villagers see the ceremony too?' Kyra asked a neighbouring student in a whisper.

'No. It is a great honour to be allowed to witness an inauguration. It is because it is part of our training in the Mysteries that we are permitted.'

Kyra was sorry about the villagers, but excited that she at

least would have a view of it. All thoughts of visiting her brother and Fern went from her mind.

In making her way with her new friends to their position beside the avenue she was amazed to see the crowd that had already gathered. The land on either side of the Processional Way was filled to bursting point with men, women and children, many of whom looked as though they had been there since the night before. Families had brought food to eat and she saw many a water skin and ale jar handed around.

She had to cling to the arms of her friends, Vann and Lea, so as not to be separated as they pushed and jostled towards the position their teacher had told them to take up. But for all the unruliness of the throng she noticed the Processional Way itself, between its tall and sombre Standing Stones, was kept completely empty. The earth between the Stones was as hallowed as that within the Circle. She herself dared not put a foot upon it, although she was sorely tempted to, to escape the pressing of the crowd upon her back.

The procession was to be at noon and she was just feeling tired and bad tempered at the length of the wait, when she heard her name called and she saw her brother Karne pushing through the crowd, carrying Isar upon his shoulders and dragging Fern by her arm behind him.

'Karne!' she shouted excitedly and flung herself at him.

In spite of the lack of space they managed to kiss and hug each other satisfactorily. She was amazed how Isar had grown and developed in the short while she had not seen him. He seemed very cheerful to be upon his father's shoulders above the crowds and banged his little fists upon Karne's head from time to time as though it were a drum.

'Oh, he is lovely!' Kyra cried, her eyes quite misty to see them all again.

Fern hugged her.

'We have missed you so much. Our home is lovely and we long to show it to you. We were talking about you last night and planning how we could possibly see you. Karne hoped we might meet you today, but when I saw the crowds . . .' She threw up her hands and laughed.

It was indeed amazing that they should find each other in such a crowd.

Kyra remembered her dream and the way her teacher had mocked her for settling so quickly for one simple interpretation. It might simply have been her yearning to see her family again that had made her dream as she did, but in the light of what Fern had just said, it could have just as easily been the flow of thought from them that she had intercepted in her relaxed dream state. On the other hand, *they* could have been influenced to think and talk about *her* at that very time because she was dreaming so vividly about them.

And there was yet another factor to consider in her dream, the interpretation of which seemed to be growing in complexity at every moment: the incredible chance of their meeting in this milling crowd this very day.

Was this a prophetic dream?

Or did their mutual longing for each other 'pull' them together through the crowds? Did they unknowingly follow a beam of thought as though it were a path?

Suddenly a hush fell upon the crowd and above it Kyra could hear the clear and haunting notes of many horns blown together in a rising cadence. The sound made a little shiver pass through her body. Even Isar looked in the direction of the horns and stopped his happy gabbling. A little frown gathered on his forehead which gave him a very wise, old look.

The procession had begun.

The High Priest, the Lord Guiron, in regalia of great magnificence, walked first. He was almost unrecognizable in his long purple robes, the great collar and crown of gold and jade heavy upon him. His face was like a mask, it was so still and cold. His eyes were gazing straight ahead like stone until he was almost level with them and then Kyra was startled to see his eyes swing to the side and meet instantly and directly those of Isar raised above the crowd on Karne's shoulders.

Kyra suddenly felt an icy wind blow from one to the other, and her own flesh caught between them raised goose-pimples with the chill of it.

But as suddenly as it had happened it was over, and Kyra, looking around, could see no evidence that anyone else had noticed, until she saw Fern weeping and pulling Isar off her husband's shoulders, pressing his face into her breast and murmuring over him sounds of great comfort but of no meaning.

Kyra noticed that Fern was shivering too.

But Karne had not noticed what had happened and was puzzled at his wife's reaction. When they spoke about it later he said he had been so busy watching the clothes of the priests he had not noticed their eyes and tried to tell the girls that they had imagined it. But his voice did not carry much conviction.

When Kyra became aware of the Procession again she saw priests of every rank in robes of crimson and in gentian, their faces framed in the unfamiliar stiffness of helmet or crown.

Behind them followed the tall figures of the Spear-lords and their wives, clad in even greater splendour than the priests.

Then came the horn players and behind them the drummers.

Further back still a small group of very old priests walked, dressed in simple white robes with no jewellery or finery of any kind, and in their midst walked the young man who was to be inaugurated as priest this day.

He too was dressed with the greatest simplicity and carried himself with great dignity.

But Kyra noticed as he passed close to them a little muscle in his cheek was twitching.

She knew how he must be feeling, and thought to the future when the procession would be for her.

When he had passed and after allowing a discreet gap to form, the students were led into the Avenue to take their part in the procession.

Just before she was pulled forward by her fellow students Kyra looked back and saw Fern still in tears cradling Isar and now Karne, aware at last that something was wrong, had his arms about them both and was trying to lead them out of the crowd.

She longed to stay with them but was pushed forward by the current of her new position in life, and had to leave them behind. As she walked the Processional Way her feelings were torn between her old loyalties and her new.

'Karne will look after them,' she comforted herself at last. He had inner strength as well as muscle, and she knew he loved both Fern and Isar most tenderly.

The ceremony in the Circle took a long time and the students who stood upon the earth bank well away from the action grew restless and began to talk among themselves.

On seeing Panora moving about quite freely among the honoured members of the ceremony, Kyra turned to Lea and asked why such a little girl of no particular significance was allowed to be among that most exclusive group.

Lea did not know, but someone who overheard the question leaned forward and joined in the conversation.

'She is no ordinary child,' he said darkly.

'How do you mean?'

'Did you not know that she is the daughter of the Lord Guiron?'

The man could not help but be pleased with the effect his words had upon his listeners. Several other students crowded round to hear more. Kyra was stunned.

'But the High Priest lives alone!' one student said.

'I have never heard of a wife!' another added.

'And Panora certainly looks more like a ragged waif than the daughter of a wealthy priest!'

'He has no wife, nor ever had one,' their informant told them.

'Only a child?' one student said with a laugh.

'Yes . . . and no . . .'

The man was obviously enjoying spinning out the mystery.

'How do you mean?' Kyra demanded.

'Well, she is not a child in the ordinary sense of the word. In fact, she does not really exist in the ordinary sense of the word!'

Now he had his listeners spellbound.

'Tell us!' they demanded.

He told them.

'When Guiron was still a young man, before he became High Priest, he fell in love most deeply, but with no hope of taking her to wife.'

'Priests are allowed to marry,' someone said, 'although it is not usual.'

'Aye,' the man said mysteriously, 'but only with real women!'

They gasped.

'He had the misfortune to fall in love with a spirit woman who lived on a lake and was only seen when the mists came down thick upon it.'

'A spirit woman?'

'Aye. As part of his training as priest he had to spend a night alone on the lake, experiencing the dark and the stars. But during the night the mist grew thick and he could not find the shore. He found instead this beautiful spirit woman. She told him she was not of flesh when she could see the way he was gazing at her, but he would not listen and *would* have her. She tried many ways to fend him off but he used his priestly powers to overwhelm her, it is said, and she bore this child we call Panora.'

'When he was young, you said,' Kyra mused, 'yet Panora is still a young child, certainly not more than fourteen summers, and the Lord Guiron is an old man now.'

'Panora never ages and comes and goes as she pleases. She is more spirit than girl.'

Kyra could believe it!

'Where is the lake? Where is her mother?'

'No one knows. When he became more powerful as a priest the lake was drained on his order, and the woman has never been seen since.'

'But how is the story known?' Vann asked. 'Surely no priest would have been made High Priest if he had such a shameful incident in his past?'

'All I know,' the man said defensively, 'is what I have been told by the old villagers who were present when the Lord Guiron became High Priest.'

'So it could be no more than an idle tale?' Lea said.

'Explain Panora then!' the man challenged.

'She could be just an ordinary waif.'

'No, she could not. She was found sitting waiting for him at his door, mocking him, when he returned from his inauguration as High Priest, and he looked as though he had seen a ghost. People tried to send the child away, but he said she was to be admitted to his house and no one was to disturb them. Before she went inside she called out loud and clear to all who were gathered there, that she was the daughter of the spirit woman of the lake and the Lord High Priest.

'When she was seen again she avoided answering questions and no more was said about it as the Lord Guiron was held in great respect. But there are some who remembered the night and the day he had been missing on the lake and how wild he had looked on his return. The legend of the spirit woman was well known and there were some who had wondered if he had encountered her even then, long before Panora's appearance. When they remembered how he had wandered about distracted and alone on the shores of the lake for a long time and then had insisted the lake was evil and must be drained, Panora's claim began to seem more real.'

'But Panora is quite plain and the spirit lady was supposed to be so beautiful?'

'She must have been like her mother in some way or he would not have recognized her and looked so horrified!'

Kyra remembered how strangely Panora seemed to appear and disappear, and the very definite position of privilege she held within The Temple. She could see her now within the Circle watching everything that went on.

'She *is* a waif . . . between two worlds . . .' Kyra thought, and a twinge of sympathy for the child disturbed her.

And then she thought of Isar.

Panora was always with him and she was the daughter of the man whose destiny it was to cross with Isar.

Fern thought he was safe and far away from Guiron in her new home, but Panora was a constant link with the very danger she was trying to avoid.

At first she thought to rush to Fern and advise the little family to return North, as far from Guiron as they could. And then she remembered what the High Priest had said: 'You underestimate the power of destiny.'

Something had to be worked out between them, either now or later, and there was no escape.

She would warn Karne to be on guard with Panora, but she would not encourage them to believe that it is possible to escape one's destiny by moving one's position on the face of the earth. Something more was required. Something from deep within the two protagonists.

As the winter progressed Kyra's interest in her studies continued to grow.

During dream study they learnt how to project images into each others' sleeping minds as she and The Lords of the Sun had already done to Wardyke in the past. But at that time she had scarcely known what she was doing or how she did it. She learned now how to control her visualizations and their projection, either as direct images or in a kind of symbolic code.

'As you learn to master the art, my children,' the teacher said to them one day, 'some of you may reach the point where you can project "cold", but most of you will never reach beyond the point where it is strength of feeling, passion, that sends the message across and manifests it in another's mind.'

Kyra was not sure of the extent of her own powers in the matter but decided one night to put to use what she had learned for her own ends.

When she had first come to The Temple of the Sun she had expected to see the young priest from the desert temple in the South as one of the teachers. In the vision she had received of her own arrival and acceptance at The Temple, she had seen him quite clearly with a group of students from his own country surrounding him.

She had seen his image in the cavern when she had called so desperately for help, but since her arrival at The Temple she had seen no sign of him, nor found anyone among all those she had questioned who had heard of him.

She knew he was one of the great Lords of the Sun, but she was not sufficiently advanced in her studies to be allowed to attend the lessons on 'spirit-travelling' in spite of her early experiences.

All the students had experienced in one form or another some unusual power before they were called for training, but once they were at The Temple these 'experiences' were ignored, and they all started from the beginning, the priesthood claiming, with some justification, that the 'experiences' had been uncontrolled and accidental.

The young priest she longed to see appeared not to be at The Temple at all. Lying in her sleeping rug that night she decided to try and find out where he was. She persuaded herself that this would be a good test of her capacities and that she was doing it as part of her training in dream travel.

She composed herself for sleep, emptying her mind of everything but the young priest, projecting her longing to see him with great passion into the dark and lonely night.

At first she wondered why the moon and stars were bobbing about in the sky and then she realized that she was on a boat and the boat was in rough seas.

A boat?

She was surprised.

She had expected the desert temple with the tall red sandstone columns fluted at the top like Palm trees.

For a moment she thought she must have failed, and then she wondered if perhaps she had not.

There must be some reason for the dream of the boat.

Perhaps it was a symbol.

Sometimes when one tried to project fear into the dream of one's partner in an experiment and used the most frightening image of a demon one could think of, the partner saw a perfectly ordinary dog. At first it seemed as though one had

95

failed but then it emerged in discussion that a dog had savaged him as a small child and ever since 'fear' was associated with 'dog' for him. The experiment had not failed after all.

She decided to explore the boat.

She passed the steersman but he did not notice her and this gave her boldness. It was a strange ship. Larger than she had ever seen. Grander. Yet made almost entirely of reeds.

She found where the crew lay and stood beside them one by one, willing them to stir in their sleep and turn their faces so that she could study them.

But he was not there.

Sad at heart she willed herself to leave the ship and try to reach the temple in the desert.

But she woke instead, restless and tossing, in her own sleeping place in the long house of the College.

She lay awake most of the night thinking about the dream, but in the morning did not mention it to her friends nor to the teacher.

The full turn of the moon later it was Kyra's time to be tested.

She was to compose herself for sleep, asking deeply within herself for some kind of guidance or lesson from the spirit realms.

No student was allowed to think of her this night and she herself was to try totally to empty her mind of all its usual images and thoughts.

A year ago she would not have been able to do this, but now as a result of the training she had received, she found it quite easy to do.

She lay totally relaxed, alone and empty of all thought. So empty indeed that she was not aware of the crossing over from wakefulness to sleep.

Next day she had to tell the class her dream and give her interpretation. On this she would be judged fit or not to move on a stage further in her studies.

In her dream she had been present in a huge temple building such as she had never seen. A building built on many levels of different kinds of wood and stone, flags and fluttering streamers blowing in the wind from every jutting peak and rib of the many timbered roof.

The Temple was built against the side of a mountain, each floor higher up the mountain, and surrounding the whole thing were other mountains of great height and beauty, white with snow and dazzling in the sun.

Within the Temple were great works of art. Wise men were studying scrolls with little markings on them which Kyra knew in her dream were symbols which they could understand within their heads.

Her own people had no such thing as writing, but in the dream Kyra understood what writing was and how it was being used to store the knowledge of a great civilization.

She walked about looking at exquisite paintings hanging on scrolls from the walls, at Statues carved with perfect precision from the hardest rock. She heard great men discussing learned ideas.

So great and splendid was this storehouse of knowledge, and so magnificent and advanced upon her own civilization, that she concluded she was seeing a vision of the future.

This was the first part of the dream.

The second part was horrible.

Suddenly from the sky came monsters in vast hordes. They dropped black rocks upon the beautiful, shining building, and as the rocks touched they roared and flashed and whole sections of the walls disappeared in smoke and flame. Pieces of roof and wall and statue were flying everywhere, and everyone was running about and screaming.

Only one group of men seemed to stay calm. There were seven of them and they walked calmly to the courtyard that was in the heart of the Temple, and went to a tree that grew in the centre of the courtyard. The leader lifted up his hand and picked a single seed pod from the tree and then the seven turned and walked away.

Through all the corridors they walked quite calmly among the screaming, running people, the falling timbers and the splinters of rock. The scrolls of paintings were in flames, the scrolls of writing utterly destroyed.

The seven men picked their way past the debris and the flames and went out of the temple by a small side door, low on the mountain and not far from a forest.

They looked back as they entered the forest and saw the last of the Temple laid flat.

The monsters in the sky were not content with that but continued their work of destruction on every living thing they could see or on any fragment, man-made or natural, that belonged to the civilization they were determined to destroy.

The seven men hurried through the forest as the demons turned their attention to the living trees and began to blast them with their fiery rocks.

As the last cover was destroyed the seven men entered a dangerous rocky chasm.

One by one they were killed.

But before each died he passed on the green seed pod they had been so carefully carrying to the next man who was still untouched.

Kyra, watching it all, was in despair.

The flying monsters were determined to destroy the men as they had destroyed everything else.

As the last man saw that there was no way out for him he flung the seed pod into the river far below him and Kyra saw it swirling off in the white and boiling waters of the rapids.

The last man stood with quiet dignity watching it go until he too was blown to pieces as his companions had been.

Kyra woke remembering the utter desolation that had once been the most magnificent civilization she could ever have imagined.

The class listened spell-bound to her story. It was a message from the spirit realm. Of that there was no doubt in their minds. None of these things had ever happened to Kyra in this life, and there were things in the dream that she could not have known about or seen.

After a long silence the teacher said to Kyra,

'What have you learned from this?'

They all knew that with spirit messages you always took the

meaning that came to you at the moment of waking. This was part of the message.

They never discussed, or analysed, these kind of dreams even if the interpretation that came with them seemed at first illogical.

'I learned that nothing is ever completely destroyed, but lives on in another form. What is past nourishes what is present, and what is present nourishes what is future, and there is no changing this.

'And I learned that the Temple I saw was not only in the future, but was also in the past. This had all happened before and would happen again. The Circle and the Spiral are the most potent symbols of Being known to man.

'The Seven men of Wisdom, the Guardians of the Mysteries, rescued the seed pod rather than any of the fabulous paintings or scrolls of writing, because it contained the tiny germ of Life that would grow again wherever it landed into another civilization. This one was finished, but a new one could grow as long as this Mysterious seed containing spirit-force was preserved.

'I realized this world, or any other world, could have had many such civilizations which had disappeared and grown again, as it were, from seed.

'And we who grow do not remember the others, no more than the seed remembers the tree from which it was taken, or the tree remembers the seed from which it grew. But the tree would not be what it is if it had not come from such a seed. And the seed would not be what *it* is had it not come from such a tree.'

The High Priest Guiron who was present at the examination of Kyra stood up and raised his hand above her head.

'You have done well.

'But remember always, graduating from a class means only that you are now fit to *begin* to learn what there is to learn, and that you have some idea in which direction to look for knowledge.'

The rest of the students drummed with their feet on the ground and looked at her with smiling faces as she passed along in front of them.

She felt very happy.

Divination

The first thing Kyra learned in the class for divination was that the power of divining was not in the object itself, but in the mind of the 'Seer', so that it was perfectly in order for them to use anything they liked as aids to divination.

'Our "surface" mind,' the teacher said one day, 'is not only crude and noisy, the most inadequate form of consciousness we have, but also arrogant and shrewd. It has been used for so long it is loth to give up its domination. For this reason, before we have the skill to change easily and accurately from it to the subtler regions below, where we are sensitive to influences travelling invisibly from person to person, Spirit to Spirit, we have to use little subterfuges, little tricks, to "outwit" our "surface" minds.

'For this reason some people throw pebbles or sticks, and make their decisions on the way they fall. Others burn bone and examine the pattern of cracks. Others kill animals and peer into their entrails, and yet others consult Oracles and are given words which can be interpreted in many different ways.

'Where you have been hindered by lack of confidence, or by trying too fast to master a skill you are not ready for, where you have been staring so hard that you can no longer see, or so long that you no longer notice, a return to the quiet within yourself, a rest from the constant harassment of the "surface" mind telling you what to do, filling your attention with irrelevant details, will be invaluable.

'Sit in front of a flower. Watch it grow.

'Relax.

'Being is easy if you do not work at it too hard.

'Understanding flows up from under the surface like a spring and brings you refreshment from times and places long forgotten by your "surface" mind. Everything you have ever learned in this life and in the ones you have lived before, is preserved, available, if only you know how to reach it.'

The students sat spellbound. Their new teacher was a vigorous and lively man who paced up and down in front of them as he spoke, using gestures energetically to emphasize each point.

Kyra knew much of what he was saying already, but if she had learned anything in the past year, she had learned how necessary it was continually to renew and reinforce one's knowledge of truth. But she wondered if the 'surface' mind the teacher spoke about with such disdain was not a protector as well as an enemy; we need to draw on inner levels of consciousness from time to time, but to live so intensely aware of so much all the time would be exhausting. We need rest, not only from our 'surface' mind, but from our 'inner' mind as well. We *need* the kind of sleep that most people call their waking life, as much as we need the kind of waking that most people would call sleep.

The students practised at first by throwing little clusters of pebbles and trying to see what they could make of them.

Kyra was amazed how often her set of pebbles took on the shape of a boat. At last, worried about this, she turned to her student neighbour and asked what he saw in her pebbles.

'A tree,' he said without hesitation and returned to his own.

'A tree? Surely not . . .'

She remembered the dream she had of the boat.

She trusted this teacher enough to talk to him about it. He quietly cross questioned her until without meaning it to happen the whole story of the young priest she was longing to see came out.

The teacher smiled.

'There are two possibilities here. Either you are longing for him to be on a boat coming towards you so that you force this image into existence. It is a wish-image. Or perhaps you have penetrated to a deeper level where you are in thought contact with him and he *is* actually on a boat coming towards you.

Both explanations may be valid simultaneously. There is no limit to the number of levels that can be operating at once.'

After they had spent a great deal of time using different methods to explore their own most secret knowledge, the students were told to each choose a partner and start to work with him. One would ask the question and the other would be the 'Seer' and try to answer it.

Each student found some things worked better for him than others and the teacher encouraged them to choose the method they felt most at home with. Belief in its efficacy and a relaxed attitude was very important.

Kyra had a set of small, carved, walrus ivory pieces, beautiful to feel and touch, that her father had given her as a farewell present.

She had always found the quickest path for her to the inner realms was the path of visual beauty. The curve of something, light touching something with unusual delicacy, the sudden harmony of two reeds moving in a breeze . . . these things were enough for her to slip from mundane consciousness to a level where depth of awareness of anything was possible.

In throwing her ivory pieces, in calmly and deeply contemplating them, Kyra drifted into a state of receptive meditation, where the bond of inner communication between herself and Vann, who had asked the question, was so close that she could 'feel' what he deeply wanted the answer to be, in fact knew himself what the answer was to be. He wanted to specialize as a Healer, but his 'surface' mind told him he should leave the College as soon as he could qualify as an ordinary village priest because his family wanted him back with them.

Kyra looked at him, her eyes misty from staring at the exquisite ivory pieces.

'You have great potential as a Healer. It would be wrong to throw it away. Your family will understand eventually and be glad.'

He knew this. He just needed to be told it.

He felt at peace at last.

One day their teacher strode briskly into their midst and asked them one question and then sent them away for a few days to think about it.

The question was: 'Does a prophet really see the Future?'

The students argued amongst themselves and went for long walks alone to think about it and when he called them back again there were almost as many different suggestions as there were students.

When the teacher had heard them all he told them to sit down and he would give them a demonstration.

He sent Panora who was hovering around as usual to fetch a man who was famous as a Seer and Prophet.

Panora vanished instantly, overjoyed to have such a mission, and returned not long afterwards with a very old, very bent man Kyra had seen from time to time about the Temple environs.

He was led by Panora to stand before them and Kyra saw that he was blind.

The teacher asked for a volunteer to question the Prophet. Several students volunteered but Kyra was chosen.

She left her place and stood before the man.

'Do not ask your question aloud,' the teacher said. 'The Prophet is not only blind, but deaf. *Think* it! The rest of you must keep your minds as still as possible so that there is no interference in the flow of thought between the two.'

Kyra was a little nervous now that she was so exposed, but seeing Panora's mocking face, she felt she had to continue. Somehow she disliked the girl. Perhaps she had never forgiven her for laughing at her that first day when she addressed that perfectly ordinary rook as 'My Lord!' But surely she would not be so petty!

She took a few moments to compose herself. She had intended to ask if she would ever meet her young desert priest in the flesh, but somehow, perhaps because Panora was staring at her so fixedly, she found herself thinking about the

High Priest Guiron, and what lay between him and Isar.

The old man took a long time to speak and some of the students began to be a bit restive. The teacher stilled them with a fierce look and there was unmoving silence again.

At last he spoke and his voice seemed to come from a long, long way away.

'A woman began the trouble and a woman will end it.'

Kyra waited, hoping he would say more, her heart beating fast.

Nothing more seemed to be forthcoming.

'Will it be the same woman?' She found herself thinking.

'A woman that was loved was there at the beginning, and a woman that is loved will be there at the end.'

And that was all he would say.

The teacher broke the tension with a sharp clap of his hands.

'That is all,' he said to Kyra. 'You will get no more.'

And then he turned to the class.

'I am afraid Kyra chose a question that will not be of much use to you as a demonstration. Whether the answer has relevance or not will not appear for many years. I should have put a limit on the kind of question to be asked.'

He looked around at the disappointed faces of the students.

'I will choose another one of you, and this time the question must have an answer that can be easily checked. Ask it aloud first, that the class may know what you ask, and then in your mind that the Prophet may know it.'

Kyra felt she had failed them in some way, and returned to her place disconsolate. It had been an 'unsuitable' question, but she *did* want to know the answer.

The student who had now been chosen cleared his throat and said aloud to the class:

'Can you tell us the exact day and time of day we will see the very next complete Stranger from over the sea in our Temple?'

This time the whole class concentrated on the question and whether it was the force of all their minds working together, or whether it was because the question was simpler to answer, the answer was given almost immediately and without any of that eerie sound of distance he had had in his voice before.

'On the third day from this, precisely at noon, a young priest, his skin much burned by the sun, dressed in white and blue, with gold around his waist, will stand with the Lord Guiron in yonder Circle,' and he pointed exactly as though he could see, directly at the Southern Circle contained as a sanctum within the Great Circle.

Kyra gasped. It was the very question she had wanted to ask, but had been prevented from doing so by Panora's disconcerting eyes. Had her mind influenced that of the student who had asked the question?

It *must* be her priest! The description fitted exactly.

She was so excited that her mind wandered far from the class she was attending and was only brought back to some kind of sense by the sharp and sarcastic voice of the teacher who could see that she was not listening and had trapped her with a question.

She blushed and stammered, but her mind was hopelessly out of tune with the class.

She caught Panora's eye and felt that she would like to shake her for the look of amused triumph on the girl's face. The thought of doing violence to her had no sooner left her mind, than the child laughed and snapped her fingers. Kyra momentarily turned her eyes away and when she looked back, in Panora's place, tugging at something in the grass for its midday meal, was a black and evil looking rook.

'Oh!' she snapped irritably, and stamped her foot.

'Perhaps it would be better if you left the class for a while, Kyra,' the teacher said to her. 'I can see you are not going to listen to a word I say.'

'Oh . . . I am sorry . . .' mumbled Kyra, contrite. 'I really will concentrate!'

'No', the man said, 'you will waste the time. Climb upon the earth ridge, and walk the whole circumference slowly. When you have done that, return to me and tell me what you have learned.'

In shame Kyra did what she was told.

'That Panora!' she caught herself thinking resentfully. And

then, 'No, not Panora. Kyra! My mind should be under *my* control, not at the mercy of every disturbing whim and influence.'

She climbed the ridge and started walking, taking deep breaths of the wonderful early summer air, feeling the warm energy of the sun stirring her spirit, its light beautiful on everything it touched.

Some people thought of the Sun as a god, but to her it was enough that it was a channel of Power for the Limitless One, as she was herself.

When she returned to the class she was peaceful and refreshed, and the words of the teacher made sense to her.

'All I ask of you is that you learn as much as you can about everything you can,' he was saying, 'keeping a mind always open and ready to receive, and yet careful and guarded enough to weigh the new against the old, the unlikely against the likely. The more background understanding you can accumulate from the past the easier you will see into the future, for the one grows out of the other.

'No knowledge, no understanding, is ever wasted. If it is not immediately needed, store it, you will need it one day.'

He gave as many examples of predictions that had failed as had succeeded, and pointed out that where the prophet had gone wrong it had usually been because he had not been patient enough to sift through all the knowledge he needed for the task.

'It is not only the present life of the man who asks for help that you must consider, not only what he *thinks* he knows about himself. You must search the inner levels of his mind and reach the real Self he might not even recognise. The time scale you must use must be as long as Time itself. He does not come into existence with his birth, nor leave it at his death. Remember this at all times.'

After the class she asked Lea about the discussion that she had missed.

Lea told her that the prophet had probably scanned far and wide among the beams of thought that he was aware of in his dark and silent world and so came upon the young stranger who was thinking hard about their Temple as he approached it. The prophet visualized him from the man's own image of himself and gave the time of arrival the young man himself estimated.

This explanation pleased Kyra.

She thought about the more difficult matter of Guiron and Isar. But the prophet again could have scanned their minds for memories of ancient experiences and guessed the natural outcome of those events.

She was content that they should all be part of a great moving, expanding harmony and play their destined part in it, but she did not want to believe that every detail of their play was pre-ordained. That she was destined by some past act of her own to be upon a ship storm-tossed at sea she could accept, but in that situation she wanted to believe and did believe that there were still many different choices she could make to affect the outcome. And if her choice should result in pain or death, it was still her choice whether she let herself suffer it in anger and despair, or whether she accepted it calmly as having some purpose in the Universe.

'We were warned about causing things to happen by predicting them,' Lea said, interrupting her line of thought.

Kyra looked at her.

'He gave us an example of a man being given the exact time of his death. It seems it is quite possible the man died at that moment not because he was destined to, but because he *expected* to. Either he gave up taking precautions because he had no hope, or he might have even done things that would lead to his death, without realizing it, convinced that it was inevitable and the sooner it was over the better.'

'So the prophet was a kind of murderer?'

'Yes. We have to be very careful what we say when people ask us to prophecy. Sometimes a whole community has been destroyed by a prophecy of doom. No doubt the prophet had good reasons for sensing its possibility, and he was right to warn them of it, but he should also have pointed out that it might very well be possible to avert by, say, a change of their way of life. Because they believed it was inevitable they gave

108

up trying. Fear, despair and self-indulgence, the predators of the mind, moved in, and the community collapsed as the prophet foretold.'

'It is a great responsibility,' Kyra said.

'Yes,' Lea agreed.

The Arrival of Khu-ren

On the third day from the day the Prophet had been brought before them Kyra took great trouble with her appearance and was late for class.

The morning seemed endless and she looked frequently at the position of the sun to establish when it would be noon.

'Kyra, the sun will not move faster no matter how much you wish it to!' Her teacher was regarding her with kindly amusement. She hung her head.

'I know you are all anxious to see if the prophecy will come true. At noon I will remind you of it and we will discuss it then, but meanwhile there is other work to be done.'

Noon came and went.

The young stranger did not appear.

Kyra could feel tears burning behind her eyes.

The teacher himself was visibly disappointed, the prophet had never been known to be wrong before.

But as it turned out, although the timing was inaccurate, the young stranger *did* appear later in the afternoon, clad as the prophet had said, standing with Lord Guiron in the Southern of the two inner Circles.

The young man *was* the priest Kyra had been waiting for. She learnt from her enquiries later that he had brought a party of his own countrymen as students for the Temple College, and was the Lord Khu-ren, one of the distinguished Lords of the Sun, who would be staying for some time to instruct those who were priests already in the highest grade known to their culture, the grade in 'Spirit-travelling'.

Kyra was full of joy and tried every trick she could think of to delay leaving the Great Circle after her class was over, but she was forced to move before the young lord finished speaking with the High Priest. Unless they were engaged in a specific training matter or part of a ritual ceremony the students were not allowed within the Circle. By using the Circle only for intense psychic instruction or for religious and mystical purposes over long periods of time an atmosphere had been built up which gave the Temple the concentration of psychic power that was necessary for the immense tasks it had to perform.

The students were only allowed in at all because their bodies had gradually to grow used to the feel of such power, for the time when it was their turn to use it. The more elementary the classes they attended the shorter the time they spent within the Circle. Those who were nearly approaching the state of the adept and had passed initiation into the Higher Mysteries spent a great deal of time in the Circle.

But none but the very high stood within the Inner Circles 'in the flesh'.

Kyra remembered when she had stood in the most holy place of all, the Northern Inner Circle, but at that time she was not 'in' her physical body, and neither was the young priest.

She had waited to meet him so long, and these few moments that were left seemed longer than all the time before!

She could not stay in the Circle, but she waited just outside determined to see him as he left.

'What is the matter?' Vann asked her.

'Nothing,' she replied, rather sharply.

'Are you not coming?'

'No. Go on without me. I will join you later.'

She thought they would never leave, but at last she was alone.

She had a long wait and had almost despaired when she heard voices and the small group from the Inner Circle appeared. The Lord Khu-ren was speaking, and his voice, which she suddenly realised she had never heard before as all their communication had been through the medium of thought, was deep and melodious. He spoke their language, but a little haltingly, with strange intonations and every now and again he hesitated for a word which the Lord Guiron supplied.

111

She was startled at the strength of feeling that surged through her as he approached, and a little ashamed. She was even trembling.

As they came nearer and nearer she found herself stepping backwards, afraid now of the meeting, her feelings were so out of control.

It seemed to her he deliberately kept his head turned away from her and kept talking and looking at the High Priest.

Within moments they were past and it was all over.

He had not seen her.

Tears came to her eyes. She had wanted him to see her so desperately, and yet had feared it. The anti-climax of it not happening at all was too much. She turned and ran and did not stop until she reached the home of Karne and Fern.

That night she spent with them.

They could feel she was troubled and unhappy but she refused to tell them why.

She rocked Isar to sleep in her arms and there were wet patches on his soft head when she laid him down at last.

Karne and Fern were very happy to have her with them, but did not question her further when they could see she did not want to tell them what was troubling her.

She preferred to talk about their affairs, to hear all their stories of village life, of the friends they had made, and of the admiration they had for their Spear-lord, Olan.

'We have been very fortunate. I believe not all the Tall Strangers are as noble as Olan,' Fern said.

'He is teaching me to fight with the long dagger of his people,' Karne said excitedly.

'Whom do you want to kill?' Kyra asked, raising an eyebrow.

'No, not to kill. It is a sport and requires great skill. And there are horses here . . .'

'We have them at home too,' Kyra said quickly.

'Yes, but here Olan has tamed them and some of the Tall Strangers have learned to ride upon their backs. He teaches me to look after them and soon he will teach me to ride as well.'

'This is a great honour,' Fern said, 'because normally it is only the Spear-lord who may ride. Olan thinks very highly of Karne and treats him with respect.'

Karne laughed.

'Other Spear-lords are not so pleased! Old Hawk-Eagle who lives over the hill to the South hates Olan and resents the fact that he treats a local peasant almost as an equal. He says it will make the other peasants restless and they will all be demanding equality soon!'

Kyra smiled.

Equality to her was something impossible on earth.

Every single person was at a different stage of spiritual evolution. There must be inequalities in this sense. There must be a kind of hierachy of wisdom and responsibility. But from what she could gather Hawk-Eagle himself would be very low down in the hierachy she had in mind, and this would not please him.

The trouble with people like him was that they thought they could impose an unnatural hierachy on the world, making sure that they (however unworthy they might be) were at the top and everyone else (however worthy) would be below.

In the morning she was up at first light and out in the cool and fragrant garden. Spider webs caught the dew and new flowers that had pushed out of their enclosing sheaths at night were turning their faces to the sun. She longed to stay in this peaceful and pleasant place with the ones she loved. For the first time she felt that she did not feel totally happy at the College. But she knew she would already be in some disgrace for not having told anyone where she had gone and for being away all night.

She ate a quick breakfast of fruit and milk and then ran as swiftly as she could back to the Temple.

She was late for class and in trouble as she expected. The teacher gave her a hard and searching look when she arrived flushed and out of breath, but said nothing. Her friends looked at her too, but there was no opportunity to question her then.

It was not until the rigours of their studies were over that they had a chance to speak to her.

'Will I be punished?' she asked anxiously.

'No, of course not. But you do owe him an apology and an explanation.'

She set off at once to find her teacher and stood before him, with contrition on her face.

'I am sorry, my lord, that I was not present last night and was late for class this morning. I went to see my brother and his family and slept the night with them.'

'You did not ask permission?'

'No, my lord.'

'Did you think it would be refused?'

'I did not think, my lord. I just ran off.'

He stared at her steadily. She dropped her eyes.

'You must learn more self control if you are to be a priest,' he said at last, quietly.

'I know my lord,' she said in a very low voice.

'Next time,' he said '"think".'

'Yes, my lord.'

'You may go now,' he said gently.

How much of what was really in her mind he had seen she did not know, but she was grateful to him for not mentioning it.

On returning to her fellow students she was given a small parcel wrapped carefully in a very fine piece of white cloth. She fingered it enquiringly and realised that it was not wool. It was a fabric she later learned was linen, unknown to her at that time.

'Where did it come from?' she asked, bewildered.

'One of the students who arrived yesterday brought it.'

Kyra looked up immediately.

'A student?' her voice shook a little.

'He asked if there was a girl called Kyra from the North with us. We said you were in our class, but were not here at the moment. We did not know where you had disappeared to!' complained her friend Lea.

'But was it one of the students from over the sea, from the

desert land?' Kyra demanded.

'Yes. He said . . .'

She was pulling it open now with trembling hands and heard no more. The others crowded round to see what it was. As the thin wrappings of linen were removed Kyra found lying curled up inside a necklace of blue faience beads of great delicacy and beauty.

She gasped, and her friends were amazed as she held it up to the light to see how exquisite it was and how subtly the colour and the light interplayed.

'What did he say?' she asked now, her voice strange and tense.

'I cannot remember exactly . . . just that it was for Kyra of the North . . . and I was to be sure you were given it.'

'What name did he give?'

'No name. Only yours.'

'I did not know you knew any of the new students?' someone said.

'How did you meet him? He has only been here a day!'

'Is that where you disappeared to last night?'

They were teasing her now and harassing her, but she was scarcely aware of it.

It would not have been from the student. She knew no students from that country. But she did know their Lord Priest.

She buried her face in her hands and started to sob.

This gave her friends pause and most of them left her alone after this, but her best friends Vann and Lea stayed behind.

'Tell us,' they said gently, but she shook her head.

At last they too left her alone and when they were gone she took the necklace out of its wrappings and gazed at it reverently. She held it against her cheek and her eyes shone. She kissed it and put it carefully over her head and stared at it lying against her breast.

She moved the pendant of jade which she had worn for so long into her carrying pouch, so that the new necklace could lie in its place.

When she joined her friends again they could see that she

was blissfully happy, but they could see also she was not prepared to speak about it.

The evening prayers came and went, and at last it was time for sleep.

She slept quietly and easily and her dream was as beautiful as the necklace.

Over the next few days she tried to see the Lord Khu-ren to thank him for his gift but there seemed no way of approaching him.

At first there was no sign of him and she was deadly afraid he had left the Temple area altogether, but then she heard he had been taken to see the College of Star Studies, the other Great Circle which was part of the complex Temple of the Sun, but built further South, away from the populous villagers and the bustle of the main Temple business.

The priests who manned the College were particularly skilled in astronomical calculations and she knew there would be a time when she would study briefly with them. But now she was anxious in case the Lord Khu-ren would settle there and it would make it almost impossible for her to see him, but she was assured by Panora, who knew everything about everybody's business, that his visit was only temporary and his main work would be done at their own College and Temple Circle.

Relieved, Kyra waited impatiently for the days to pass and at last was rewarded by the sight of him walking in procession with the Lord Guiron for the Harvest Ceremony. She could not approach him, of course, but she hoped at least to catch his eye.

As he came level with her on the processional route she would not have been surprised if the whole concourse of people had not heard the loudness of the thoughts of her mind *willing* him to look at her.

Whether the others noticed anything or not she did not know, but he did.

His eyes met hers very briefly and then dropped to the chain

116

of beads around her neck. If she had had any doubts before that he had sent them to her they were dispelled now. There was a warm shine of recognition in his dark eyes and pleasure at seeing his gift upon her breast.

But the look, though intense, was very fleeting.

The priest that walked beside him came between them and he was carried past. He did not turn his head to look at her again, but then she knew that no priest upon the Processional Way was supposed to look anywhere but strictly ahead at the approaching Sacred Circle.

The Lord Guiron had broken that ancient law by looking into the eyes of Isar.

And now the Lord Khu-ren had looked at her.

She was flushed with pleasure and confusion.

After this she accepted the fact that she would see very little of her lord and that it was probable that they would have no means of meeting for a long time. He was very much among the more important of the priests and none of his duties took him anywhere where she was likely to be.

She managed to convince herself, because of the look she had received from him during the procession, that some day, some time, the moment would be right and they would be together.

Meanwhile she kept her feelings secret from her friends and apart from occasionally teasing her about the mysterious student who brought the necklace and then never called again, they allowed the subject to fade away.

The necklace became so much a part of her that they almost forgot there was a time when she did not have it.

The first time the Lord Guiron noticed that his jade sign had gone from her neck and she had faience beads in its place, he gave her a strange and penetrating look that made her heart beat anxiously. But he said nothing. And his thoughts she could not fathom.

Because she was anxious to make as much progress as possible, as fast as possible, towards the time when she would be ready for 'Spirit-travelling', she worked harder than any of the other students.

It seemed to her at times her teacher knew what she was trying to do and deliberately held her back.

'These things cannot be hurried, Kyra,' he said to her one day, noticing the look of impatience on her face when she thought she was ready for a particular graduating test and was refused permission to take it. 'Each stage of learning must be fully absorbed into the system of the student before he moves on to the next one.

'Think?. What are your motives for taking this test now. Is it because you know you are ready, or is it because you are impatient to reach the next stage because of reasons quite unconnected with the growth of understanding?'

Kyra was silent.

She remembered a dream she had had the night before.

She was a small child and saw in the distance amazingly tall and beautiful Shining Beings. A feast was being prepared for them, and as a great honour she was allowed to help prepare the feast although all the other children of her age had been sent to sleep.

Excitedly she rushed about doing everything her elders told her to do, but as she laid each delicious bowl of food upon the place of the feast she sampled a little of it. It was legendary food. Nothing like it had ever come her way before. She ate from every bowl a morsel, no more, thinking all the time how lucky she was to be allowed to stay awake and serve at the feast. She would see the Shining Beings and hear their talk while all the rest of the children were asleep.

But before the Shining Beings arrived to eat, she was in pain and ill with all the bits and pieces she had swallowed, and she was sent home.

She missed the feast. She missed the Shining Beings.

'You see?' her teacher said, looking at her closely.

She flushed.

'I see,' she said.

And she tried to be patient.

When her teacher thought she was ready, she took the test, and passed.

The next few years passed very fast and very busily.

There was much to learn and as long as Kyra knew the Lord Khu-ren was still at the Temple College and she had his beads about her neck she was content.

Of course she listened with great attention whenever he or anything concerned with him was mentioned and it was in this way she learned that in his own language 'Khu-ren' was a reminder of the Being's radiance in eternal life and its secret and Spiritual name.

She sat one night watching the stars and thinking about this for a long time. Names were important. His parents and the priest who named him at his birth must have known that he would be a special person, with spiritual powers well above his fellow men. To be a Lord of the Sun so young he must have travelled a long way on the journey of enlightenment before his present birth.

She thought about her own name, Kyra. It was not easy to put into common words but it meant in the ancient language of their people which was now almost forgotten, 'balanced for flight on the point of beauty'.

Maal had told her this and Karne had laughed.

'What does Karne mean?' she demanded.

'Axe-head,' Maal had said, and she remembered how Karne had not been sure whether to be pleased or insulted.

Her studies in the Mysteries grew deeper and deeper and ever more difficult, but the College policy was sensible and their concentrated sessions of deep meditative work and spiritual discipline, were interspersed with periods where different but related faculties were called into use.

Kyra's favourite of all these periods was the one when she was taught the whole process of making pottery, from finding the most suitable clay, cleaning it of impurities, kneading and thumping it to remove the air bubbles trapped within it which would make the pot explode when it was heated, to working it with her hands into beautiful and pleasing shapes.

She learned to build the little stone and earth oven and how to keep it burning at the right temperature.

She learned to scratch designs upon the surface of her pots before they were fired, and even how to use salt and ash and certain powdered rocks to change the colours of the clay.

The teacher encouraged them to become totally immersed in what they were doing and to forget everything else.

'*Become* the pot you make', he said. 'You are not making a pot. You are making yourself.'

One Spring Kyra moved to the College of Star Studies further South and learned to calculate the movements of the Sun and the moon and the Stars.

She was privileged to be present at the ceremony at dawn on Midsummer's Day when the great, dazzling orb of the Sun rose directly above the Sun Stone and shafted light like a knife straight into the eyes of the High Priest who stood in the dead centre of the Great Circle.

It was at this moment that he lifted his arms and spoke in a loud and awe-inspiring voice.

And it was at this moment that he saw Visions.

It was from these visions that the whole wisdom and teaching of the Temple of the Sun took its form.

Around him the highest priests of the community stood and listened to his words. Beyond them were the ring of Standing Stones brought in the ancient days from a Temple of great Sanctity in the far West, the giant Tri-lithions and the Circle of the Immense Stones from the Field of the Grey Gods, each linked to each with a lintel of finely worked stone.

The students and lesser priests stood outside the Stone Circle but were no less moved by the impressiveness of the occasion . . . The darkness bursting into light, the inspired voice from the Spirit Realms speaking through their High Priest, the huge, oppressive rocks . . .

Kyra's heart beat until it hurt against her ribs.

She knew she was present at the meeting of great forces and the men within the Circle at that moment might well be possessed and in great danger.

She knew one of them was the Lord Khu-ren and as it grew lighter she could see him, his eyes shut and his face lifted to the sun, an expression that was not his own transforming him.

As the words finished issuing from the mouth of the High Priest, all the spectators found themselves singing, starting with a hum, the sound rising and rising until it seemed to reach the highest point of the sky where the last star flicked out as their eyes followed the sound upwards towards it.

And then the sound burst and from hundreds of throats the hymn to dawn on Midsummer's Day rose and spread outwards until the whole landscape was in light and sound, even the sombre burial mounds that ringed the Temple at a discreet distance transformed to something beautiful and joyful.

The air was suddenly full of birds, flying and swooping and arcing in time with the hymn.

Kyra was moved to tears. She wished the moment could last forever. She felt great thoughts within her, great feelings of wanting to help the world, to lift all human spirits up to join in light and love and absolute understanding.

The love she felt even for the Lord Khu-ren seemed almost a little thing compared with the love she suddenly felt surging in her for all of Creation. It seemed to her there were no divisions. No one to love and not to love.

All was One and all was taking wing at this moment into timeless ecstasy.

She too shut her eyes.

And with Khu-ren she stood as though enclosed in a crystal of light, the walls of which were fading even as she became aware of them, the light from outside breaking through to them.

As its unbelievable brightness touched them they both faded from sight.

She knew they were still there. She felt herself aware of herself and yet she could not see any part of herself. Only light. She felt herself aware of him, and yet she could not see him. Only light.

She remembered thinking with great joy, 'We exist
. . . although all our visible and physical parts are gone! . . .'

And then . . . and then . . .

Someone pressed her arm.

It was Lea.

She opened her eyes and stood dazed upon the grass outside
the Great Circle. Her body visible again.

'Come on,' said Lea, 'it is over. We have to go now.'

But there was something more.

She could feel the pull.

She looked into the Circle and the Lord Khu-ren's eyes were
looking deeply into hers, gravely and with concern.

She was shaking uncontrollably from her experience and
was very pale.

Lea put her arm around her.

'What is the matter? It is not cold.'

'No . . . not cold . . .' muttered Kyra with her teeth
chattering.

'What is it then?'

'Did you not feel anything?' Kyra asked, her eyes lost and
bewildered in this ordinary world of moving people and pale
sunlight on grass.

'It was very moving,' Lea said. 'The High Priest spoke with
Spirits.'

'And you?' asked Kyra.

'I?' Lea said surprised. 'Nothing happened to me.'

And then . . .

'You mean the singing? It was wonderful.'

'It was beautiful,' Kyra said, her voice quite faint with
awe.

'Yes, it was very beautiful,' Lea agreed, thinking of the
singing.

Kyra said no more but allowed herself to be led away.

About noon, the morning ceremonies over, the students were
spread out upon the grass well beyond the outer circumference

of earth ridge and ditch, resting and talking amongst themselves about the experiences of the day.

Kyra was apart from the others and was lying flat on her back with her eyes shut, trying to recapture that marvellous moment of somehow being united with Khu-ren as though they were the two halves of the same Being enclosed in Light, when she felt a shadow fall across her. She opened her eyes and looked straight up the tall body of the Lord, to his face leaning over her, his dark eyes, made darker by the lines painted around his lids, looking into hers.

She jumped up instantly, colour flooding to her face, and then stood awkwardly in front of him.

Three midsummers had passed since he first came to The Temple of the Sun and in that time they had seen each other occasionally but had never spoken.

Now they stood together and did not know what to say.

She had grown taller in those three summers. She wore her hair coiled on the top of her head now instead of in a long and untidy plait as she had the first time he had seen her.

The cord she wore around her slender waist was black with a thread of gold to indicate that she had reached the level of studying the dark of the night sky and the gold of the stars.

'I wish to apologize,' he said at last, very gently.

She looked surprised.

'I should not have taken you with me into the Light. But . . . I could not stop myself.'

She lowered her eyes and stood very still, afraid that he would see her thoughts.

So it had really happened, and she had not imagined it!

But it was the fact that it was his longing for her that had brought them together that was the most wonderful thing of all!

They stood awkwardly and silently for a while and then he touched the beads he had given her which she still wore. She felt his hand lightly on her throat and currents of feeling passed through the whole of her body.

She looked up at him and her eyes must have shown it all.

He withdrew his hand and stepped back a pace from her.

There was a tense silence between them.

But when he spoke again his voice was well under control.

'The Lord Guiron tells me you are making good progress,' he said.

'So he has asked about me!' she thought joyously.

The Lord Khu-ren smiled.

'Yes, I have asked about you,' he said.

She blushed.

'And there has not been a time when I have not been aware of you,' he said gravely, and she sensed a touch of bitterness and self-reproach in the gravity.

She thought he would hear her heart beating. Was this really happening?

'Kyra,' he said, and her heart lurched with anxiety, 'you know this cannot be.'

'Why not!' the words burst out from her pent up heart with such violence she startled herself.

His eyes looked even darker now, and there was pain in them.

It was his turn to drop his gaze and turn away from her.

'It is not possible,' he said firmly and harshly. 'We must both accept it!'

And he turned and strode away.

She was devastated.

'No!' she shouted, but it was unlikely he could hear her. 'I will *not* accept it. I will *not*!'

She found herself stamping her foot and shouting like a small child and then she ran into the woods and sat weeping with her arms about a tree.

Priest? How could she be a priest with such longings in her, with so little self control.

She *would* not be a priest!

Why should she be a priest?

If she said today she was giving it up, would anyone stop her?

It was too much to bear.

She was not fit.

She wanted only one thing and that was to be with the Lord

Khu-ren.

But — Khu-ren was a Priest. One of the highest. Would he give it up? Would he *have* to give it up?

Oh, how she needed comfort and advice.

But who could she turn to?

She had told no one of this love of hers. She had not wanted anyone, not even Karne and Fern to know about it. Somehow the very secrecy of it kept it safe. As soon as someone else knew, it was vulnerable, *she* was vulnerable in some way. She could not explain.

Even that it had become verbal and definite between Khu-ren and herself had brought about this danger now.

Before, when it was still secret, everything was still possible.

But now his words made her choke with sobs.

'It is not possible,' he had said with such finality. 'We must both accept it.'

Sometimes she thought the Lord Guiron suspected. Ever since he had noticed the faience beads!

And then Khu-ren had said he had asked after her.

Should she go to the Lord High Priest now and ask his advice? But something held her back from him always.

She admired him. He was a great, great man. But . . . the story of the spirit lady of the lake and Panora always haunted her somehow. It did not fit with his honoured position as High Priest.

And there was always the shadow of the mystery of his relationship to Isar between them.

But . . . on the other hand . . . if the story of the lady were true . . . he must know better than anyone what it was to love someone more strongly than one's duty to the Priesthood.

She would speak to him.

She would tell him she was giving up the Priesthood. Of that at least she was certain.

And she would ask him if it would be possible for a priest of Khu-ren's standing to take a wife.

She felt better when she had made this decision.

She washed her face in a stream and returned to the others.

The Labyrinth and the Test of the Star

On her way back to the Temple College her friends noticed that she was very tense and silent.

'Tell me!' Lea said gently, and Vann took her hand and showed that he too would like to help.

'There is nothing!' Kyra said defiantly.

Vann and Lea looked at each other.

But they loved her enough to leave her until she was ready to tell them.

She could not at first find the Lord Guiron and, as she was weary from the travelling and the emotions she had been through, she fell down on her sleeping rugs and shut her eyes before she had even eaten the evening meal.

Her dreams that night were restless and disturbing. She tossed and turned so much that Lea who slept next to her woke her once and tried to quieten her with soothing words. After this she did not move about so much, but in her dream world she wandered hopelessly through a labyrinth.

It seemed to her that beyond every turn she would find the Lord Khu-ren. On and on she searched through the dark and hostile passages, but he was always just out of sight, just out of reach.

As she reached the same point at the Centre time after time, she sat down on the cold stone ground and wept. Around her the labyrinth crouched, in silence and in mocking emptiness.

She would never find the Lord Khu-ren. She would never find the way out. There was no way!

But as there is a way in, there is always a way out of a labyrinth.

Despair had closed her eyes to it.

She thought of conjuring up his image as she had done in the great cavern.

But he had spoken of 'the illusions of love' in the same breath as 'the illusions of fear'.

And she was weary of illusions now. She had felt his touch upon her neck and it was this kind of reality she wanted now.

'I cannot help it!' she said defiantly to the invisible Spirit realms that she knew were always present, occupying the same 'space' she occupied but in different form, in a different 'reality'.

'I am not like you! I have a body and my body has needs as well as my spirit. Why do we incarnate on earth if it is not to experience earth reality, earth love!'

She lifted her tear stained face and stared around her in the dark, defying the bodiless, formless Beings to answer her this riddle.

'The answer is . . .,' a gentle voice spoke behind her, and she spun round to see the girl she had twice seen before in vision form, the girl from the Island of the Bulls, the lithe, naked acrobat who danced with bulls and somersaulted over their fearsome horns and yet, at the same time, was one of the noble Lords of the Sun. 'The answer is, my friend, as you would know if you stopped weeping and stilled your mind as you have been taught to do, that we incarnate on earth indeed to experience earth reality, earth love. Spirit and body must both have fulfilment on this plane and the love that can satisfy both is worth a great deal and must be cherished.'

'Then *why* did he say the love between us was impossible?'

'He too is body remember, great Lord of the Sun though he may be. He does not know everything!'

'Then . . .?'

'You must both learn to accept the *pace* of destiny. Because you cannot have what you desire *now*, this moment, does not mean that you may never have it. There are other lives than yours woven into the fabric of your fate. Each may have to take its course before the time is right for you.'

'If only I could be *sure* I would have him in the end!'

'If it was sure that I would not get gored by those horns I

leap over in the palace games, I would not leap.

'You ask for certainty! You ask for the end of challenge and excitement, of development and the joy of achievement.'

Kyra was silent.

Then said in a very small, sad voice,

'I really do not think I am strong enough to be what everyone expects me to be.'

The beautiful girl smiled and there was an element of mocking mischief in her eyes.

'If you are not, then what makes you think you will be worthy to be the wife of the great Lord Khu-ren?'

Kyra was trapped.

She sat, thinking very deeply, for a long, long time.

When she became aware of her surroundings again she was no longer in the dark and oppressive labyrinth.

She was in the palace enclosure on the Island of the Bulls, amongst the crowds she had encountered once before while 'travelling in the spirit'.

The crowds were shouting for the young acrobat to risk her life against the monstrous stamping beast that tossed its horns and raised red dust with its hard hooves.

The beautiful queen with the bare breasts and gold snake ornaments and her court retinue were seated, as before, on the dais raised above the dust and sweat of the enclosure.

She raised her arm and, from a wall of translucent alabaster, the young girl Kyra had been speaking with in the labyrinth leapt gracefully into the arena of the bull, and as before danced to him while the crowd chanted and stamped and clapped, the rhythm quickening as the girl's movements flickered faster and faster.

Kyra stood paralysed with fear for her as the beast suddenly lunged foreward. Quick as light the girl leapt, seized the horns and was over the fierce head and back almost before the creature was aware of it. Perfect agility. Perfect timing. Perfect sense of inner communication with the bull to judge its every twist and turn. In the split moment she was arcing across its back Kyra saw the two disparate beings as one. Harmony and beauty were there in that moment where danger and suffering should have been.

Once on the other side of the bull, separate from him again, the girl leapt up on the wall and stood arms raised, her face transformed with triumph and excitement as the crowd cheered and cheered.

Kyra felt tears of pride and emotion for her beautiful friend pricking behind her eyes.

And then she was awake and had the day to face, but she had made a decision. The way through a labyrinth, Maal had said, could as easily be the way of unfolding enlightenment as the way to confusion and despair.

She would not go to the Lord Guiron for his advice, nor to tell him that she was giving up her studies.

She would keep her love secret as before and she would demand nothing of the Lord Khu-ren or of Life.

She would concentrate on making herself worthy to be a priest.

And then . . . maybe . . .

But of this she was no longer prepared to think.

By the end of the Summer she was ready to take the Star test. Although her studies had been at the College to the South, her test was taken in the main Temple of the Sun.

On a clear, moonless and cloudless night, she entered the great Stone Circle of the Temple and lay upon her back on the grass, her feet towards the East where the Sun would rise.

She was alone and the whole night was hers.

This night she must not let her attention wander for an instant.

The Star the High Priest had chosen for her was rising at the moment she lay down and she must watch its progress across the sky, unwaveringly the whole night long. No matter how tired her eyes became she must not let it out of her sight for an instant.

The effect of the high earthen ridge around the Circumference was to cut out all sight of the landscape and the villages around. She was isolated in a Circle of Power in complete darkness, alone with the Stars.

As the night progressed she totally forgot herself lying on the grass. All that existed was the one star she followed, brilliantly in focus, while an incredible pattern of subtly changing points of gold moved round in the background of her vision.

The star she watched not only moved with slow but inexorable majesty across the dark forever hole of the night sky, but grew in brightness and in power until she felt it like a sharp needle point actually penetrating the centre of her forehead.

It seemed to her the earth bank and the Tall Stones surrounding her not only kept the rest of the world out, but concentrated the power of the stars and whatever realms of Reality that lay beyond her normal consciousness, until they grew in strength and became the only Reality of which she was aware.

It seemed to her the needle of the Star she watched pinned her through the centre of her forehead to the earth and she could not move her body. In her stillness she could feel the earth moving. She was no longer loose upon its surface but was joined to it by this thin, sharp beam of force that passed from the Star to her, through her into the earth, and through the earth until it came out the other side to continue its journey . . .

Her mind ached with the strain of thoughts that were coming to her.

Her forehead ached with the pain of the sharp beam passing through it.

She felt very strange as she turned with the earth, feeling the earth move, and the Star stand still.

But the thought she was trying to grasp kept returning until at last her mind *could* encompass it.

It was the realization that the beam of force from the star that was passing through her and through the earth, and through the universe beyond, was returning to the Star of its origin from the other side!

As though the Whole Universe was a sphere, yet of such a kind that there was no material solidity to it whatever, and therefore no bounds of inside and outside.

She was like a bead on a necklace, threaded through the line of force that was curving with the Universe.

As she grasped this there seemed to be a kind of brilliant explosion in her mind, or was it in the sky?

But suddenly, from every star in the sky, there seemed to be the same fine beam of light, and each one was threaded through the pain in her forehead, through the earth, and through the Universe beyond and back again to its original Source.

The sky now instead of being black with separate points of light, was criss-crossed with fine arcs of light, each starting in a star, or . . .

Did they start in her head?

She could no longer tell if she was the centre from which all the beams were coming, or whether she was the passive recipient of the beams from the stars.

Was she the beginning of all things?

She?

Who was she?

She could not remember her name.

She thought and thought in a sudden kind of panic . . .

'What is my name?'

But she had no name.

The more she tried to remember the more the beams passing through her head hurt her.

At last exhausted and in agony, she accepted that she had no name.

And with that acceptance the pain ceased, and she lay in wonder, watching the cycles of light weaving their magnificent pattern all around her and through her.

The beauty of it! The blissful peace and happiness she felt that anything could be so perfect occupied her for the rest of the night.

And when the sun slowly rose and the vision faded, she remembered her name.

And with the remembrance she moved and felt pain in every limb.

Slowly she dragged herself to her feet and looked round her with weary and bewildered eyes.

The dawn light revealed the Circle as she had known it before, the grassy bank, the giant Stones. Above her the first flights of birds called cheerfully to their fellows.

Around her stood a circle of the highest priests in the Temple.

She looked from one to the other with aching, bloodshot eyes.

The Lord Khu-ren was amongst them, but she was too tired even to react to him.

The Lord Guiron spoke at last.

'My child,' he said gently, 'you must tell us all that happened to you in the night.'

She began to shake her head, thinking how impossible it would be to put all that into words.

'You must try,' the High Priest said. 'It is important.' He spoke quietly, but with great authority.

Stumbling for words the young girl started the story.

The priests around her stood silently, impassively, listening.

No one helped her when she could not find the words, but gradually, clumsily, the story emerged exactly as it had happened.

As she finished speaking, she could feel herself slipping into darkness, her body cold and infinitely weary.

Then for the first time one of the priests moved.

The Lord Khu-ren stepped forward and caught her in his arms as she fell fainting.

The Haunted Mound

The Winter passed in training for Healing.

They learned a great deal about the body and the natural ways it had of healing itself. They learned how the mind, clouded by fear and doubt, could hinder these natural ways, and how they as priest-healers could bring back confidence to the patient so that the ways of nature could work again freely.

It seemed the mental image a person held of himself had great power to influence his body. They were taught to change with great tact and skill the self image of illness the patient held tenaciously within his mind, to one of well being and health. The image changed, the patient visualizing himself well, the healer's work was done. Nature did the rest.

They learned that when the illness had gone too far for the patient's own body to heal itself, they could transfer the strength of their own life-force, to aid the natural healing processes within the patient.

They learned to do this by laying their hands upon the sufferer and directly 'willing' the strength which they knew flowed through them from the Great Source of Life, to enter his body and make him whole again, to by-pass, to push aside, the impediment within the patient that was preventing his natural supply of life-force from entering.

They also learned to use the power of thought to do the same thing when they were too distant from the sufferer to touch him physically.

They studied how to prevent illness, what to eat and how to exercise. The movements they practised were always simple, slow and effective, control of body built up gradually stage by stage until it became a perfect instrument for the use of its owner on earth.

Kyra enjoyed the classes and worked hard.

But one day in early Spring when she was in the middle of a set of rhythmic movements, her concentration was broken by the sudden stinging of the thought that Fern needed her.

She had seen very little of Karne's little family lately as they had been busy having another child and she herself had been occupied with her own determination to make good and fast progress in her studies.

As the thought from Fern reached her, she stopped in mid-movement, and a look of puzzled concentration came to her face.

'What is it, Kyra?' her teacher asked.

'I am sorry,' Kyra said hastily, 'but I must go. I am needed.'

The teacher did not question further but let her go.

She ran faster now than she had ever run. Her body was at its most proficient because of the training she had undergone, and the distance between the College and Fern's little house seemed much shorter than usual.

She found Fern alone with the new baby, weeping, Karne away from home with Olan, and Isar lost.

'Oh Kyra!' she cried when she saw her. 'You have no idea how I longed for you!'

'I felt it,' Kyra said gently. 'Now tell me.'

She put her arms around her.

'Tell me.'

'Isar has wandered off somewhere and has been gone for ages. I have looked everywhere and all my friends have been helping, but no one has seen him.'

'Was Panora with him?'

Kyra knew the girl spent a great deal of time with Isar.

'I have not seen Panora for a long time. I was cross with her once . . . Oh Kyra . . . I did not mean to speak so harshly . . . I think I was jealous because Isar seemed to prefer her to me . . . and I told her to go away. She did, and I have not seen her since. I thought perhaps Isar had wandered off to look for her. I know he missed her. I feel so ashamed! If only I could unsay those words!'

'Calm yourself. No words can ever be unsaid, but new ones

can be spoken. Come, I will help you find him. But first you must be quiet. I must try to "feel" where he has gone.'

'Oh Kyra!'

'S-s-sh,' Kyra said softly, stroking Fern's head. 'Gently . . . you will make your baby upset.'

Fern buried her face in her second child's soft body and rocked backwards and forewards, her cheeks wet, but her sobs stilled.

Kyra moved outside the house and sat in the garden, first letting the beauty and the peace of the Spring leaves and flowers distance her from the disturbing anxiety and fear of Fern.

Then she began to empty her mind as she had been taught to do.

Dark and disturbing impressions began to come to her and at first she thought she was witnessing a burial, and her heart jerked to think it might mean Isar was dead.

She struggled to regain her concentration and this time received impressions of a lake, a mist, the shadowy figure of a woman.

'Guiron's lover!' she thought with shock.

Again her own thoughts having intruded she had to force her way back to meditative calm again.

But no more impressions would come to her.

She would have sat longer, trying yet again to see Isar, if Fern's anxious face had not appeared.

'Did you learn anything?' she asked, her eyes so full of pain, and yet so trustful that Kyra could work miracles.

'Something,' Kyra said guardedly, 'but I cannot work it out yet. I need more information.'

'Try!' Fern said, tears beginning again. 'Oh Kyra, I *love* him so!'

'I know,' Kyra said soothingly. 'I know. We will find him.' 'Is it possible for a neighbour to look after your baby while we go and search?'

'Of course. They have been wonderful to me. Someone has even gone to fetch Karne and he is a long, long way away with Olan.'

'Good. Find someone to take the baby, then find me an old and reliable villager who has a good memory for the old days.'

Fern did not question the commands, but obeyed immediately.

The baby was happily settled. The oldest woman in the village was brought to Kyra.

'I believe,' Kyra said to her, 'there used to be a lake somewhere not far from the Temple, which was drained many years ago. Do you remember it?'

'Oh aye!' the old woman said, 'I remember the lake.'

'Where was it?'

'It were on the other side of the haunted mound,' she said darkly.

Kyra looked enquiringly at Fern.

'I think she means that enormous mound we saw first from the ridge way when we arrived. It is supposed to be haunted. No one will go near it.'

'Oh yes,' Kyra remembered. 'And the lake was there?'

'I suppose,' Fern said, shrugging.

'Thank you,' Kyra said to the old lady. 'Come,' she said to Fern.

They went as swiftly as they could but it was a long way and the sun had passed its zenith when they came within close sight of the weird man-made mountain.

'What makes you think he will be there?' Fern asked, still worried.

'I am not sure . . . but I kept getting a picture of that lake . . . so it is possible . . .'

'I am glad it is no longer a lake,' Fern said, out of breath from trying to keep up with Kyra.

Kyra did not mention the other impression she had had, of a burial.

'Are you sure it was not another lake?' Fern suddenly felt anxious again. 'A lake still filled with water?'

'No, it was the one that is now dry land. Of that I am sure. Do not be afraid.'

As they approached the strange mound they noticed the signs of village life had ceased. It stood very much alone in a

136

great bare space and they could see the flat plain to the West, now overgrown with reeds and marsh grasses, that had once been a lake.

They were just about to bypass the haunted hill and make for the area where the lake had been when Kyra's eyes were drawn to the top and she saw standing there a tall and impressive warrior figure. The sun was behind him, his silhouette black but surrounded by fire. His arms were raised and in one a battle axe caught the sunlight and flashed malevolently.

Her heart missed a beat.

She knew who it was with a strange and terrible certainty.

'Fern!' she cried.

Fern looked at her.

'I want you to promise me something.'

'What?'

'You will stay here and not move until I return. If you do this I will bring Isar unharmed to you.'

Fern looked as though she were about to promise, though puzzled, when a movement or a flash of light drew *her* eyes upwards to the summit of the mound.

'Isar!' she cried in delight and she was off towards him before Kyra could stop her.

To her the figure on the top of the mound was that of a small boy with red hair, no more than about five summers old, waving a bullrush from the marsh over his head.

Her mother's love propelled her up the side of that steep and forbidden mound faster than Kyra could manage, and when Kyra arrived at the top mother and son were happily sitting side by side, arms around each other, kissing and laughing.

Kyra stared at them.

She knew she had not been mistaken in what she had seen, and she just as certainly knew that this was the child Isar with his mother and a bullrush in his hand.

The harsh, mocking sound of a rook as it flew off from the long grass on the side of the mound brought back the chill to Kyra's heart.

There were things she *must* find out before it was too late!

Isar offered no explanation for his actions and his mother asked for none. The three of them made their way back to Fern's home as quickly as possible, there to find Karne returned, just about to set off with torches to look for them.

Kyra did not disturb their happy reunion with any of her own forebodings and when they had eaten and put the children to bed she kissed them both and returned to her College.

The next day she started enquiring about 'the haunted mound' and tried to find out as much as she could about its history. The first people she asked knew nothing more than that it was haunted.

'What kind of ghost haunts there?' she asked. But no one seemed to know. She could find no one who had ever seen the ghost, nor even spoken to someone who had. The legend of its haunting must be very far back in the past.

From one of the oldest priests she managed to establish that the mound had been raised before the building of The Temple of the Sun.

'There is a legend that a great and powerful king from over the seas came to this land in the ancient days, conquered its people and lived in great splendour for many years. Some say it is his burial mound.'

'He must have been very powerful indeed to command such a burial,' Kyra said, looking round and comparing the not inconsiderable mounds around the Temple which housed the dead of many noble families from many countries in the world.

'Aye,' the old priest said. But that was all he knew.

And with this she had to be content for some time.

The lake that used to be beside the mound some old people remembered.

It had been drained during the lifetime of the present High Priest and she longed to ask him about the lake and the mound, feeling strongly that the two were connected, but she was still too much in awe of him to attempt a confrontation.

The Field of the Grey Gods and the Return of Wardyke

At last the time arrived for her to study the choosing of the Stones.

The day their teacher chose to visit the Field of the Grey Gods was a bright and sparkling one. A day on which it was hard to believe in the dark side of life.

The students chattered happily as they wandered up the long path to the ridge way from the Temple. Vann picked some daisies and made little crowns for Lea and Kyra.

Kyra laughed and let down her hair which was now almost to her knees. She looked like a nature spirit as she began dancing along ahead of the others, her eyes shining, her crown of daisies slightly lop-sided, her gold and shining hair flowing out around her in the breeze.

She felt something good was going to happen today, and if it did not she would *make* it happen!

'Kyra!' called Lea laughing, but Kyra did not hear.

She knew the way to the Field and she had waited a long time to be allowed to visit it. There was no holding her back now.

At the point where the path from the Temple joined the ridge way some young trees had grown up since she, Karne and Fern had first stood hesitating there, and she did not see the figure resting in their shade until pirouetting happily, she arrived among them.

And then she stopped. Before her stood the Lord Khu-ren.

He had not seen her since the time she took her Star test and had fallen so wanly into his arms. It was difficult to believe it was the same girl, she was now so full of light and life.

Even the sudden shock of his appearance where she did not expect him could not discomfit her this day.

She met his dark eyes with a sparkling blue, and bowed to

him with a slightly exaggerated and mocking movement, glancing up immediately to see how he was reacting.

He was smiling.

'My lord,' she said, 'I think this is one of the good days in the world!'

'I would agree,' he said, his eyes following the light that glanced off her long hair.

'I think, my lord,' she said, her face alight with mischief, 'this day I am going to dare the gods to do their worst!'

And before he could grasp what she meant, she darted forward, flung her arms around him, stood on tip-toe and kissed him passionately on the mouth.

She had meant to dart away again and disappear along the ridge way before she could pay the penalty for her audacity, but she reckoned without his own feelings in the matter, and when the other students arrived several moments later they found the golden Kyra locked helplessly in the close embrace of the tall dark Lord from over the sea, both of them oblivious to the amazed crowd of onlookers.

The students of course were delighted, but their teacher was old and sour and might not have the same reaction.

When Lea heard him puffing up the hill almost within sight of this astounding scene, she hastily touched Kyra's arm and called out to attract their attention.

And then it was for the first time the two dazed people saw that they were not alone.

Scarlet, Kyra drew back from Khu-ren, and he in his turn went a deeper shade of sunburn.

They would have stood there confused and shaken forever if Lea had not take the situation in hand and led Kyra away.

When the teacher-priest finally came to the trees he found only the lord Khu-ren standing there, the others running like children and laughing as they ran along the ridge path to the Field of the Grey Gods.

The hot and puffing priest bowed to the tall young man, mentioned the heat of the day and passed on.

'Peculiar look he had on his face,' the old man thought, but then thought no more about it.

Khu-ren stayed there a long time, watching the landscape as it stretched below him in every direction, carefully winding several strands of very long and very golden hair about his finger until it became a ring.

The knowledge concerned in the choosing of the rocks followed naturally from all the other classes they had attended over the years.

The students had grown sensitive to the inner forces of themselves and of the world around them. Those who had not had left the College and returned to their homes.

Of those who remained some would study to be village priests, leaving the College when they had a certain standard of general knowledge in the different disciplines. Others would stay on and specialize, rising higher in the priesthood. Vann wished to stay on and specialize in Healing. Lea in Dream Interpretation, while Kyra looked to be a 'spirit-traveller' and perhaps, eventually, a Lord of the Sun.

The choosing of the rocks suitable for the Tall Stones of a Sacred Circle was a specialization in itself, but they were all to attempt at least to understand a little of what was involved.

Kyra had seen the strange Field of grey rocks before on her original journey to the Temple, but many of the other students had not. They were amazed and somewhat apprehensive when they heard the legends that were associated with the Stones.

Not one of them dared approach the Stones until the priest, their teacher, had finally arrived, very red in the face and out of breath.

He allowed himself to cool down in the shade of the trees that edged the field while he discussed with them the method he proposed to use in training.

Today they would wander in the Field and each try to find a rock that gave them a particularly strong 'feeling'.

'You may find a rock that has vibrations for one of you, has none for another. This we will discuss later. The first stage is for you to get the "feel" of the rocks.'

'Now go!' he said, and waved his plump hand at the field.

The students scattered like feathers before a wind across the Field.

At first they darted from rock to rock, putting their foreheads against the cold stones, sensing nothing, and moving off immediately to another. But after a while they began to realize they were being too hasty. None of them was getting *anything* from the rocks, and it was apparent the teacher expected at least some of them to get *something*.

So they slowed down and gave each rock a longer time to respond to their overtures.

Kyra remembered her old village and the Sacred Circle there, and the training she had already received from Maal to feel the power in the Tall Stones. She had an advantage here over the other students and it was she who first found a stone that she was sensitive to in the Field.

It was a strange shape, almost like a throne.

She felt tempted to sit on it and pretend to be a Queen, with Khu-ren at her side as King. But she restrained herself and knelt beside it instead, her head resting on the hollow time and the weather had excavated.

There was something about it.

Several times she left it, not sure that she could feel anything from it, but several times she returned.

There was something.

She closed her eyes and concentrated, tried to feel deep into the Stone, to *become* the Stone in a sense, to feel it feeling *her*.

There was certainly something between them, but she could not explain it.

After a time she stood up and moved away.

'I do not feel vibrations,' she said to herself, 'I just feel a sort of sympathy. That cannot be what the teacher meant!'

And she firmly walked away from the Stone.

But whatever other one she tried, she could not get the one like a throne out of her mind, and so eventually she returned to it and sat upon it, waiting patiently for the elderly priest to work his way right round the field from student to student until he reached her.

She would tell him what she felt, though she was not at all

142

sure that it was what she was meant to feel.

After a while she began to feel strangely drowsy . . . or was it dizzy?

The others seemed to be getting further and further away, the sounds of the birds and the talking of the teacher and the students fainter and fainter. She looked around her, slightly puzzled, but not alarmed. Even the colours around her seemed to be changing subtly and those that had been dark now seemed to be light, and those that had been light seemed now to be dark.

'How strange,' she remembered thinking, and then she was conscious of nothing more.

When she awoke she was lying on the grass of the ridge path, away from the Field, the anxious faces of her teacher and her fellow students gathered closely around her and staring at her.

Vann who had great natural powers of Healing in his hands was holding her head. She felt life and consciousness mercifully flowing back into her body.

'What happened?' she murmured, her lips very dry.

'You must have found a powerful stone,' the teacher said, and then to the others, 'Stand back and give her some air.'

Looking considerably relieved at her recovery the others moved back, only her special friends, Lea and Vann, staying close to her.

'Stone?' she muttered stupidly, not remembering anything clearly.

'One of the special Stones we were looking for,' Lea said softly. 'Remember?'

'You see you should not have spent so much time on it,' the teacher scolded. 'I meant you to locate one and then call me. I found you lying all over it!' he accused, 'No wonder you fainted!'

She was amazed.

She began remembering now.

'But . . .' she began.

'You see,' the teacher went on scolding, 'the forces in the

earth are very strong. In certain places stronger than in others. In certain rocks stronger than in others. In certain people stronger than in others! You must be very sensitive to energies and forces hardly felt by others, and you must have found a rock particularly charged with Special Power. You should have been more careful!'

'Oh,' said Kyra.

While she was recovering the students went to the special stone Kyra had found and tested themselves against it. Some of them could feel strangeness in it. Others could sense nothing.

The teacher pointed out that this was why certain priests who had the aptitude for sensing power in rock, travelled sometimes days and months to places where a new Circle was to be built.

'Not everyone can feel the natural currents in the earth. Those who can, pick out the Stones and the places of natural energy where they are to be erected. Once they are raised in their correct places by the correct ceremonial procedures and are used in a community as a Sacred Circle, the natural energies in the Stones and in the earth combine with the forces generated by the ritual worship of the people to become very powerful indeed. The Inner Circle of our Temple has power to transport the spirits of Initiates across the world.'

Kyra remembered the meeting of the Lords of the Sun in that very Circle many summers ago when she was a desperate, half-tutored girl, asking for their help.

When she was strong enough to stand and walk, one arm linked through Vann's and one through Lea's, the teacher led the whole group back to the College.

As they walked they talked in little groups about the unseen threads of force that were woven through the fabric of the earth.

'Sort of keeping it together,' one said.

'Alive,' another said.

'I have heard,' a third joined in, 'that over great periods of

144

time the pattern of flow sometimes changes and Sacred Circles have either to be abandoned or moved to find the new route of the energy flow.'

'Almost like a river that changes its course?'

'Almost like that.'

As they reached the crossing of the ridge way and the path leading down to the Temple, Kyra's attention wandered from what the others were saying and relived the moment of great happiness she had spent in the arms of the Lord Khu-ren such a short while before.

There was no sign of the young Lord now, but she noticed the daisy crown Vann had made for her lying on the grass where it must have fallen from her hair.

She smiled, relieved.

So strange had been the happenings since, she would not have been surprised if that incident had proved to be a dream or a vision.

It was not always easy to be sure which one of the different types of Reality one was experiencing.

She longed to see the Lord Khu-ren again, but it was not to be for some while.

Soon after the incident of the rock in the Field of the Grey Gods she visited Karne and Fern.

She found children in the garden playing happily, but Fern and Karne in some distress.

Isar ran up to her at once and took her hand and led her off to see the dam he was building in the stream. Seeing him today so full of childish fun she could not believe he was the same tall and vengeful warrior she had seen on top of the haunted mound.

After she had spent some time with him and helped him move a boulder or two, she managed to withdraw and visit his parents.

'What is the matter?' she asked at once, on seeing their faces.

'Wardyke!' Karne said immediately, and her heart sank.

'He arrived here yesterday and wanted to see Isar,' Fern said miserably.

' "His son" he called him,' Karne said bitterly.

'Oh no!' Kyra looked distressed. She had hoped they had heard the last of Wardyke when they banished him from their community and stripped him of all his powers as magician-priest.

'What did you do?'

'I told him to go, there was no son of his here!'

'And . . .?'

'He just smiled . . . and went.'

Kyra looked surprised.

'But oh, Kyra,' said Fern, 'if you had seen his smile! I know we have not seen the last of him!'

'How was he? Do you think he has regained his powers in some way?'

'No, I do not think so,' Fern said thoughtfully. 'When I first saw him I felt almost sorry for him . . .'

Karne snorted and it was clear he had not felt the same.

'He has aged a great deal. His hair is quite grey and he is very thin and ragged looking. He must have been wounded in some way because his left arm and his left leg are sort of . . . well, he sort of drags them . . . he does not use them properly.'

'Has he seen Isar at all?'

'No. Nor will he!' said Karne fiercely.

Fern looked less certain.

'Do you think he has?' Kyra asked her.

'It is possible . . . I cannot keep him with me in the house all the time. He runs about the village with the other children and plays a great deal down by the stream. It would be easy for Wardyke to come upon him one day.'

'Of course his unusual red hair would give him away as your son,' Kyra said musingly.

Karne looked at the long dagger Olan had given him that was hanging on the wall behind them.

'No, Karne. That is not the answer and you know it.'

Karne knew she was right, but down here in the South ways were different, and many quarrels were settled with violence where in their small quiet Northern community it would have been unthinkable.

'Settled?' Kyra asked, seeing into his mind suddenly with great clarity. 'Nothing is "settled" that way. You just move the problem to another time, maybe another life, and have to undo what you have done in ways that may well be more unpleasant for you than the original problem.'

'I know!' Karne said impatiently. 'I know.'

And he left the house muttering that there was much work to be done.

'He is very worried,' Fern said gently in his defence.

'I know, and it is easy for me to talk about keeping feelings under control . . .!' she said wryly.

Fern could not catch the implications of the remark as she did not know about Kyra's love for the Lord Khu-ren.

'What will I do, Kyra,' she pleaded, 'if he were to take him away from me?'

'He has no right!'

'Of course not. But he might still do it.'

Kyra was silent, thinking.

Fern went on talking.

'The garden and the trees watch over him and I can "feel" when he is in trouble. But I fear one day it may be too late before I reach him. The feelings I get are not specific. I feel danger and pain and love, but exactly *where* the danger is is not so easy.

'I have made friends with Panora again. I called her back and apologized. She is with Isar a great deal and I will warn her to watch out for Wardyke.'

This did not comfort Kyra much. She had never been able to shake off the feeling that Panora was somehow malevolent.

She had told Fern of Panora's connection with the Lord Guiron, but for some reason Fern refused to accept it as a warning. She pointed out Isar was Wardyke's son and yet had nothing of Wardyke in him.

The two young women spent a great deal of that day

discussing what to do for the best, and it was decided that Fern should try to talk to Wardyke about Isar and to Isar about Wardyke, and to let them meet, but at first only in her presence.

'If you forbid him to see Isar he will do everything in his power to take the boy from you. You must be subtle. You must be cunning. You must be watchful. Isar is held to you and Karne by bonds of love and trust that nothing can break. Wardyke will accept this when he has tried and failed, but never if he is prevented from trying.'

Fern admitted to still being very much afraid of Wardyke.

'But he has no powers as magician now,' Kyra said.

'I know, but I still fear him and I cannot bear to speak with him. When he came yesterday, I hid, and Karne did all the talking.'

'I think that is unwise. Karne is anxious and impatient, and does not always consider the full implications of what he says or does. You must discuss the matter with him before Wardyke comes again and make Karne understand it is the only way to keep Isar. You cannot hide him forever.'

Fern nodded sadly.

The work at the College was becoming more and more demanding and Kyra had little time to visit Karne and Fern again.

Her experience with the rock in the Field of the Grey Gods, combined with the remarkable advances she had made in all her studies, earned her a special meeting with the Lord Guiron.

'I have been watching you, my child,' he said, 'and have decided that if you wish it you may enter now the first stage of priesthood.'

This meant she would be qualified to be a village priest and would have a ceremony of inauguration.

She gasped.

'But my advice to you is not to leave the College at this stage, but to study for the higher grades. I think,' he said,

148

looking deeply into her eyes, 'you have the capacity to enter the highest grade of all.'

One of the legendary Lords of the Sun!

She was overwhelmed.

She had dreamed and longed for this, but it had seemed so impossible.

'I remember you had experience of "spirit-travelling" long before you came to us as student. You still have much to learn as I am sure you realise, but the Lord Khu-ren tells me, and I have noticed, that you learn fast.'

Kyra blushed with pleasure and her hand went involuntarily to the faience beads about her neck.

She saw Guiron's eyes follow the movement of her hand and smile with amusement. How much did he know?

There was an awkward silence between them for a moment, Kyra's heart beating fast with joy at the implications of what she had just been told.

'Your inauguration as a priest will be at noon six days from now. Prepare yourself.'

She bowed, but did not turn to go as was expected of her.

He raised an eyebrow enquiringly.

'My Lord,' she stammered, and stopped.

He waited patiently, a very impressive figure.

She trembled with the audacity of what she was about to ask.

'My Lord . . .' she brought out with difficulty again . . . 'is it possible . . . I mean . . . is there a law against the marriage of priests of the highest grades?'

She had said it, and she was scarlet!

He turned away from her and walked two or three times across the room, his face lowered and in shadow.

She was alarmed.

'I . . . am sorry . . .' she muttered.

He came to stand at last before her and his face was hard and composed as she had never seen it before.

'There is no law,' he said, 'but it is not the custom, nor is it advisable.'

She bowed hastily and retreated backwards from his

presence.

Outside, she stood in confusion. She felt she could not face her fellow students and went for a long walk by herself.

She followed the path from the Temple to the ridge way, not noticing the quiet fields on either side, the silent burial mounds, the woods and houses that stretched beyond.

Her journey was in the past, marking the moments in her life that had led her to this point, and wondering about the moments in her life that would lead her on beyond it.

So absorbed was she that his arms were about her and his lips on hers before she even knew he was there.

'My lord!' she gasped, and then gave up everything of past and future to the beauty of the present moment.

When they at last had drawn apart and were sitting close together on the grass, she said,

'The Lord Guiron said it is not the custom, nor is it advisable, for priests of the highest grades to marry.'

He untied the coil of her hair and shook the golden shower of it about her shoulders, twining his fingers in it to pull her head back to kiss her lips again.

'It is not advisable, nor is it the custom, but it is not against the law,' he said.

'You mean . . .?'

'I mean . . . take one step at a time, my love . . . You are entering my class as a student . . . not as my wife . . .'

She flushed and turned away, ashamed that she had presumed so much.

'On the day you have learned all that I have to teach and we stand equally within the Inner Circle of the Priesthood, I will ask you *then* if you wish to defy custom and ignore advisability. I will not take you as master to student, lord to awestruck girl!'

She buried her face in her knees, not wanting him to read in her eyes how much she wanted to be taken now. 'Dignity' and 'Equality' were cold, hard words in the turmoil of her present feelings.

He must have felt it too because he suddenly stood up and said sharply, 'Come. The sun is setting.'

They did not touch again, nor speak, as they walked down the gradually darkening path towards the Temple.

Kyra's Inauguration

In the next few days Kyra had many formalities to attend to, and most of them in the pouring rain.

Her student friends were delighted with her success but sorry to see her move out of their immediate circle. She would now live on the other side of the Temple among the other priests who were continuing their studies, and would be cut off from her old companions in many ways.

The last but one night before the ceremony, they made an enormous bonfire in a field some distance from the College and had a wild party, all their years of serious study forgotten, and they danced and sang as they used to dance and sing in their home communities when they were still carefree children.

Someone smuggled in strong ale and at the end when the rain that had been threatening all evening started to fall really heavily, the party became a disorderly but cheerful scramble in the mud.

The dawn found many a bedraggled student fumbling his way home to the College sleeping quarters, and the classes that day were very subdued.

If the teachers knew of the event, they gave no sign. It is possible such parties were not unknown in the College.

They had chosen the last night but one for the party, because the actual night before had to be spent by Kyra alone in the Sanctuary, meditating.

Her head ached from the previous night's revelries, but she had learned to ignore natural pain in herself and soon had it under control.

Much more difficult it was to control her thoughts.

But she had not come this far without learning anything and, difficult though it was, it was not long before she was in

152

deep meditation.

This night she must speak with Spirits and listen to their guidance and advice.

With the dawn the priests of higher rank arrived to prepare her with prayers and incantations for the day. She had special oil from an exquisite gold jar rubbed gently into her forehead, and she was dressed in a plain white robe with no decoration or ornaments. It seemed to have been woven in one piece and was beautiful in its elegance and simplicity.

They made a move to take the necklace of faience beads from her throat, but she put up her hand to protect it from them with such fierce determination that the priest in question drew back his hand in some alarm and looked for guidance from his fellow priests.

No words were said, but the Lord Khu-ren stepped forward and took her hand away from the necklace, lifted it slightly and dropped it down underneath the white robe so that no sign of it showed. But she knew it was still there.

He avoided looking into her eyes when he did this or giving any sign to the others that there was anything special between them, but she felt his hand as he moved the beads, and her heart quickened.

They both knew that wearing the beads on the day of inauguration was breaking with an ancient custom and they both took it as a kind of secret sign that this would not be the only custom they would break.

When it was time to leave the Sanctuary she was stunned to see how many people had gathered to watch the procession . . . *her* procession! She wondered if Karne and Fern were there. She had sent a message by Panora, but had been too busy to visit them herself with the news. How proud and pleased they would be to see her walking in such a noble throng!

How she wished Maal could be there and all the people of her home community.

And then she felt ashamed.

The messages she had received in the night had made it clear to her that she was an instrument of the Spirit Realms and the God from which All things come.

Her only power came from them, her only skill was to open herself and allow their energies to work through her. She was nothing but a willing channel through which the innate life Force of the Universe could be concentrated where it was needed most.

The force and meaning of this suddenly struck her as she walked the long, long avenue to the Sacred Circle.

The crowds that pressed in on every side became a blur. The tall and magnificently robed figures of the men and women of the priesthood ahead of her became strange and alien.

What were they doing with such finery?

They were not gods to be worshipped and obeyed.

They were servants of the Great Spirit and were there to obey.

And then another thought struck her with the suddenness of pain.

The Lord who walked ahead of her, a cape of blue and gold sweeping over his bare shoulders to drag upon the ground behind him . . . what of him?

If she had given up her selfhood, would he be taken from her too?

She had felt so sure that day upon the ridge way when he had talked of the time when she would stand equally with him and he would ask her to be his wife that there would be no question but that she would say yes.

What if at that point she was told by her Spirit Lords that she must not join with him.

What then?

Would she obey?

The procession she had thought would be a triumph and a joy, now oppressed her heart.

She kept her eyes lowered, watching her bare feet walking the cold, damp earth.

The sun shone but it had not yet dried up the moisture of the past few days.

154

Her old misgivings began to trouble her.

Was she fit?

Could she possibly carry the burden of being a priest?

She had enjoyed the dancing at her party.

She had enjoyed the touch of the Lord Khu-ren's hands and lips.

She knew he suffered too. She had seen the shadows in his dark eyes. But he was stronger than her and accustomed to being a priest.

Perhaps . . . and here she looked up quickly to see how far they were away from the entrance to the Circle . . .

Perhaps it was not too late . . .

She had not spoken the words of vow yet.

She had not received the Mark of Power.

And then . . .

And then . . .

She remembered the girl acrobat's words in the labyrinth when she had said she was not worthy to be a priest . . .

'If you are not, then what makes you think you will be worthy to be the wife of the great Lord Khu-ren?'

And he had said: 'I will not take you as master to student, or lord to awestruck girl.'

And the more she thought, the more she knew that their meeting and everything in her life so far had led step by step with ordered certainty to this place, this ceremony.

She *must* trust the overwhelming feeling that she had that there was reason in it.

The Spirit Lords had let her keep her faience beads in spite of ancient custom decreeing otherwise. She would take this as a sign he and she were meant to be together.

She would go on.

She felt the power of the Great Circle as she had never felt it before, closing in around her as she entered it. She was exhilarated, but afraid.

There was now no going back.

The ceremony was long and impressive.

The low drumming of the musicians, the chanting of the ancient words of initiation, the careful circling of the priests in their ceremonial robes, the occasional sips of a special and potent drink from a golden cup held by the High Priest himself, all served to make her feel less and less like Kyra and more and more like some strange and supernatural being.

She hardly felt the new robes being put upon her, the heavy pendant about her neck, the cloak of blue and gold, similar to Khu-ren's but not as grand, and finally the circlet of jet beads that fitted around the high gold coil of hair that sat upon her head already like a crown.

When this point was reached she thought all must surely be finished, but there was one thing more.

The others retreated from her, bowing, leaving her alone with the Lord Guiron, the Lord High Priest.

'My lady,' he said quietly, 'I once took something from you and promised to return it to you when you were ready for it.

'The time has come.'

And he stepped forward and held out his hand palm upwards to her.

On it lay the stone sea urchin she had found in the great cavern.

It was hers.

She bowed her head and took it, feeling strength and confidence coursing through her as she did so.

'Use it well,' he said gravely, 'you have now the mark of the priest upon you.'

He too bowed and retreated from her.

She stood alone as the sun sank and the crowds faded away.

Ancient Relationships made clear

Some while later when Kyra was greatly absorbed in her new studies she felt another call from Fern that could not be ignored.

She asked permission to be absent and went at once to the home of her brother and his family.

As before Isar was missing.

She questioned Fern about Wardyke and whether they had followed her advice. It seemed they had and all had been going fairly well.

Wardyke was allowed to meet the boy. He had settled in the neighbouring village under Olan's old enemy, Hawk-Eagle, and came only occasionally to visit. The visits were not pleasurable for any of them, but they passed uneventfully enough and Wardyke seemed content with the way things were.

'And Panora?'

'Oh, she has been a great help to me,' Fern said warmly. 'She always stays with Isar when Wardyke is with him. He never sees him alone even if Karne and I are not present.'

Kyra was thoughtful. This news did not comfort her.

'How long has he been missing this time?'

'He was not in his bed this morning. I do not know if he left in the night or in the early morning before I woke. He often goes out into the garden or down to the stream as soon as the first light comes, so I did not begin seriously to worry until he missed his midday meal. He never misses that!'

Kyra could see she was very worried.

'I was feeling ill at ease all morning. My garden seemed to be trying to tell me something, but somehow I did not associate it with Isar.'

Kyra knew the difficulty of interpreting 'feelings' where

there are no words to act as guide lines.

She noted this second disappearance had also occurred while Karne was far from home.

'I have already looked at the haunted mound and the lake,' Fern said despairingly.

'You must not worry any more now,' Kyra said firmly. 'I found him the last time and I will find him this time.'

She wished she felt as confident as she sounded.

She left Fern to attend to her other child and as before sat in the garden and tried to 'feel' the presence of Isar. Her mastery of this technique had developed since the early days and she slipped into meditative silence almost immediately, her inner senses scanning the surrounding landscape for any traces of Isar's thought flow.

The impressions she was receiving were from the other side of the temple, from the Field of the Grey Gods.

They were not very definite, she could see nothing of Isar, but she kept remembering the Field of the Grey Gods and could not put it out of her mind. There was always the danger that her mind had wandered into a memory of her own or was even picking up the thought flow of someone else, but this impression was persistent and the only one she had, so she decided to act upon it as she had before.

She told Fern that she thought she had located Isar, that he was quite safe and she was not to worry.

'I will come with you,' Fern at once insisted.

'No,' Kyra was firm. 'It is a long way and you have another child who needs you. I will bring him safely to you, but you must not worry if it is not before the sun sets. He had wandered further this time and it will take longer to bring him back.'

Fern's eyes were full of tears as she watched Kyra leave, but she had great confidence in her and knew that if anyone could find Isar and bring him safely home, it would be Kyra.

As Kyra hurried back to the Temple she wished she had Fern's confidence in herself. She fingered the stone sea urchin in her carrying pouch and it seemed the strength it gave her lent her speed and she covered the ground much more swiftly than she normally would have done.

She bypassed the Temple and came along the ridge way from near the Sanctuary, passing the junction of the Temple path and the ridge way that meant so much to her in terms of personal happy memories, without even a glance.

The evening light and long shadows were upon the Field of the Grey Gods when she arrived, and the scene that she saw before her struck a real chill into her heart.

Seated on the throne of rock that she had found was a great King clad in strange and foreign robes. He was dark as the Lord Khu-ren was dark, but there the resemblance ceased. Where Khu-ren was tall and slender, his features fine and chiselled, the King was huge and broad, his features handsome but coarse.

Kneeling in front of him was a slighter man, dressed all in black, apparently from the splendour of his garb, a man of importance in the court, but from the way he knelt, something in the way he moved his hands and head, even from this distance, Kyra could sense there was something obsequious and sinister about him.

It seemed to her (strange that she had not noticed this before!) they were not in the field of scattered rocks at all, but were in a great hall built of giant slabs of uneven rock fitted skillfully together. The King's throne, which at first had seemed to her the rock she had sat upon and fainted, was larger than she remembered it, and carved with unusual devices.

Upon a stone pillar beside the two men was the carved statue of a huge bird, watching the scene unblinkingly.

The same feeling she had had when she had sat that first time upon the rock came over her now. A sort of drowsiness, a sort of dizziness, as though she were not seeing what she was seeing.

She gripped her stone sea urchin and prayed for help not to lose her senses as she had done before, and feeling strength returning to her limbs she took a bold step forward.

With that movement, in that instant, the scene before her

shattered like a dream on waking and she was staring amazed at the Field as she had known it before, full of scattered random rocks, and on the one she thought of as a throne sat the small boy Isar, with Wardyke kneeling in front of him and Panora perched on a rock beside them in the very place where the stone bird had been.

Kyra gasped and rubbed her eyes.

The scene did not change again.

The three had turned towards her and Isar called out delighted to see her. He jumped off the stone and ran to her.

'See what a great place this is, Kyra,' he chattered happily as she put her arms about him. 'We have been playing games.'

She looked into his guileless eyes and looked beyond him at the half crippled Wardyke now standing stiffly waiting for her approach, Panora smiling her unpleasant, secret smile.

'Games?' she asked, looking directly at Wardyke and Panora.

'Yes, games!' Isar answered, but the other two said nothing.

'Your mother is worried about you,' she scolded the boy. 'You must not run off like that without telling her where you are going.'

'Panora told her,' Isar said confidently.

Kyra looked at Panora.

The girl shrugged shamelessly.

Kyra knew now that she could never trust her again.

She sighed.

'Come,' she said, and took the boy's hand.

The other two remained behind watching as Kyra and child became smaller and smaller in the distance.

The moon was out before Isar was safely home.

'Do not trust Panora or Wardyke again,' Kyra said to Fern. 'Keep Isar close to you. I cannot tell you yet what is going on because I am not sure, but I am going to seek help now and we will soon know what is best to do.'

She left Fern worried, but Isar promising never, never to leave his mother's side again until he had permission.

In the morning she went to the Lord Khu-ren and told him gravely that she must have his help.

They had treated each other with great formality since she had entered his class and nothing had passed between them that would have made any of the other priests present suspect they had anything more than a teacher-student relationship.

They had avoided each other away from the classes as well, not trusting themselves.

This was the first time she had approached him privately. He looked into her eyes and knew it was a matter for a priest and friend, not for a lover.

'Come to me after the lesson is over today,' he said.

She nodded, but hesitated before she turned to leave.

'I would like to meet you beside the Field of the Grey Gods,' she said tentatively but earnestly.

He looked surprised, but he agreed.

And so it was that they met that afternoon beside the field of scattered rocks and Kyra talked and talked, telling him everything she could think of that would be relevant to the situation.

He knew already of Wardyke's role in her former life but he had not known he was Isar's father.

She told him of the strange destiny that seemed to link Guiron and Isar. She told him of the haunted mound incident, and what she felt about Panora. She described the strange scene she had witnessed in this field the day before and of her own experience with the 'throne' rock.

He listened very attentively to it all.

'I did not know who to turn to,' she said apologetically at last. 'The only other possibility would have been the Lord Guiron, but he is somehow involved . . .'

'You were right to come to me. I understand.'

'I hope you do not think . . .' she stammered a little, embarrassed that he might think it was an elaborate way of attracting his attention to her again.

'No, I do not think . . .' he said gently, amused.

He raised his finger to his lips to indicate that now he wanted to be in silence to think it through.

They sat beside each other, silently, not touching, for a long time.

At last he stood up.

'I want you to stay here,' he said. 'Do not interfere in any way whatever happens—unless I specifically call for your help. Understand?'

'What are you going to do?' she cried, alarmed.

'There is nothing much I can do until I know how everything fits together. I am going to sit upon that throne myself and see what happens.'

'Oh no!' she cried. 'I fainted. It was horrible!'

He smiled and touched her on the nose.

She felt very foolish suddenly.

He was a Great Lord of the Sun, and she had been a green student on her first lesson about rocks.

She sat down on the bank and watched him walk into the field.

He sat upon the stone shaped like a throne and became very still.

He sat for a very long time.

Nothing changed. The field remained a field of scattered rocks. He was still the Lord Khu-ren whom she loved.

But he was as unmoving as stone.

The sun set and she began to shiver with the evening chill. She wondered what she would do if he sat there into the night. He had made her promise not to do anything unless he called to her for help.

She went into meditative silence herself, but could hear no call for help.

Nothing at all.

At last he moved, stood up and stretched himself.

She was so happy the anxious vigil was over she ran across the field to him and flung herself into his arms. She was bitterly cold now and he held her close to warm her. She was so thankful to have him back that she kissed him again and again on every bit of his face that she could reach.

He laughed and tried to hold her off.

'Wait,' he said, shaking her and laughing, 'you will make

me forget all the important things I have learned while sitting here.'

She jumped back immediately.

'Oh . . . I am sorry . . . please forgive . . .'

'All right! All right!' he laughed, 'you do not need to go so far away.' And he put his arm round her shoulders to give her warmth and comfort as they walked back to the Temple and he told her all that had come to him while he was seated on the 'throne'.

It was a story almost complete in every detail that seemed to make sense of all the bits and pieces Kyra had been worrying about.

It seemed that in the ancient days, before their Temple had been built, a great warrior King had come from over the seas, indeed from Khu-ren's own country, and had conquered much of the land around them, which at that time was full of wandering tribes, each under the leadership of a chieftain.

The King set up court in that very place. Many of the rocks that they could see scattered about the field were in fact part of the walls of his great palace. Kyra had not been wrong in her vision.

The stone that looked like a throne had indeed been a throne, but the weather, time and conflict had reduced it to its present ambiguity.

His god had been in the form of a large black bird, and it was he whom Kyra had seen upon the column.

Both his close friend and adviser and his beautiful queen he had brought from his own far country, the three sustaining each other against the alien nature of the land to which they had come.

All went well for many years.

They lived in a luxury that no one in the land had ever seen before, and the queen and he were idyllically happy in their love for each other.

But a shadow was not far from their lives.

One of the most powerful of the local chieftains, who had

163

been befriended by the king and invited to his court as an equal, fell in love with the beautiful dark queen.

For a long while he watched her, in the movement of dance, in the stillness as she sat beside her lord.

But one day he could bear it no longer and he approached her.

She turned her head towards him slowly as he spoke the words that had for so long been burning in his heart.

Her almond eyes were dark with scorn.

Bitterly he retreated and did not rest until he had devised a way of killing the king and his friend-adviser. So cunningly did he do his work and dispose of the bodies that no one but the queen suspected it was he, and she was helpless and unable to convince others.

It was not long before the murderer, mourning apparently so sincerely the disappearance of his friend, had managed to take his place as king.

On the day he was crowned he asked the former queen to be his wife.

She refused.

He raped her.

And later when he was asleep she left his side and flung herself into the lake where she and her lord had been happy to sail on many a peaceful summer afternoon.

From that time on nothing went right for the new king.

He was broken with remorse for what he had done to the woman he loved and gradually his enemies destroyed him and the palace he had taken as his own.

He died in battle and through many other lives on this earth and on others he paid for his lust, treachery and violence, until at last the guilt was worked off.

He was born again on this earth, at this time, and led a good life.

'He became,' and here Khu-ren paused and looked hard at Kyra, 'the High Priest of this Temple, the Lord Guiron.'

She gasped.

'Everything in his life went well until the night he spent in the mist on that lake. He had no surface-memory of the story I have just told you. The whole debt had been paid and he was clear to live now an enlightened life.

'But there were other threads of destiny woven into this tale that had not yet been worked through. The friend of the King still harboured malice and feelings of revenge. The Queen had never been reborn but had haunted the lake waiting for the return of her lord.

'Guiron was confronted by the image of the woman he had loved and he made the same mistake again! She refused him and he forced himself upon her.'

They had stopped walking and were standing in the dark, Kyra almost not breathing with the interest she had in the story.

'And so the whole cycle of purgation has to start again.'

'How do you mean?' Kyra asked breathlessly.

'Guiron, horrified at what he had done, drained the lake and destroyed the image of the woman, thinking once again to escape the consequences of his action.

'Whether he remembered now the whole story from the past I do not know. But it is possible.'

'Isar?' asked Kyra anxiously.

'The murdered King.'

'Wardyke?'

'The murdered King's friend.'

Kyra remembered that the demon figures associated with Wardyke had reminded her of the gods and demons of Khu-ren's land.

'Panora?'

'A kind of half-human creature, half-spirit.'

It seemed to her now that Wardyke and Panora were there to play their part in arranging the vengeance of Isar against Guiron, whether the two protagonists wished it or not.

Kyra was silent in the dark, clinging to Khu-ren's arm.

When would it end? If Isar carried out this act of vengeance the cycle of purgation would have to turn for *him* through aeons of pain.

How long the threads of cause and effect that wove about their lives!

How strangely they played their parts in other people's dramas.

That Wardyke should father Isar and that *she* should be instrumental in bringing him face to face with Guiron after all that time!

Khu-ren put his arms around her.

'You are shivering, my love.'

She clung to him and without either of them intending it they found themselves together in Khu-ren's warm sleeping rugs for the night.

A Wounded Friend and a Lake that is not a Lake

As soon as she could Kyra told everything she knew about Isar to Karne and Fern. They sat for a long time discussing it and their suggestions ranged from leaving the Temple environs and moving back to their old home, to facing it out here and now.

In the end they were all agreed that moving their location on the face of the earth would do no good whatever, nor would trying to destroy Wardyke and Panora physically. It was decided that the only reasonable course they could take would be to watch the relationships between Wardyke, Panora and Isar closely and try and counteract their influence on him in every way possible. They all knew that not much purpose was served by forbidding someone to do something. Their only hope in saving Isar from the consequences of a course of vengeance was to influence him with their love and convince him of the beauty and necessity of forgiveness, so that when the final confrontation came he would not choose to go the way Wardyke and Panora wanted him to and he would be strong enough in himself to withstand their pressures.

Kyra left them soberly and sadly considering the future, with promises of help from her at any time they needed her.

She told them also of her love for the Lord Khu-ren and of his assistance in the matter.

Fern looked at her with tears in her eyes, knowing what it was to love.

Whatever the plans of Wardyke and Panora were at that time they seemed to leave Isar alone for a while. Perhaps they feared Kyra's interference. Perhaps they knew the powerful Lord Khu-ren was now involved. They may have even thought to lull Isar's family and friends into a feeling that all danger was past. At any rate Isar was still very young and they could afford to wait.

Isar grew daily closer to his mother and her gentle teaching.

Karne too spent much more time with him and when he went on journeys for Olan, riding on a horse, he took Isar with him sitting in front of him.

The boy had an amazing knowledge of the countryside and many times set Karne on the right path when he was about to stray. Apart from this, which could have been explained by the fact that Isar had lived in this area before, there was not much sign that there was anything unusual about him. He loved to ride, to run, to jump, to play fighting with cudgels as other boys did. But his greatest joy of all was to carve wood into beautiful and fantastic shapes. With this skill he gave both Karne and Fern great pleasure, especially as he chose the wood with care and never harmed a living branch.

Meanwhile the Lord Khu-ren and the Lady Kyra struggled to keep their love for each other under control.

Apart from that one night when Isar's story was revealed, they did not see each other except as master and student in the class among the other priests.

Kyra could see, when she was thinking sensibly, that a priest of Khu-ren's stature could not live a normal family life without jeopardising his work as Lord of the Sun.

The control of the subtle and complex inner forces of his Being necessary for the great work he had to do across the world in 'spirit-travelling' would be endangered by. family distractions and worries.

The only way they could be together would be if they had equal powers and worked in unison. Their bond of love would then aid and strengthen them. But as long as she was still a feeble and unformed girl, demanding his attention away from his work, instead of aiding him in it, there would be difficulties.

She knew also that if she chose this way, graduated to stand beside him as an equal in his work, she would have to give up any idea of having children of her own.

A mother with children could surely not be a Lord of the Sun.

A mother with children must be a mother.

These were not easy days for her.

One night in sleep she had a dream that she knew at once was not a dream, but a cry for help.

She could feel great pain but at first could not locate the source or cause of it. Then impressions of noise , of shouting, heat and dust, and blood. Pain seemed everywhere in her, but visually she could see nothing but a sort of whirling reddish fog. Then she felt hands pulling at her and the pain grew worse, until she could hear herself screaming . . . then through the sound of screaming and people's harsh voices shouting in a language unknown to her, she struggled to interpret another sound which she knew was of great importance but which she just could not grasp with her mind.

The pain passed through her like a wave and her whole dream went black.

She was awake, sitting upright, feeling no pain but an overwhelming sense that she was needed somewhere.

But where?

If only she could isolate the other sound and recognize it she would know where she was needed.

She tried to calm her mind.

'Slowly,' she chided herself, 'you must go into the Silence if you want clarity of thought.'

Her mind was at first quite blank as she removed the disturbances of her own life from it and then she deliberately put herself through the dream again, but this time she kept consciousness.

She knew she was succeeding when the terrible pain began to return to her body. She almost wavered then and backed away but her training stood by her and she forced herself to go on and feel all that she had felt before, hear all that she had heard before. This time she recognised the other sound, the sound of thundering hooves.

The Island of the Bulls!

Her friend, the beautiful acrobat.

For a few moments her mind was in complete disorder as she tried to cope with the emotions of worry and fear for her friend, and the decision as to what to do.

The Lord Khu-ren this night was on work of great importance in another country. He had entered the powerful Northern Inner Circle of the Temple at sunset and must not be disturbed until dawn. It would be dangerous both for him and for the situation he was at this moment helping in his 'spirit' form.

She alone must help her friend.

She pulled her long woollen cape around her and left the room of sleeping people. She entered the Great Circle of the Temple.

She held her sea urchin talisman tightly in one hand, asking for power to 'travel' and her faience beads she touched for comfort with her other hand. Her forehead she laid against one of the Stones in the Outer Circumference of the Circle she had on several occasions found had special significance for her.

The night was very dark and she felt very much alone.

'I must not be afraid,' she told herself. 'Fear will prevent my "travelling".'

And indeed while she thought about herself and her fear she stayed where she was, but when she started to think about the girl, the force of her affection for her made her forget herself, and suddenly she was no longer in the The Temple of the Sun.

She was in a high walled room in the Palace on the Island of the Bulls, wall paintings flickering in the firelight of torches, her beautiful friend lying very still and covered in blood upon a cold slab of stone.

Around the walls people were gathered weeping, but near her two priests of her own culture were working upon her, one

170

washing the blood away from the wounds, the other sprinkling herbs into the cleaned gashes and uttering incantations.

Kyra moved forward to stare down upon the pale face of the girl. The people in the background showed no sign that they had noticed her arrival or were aware of her presence. Only the two priests reacted in amazement at the sight of her.

In appearance she was very different from the people of their land. Her long cloak of fine gold hair flowing loose made her appear to them like a shining being from another realm.

Bowing slightly, they retreated, and it was clear to her they now expected her to save the girl.

As soon as she had established that the life force had not yet left the bodily sheath entirely, she indicated to the priests that the mourning, miserable people were to leave. This they did at once, though under protest.

When the room was clear except for the two priests who stood well out of the way and projected only confidence, Kyra leant over her friend again.

Remembering how Maal's little stone sphere of power placed upon his chest had revived the pumping of his heart when it had almost stopped, Kyra now placed her sea urchin talisman between the girl's breasts, folded her limp hands over it and then placed her own hands upon the girl's forehead. All that she had learned in Healing came to her now and her love for the girl, her longing for her recovery, gave impetus to the forceful flow of life that she willed through herself to the girl from the great Source beyond.

When she could see the pumping of her heart was gradually becoming stronger she began to massage her limbs, forming a strong visualisation of the acrobat refreshed and renewed, energetic and healthy again. At the same time she never ceased to will the force of life to flow through her.

When she was sure the immediate danger of death was over, she looked to see what the wounding of the bull's harsh horns had done to her. She found deep gashes and broken bones.

She called the priests back to her side and asked for clean cloth, more water and more healing herbs.

Together they staunched the bleeding, set the bones, bound the wounds with clean linen and healing herbs.

And only when this was done did Kyra dare to remove the talisman of power and call the girl to wakefulness.

As she opened her eyes and saw Kyra's loving face above her, she smiled a very small but very happy smile.

'I called you,' she said, and shut her eyes again.

Kyra dismissed the priests and sat beside her friend, holding her hands, loving her.

Kyra was moved and touched that she had been called. It would have been more likely that she would have called one of the great Lords of the Sun, of which, after all, she was one.

'No,' the girl whispered, as though Kyra had spoken this aloud. 'I wanted you. I wanted to show the Lord Khu-ren that *you* could do it.'

Kyra looked her surprise.

'Ah yes,' the girl smiled wanly, 'I have loved him too. But that was long ago. I did not wish to give up the excitement of my life here and so I let him go. It was meant to be. You and he are for each other. I have seen it and I accept it.'

Kyra did not know what to say.

The girl shook her head very slightly. It still pained her greatly to move in spite of the numbing herbs.

'Nothing,' she breathed. 'Say nothing.'

Kyra sat still holding her hands, feeling all that was between them and between them both and the Lord Khu-ren.

Yet another strange thread she had not been aware of in the fabric of her life.

'I will sleep now,' the girl whispered at last. 'You must go. I will be all right now.'

'What about . . . ?' Kyra did not like to say anything about her future as an acrobat, but the thought came unbidden and the girl caught it.

Again she moved slightly. This time it was almost a shrug of the shoulders.

'My name is Quilla, which means in my language, "flight",' she said.

Kyra leant forward and kissed her on her forehead.

172

'You will fly again', she said gently, 'and I will visit you again.'

'Who knows,' and here Quilla's lips formed a smile with a touch of mischief in it. 'I may come to your wedding!'

Kyra smiled too, also with a hint of mischief in her eyes.

'You are welcóme!'

On that warm note they parted, Quilla to sleep and Kyra to find herself in the anxious arms of Khu-ren who had returned at early dawn from his exhausting night of 'spirit-travelling', to find Kyra lying in a dead faint on the cold dewy grass beside one of the Stones of the Great Circle.

When he had taken her home and warmed her and scolded her roundly for being there at all, he listened to her story with great interest.

When she had finished he sat so gravely thinking that Kyra began to grow alarmed.

'Is it her you really love?' she burst out at last.

He looked at her as though she had said something stupid and childish.

She *felt* stupid and childish.

But when he took her in his arms and covered her with the warm fur of his sleeping rugs she felt very different.

When Kyra had first entered the class of 'spirit-travelling' she had made amazing progress, partly because she had had some experience before, and partly because she was determined to master it as fast as she could.

But after this time with Quilla both Khu-ren and herself began to notice a disturbing thing. She tended to faint a great deal during and after 'travelling' and many times failed to achieve separation from her body in spite of every sign that she was doing it right.

She managed two visits to the Island of the Bulls before it became too obvious for them to ignore that something was wrong.

Quilla was healing slowly but surely. Her quicksilver personality was impatient to be at her old trade, but there was no way she could be allowed to, or even be capable of it, for a long time.

'I have always been short on patience', she said gloomily, 'and now I suppose I will *have* to learn it!'

It was after this visit that Kyra took so long to come out of a faint and felt so ill when she did that Khu-ren decided to think seriously about allowing her to go on at all with her training.

She was in despair.

It mattered so much to her to marry Khu-ren, and she was as determined now as he had originally been, that they would not marry unless they could work together as well.

'Perhaps your real role in life is to be a Healer,' suggested Fern when Kyra poured out all her troubles to her, 'and not one of the Lords of the Sun at all.'

But Kyra would not accept this.

'I know I can "travel". I know it is in "travelling" I can be of most use to Khu-ren and my fellow beings.'

'But you cured your friend Quilla . . .'

'But I "travelled" to do it!'

Fern sighed. She was very fond of Kyra and knew how she felt.

And then her new baby stirred inside her own body and she looked at Kyra with a look of revelation.

'You are with child!' she almost shouted.

Kyra looked astounded, and then she remembered the night when Khu-ren had told her the full story of Guiron and Isar and she had not returned to her own sleeping place.

The two girls stared at each other.

The realization of what this meant slowly dawned on Kyra.

The joy that she first felt to be carrying his child turned to despair as she realized she would now have to give up all thoughts of 'travelling' and being his equal and his wife.

'I will not chain him to me with this child! Oh Fern! What am I to do!'

It was a cry from a very deep source of pain.

Fern held her silently in her arms, as once Kyra had held

174

her.

'There must be a meaning in it, my love, there must be a way!' she said gently.

'What meaning? What way?' sobbed Kyra.

Fern stroked her hair.

'How many times did Maal tell us there is no way in the confines of our bodily existence that we can see enough of the picture to know what the meaning is?'

'I know . . . I know . . . but . . .'

'But this has happened now. It is a child of love at least.'

And Kyra felt a twinge of shame to be so complaining to Fern when Fern's child had been forced on her in fear and hate, and she had carried it bravely and cherished it with love.

Yes, her child was certainly a child of love.

It would change the course of her life, but who was to say this change was not meant to be.

'You will speak to the Lord Khu-ren about it?' Fern asked after a while, when Kyra was calmer.

Kyra hesitated.

'Yes!' Fern said firmly.

'Yes,' agreed Kyra.

When Kyra left Fern she knew that she must walk and think alone for a while before she faced her Lord.

Without realizing it she found herself following the tracks that led to the Haunted Mound and the one-time Lake. So deeply was she engrossed in thought that she had climbed the mound before she realized it and was sitting on the top gazing at nothing, her thoughts all of the child within her and what role it would play in the world when it was released from her body.

She felt at peace now as though Fern were right.

It was meant to be and its influence would be for good.

She began to feel very drowsy and very happy.

She noticed a flight of water fowl across the sky and heard the splash as they landed on the lake.

Smiling, she looked down at the shining waters and the

175

birds swimming elegantly beside the reeds. She picked up a pebble and threw it hard so that it reached the water and she watched the circles as they grew out from the central impact.

And then the warm peacefulness of the scene began to change and she felt a little cold. She noticed mist was beginning to gather on the far side of the lake and drift across towards her.

'I must go,' she thought, but she was so happy and comfortable where she was she did not move.

She lay back and watched the drifting clouds pass by for a long while and then told herself again that she must go.

She sat up and noticed with some alarm that the mist had completely covered the lake now and was creeping up the mound on which she was seated.

Startled, she stared into the uncertain moving cloud, and saw the faint figure of a woman emerging towards her.

For what might have been an instant or a million sun cycles the two women stared at each other, Kyra and the beautiful wife of the long dead King, and then with a sharp intake of breath Kyra realized where she was and what was happening.

She jumped to her feet, a sharp pang of fear stabbing through her heart.

'There is no lake!' she cried aloud, 'No water birds swimming on water, no mist, no beautiful living Queen!'

And with that cry the whole scene changed and she was alone and frightened on the mound, with a dry plain beside her, and a cloudless sky above her.

She scrambled down the slope as fast as she could.

What further role these ancient actors were to demand of her she did not wish to think about.

Khu-ren was almost knocked down by the force by which she flung herself upon him as he emerged from the Temple.

He tried to hold her off and steady her at least until they could reach a place of greater privacy, but she was in such a state of perturbation, he could do nothing but put his arm about her and lead her boldly off in front of everyone.

So disturbed was she that the story came out backwards and the news about the lady of the lake came before the news that Kyra was with child.

Khu-ren was bewildered at first, but eventually made sense of it all.

'So,' he said calmly, 'we are to have a child.'

'Yes!' shouted Kyra as though he should have grasped this point a long time ago.

'This probably explains why you have not been too successful with your "travelling" ', he said with maddening self-control.

'Forget the "travelling" !' cried Kyra in exasperation, her own feelings in the matter having changed since she had spoken to Fern. 'That is not important! What is important is that our love has given us a child!'

'Hmm,' he said, but he could not keep the act up much longer and when she threw something at him his face broke into the expression of delight he was really feeling.

'I have decided everything,' Kyra said later. 'I refuse to let this interfere in any way with your life.'

He looked at her and laughed.

'And how do you propose to manage that, my love?'

'Well, I will leave the Temple and become an ordinary mother living in Fern's village. You will continue with your work here as though nothing has happened . . . but perhaps . . . you will visit us from time to time?' Her voice had started very briskly on this proposal but by the end it had trailed off somewhat into a kind of pleading query.

'Oh,' he said, his dark eyes sparkling with mockery. 'That is very kind of you.'

'Seriously . . .' she said.

'Seriously?' and he laughed again.

'Well . . .' she began to wriggle a bit with embarrassment. 'What do you suggest then?' She demanded at last, quite flushed.

'I suggest we marry. No!' he said and put his finger to her

lips to stop her interrupting. 'Listen for once. You will leave your studies for a while and when you are ready to take them up again we will continue with them until you join me as Lord of the Sun.'

'But . . .'

'Our child will live within the Temple community and have great advantages. If he shows signs of power he will be trained as priest. If not he will choose whatever else he wishes to do . . .'

'But . . . how will I look after him properly if I am working as a priest?'

'You will find a way.'

'You make it sound easy.'

'It will not be easy. I do not promise you that. We will have strains upon us that at times will be hard to bear, and he will have pressures that perhaps a child in an ordinary family would not have . . . but . . . I am sure for all that he would not wish that he had not been born, nor us that we had not brought him into Life.'

'And what of the others?'

'What others?'

'Other children if we marry?'

Khu-ren was silent for a while.

'We have started on a course we both knew we should avoid. We did not avoid it. Now we must follow it through and make of it what we can.

'If it means giving up everything we expected of life, then that is how it must be. There are many ways to live a life and there is no going back now.'

She was silent at last.

He was wise, and she loved and trusted him.

Wardyke's War

Kyra slipped into the new way of living quickly and more easily than she had thought she would.

She left the classes of 'spirit-travelling', but there were a great many other things she still needed to learn and for some of them she joined her old friends Lea and Vann again. Both had been inaugurated as village priests and both had chosen to remain at the Temple for further training. Most of their original class had left and the three grew closer together than ever before.

Her husband had a great deal to do but they had many times of tenderness and peace together.

The Lord Guiron had blessed their marriage in a formal but simple ceremony, but Kyra could not shake off the feeling that he had some kind of premonition or foreboding about it. His words almost took the form of a spell to avoid harm rather than of the usual marriage blessing, and she noticed him many times looking at her in a strange, gloomy and penetrating way.

She tried not to worry but knowing the extent of his powers as a prophet and priest, she was very ill at ease and found herself trying to avoid his presence.

As the child came nearer to birth she had to face another problem.

Day after day she had an overwhelming longing to visit the Haunted Mound and the site of the old lake. She was determined not to go there again after her last experience, but she had to fight something in herself to stay away.

Fern and Karne were having their troubles too.

Isar was no longer young enough to keep under surveillance all the time. He had grown very tall for his eight summers. He was handsome and proud and did not care to be told what he should do or not do. Both Karne and Fern respected him for this, but given the circumstances of his past it made it more difficult for them to keep him from harm. They fortified him as best they could with the beliefs and understandings that they had of life, but they had the impression that he did not always agree with them. Other influences were at work upon him at the same time and he was young and impressionable, not always capable of seeing things as clearly as an experienced person might.

Wardyke became the right hand of his Spear-lord, Hawk-Eagle, and encouraged trouble between his master and Olan. The two land owners were constantly quarrelling, the ownership of the lands bordering each other always in question.

Fern was concerned to hear the men talk of fighting for the land, the one determined to oust the other.

'But this is foolishness!' Fern cried to Karne. 'There is enough for both.'

'Try telling that to old Hawk-Eagle! It is he who is always taking more. Olan has given in many times to keep the peace, but he is gradually being squeezed into a position where there is not enough land to feed his own people. We cannot let Hawk-Eagle take any more. *That* would be foolishness!'

'Surely you can talk to him?'

Karne laughed.

'Of course we have *talked* my love! But Hawk-Eagle does not understand our language, and of course now he has Wardyke at his elbow all the time there is even less chance of a reasonable settlement.'

'What about the priests at the Temple? Can you not ask them to settle it?'

'I am afraid, my sweet innocent, the priests at the Temple are so busy reaching for the other kinds of reality, they do not pay much attention to this one!'

'I am sure that is not true!' Fern said indignantly.

'True or not, it is none of their affair. We must settle this between ourselves.'

Karne had become Olan's most respected friend and tenant, and Wardyke Hawk-Eagle's. It was strange how another confrontation between these old enemies seemed now inevitable.

Fern thought of calling on Kyra for assistance, but knowing that her time for delivery was near and having heard that she had not been at all well of late, she thought she had better not worry her.

Isar spent more and more time away from home, and when questioned where he had been boldly refused to answer.

One day Karne came storming home, his face a study in the conflicting emotions of anger and anxiety.

'Do you know where that boy is this very moment?' he demanded of his wife.

She looked startled.

'With Wardyke! And that is where he has been every time we have asked him for his whereabouts and he has not replied.'

Fern felt sick with worry, more for the fact that the boy was keeping his meetings with Wardyke secret from them than that he was with the man. After all, they had not forbidden him to see him.

Such a little while ago they had been so close and happy together, but recently she had noticed a sullen streak, a secretive look. She might have guessed Wardyke was behind it.

When he returned that evening she contrived to speak with him without Karne being present. She did not want the confrontation to be an angry one.

'I hear,' she said gently, 'you have been spending a great deal of time with Wardyke and Hawk-Eagle lately?'

The boy looked at her with expressionless eyes. He neither denied it, nor agreed with it.

'You know, of course, that Hawk-Eagle and Olan are enemies?'

'I know.'

'Do you know the reasons?'

181

'Olan tries to keep land that is rightfully Hawk-Eagle's away from him.'

'That is not so, but we will not discuss that now.'

'What then?' the boy said coldly.

She hated the way he spoke and how he had changed. She thought back to the time when he used to sit peacefully creating beauty with his wood carving. He had not touched his tools for a long while now. Wardyke had always had the power to destroy what was good and creative in people and bring out what was destructive and restless.

'You know Karne and I do not like Wardyke, nor trust him.'

'I know.'

'And yet you still see more of him than of us?'

'He is my father,' the boy said, lifting his head defiantly.

'Yes,' she said and her voice had lost its gentleness and had an edge of great bitterness to it. 'Yes, you can call him that, if that is what you mean by "father"!'

The boy was silent.

'You know he forced himself on me and I hated and feared him?'

Again Isar did not reply, but she thought she detected a slight uncertainty in his eyes. This was not quite how Wardyke told the story.

'Karne has brought you up, fed you, protected you and loved you. To me *that* is fathering!'

'What if Wardyke is sorry for what he did and wants to make amends?' Isar's voice was less cold now, less sure that he was right.

'Then we will welcome him as friend,' Fern said, 'but do you think this is how it is? Think.'

Isar thought.

'He does not visit as a friend, but entices you away and makes you lie to us and keep secrets from us. He encourages a man to rise in violence against another man, knowing that in the process Karne who has cherished you, and even your mother, may very well be killed. Does this seem like "trying to make amends" to you? Or does it seem like vengeance?'

Isar was still silent, his face dark and confused.

'I will say no more about it, nor will I forbid you to see Wardyke. See him, but *think* about what you see. You are old enough now to judge for yourself.'

She left him alone and went for a walk in her garden, trying to regain her peace of mind, trying to calm the anger and the hate that still burned for Wardyke in her heart.

She did not know how to break the link between Wardyke and Isar. It was of double strength if Kyra's amazing story had any truth in it. Not only was Isar Wardyke's natural son, but they had been friends for long ages before she or Karne had ever come between them.

In a moment of despair she thought she would abandon all efforts to interfere in what must be a very strong and significant liaison and then her love for Isar, the boy, her child, and the thought that whether she liked it or not she *had* become involved in this ancient drama and must have some role to play, decided her to keep trying, keep loving, keep interfering.

The day before Kyra's child was born the longing to visit the Haunted Mound grew so overwhelmingly strong that she slipped away from the Temple College without Khu-ren's knowledge and walked the distance as though in a dream, all rational control gone.

She was not well, and had not been for some time, but she *had* to reach the mound!

Busy about their own affairs, no one paid particular attention to the young priestess, heavy with child, and clad in a long, flowing blue cloak, passing their way and climbing the steep sides of the forbidding man-made mountain.

Out of breath and dizzy with the strain of it she flung herself down on the top and sobbed with relief. She did not know why she felt so relieved, she knew only that those long days of fighting and struggling within herself to stay away from this place were over and she was where she was meant to be.

After a while she fell asleep with exhaustion and the dream (or vision?) that came to her was not a comforting one.

She was lying on a couch somewhere in a strange and foreign place and her body was racked with the most terrible pains she had ever felt. This time she knew it was her own pain she was suffering and not that of anyone else. There was no cry for help except from herself and, although she could feel the pain, she could not move her limbs, nor open her mouth to utter the cry for Khu-ren that she longed to give.

In the dark recesses of the hall around her she saw her old enemies, the demons, half-animal, half-man that had haunted her before. They were crouching and leering, occasionally taking a darting step forward and then retreating to the shadows again, as though they were waiting for the pain to increase and she to become weaker before they dared approach too near.

Fear and pain occupied her entirely and she felt desperately alone.

She called in her mind for Khu-ren, for Maal, for all her Spirit Lords and at each call the demons cringed as though they had felt a lash. But she began to feel weaker and weaker with pain and even her mind-calling began to fade, and her tormentors, noticing this, drew nearer.

Suddenly, through an archway that she had not noticed before two figures came and stood one on each side of her.

Through her agony she recognized the tall and bulky figure of the ancient King she had seen in the Field of the Grey Gods and the tall and elegant figure of the sad Queen of the lake mist.

They had walked into the room together, but as though they were not aware of each other's presence. Now, standing on either side of her, their eyes met and it seemed as though they noticed each other for the first time.

Great joy came over their faces and they took each other's hands and held them over her and then, as silently as they had come, they walked away, but this time hand in hand and very much aware of each other.

While they were present the demons held back, but as soon as they had disappeared through the archway, they surged forward and, screaming with agony, Kyra was torn apart.

As darkness and pain overwhelmed her, she was shaken awake by a hand and she found a startled Isar looking into her eyes.

'Kyra!' he was calling. 'What is the matter? Why are you screaming?'

She sat up at once trembling with the horror of the experience and flung her arms around her young nephew.

'Why are you crying? What is the matter? Are you in pain?'

She heard his anxious questions, but could not answer them.

'I am going to die,' she kept thinking. 'That dream means that I am going to die!'

And now she knew why she had come to the Haunted Mound.

The child she was bearing would be Isar's Queen, but in bearing her she was going to die.

'No,' she sobbed, 'no! I will not! I will not!'

'Kyra, let me take you home to mother,' the anxious boy pleaded, pulling at her arm.

'No!' screamed Kyra and with astounding force she pushed him aside and stood as tall as she was capable of upon the very top of the burial mound.

She shook her fist at the sky.

'I will not die!' she shouted fiercely. 'I will play my part if I must, but I *will not* die!'

'I am *Me*! Kyra. I have my own destiny . . . not yours alone!'

'What are you talking about?' the bewildered boy thought she had gone mad.

She looked at him suddenly and there was hate in her eyes.

'I do not see why I have to die for *you*!' she spat out.

'Kyra!' he gasped.

And then she fainted.

He stared at her in horror for a few moments, convinced that she was dead, and then turned and ran to fetch help.

When Kyra became conscious again she was in Fern's house and in extreme pain. She remembered the dream and it was as though the pain she was feeling was the same. The terror on her face startled Fern.

'Do not be afraid, my love, it is only the baby coming. Nothing to be afraid of.'

'Khu-ren,' sobbed Kyra, sweat pouring from her.

'He is coming,' soothed Fern. 'Isar has gone to fetch him.'

'Fern, I am going to die,' Kyra burst out.

'Nonsense,' said Fern calmly. 'There is a new life coming here, not an old one going!'

'I had a dream . . .' gasped Kyra.

Fern wiped the sweat and tears gently from her face.

'I do not know anything about a dream, but I do know a great deal about having babies. You are having a bad time, but you are not going to die.'

'But I dreamt . . .'

'I do not want to hear about any old dream!' Fern said sharply. 'You priests know a great deal, but not everything. Dreams can be misinterpreted just like everything else, and you know as well as I do that if you believe you are going to die, you lessen your chances of living.

'Now stop being a priest for a moment and be a *woman*. Push!' she commanded.

Kyra pushed.

Meanwhile Isar had found Khu-ren and the two were hurrying back to Isar's home. As they went the boy told Khu-ren the circumstances of how he had found Kyra and the strange things that she had said.

Khu-ren's face grew darker and darker.

'Boy, I am going to run and my legs are longer than yours. I would be grateful if you would return to the Temple and find the Lord High Priest, and bring him to your home.'

Isar turned instantly and was gone.

He was really troubled by Kyra's insistence that she would have to die for *him*.

By some strange quirk of fate Hawk-eagle and Wardyke chose this night of all nights to attack the village of Olan. Of course they had no way of knowing about the drama that was being acted out in Fern's little house. Karne himself was unaware of it as he had been all day with Olan preparing defences, knowing that the time was near when the talking and the insulting would stop and the violence begin.

Fern had been too occupied with the crisis of the moment to send word to him and could think only of fetching Khu-ren and seeing Kyra safely through the delivery of her child.

It was obvious to her the birth was not going as well as her own had done and that Kyra and her child were in very great danger, but she managed to keep her fear from showing and continued to help her friend in every way she could, with calmness and fortitude, praying all the while for the arrival of Kyra's husband.

The dream Kyra kept muttering about seemed to be their worst enemy. There were times when Fern felt Kyra was so sure she was going to die, she just seemed to give up trying to live. At those times Fern used all her energy of love to sustain her, but if Khu-ren did not arrive soon she did not know how much longer she could keep her going.

The attack Hawk-Eagle and Wardyke had planned to launch that night was delayed a while because Wardyke had intended Isar to be at his side and Isar had disappeared. He had been in the village all day seeing the preparations for the attack. Wardyke had thought the boy had seemed a bit restless and unsettled and if he had not been so busy himself he would have worried about it. As it happened it was only when the moment for attack arrived that Wardyke realized Isar was missing and something was wrong.

He tried to stall Hawk-Eagle for as long as he could without telling him his reasons, torn between the two fears, one that the boy was in the victim village and would be destroyed with the other villagers, and two that he had betrayed them and the other village was prepared for the attack.

Isar had been very uncertain of his loyalties since his talk with his mother. He had grown very close to Wardyke with the help of Panora and had thought his loyalties lay with him, but since his mother had commanded him to think for himself, he had been noticing things about Wardyke that he had not noticed before. Things he did not like.

Wardyke himself had been so busy plotting with Hawk-Eagle he had not noticed the change in the boy.

Confused and distressed by the violence that was threatening to break upon the people he now realized he truly loved, the boy left Hawk-Eagle's village determined to warn Karne, but en route for his home he had seen Kyra upon the Haunted Mound and had become enmeshed in that particular crisis, totally forgetting the other.

In some ways he had always felt the talk of attack was just talk. He never really believed Hawk-Eagle and Wardyke would do it, though within the last few days he had realized Hawk-Eagle's greed for more land and power was very strong indeed, well matched by Wardyke's greed for vegeance against Karne who had been the instrument of his downfall as magician-priest.

It was when he finally grasped that real violence was to occur that Isar knew that he had to choose, and he chose to return to Karne and Fern.

But it was perhaps his former affection for Wardyke that made it easier for him to forget the urgency of the message he should have delivered to Karne and Olan when another crisis arose.

Wardyke thought he had some control over the situation but he reckoned without Hawk-Eagle's own personality. Having decided to attack, and this had been largely on Wardyke's recommendation, he would not be held back.

If the boy had gone back to his old friends, too bad for the boy. All the more reason to start advancing before they had too much time to prepare a defence.

Wardyke was torn between his love for Isar and his hatred of Karne and Fern.

But his wishes no longer carried any weight. As before, he had unleashed forces of hate and violence in people he no longer could control.

The attack was launched.

Fern struggling with Kyra was horrified to hear the sound of shouting, fighting, screaming, the roar of flames, distant at first but coming nearer all the time.

She feared for Karne, for her children sleeping snugly in the other room, for Kyra struggling to give birth. She feared for Isar somewhere on the road to or from the Temple and prayed now that he would not return, but that someone would see their plight and come to their aid. But she knew these villages were small and the wooden houses easily burnt. Before help could reach them there would be nothing left but cinders and charred bones.

She had a terrible choice to make, to seize her children and run, leaving Kyra who could not be moved to face death alone.

She screamed to all the Spirit Lords that ruled the world to help her in this, the worst moment of her life. She could not leave and yet she could not stay!

As though in answer to her prayer the hanging rug that covered the doorway to her house was swept aside and the Lord Khu-ren strode into the room.

'Go!' he shouted at her. 'Take your children and go!'

She gathered them up and ran, as she saw him bending over Kyra.

Outside was chaos and confusion.

The men were fighting as best they could, but fire arrows were being shot by skilled bowmen at the straw roofs of the houses and the men were hindered by the smoke and flames, and the fleeing, screaming women and children.

Briefly, in the light of flame, she saw Karne and Wardyke locked in battle, both using the long daggers the Spear-lords had introduced into the country.

Olan was on the ground with Hawk-Eagle's spear through his stomach.

She looked no more, but ran, her heart breaking.

In Fern's abandoned house, the roof on fire, Kyra gave the last push that brought her baby into life.

Guiron and Isar entered and it was Guiron who seized the child and ran with her to safety.

Khu-ren lifted his unconscious wife.

Isar seized a cudgel that he used for practice fighting and ran wildly towards the battle, his eyes ablaze.

'Wardyke!' he screamed seeing Wardyke about to drive his dagger through Karne's fallen body.

Wardyke looked up and saw his son, his ancient friend, with cudgel raised in hate and anger against him.

'My King!' he cried.

'No!' Isar shouted. 'That was another time. Another place. *Now* Wardyke . . . *now* is the time to live!'

And he stood so fiercely strange, this boy who was at once a boy and yet a King, that Wardyke fumbled with his dagger and dropped it, and stood staring, not knowing what to do.

And in that moment one of the fire arrows loosed from the bow of one of Hawk-Eagle's men, passed through his heart and he fell in death.

'No!' cried Isar, and a boy again in tears, he flung himself upon Wardyke's body, but there was no way he could bring him back to life.

Karne staggered to his feet in time to see Hawk-Eagle raise his dagger against the boy and with a cry of rage he stepped between them, his love for Isar giving sudden strength to his already wounded body.

Hawk-Eagle fell and rose no more.

The new Spear-lord and the new 'Traveller'

Many days and nights passed before Kyra regained consciousness, but when she did she was amazed to find herself still alive.

Ashen and pale and thin she was, but still very much alive.

She looked around her room savouring each familiar thing.

'I did not die!' she whispered to herself with joy. 'I did not die!'

And then she remembered her baby, and her head turned with anxiety to look for her.

'Yes,' Fern said gently, sitting beside her. 'Your baby is safe too.'

Kyra smiled with great joy.

'A girl?'

'A girl,' Fern confirmed.

'I will call her Deva. It means "shining one" in a language I once heard in a dream.'

'You and your dreams!' teased Fern. 'I thought you said you dreamed you were going to die?'

Kyra was too weak to say any more, but she smiled a very little ashamed smile.

Fern kissed her.

'Yes,' she said, 'I know your next question. He has been with you day and night all the time. He will be back in a few moments.'

Kyra shut her eyes, this time to sleep in peace.

When she awoke the Lord Khu-ren was beside her.

When Kyra was a little stronger they had a simple ceremony to bless and name the baby in the room where she lay, as she was still too weak to move.

Karne was there, bound with bandages but in reasonable health, and Fern with their children, Isar standing separately like a man in his own right looking with very shining and loving eyes on the new baby who was dark of complexion like the Lord Khu-ren and the original Queen who had lived so long ago and had been his wife.

The Lord Guiron performed the ceremony and the blessing with humility and warmth.

There seemed to be no shadows present except perhaps for Panora who watched from the background with a peculiar brooding look in her eyes, unnoticed by the others.

Deva smiled when she was named.

Indeed a shining one!

'Is she not beautiful?' Kyra whispered to Khu-ren.

'You are both beautiful,' he said with a smile and put his arms around the two of them.

'Come,' Fern said firmly to the others, 'we must leave Kyra to rest now. She is very weak and if Deva is anything like my children she will need a great deal of looking after.'

Kyra was too weak for a long time to take care of Deva properly. Fern stayed with her, glad of the temporary home for her small family since their own had been burned to the ground.

When Karne and Isar returned to the village the day after the birth of Deva they found a desolation worse than they had expected. There were very few houses still standing but fortunately there were fewer dead in either village than Karne would have thought possible in such a fierce battle. The survivors who had fled in the night had returned to wander aimlessly among the ruins of their homes, uncertain of what to do next.

Isar slipped away from Karne and sought out the body of Wardyke. It was lying where it had fallen, so burnt and charred it was almost unrecognizable.

The boy squatted beside it and wept, his heart almost breaking. There had been so much of Time and Mystery, love and treachery and pain in their relationship and now Isar knew in a way he could not have explained that his path and Wardyke's would not cross again.

In the moment he had denied the past, he had broken free

192

of Wardyke's spell, a spell that had been upon him since before he left their home in the land of the Long River and the desert that flowered after every flood. It was his friendship for Wardyke who was in trouble and was sentenced to death that had made them flee across the sea and come to this strange and barbarous land.

It was Wardyke's idea that he should set himself up as King and Wardyke who organized the ignorant wandering tribes to pay tribute to him and build his palace and supply him with his wealth. Wardyke who sniffed out gold like a dog sniffed excrement. Wardyke who destroyed his enemies, manoeuvred his friends, while he and his beautiful Queen lived in love and joy, thoughtless of anything that could harm them or change their earthly paradise.

When a certain chieftain had come to their court, joined the feasting and the hunting, it was Wardyke who had warned that he was not to be trusted. But thinking that it was jealousy because this man was the first he had loved beside Wardyke himself, Isar had taken no notice.

For the first time he had not taken Wardyke's counsel and it was his undoing.

Many times since then the three of them had been reborn in other lands, in other worlds. The old score had at last been settled and he had been at peace upon a world in another galaxy, a world of many suns where light was danger and they had lived in darkness underground, seeing with their minds, peaceful amongst themselves.

The ache of longing for his Queen who had never been reborn, but had clung tenaciously to the place where she had died, had at last healed. He lived with no memory of this ancient wound.

And then, in the darkness that was not darkness to him, he had suddenly felt a shaft of pain through his heart and his friends mourned his death.

In that instant he was conceived in the womb of Fern, called thither by Wardyke's relentless spirit.

The stirrings of these memories had been with him since his birth, like dark shadows at the corner of his eye which, when he turned his head, he could not see.

In dreams images haunted him from the past, but he only partially recognized them, and the soft arms of his mother had dispelled many of the dark traces from his mind.

Standing on top of that ancient hill, surveying the lake, he had remembered, fleetingly, and again on his one-time throne . . . but in each case the memory had slipped like a dream slips, like an adder slips under rocks, to lie in darkness biding its time, but out of reach of the conscious mind.

It was only at the moment when he faced Wardyke in battle and saw his weapon raised to kill Karne whom he loved, the moment that Wardyke called him King, that the whole memory had come flooding back and he knew he had to make a choice.

The choice was made in an instant from deep inside himself and there was no going back.

But now beside the body of his friend his heart ached and he wished life's justice was not so long and so inexorable.

He felt a hand upon his shoulder and looked up to find Karne beside him, looking on him with great tenderness and understanding.

He stood up.

'We have to attend to the burials and the rebuilding,' Karne said quietly. 'No one else seems to know what to do.'

He looked at Isar deeply.

'I need your help,' he said with humility.

Isar looked from Wardyke's body, to the living warmth of love in Karne's eyes.

'You have it,' he said with dignity.

Karne bowed his head slightly and the two began the task of making order out of chaos.

As soon as someone took the initiative the helpless villagers were willing enough to work. They had been used to a Spear-lord and an ordered routine and they seemed to need someone to tell them what to do. Without meaning to take over Olan's place, Karne found himself issuing orders.

In the bustle of work Isar's painful memories faded and he found comfort as a boy again, running messages for Karne, organizing the clearing of the old burnt wood away and advising where new timber suitable for building could be found.

Karne noticing that many of Hawk-Eagle's villagers were wandering among his own with as much despair upon their faces and with expressions that showed they were equally at a loss to know what now to do with their lives, and, suspecting that the villagers themselves had not had much to say in the attack but had just been doing what they had been told to do by their Spear-lord, he gathered them together and made a great and moving speech suggesting they all forget the past and join together to rebuild the future. There were not many dissenters to this idea. Quite a few of the villagers had sons or daughters who had married into the other village, and relatives and friends had been involved in the fighting, caught up by Hawk-Eagle and Wardyke in a war that was not really their war.

Isar stood beside Karne on this, and Hawk-Eagle's people, recognizing him as Wardyke's son and hearing him join with Karne to plead for peace, agreed.

Sadly not only Olan had been killed in the fighting, but his beautiful daughter as well, and Olan's widow was now alone.

The bodies of the dead of both sides were gathered and a great funeral pyre was built.

But those of Olan and his daughter and of Hawk-Eagle were kept separate for they were of the tribe that had separate burial mounds.

That night there was great sorrow and mourning.

Priests from the Temple arrived and the High Priest, Lord Guiron, said words of comfort and prayer to the bereaved from his own heart, as well as the ritual words that were expected of him.

Karne watched him very closely, wondering what he was thinking and if he remembered anything of his old connection with Wardyke and the young boy who stood beside him, mourning.

But if he did, he gave no sign.

The words were simple, moving and sincere.

When the ashes the following dawn were gathered and placed in pottery urns for burial, Panora slipped forward and placed a garland of flowers around Wardyke's urn. Karne could see that she was weeping and as she turned to leave he caught a look in her eye towards the Lord Guiron and the boy Isar that chilled his blood.

The old score was not settled as far as she was concerned and she would not let it rest.

But Isar did not see it. He carried Wardyke's ashes to the burial place and laid them down with the others killed in battle, Panora's flowers still upon the urn.

That day passed in raising the burial mounds.

The next in clearing the ground for rebuilding.

And the third day they started serious work on reconstruction.

While Khu-ren was with Kyra, and Fern was temporarily released from her duties as nurse, she returned to see what she could salvage of her old home.

Olan's wife found her there sad among the trampled ruins of her garden, thinking of Wardyke and how years ago he had destroyed with fire her beautiful living wood. She sat on the ground and lifted broken fronds and branches gently, seeing how much she would have to cut away to let the new growth through, speaking words of comfort and tenderness to them.

Olan's wife watched her for a while and then moved closer to her.

'Have you words of comfort for me too?' she said with pain. 'Olan and my daughter have no roots hidden in the earth to send up leaves again in Spring.'

Fern looked up at her and opened her arms. The proud, tall woman, the warrior Spear-lord's wife, sat upon the earth and buried her face in the peasant girl's breast.

Fern kissed her and stroked her hair.

'*I* have no words,' she said softly. 'The words are in your own heart. Listen to them.'

The older woman's tears fell upon the young woman's arm.

'Sssh,' Fern whispered. 'Listen to them.'

Gradually Olan's wife quietened and she lay listening to the beat of Fern's heart, puzzling a little about what Fern meant, wondering what she was supposed to hear.

She began to feel drowsy and at peace. Sleep had not come her way since that terrible night. Fern rocked her gently and whether she was asleep or not she did not know, but she felt a calmness come over her, a calmness which seemed to shade into a feeling first as though there were a glimmering of hope and then growing into the strength of a conviction.

Wherever she looked in Nature there were correspondences that ran through the lives of everything, a cyclical pattern, a constant ending and beginning, destroying and renewing, and wherever she looked she saw *no waste*. Everything that existed continued, even if in another form. She thought about the caterpillar and the butterfly. She thought about the fallen dead leaves in a forest, nourishing the new and living tree. If such things were without exception in Nature, Man, the most complicated and subtle creature of all, the most difficult to bring to maturity, would hardly be the only one to be denied renewal, the only one to be *wasted*. The slow and painful struggle he had to reach complex consciousness *must* be for some continuing purpose.

Olan's wife opened her eyes and there were now no tears in them.

She looked at Fern and Fern knew she had heard the words in her own heart.

'You see!' she said gently, releasing her from her embrace.

'I see,' the woman said.

With Karne's supervision and energetic work the stricken homes began to rise again, but almost without anyone realizing it the two villages that had been so separate and so

197

different began to merge into one large straggling village with a great deal more open space between the houses than there had been before. Not everyone rebuilt their homes in exactly the same place, relatives in one village moved nearer to relatives in the other, some chose new land but some stayed with the old.

Also, without anyone realizing it, Karne was increasingly consulted on every decision that had to be made. At first he turned always to Olan's widow for the final permission for any move, but she knew as well as he did that the decision was always his, and she agreed almost without thinking to whatever he proposed.

At last she said he need not consult her any more but do as he thought fit.

Hawk-Eagle had no wife, nor heir, and so his people tended to turn to Karne too.

On the day the last house was rebuilt the villages decided to hold a celebration.

Kyra was still too weak to attend, but Fern and her whole family were there and all the people from both villages gathered round one central fire and drank strong ale and feasted well into the night.

At the height of the festivities Olan's widow called for silence and was placed high upon a rough platform of wooden beams.

The tall woman stood beautiful and elegant in the firelight and the villagers gradually became silent, all faces turned to her.

'It is not easy for me to speak without my husband at my side,' Olan's widow said, 'but what I have to say I say with his authority behind me.

'Before he died,' and here her voice broke slightly, but she resumed in clear and ringing tones within moments, 'his most trusted friend and confidant was Karne whom I think you all know.' She turned and pointed to Karne who was standing near the platform with his arm around Fern and his latest baby on his shoulder.

A cheer went up that rang so loud the very sky seemed to

receive it!

Fern flushed with pride and turned her face into her husband's shoulder.

He looked embarrassed.

'With your permission,' and Olan's wife looked around smiling at the happy, friendly faces around her, 'I would like to ask Karne to be Spear-lord of this fine new village in the place of both Hawk-Eagle and Olan.'

Another cheer went up.

She held up her hand for silence as the cheering seemed to be getting out of hand.

'You will know it is not the custom for one of the local people to be the Spear-lord of a village. In asking this I am breaking with long years of history and there are many people who might object most strongly to this move.'

Cries of 'No! No!' came from the crowd.

'Other Spear-lords in other communities,' she reminded them, and the crowd grew silent to think about this. This could be dangerous.

It was indeed a break with custom and with history.

Karne thought about it too and knew that it was honour beyond his dreams, but responsibility and challenge as well.

He looked at Fern.

She shook her head slightly.

'It must be your decision,' she said softly but firmly.

He looked around at the faces of the villagers. He knew they wanted him. He knew he was capable of the task. But . . . Hawk-Eagle was not the only member of the Spear-lord race who wished to keep their ancient privileges to himself.

'What do you say, Karne?' Olan's widow looked at him straight and steadily. 'My husband believed your people were ready for responsibility and this made him many enemies. What do you say?'

Karne took a deep breath and stepped up to join her on the platform.

'I say Olan was right and I will stake my life to prove him so!'

The roar of approval that went up this time could be heard

199

far and wide and could not be stopped by any one until it had spent itself naturally.

The dancing and the singing that followed this was truly wild and joyful.

Dark destruction past, the moment of regneration is always one of joy.

Within the next few days calmer discussions were held both with the villagers and the Inner Council of the Priests at the Temple.

It was agreed after some small dissension, that though unorthodox, the move was a good one.

Karne was installed as Spear-lord in a ceremony presided over by the Lord High Priest, and given official authority by the highest powers in the Temple. They hoped by this means to avert angry reaction from other Spear-lords who feared their positions would be usurped by commoners and local peasants.

Messengers were sent across the land where the rule of the Spear-lords had most hold, to explain that it was now possible in certain very specific circumstances, for a local man held in great respect by the community, to succeed a Spear-lord, but only at the discretion of the Priests of the Inner Council of the Temple, and after rigorous investigation.

He would hold his authority in trust for the Temple and it would be removed from him if he abused it.

Olan's wife bade farewell to the village she had lived in for so long and returned to the house of her parents.

Fern and Karne moved into the Great House and within days Isar began carving every wooden post and beam he could find in it with beautiful designs.

Karne took charge of the running of the village and Fern set about creating another garden that would bring delight and peace to all who walked in it.

Meanwhile Kyra gradually grew stronger, but Vann who attended her as Healer had to tell her that in bearing Deva she had suffered such damage that she would never again be able to bear a child.

When she heard this she dropped her face into her hands and sobbed, but the Lord Khu-ren who came to her soon after this took her hands and lifted up her face.

'My lady,' he said tenderly, 'we have Deva and we have each other. Why do you weep?'

She felt ashamed and dried her eyes.

Deva fed upon her mother's milk and grew delightfully round and rosy.

When Kyra could walk again she carried her on her hip everywhere she went and talked to her as though she could understand all the things her mother said. Deva chuckled and looked around with large, dark eyes as though she were surprised and joyful to be alive.

'Do you think she will have powers to be a priest?' Kyra asked Khu-ren eagerly. 'She should, with both of us so deeply involved.'

He smiled and shrugged.

'She is herself,' he said.

A shadow crossed Kyra's face.

'Is she?' she asked sadly. 'Remember the dream I had upon the Haunted Mound the night she was born? I sometimes wonder,' and her face was pensive, 'what claim we have upon her if she is that ancient Queen . . .'

Khu-ren kissed her into silence.

'She is Deva now . . . our child . . . enjoy her . . . love her. When she is grown to be a woman it will be her decision what place she takes. You know as well as I do that no one is born exactly as they were in a previous life. The differences in Deva and in Isar now may change the destiny that seems to us so closely and inevitably linked.'

'But the dream?'

He smiled.

'You thought it meant that you would die in bearing her!'

Kyra laughed.

'Oh well,' she said, 'I see I am not to be allowed to worry!'

'That is right,' he said, and left her.

Gradually Kyra resumed her studies and her work. Deva was looked after by Fern while her mother was busy, and the great house of the Spear-lord Karne became a second home to her.

Isar was always at her side and it was he who taught her how to walk and how to say her name.

Kyra had made it clear that Panora was not to be allowed anywhere near her daughter and if Panora was at Fern's house Deva was to be brought instantly back to her mother.

Fern's first trust in Panora had disappeared, but the girl still came to the house as though she were welcome, and Fern could not bring herself to be unkind to her. She was always ill at ease when the girl was around and kept a close watch on the children, but Panora showed no signs of harming them. She was in fact most helpful and kind, singing to them and playing with them as often as they wished.

Fern kept her word to Kyra and kept Deva out of her way, but Isar was often off with her, apparently visiting other villages far afield.

It was after such a visit when Deva was three summers old that Isar brought news to Karne that Hawk-Eagle's brother, who had been living all his life on the other side of the Western mountains, had at last received word of Karne's position in Hawk-Eagle's old village and was intending to do something about it.

'What is he intending to do?' Karne asked Isar curiously.

'That I do not know. I heard it as a rumour from people who had not even met him.'

At the time of Karne's installation as Spear-lord there had been a certain amount of restlessness amongst the warrior race, but as no one had a personal stake in the village concerned and the Priests of the Inner Council of the Temple of the Sun had great authority, nothing had been done about it, but Karne knew it would not take much to rouse them if they had a specific leader who had a claim on the village.

He was loath to give up his position now, not only because he enjoyed the responsibility it gave him, but because he felt he had really made a positive contribution to the wellbeing of his people. The village economy was healthy, the people happy and well fed. Other villagers came to admire his work, and the carvings of Isar upon the houses were becoming famous.

He had introduced the system of the Seven Elders from his home community and the villagers really felt it was their village and took great pride in it.

His greatest triumph was that several Spear-lords in the district, on seeing how well the community was run, had allowed their villages the privilege of the Seven Elder system. They still retained ultimate control, but many matters were turned over to the Elders, and the Council of Elders could bring to the attention of the Spear-lord any problem the villagers had that the Spear-lord might have overlooked.

On the other hand, other lords, those who had been Olan's enemies in his lifetime, turned the other way and became more self-assertive, determined not to relinquish the smallest part of their power and privilege.

During the first processional Karne and Fern attended, walking with the traditional splendour of the warrior caste behind the priests along the Sacred Way, they could feel the antagonism building up around them, particularly as the crowd cheered incessantly whenever they appeared.

Fern was afraid and her heart was very low. She had no wish to be a great lady walking in grand robes and living in a house too big for her needs. She had no wish to stir up change and restlessness. To her each person's life should be spent in perfecting his private relationship with the Universe. From this all else followed. Pushing and jostling for power positions relative to each other to her was a waste of precious time and energy, and could lead nowhere but to sterility of Spirit and thence to the destruction of the material world around.

To know one's true Self and one's position in the scheme of the true Universe could be compared to a person, seeing clearly, walking forward and attending efficiently and steadily to the real needs of his fellow human beings and the natural world of which he was an integral part.

Not to know one's true Self and one's position in the scheme of the true Universe could be compared to a blind person blundering and stumbling about in a room full of unfamiliar things, knocking them over, breaking them, and achieving nothing.

Karne would have agreed with much of this but he was caught up in action now that was running too fast to be stopped. His strength was that he had been long enough with Maal, Kyra and Fern to know the value of deep thinking, and to have a reasonably clear idea of who he was and why he was, and yet enough joy in physical and challenging action, enough excitement in quick decisiveness, to ride the coming storm with some elation.

He held his head high in the procession and his eyes sparkled to meet those of his adversaries.

He believed what he was doing was right. The old warrior caste and the old ways had served their purpose. His people, or at least some of them, were ready now to think for themselves and be more than chattels.

At the same time as these thoughts were occupying the minds of Karne and Fern, Kyra was facing the most difficult part of her training.

For years they had been trained to sense the inner levels of their own thoughts, to use them for greater understanding and awareness. They had been trained to go beyond even the innermost levels of their own consciousness and join with the great flow of spirit-consciousness all around them, again to use what they found there for greater, deeper awareness and understanding of everything, great and small, that comprised the Whole, the All.

She worked hard, struggling many times and through many difficult trials to reach the state when she could feel that she was as ready as it was possible for a human being to be to take the final step to become Lord of the Sun.

At noon on one never-to-be-forgotten summer's day she passed from Tall Stone to Tall Stone in the Northern Inner Sanctum of the Temple, touching her forehead to the Sacred Rocks until she felt their power working through her. And then, standing in the centre of the Sacred Inner Three, she closed her eyes, feeling the throbbing of their energy through her body and the strength of the earth through the bare soles of her feet.

Around her she could hear the faint swish of sound as the priests, touching hand to hand to form a continuous circle, walked round and round the outside of the Stones, adding the strength of their spiritual experience to the forces in the Circle of Stones.

She began to feel stranger and stranger, as though all the blood, all the life force in her was draining out. She briefly remembered the first time she had felt this and had thought she was dying. This time she knew better but she could not quite dispel a tiny thrill of fear as finally her body went cold and numb and she could no longer move a limb or command a single bit of it to do her bidding.

She tried to concentrate on the feeling that was coming to her from the stone. Tried to concentrate on the words that were forming in her mind that she had been taught to use at the moment of separation.

'I am not Kyra. This body I lend back to the elements from which it came. It is nothing to me. I am Nameless, Formless. I am the point of consciousness on which everything rests. I am conscious of Everything and am no longer limited by that discarded shell I see below me. I AM.'

It worked!

She could see her body surrounded by the Three Stones that symbolized the God-Spirit, its manifestation in matter, and the human Spirit which formed a bridge between the two.

She could see the priests moving and murmuring, round and round the Circle. She could see the outer Rock Circle, the earth bank beyond, the Colleges, the priests' houses, the burial mounds, the forests, fields and villages . . .

She was high . . . high . . . high . . .

She knew this time she had a particular mission. It was not enough as she had done before to blunder accidentally into far-off lands. It had been decided where she would go and whom she would meet, and her journey must be controlled and her arrival must be accurate.

She deliberately blanked her mind of any distractions, and visualized in passionate detail the mountain area her teacher, the Lord Khu-ren, had described for her.

First she saw in her mind's eye a terrain of enormous dimensions, plains that seemed to lie in baking sun forever and ever, and beyond them the rising foothills and then the mountains themselves. The greatest mountains on earth.

She visualized herself as an eagle flying closer, and as she approached the range her vision became more restricted in scope, but in detail more and more explicit.

At last she stood upon the mountain side and saw around her a proliferation of beautiful plant life, from the enormous bushes richly decked with clusters of waxy purple flowers to the tiniest ferns and mosses.

She looked around and could see for a great distance in every direction and there was no sign or mark of man anywhere.

She lifted her gaze and beyond the mountain where she stood she saw, rising to the blue immensity of the sky itself, a giant peak of virginal crystal, the sunlight glancing off the sharp facets of its sides, the rock she knew to be below the ice and snow darkly silent and brooding.

She stood very still and watched the eagle whose body she had borrowed lift off and fly to a craggy place a long way to the East.

She felt the mountain silently about her and its power was greater than the puny Stone Circles her people built to lend them strength for their little excursions into Reality.

This Rock seemed Conscious. She felt its Thought examining *her*. She was afraid of the force she felt, the unusual strength of the thoughts that came into her mind.

The air, the watching plants, the invisible rays from the mountain itself seemed to be working on her, purifying her, clarifying her mind until she could see everything, not only the things around, but everything in great and perfect detail from every angle simultaneously.

Vision upon vision of incredible intricacy arose for her and she saw the beauty of her earth contained like a leaf in amber, its own beauty far outdone by the beauty of that which contained it and was everywhere around it.

Even the crystal giant above her she could see now was just one peak in a series of peaks, each shimmering with a richer and more brilliant light.

She felt her heart would burst, unable to contain so much visionary splendour, so many feelings crowding into her of understanding and awareness. She wanted to cry to the Lord Khu-ren for help, to escape from this throbbing, powerful place. If what she had been taught about earth currents was correct this place must be the centre of them all.

Her people were right to send her to these mountains to test herself against them.

The vast energies that had formed them were still within them and she knew that now and for as long as they stood they would be a challenge worthy of any man's acceptance. Some would test themselves bodily against the rock faces and the ice and ultimately against the peak of peaks. Others would stay in meditation and in silence absorbing the spiritual energies to the limit of their endurance and capacity.

Feeling herself almost at that point she began to tremble and as though in answer to her unspoken plea for help she noticed that a man had joined her.

He came crawling out of a hole in the rock face of the mountain and stood before her blinking owlishly in the light.

He was the thinnest man she had ever seen, a skeleton with a fine white pall of skin drawn over his bones, but his eyes were alive and dynamic.

She remembered now she had seen just such a ragged, ancient, bony man amongst the grand Lords of the Sun.

'Yes,' he said smiling, and when he smiled his hideous skull face became beautiful. 'Yes, we have met before.'

She felt better now that she was no longer alone. She knew also she had succeeded in her task, because he was the man she had been sent to meet.

'My lord,' she said reverently, bowing, 'I am greatly honoured to be in your presence.'

207

He moved his bony hand to indicate the beauty of the mountains around them.

'It is not I!' he said, and she understood he meant her to be reverent towards the mountains, not to him.

'I have been sent, my lord,' she said softly, humbly, 'to learn from you.'

He smiled again, this time amused.

'And what is it that you have been sent to learn?'

'If I knew that, my lord, I would not still need to learn it!'

He nodded, pleased by her reply.

'But I can teach you nothing,' he said gravely.

'Could I at least ask you a question?'

'You may ask, of course, but whether I can answer it is another matter.'

'I must ask it. It is something that has worried me from time to time but I have never dared put it into words before.'

'Ask it then.'

'You are a man of great understanding . . . perhaps the greatest in the world . . .'

He stared at her expressionlessly, neither denying nor accepting the compliment.

'Would it not be better for the world if you were among people giving of your understanding to them . . . helping them with their lives . . . rather than staying locked up in this cave . . . in this mountain . . . benefitting only your own spiritual development?'

She poured out the words, horrified at herself, hardly realising what she was saying until she had said it.

He looked at her long and unblinkingly. It did not seem that he was offended. Nor did it seem that he intended to answer her question.

'I am sorry . . .' she stumbled out, trying to break the silence somehow.

He lifted his hand to make her silent, and then carefully chose a flat stone and sat upon it cross-legged, going almost immediately into a kind of trance.

She watched him for a while, puzzled and ill at ease, at a loss to know what to do next.

At last she felt the need to sit beside him, cross-legged too, and so she did.

She stared at the scenery around her, wondering at its beauty and its remoteness from any other living human being, and wondered about the question she had asked. She was not even sure why she had asked it because the training she had received at the College of Priests had stressed again and again the power of the flow of thought from one person to another, so that it was quite acceptable to her that a holy man or hermit, while taking no apparent part in the world's affairs, could indeed have a profound influence upon them by the strength of the beam of his trained and concentrated Thought directed into the minds of certain receptive people who were concerned in the world's affairs, and who were affecting men's lives every day, and yet had never themselves had the time or opportunity to develop their own minds to the point to which they should have been developed if they were to bear such responsibility and wield such power.

She knew also that immature and receptive people were also open to influences from unscrupulous and evil sources, and a man such as the hermit beside her had valuable work to do in intercepting and counteracting such influences.

Because he could not be *seen* to be doing anything in the Outside world most people accepted as the only world, it did not mean he was doing nothing in the worlds that existed out of sight but were just as significant.

She realised she had asked the question because she had accepted the answer when it had been given to her at the College with only part of her mind. She needed the actual experience of sitting beside this man on this mountainside (and yet in 'spirit' form only!) 'feeling' his thoughts within her head, to know that what she had been told was indeed true.

They sat in silence for a long time and Kyra had never experienced before such profundity and clarity of understanding.

She would have liked to have stayed forever, but something was pulling her away.

As though he sensed it, he looked at her and the strange,

silent spell that had been on her and in which she had understood so much was broken.

He stood up, bowed slightly to her, and returned to his cave.

She saw that the afternoon must have progressed a great deal since she arrived, and a long purple shadow from the immense peak was lying across the land almost to the horizon. Everything in its path had a strange softness as though it were dissolving.

She too stood up and forced herself to shut her eyes and remember who she was and where she had left her body.

She longed to open her eyes again, to stay in this powerful, beautiful place but she knew she was not ready to leave forever her husband and her daughter, no matter how much beauty and understanding were offered in their place.

With this thought she was home and she opened her eyes to the encircling stones of the Northern Inner Sanctum of The Temple of the Sun.

Before her stood the Lord Guiron and the Lord Khu-ren, and behind them many faces she knew of the Temple Priesthood.

She was shivering and very, very tired, but before the minutest detail of it could fade she was forced to give a description of everything in absolute completeness.

At the end she was allowed to go and she knew by the faces around her that she had passed the test.

The day of her inauguration as one of the select group of Lords of the Sun was a very great day for her.

This time after the long procession down the Sacred Way a great many of the community around were allowed into the Sacred Circle in orderly groups.

To call all the Lords of the Sun together needed great power and the Outer Circle was filled with concentric Circles of people, male and female alternately, each turning rhythmically within the next, until the Northern Inner Sanctum itself was reached and that was surrounded only by the highest priests.

Deva and Isar hand in hand were among the outermost children's circle, and Fern and Karne were with the Spear-lords and their ladies.

The fact that Karne's sister was to be inaugurated as Lord of the Sun gave him extra status in the eyes of the ruling caste, and many who were wavering which way to go now joined his side against the dissidents.

The low and vibrant sound of drumming set the pace of the circling figures.

The Lady Kyra, the Lord Guiron and the Lord Khu-ren, being the only three Lords of the Sun present, were alone in the Inner Circle, each standing regally against one of the Standing Stones, facing the great Central Three, the focus of power, their backs to the moving rings.

As the drummers increased the speed of the beat, the speed of the circling figures increased, and so did the build-up of energy.

Gradually, as the humming, vibrating note that issued from the throats of the encircling people and the drums of the drummers grew louder and louder, and the energy generated by their bodies and thoughts grew stronger and stronger, Kyra noticed changes happening within the Inner Circle.

At first a kind of flimsy shadow appeared before each unoccupied Stone, hardening at last into what appeared to be the full bodily forms of the other Lords of the Sun.

She felt great joy to see Quilla from the Island of the Bulls, now quite healed, standing straight and tall in her traditional dress, supple and graceful as ever. Kyra was glad the bull's horns had left no scars to mar her beauty, but even as she thought this a little thought that should not have entered her head as one of the Great Lords of the Sun entered hers, and she looked quickly at the Lord Khu-ren to see if he was looking at the girl of flight with more than ordinary interest. If he was, nothing showed upon his face and Kyra was ashamed to have even entertained such a thought for an instant at a time like this.

She met the eyes of the old hermit from the great mountains and she knew he at least had seen her thought. She flushed.

But his eyes were amused, not accusing.

Then there was no more time to think irrelevant thoughts. She 'left' her body against the rock and in 'spirit' form moved slowly around the Circle bowing to each Lord in turn, receiving each one's blessing, each one making a sign particular to his or her race or culture on the newcomer's forehead.

She received the sign of the Circle, the sign of the Star, the sign of the Crescent Moon, the sign of the Tree of Life . . .

The ancient hermit of the mountains made no sign at all but looked deeply into her eyes and she saw a vision of her world, among a myriad other worlds, all reflected in the small black circle in the centre of his eyes.

When she had completed the round she knelt in the centre of the Stone Circle and bowed so low that her forehead rested on the earth.

From the earth, through her forehead, she heard the drumming and the throbbing of the vibrations set up by the people of her community and she was filled with great love and a feeling that all that she heard was the beating of her own heart. She loved all things as she loved herself because they *were* Herself.

She did not know how long she stayed thus.

At last she lifted her head slowly and looked around.

The Lord Guiron, the Lord Khu-ren and the Lady Kyra were alone in the Inner Circle.

No one else was in sight.

The great Outer Circle was completely empty.

She looked dazed.

'Come,' the Lord Khu-ren said, and took her hand.

They followed the High Priest, Guiron, out and across the little wooden bridge.

The Circle of Power lay behind them, dormant.

Panora's War

Panora was not at the inauguration of Kyra as Lord of the Sun. She was in the far West visiting Hawk-Eagle's brother, Nya.

Nya had not seen his brother since they had been children and he knew nothing and cared nothing about him, his land or his people. Nya's people were mountain nomads and lived wild and scattered, coming down to the settled communities in the valleys only to raid and take what they needed for the winter months, sometimes trading their furs, sometimes not.

It was Vann, Kyra's friend, who had first brought Nya to the notice of Panora. His own family had suffered greatly at the hands of Nya and his rough people, and it was in telling the story of one of Nya's raids that Vann mentioned he was one of two sons of a man called White Hawk. Panora knew that Hawk-Eagle's father had such a name and knew also that he had died in the clutches of a bear when his sons were very young, one coming East with a relative, the other staying in the mountains.

No sooner had she skilfully extracted from Vann the exact location of Nya, than she had sent a series of messages to him bringing to his notice that his brother had been murdered and his village taken over by his murderer.

When she could slip away unnoticed herself she travelled West to seek him out, stirring trouble against Karne all the way, and promising the anxious Spear-lords a leader who would restore their threatened privileges to them.

Nya's camp was in a forest by a waterfall and Panora was treated with great suspicion when she first appeared, but so unafraid was her carriage and so flattering her words of welcome to Nya and his untidy band of ruffians that she was soon accepted and was squatting with the lord himself, tearing at a boar steak and swilling ale as though it were her usual drink.

'What is your interest in this?' Nya asked at last, when he had listened at length to Panora's speech on how it was his duty to march East and seize back his brother's land.

Panora was careful how she answered.

If she were truthful she might have said that she had no interest in the particular case at all, but that she was tormented by an ancient spite which she saw a way of satisfying by using Nya.

She was tired of the kind of servant-to-master relationship she had with her father, tired of the settled orderly existence of the Temple and the communities around it. She had a kind of aching itch deep inside her that would not be cured until everything the Lord Guiron and the Temple stood for was overturned, and Isar was King again, her mother Queen, and she a princess treated royally.

Until Wardyke's coming she had not even known what it was that ailed her and made her so dissatisfied. He had filled her head with stories of ancient times, the splendours of her mother's palace and the wrong Guiron twice had done.

He had poisoned her mind against Karne and Fern whom at first she had felt to be her friends. And when Wardyke was killed Panora had brooded long and bitterly on how she could avenge not only his death, but that of her ancient royal mother as well.

On hearing of Nya, and feeling the stirring of anxiety among the Spear-lords that their long established powers were being undermined by changes and decrees from the Inner Council of the Temple, she saw her chance.

A war would relieve her restlessness.

A war would ease her dissatisfaction. It would destroy the upstart Spear-lord and the treacherous priest.

The Temple would be razed to the ground and she would build a palace for her mother, the Queen, and her mother's chosen husband, that would out-rival the ancient palace that had stood upon the Field of the Grey Gods.

She would be powerful and grand instead of a servant-messenger, a half-grown child tolerated everywhere, but nowhere loved.

She would be the instrument of vengeance, the instrument that would change the balance of power in the whole country.

The more she thought about it the more grandiose her schemes became.

But to start them she needed to use the weapons of a band of violent men, and then she needed violence to breed violence, hate to breed hate, and in the final holocaust she needed power to destroy what she wanted to destroy, and build what she wanted to build.

She must not lose control as Wardyke had lost control.

But these thoughts she did not express to Nya.

'Justice is my interest,' she said sweetly.

He snorted. It was not a word much used in his vocabulary.

'All right,' Panora tried again. 'Hawk-Eagle was my friend. I want vengeance.'

That he understood.

'And you,' she added, 'will get his lands, his riches, great honour and power as Spear lord. No longer will you have to live from day to day in the mountains, killing for every scrap of food. Food will be plentiful all the year round. People will respect you and you will live in a great house with furs upon the floor. Your lady,' and here she looked at the filthy ragged crone at Nya's side, 'will wear jewels and soft clothes and drink sweet wine instead of goats' milk and bad ale.'

Nya's woman showed her rotten teeth in a greedy smile.

Nya looked with disgust at her and this point did not seem to attract him.

'Perhaps,' Panora said to him softly, 'you would prefer another woman. One of the East, bred among the Spear-lord caste, fine of feature, tall and straight of limb.'

This pleased him better and he smiled at last.

'You say there are many who will join us on the way?'

'Yes.'

'I will serve under no other man!'

215

'No,' Panora said, 'you will be leader. They will follow you.It is your vengeance that will be done, your land that will be reclaimed. They will help you because your cause helps theirs.'

Nya thought about it from every angle. It seemed a good enough proposition to him. He and his men enjoyed fighting and to gain so much this time would add to the attraction.

But being treacherous himself he was always on guard against the possibility of treachery in others.

'And what do you take when all the fighting is done?'

'Nothing of yours.'

'What then?'

'I take what is rightfully mine.'

'And what is that?'

Nya was not entirely a fool. He wanted to know exactly where he stood before he committed himself.

'A place of honour too.'

'Aha!'

'But it will not conflict with yours. I promise. You will have your brother's land and much besides that you have conquered. I will have vengeance for my friend and a place of honour I have always been denied.'

'Hm-m,' Nya thought about it.

'Surely if I show you the route to take where the most will join your force, give you aid in every way from my knowledge of the Temple area, a small reward of land or honour from your bounty would not be too much to ask?'

Nya shrugged.

'We will see. I will think upon it this night. In the morning I will give you answer.'

Much time that evening was spent in drinking and carousing.

When they finally retired to sleep Panora could not imagine any one of them being in a fit state to think anything through!

She settled under a hide tent in a ragged sleeping rug beside a badly smelling woman and her four children, and thought about the future and the palace she would build, riches, power and glory

In the morning Nya gave the answer 'Yes', and voices and fists were raised with gutteral shouts of affirmation.

At the turn of the next moon cycle the band moved off, pillaging as they went the villages that would not join with them, growing in strength with the ones that would.

Back at The Temple of the Sun little Deva, the Shining One, sleeping beside her mother, woke screaming in the night, and spoke of horrible hordes marching upon her loved ones with death in their eyes.

Kyra was troubled but rocked her to sleep pretending that there was nothing to worry about.

This was the first time that Deva had revealed a dream and Kyra was not sure if it was the result of far-sight or of the usual childhood fears when faced with a new and inexplicable world.

She and Lea and Khu-ren discussed it, but could find out no more about it as in the morning Deva had completely forgotten she had suffered it at all.

'Let it rest at that,' Kyra said. 'I do not want to raise these fears again by probing. She is too young.'

But Khu-ren spoke to Isar and asked him to keep his ears and eyes open for any more rumours like the one he had brought about Hawk-Eagle's brother.

Isar's fame as a wood carver was growing rapidly and he often spent time in distant villages carving for people who admired his work. He had great pleasure and satisfaction in this and Karne saw that he had training with the best craftsmen in the Temple area.

It was on a day that he was very far from home that he heard the first rumours of a vast army that was moving across from the West, devastating everything in its path. He even saw straggling groups of refugees, carrying what possessions they could upon their backs and telling horrifying stories of murder and rape, burning of homes and stealing of crops and cattle.

'Their leader is a giant with long black hair and beard, his eyes like the dead,' someone told Isar.

'And at his side is a strange creature, half demon, half little girl. He seems to do everything she tells him, and yet great warriors tremble at a look from him!'

'Sometimes flocks of giant black birds follow them for great distances and eat any crops that have been left behind or hidden. The villagers are starving!'

Isar was horrified. He mounted Karne's horse and rode as hard as he could to the Temple. Arriving there he found others before him bearing the same kind of tale.

Some of the Spear-lords who had taken to the new ways and appreciated the help of the Elders, and were loyal to the priests, had come as soon as they heard of the trouble, and the whole Temple community was in an uproar.

The Lord Guiron called all the messengers together and he and his chief priests listened gravely and silently to all the differing accounts. Through the exaggerations and the distortions he managed to build up quite an accurate picture of what was happening.

So it was coming about as he had feared!

Kyra remembered her daughter Deva's dream.

She also remembered she had not seen Panora anywhere for a long time. She started to make enquiries and it soon became clear that no one, not even the Lord Guiron had seen her. Nor had anyone missed her.

Kyra was convinced 'the strange creature, half demon, half little girl' with the advancing hordes was Panora.

This was Panora's war.

The Lord Guiron and his priests called a meeting of all the friendly Spear-lords and the Elders of their villages and sent them back to their communities with words of strength and comfort, advising them to prepare defences but to do nothing until they heard from the Council of the Priests.

'You will have protection from us,' the Lord Guiron told them. 'It is only in the last resort you will have to fight.'

He then called upon the Lord Khu-ren and the Lady Kyra to visit him in the privacy of his own house.

'There is much that has been unspoken between us in the last few years,' the Lord Guiron began.

Khu-ren and Kyra were silent, not sure what was coming next.

'I speak of the story that began in the Palace they now speak of as the Field of the Grey Gods.'

The Lord Khu-ren nodded. How long had he known that they knew? There had never been any sign.

Guiron's face seemed very tired and old, as though he were oppressed with memories too sad to carry further.

'I have paid for that ancient guilt many times and now it seems not only I, but those I love and cherish, will have to pay again.'

Kyra put her hand upon his arm with warmth and sympathy.

He was such a great Lord and yet at this moment to her woman's heart he was like a lost and desolate child.

'This war,' Khu-ren said, 'has roots in other matters than your guilt. People used to privilege are fighting to keep it against the tide of change. This is an old story, nothing to do with you or what you have done.'

Guiron sighed.

'There is no time for games. What you say is only partly true. The flame that sets this mess of straw on fire is Panora. She lives only as long as my guilt lives. She plots only as long as my guilt is not expurgated.'

'I have often wondered why you have kept her by your side,' Kyra said thoughtfully, 'was there no way . . .?'

'No way,' Guiron answered gloomily. 'Nya thinks he comes to reclaim his brother's land. The other Spear-lords fight because they think they are being threatened by a change that is to their disadvantage, but none of these made a move until Panora drove them to it. They are her warriors, her minions, whether they know it or not.'

'What does she hope to gain? Killing Karne and his family will not satisfy her vengeful nature.'

'Karne must go because he was the enemy of Wardyke. I must go because of what I did to her mother. But with us must go all that we stand for, the good and gentle changes Karne has made in village life, the Temple and its mighty power.

'I have "travelled" to her camp and looked into her eyes, and seen there the destruction of this whole Culture, the Temple laid to waste and in its place a palace of great magnificence in which the King Isar and his Queen Deva rule, their Warder and their Guardian, the Princess Panora.

'The Princess Panora grown in power beyond all belief.

'The Princess Panora ruling her King and Queen of Straw, and her kingdom of devastation!'

Khu-ren and Kyra were silent, the realisation that what he said was true bringing a chill to their hearts.

'What can we do?' Kyra spoke at last, her voice trembling.

Guiron's shoulders were hunched. He was tired and he had lost all will and hope.

'She is no ordinary girl and she has been learning from The Temple all these years,' Khu-ren said. 'She has been feeding on us, biding her time and now she is more deadly than a viper between the breasts of a girl.'

Kyra shuddered.

It was no satisfaction to her now that she had never liked or trusted Panora.

'I think,' the Lord Khu-ren said, 'we should go into the Silence and seek the answer there.'

The Lord Guiron suffered himself to be led to The Temple and thence to the Northern Inner Circle of Great Power.

There the three who were Lords of the Sun stood until dawn, deep in the Silence within themselves, seeking guidance from the Spirit realms around them and within them.

It took Panora more than a moon cycle to gather the army she thought sufficient for her purposes and move it within striking distance of The Temple.

Nya's men, unruly and greedy, were overloaded with the feasting and the pillaging on the way, but Nya still thought he was the leader of the expedition.

Panora moved among the gathering armies, her strange hypnotic power strengthening their purpose and confidence whenever it showed signs of wavering, feeding their fears, their hates, their greeds.

She was everywhere and nowhere. No one could find her, but she could find everyone. If a group of Spear-lords began to have their doubts when they noticed it was against The Temple itself they were making their advance, and not just against the upstart Karne, and held a secret meeting, Panora was suddenly and mysteriously in their midst making them see that it was the Temple and the Lord High Priest who were their enemy after all.

'Karne may be killed by one spear thrust, but if The Temple is determined to break the power of the Spear-lords and promote the common people to their ancient privileges, a hundred Karnes will spring to life whenever one is killed!

'You must destroy the Lord High Priest and The Temple at his back if you are to keep your way of life.

'You see that. You are not blind. You are men of action and of power. Use it! No priest living in his dream world can stand against you.

'Take the Temple! Make it yours! Instal it in *your* people who will look out for *your* rights!'

She stood amongst them strangely grown in height, a spear raised in hand, eyes like demon eyes enflaming them to action.

On the day when she thought the time was near to strike she vanished inexplicably from their midst and reappeared in the garden of Fern's house where Deva was playing happily unaware of all the threats of violence and of war.

The child looked up to see a strange girl standing beside her. Before she could utter a sound, Panora had seized her and whisked her away.

Isar, coming at that moment out of the house, saw it happen and ran like a deer in the direction they had vanished. They had moved so fast that by the time he could see clearly the trackway he thought they had taken, it was already empty.

Distraught with fear for Deva's safety he rushed to the field where Karne kept his horse and forgetting that his father would need it, he leapt upon its back and galloped off in the direction in which he was sure Panora had gone.

Panora meanwhile made sure that she kept just out of reach of him but left enough evidence of her passing for him to follow easily. It was part of her plan that he would be with Deva away from the battle and out of reach of any of their family or friends.

It was nightfall when Isar finally tracked Deva down. She was sitting in the doorway of a derelict house far from any other habitation and crying for her mother.

When she saw Isar she flung herself into his arms and clung to him sobbing with relief and joy. Gently he soothed and comforted her and then, when at last she was quiet and he looked around for the horse, it was nowhere in sight.

He asked Deva about Panora but the little girl just shook her head and looked so full of fear he left the matter alone. There was no sign of her. It was clear she meant Deva to stay there, far, far from possible help.

As darkness was fast closing in upon them he decided the most sensible thing would be for them to stay in the half-ruined house overnight and try to find their way home in the morning.

He told Deva this and spoke with such calm authority that she who loved and trusted him was quite content and began to look on the whole thing as an adventurous game. But she was very careful never to leave his side and, weary as she was, she followed him everywhere as he gathered straw and built a soft bed for them in the most sheltered part of the almost roofless house.

When she complained that she was hungry he promised her he would find her food in the morning, but meanwhile she must sleep and he would tell her a story to lull her off to dream land. She settled down happily in his arms and he told her story after story until at last he felt her go limp and her breathing settle soft and rhythmically.

222

But he could not sleep himself. He lay cramped and troubled all the night with thinking upon the matters that had occurred, the war that was brewing and the part his one-time friend Panora was playing in it.

Many thoughts came to him in that long, long night and many decisions were made.

Meanwhile Panora had returned to her army and, finding her commander-in-chief, Nya, lying in a state of drunken stupor, gave the command to advance herself, in his voice. The moon rose full and brilliant above the plain and the hastily constructed defences of Karne and his Spear-lords showed up clearly.

The priests had sent word that this would be the night of the battle and Karne, lying in a ditch waiting with his men, could feel it in the air. If the sky had not been so clear he would have been sure there would be a storm, so hot and breathless and oppressive it was.

He was momentarily surprised and anxious that Isar had not brought his horse to him in answer to the message he had sent, but as everything was in such tension and confusion, he dismissed the worry by telling himself Isar could probably not find him. He had indeed moved his position several times.

The priests had sent word that no one was to attack, only hold themselves ready to defend. They had hinted before that there were other ways of defeating enemies than by force of arms, and weapons were to be used only as a last resort.

Karne and his friends, remembering the legendary powers of the priests of the Temple of the Sun, were thankful that they at least were on their side.

There was something non-human and supernatural about Panora, but the rest of their enemies were ordinary men like themselves, and this was a relief.

The enemy had no such comfort.

Now that the moment of confrontation had come not a few

of them had misgivings about raising arms against the Mighty Temple priesthood.

Panora seemed to be everywhere at once and it was her energy that flowed through them like strong ale.

As the moon reached a height sufficient to flood the whole battle plain with eerie light Panora gave a shriek that made every one of her enemies' blood run cold.

It was the sound of Vengeance and with it the whole dark plain seemed to come alive, bushes and stones moved, the very earth itself heaved to spew out a dark horde of fighting men.

As they advanced they chanted a savage and relentless chant that added to the chill already in the hearts of the defenders.

They knew they were outnumbered beyond belief and as they lay helplessly in the ditches and behind the hastily erected banks it seemed to them their case was hopeless.

But even as the first line of attackers came within spear throw a wondrous thing happened.

Upon three burial mounds, and clearly visible in the moonlight, three figures suddenly appeared, luminous and larger than life. The Lord Guiron in the centre, flanked by the Lord Khu-ren and the Lady Kyra.

The advancing army paused, its derisive and impressive chant cut off in mid breath. Ten thousand men stared at the three upon the burial mounds and as the centre one raised his arm and pointed they raised their eyes to follow it.

Above them the moon that had signalled their attack and had been showering its light upon their enemy now seemed to have a weird shadow of blood creeping across its face.

They stared horrified, as gradually the shadow spread, the light dimmed, and the ghost of the moon, each detail of its pock-marked face clearer than it had ever been, looked down upon them in a sombre and ominous silence.

Even Panora was momentarily stunned and in that moment Guiron spoke with a voice of thunder that carried across the plain with more than human strength.

'You have dared to challenge the authority of The Temple of the Sun.

'You will advance no further.

224

'Between you and the innocent people you wish to destroy is a wall of power. If you touch it *you* will be destroyed. If you go back to your homes and live as you have always lived in peace and harmony with your neighbours, no harm will come to you.'

'Do not listen to him!' screamed Panora. 'He is no more than a priest frightened of losing power.

'We are the power now!

'We take!

'We break!

'We make a new world that will be ours!

'Advance!'

Her voice, like Guiron's carried with an unnatural force across the echoing plain. Her power of personality, like Guiron's, was more than natural at this moment.

Half of her dark force moved forward under the strength of it, the other half hesitated and stayed where it was, confused and dismayed. But in the section that moved forward there were more men than the defenders had at their command.

As they advanced the two figures standing on the burial mounds to the North and South of Guiron raised their right hands and pointed dramatically. Between their pointing fingers a lightning bolt seemed to shoot across the plain.

Again the advancing army paused.

Again Panora drove them on.

'Beware of the wall of power!' Guiron roared. 'No man may pass unscathed!'

'It is a trick!' Panora screamed. 'You can see there *is* no wall!'

The moon had come clear of its ghastly shadow now and the light shone full upon the plain.

There was no wall visible.

The horde advanced again.

'Now!' shouted the three great Lords of the Sun with one voice and in that instant total confusion broke loose upon the plain.

Some screamed as though they had been burned as they touched an invisible wall of fire. Others shrieked with fear as the sky rained vipers and poisonous adders. Yet others leaped back from demon figures burning with unearthly light. Some saw long dead relatives raise spears against them. Others were engulfed in a black and suffocating fog. Leaping flames chased others back.

In the days to come each one who survived this terrible ordeal had a different tale to tell.

No one saw the same enemy.

No one penetrated the invisible wall.

'Advance! Advance!' shrieked Panora, mad with disappointment at the frustration of her plans.

'There *is* no wall. It is a trick!'

But her voice was lost in the shrieking of the damned and the stampeding of terrified men.

The battle that was no battle was a rout.

The defenders, still untouched behind the lines of their defence, gazed with horror and with awe at what they saw.

They saw nothing of wall, or fire, or fog or vipers . . . nothing but men screaming in fear and agony and falling about in the dark and running back from whence they had come.

They stared amazed.

And when they turned to look upon the three burial mounds there was no sign of the three Lords of the Sun.

And when they looked at the moon it was as bland and pale as ever.

Weeping with rage Panora watched the scene and knew that she had lost.

Never again while they remembered this night would any man rise against the power of The Temple.

But even as she despaired she remembered she had one last trick to play.

She had the children. Deva, the beloved of Kyra, Khu-ren *and* Guiron, and Isar, the beloved of Karne and Fern.

226

Swiftly she left the shameful scene of her defeat and travelled to the derelict house where she had left her captives.

She would triumph yet!

But even this victory she was to be denied.

Dawn light was breaking as she came upon the place and the children had left.

Above the house a wheeling flight of enormous black birds were screeching in the sky.

Panora shook her fist at them.

'Why did you let them go?' she screamed.

The birds wheeled once more and flew off across the horizon. Even her familiars had deserted her.

Bitterly, but still determined to salvage triumph from the wreckage, she set off in search of the children. She knew the horse had left them and they would not be able to go far on Deva's little legs.

But what she did not know was that Kyra's love had located them and even at that moment the Lord Guiron and herself, now in their bodily form, were hastening to the place where they knew the children would be.

Weary and bedraggled from journeying and hiding, Panora was in time to see their reunion in a little forest glade.

Kyra gathered both children to her breast, tears of relief falling upon them. She had played her part as great Lord of the Sun as it had been required of her, but now she was woman and mother, desperate with weariness and weak with relief after the long anxiety.

The High Priest stood aside and watched them, his face filled with remorse and love.

When Kyra had welcomed them enough and they turned to him, he stepped forward and knelt upon the grass, taking Deva's little hand in his and bending his large head to kiss her fingers.

Isar watched him warily.

'My lady,' the Lord Guiron said with great humility, 'I ask your forgiveness for all that I have done.'

Deva, dark and beautiful, with the light that she was named for shining from her eyes, smiled not like a little girl but like a great Queen.

She raised him with a gesture and said softly and graciously,

'Go in peace, my lord, there is no longer anything to forgive.'

And as she said this they heard a cry from behind them and looked round to see Panora crouching beside a tree, her eyes still dark with pain and hate.

Deva took a step towards her, in spite of Kyra's warning hand.

'You must go,' she said with authority in her voice. 'You have wandered too long between two worlds. I know myself how fruitless and lonely this can be.'

'Choose spirit-world or earth-world, one or the other, and learn to live there without hate or bitterness. When you are ready, age and die as other people do. When you are ready, be born again as other people are.'

Panora stared at her. It was as though the figures in the forest glad were frozen in time.

The old man, the young woman, the boy, the girl child and the girl demon were all poised on a moment of change, Panora's decision affecting all their lives.

At last Panora moved and it seemed to them that the hate and bitterness had gone out of her eyes.

She bowed her head to Deva, her one-time spirit mother, and Guiron, her earthly father, and before they realized she had it on her, she seized a dagger that was hidden at her waist and plunged it into her own heart.

They all gasped in horror as she fell.

Kyra held Deva and Isar back, and only Guiron moved forward swiftly and cradled the strange limp creature in his arms. He had to lean close to hear the words that she murmured as she died.

'If my mother forgives you, so do I,' she whispered and the ancient feud died with her.

Guiron turned and looked at Isar with a question in his eyes.

'We have much living to do without bothering about old

228

tales,' Isar said, looking at him straight.

'So be it,' Guiron said, bowing his head. 'I thank you, and I will not cross your paths again.'

At the time they did not know what he meant by this but when they returned to The Temple he told the Inner Council of Priests that he intended to resign as High Priest and recommended that they accepted in his place the Lord Khu-ren.

He would not explain his reasons, but neither would he be diverted from his decision.

Kyra and Khu-ren understood but said nothing.

He told them that it was his intention to leave his country and wander a stranger in strange lands for the rest of his natural life, teaching and healing where he could.

That way he hoped to atone for all the years he had worn the Crown of the greatest Priest in the land, knowing that he was not worthy of it.

Khu-ren's Inauguration

The inauguration of the Lord Khu-ren as the High Priest of the Temple of the Sun took place in two separate ceremonies, the first at the Southern College of Star Studies at the moment of the Spring Equinox, when day and night were equal in length and all nature was poised ready for the great surge of Summer growth.

At the moment of sunrise the Lord Khu-ren stood at the Standing Stone that marked the Spring Equinox and was transformed by the beams of the rising sun as it touched the gold that was everywhere upon him, from the band around his forehead to the sandals upon his feet. He seemed to be made of light and as the reflection of the sun from the gold upon his body reached the priests who were gathered around him they all bowed to him and then rose to full height to sing a song of praise and glory to the Sun and to its father, the Spirit of Light, and its servant, the Lord Khu-ren.

Deva, the Shining One, had the task of bringing the High Priest's crown solemnly along the processional way from the Midsummer Sun Stone to the Lord Guiron, whose last work as Lord High Priest was to place it upon the head of his successor.

Kyra, in long blue robes, threaded with white and gold, watched proudly from her place at the head of the Inner Council of Priests.

Deva, small as she was, carried herself like a queen, and her father, tall and handsome, bore himself with dignity and humility as the greatest power in the land.

From the ceremony at the Temple of the Star Studies the procession moved solemnly and sedately the long distance back to the main Temple of the Sun.

Night was passed at the Sanctuary, the other priests and

Spear-lords camping on the hills around, while the new High Priest sat alone in the centre of the Sanctuary and communed with Spirits.

At dawn the procession moved off again to the Temple along the Sacred Way, the Lady Kyra walking beside the Lord Guiron, a few paces behind her Lord, the High Priest.

Within the Great Circle concentric rings of people were moving to the sound of drums . The Lords of the Sun were to be called to take part in the final ceremony.

As Kyra took her place in the Inner Circle with the Three Great Stones at its centre and waited for the Lords from across the world to come and pay their respects to her husband, her mind went to the stone sea urchin she had found so deeply buried in the earth.

It lay in her chamber now and was not with her in the Circle, but so vividly did she think about it, so accurately did she visualize it in every detail that it was as though she held it in her hand and gazed upon it.

Its centre became the centre of the circle she was in.

Her husband was waiting, crowned and magnificent, in the very centre of both the Stone Circle and the Stone talisman she held in her mind. From him radiated out beaded lines of power reaching to every point of the universe, and from every point of the universe beaded lines of power reached back to him at the centre.

The simple sea creature, immortalized in stone, was a symbol of the Universe!

She looked up and wherever she looked and wherever she turned she saw each and every thing joyously as itself and yet, at the same time, in its role as symbol, pointing to everything else.

The bird that rose in flight was the developing Being who sees everything from a new angle as it rises.

The blade of grass was the living Being who draws its nourishment from earth *and* sun, from dark *and* light, from matter *and* spirit.

The Tall Stones that surrounded her reached for the sky, but were embedded in the earth, and formed a circle that was at once closed *and* open.

The sunlight sparking off the faces of the minute crystals in the Stone reminded her of the flashes of inspiration she had experienced throughout her life which had led her spirit to rise, her vision to lift and follow the tall and magical Stones until she was carried up and up to be absorbed in one of those moments of amazement at the blue depths of the sky and the immensities she knew were beyond it . . . One of those moments when, balanced on a point of beauty almost too great to bear, she could sense the presence of an Intelligence and a Love so overwhelming that she could only presume it was what men called 'God'.

The words 'Magnificence' and 'Purpose' burst in her mind like exploding Suns.

She lifted her arms . . .

and her heart sang . . .

Book 3

SHADOW ON THE STONES

Contents

The Messenger

The traveller was exhausted. It had been many days and nights since he had eaten or had rested. His clothes were torn, his body filthy and his eyes wild and red. He knew that if he followed the ancient customs it might be a long time before he received an audience with the High Priest. There was no time left for such formality.

He had heard good reports of the dark Stranger Priest from over the sea and knew that his wife, the Lady Kyra, was noted not only for her exceptional powers as priest and Lord of the Sun, but for her sympathy and understanding of all who came to her in trouble. He knew also that she was of his own land, and no stranger to its problems.

It was not easy to find his way within the maze of wooden priest-houses and long student huts that clustered closely around the great Temple of the Sun, but he was desperate to deliver his message and his desperation gave him courage to dodge and hide. He came at last to the High Priest's home, set back among trees and separated from the others, but otherwise hardly distinguishable from them, and not of the grandeur he would have expected.

There was no marker of crossed feathers above the skins that hung over the doorway, to indicate that entry was not permitted, and indeed they were drawn aside and fastened so that the cool air and the light could pass into the interior.

He crossed the threshold swiftly before he could be seen or stopped.

'My lord, I must speak with you,' he cried in a voice breaking with weariness and urgency, and then almost stumbled and fell at the contrast between the vibrancy of the light in the outside world and the inner, still, darkness of the chamber.

He could see nothing.

1

Watching him in some alarm stood Deva, now thirteen summers old, alone in her mother's chamber, dressed in her mother's robes, her face painted with ceremonial paint, the crown of the Priestess upon her head. She knew that she was not allowed to wear this even in play, but there had been no one to see her and the temptation to try it on had been too great.

Frightened, she stared at the rough, uncouth intruder. Was he human robber or demon drawn to her from the hidden realms by the sacrilege she had just committed?

To the man standing in the doorway, his eyes gradually adjusting to the dim light within the house, she was a priestess in full regalia, standing impassively and calmly, waiting for him to deliver his message.

'My lady,' he said softly, stumbling forward a few steps to fall on his knees before her.

'I beseech you . . .' he continued in a low voice. He found himself trembling and the words catching in his throat.

He had thought about this meeting many, many times as he had travelled the long, weary way from his home in the west country, but never had he imagined he would feel such awe in the presence of another human being. This must be the great Kyra, the Lady who had repelled an army with power from her slender hand. She was looking at him now with dark eyes, eyes as bright as jet, and the words he had rehearsed so many times would not come to his tongue.

She did not move.

'My lady,' he tried again at last. 'Forgive me that I break in upon your home . . . that I come to you with no preparation, no ceremony . . . forgive me . . . my appearance . . . I would not have had it so, but the matters that I would bring to your attention are urgent beyond all ceremony, all appearance . . .'

His voice trailed away. She was so beautiful and there was a scent so strong and so holy about her that he could hardly bear it.

He dropped his eyes from her black gaze and stared helplessly at the point where her long cloak of white and blue touched the ground.

It would be easier to talk to the High Priest, her husband. He had never been at ease with beautiful women, and this one was beautiful beyond any he had ever seen.

Meanwhile Deva in her borrowed robes was puzzling what to do. She knew she should acquaint the man at once with his mistake and lead him to her mother, but . . . and here the little thread of mischief in her gave a tug . . . she was enjoying the role of priestess and she saw no harm in playing it a moment or two longer.

She raised her hand with a graceful and imposing gesture.

'Rise,' she said as imperiously as she could. 'There is no need to kneel to me.'

At least that was no lie, Deva told herself.

'My lady,' the man almost crawled forward. 'May I touch your hand?'

Deva found herself lowering it to him grandly, flushing slightly at the thrill of power she felt stirring within her.

Instead of touching her fingers briefly as she had thought he would, he seized her hand and started covering it with kisses, tears streaming from his eyes and down his rough and dusty face.

Fear and pleasure fought for control over her. She was at once horrified at herself for allowing this to happen, and for enjoying it.

She pulled back her hand sharply.

The man gave a kind of sob and fell fainting at her feet.

Terrified, she stared at him.

She thought she would remember until the end of her days the tears in his eyes when he thought he was kissing the hand of the legendary Kyra. The story of Kyra's part in Panora's War had spread throughout the land and was sung by many a poet on feast days. She had become worshipped almost as though she were a god. Indeed Deva had heard her mother complaining about this to her husband, the Lord Khu-ren, and protesting that it was wrong for anyone to set her aside so from other people. Her powers were no greater than his or those of the former High Priest, the Lord Guiron. Together they had tricked the enemy into defeat, using what skill they had as human beings trained to work with the Spirit Realms, the Lords of Light.

Her mother would not have allowed the man to grovel so, and Deva felt tears of shame in her own eyes for her part in the embarrassing scene.

With shaking hands she lifted the crown of the priestess off her head and struggled to unpin the robes about her shoulders. She was determined to be out of the clothes before anyone else saw her. Her mind was racing with thoughts of how she could undo the harm that she had done.

As soon as she was clad once more in her own tunic, she reached to fetch water for the man, spilling it from the earthenware beaker in her haste.

His eyes opened and he stared bewildered at the dark haired girl child leaning over him.

He shook his wet hair free from the water she had poured upon it, and dragged himself in confusion to his feet, gazing around himself, only half remembering what had occurred.

'You must have had a vision,' the girl was saying breathlessly. 'A dream . . . a vision . . .' she gabbled, 'you fainted . . . you are better now!'

'My lady . . .' the man murmured, looking around the chamber, thinking of the stately priestess he had seen with gold upon her head.

'No, she is not here. You had a vision,' Deva insisted, her heart cold with the lie she was telling, and yet still telling it.

The man was silent.

He was tired, so tired he feared he might not be able to keep upright much longer.

'I must . . .' he said at last, painfully, pulling the words out of an aching body. 'I must see her . . . I need . . . we need . . . help . . .'

'You will have it!' promised Deva hastily. 'Just do not fall down again.'

She pulled his arm and seated him upon a wooden bench.

She thrust a beaker full of water into his hands.

'Drink that,' she said with a semblance of control returning to her voice. 'I will fetch the Lady. Do not fall!' she added commandingly as he swayed.

He forced himself to remain upright.

'Hurry . . .' he whispered.

But she was already gone.

He saw the skins at the doorway still moving from the touch of her shoulder.

He thought it was a breeze that made him feel so cold and every moment colder.

When an agitated Deva returned with her mother they found him lying on the floor, the earthenware beaker smashed to pieces beside him and the spilled water already seeping into the clay floor.

'O no,' cried Deva, 'he has fainted again!'

She rushed for more water as Kyra kneeled beside him.

When she returned her mother was standing very tall and still beside the figure on the floor.

She lifted her hand to stop her daughter approaching any nearer.

'He is dead,' she said quietly.

Deva stood stunned.

She herself was near to fainting with the shock.

What had she done?

She had deceived a dying man and wasted precious moments in foolery when they were the only ones he had.

Kyra straightened the stranger's dusty, crumpled body and asked Deva to join her in lifting him to lie with greater dignity upon the soft rush bed.

The girl shuddered as she touched his cold skin.

'What will we do my lady?' She whispered. 'He asked for help but we know nothing of the nature of the help he wanted?'

Kyra was deep in thought.

'Leave us,' she said to Deva.

As Deva withdrew Kyra sat quietly down beside the stranger, the stone sea urchin that was for her a talisman of power in one hand, the other upon his forehead.

There was no way she could call him back from the dead, he was not a priest who knew how to die in stages and with control, but a rough man of action who had fallen into death unwillingly and unprepared. Her only chance was to draw from the air around him the last vibrations of his thoughts before they moved beyond her reach on to another level of reality.

The Shadow of Fear

Isar made camp in a small cleft between two hills. It would perhaps have been more sensible if he had chosen a position nearer the top of the hill where the view of the surrounding countryside would have given him warning of any approaching danger, but he foresaw no danger.

A spring bubbled from lichen-covered rock and the green fronds of ferns enclosed the place as though it were enchanted.

He set his fire carefully so as to disturb the harmony of the place as little as possible and the scent of wood smoke rising through tall trees and leaning bushes, tugged gently at his memory of other places and other times that had been so wreathed in peace and quietness that they had become special times, times that brought renewal and refreshment.

He enjoyed being alone and never felt lonely. In the silence amongst growing things he had often felt the subtle stirrings of communication between all that existed and himself. This was a gift his mother, Fern, had given him for a birth present as other mothers give sun-metal or moon-metal discs. Growing plants did not speak to him quite as they did to her, but his sense of vision was more than ordinarily developed and an arrangement of leaf and twig that would pass unnoticed by others could be a potent source of joy and revelation to him.

No one knowing Isar would associate him with his natural father, the cruel magician Wardyke. He had all his mother's features and qualities. He was slender and lithe, his hair the colour of copper, his face gentle, his eyes light hazel with flecks of gold. His tallness might be inherited from Wardyke, but that was all. The Spear-lord Karne had brought him up as his own son, and it was Karne he respected as his father since Wardyke's death.

He was sitting now with his back against a rock, relaxed and sleepy, watching the night shadows gradually snuffing out the distinctive patternings around him, pleased by the graceful and sinuous dance of the thin thread of smoke from his small fire, when he fancied he saw a shadowy figure standing in the darkness behind the smoke. So tenuous was the impression that he narrowed his eyes to afford a better focus, but did not move a limb in case the disturbance either dispelled the vision (if it were a vision) or caused the animal to charge (if it were an animal).

As he stared and his eyes began to smart with staring, he began to 'feel' that it was Deva.

His ordinary senses gave him no evidence of this, but he began to have the feelings in himself that he always had when Deva was near, stirrings of happiness and warmth, protectiveness, and also, sometimes, a touch of amused irritation.

But now he felt that she was worried and afraid. She seemed to be weeping and reaching out to him.

Forgetting momentarily where he was, he moved to take her in his arms, but even as he did so he realized that she was not there and it was the night held at bay by the last flickering of his fire, that waited under the trees.

In the morning, after a restless night of bad dreams he could not remember when he woke, he decided to return home. The impression he had received of Deva in trouble had been strong, even though it had been indistinct. He was determined to find out more about it even if it did mean he would not meet Janak, the great man he was travelling to meet, the man who could make dead wood live again in new forms.

As he packed his few belongings in to the leather pouch he carried slung over his shoulder, and returned the ashes of his fire with gratitude to the forest from which they had come, he argued with himself about his decision. He knew Deva would have tried to stop him had she known that he was leaving upon such a long journey, however innocent, and it was for this reason that he had not told her of it himself. He knew she was spoilt in many ways and had innumerable tricks to twist events the way she wanted them. By now she would have found him gone and would be wanting him at her side again to torment and delight. As the daughter of two priests it would not surprise him if she had ways of reaching him not available to ordinary people.

And yet . . . and yet there was something more to her pain this time . . . something deeper . . . more urgent . . . more serious.

He would turn back.

As he reached the top of the eastern of the two hills that had sheltered him in the night, the one he had climbed down to find his camping place, he took a last yearning look to the west.

On the horizon he could see a dark and ominous cloud of smoke. At first he thought it might be an accumulation of cooking fires and was about to turn away, when something made him stay.

He was never afterwards sure whether it was the scent of fear in the air, the sense of someone standing beside him pointing to the smoke, instantly gone as he turned his head, or curiosity within himself, that made him travel towards the west and not the east that day, forgetting Deva.

He journeyed far into the day before he neared the place where the fire had been. The smoke had died down long before he reached it but he had marked its position in relation to rocky outcrops and free standing trees, and thus had no difficulty in finding it.

Several times he saw groups of strangers carrying weapons and an instinct made him avoid them. He had never been as far west as this before, but the descriptions he had had of the gentle people who lived in the country did not tally with those he saw. In each case the sound of their voices, talking in an unknown tongue, was aggressive and harsh. But it was only when he saw one shoot a bird and laugh to see it fall, drawing his arrow callously from the broken feathered body, that he knew for sure these were not his people.

He took greater care in his journeying, keeping to the bushes and the trees, avoiding open places, his heart heavy and anxious.

When he caught sight of the silhouettes of a group of Tall Stones upon a rise of ground his spirits leapt. Here at last would be the real people of Klad, the people who worshipped the Lord of All, symbolized by the burning disc of the Sun and the Sacred Circle of Stones.

Although he was tired, his pace quickened and he ran the last part of the way.

Where there was a Circle there would be a Priest and a village community. He would settle at last the questions that tugged and scratched at his mind.

But as he came within clearer sight of the Stones he went cold.

This was not as it should be.

The whole area was blackened and charred by fire. The village that had been sprawling comfortably around the base of the knoll was now no more than smouldering embers and a broken cooking pot or two.

There was no sign of life and the air carried an acrid stench and a dry warning of hurt and danger.

He turned to the Stones and nausea and horror overcame him.

The beautiful Circle that had stood since ancient times for communion amongst all the Realms of Being, was desecrated beyond belief and seemed to crouch like a wounded and despairing animal waiting for death.

Slowly Isar's eyes moved from Stone to Stone and at every one he saw the burnt and mutilated body of a man, in some cases the hide ropes that had bound them to the Stones not quite burned through.

Their pain was still present and he fell to the ground with the weight of it.

'O God,' he sobbed, 'O Lord of All that Is! How *could* you let this happen?'

A small breeze drily stirred the ashes.

No answer came to him from the blind Circle of Stones.

After this . . . long after this . . . he gathered himself together and turned back towards the east.
Now he would go home.
He would walk through the night.
He would not rest until he had left the pain and evil he felt in this place, far, far behind.
Night creatures called shrilly from the darkness.
Moonlight drew grotesque shadows from the trees.
Twigs cracked where no one walked.
The world that had enclosed him up to now with such loving care, had turned hostile.

At the dawn he found himself further west into the land of Klad than he had been the evening before, and no matter how fervently he wished it, he could make no progress towards the east.

It was a long time before he came upon a village that was inhabited.
He paused upon a neighbouring hill and watched it closely before he approached.
He longed for friendly human contact and a warm and comfortable place to sleep, but caution held him to his post and he lay still, marking all who came and went with close attention.
The village itself seemed unremarkable enough, a cluster of small homesteads of wood and turf, smoke from cooking fires rising steadily, the cattle and sheep driven to their separate enclosures of banked earth and thorn-brake by village lads. He saw girls drawing water from the stream and carrying it in leather bags and earthenware pots as in his own

village. If he had not seen what he had seen, nor sensed the menace in the air, he might not have noticed that all he saw were moving sluggishly like a stream choked by weed in time of drought. Even the young girls carrying the water had no spring to their walk and instead of chattering and calling to the boys as girls in his own village used to do, they kept silent, with eyes down, and there was no whistling with the cattle drive or singing amongst the shepherd boys.

He moved closer, every sense alert. He noted heaviness of heart, slowness, inertia, lack of any kind of hope or will to live, but there seemed to be no immediate danger.

He looked at the sky and knew that heavy rain was very close.

He decided to trust the village and, light as a deer attuned to danger, he sprang down the hillside scarcely dislodging a pebble from its resting place.

He stopped at the edge of the village, facing an old man milking a cow.

As soon as the man became aware of Isar's presence, he stiffened as though expecting some harm to come to him, not believing that there was any way to avert it. He stopped his milking and stood up, arms hanging limply at his sides, head bowed, waiting.

Isar stared at him.

It seemed that he, Isar, was the one to be feared.

He noticed that the man had an ugly sore at the centre of his forehead, but otherwise, apart from his weary docility, was not unlike a number of old men Isar had seen in his own community.

Isar waited for the customary greeting of host to traveller, but it was not forthcoming.

He was plainly expected to say the first words and, although it made him uncomfortable so to break with tradition, he felt obliged to do it.

'I greet you, sir,' he said gently, 'and may the Spirit Helpers of the Lord Sun be with you, teach you their ways and keep you from harm.'

The age-old form of words that Isar had used so often as

greeting that they had become commonplace to him, seemed to shatter the mood of waiting resignation in the man.

He looked up startled, his eyes instantly going to Isar's forehead as though seeking something there, and being surprised that he did not find it.

The man was plainly confused, not knowing whether to return Isar's greeting or to run for cover.

Isar slowly raised his hand in the salute to the Sun his mother had taught him before she had taught him to speak.

Fear in the man's face began to give way to hope.

He opened his mouth, but no words would come.

Slowly, tentatively, he raised his own hand in answer, and then in terror looked around to see if it had been observed.

'Do not fear me,' Isar said, 'I am a traveller. I know nothing of this land or what it is you fear. I seek only lodging for the night.'

Other villagers joined them, and stood behind the man, staring at Isar. His eyes went to their faces, seeking the one who was their Priest or Elder and who would speak for them without the fear the rest so plainly showed.

On each face, on each forehead, in the centre, was a sore still festering, or a scar that bore witness to a sore that had once been there.

His hand went involuntarily to his own forehead and he felt the smooth skin with relief, momentarily experiencing a twinge of fear that the mysterious power that seemed to hold this people subject, had pierced his own forehead in some way since he had entered its realm.

The villagers watched him warily.

The man he had greeted turned to them and spoke at last.

'He used the old greeting,' he said with awe. 'He is not one of Them, nor of Us. He is a traveller.'

The villagers moved closer, still wary, but their curiosity and the dawning of hope in their hearts, driving them on.

'Where are you from, traveller?' The old man asked.

'From the east, from Haylken, the Temple of the Sun.'

'Groth?' The man said.

Isar looked puzzled. He did not understand the word.

The blankness on his face worked on the people like rain on a parched land.

Suddenly there was movement and sound.

He was seized and bustled and jostled until he found himself in a small and crowded house. Some of the people had pushed in with him, but the rest had scattered like frightened birds from a farmer's field-strip when the farmer's son shouts and bangs sticks together.

The old man he had first approached seemed to be the one most in charge. Silent as the people had been before, now questions poured from them and their eagerness to hear his answers pulled him from side to side until he was dizzy.

'How did you escape from the burning?'

'How is it that the guards did not see you?'

'Are you from the Temple itself?'

'Were you sent?'

'Do they know that we need help?'

'Are they coming to help us?'

They touched him. They kissed him. Time and again hands stretched to his forehead and trembling fingers felt the smoothness of his brow.

'Stop, stop!' He called at last. 'I cannot answer all your questions until I have asked you some of my own.'

'Ask!' They cried, eager now to communicate in any way possible.

They knew he was from the east.

They knew he did not understand the dread word Groth.

'Why is it that you all have wounds upon your foreheads?'

'It is the Mark,' they said, 'the Mark of Groth. We are slaves of Groth.'

'This word "Groth"—what does it mean?'

The daring of his question silenced them for an instant and then they all tried to talk at once.

'No,' he laughed, holding up his hands to fend off the confused and flying words. 'One at a time. I have not as many ears as you have voices!'

They looked at each other.

The old man Isar had first encountered, whose name he

learned was Keel, was tacitly chosen to be their spokesman.

'He is the new god,' he said, and his voice carried fear even at his daring to speak the words so, without reverence.

Isar looked amazed and sceptical.

'How can there be a *new* god?' He said scornfully. 'God has been from Always. There is no Before and no After.'

'Ah yes,' Keel lowered his voice and he spoke in the way a man speaks who has been told something, has accepted it, but has not understood it. 'It is the same god — but before we did not know about him properly.'

'And now you do?'

'Na-Groth tells us about him.'

'And who is this Na-Groth?'

Isar could feel the thrill of cold fear that went through the people at the tone of his voice.

'He is Groth's spokesman. Groth speaks through him.'

Isar was silent. It was plain that no amount of sceptical mockery from him would counteract the fear with which these people regarded Na-Groth and his god.

'And what of the Spirits?' He said at last. 'Do they not speak to your hearts in the Silent times and tell you of your God and His ways?'

'Na-Groth says we must not go into the Silence. He says that only he knows the ways of Groth. He says the Spirits do not exist. He says that nothing speaks to us in the Silence but our own desires and fears.'

Isar's heart was beating fast. He began to see what had happened here and how far it had gone.

He too began to feel the fear and the despair.

Fear and despair! Were these the inward marks of the new religion, as wound and scar were the outward?

Was it possible his own people had misunderstood the nature of God?

He thought back to the quiet field-strips and villages he had left behind so recently, which now seemed locked in some bygone age, with his childhood. He thought of the confidence he used to feel that all the great and distant stars above his head and the familiar grains of sand beneath his feet, were contributing with all the Realms of Being, visible and invisible, to a pattern of great magnificence, each in harmony with each, each dependent on the other.

His silence worried the villagers. They began to move about uneasily. A look-out was posted at the doorway, and there was murmuring amongst them. Was the traveller a spy of Na-Groth after all? Had he falsely led them on to trap them?

Isar felt helpless.

Their anxiety preyed on his spirit. He felt it consuming him, and he had to work hard to regain his own inner strength.

'No,' he said at last, 'I am no spy. I am a traveller and I am weary. Does this village not sleep when night comes to it?'

Keel took his arm, remembering suddenly with joy, the old ways of hospitality.

'We sleep indeed, though dreams are not welcome to us these nights. But first we eat. Woman, what are you about that you have not prepared the evening meal?'

Isar felt the injustice of Keel's remark for the woman, but she did not seem to mind.

Soon the bustle of preparing the evening meal did away with all the tension.

By the time they came to roll up in their rugs there was peace in the house and there were some who did not remember Na-Groth in their sleep.

Isar slept long and soundly, weary beyond any weariness he had ever felt before.

The priests of the Temple of the Sun were able to turn Isar's journey to meet the wood-carver Janak, to their advantage.

Through Kyra's reading of the messenger's last thoughts, they were now well aware of the situation in Klad, and the Inner Council decided that Isar was not to be brought home to safety, but was to be sent farther into Klad to seek out Na-Groth and destroy him.

16

The priesthood had great powers, but they were still limited to human frames and needed human channels for their work.

The priests of Klad had been killed, and though they might still be capable of helping in certain subtle ways within the deepest levels of consciousness, they too could only work through someone still physically upon the earth.

Isar, although not a priest or a novitiate, was sensitive to more levels of reality than most men. He could be of great help to them.

The Lady Kyra and the Lord Khu-ren worked far into the night among the Tall Stones of the Temple to contact his spirit, to strengthen and instruct it in the task it had before it.

They called on the Spirit Realms and were given Isar's secret name, the one he had through all time and which was known only in the Spirit Realms. There were times of crisis when it was possible for humans as highly evolved as the Lords of the Sun to call on the Spirits for this knowledge and be given it to hold in trust until the crisis had passed.

These secret names were not given lightly, for the knowledge of them carried great power and humans were not on the whole to be trusted with such authority.

Kyra and Khu-ren knew that when they had reached Isar his secret name would fall so deep into the hidden places of their minds that they would never again remember it with their surface consciousness. Nor would they forget it, for nothing that is experienced is ever totally forgotten.

It would be hidden until they too entered the Spirit Realms and were capable of remembering it without danger to Isar.

Now, murmuring his names, his given name and his secret name, they passed from Stone to Stone of the Inner Sanctum, touching the Sacred Rocks with their foreheads, with each touching, the humming and vibrating of the rocks that was imperceptible to ordinary people, growing in their consciousness until it seemed to them the Universe was filled with noise and energy through which the two names of Isar reverberated like giant drums.

In their home beside the Temple their daughter Deva lay staring into the dark, her eyes stubbornly open against sleep, daring the darkness and the evil god called Groth to touch her lord Isar. Her thoughts were fierce and protective but they were only the selfish thoughts of a young girl in love, and went no further than the chamber in which she lay.

Groth and Na-Groth were not aware of them.

Nor was Isar, lost to consciousness, deep in Kyra's strangely refreshing sleep.

Nor were the villagers of Klad tossing uneasily at his side, worrying about the morning and what it would bring.

Towards dawn Deva's body refused to obey any longer the commands of her mind to vigilance. She fell asleep like a grey feather from a bird and lay snuggled in her fur rugs, a child again.

She had not been asleep long when she began to notice that she was in a place she had often visited before in dreams, particularly when she was troubled. It was a place she recognized when she was asleep, but not when she was awake. If she had been there at all, ever, during her waking time, it must have been in a former life.

The place was a garden. Flowers grew there that did not grow near her waking home. The earth was sandy and reddish and a ring of small fountains, catching the intense sunlight and reflecting it like silver, arose from a circular pool curbed with slabs of pure white stone.

Sometimes she stood on the stone pavement gazing down into the white slabs, noticing that they were of a crystalline structure so fine that she could look into them and see the crystals in the depths as easily as those on the surface.

At other times she looked towards the pool and through the veil of spinning, moving drops of silver liquid she could see purple water flowers growing, glowing with such intensity of light that it seemed they were alight themselves and were not reflecting the sun.

During one 'dream' she looked up and thought she saw a roof of transparent rock crystal held up by a ring of tall, slender white columns. The sunlight was concentrated through the rock crystal canopy in such a way that a beam of brilliance that hurt the eyes shone down upon the water flowers so that they seemed to dissolve in light and she could only 'feel' that they were there, 'remember' that they were there, but she could not see them.

At such times she felt great reverence and awe as though she were in the presence of something beyond our Reality.

But there were times when, although the place was beautiful, it seemed ordinary, and she found herself playing among the trees and shrubs with a small, sleek black cat.

She was a child. This was her garden and her cat.

Once, enclosed in green shrubs, unseen, she watched two men walk in the garden. One was tall and vigorous, speaking with his hands to emphasize his words, the other a calmer, older man dressed with careful elegance.

She knew the older man was the king and the younger man was her father. She was proud of him. He was a great philosopher and architect, at this very moment engaged in supervising the construction of a remarkable building . . . a building that pierced the sky with one sharp golden point, drawing power from the mysterious Spirit Realms and dispersing it down the sloping triangular sides of stone into the earth, north, south, east and west.

This night when Deva, who lived now in the body in another time and another place, visited the ancient garden in her sleep, she carried with her the faint remembrance of Isar and his dangers. The beauty of the fountains and the water flowers could not hold her. She was impatient with her playmate cat and walked distractedly among the green bowers, searching for her father.

The parents of her present body would not bring Isar out of danger, but expected him alone to challenge the might of Na Groth and his god.

She would ask nothing of them again.

Something in her longed for former times and homed upon an ancient love.

But she was too anxious, her mind too active and demanding. Instead of allowing the 'dream' to take her into the garden and make its own shape, she tried to force the image of her former father to appear, and he eluded her.

Dismayed she saw the lovely place dissolve around her and found herself awake with only longing in her heart and no comfort to sustain her through another day of anxiety.

The Chase

Isar was awakened by a girl shaking his shoulder. He remembered her among the group of villagers who had surrounded him in the house the evening before, but she had kept silent while the others had been questioning him. She was a little older than Deva, pale and thin, her bones almost protruding through her skin, her eyes large and expressive.

Struggling with the unnaturally deep sleep that had fallen upon him and was now so rudely being dispelled, Isar opened his mouth and tried to muster his thick and sluggish tongue to ask what the matter was. He felt as though part of him was awake and the rest was struggling behind, trying to catch up.

Seeing his lips move, her thin fingers went to her mouth and she shook her head. He stared stupidly at her. She pointed to the figures lying around him still locked in sleep and again indicated that he should make no sound. First light was creeping through the doorway and he could see the shapes of the other occupants of the house like humps and hillocks in the half dark.

She tugged at his arm, determined that he should wake and follow her.

His eyes began to close again. He was still weary and confused.

She pulled his rugs from him and roughly poked and tugged at him to force him awake. Through the haze of his sleepiness he caught an impression of fear and urgency in her movements. He began to realize that he might be in danger and that she was trying to warn him.

Suddenly he was fully alert.

So urgent was her insistence that he had barely time to gather his belongings together before she had him stooping and crouching and creeping to the door of the house. She went ahead of him and held him back with her hand while she made sure all was clear outside.

He followed her unquestioningly when she gestured him on.

It was very early indeed and the village, half hidden in mist, its inhabitants still lost in sleep, seemed ghostly and unreal.

The air was chill and the grass wet from the night's rain.

He held her hand and allowed himself to be led away from the village, first to a clump of trees and then, stumbling and slithering a bit, up a muddy hill.

Every time he tried to open his mouth to ask a question she put her finger on his lips and he was silent.

When they reached the top she pulled him down beside her amongst the long wet grass and pointed to a winding path, barely visible, to the south west of the village.

At first he saw nothing but the track threading brown amongst the grass and bracken, but soon he caught a sound followed almost immediately by the sight of a group of men emerging from the mist and bearing down upon the houses.

As they drew nearer Isar noticed that they were led by one of the villagers, one who had not joined the others in sleep but had crept from the house when the questioning was at its height. The men behind him were larger than he, dressed in dark leather, carrying staves and armed with axes and swords. They stepped in time with each other in a way that made Isar shudder. It was as though by giving up their individuality of movement, they gave up their humanity.

He looked at the girl's tense face and knew that she had saved his life.

'Thank you,' he whispered, 'may the Spirit Realms keep you as safe as you have kept me.'

She shook her head slightly and there were lines of anxiety still upon her pale face. She pointed away from the village.

He followed her gaze. Was there further danger there?

She tugged his arm and he knew he must follow her yet again. The men were out of sight now, but it was not safe to stay so near the village. If the informer had convinced them that there was a traveller from the east present without the

Mark of Groth upon his forehead, they would certainly scour the countryside until they found him.

'Where can we go?' He whispered to the girl.

Again she put her finger on her lips. Again he fell silent and followed her.

They had travelled a long way and the grass was already dry in the morning sunlight before she allowed him to rest.

Sitting with his back against a mossy rock he turned to her and said: 'I owe my life to you, but I do not know your name.'

A sad shadow flitted across her face and she turned away from him, staring out across the wild and rocky moor that stretched to the south of them.

Thinking that she had not understood, he repeated the question more slowly, emphasizing every word, as he would for a person who did not speak his language.

'Your name?'

She was silent still.

He took her arm and turned her to face himself, and then he put his hand on his own chest.

'My name,' he said distinctly, 'is Isar.'

And then he pointed to her and his expression was questioning.

'Your name?'

She shook her head sadly.

He looked at her, unsure what to do next.

She looked at him long and thoughtfully and then half opened her mouth as though she were about to say something, but shut it again before she did.

His eyes on her were so intense and curious, so gentle and so warm with friendliness she seemed to take heart to try again. But this time she opened her mouth wide and pointed to the inside of it.

Puzzled, he leaned forward and looked into her mouth.

And then he understood.

'O no!' He whispered.

Na-Groth had not only put the mark of slavery upon her forehead, he had cut out her tongue as well!

He drew back in momentary revulsion at what he had seen

and then he realized that her eyes were still upon him and she had noticed his reaction and had been hurt by it.

Tears were welling up in her eyes.

Filled with regret for the tactlessness of his expression and bitterness at the cruelty of Na-Groth, he took her hands, pulled her tenderly towards him and kissed the scar on her forehead.

She smiled for the first time since he had seen her and with that smile her thin, gaunt face became beautiful and full of light.

'But you can hear and understand?' He asked.

She nodded vigorously.

He thought about the situation.

He did not know how she had known that his presence had been betrayed, but it would be clear to Na-Groth's men that she had helped him to escape.

There could be no going back to her home village.

She would have to come with him.

But where was he going?

He looked at the open moor to the south, the hills behind him and to the east. The east was where he longed to be, but between him and his home lay unknown country filled with alert and hostile men.

He looked at the girl and his brow was creased with worry.

She was sitting with her knees drawn up and her chin resting upon them, staring unseeingly into the distance. The light had gone out of her face. She was exiled from her home and friends, companion of a fugitive.

Isar shut his eyes tightly and then opened them wide, hoping to find that the whole thing was nothing more than a bad dream.

But it was not a dream.

'We cannot sit here forever,' he said at last, decisively. 'You have saved my life and taken me from danger and it is now my turn to do this for you. It will not be easy, but we must return to my people and fetch help.'

To his surprise the girl shook her head.

'What do you mean? You will not come with me?'

She shook her head.

'You *will* come with me?'

She nodded affirmatively.

'What then? Why did you shake your head?'

She pointed to the west and nodded, pointed to the east and shook her head.

He frowned. Was she saying that they must go deeper into Klad?

She pointed yet again, vigorously, to the western hills.

'But why?' he demanded, frustrated that she could not answer.

She shrugged helplessly, but pointed yet again and her face showed her determination.

'No,' he said, 'you are wrong in this. There is nothing we can do against Na-Groth by ourselves. No, do not nod your head at me! Believe me, there is *nothing* we can do. We *must* go east and bring help from the Great Temple.'

He could see she was going to be stubborn about this, but he decided it was up to him to make the decisions. He pulled her up by her arm and turned her towards the east.

In order to make her come with him he had to hold her roughly and drag her along. She tried many times to break away and turn them back and her determination began to make him doubt that he was doing the right thing.

What if she had some good reason for going west?

But if she had she could not tell him, and he chose to believe that it was her fear of the unknown that kept her tied to her own country in spite of everything.

After a while she tired of fighting him and walked beside him without being held, but her face was sulky and her eyes were downcast.

They made good progress although sometimes they had to weave backwards and forwards across the country to avoid groups of Na-Groth's warriors and villagers they could not trust.

The sun had just passed its zenith when she held him back and began to look around her nervously like a young doe sensing danger.

At first he could hear nothing, but he remained still, respecting her superior sensitivity to danger.

And then, borne on a breeze, he heard distinctly what she had already heard, the distant bark and howl of dogs on the hunt.

He had heard packs of wild dogs in the forests and had feared them and pitied their hapless prey, but there was something mingled with the sound this time that made his body suddenly cold.

The throats of men were uttering sounds as savage as the dogs. Together they were hunting and together they were coming nearer.

The girl and Isar looked at each other and knew, without any doubt, that they were the prey.

They looked around desperately.

Where was there to run?

Where to hide?

It was the girl who made the decision.

She seized Isar's hand and they ran and slid and stumbled back down the hill they had just climbed so laboriously in the heat of the day, she turned him into the wood at the foot of the hill, through it and out the other side. She was making towards a gleam of water she had noticed earlier.

His lungs were aching with the effort, his blood hammering in his ears, but, louder than the hammering was the ghastly howl and jabber of the hunters as they came nearer.

The girl gave his hand a sudden tug and before he knew what was happening he was plunging off a low cliff into a lake. The shock of the cold water banged all his breath from him and, gasping and choking, he allowed himself to be pulled by the girl, who so much smaller and frailer than he, could swim with the strength and precision of a fish. She guided him under an overhang of rock and they hid close to the slimy, muddy bed of the lake edge, their heads obscured in water reeds and shadowed by the overhanging cliff.

They could still hear the dogs, but they could not see them.

Isar struggled to regain his breath. Mud and water weed plastered his head and the girl herself looked uncommonly like a rat, her face was so pinched and thin, her hair so closely bedraggled about her face. At another time he would have laughed, but now it was all he could do to keep hidden and prevent himself coughing.

The dogs were confused by the lake and led their human counterparts in several directions. Isar could hear the angry shouting of the men and thought perhaps they would be safe at last, but then he noticed that they had found a way down to the water's edge and were beating the reeds to find them. Startled water birds sprang up screeching and flew off in every direction. The air was noisy with shouting, barking, howling, yelping, screeching and the beat of stick on reed and wing on wing.

The girl pulled him under the water and started to swim towards the centre of the lake. He followed, though swimming did not come easily to him. His movements were clumsy compared to hers, but he managed somehow, his lungs almost bursting with the effort of holding his breath under water.

They had to surface.

There was no way to hold their breath longer.

In fear and dread they broke cover, took deep gulps of air and plunged again.

So quickly had they dived they had no time to ascertain whether they had been noticed by the hunters.

They had to swim on, not knowing if their pursuers would be waiting for them when they reached the shore or not.

Everything had happened so quickly Isar had not had time to grasp the full reality of the situation.

Now, in the murk of the cold and clouded water, his aching lungs told him that death could be very near.

A wave of longing to live flowed through him like pain.

Why had he let the days pass by so casually?

Why had he not shot each moment like a golden arrow, using to the full, the bow of life he had been given so freely as a gift.

He knew death was not final, but only the entrance to other Realms of Being . . . but . . . he enjoyed being Isar. He did not want to change . . . not yet . . .

'O Lord of Spirit, Lord of Sun, Lord of the Circle out of which there is no passing . . . give me longer as Isar . . . longer to love those that I love . . . longer that I may bring help to the people under the shadow of Groth!'

His head broke the surface of the water . . . the sun burst with light into his eyes and he could see nothing but brightness and gold.

Blinking and dazed, he could feel the young stranger's hand in his and his clothes dragging on him and the mud of the lake bed sucking at his feet as he stumbled and struggled out on to the pebbles of the shore.

The voices of his enemies were in the distance.

He looked back and saw them still beating the reeds on the other side. Unquestioningly he followed the girl into the woods that bordered the lake and that mercifully hid them from their pursuers.

But she would not let him rest until the sun was setting, and then they fell upon the hill side, aching in every limb, caked with dried mud, scratched and torn by briars, but alive, and safe at last from the hounds who had lost their scent.

Isar, lying on the ground, staring up at the strange luminous blue of the sky just before night fall, saw a lark soar high above them and heard its sweet call as it turned to find its nest.

'I shall call you Lark,' he said. 'You remind me of a lark.'

The girl looked at him, puzzled. A lark is noted for its song, and she had no voice.

He smiled and understood her thought.

'You are small and light and swift. You ride high and see further than most of us. You do not sing with words, but I hear the sweetness of your voice in my head,' he said, and he closed his eyes sleepily. 'Besides,' and his thoughts seemed to continue in his dreams, 'the lark is a sacred bird and leads men to the safety of the Spirit Realms.'

The Sacrilege

Slowly the Spear-lord's wife, Isar's mother, Fern, walked amongst the green profusion of her garden. The sunset had been magnificent, but for once she had not bowed her head to it, nor murmured the customary words of evening prayer.

This coming darkness brought one more night of danger to her much loved son and the prayer she must say must not be one of custom, but of power and sincerity.

As she walked she gently touched the darkening branches of her Rowan tree, called with her heart that all that lived and grew, rooted in the earth and drawing strength from sun and air, would hear her and convey wariness to Isar, strength of purpose, sharpness of senses.

She sank upon her knees and lowered her forehead to the earth.

She listened to the minute earth sounds of growing roots, of burrowing earth worms, the slow suck and slither of slug and snail. Deep in the earth she felt the process of decay and renewal as once dead matter was slowly changed into a new cycle of life. Below that she could detect the restless shift and grind as strata of rock deep buried sought new levels and re-adjusted to old. Nothing stayed the same.

She could not hold Isar immobile, to be broken by the slow chisel of time. She did not ask that.

But tears nevertheless fell on the soft grass for what could never be.

'What are you doing?' a deep voice spoke above her, and she looked up the full length of Karne, her husband, who seemed, from this angle, to be a giant.

He took her in his arms and lifted her up. He saw the tears on her cheeks. Gently he wiped away the small shreds of grass and stick that adhered to her soft skin.

'I was praying,' she whispered with a catch in her voice as she tried to stop herself weeping.

He held her close.

He kissed her deeply on the lips.

At first she surrendered to the kiss and felt comforted by its intensity. But a cold feeling began to come over her and she pulled herself sharply back.

Had she imagined there was the taste of parting in the kiss?

She looked at him.

He was in his travelling cloak, a broad leather belt fastening his sword to his side, leather on his arms for protection, and, over his shoulder, the fighting bow he had not used since Wardyke's war.

He put his fingers to her lips.

'I know, I know,' he said softly. 'But it has to be. You must stay at home and pray, but I must go and seek him. I will bring him back to you. I swear it!'

'How can you swear it?' she said fiercely, weeping, her voice harsh. 'Do you know all that the Spirits know? Are you God Himself that you can order a man's destiny?'

'Destiny comes from men's thoughts and men's actions working within the limited Circle of our Existence. The Lord who wears the whole of our universe as though it were one bead upon a necklace, will not deny my right to use my body and my mind while I have them, in the way that seems right to me.'

Fern wanted Isar safely back more than anything in the world and she trusted Karne greatly, but, what if Karne were lost to her as well as Isar . . . how would she live?

'You must not think those thoughts,' chided Karne, seeing her expression. 'I will take care. There are other men coming, but I cannot wait until they are all assembled and ready.' Karne had never been noted for his patience! 'I will go ahead and when they arrive I will know the situation exactly and what the plan must be.'

'Does Kyra know that you are going?'

Fern dried her eyes, knowing that it was useless to continue fighting the inevitable.

'No. You will tell her my love, when I am safely gone.'

'But . . .'

'I am going. The Temple is slow to resort to arms and busy with the devious ways of mind and spirit. In case they do not work, I and other armed men, will be ready.'

'It is a long way to Klad,' she said forlornly, 'the methods of the Temple may be the only ones that will be effective and in time.'

'No one will be more pleased than I if their methods work. I go only in case they do not.'

'And because you cannot sit around and do nothing no matter how many priests command it!' A flicker of amusement passed through Fern's eyes.

He smiled broadly and touched her under the chin, looking down into the golden brown depths of her eyes with amused tenderness.

'I love you,' he said and then, suddenly solemn, 'I *will* take care.'

She watched him go, the green curtain of creeper that hung from tree to tree making a kind of archway, hiding him from her sight almost immediately.

The night would be soon upon him. A patient man would have waited until dawn. But Fern knew that every man must do things in his own way, at his own pace.

His way was not her way, nor the way of the Temple, but that did not mean it was wrong.

The same night that saw the beginning of Karne's journey, and Isar sleeping upon the hillside in Klad worn out by the pursuit of the hunting dogs, found Deva in sleep far away in time and place, walking in the garden of her former life.

After the experience of the night before she had not tried to come to the garden, but had deliberately tried to think of other things at the time of going to bed.

She lay flat on her back in her rugs and thought about Isar, not the danger he was now in, but the happy times they had had together.

She remembered how she used to sit beside him while he carved figures in wood, sometimes for her and sometimes for other people. Grown-up people made a great fuss over his work and took it for their homes.

She had been with him a few summers ago when he had been carving the Sacred Symbols into the wood of the great columns that lined the entrance to the Temple from the ceremonial avenue.

There had always been wooden columns marking the entrance, but it was Kyra who suggested to the Inner Council that Isar should mark them with the Sacred Signs.

'I have seen those marks on houses,' Deva said.

'You have seen them everywhere.'

'And on stone . . .' Deva continued thoughtfully.

'Everywhere!' he said vaguely, pausing briefly in his work to wave his hand, his gesture taking in the Circle of the great Temple, the low hills studded with burial mounds surrounding it, the sky surrounding the hills.

She looked around, puzzled.

'You mean everything seems to go in circles, and the signs are circles within circles?'

He nodded abstractedly, concentrating on pressing his blade into the hard, dark wood at just the right angle, to draw it with all his strength against the grain.

'Is it because our eyes are round that we see round?' she demanded.

He did not answer.

'Or does everything go round anyway, quite apart from how we see it?'

He was still silent, concentrating on his work.

She stood beside him, a small figure determined not to be ignored, silent for a few moments, but soon with another question.

'Why do you put that sort of path from the inside to the outside?'

'Or from the outside to the inside,' he said enigmatically.

She was beginning to get very irritated with him.

'I do not think very much of our secret symbols,' she said boldly, lifting her chin, her black eyes flashing at him.

This gave him pause and he looked at her shocked.

Pleased with the effect of her last words she decided to give him something else to think about.

'I have seen much more interesting symbols carved on stone columns in a garden I go to sometimes.'

He was silent for a few moments.

He stood up and looked straight into her eyes.

He knew Deva was mischievous and could not always be relied on to tell the truth, specially when she was trying to attract attention to herself.

'What sort of symbols?'

'Birds and animals and . . . men looking sideways . . . sometimes men with animal heads . . . all sorts of different things!'

'Where is this garden?'

'It is a secret.'

'I thought as much,' he said. 'You are making it up.'

'I am *not*,' she said hotly.

But she had lost his attention and he went back to his carving, an irritating expression of disbelief on his face.

She was furious and stood silent and fuming for what seemed a long while, and then she took one of his best knives and while he was not looking carved some of the tiny figures she had seen in her 'dream' garden on a sliver of flat chalk stone she found beside her on the ground.

They both worked silently, completely absorbed in what they were doing. It was the arrival of the Lord Khu-ren, her father, that shattered their concentration.

Deva would never forget the next few moments. In them she learnt how painful it was for her when Isar was angry with her, and also that her 'dream' garden might very well have a reality she had not before been sure about.

Khu-ren found the two young people apparently peacefully and harmoniously at work together, and he greeted them lovingly.

Isar looked up and saw Deva using his best wood carving knife on stone, and with an unaccustomed shout of rage seized it, cutting her finger accidentally as he did so.

She screamed as blood spurted out.

The peaceful scene was instantly transformed to one of chaos. Isar was shouting, partly with anger about his knife and partly with horror at what he had done.

Deva had the attention she wanted and used every trick to keep it. The cut was not really very painful but she made a great fuss and was carried off by her father to have it bound with healing leaves and cobweb.

Isar trailed behind, distraught and anxious, convinced he had maimed her for life.

When Khu-ren straightened out her clenched hand to bind the finger, the piece of carved chalk stone, now stained with blood, fell on to his knee. He put it aside while he was working on her hand, but when the bleeding was staunched and the two youngsters started grumbling at each other again for what had happened, he picked up the chalk stone in order to distract their attention from their grievances.

'What is this?' he asked, holding it out and looking at it carefully, expecting to see that Deva had been copying the Sacred Symbols Isar was carving on the wooden column.

Instead he saw, carved crudely but unmistakably, the symbols of his own land, the land of the desert and the Great River, that he had left so deliberately behind when he was a young man.

His face grew grave and he stared at the carved stone long and intensely.

Deva and Isar became silent.

They could see his change of mood and were at a loss to understand it.

He repeated his question, but his voice was now stern and serious.

Deva was a little frightened. Her father could be very formidable at times.

Seeing that she could not answer, Isar spoke quickly for her, as he had often done before when her mischief had led her into trouble.

'It is nothing,' he said.

'Nothing?' Khu-ren said pointedly, holding out the piece of stone for Isar to see.

Isar saw some extremely clumsy scratchings, one of which resembled a bird with very long legs, and one that could have been a man but he seemed deformed. His body was facing forwards, but his feet and head were facing sideways.

He looked puzzled. Why should this make Khu-ren so grave?

'Where have you seen these things?' The High Priest demanded of the little girl.

Nervously she shook her head.

'Nowhere,' she whispered drily.

He looked at her with the same black eyes as her own, long and penetratingly. Then he looked at Isar.

'She . . . she said she saw them in a secret garden. But I think she was just making up stories as usual,' Isar said.

Deva flushed with the injustice of this remark, but was not sure enough of herself to contradict it. She seemed to be in some kind of trouble because of the scratchings, but she did not know why. She decided to stay quiet until she was certain of her position.

'They . . . they are very good,' Isar ventured now, feeling sorry for her. 'Do you not think so, my lord?'

'No,' said Khu-ren, 'I do not think so. And I do not like lies either.'

Isar put his arm around Deva and she snuggled up to him.

'My lord!' He lifted his chin to speak defiantly, but before he could say more Khu-ren held up his hand to silence him.

Isar was silent, not because of the authority of the High Priest's gesture, for he would have dared anyone to protect Deva, but because he could see the man's mood had changed again.

'Never mind,' Khu-ren said. 'We may be making too much of this. They are just the idle scratchings of a little girl after all. I am sorry I frightened you,' he said to Deva and kissed the top of her head. 'Run along now!' He waved them away and went off himself, but Deva noticed with rage that he took her piece of stone with him.

'Idle scratchings!' she said bitterly. 'I will have you know that they are copies of symbols I have seen in the most beautiful garden in the world. They are from columns that hold up a roof to make a shady walk around the garden because the sun is very hot there. Much hotter than here!' she said fiercely to Isar. 'Your fair skin would be burnt to ashes there. But mine would be all right!' she added proudly.

Something stirred in Isar's memory, something from his childhood. He had known once, but the knowledge was as vague as dream knowledge, that he and Deva had lived and loved before in ancient times and the garden she described seemed fleetingly familiar to him too. But the image was too unclear. He could not be sure.

'You must tell me more about your garden,' he said gently to her, stroking her black silky hair soothingly.

'You said I was making up stories!' she said sulkily.

'I was wrong,' he said humbly. 'It is very easy to be wrong about things.'

They found a bank to sit upon and she told him about her 'dream' visits and what she had seen there.

He listened intently but could not say truthfully he believed she was really visiting an ancient garden (in memory), or whether she was dreaming about an imaginary garden.

But then he thought about the scratchings on the stone and how disturbed Khu-ren had been.

It was strange.

Midsummer had come and gone four times since then and now he lay upon an alien hillside with danger all around him, a girl who could not speak beside him, and Deva wrapped in her rugs in the High Priest's house, and yet walking in a garden half a world away in a time long since passed.

This time Deva had drifted into the garden while she was thinking of Isar and the occasion when he had cut her finger. Surprised, she still felt pain in the same finger in her dream, and looked down at her hand. A small snake was slithering away across the hot paving stones and she knew she had been bitten.

She screamed.

Someone came running.

It was a boy, slightly older than herself. Someone she had never seen before. Someone lithe and muscular and dark, someone who excited her so much that she stood still, holding her finger tightly to stop the poisoned blood flowing, but making no sound.

Within moments he had a dagger in his hand and was cutting her finger. He seemed so sure of himself she made no murmur though she expected the pain to be extreme. Having cut, he sucked and spat the mixture of blood and venom on to the smooth white crystal of the paving stones. She stared at it with horror, dazed by the suddenness of it all.

He was still sucking and spitting when the king's guards came running and seized him, beat him and dragged him away.

'No! No!' she screamed, but they did not listen to her. She tried to run after them, to explain, but she began to feel as though she were falling and everything was growing dark around her.

She must have fainted.

Time in that ancient land must have passed, because when she became conscious again she was lying in a strange room on a bed of black wood with four gold panther heads at each corner.

Men were bending over her.

One was her father.

She lifted her arms to him at once and struggled to tell him of the boy who had saved her life, and must himself be saved.

He soothed her with his large and finely shaped hands, he gazed at her with loving concern, but he did not understand a word that she was saying.

Desperately she sought the right words.

The words that came made sense to her, but not to the men who surrounded her.

She looked around in despair.

She was caught between two life times.

She was at once the girl of the garden, the daughter of the architect, who had been bitten by a snake and rescued by a boy who should not have been in the king's garden, and yet she was speaking in the language of Deva who lived now in another life and in another time.

Weeping with frustration she found herself awake in Deva's own time, Kyra at her side questioning her gently about her bad dream.

'It was not a dream,' she sobbed. 'It was not a dream!'

'The garden again?' Kyra asked softly.

Deva did not answer, but her mother knew by her face that it was so.

'Tell me,' she commanded softly.

Deva was wide awake and sitting up fiercely.

'I will tell you *nothing* lady, until you bring Isar home.'

Kyra shook her head sadly.

'You do not help Isar this way, daughter,' she said. 'Nor yourself.'

'*You* do not help him lady! You do not help him!' she cried bitterly.

'There is no help in former times. "*Now*" is the material we have to work with. *Now* we try everything in our power to help him and ourselves.'

'Have you spoken with him? Have you found him?'

Deva clasped her mother's hands for the moment forgetting that she had sworn to ask her nothing until she brought Isar home.

Kyra's face was grave.

'We think we gave him deep and restful sleep . . .'

'Is that all!' Deva cried in anguish.

'A rested and refreshed mind and body could make the difference between life and death in such a situation of danger.'

'But have you not *spoken* with him?'

'I was on my way to the Temple when I heard you cry out,' Kyra said.

'O no!' Deva was in despair again.

Her mother rose.

'Gently, my love,' she said tenderly. 'Tonight the moon is full, the stars are right, and the powers of the Stones will be at their greatest. Tonight we will reach him. Do not fear.'

But Deva did fear.

Their communication with him could only mean greater danger for him. They were not going to call him home. They were going to 'use' him to do their work in Klad.

She lay in the dark tossing and turning, sleep impossible, reasonable trust and patience far from her. The darkness seemed to press upon her like a suffocating incubus mocking her helplessness, whispering to her of Isar's danger.

She had failed him once long ago when he had been flogged and imprisoned for trespassing in the king's garden, and she was failing him again.

Where Kyra had moved the door skins to allow her exit, a wedge of blue-grey remained, drawing Deva's eye.

There was a way out of the darkness if only she had the nerve to take it.

The dark hole of her chamber had a doorway. Outside the doorway the full moon was climbing steadily above the Temple, the Sacred place of Tall Stones, the Inner Sanctum which was forbidden to non-initiates.

She sat up, cold and rigid with fear at the daring idea that had come to her.

She rose instantly, her decision made.

She took light from the torch that burnt all night beside the entrance to their house and lit several little chalk-stone oil lamps.

She searched her mother's chamber for the robes she had worn when the messenger from Klad had arrived.

With trembling hands she transformed herself into the semblance of a priest and set upon her head the diadem of jet Kyra had worn at her inauguration.

Time was passing and she must not be late.

Where was the long blue cloak that would complete the image?

Her mind was racing.

There was a kind of justice in the fact that to save his life she had to trespass in a forbidden place just as he had done at their first meeting in that other life so long ago.

There was no doubt that she would be punished too.

But nothing mattered to her except his safe return.

She found the cloak at last and drew it about herself.

The moon was high enough for her to need no torch and she flitted unseen from shadow to shadow until she neared the Temple entrance. Then she walked boldly forward as though she had the right to pass into the Sacred Circle.

The young priest who had been set at the entrance to warn away anyone not part of the night's work, half raised a hand to stop her, but let it fall again as she swept elegantly past him.

Once within the Circle she came to rest in the shadow of one of the Giant Stones that rimmed the outer bank. From there she could see without being seen the ceremony taking place in the Northern Inner Sanctum.

She wanted to be sure she knew the position of everyone before she moved.

Up to now she had been so intent upon her purpose she had had no warning pangs to give her pause, but now the majesty of the scene before her filled her with the beginnings of doubt and fear.

The Great Temple was always an impressive sight and held within its high sloping banks and its circle of giant Sacred Stones, a kind of powerful energy, that ordinary people found almost too strong to bear. Deva could feel it now. The whole scene seemed charged with significance and power. The shadows of the rocks were blacker than ordinary shadows and lay at the feet of their masters like deep holes leading into the earth. The Stones themselves gleamed eerily in the moonlight and the figures of the priests moving around the Sanctum seemed at once very small next to the Tall Stones and yet very large compared to their normal selves. The darkness of their cloaked bodies was like the darkness of the shadows, as though she was looking not *at* them, but through them into . . . unimaginable depths of Being . . . pure consciousness, without form . . .

Deva tried to stop herself trembling by reminding herself that she saw these men and women every day and they were not much different from herself.

But even as she told herself this the power of the Temple began to work on her and she began to see the contrast between her own selfish, short-term desire to rescue her love, and their greater and more comprehensive one, to rescue a whole people.

She put her hands to her ears as though the words were reaching her from outside.

'I *will not* listen,' she hissed. 'He *must* be brought back. There *will be* another way to save our land!'

Afraid to wait a moment longer she made her move and slid across the grass like the shadow of a snake, until she was just outside the inner ring of Stones where the priests were working.

The priests stood just outside the Circle, each marking a Stone, each with his eyes closed, deep in concentration.

At the very centre the two Lords of the Sun moved from Stone to Stone of the Sacred Inner Three, murmuring softly and touching their foreheads reverently to the ancient channels of power between Earth and Sky, Body and Spirit.

Deva leapt into the Circle and stood as though frozen in Time, hearing as loud as thunder what had been incomprehensible murmuring to her a moment before, the given name of Isar and following it the Secret Name she had no right to hear.

With the hearing of it the Moon that rode in the white light above them seemed to explode and lightning burst from it, touching the tip of every Stone in the Great Circle.

Horrified, Deva saw herself in a cage of white fire, the faces of the priests huge around her, their eyes like black sockets in their heads.

'Isar!' she screamed and then, with all the passion in her body, the Dread Name she was never meant to know.

With the speaking of it pain went through her like a sword and she fell into darkness like a pebble into a bottomless pit.

'Deva!' screamed Kyra, priest no more, but mother rushing to her child.

'Deva!' gasped Khu-ren.

The priests outside the ring opened their eyes and stared astonished at the scene before them.

They had heard and seen nothing, but had felt the sudden shattering of the vibrations that had held them locked into trance.

Now they saw the two Lords of the Sun stooping over a third figure, lifting it to the moonlight. For a moment they fancied it was Isar returned magically in some way by the power of the incantation, but as the pale light fell on the face of the limp figure they saw it was the beautiful girl child of the High Priest and the Lady Kyra, Deva, who charmed and plagued them as they went about their business in the Temple community.

They drew closer, but did not dare to cross the invisible line that divided the Inner Circle from the Outer.

In Klad Isar jerked awake, his name exploding in his head.

He sat up and looked around him, bewildered, his heart pounding. He half expected to find himself at the centre of a thunder storm, but everything was strangely calm. The moon was full and brilliant, throwing the landscape into relief, picking out with light the beaded threads of streams and flat surfaces, darkening the shadows of cliffs and trees and rocks.

Awake he was not sure that it had been his name that he had heard. Asleep it had seemed to belong to him and he had responded, but now he knew it was not Isar. He struggled to remember it more clearly but already it was slipping away from him like water draining into sand.

He looked at his companion. She was curled up, her knees drawn up to her chin, sleeping soundly.

Should he wake her and suggest that they travel on? He was refreshed and restless now, anxious to move, troubled by the strangeness of his experience.

It was light enough to find their way and probably safer than by daylight.

He began to long for home with a desperation that was almost an ache . . . Home where there was quiet and peace, long hours to sit carving or dreaming, helping his mother tend the growing things of the garden, carrying the water from the spring for her. She always wanted water from the spring rather than from the stream which was nearer.

'It comes from deep in the rock. It is fresh and clear and full of earth energy. Drink. You will see what I mean.'

Thinking of that water now gave him a thirst.

He touched Lark's shoulder and she sprang up, instantly on the defensive, fear and the moonlight making her eyes gleam unnaturally in the dark.

He was sorry that he had woken her and tried to tell her so. He tried to explain the name he had heard in his head.

'I am certain I was being called home.'

He could not see the expression on her face.

'We will move on now. It will be safer at night. Easier to hide from Na-Groth's men.'

She nodded and gathered herself together turning towards the west.

'No!' he said. 'I am going home. I have been called home. They know there is nothing I can do against Na-Groth.'

She did not turn, but continued to gaze in the direction she wished to go.

'What do you want me to do?' he burst out angrily. 'What could I possibly *hope* to do!'

He hated her silence. How he longed for talkative little Deva!

The girl's quiet was confronting him with a decision he did not want to make.

'Well, I cannot help it,' he said at last, 'if you want to go and throw yourself at Na-Groth's feet I cannot stop you. But *I* am going home!'

He picked up his carrying pouch with determination and slung it over his shoulder.

He looked at her.

43

She had not moved.

Her small face was set and cold.

'You would do well to come with me. You will be safe with my people. Here there is nothing for you but pain and death.'

She looked at him with her large eyes, but she gave no sign that she had changed her mind.

'I am going now,' he said. 'Are you coming?'

She shook her head.

'Goodbye.'

She stared at him in silence.

'Thank you for saving my life.'

He waited a few moments longer, but she did not move.

'Goodbye then,' he said again and turned to go.

He looked back at her, but she still did not stir.

He started to walk, looking over his shoulder time and again, hoping she would follow him, not believing for a moment that she would not.

Deva often played tricks like this, but he always won in the end. She hated to be left alone and when she saw she was not going to get her own way she always gave in.

But Lark was not Deva.

Suddenly the dark smudge of her figure on the hill disappeared.

His heart leapt. She was coming.

But when some time had passed and there was no sign of her he was worried. He stopped where he was, standing in as much light as he could, hoping she would find him.

'Perhaps she is playing a trick on me and will stalk me in the shadows, making me think that she has gone the other way.'

He still could not grasp that she would dare Na-Groth's country, alone.

He walked on, slowly, thinking to give her time to catch him up.

The night wheeled slowly past.

He strained to catch the smallest sound of breaking twig or rustling leaves that would betray her presence, but gradually it became clear to him that she was not going to join him.

With an exclamation of irritation he stopped in his tracks

and sat down upon a boulder. He had to think.

A dark feeling of despair took over his heart. He was lonely, afraid, anxious. He did not know what to do.

All he knew was that the thing he most wanted to do, to go home, was somehow impossible.

He had never felt so lonely in his life.

He, who loved to be alone, was now lonely and afraid.

Almost without realizing he had made the decision, he stood up and turned on his heel.

He ran, clambering and scrambling over the moonlit screes, trying to retrace his steps to where he had last seen her.

When he came to the place where he thought they had slept, the shadows around him were different and he was not at all sure that it was the place after all.

He pressed on and on, the night riding beside him like his own shadow.

The pale glow of dawn found him deep into Klad with no sign or trace of Lark to comfort him.

Deva was not dead, but she lay in a coma so deep that all the healing arts of the Temple priesthood could not penetrate the dark shell that enclosed her.

Kyra watched by her bed until she was too weary to lift her hand in protest as Khu-ren carried her off to her sleeping rugs. Of all the powers she had, the skills she had developed in the long hard years of training not one would come to her aid now that she most needed it.

Sitting beside her daughter, the only child she had or could ever have, her thoughts were dark and sad, weights holding down her winged spirit.

Gently Khu-ren reminded her of the dangers of an invasion from Klad and the urgency of their work with Isar to prevent it happening, but she could not listen. She understood the selfishness of Deva's love for Isar now. She experienced it herself. Nothing mattered to her if Deva died. And if Deva died it would be her fault. She had been too busy to realize how desperately her child had wanted Isar and how incapable she was of controlling that want. She should have helped her to understand, helped her to hold herself in check.

Tears flowed freely down her pale cheeks, worry gripped her mind like a cold hand, holding it immobilized so that she could not seek help from the deep inner levels of her consciousness, nor climb to the Spirit Realms to ask their help.

Khu-ren loving them both, knew that there were things to be done. He had tried to use the power of the Inner Sanctum without Kyra's presence, but the place had been so disturbed by Deva's act of sacrilege, the great priest found himself curbed and limited.

The way the priests worked with the flow of energies from Nature had always been dependent on a subtle balance of their own spiritual vitality, concentration and respect.

No one *demanded* anything of the Spirit Realms.

No one carried his own desires into the Circle or took knowledge that was not freely given.

Khu-ren feared for Deva's life and sanity.

She had heard the Secret Name of Isar. She had spoken it loud and clear.

Would she be allowed to walk the earth again in the body of Deva, having that knowledge?

Would Isar suffer for it?

There was much a High Priest did not know, and Khu-ren sighed to think of it.

He went to a little wooden chest in which he and Kyra kept many precious things, and he took out the flake of chalk-stone stained brown with Deva's blood and scratched with the signs of his own country.

He read them aloud.

'The Spirit of Man is many . . .'

He pondered long and seriously.

Many summers ago Khu-ren had left the place of his birth, the Two Kingdoms of the Desert, fed by the Great River, and had come to Kyra's small forest country. In his own land he had been dissatisfied with the changes in the teaching of the

Ancient Mysteries brought about by corrupt priests and kings who had forgotten how to be channels for the divine.

He had studied long and hard to reach his present position, dared initiation rites that had killed other men, learnt truths almost too heavy to bear, but during this time he had also grown in wisdom and sensitivity. He joined the secret Lords of the Sun and learned to travel the world in spirit form and commune with peoples he would never see in the flesh.

He had met Kyra in spirit form when she was an anxious child, frightened of the powers she had but did not yet understand. She came asking the mighty Lords of the Sun for help for her small, unsophisticated community in the far north of a green island country. A country which had no writing as his people knew it, but which read all natural things as though they were hieroglyphs. Trees, stones, the stars . . . all spelled out for them the words of their god.

Partly he had felt the natural pull of man to woman with this golden child, but more strongly he had felt the attraction of a new culture that seemed to answer all his doubts about his own.

Her people did not capture Truth in words, paint it on papyrus or hammer it on rocks until it was so fixed and dead, it had nothing of itself left.

Truth for them was caught in flight, glancing from mind to mind. Always set free again. Never caged.

All their hidden resources of spirit were used to gain wisdom, and when a Truth was accepted it was accepted because it had been *experienced*, not because it was written down.

For many years after Khu-ren had met Kyra he was restless and undecided.

There was much that was great about his country, but he had a terrible foreboding of its end as he travelled the countryside and saw carved on every Temple wall static words, fixed and inflexible against change, monstrous texts boasting of royal deeds that never happened, glorifying war and killing, perpetuating the small thoughts of small minds for other small minds to copy without understanding. Symbols of gods and

47

spirits accepted as the gods and spirits themselves.

Kyra's country became for him a place to start again, to try another way to Truth.

He had found it a hard way, exacting and uncompromising. But it had excited and satisfied him.

He knew that Deva had once, in another life, lived in the country he had left, but he had not realized she still visited it until he saw the stone she carved. Seeing it had stirred old memories, old anxieties. In many ways the country that was now his own would benefit by writing. In many ways it would not. It had been an issue he had considered long and seriously, and had decided that their civilization was to be left to change in its own way, in its own time. Neither he, nor Deva, nor any of the carefully chosen students he had brought with him, would change the pace or nature of its slow but subtle progress.

Was she there now, his daughter?

He turned the dusty stone over and over in his hand.

There was something else he knew about her past.

She and Isar had come to this country, immigrants like himself, man and wife fleeing from their homeland with a friend who had been threatened with execution. They had lived in this very part of the country, before the Great Temple had been built, and the man, who was now Isar, had been murdered here. But he had been born again many times since he had lived with Deva in those ancient times and had evolved, while Deva had taken her own life and refused to leave the place where he had been killed.

She had stayed, a shade, waiting for him, desperately clinging to her passion for him, refusing all change, all other destinies. It was she who chose Kyra to give her entrance to the time and place that would coincide with Isar's return.

The cord that bound them together was long and strong indeed.

Deva's eyelids stirred and Khu-ren stooped swiftly to massage her limbs.

How he longed to see into her mind!

Her long memories stretched to times before the corruption and her former father had been a man so great in wisdom that he had become a legend by the time Khu-ren was born.

Deva murmured something, but the word was unfamiliar to Khu-ren. A name perhaps? The name Isar had once been called?

Her eyelids were still again and she was lost to him.

Sadly he sat beside her until Kyra came to join him and then together they prayed for her return.

It was known by the priesthood of the Temple of the Sun that when a Stone had become defiled in some way and weakened in its power, there was a way of returning it to its former strength by certain rituals.

To begin with it was touched by the hands of priests circling in the direction opposite to the normal one, as though unwinding an invisible cord from it, and then a visible cord was wound spiralling around it by the High Priest from ground level to tip and down again to ground level.

The cord was a special one, kept only for this purpose, in a stone jar with a lid, brought from over the sea in the ancient days.

It was made of three long and unbroken threads. One of the purest white wool, one of flax dyed with blue indigo, and one of fine gold wire. Where the cord had come from could no longer be remembered, but they all knew it was very precious and very sacred and must never be touched for purposes other than the Cleansing of the Stones. Prayers to accompany the winding process had been handed down by tradition, many of the words strange to the present priesthood, but intoned nevertheless with great care and reverence. There were some mysteries it was not wise to question. Belief had proved itself

49

many times to be a powerful energy. Doubt was always destructive.

After the winding, came the unwinding, and the ceremonial return of the cord to the jar.

The cord and its beautiful container were then taken to the centre of the Circle of which the Stone was part, set upon the ground, three priests walking in measured steps around it, while drummers played an ancient tune, the beat of which was alien to the tunes of the usual Temple Ceremonies.

On this occasion it was not only one Sacred Stone that had been defiled, but the whole Inner Sanctum.

The ritual had to be repeated for each Stone of the Circle and three times for the three Stones that stood in the centre.

> Beautiful the gold, the blue and the white.
> Beautiful the Sun, the sky and the moon.
>
> Beautiful the man who stands on the earth
>   and reaches to the Sun,
>   and reaches to the Sky,
>   and reaches to the Moon.
>
> Beautiful is the sun that speaks to Man of the Source of
>   All.
> Beautiful is the sky that speaks to Man of the Spirit that
>   encompasses All.
> Beautiful is the moon that speaks to Man of the Earth
>   that reflects the All.

Softly the reverberations of the drums and the ancient words wove their spell about the place.

Softly and subtly the light around them seemed to change.

The Storm

Isar journeyed deeper and deeper into danger searching for Lark.

Having been betrayed once he was cautious in his approach to other people, and it was not until he reached his third village that he was so tired and hungry he decided to risk showing himself.

He heard music coming from one of the houses and took this as a sign that the people had not yet been completely demoralized by Na-Groth's rule.

He slipped silently from the shelter of the woods and made for the house with music.

His heart ached for the old ways of his people, so suddenly changed. Now a man must look continually over his shoulder and on no day could he assume a tomorrow.

The music was sweet and sad, made partly by the plucking of strings, partly by the blowing of pipes. He stood in the doorway and looked into the dim interior, his eyes slowly adjusting from blindness to shadowy sight.

To the people crowded into the house his presence brought fear and confusion. They were gathered about one of their number who had been brutally murdered by Na-Groth's men. They were secretly praying for him in the old way, which was now forbidden, and while they were doing so the light from the doorway was suddenly eclipsed, and the darkness of a long shadow fell upon them.

With his back to the light Isar's face could not be seen.

The music stopped.

For a long moment the air was heavy with shock and uncertainty, and then the son of the man who had been killed seized a heavy object and threw it with all his might at Isar's head. As it struck him with sickening force on the forehead he

51

began to keel over and in that instant the man's son fell upon him with a howl of hate and beat him to the ground with all his strength.

In the darkness and confusion Isar tried to defend himself, but within moments other men had joined the boy and he was being kicked and punched from every direction. He was dimly aware of women screaming and men shouting, and then the pain of the blows upon him became too great and he fell into the deep hole of oblivion.

'He is dead!' one of the villagers said.

They stopped hitting him and drew back to look at him.

He was cut and bruised and bleeding, but in the light from the doorway they could now see he was not one of Na-Groth's men. His hair was long and the colour of copper, his skin pale and fine, his face and hands gentle and sensitive.

Another silence filled the house, different from the first.

'What have we done?' was in everyone's mind.

Killing had never been their way. Once the passion of anger had passed, they would have regretted this act even if it had been one of Na-Groth's men.

They took Isar in and brought water to wash his wounds.

They laid him beside the man whose funeral this had been, and begged his forgiveness for making the ceremony of his passing ugly with hatred and violence.

Isar lay still.

In a far country in a long ago time he remembered another boy who had been unjustly beaten, and lying in his cell, had waited for death. He had been freed by a young girl and her father.

She was with him now in a garden of great beauty, and he lay on thick grass with his head upon her lap. A pearl grey crane stooped to stalk a grasshopper close by them, and he could hear the soft hush of water falling from fountains. He wished time could stand still and this moment could last forever. Her hand was cool against his cheek. He could even feel the pulse in her wrist.

But time did not stand still and the crane, stretching its long, slender neck, flew away, as a voice called his name.

He heard it now as though it came from a great, great distance and he knew that there was something he must do. The girl's hands were holding him back. The voice was calling him away.

Struggling to regain consciousness Isar caught words the source of which he was not certain.

'. . . you must leave the garden when you are ready . . . or the garden will leave you . . .'

Isar opened his eyes and looked into the anxious faces of strangers.

He lifted his hand to his head and felt the painful cuts and bruises.

'We are sorry,' the people said humbly, 'we thought you were one of Na-Groth's men.'

'They killed my father,' Gya, the young lad who had struck him first, explained.

'It is no matter,' Isar said gently. 'I should not have come upon you so suddenly. These are bad times.'

'Bad times indeed,' sighed several voices together.

'We are thankful you are not dead,' someone said fervently.

Isar smiled faintly.

'So am I!'

The people laughed nervously and pressed food and drink upon him, and propped him up with rolls of rugs so that his aching back would be supported.

He stayed a while with these people, his wounds being dressed tenderly, his every wish anticipated.

They hid him from the wandering bands of Na-Groth's men and found new clothes for him so that when it was time for him to move on he would not be so conspicuous.

The blow he had received on the forehead turned out to have been for the best after all. It left him with a scab that could almost pass for one of Na-Groth's marks.

'Why does he do this to people's foreheads?' Isar asked the woman who was dressing his wound, and who had commented

53

that it would help him with his disguise.

She shrugged.

'It is the sacred place of the head, the Seeing place. In ancient times it is said that people had three eyes, and this is where the third one was. I do not know if that is true, but I have noticed that the priest used to place this part of his forehead against the Tall Stones of the Sacred Circle.'

Isar looked thoughtful.

Na-Groth was symbolically blinding the conquered people as well as making them slaves.

In killing their priests he had truly blinded them, for the priests linked the community to the rest of the world and to the helpful Spirit Realms. Without them the community was limited and confined.

When the woman left him alone he prayed for help from Kyra and Khu-ren and the other mighty priests. His prayer was profound and sincere, but strangely seemed to make no contact.

His mind wandered to his mother and the man he accepted as his father, Karne. Their love still encompassed him and gave him comfort.

A small boy with straight ash white hair was sitting cross-legged on the floor of the chamber playing with pebbles, moving them around and talking softly to them as though they were people and he were acting out a story with them. Isar was sorry to break into his private world, but the thought of Fern had brought another thought with it.

He called to the child several times before his voice broke through the hold of his game.

At last he looked questioningly up at the tall stranger, with his innocent, wide blue eyes.

'Is there a Rowan tree near the Sacred Circle in this village?' Isar asked the boy.

The child stared at him.

'A Rowan tree?' Isar repeated.

The recognition in the boy's eyes showed that he knew what Isar was talking about, and that he knew where there was such a tree.

'Can you take me to it?' Isar pressed gently on.

Fear and darkness came to the boy's eyes and he shook his head vigorously.

'Why not?'

The boy did not answer, but Isar did not give up.

'Why not?'

'It is bad magic,' he said.

'Nonsense!' cried Isar. He remembered when he was a child how on a certain day travellers had arrived from the North and were greeted with singing and joy because they brought the gift of a Rowan tree. It was carried in a leather bucket full of earth and was planted with joyful ceremony amongst the grove of Special trees the priests cultivated for medicinal and magical purposes.

'It is good magic!' he said to the boy.

The boy shook his head gloomily.

'Show it to me and I will tell you if it is good or bad magic.'

The child looked at him intently as though trying to decide whether he could be trusted or not.

'You need not come near it yourself. Just show me where it is,' wheedled Isar.

At last the boy agreed to help him.

Isar was weak and dizzy and had to lean upon his small shoulder. Haltingly they left the house and stumbled along a path half overgrown with brambles. It seemed a long way from the village, but when the child at last paused and pointed, Isar realized why he had been so afraid.

The Sacred Circle had been desecrated just as the first one he had seen in Klad had been, the rotting carcases of men were still hanging from the Stones, and a wave of such fearful evil wafted from it that Isar reeled back.

Not far from it grew the Rowan trees, but even they were mutilated and almost unrecognizable.

Na-Groth had evidently known something of their reputation.

The boy was cringing, his eyes big with horror.

'Go!' Isar cried, pushing him away, regretting that he had exposed him to this. 'Go back to your home. I will try and change the bad magic to good magic.'

'The Circle?' the boy whispered.

'No. That is beyond me. But I will try what I can do with the trees.'

The boy retreated.

With a great effort of will Isar forced himself to go nearer the dread place, hoping that at least one of the trees was still alive.

Fern had told him once that all things were aware of each other in secret and subtle ways, time and space being no barrier to this kind of awareness. He knew that people could communicate in thought across the world, even though sometimes they did not realize they were doing it, but Fern had taught him that natural things could do this too. There was a Rowan tree in her garden and she had spent a great deal of time teaching him to know its ways.

'One day when you are in trouble, far from home, remember this tree. Find one of its kind and speak your heart to it. This one will hear it and bring me the message.'

At the time he had not been sure that he believed her, but now he was in trouble, far from home, and he needed help.

He searched among the sad charred remnants of the once beautiful trees, and found to his joy one pushing healthy shoots of green from scarred bark.

He stood beside it, holding the feathery leaves tenderly in his hand, stroking the deformed wood.

Deep in his being he called to Fern, told her of his danger and the suffering of the people he was amongst.

Then he stayed quiet for a long time, listening.

The air around him seemed to go very still and the boy who had retreated to the shelter of some bushes, but had not left him, fancied he could *feel* magic happening. His skin prickled cold and he looked around him apprehensively, but he was too curious to leave.

Slowly, Isar seemed to gain strength and comfort from the fresh life of the tree that had defied Na-Groth.

He could not say that he heard voices, but within himself he seemed to know what had to be done.

He was to find Lark and together they might have the strength and cunning to challenge Na-Groth and his god.

So be it.
  He would not try to run away again.

As soon as he was fit enough to travel Isar set off, the villagers half sorry to see him go, half glad that they would no longer run the risk of hiding him.

The boy Gya, brown and lean and muscular, went with him, eager to help in any way he could. His mother and sisters watched him go and held back their tears until he was out of sight.

Danger was everywhere now and to walk into it with head held high was no more foolhardy than to try to hide from it.

When they travelled the well worn paths they kept careful watch for Na-Groth's men, but when they took to the forests there were other dangers. On the third day Isar narrowly escaped being gored by a wild boar. It was only Gya's presence of mind and skill with the bow that saved him.

That night they roasted boar steaks over their small fire and laughed about the incident, Gya much amused by the look of astonishment on Isar's face as the boar charged, and the clumsiness with which he fell about in the undergrowth trying to avoid the beast's tusks.

'You are good with that bow,' Isar said with admiration, 'are you a hunter?'

'My father was. He taught me much. I used to go hunting with him sometimes, but more often than not we used to shoot just for the joy of it, not at living things, but at targets. Some of the boys would throw things in the air for us to aim at. My father never missed, but I cannot say the same for myself.'

'I am glad you did not miss this time,' Isar said with feeling.
Gya smiled.

'It is a matter of time and practice. I have had a bow so long it has become part of me. My father used to say that the bow is an extension of your arm, the arrow of your eye. It should become one action to look, to shoot and to hit. When I have shot well I feel I *am* the arrow. When I do not feel this I know I am going to miss the mark.'

'Do you not feel pity for the life you end when your arrow reaches a living creature?'

Gya's brown eyes clouded slightly.

'I do not shoot for the pleasure of killing. I shoot to keep alive — and to save life!' he added, looking reproachfully at Isar.

Isar acknowledged the rebuff and bowed his head slightly.

The meat was good and he was very hungry.

As they came nearer to Na-Groth's stronghold, they kept more and more under cover and asked fewer questions of the villagers they met.

Eyes became increasingly unfriendly and wary, words were short and unwelcoming, fields were unworked, children thin and hungry. The men were mostly away, busy with Na-Groth's work, and the women and children were left to tend the land. In normal times this would not have been so disastrous as the women and children had always worked side by side with the men in anything that needed doing, but now the will to work had gone. Whatever they made or grew was taken from them. They were lonely, afraid and resentful. They could no longer feel the presence of invisible helpers, no longer believe that everything they did had meaning and purpose.

Na-Groth had told them the Spirit Realms did not exist.

They were alone but for Na-Groth and his fearsome god.

So shaken was Gya by what he had seen and heard, that he railed against their ancient God that he should let such monsters as Na-Groth exist and flourish.

Isar was silent at first, remembering how recently he had felt the same way, but thoughts were struggling to take shape and he felt bound to share them with Gya.

'You cannot drink from a stagnant pool without being sick,' he said. 'The clear stream fed by a healthy spring is constantly moving, fighting obstructions, changing and causing change. Do you not see, Gya, our way of life was good, but if it were never challenged, it would become stagnant?'

Gya had come to respect Isar in the time they had been together. At first he had been amused that Isar knew so little about the things that came easily to himself, but now he was beginning to see that physical prowess was not the only defence against evil.

'Our God gives us the dignity of free choice. Na-Groth chooses one way, and we another. *Ours* is the responsibility, and it is *our* efforts that will have to set the wrong to rights. Do you not see that?'

Gya could feel Isar's convictions strengthening his own. He felt inspired to leap up and attack the armies of Na-Groth single handed.

'No,' laughed Isar. 'That is not the way. No man has enough arrows to kill the armed men of Groth. They will spring up again as fast as they are killed if the idea that feeds them is not first discredited. We must use our minds before we use our arms in this battle.'

The two young men sat together on the hill, shadowed by trees, the sun sloping to the Western horizon, where dark clouds rose to meet it.

They sat silently for a long time, Isar deep in thought, Gya flicking little bits of twig at a particular stone. Even at rest he was flexing and training his muscles and his eyes to accuracy of aim.

The night brought heavy rains and harsh winds.

Karne, making his way westwards was gathering fighting men to his side.

'I do not say that we *will* have to fight, but we will form a barrier as long as is needed between the troubled land of Klad and our own houses. This will give the priesthood of our Temple time to work their magic on the enemy and drive it from our shores.'

The story of Panora's war had become legend, and the defeat of a mighty army, on the plains not far from the Great Temple itself, by the sole use of priestly Mysteries, was told around the cooking fires from one end of the country to the other.

The people had great faith in their priesthood and Karne did not choose to tell them that the priests of the Tall Stones and the Sacred Circles in Klad had been destroyed as easily as ordinary men.

Not all the men he spoke to joined him on the march, but enough to make a sizeable force grew steadily as they approached the menace in the west.

Villagers near to Klad were already in a state of agitation. Friends and relatives had disappeared on market journeys to the west. They were beginning to realize that something was very wrong, but had not been sure what it was.

The night of storm and rain that beset Isar and Gya on their hill, doused the cooking fires of Karne's army and hid their approach from Na-Groth's spies.

In the Temple of the Sun the Sacred Inner Sanctum was gradually restored to power. Kyra could feel the coursing and the spiralling of its energy as she leant her forehead to the Stones.

'Now,' she called in a ringing voice, 'let us begin!'

The priests took their positions around the Circle, the two Lords of the Sun stood within the triangle of the Holy Three at the centre.

'Now!' Khu-ren cried, and as the wind of the coming storm rose soughing in the trees, the sound of their incantation rose to meet it.

Round and round the priests went, stirring the invisible energies of the air.

Still stood the two tall Lords of the Sun, male and female, concentrating their energy and their will to reach Isar in a distant and desolate land.

In her garden Fern stood with her arms around her Rowan tree, her cheek against its trunk, which pulled against her, as above, its branches were torn and buffeted by the wind.

She thought of Karne and Isar, and prayed that all the strength of the Spirit Realms there to help them, would be wisely used.

'Remember,' she whispered, 'you are not alone. No one is alone. Remember it!'

Deva's eyelids flickered and for the first time since she had fallen into unconsciousness she opened her eyes and looked around her.

She was alone in Kyra's chamber, the flame of a lamp flickering beside her, the sound of wind and rain howling and beating against the wooden walls of the house, the door covering flapping like the wings of a trapped bird.

Slowly she sat up, looking around her at the shadows, everything unfamiliar. Where was the hot sand of the desert, the green lush lands of the flood plain of the Great River, and her father's Pyramid gleaming in the sun?

Slowly her eyes adjusted as her mind accepted what she saw.

She knew that she was Deva, the daughter of Khu-ren and Kyra.

The storm drove Isar and Gya to shelter under a ledge of rock, squeezed between the rough earth and the hard stone, their hands scratched from the bushes and plants they had pulled aside in their haste as the wind drove a sudden squall of rain upon them.

As the night wore on the two young men fell uneasily into dark pits of sleep, only to find themselves, unrefreshed, struggling to wakefulness again. So savage was the night Isar found himself fearing that it would go on forever, that Groth had somehow extinguished the God of Light, and nothing but darkness and despair was left to contemplate.

It was during one of these moments of half sleep that Isar

was startled to see the dark outline of a figure standing on the hillside beside him.

Illuminated in the sudden splendour of a flash of lightning he recognized the Lady Kyra.

He gasped and struggled to free himself from the encumbrance of the branches and turfs he had laid upon himself.

'My lady!' he cried and wrenched himself free, half tumbling out of the cleft of rock into the stinging night.

But she was gone.

The next lightning flash revealed a hillside empty save for the thin trees struggling in the clutches of the wind and a distraught Isar streaming with icy water.

'What are you doing?' shouted Gya. 'Have you gone mad?'

'The Lady . . . I saw the Lady Kyra,' Isar babbled frantically, searching into the darkness for the figure he had seen so briefly but so tantalisingly close.

'There is no one there. You are crazy!' growled Gya. 'Come back before you fall and break your neck.'

Isar looked around him as lightning flooded the scene once more with its eery, sickly light.

There was nobody there.

Gya was right. He was crazy.

He crawled back under the ledge, shivering and soaked, his heart aching with disappointment.

'Rub yourself, beat your arms . . . you will freeze to death if you do not.'

Gya began to pummel him and he rubbed himself as best he could with his stiff, icy hands. Warmth came gradually to him, but sleep was gone and for the rest of the night they talked, Isar telling Gya about his home and the Temple of the Sun, and the woman he thought he had seen on the hillside.

'From what you say,' Gya said, 'it is quite possible she was there . . . in spirit form I mean.'

'Which means . . .' Isar's face lit up, 'we are not alone and lost. They know where we are and will help us.'

Gya slapped him on the back.

'That is good news indeed, and I will tell you some more!'

'What is it?'

'Listen.'

'I am listening.'

'Does it not seem quieter to you? The storm has almost passed.'

Isar was so thankful, he did not reply, but buried his head on his knees to say a prayer of gratitude. He was so cold and wet, he did not think he could endure much more of such a night.

As he shut his eyes he seemed to see the Temple and its priests around him, faintly, as one sees an after image, fading even as he tried to hold it. The Lord Khu-ren's face was the last to disappear and Isar could see his mouth moving, but he could not make out what the words were.

Gya was shaking his shoulder.

'First light is on its way,' he said urgently. 'We should move. We will never be dry and warm until we do.'

Isar was so dazed and unresponsive, Gya took the initiative and hauled his friend up by the arm and pushed him into the open.

Isar looked around him, the first greyness of dawn was giving shape slowly and imperceptibly to the landscape. The wind had already dropped and the rain was falling only lightly.

They gathered their few belongings together, Gya tenderly testing the gut string of his bow and rubbing it with fat from a small pouch, before he was prepared to move.

Shuddering and shivering with cold they set off down the hill away from the rising light. When they reached flat ground they started to run, rejoicing in the warmth the exercise gave them.

The visions Isar had seen had given him courage. He had begun to feel there was no way out of Groth's dark clutches, but now he knew he was wrong.

The Sun was not dead.

'And even if the Sun did die,' Isar thought, 'what is the sun but one form of created light? The Source of All, the Creator, is still there.'

Groth could only at his most powerful put out the light of one small sun. He could not challenge the Whole, for he himself was only a small part of the whole.

Comforted, Isar began to make plans.

He saw Gya and himself, the saviours of a whole people, striding down into Na-Groth's dark domain, challenging him . . . Gya felling him with one swift arrow, while Isar of the silver tongue, made speeches to the cowed populace and renewed their faith in the old ways.

He caught himself smiling as he jogged along.

He saw his triumphant return home and Deva running to meet him, excited by the stories she had heard of his victory. He saw his mother putting a garland of leaves about his head, and Karne, the great Spear-Lord, bowing to him.

There would be a festival of thanksgiving and Gya and he would be honoured guests, taken to the very heart of the Temple.

'What are you laughing at?' Gya's voice broke through his dream.

'O . . . nothing,' Isar replied, flushing slightly, glad that Gya could not see into his thoughts.

'I see the rain has soaked into your head and your thoughts are floating in it,' Gya said sourly. 'I will have to do the thinking for both of us.'

This pulled Isar up short.

'I am sorry, friend,' he said soberly. 'I was floating as you say, but now I am on dry land. How far do you think we are from Na-Groth?'

'Not far. We had better avoid all tracks and villages.'

The dim light of a grey damp day was around them. The landscape was sodden and heavy, as though from prolonged weeping.

'Poor earth,' Isar thought, 'she feels the tread of Na-Groth's feet as heavily as the people do.'

'You are thinking again!' accused Gya.

Isar had a way of withdrawing into himself from time to

time that disturbed Gya. He could not follow and he could not understand. He himself never felt the need to retreat from the world. He was always present, always eager to sample what it had to offer and to test his skills against it.

Fear and despair were not feelings that came easily to Gya, though he had known them briefly when his father died. Deep thoughts about the meaning of life were also rare for him.

He listened with interest to Isar's description of the Temple and the beliefs that sustained it. He knew there were many in his village who shared these beliefs even though Na-Groth had worked hard and harshly to destroy them. But for his own part he was prepared to leave the Ultimate Question unanswered and busy himself with matters of more immediacy.

When he had said this to Isar, his friend had been shocked.

'But you cannot separate the two,' he had cried, 'awareness of the total shape of things affects the way you live your life. A traveller walking through a marsh, treads differently from one climbing a rocky mountain, and a man going nowhere, treads differently from a man going somewhere.'

Gya could not deny it.

'I will think about it, one day,' he said, 'but now all that I can think about is finding Na-Groth.'

The two young men journeyed on, keeping to the wild places, but always bearing to the west.

By midday the sun was breaking through the clouds in fitful patches, and their bodies told them that they were hungry.

Fern's training had given Isar a wide knowledge of plants, and it was Isar, the dreamer, who provided their meal, while Gya, the hunter, came back empty handed from his search for food.

'I am glad to see you are good for something in this world,' teased Gya.

Isar punched him and laughed to see him roll with exaggerated movements and much hilarity down the slope he had just climbed up.

'Catch,' he called down to him and threw a bundle of edible leaves and roots after him.

And so it was that Gya was halfway down the hill, and obscured by bushes, when Na-Groth's men suddenly appeared and seized Isar.

The Capture

When Kyra and Khu-ren returned to their home early in the morning after the storm, they found Vann, the healer-priest, with Deva. She was sitting up and sipping broth from her favourite earthenware bowl, made by Kyra when she was a young girl.

The weariness that made Kyra ache in every limb, lifted, the instant she saw her daughter so recovered.

'Deva!' she cried and flung her arms around her, tears she had kept back all night, welling from her eyes and falling on the girl's dark hair.

Khu-ren stood beside them, no less relieved and pleased, though he did not show it quite so openly.

'I have good news for you my love.' Kyra was smiling through her tears.

Deva who had coldly held herself back from her mother's embrace now turned to her, her eyes blazing with the question she dared not ask.

'No. He is not back, but he is safe and we have seen him.' Kyra said. 'He has a friend with him. No, I do not know who it is, but there were two young men sheltering from a storm, and one of them was Isar. He saw me for an instant, but the air was too wild with lightning fire for the vision to hold steady. But we know where he is and he knows we are giving him support. Everything will be much easier now.'

Deva buried her face against her mother's breast and sobbed.

'I miss him so!'

'I know. It will not be long.'

Khu-ren took his daughter's hands and turned her slightly away from her mother.

'Where have you been?' he asked quietly, but in a tone that carried authority.

Deva did not answer.

'Not now my lord,' Kyra said gently. 'Not now! Is it not enough that she is back with us?'

The Lord Khu-ren straightened and looked down upon the girl thoughtfully, and then he drew Kyra aside to speak to her privately.

'It is not good to let her escape to the past all the time. She will never learn to grow with this life and be ready for the next.'

'But surely not now! There will be time enough to discuss these matters with her when Isar is safely home again.'

Khu-ren's face looked dark and doubtful.

'Who knows what time we have left,' he said somberly. 'Now is the best time for everything.'

'I beg of you,' Kyra whispered. 'She is not strong. See how pale she is.'

The girl indeed was pale, her black eyes and black hair startling against the pallor of her skin.

'She needs rest,' Vann now spoke for her and because Khu-ren had great respect for him as friend and healer, he allowed himself to be persuaded.

'Let her rest then,' he said briefly, 'but watch her well and do not let her drift away again.'

Vann nodded, and wiped the girl's damp face with a soft cloth he had by him.

Kyra sat down beside her, enfolding her in her embrace and rocking her slightly backwards and forwards as though she were a very young child again.

The Lord Khu-ren watched them for a while, his face tender and loving, though there was still a line of anxiety between his brows. Then he left the room and sought sleep for himself elsewhere.

The weariness that had temporarily left Kyra when she saw Deva was so much better, returned, and her limbs grew heavy and her eyelids longed to close. Vann, seeing this, gently moved the rugs around the two women so that they were warm and together, and together they drifted into sleep.

Before he left the chamber Vann leant down and listened to

Deva's breathing. He was content that she was deep in natural sleep and not in trance.

As they slept it was the mother who slipped back in time, but to memories not far distant from the present, to her life as a child in a far northern community amongst heather and rocks, a circle of Tall Stones upon a hill which was the testing ground of a friend called Maal, and an enemy called Wardyke.

At midday the two women woke, Deva forming a question even as Kyra emerged from the dream.

'My lady, who is Maal? I sense great love for him in the way you call upon him in your sleep.'

Kyra woke slowly, sleep falling from her like soft mist from a hill warmed by the sun. But she seemed to be still part mist, part woman, listening for something, stretching her senses to catch something Deva could not hear.

Deva waited with patience beside her, but after a while Kyra seemed to stop trying to hear the inaudible and see the invisible.

'Maal was the priest of my village before I came here,' she said. 'Karne, Fern and I loved him greatly. He taught us to see in ways we did not think it possible to see, and hear in ways we did not think it possible to hear.'

There was a sad catch to Kyra's voice.

'You speak of him in the past,' Deva said. 'Did he die?'

'Yes, he died.'

Kyra was listening again, a frown of concentration gathering on her forehead.

'What is it?' Deva whispered. 'What do you hear?'

'I do not know. It is just that . . . it may have been the dream that brought him back so vividly to my mind that I think I hear his voice . . . or perhaps he brought the dream to me . . . He promised me . . .' Her voice trailed away in silent memories.

'What did he promise you?'

'He promised to come back to me when I really needed him. And now . . .' Kyra stood up with sudden conviction. 'There could not be a time I needed him more!'

Deva was wide eyed.

'Do you think he is alive?'

'Alive yes — but on what level I do not know.'

'How will you know him if he has come back?'

'I will know,' Kyra said confidently, and then laughed. 'He always used to say "You will know when the time comes," and it annoyed me! I always asked for explanations, signs, proofs, but he would never give them to me. And yet he proved right every time. I *did* know when the right moment had come for things that he foretold. And I know now, somewhere, somehow, he is trying to reach me.'

Kyra's beautiful face was alight with joy and hope.

'I long to meet him,' said Deva, a shade envious of her mother's love for him.

'Maybe you will!' Kyra cried. 'Come child, let us comb your hair and wash your face. Make yourself bright for the new day. Everything will be better now that Maal is near!'

Gya watched helplessly as the brutal warriors of Groth beat Isar and dragged him down the other side of the hill and out of sight.

His first instinct was to seize his bow and his arrow and let fly at them, but foolishly he had laid them down beside Isar when he had returned from the hunt. The men had taken them.

He knew that it would be hopeless to try to fight unarmed. He was heavily outnumbered.

He stayed hidden, his heart pounding with frustration, and decided that the only thing he could do was to follow and see where they took Isar.

It was strange that they had not killed him outright. They must have received orders about him.

Gya crept as silently and as swiftly as he could around the base of the hill, guided by the sounds the men were making as they crashed through the long grass and the bushes. They were shouting to each other in their guttural foreign tongue and some of them were singing a sombre song.

Gya came near enough to ascertain that Isar was still with them and still alive, and then he kept well back and out of sight. His thoughts were bitter with regret that he had left his bow unattended.

He would get it back whatever the cost, and he would rescue his friend!

But meanwhile he needed patience and skill at keeping hidden. His hunting experience helped him greatly and Na-Groth's men caught no scent of him.

After several pauses to drink at streams, and once to terrorize a village and demand food, the group began to climb a steep ridge and make for a cleft that seemed to offer easier passage.

Gya was still with them, weary and scratched and desperately hungry, but the sight of Isar, bound and staggering and constantly beaten, kept him going.

Half way up the ridge he realized with dismay that the pass was heavily guarded.

This gave him pause, and, for a moment, he thought he would have to turn back, but his friend and bow were in the hands of the enemy and were being carried inexorably nearer to the stronghold of the dread Na-Groth. He was determined that he would not desert them.

Keeping close in the wake of Isar's captors, he passed the guards unseen while they were still joking and shouting friendly insults at each other. He was so close to the bird of danger that he could hear its heart beat.

Pausing at the lip of the ridge overlooking the plain to the west, Gya could scarcely refrain from gasping.

Night was close to falling and its dark stain was already over the land below, although the ridge was still in light.

As far as he could see the natural green of the earth had been destroyed. Ragged black tents and shabby wooden shacks were sprawling everywhere, cooking fires were so numerous it almost seemed that the whole plain was smouldering, and a suffocating lid of smoke hovered over the place cutting off fresh light and air from the inhabitants.

Gya wondered if they ever saw the sky and marvelled at the stars.

Hastily he ducked behind some hawthorn bushes as the guards and Isar's captors finished their fraternizing.

Gya wondered what Isar was thinking as he lifted his head to look at the scene below.

He must have been in despair.

Na-Groth's people outnumbered the people of the villages many times, and nothing held them back from cruelty and killing. Their leader preached it. Their god demanded it. It was difficult to keep in mind that they were also human, and so subject to natural laws of change.

Gya knew that he could not afford to lose sight of Isar now. Amongst those innumerable hovels it would be impossible to find him.

He kept close, silent as a wild cat stalking its prey, glad of the falling dark.

Isar's captors lit torches and their acrid smell and guttering flames led Gya on. It was completely dark by the time they reached their destination.

Drawn back in the shadows, Gya stared aghast at the vast palace of Na-Groth, its wooden columns hung with skulls, flickering white in the light of the fires that burned on the open ground before it.

In the centre of this open space stood a giant figure.

The hateful Groth himself.

Gya shuddered and drew back.

Isar was dragged before the palace of Na-Groth and pushed down upon his knees.

The leader of his captors shouted and struck his spear loudly upon the ground.

From the dark chasm of the entrance a man appeared, robed in red, the colour of death.

Isar could see his eyes glittering in the flame light and his cheeks shadowed and hollowed like a skull's.

He carried a tall staff and thumped it on the earth imperiously.

Dust rose.

He spoke words Isar did not understand and was answered in the same language.

Isar was hauled up and pushed forward, so that he fell on his knees in front of the man.

His mind told him to rise, his pride as a free being cried out against the indignity of kneeling to this creature, but his body was weak from the rigours of the day and it would not obey his command.

The man, noting the struggle in the boy's face, smiled, and the smile was the most chilling thing Isar had ever seen.

'Come!' he said suddenly in Isar's language, but with a stranger's intonation.

The soldiers pulled Isar to his feet and pushed him to follow the robed figure. In the darkness of the monstrous building he struggled to think of ways of escape, but his weariness robbed him of all his initiative.

The passage, dimly lit by an occasional sputtering torch, gave way at last to a huge chamber, where impotent and lifeless trees formed the columns that held the roof of wood and hides high above them.

All the wood in the building had been charred and polished in some way so that it had a dull, dark gleam.

Fires in small stone enclosures were burning at intervals around the hall, and torches were leaning from the columns above the height of a man's head. The atmosphere was hot and thick with a sickly sweet smell. Near the roof, the smoke gathered and hung oppressively.

At the end of the chamber and focussed in most of the light, Na-Groth and his Queen sat on high thrones of the same dark polished timber.

Isar was led before them and, again, given a push from

behind that precipitated him on his knees before his enemy.

The man who had brought him spoke long and eloquently. Although Isar could not understand the words, he caught the boasting drift of it. It seemed that he had been specially sought and that his capture was regarded as a great achievement.

Fleetingly he wondered why this was so, but had no time to think the question through.

All his effort was concentrated on bringing himself to his feet.

He was bound and his body weary to desperation, but he was determined not to kneel to Na-Groth.

Around him the court of Na-Groth was gathered, warriors and guards, old men in long robes like the one who had greeted him at the entrance, women in garments the like of which he had never seen and, behind the Queen, two lines of young girls, her personal attendants.

The Queen was magnificent in form, her hair sloe black but her skin pale. Her eyes were like black diamonds and it was she who commanded his first attention. It was the curl of her lip that goaded his flagging strength to one last effort.

Clumsily he staggered to his feet.

'Kneel before the great Na-Groth and his Queen!' commanded the skull faced man, pointing his staff at him, his eyes blazing.

But Isar stood precariously on his feet, lifting his chin and daring to look directly into the eyes of the deadly Queen, and then into those of Na-Groth. There he met such a look of crazed greed that he almost reeled back. The man was either drugged or mad. His eyes were blurred and bloodshot, but the muscular hand that gripped the side of his throne was endowed with almost superhuman strength.

Isar had the feeling in those few crowded moments that Na-Groth was not in charge of himself.

Someone, or something, else, ruled his dark soul.

Isar looked back to the Queen.

Was it she?

But he did not think so.

Both of them were looking out from the dark holes of their eyes, using the splendour of their surroundings to hide their own inadequacy.

Kyra could command respect and speak with authority, standing barefoot in a field, with nothing more than a peasant's loose woollen shift about her.

But these people had to use tricks to give them stature.

The skulls, the fires, the dark wood, the towering columns, even the use of giant shadows in the spaces between the columns, were all part of the illusion.

The warriors' swords and spears, however, were real, and he had felt the harshness of their knuckles.

He thought back to the Temple of the Sun and asked for strength to outface his enemies.

Behind the Queen's throne he noticed a slight movement and turned his eyes towards it.

His heart leapt.

Lark was there, her deep, expressive eyes willing him to silence.

Joy at seeing her was extinguished instantly in anxiety for her safety as well as for his own. He knew without any doubt that she was there because she was forced to be there. Most of the other attendants looked as though they had come to accept the advantages of their situation, but Lark's eyes had not changed since he had seen her last, and he knew she was still loyal to the old ways and the overthrow of Na-Groth's power.

He looked away from her, knowing that he must give no sign that he recognized her, or she too would be lost.

'Kneel!' the command was given again, harshly.

He stood his ground.

A guard whipped him until he at last fell down.

'I see . . .' he managed to bring out from his bleeding mouth, 'Na-Groth does not want the respect of free men, only the fear of slaves!'

This time the whipping he received made him lose consciousness.

The Invisible Enemy

Karne was hoping to keep his small army well hidden from Na-Groth. Surprise was his greatest strength, for the men he had with him were greatly outnumbered and, most of them, unused to conflict.

But Na-Groth was no fool.

Even as Isar lay bound and bleeding on the floor of one of the dark chambers of the palace, and Karne was surveying his men and speaking to them of surprise, one of Na-Groth's spies was kneeling before the two thrones and speaking of the puny force the Temple had managed to muster.

Na-Groth laughed hugely at the description.

'So be it!' he roared, still laughing. 'If they want to die as heroes, let them die as heroes! We will not disappoint them.'

The place was filled with the noise of people stamping their feet in approval and Na-Groth's humourless and rasping laughter.

It was the Queen who raised her hand at last for silence, and on the instant, everyone froze as though a sudden chill wind had swept over them.

She glared at everyone in front of the thrones, her venomous eyes subduing them, compelling them to their knees.

When the whole vast hall was full of silent, kneeling figures, she rose to her feet, drawing her lord with her.

The two stood on their dark platform, high above their subjects.

Na-Groth was not laughing now and his face was gathering darkness like the sky before a storm.

He waited long enough for the silence to become intolerable

and then he raised his fist above his head and brought it down
like an axe, his voice spitting out the words:

'Crush them like flies!'

'Like flies!' screamed his minions at his feet.

'Like flies,' said his Queen with satisfaction in her cold and
deadly voice.

'Let the beacon fires be lit and the warriors be sent!' roared
Na-Groth.

It was as though a dark wind swirled through the hall and
gathered all the people up like winter leaves.

No one but Na-Groth and his lady Maeged remained.

Khu-ren and Kyra were very near to despair.

For all their skill they could not reach Isar.

The black malevolence of Na-Groth's rule produced
powerful vibrations, stronger as they centred on the persons of
Na-Groth and Maeged.

Their palace was impregnable to the priests of Light.

Khu-ren, in spirit-travel, could visit the ridge that
overlooked the encampment and could see quite clearly the
distant dark palace, but, when he tried to move towards it, the
air broke up around him in swirling currents, and he had to
use all his psychic strength not to be sucked down into the
vortex of Na-Groth's destructive will.

'We need someone inside the palace to reach out to us,' he
explained to Kyra.

'If only Isar were strong enough!' she said sadly.

Khu-ren looked at her closely and his voice took on the
tenderness of warning.

'You must prepare yourself my love,' he said gently.

'For what?'

She looked at him with frightened eyes, for she knew the
answer.

'Isar may be dead.'

'No!' she cried.

'It would be surprising if he were not. We have lost contact with him completely, which means either he is dead already, or he is well within the range of Na-Groth's power. We could not expect that Na-Groth would not have killed him as soon as he found him.'

Kyra was silent, her shoulders bent and her face desolate.

Khu-ren put his arm around her and they sat together, deep in thought.

Gradually Kyra began to straighten up and pull away from her husband.

She had that look upon her face that she had when she was listening for something ordinary ears could not catch.

He drew back at once and waited beside her, hardly daring to move in case he disturbed her concentration.

Slowly . . . slowly she turned to her husband.

'What is it?' he whispered.

'It is Maal,' she said, her voice shaking, 'I am sure it is Maal!'

He kissed her and held her tight.

'Where is he?'

'I do not know . . . the impression was very faint and strange. There was a girl and he was a shadow behind the girl . . . and his voice came from the mouth of the girl . . . and yet . . . and yet I did not get the impression they were the same person . . .'

Kyra strained to recapture the experience, but it was gone.

'What did he say?'

'Karne . . . is . . . in danger. His position is known to Na-Groth. There was something about flies . . . but I did not understand that.'

'Never mind what you did not understand. We have enough to know that Karne is in danger, and him, at least, we *can* reach.

'Come.'

He took her hand and they prepared again for the adventure of spirit-travel.

Karne posted the watches for the night and took one of the positions himself.

He was restless and knew that he would not be able to sleep though his body was weary from the effort of the day. At times he felt it was only the strength of his own will that sustained this crowd of men and drove them away from their families and into danger.

It was not an easy burden to bear.

Up to now his determination to gather an army and move it to Klad had kept him going.

But now they were in position as near to Na-Groth as they dared to be, he was not sure what to do next. He did not want to fight if it could be avoided.

On their way he had made constant inquiry of villagers about the passage of a tall, red haired youth, and was convinced from what he had heard, that Isar was too far ahead of them for their paths to cross.

He sat in the darkness, watching over his men, and thinking anxiously about Isar.

He looked up into the clear sky above him, and it was as though a sudden reversal of his normal thinking occurred.

From being Karne, master of his own actions, leader of men, proud Spear-Lord on whose shoulders rested the cares of his people, he had become a minute point in an immensity of Nothing.

Confidence in himself, his people, his god, trickled away. He felt as though a suffocating black cord had settled round his chest and was somehow drawing tighter and tighter.

At first he abandoned himself to the desperation of the experience, and then his old habits of thinking and believing began to return.

He broke from the clutches of despair and shook his head fiercely to clear it of its dark thoughts.

He thought of his sister, younger than himself, but often wiser.

'Help me,' he cried deeply in himself. 'I cannot see the way!'

Was it possible there *was* no way?

'Karne!'

He heard his name called and turned his head.

Kyra was standing before him, faintly luminous in the darkness.

He sprang up and made to move towards her.

'No!' she said sharply, holding up her slender white hand.

For a moment she seemed to disappear and Karne felt a choking lump rising in his throat.

'Fool!' he cursed himself.

But she returned, and this time he remained as motionless as the still night air.

'Listen to me . . . there is no time . . . Na-Groth knows you are here . . . Try to . . .'

But before she could complete the sentence the noisy approach of one of the men complaining that he had watched long enough and was ready to sleep, broke the tenuous thread of the vision.

Kyra was gone.

Karne rounded angrily on the man.

'No one will sleep tonight,' he roared, 'wake everybody up!'

'What?' gasped the fellow, staring stupidly.

'You heard me! Wake everybody up and tell them to report to me at once.'

As the oaf still stared and gaped, Karne punched him in the chest.

'Move!' he shouted. 'We are about to be attacked!'

This made the man move.

While the men, confused and grumbling, were gathering around him, Karne was planning.

All doubts of purpose and meaning were gone.

He enjoyed action, and action they were about to have.

Meanwhile Gya who was hiding among the hovels of Na-Groth's encampment was needing all his cunning to stay alive, and had not yet found a way to reach his friend in the Palace or retrieve his bow.

He had managed to steal some food and was sitting in the dark shadow of an untidy pile of wood, when he had the sensation that he was being watched. His hands went automatically to his weapons before he remembered that he no longer had them.

He stayed tensely still and looked carefully around him.

At first he saw no one and then there was a slight movement to the left.

Turning his head swiftly he looked into the watching shadow of a small girl. She seemed no more than seven or eight summers old and so thin and sickly it was not likely that she would see the ninth.

He crept towards her holding out what was left of the meat he had stolen earlier from an unguarded spit.

She did not move back in fear as he half expected her to do, but continued, unmoving, to stare at him.

Her scrutiny began to make him feel uneasy.

He was shocked to see her face and limbs were marked with festering sores.

For the first time Gya felt great pity for these people, particularly for the children, who were caught in a trap as surely as were his own people.

There was no malevolence in the eyes of the child as she stared at him, only curiosity.

'Here,' he said softly. 'Take this. Eat.'

He imitated the motions of putting the meat to his mouth and eating, and then he held it out to her.

Briefly her eyes left his and moved to the meat, and then back again to his.

'It is yours. Eat,' he whispered.

Whether she would have taken it or not he would never know, because a woman's voice called out 'Berka!' and instantly she turned and ran.

Gya was in a quandary.

He was not sure if the child would give him away or not, but he could not risk it.

He must move.

He stuffed the last of the food hungrily into his mouth and

looked around for somewhere new to hide.

It was late and most of the fires had died down.

There were more dark places than before in which to hide, but also more risk of tripping over or bumping into something.

By this time of the night his own people would have been soundly asleep, but a great many of Na-Groth's people seemed to be still awake.

Groups of them were gathered, drinking barley ale. Their laughter came in strangely regular little bursts, as though the laughter had nothing to do with the way they felt, but was expected of them.

Others were wandering about, poking around other people's cooking fires, as though hoping to pick up leftovers. He saw one or two find something and instantly pounce on it, looking furtively from side to side.

They did not see him.

One ate whatever it was, and then slithered away into the shadows, while the other hid what he had found in his clothes, and ran from the place.

Gya smiled wryly to himself.

Who would have thought, he, swift, proud Gya the bowman, would have become a nocturnal scavenger no better than these other human dogs?

Again a fleeting ripple of pity touched his heart.

Had these people once been as carefree and as kindly as his own people had been?

His face darkened.

He remembered how he had attacked Isar, a harmless stranger.

Was Groth's dark taint already upon them?

Just before the first light of dawn, Na-Groth's warriors crept up upon the position their spies had given them for Karne's motley army. They could see the humped shapes of sleeping figures, just faintly where they showed against the sky, or in the last dying glow from the watch fires.

Swiftly they moved, their weapons ready.

Clubs were raised, axes and knives lifted to position above unsuspecting bodies.

No sound was made.

The leader held his breath for one long and fateful moment and then, with a short, sharp exhalation, plunged his blade into the first of the sleeping figures.

Instantly his men were about their grizzly work.

No one was spared.

Violence and hate had won.

Strangely the enemy did not fight back.

No sound came from the camp.

Na-Groth's men would have expected some screams and groans, if not resistance.

Could they have killed the whole army in one instant?

Na-Groth's captain stood up and stared into the dark.

His men stood poised and uneasy.

Not sure what they had done.

Not sure what there was still to do.

And as they listened, they began to hear, fine and eery, a high pitched note, that seemed at first so faint that it could have been one of their own body-sounds, and then, gradually, gradually becoming so strong that they were aware of it outside themselves, and everywhere surrounding them . . . above them . . . in the air . . . in the sky . . .

It was unearthly.

It was like nothing they had heard before.

It chilled their hearts.

Some flailed about with weapons trying to find the source, but there seemed to be no source.

The sound was everywhere in equal intensity . . . strange,

thin, hollow, inhuman . . . It seemed to pervade the universe, and grow stronger every instant.

The warriors who had been so bold and confident, part of a well disciplined unit, began to break up in panic.

Each man suddenly seemed to be alone, in the dark, with some mysterious and unknown force homing in on him.

Terrified, Na-Groth's rabble scattered, stumbling and fleeing, the sound pursuing them, rising in pitch, until it seemed to be the sound of mockery and of triumph.

Above them the sky slowly reddened, appearing menacing to Na-Groth's men, but friendly to the men of Karne who were merry as they climbed down from the trees, holding the small reeds through which they had been blowing, high above their heads as an offering of gratitude to their God and his hieroglyph, the Sun.

The torn and gashed condition of their sleeping rugs was a small price to pay for their lives, and they sang as they prepared their breakfast, already incorporating the name of their leader, Karne, into a hero's song.

The coming of dawn brought more problems to Gya. Grey faced with weariness he looked helplessly around him, wondering how he could possibly escape notice during the daylight hours.

The palace was so heavily guarded it seemed an impossible task to approach it, and he was beginning to despair of ever helping Isar.

He must find somewhere to hide.

Even as he reached desperation, he found Berka, the ragged child of the night before, staring at him again. She seemed to have an uncanny way of seeing him when he thought he could not be seen.

He stared back at her, unsure whether she was friend or enemy.

He tried smiling to put her at her ease, but the smile was not as relaxed as he had intended it to be.

She did not smile back, but after another prolonged stare she suddenly beckoned to him to follow her. He hesitated. There was still no overt enmity in her eyes, but he could not be certain that there was friendship there either.

He decided to allow his intuition to guide him, and followed her. The fact that she led him from cover to cover and was constantly darting looks, not only at himself, but in every direction, convinced him at last that he was right to trust her. If she were going to give him up to his enemies she would surely have led him straight to them.

They had a few narrow escapes, and each time, it was the presence of mind of the child, that saved him. She seemed to be used to this kind of secrecy. She knew the movements of her people, and how to avoid them.

She brought him eventually to a halt, beside a pile of wood and rotting hide, that must once have been a shack. The best timbers had been removed, and rubbish of all sorts had been piled up against the remainder. The smell was sickening, and Gya could not imagine what she intended. He was startled when, with calm assurance, the self-possessed little girl began to move some boards and revealed that the whole heap was hollow inside and would afford adequate shelter.

Obediently he crept past her as she indicated, and she nodded with satisfaction as he took up his cramped position inside.

She pointed at him and mimed sleep.

He nodded, and whispered 'thank you', but, as he was still not sure if she understood his language, he blew her a kiss. This place was bad, but it was better than being captured.

She seemed to understand the kiss and, for a moment, something like unguarded warmth flickered across her wary eyes.

Then she replaced the wood, and was gone.

He was in darkness.

Inside the palace Isar had waited miserably for the dawn, but saw nothing of it when it came.

The small room he was in had no opening, except the one heavily covered with hides and carefully guarded.

The air was stuffy and oppressive, and his one comfort, a small chalk-stone lamp with its flame guttering in a pool of oil, had been removed by the guard not long after he was brought to the place.

The little chalk-stone lamp had reminded him of his home and he ached to see the smooth, gentle, feminine curves of the chalk-stone hills around the Temple. This was a harsh and rugged land, the hills high and craggy, Na-Groth's plain, a stronghold.

Would he ever see his home again?

He doubted it.

He fell to fitful sleep about the time Gya was being shown to his hiding place by Berka, and Karne's men were celebrating their victory. He did not wake again until he was roughly shaken and dragged out of the room.

He was taken to a larger one where he was pushed on to his knees before the same old man who had originally led him into the palace, the priest of Groth, Gaa-ak.

This time he was too tired, too dazed and too much in pain even to contemplate defiance.

He remained kneeling, looking around him with blood-shot eyes, amazed at the richness and variety of furs that hung upon the walls.

'I trust you are well rested,' Gaa-ak said.

Isar looked at him stupidly.

The guard poked at him.

'I slept a little,' Isar muttered with a dry throat, thinking of water.

'You are a carver of wood,' the old priest of Groth now said, more as a statement than as a question.

Isar showed surprise.

'We knew of your coming,' Gaa-ak said in reply to Isar's unspoken question. 'We were waiting for you.'

'How?'

'We knew.'

'I was coming . . .' Isar started to say and then stopped.

'To see Janak, the greatest wood carver this side of the Great Ocean,' prompted the harsh voice of Gaa-ak.

Again Isar looked surprised.

'Is he . . .?'

'He is dead,' the old man said coldly.

Isar was shaken. Janak was a great man and there was no one to match him in his skill.

'Na-Groth ordered his death before he knew who he was. A pity. We need him now.'

Isar stared at the man.

'We will just have to use you instead,' Gaa-ak added coldly.

He was watching the boy closely.

'Did you hear what I said?' He said sharply.

Isar looked at him again, but said nothing.

'We need someone skilled at wood carving. Your life has been spared only because of this.'

Isar had wondered why they had not killed him.

He looked around gloomily at the sombre walls, the dark columns.

He had seen no carving in the palace. What did they want carved?

Gaa-ak was pacing up and down, a muscle twitching at the side of his eye, giving him the appearance of a ghoul, winking with a kind of dreadful and deadly bonhomie.

Isar shuddered and looked away.

'Do you not want to know what it is that we must have carved?'

Gaa-ak prodded him with his staff as he said this.

Isar looked at him wearily.

'I want to know,' he said obediently, but with no enthusiasm.

The priest of Groth looked pleased and conspiratorial.

'Follow me!' he commanded, a gleam of excitement in his eye as he strode from the chamber.

Isar looked questioningly at his guards. They shrugged and hauled him to his feet, keeping a spear at his back as he followed the old man along the dark passages, through the great hall, now empty except for guards, and out through the main door, into the daylight.

Although the sun shone, it was not as it was at Isar's home, flickering through leaves on to the heads of children playing. It was sifted through layers of dirty air to fall dully on dull surfaces.

Isar was marched forward until he stood before the enormous mass of the Statue of Groth. There he was pushed roughly to his knees again.

He noticed that many people were on the ground before the Statue, crawling or kneeling, praying in whining, wheedling voices for favours.

The boy who had been used to the Temple of the Sun looked around him in amazement.

The movement of his head elicited a sharp blow from Gaa-ak's staff.

'When you are in the presence of Groth you look at no one but Groth,' the old man snapped.

Isar looked at Groth.

Groth had no face.

'Pray. Pray for your life,' hissed the old man giving him another push with his stick.

Isar prayed. But not to Groth.

'Aloud!' snarled Gaa-ak.

'I do not know the words,' stalled Isar feebly.

'Speak after me,' the man said, and bowed his stiff neck reverently to the wood and straw.

Isar felt more sick and more afraid than he had ever felt before.

'I will not pray to a false god,' he thought bitterly.

But if he was to live . . . ?

And if Groth was nothing but wood and straw what was the harm in it?

Words Kyra had spoken long ago came back to him.

'Thought has power. Belief has power. If people believe in a thing strongly enough they invest it with power.'

He was afraid.

Had this monstrous creation been given power by the people's belief in it?

He heard the old man intoning words in a loud, high pitched, unnatural voice.

'Lord Groth, mightiest god in the universe, hear my plea . . .'

It was clear he expected Isar to repeat them, and when he did not, the guards struck him savagely.

'It is only wood and straw . . . nothing but wood and straw . . .' Isar told himself over and over again, and then, swallowing hard, the pain of the blows bringing sweat to his brow, he said with his mouth the words the priest of Groth wanted to hear, but inside the sanctuary of his own mind he cried to his own God, his own Helpers in the Spirit Realms, his own people.

He shut his eyes and tried with all his might to visualize the Tall Stones of the Temple of his homeland, and the priests who served there. A picture of it came to him, and, instead of the dusty forecourt with the monstrous statue, he saw Kyra and Khu-ren and the priests of the Inner Council walking from Stone to Stone, touching them and intoning the words of the ritual to fend off harm.

Loud and clear he suddenly echoed their words and stood upright, all pain gone, his face transformed.

The old man beside him appeared momentarily to falter and crumple. The supplicants grovelling in the dust at the feet of Groth, looked at him with glazed eyes.

'Spirits of the Realms deeper than man's heart, rise to our aid.

Spirits of the Realms higher than the Sun, visit us now at the time of our need.'

'Enough!' shrieked the priest of Groth regaining his strength. 'You are faced with the greatest god the world has ever known and you blaspheme!'

Isar stood his ground watching impassively as the old man frothed and ranted.

He knew he would not be killed. They needed him.

Behind him there was a movement and a sound.

Groth's beautiful, cold Queen, with all her entourage, was emerging from the palace. They seemed to glide across the forecourt with the rhythmic motions of a snake, and came to rest not far from him.

'What is it you want of me lady,' Isar said boldly, meeting her gaze.

She smiled, a small and ominous smile, and her eyes flicked over him like a whip.

'Has my lord priest not told you?'

'I am to carve something — but what it is I do not know.'

She looked at the old priest.

'He is an old fool and not long for the world,' she said icily.

Isar could see the fear in the old skull face, and felt almost pity for him.

Behind the Queen he sensed Lark's presence, but dared not look at her.

'Why,' the lady Maeged said, jerking her long robes about her as she moved imperiously nearer to Isar, 'you are to give our god his face. There is no greater honour than that!'

Isar was amazed.

He looked up at Groth's faceless head.

Until now he had felt the vast statue's presence and menace, but had not paid much attention to the details of its construction.

He studied it now with the eye of an artist, and noticed that, apart from its immense size, which was impressive enough, it was built with great skill. Trunks of trees, branches and twigs, were all woven in a way to give it bulk and solidity, the finer details supplied by woven straw.

He wondered why Na-Groth had not seen to the matter of the face before. There was no doubt that the right mask would add much to the image.

Maeged was standing before him, studying him, as he studied Groth.

'You will do it,' she said, 'or you will die like the man who destroyed the last face.'

Isar looked his question, and shivered to see brooding

pleasure in the Queen's eyes.

'It was in another country . . . before we came to Klad,' she said. 'He was killed piece by piece . . . by Groth himself. His face was the last to go.'

Isar felt ill and could not resist a quick look at Lark.

In meeting her eyes, he was filled with such strength and comfort, it was almost as though they were free and together again.

He forced himself to look away from her in case the fell Queen intercepted their communication.

'You will do it?' Maeged asked, but the tone of her voice was such that there was no question of his refusal.

'I will do it,' he said.

Her eyes flickered like those of a snake darting at its prey.

Swiftly she turned on her heel and snapped her fingers.

Her attendants lifted her trailing robes from the dust and she swept off across the forecourt, back to the palace.

Isar noticed that Lark had taken advantage of the disturbance of the Queen's going, to slip away. The people in the forecourt had fallen upon their faces, the guards were concentrating on Isar, and the old priest, Gaa-ak, was occupied with his own worries.

Isar had the presence of mind to turn away from Lark, so that his following eyes did not give her away. But his heart went with her.

Only Berka who was watching everything that happened from the shelter of the houses that bordered the place, saw her go and slipped forward to join her.

The Lords of the Sun

The Lord Khu-ren had decided to call together the full power of the Lords of the Sun. This was not lightly nor easily done, but he felt it was justified.

The Great Temple was full of people, men and women alternating, hand in hand, moving rhythmically in circles, the life energy of their bodies helping to increase the power needed for the transfer of Spirit-Forms from across the world.

Within the northern Sanctum the Lord High Priest and the Lady Kyra waited for their peers, feeling the pulse of energy build up around them.

Gradually the beat of the drums and the throbbing of the earth seemed to come from within them.

They felt themselves to be in a vortex where Time and Space and Physical Reality had no meaning. The singing in their heads was the singing of the Spirit Spheres, the myriad Realms of God, each sphere spinning with its own energy, each humming with its own voice, the full and separate syllables of each sound making up the Secret Name of God, only one letter of which was entrusted to each Sphere, and our whole universe contained, with other universes, in only one of the Spheres.

The name of God was complete.

It had no end, and no beginning.

Kyra was filled with awe at this paradox, and prepared to abandon herself to the vortex.

What she was experiencing now could not be expressed through words available to man. She knew she must let go, let go of the world, of reality as she knew it . . . whatever came she must allow to come, without filtering it through the comforting, but limiting, mesh of her mind.

She could hear the thundering of Presences, feel the pull and tug of light as it spiralled past her, the abrasive wing of darkness as it swooped into the eye of the Vortex.

There was no way back . . . only through . . .

Kyra let go . . .

and in that act of relinquishment so changed the mode of her Being that she burst into the Spirit Sphere in a myriad fragments of Light, each fragment experiencing a form of existence she had never known before.

But the human frame cannot hold such transformations for long, and, trembling with the strain of it, her body in pain from the unusual demands made upon it, she had to return to being Kyra.

Around her in the Inner Sanctum of the Great Temple of the Sun were grouped the Spirit-forms of the Lords of the Sun.

'Is this Reality not enough that I have to take on the knowledge of others?' she thought wearily.

Sometimes the awareness of the immensity of Existence, its complexity and its beauty, was too much to bear.

Sometimes she longed to be an ordinary person, content with the immediate and the visible.

And then she looked around her at the figures of the spirit-travellers from distant places on the earth, and the excitement of knowing that she was part of a growing and limitless process of understanding, filled her with joy.

Khu-ren was communicating their problems to the Lords of the Sun.

They shared, in vision, what he knew of Na-Groth.

One, a tall man in a long feathered cloak, responded with recognition.

He knew of Na-Groth.

Instantly all attention was upon him and Khu-ren's mind was incisive in its questioning.

It seemed that in this particular Lord's country a certain plant grew that was used for making dreams.

In their underground Temple there were bare stone cells where supplicants slept after having inhaled the smoke of the burning plant.

In the morning they would tell the Seer-priest of their dreams and he would interpret them.

Kyra thought about her own priests who had great respect for dreams, but would not have confused illusion with inner reality.

It seemed Na-Groth had been one of these Seer-priests, and, at first, had done his work well and conscientiously. But, as priest, he had free access to the sacred plant and began to use it more and more for his own purposes. At last he claimed that he, and only he, was in touch with God, and God was ordering him to take command of all mankind to lead them to worship him as he had always wanted to be worshipped.

The first indication that the feathered priesthood had that all was not as it should be, was when they began to notice that people were leaving the Temple of the Sacred Smoke tense and worried, instead of relaxed and happy.

Some took their own lives, some the lives of others.

The priests at first were loath to doubt one of their own, but there came a time when Na-Groth's excesses could be ignored no longer.

Their land was in darkness and fear, much as Klad now was.

'You speak of the past. Is your land now free and happy once again?'

'Yes . . . and no. Yes, we defeated Na-Groth. But no, we have not returned to our former innocence, for our people no longer trust the Smoke and our Temple has fallen into disfavour. Our priesthood lives in the hills and is consulted by only a few people. The others prefer to live without a god, than with one they hate. They blame us for Na-Groth's god. You see it was our Sacred Smoke that conjured him to life.'

The Lords of the Sun waited patiently for the continuation of the story, their hearts heavy with what they already knew.

It was Kyra who asked the next question.

'How did you defeat Na-Groth?'

The feathered priest looked at her.

'I am ashamed to tell you.'

'Tell us.'

There was a long pause.

Faintly Kyra was aware of the drumming, the pulsing, the turning of the people in the circles beyond their Inner Stone Ring. She knew they could not hold the spirit-travellers for long, the thread was fine and fragile, and time was already straining it.

'We used his mother against him.'

The regret in the priest's mind touched all the Lords of the Sun with sorrow.

'How?' prompted Kyra.

'She lived in a village a long way from the temple. Na-Groth had long since abandoned her and she was bent with age and loneliness. We visited her and probed her memory for anything we could find to help us against her son. She was not aware that that was what we were doing.'

Again they could feel the pain of his remorse.

'We felt it was justified at the time, but when she found out what we had done, and that it was her words that had helped us to it . . . she killed herself. She still loved her son.'

The man's mind was full of grief, and they could all feel the suffering of the mother.

Gently Khu-ren turned their attention from the mother to the son.

'We must know what she told you, and what was done.'

His thought was steady and urgent.

'There is not much time!'

'As a young child,' the feathered priest continued, 'he was savaged in the face by a wild cat, and this has so scarred his memory that he is consumed by dread of these animals.'

The memory of the young Na-Groth's ordeal came to them with terrifying clarity. They lived again the pain as the animal tore at his face. They felt his fear of blindness as he struggled to protect his eyes. They experienced the surge of hate and vengeance that was his as he picked up a stick and flailed at it. When it was felled at last they shared his terrible, cruel joy as he reduced the living creature to a mass of blood and bone and sticky fur.

'We sent our people out with traps and caught two wild

cats,' the priest of the Sacred Smoke continued, 'and then we released them in the temple when Na-Groth was alone.

'I can hear his screams still!'

The great Lords were silent as the tale ended.

But the energy in the Sacred Circle was beginning to dissipate as the weariness of the people circling grew.

Kyra could see the images of those around her beginning to break up and fade.

'We thank you,' Khu-ren managed to project. 'Perhaps you have helped us to save our land.'

The priest of the Temple of Smoke was the last to go.

Khu-ren and Kyra bowed to him.

When he was gone Khu-ren looked at Kyra.

'And so the mother will destroy her son again?' she said regretfully.

'No,' Khu-ren said. 'The son destroys the son. He was entrusted with a Mystery which he has misused. It is only fitting that fear should destroy the one who rules by fear.'

The people of the circles were dispersing, the priests supervising their orderly exit from the Great Temple.

The Inner Council gathered round Khu-ren and Kyra and were told what had taken place.

'How will we use the knowledge?' they asked at once.

But Khu-ren and Kyra were exhausted.

'We will think on it and meet again. This is too important a matter to be decided by tired minds, in haste.'

Birds flew down and sat upon the Stones, and in the very place that Kyra had had her experience of the Vortex, a cricket began its familiar song.

The Preparation

Lark looked deep into Berka's eyes and knew that she had found a friend.

Without questioning, she followed the child into the depths of the sprawling, ugly township, Berka's ragged cloak over her shoulders so that she would not be so easily recognized as one of Maeged's slaves.

She was led to the broken wreckage of the house in which Gya lay hidden, and the makeshift entrance door was pulled back.

Inside Gya woke with a jerk from his long and restless sleep, to find himself observed by Berka and a stranger. He was on the defensive at once but the smile of the older girl put him at ease. She put her hand to her lips to indicate that he must make no sound and sat down beside him. Berka remained standing, the cramped conditions not affecting her small frame.

Gently Lark put her hands on Gya's head and shut her eyes.

She seemed to be concentrating deeply.

Puzzled, he stared at her.

So far no words had been used, but he could feel that she was to be trusted.

He found himself thinking about Isar and the adventures they had been through together. Suddenly he had a flash of inspiration. This must be the dumb girl, Lark, Isar had spoken so much about!

As soon as the shock of this registered in his mind, she smiled and opened her eyes, looking straight into his.

'You are Isar's Lark?' he whispered.

She nodded.

He looked shaken.

Berka stood in her customary way, watching and listening.

'Have you seen Isar?' Gya whispered next.

Lark nodded.

'Where?' he almost cried aloud, thinking that if Lark was free, Isar might very well be free too.

Lark could not answer and looked to Berka for help.

'The tall one . . . hair like . . . sun?' the child asked

Lark nodded.

Berka turned to Gya.

'Groth,' she said, haltingly in a language she did not find easy to speak. 'He make Groth face.'

Gya looked bewildered.

'Groth no face,' Berka repeated using her hands to mime what she was trying to express. She hid her face in her hands and then suddenly revealed it, pulling her features into a fierce and ugly shape. Gya in spite of the circumstances, could not help laughing.

She pointed to her face as it was now.

'He make. He make,' she said.

Gya was still very puzzled, but he decided not to pursue this line of questioning. It now seemed clear Isar was still in the clutches of Na-Groth.

'Will you help me to free him?'

Lark did not know how to mime the answer to this. She wanted to say that she would help him to destroy Groth, and that way he would eventually be free. She wanted to say that it would help neither Isar nor his people if he were taken from the palace now. But she had no tongue to say all this.

She looked at Berka.

The child shrugged. She too did not know how to put into the words of his language the complex thought she had only half caught from the mind of the dumb girl.

It began to dawn on Gya that they were not going to help him.

He gripped Lark's thin wrist roughly.

'You *must* help me!'

He was met with a look of gentle reproach, and he dropped her wrist, ashamed.

But what was to be done?

Now that he was rested he was determined not to stay idle another moment. He would find a way into the palace of skulls and shadows, and out again, without their help!

As he began to gather himself together, the girls could see from his eyes that he was desperate and impatient.

Vigorously Lark shook her head and put a restraining hand upon his arm.

He shook it off angrily.

'You will not help me. I will do what has to be done alone!'

Again she shook her head, her eyes worried.

Berka now took his arm, but he instantly pulled himself free of her small grip.

The two girls looked at each other, and then, together, they looked at Gya.

Their eyes were strange.

It was almost as though they were no longer separate entities, but had become One, and that One was an ancient Being, familiar with the Mysteries.

He drew his breath in sharply as he met the unexpected power in their eyes.

He could not move.

It was as though a voice in his head made it clear to him that he was to follow Berka and that she would show him what he must do.

Isar must be left in the care of Lark.

He bowed his head slightly.

The force with which they held him, left them as suddenly as it had come.

Berka lifted the boards at the entrance and looked out.

'Come!' she said to him in her child's voice.

Still shaken by the experience of what he had seen in the girls' eyes, he followed her.

She led him skilfully between the shacks until Gya became uncomfortable at the distance he was from the palace and his friend. Several times he almost pulled away from her, telling himself he must be crazy to put himself into the hands of a sickly child, an enemy child, but the memory of that special look returned to him, and, although he now began to doubt that it had happened at all, he could not be sure.

. She came to a standstill at last before the doorway of a house.

She gave a low call which was immediately answered from within. Gya found himself pushed gently but firmly through the doorway.

Inside he was startled to find himself surrounded by enemies. He clenched his fists and tensed his muscles ready for a fight, but he was not challenged.

Silently the gathering of strangers considered him.

Berka spoke long and persuasively to them in their own tongue and Gya could feel the hostility in their gaze lessening.

When she had stopped speaking, one moved forward and took Gya by the arm to show him where he was to sit amongst them.

Gya looked from face to face and everywhere he saw scars, hollow cheeks and haggard eyes. He could almost smell desperation in the air. These people were not the arrogant master race he had seen swaggering about the place, they were hunted animals like Isar and himself, though of the same race as the hunters.

Berka had brought him to a meeting of conspirators, dissidents, who were tired of being party to killing and repression, who had finally turned against the laws that took people's loved ones forcibly from them, and forced them to shed their blood in Groth's name.

Many of their number had been discovered and destroyed.

These were the ragged remnants.

They welcomed Gya with reservation. They had been taught to believe the local inhabitants were ignorant savages to be used as a work force, but good for nothing else. They no longer believed this, but it was still not easy to accept one as their equal.

'Berka tells us that you want to join us?'

Gya hesitated, not sure if this was true.

'What is it that you have to offer that would be of use to us?'
The slight edge of scorn to the man's voice stung Gya's pride.

'I am a bowman,' he said, drawing himself up tall. 'Probably the best in the land.'

A disbelieving snort came from a man crouching in the shadows.

'Then where is your bow, bowman?' asked the man who had spoken first.

'It was in the possession of a friend when he was captured by Na-Groth's men. It is within the palace.'

A murmur went round the group.

'Then it is lost forever!'

'No!' Gya said with conviction.

'Nothing that is taken by Na-Groth is ever free again.'

'Na-Groth is a man. He can be outwitted.'

There was a tense and uneasy silence in the room.

'Na-Groth is the right hand of Groth. He is no ordinary man.'

'Na-Groth is a man like any other man!' insisted Gya.

'He sees everything!'

'He hears everything!'

'He knows everything!'

The voices came whispering out of the shadows and the smell of fear was strong in the room.

Gya suddenly knew why he had been brought here.

He knew what his role was.

These men had been so conditioned to fear Groth and Na-Groth that they were helpless to carry their rebellion through.

They needed a leader from outside the conditioning, outside the fear.

Gya could be that leader.

He knew it, but whether they would follow him was another matter . . .

He stood straight and proud.

'If I prove to you that Na-Groth does not see everything, does not hear everything, does not know everything . . . will you follow me to destroy him?'

Eyes stared at him.

For a long while no one said a word, and then one spoke for all of them.

'If you can prove it,' he said, 'we will follow you.'

Berka smiled with relief and slipped unnoticed from the room and was gone.

Lark had not followed Gya and Berka, but had gone straight back to the Palace.

In her dreams a wise and beautiful old man had come to her and through his eyes she had seen many things.

She knew that he was of the Spirit Realms, but whether he was one of the free Spirits or one of those awaiting rebirth on this earth, she did not yet know. Much would have to happen before she would learn that he was the Spirit form of Maal, the priest-friend of Kyra, Karne and Fern, who had been killed by Wardyke, but who had promised to return when his help was needed.

It was he who had led her to seek for Berka and Gya, and it was he who had given her strength to speak with thoughts and to quell with looks.

On her return to the palace she learned that men had been sent to bring timber for the huge mask that Isar was going to carve.

The place was buzzing with speculation about the Face of Groth.

'It is a sacrilege that a local savage is to be given the privilege of carving it!' Lark heard someone say as she passed by.

'No, it is better so,' someone else replied. 'Whoever carves it cannot live to say he carved the Face of Groth. He will be killed.'

'I expect Na-Groth will make a festival of the killing,' another voice joined in.

'It will be slow!'

'My woman loves festivals of sacrifice.'

'You are lucky. Mine wept for hours after the last one. I had to keep her hidden in case Na-Groth was offended.'

'You had better keep her out of sight this time. He does not like people who do not enjoy his festivals.'

Lark passed the group and her heart was heavy for Isar.

In her dream everything had seemed possible.

Now, she was not so sure.

To Deva precious time was passing and the great priests of the Temple of the Sun seemed to be doing nothing to help Isar. She began to wonder if they had any power at all. She began to wonder if Groth was indeed the true god.

'At least he gets results!' thought the girl bitterly.

Kyra had tried to teach her the difference between force and power, between slavery and freedom, but it seemed she had not accepted the lesson.

Groth was holding her love.

It began to seem to her that it was to Groth she should turn for his release.

She searched her mind for all that she had heard about the dark god, and when she had found what she was seeking, she closed her thinking to all else.

Secretly she searched for the little white kid that her favourite goat had delivered to her at the last full moon. It had been living with her in her chamber until her recent illness, and had been fed with choice scraps from her own food.

She found it in the home of Lea, her mother's friend, the priest of dreams.

From her father's chamber she took the ceremonial knife with the blade of sharp jasper and the wooden handle studded with gold pins. It had never drawn blood, nor was it ever intended that it should. Its function in the Temple rituals was purely symbolic.

Deva hid it now in her tunic and ran with the kid bleating pathetically under her arm, away from the Temple of the Sun

103

to the dark hump of the Haunted Mound that rose so mysterious and high above the low plain to the south west. She had heard that in ancient times it had been used for ceremonies to a strange god and dark ghosts of blood sacrifices were said to haunt the place.

She must not be afraid.

Groth had her lord.

He had the power to release him.

What did her parents know?

Times were changing and a new god was supplanting the old.

She was out of breath when she at last struggled up the steep slope of the Haunted Mound. The animal in her arms struggling to escape, was much heavier than she had thought it would be, and the knife at her waist seemed to add its strength to drag her down.

But at last she was at the summit and the sun's dark red orb had not yet sunk below the horizon.

'At this moment,' she thought, 'it is probably touching the head of Groth.'

She had started to think of him as associated with the setting of the Sun. The rising of the Sun belonged to the god of her mother.

There was no time to lose.

She gripped the small white animal that she loved, and raised the ritual knife high, fear and guilt singing in her ears to drown the cries for mercy that were welling from deep within herself.

'Groth! Powerful new god of Klad . . . accept the sacrifice of this life I love in return for the life of Isar!'

The animal screamed as she plunged in the knife . . . and screamed again.

It was not dead. The sacrifice was not complete.

Sobbing, she stabbed and stabbed.

The creature screamed and struggled.

Blood was everywhere on its white fur.

Its eyes were full of pain.

They would never leave her.

Sweating and weeping and now screaming herself, she finished the deed at last and stood shuddering over its pathetic little corpse.

The cold shadow of the night crawled across the landscape towards her.

'O God,' she sobbed, 'what have I done!'

But the God she called was not called Groth.

Karne had a difficult decision to make. He knew he must take advantage of the confidence his men had gained by the success of their subterfuge, but he was not sure how to do it.

To move deeper into enemy territory without a clear and workable plan was foolhardy. To retreat was unthinkable.

He needed another scheme like the last, something amazing and unexpected.

He walked away from his men and sat upon a flat slab of rock on the top of a hill. From that position his view over the surrounding countryside was wide and clear. Something tugged at his memory but he could not bring it to the surface.

Far below him the trackways that criss-crossed the land looked like the outlines of a pattern. Above him a kestrel hovered a long time and then drifted off on a current of air, to hover again, and this time to plunge and kill.

The two separate images came together in his mind and, in a flash, he found what he had been seeking!

Kyra had travelled in spirit form many years ago to a distant land and had told him how she had found a people there to whom flying was a sacred act, a form of meditation. Karne had been sceptical, but her description had been so detailed and so vivid that by the end he was half inclined to believe her.

It seemed the fine dry sand of a vast plain was used by the priesthood to hold huge symbolic patterns, which meant nothing when you stood on the ground beside them, but which took shape and meaning if you were far enough above them. To get above them initiates launched themselves from the high cliffs of a mountain range that ran down the west side of the plain, strapped to a frame which held huge sails of thin hide. Instead of crashing to the ground as she would have expected, they drifted out over the plain, slowly and gently, curving to the slightest movements of the air, gazing down upon the sacred markings and drawing strength from them. They came to land a long way from their launching place, unstrapped themselves and walked away unharmed.

'Why not?' Karne thought. When she had told him of it he had longed to try it out. But the longing and the opportunity had not come together. Now they had, and his determination and his need were going to make it work.

When Gya had said so boldly that he would prove that Na-Groth was fallible, he had no idea how he was going to do it. But his chance came sooner than he expected.

News that one of Na-Groth's armies had been defeated inexplicably by spirits, began to be whispered amongst the inhabitants of the dark plain.

The indiscreet villager who had started the rumour had been instantly put to death as an example to others who might consider undermining Na-Groth's image, and the troop of soldiers who were reputed to be the ones who had fled before the vengeful spirits, were slaughtered as well.

A fresh troop of warriors was despatched at once to the scene of the rumoured battle.

Gya saw his chance.

'We will go with them,' he cried. 'We will march with the warriors as though we are part of Na-Groth's army. And when we find Isar's people, we will join with them and turn on Na-Groth's troop.'

The rebels were doubtful. They had been waiting so long they could not believe the moment to act had really arrived.

'What would we do for weapons?' one asked.

'Did not the troop who were just massacred have weapons?'

106

Gya demanded.

'Yes, but . . .'

'They must be somewhere. Find them!'

He spoke with such authority the men found themselves accepting him as commander without question.

Berka watched with shining eyes, proud of her protegé, and when he shouted 'Find them!' she was the first to dart away.

The weapons were found and stolen, the men dressed in the dead warriors' clothes, and ready to march with Gya at the head.

As he raised his arm to start them off Berka returned, out of breath, dirty and badly scratched, but in her hand she carried triumphantly his precious bow and arrows.

In the palace Isar was choosing the wood for the Face of Groth. This was perhaps the most important part of the whole process of carving. The wood must be right. The wood must contain the image. The knife's work was to release it to the vision of others.

Groth's skull-faced servant Gaa-ak had led Isar into a room much larger and lighter than the one in which he had been confined. Near the roof were slits where the spaces between the beams had not been completely sealed over with reed and hide. Shafts of sunlight speared the gloom and picked out in grotesque detail the faces of Groth's servants surrounding him, and the twisted, gnarled wood they had chosen to bring for him.

Slowly Isar paced up and down looking at the wood, Gaa-ak watching impatiently.

'Take your choice!' the old man commanded at last. 'Groth cannot wait forever for his Face.'

'Cannot?' questioned Isar, raising his eyebrows.

'Will not!' snapped Gaa-ak.

Isar smiled briefly, but his attention had already left the man and he was thinking about the wood.

Usually when he was about to make a carving he stayed alone with the wood for a long time, studying it, feeling where the image lay and how it could be released. With so many people standing about watching him, the pressure of time upon his back, the smell of danger in the air, his inner senses would not function properly and he could see nothing in the wood waiting for his blade.

He delayed as long as he could, picking up first one piece of timber and then the other, running his fingers over each one in turn.

What was he to do?

On Gaa-ak's nod a guard prodded him painfully with a spear and he decided he could stall no longer. He took the first piece of wood that he touched and looked with gloom at it as the other pieces were taken away.

It was a huge, ugly, shapeless piece, with no character and no life.

He felt no urge to create anything out of it.

'Good!' Gaa-ak snapped.

He nodded sharply at one of the guards and the man left the room.

'You will be given your tools, but do not think that as soon as you have a blade in your hand you will be able to escape!'

The old man's eyes glinted dangerously.

'The guards will be doubled and they will all be picked men with instructions to kill.'

'But if I am killed . . . ?'

'Groth will have to wait longer for his Face. That is all. It is of no great matter.'

Isar was silent and depressed. He felt no joy in taking his carving tools into his hands again, though he had longed for this many times in the past dark days.

Khu-ren and Kyra were on their way to the Temple refreshed and ready to take the next step in their difficult task of defeating Groth, when a disturbance near their home gave them pause. People were shouting and weeping and crowding round something that was carried in the arms of one of them.

The first reaction of the two priests was to continue on their way to the Temple as their work there was urgent, but Kyra's instinct told her that she was needed.

It was her scream that brought Khu-ren swiftly to her side.

The noisy crowd instantly became quiet and drew back, leaving the two great priests kneeling beside the pale, dishevelled figure on the ground. It was Deva, unconscious and covered with dried blood, her face streaked with dust and tears.

Kyra wept for her child, but Khu-ren gently pushed her aside and put his hand on the girl's breast.

'She is alive,' he said softly. 'Kyra, she is alive.'

And then to the silent crowd commandingly:

'What happened? Where did you find her?'

'Beside the Haunted Mound, my lord,' the man who had been carrying her said in a low and respectful voice. 'She was lying on the ground.'

'What is this blood? Where is she wounded?'

Khu-ren searched for the source of the bleeding.

The man who had found her shook his head helplessly.

'I do not know my lord, I brought her here as quickly as I could.'

Khu-ren was puzzled.

There was no wound, but a great deal of blood.

'Fetch the Lord Vann,' he commanded, 'bring him to our home.'

His face was grave.

Several people ran for the healing priest.

Khu-ren prised Kyra loose from her child and lifted the girl in his arms.

'Come,' he said, 'we will take her home.'

Deva walked again in the hot sun of the desert land she had left so long ago. There was the shadow of a horror at the back of her thoughts.

'I will not think of it,' she told herself. 'I *will* not think of it!'

But although she refused to recognize it, it coloured everything she saw. The garden that had once seemed so beautiful, full of deep green peace, now carried menace in the shadows.

Time had passed in that half-forgotten, former life of hers. She was no longer a child. She was a young woman waiting for news, news on which a life depended.

She paced the white stone paths and stared at the fountains and the lilies which once had seemed so transcendent, but this day she saw nothing but water that was slowing to a trickle and lilies that were dying.

She heard someone approaching and spun round to find her love running towards her, his face distorted with anger and bitterness.

'They are going to execute him!' he cried. 'We must rescue him!'

She knew now what the horror was.

She had seen his greatest friend kill the commander of the King's guard in anger.

She had seen the stabbing . . . the blood . . . heard the screams . . .

But what she would never forget were the eyes of the commander at the moment of death!

Deva in her sleeping quarters, Vann and Kyra at her side, tossed her head, her eyes flickering, memories passing through her mind . . . her lover fighting the guard, herself drawing back the bolt of the prison cell, their friend escaping . . . the three of them at sea . . . going to a new land to start a new life . . .

But the dying eyes of the commander followed her there.

And later she saw the same look in the eyes of her love, as he was murdered, and in the eyes of the white kid as she sacrificed him . . . the same blood spilling . . .

Would it never end?

She screamed and sat up.

Kyra's anxious face was beside her, her comforting arms around her.

The kindly, grey haired healing priest, Vann, was behind her mother.

She could smell herbs burning in the brazier.

Fully awake now, she looked with wide and frightened eyes around her.

She had killed a living thing, an innocent gentle animal she loved, and she could hear Groth's laughter like thunder over distant mountains.

She looked down at herself. The blood was gone. She had been bathed in sweet smelling water and dressed in fresh robes.

But the questioning eyes of the dying creature were still with her.

Why had she done it?

Kyra stroked her head and the girl pulled away from her.

If her mother only knew . . . ?

'I know,' Kyra said gently. 'The body of the kid was found.'

Deva looked at her aggressively, ready to defend herself.

Kyra looked back at her steadily. There was no accusation in her look, only love.

Deva lowered her face, so that her mother could not see her eyes.

How could she bear it?

'Did Groth hear your prayer?' Kyra now asked quietly.

Deva lifted her chin and her eyes were defiant.

'I do not know,' she said. 'Did your god hear yours?'

Kyra was silent.

Things had gone further even than she had feared.

Was it now 'your god' and 'mine', she thought sadly.

Her heart ached.

They were trying to defeat Groth in far away Klad, when he was already stalking in their midst.

Vann held up his hand to prevent her saying anything.

'The child has been through a great deal. She must rest now. Leave us.'

Kyra hesitated, but Vann was right.

The expression on the girl's distraught face was enough to show her that the time was not right for teaching or for learning.

Kyra bowed and left the room.

Vann offered Deva a soothing potion.

Her face distorted bitterly as she dashed it from his hand.

'I am not a child,' she snapped. 'I do not need you. I do not need *any* of you!'

He looked at her long and searchingly and then he too bowed and took his leave.

Alone, Deva flung herself down and sobbed as though she would never stop.

In the palace of Na-Groth, Lark was asleep.

Her sleep was deep and restful at first, and then, slowly, a vision began to form for her.

She tried to ignore it, too tired to accept anything from anyone any more.

But the vision was persistent.

She had to let it come.

Kyra's teacher, the spirit Maal, helped her once again to see what it was necessary for her to see.

She saw the Temple of the Sun, the Tall Stones vibrant with the energy of the priests who stood beside them, Maal pointing to one strange regal figure in feathered cloak. It seemed as though she entered his body and there experienced his memories and his thoughts.

Screaming, she turned to fight off the attack of a ferocious little animal. She felt fear, agony, saw the malevolence in the creature's eyes!

Terrified, she sprang awake.

And as she looked around the crowded room of sleeping slaves she remembered Na-Groth.

The scar that he had so prominently under his left eye was exactly where she had felt the pain on her face in the dream.

When Karne's men were first told that they were going to construct wings and fly like birds they argued fiercely.

How could this be possible?

It was in the nature of man to walk on the earth and in the nature of birds to fly in the air. To break the laws of nature could lead to nothing but disaster.

'True,' Karne said, 'but we are not going to break the laws of nature. We are going to use them. A great priestess told me that it can be done, and she will help me now. Trust me. We cannot defeat Groth by ordinary means, we *need* to take him by surprise, to use means unfamiliar to him. Remember the last time?'

They remembered.

They had argued then as well.

Their doubting tongues became still and they worked as Karne commanded them, harder than they ever had before.

Karne would have preferred to have had longer to prepare, better hide available, time to practice the technique — but he knew life had to be taken as it was and not as we would have it.

He was thankful for his curious and questioning nature. When Kyra had first told him about the bird-men he had questioned her about every detail and had drawn from her mind things she had not realized that she had noticed. He had pestered her so much with questions that she had grown impatient, but not before he had formed a very clear picture of how the gliding-frames were constructed.

Now was the time to test her powers of observation, and his own understanding and memory.

A thrill of excited fear passed through his body, but he did not let it show to the men who were now so willingly working for him.

They had found a friendly and courageous village to house them while they worked and many of the villagers insisted on joining in the project, some visiting neighbouring villages to barter and borrow hides from friends.

He knew they did not have much time, so he divided them into two groups, making sure that the one rested while the other worked. He even kept them going through the night, huge fires lit by the villagers to give them light. It was fortunate that this particular village was so tucked behind a hill and forest that it was not easily come upon by Na-Groth's men.

The children were only too happy to keep watch, thoroughly enjoying the bustle and the daring of the situation.

When the first sail-glider was finished, rough and crude, but possibly ready for flight, the question of testing it arose.

The villagers and Karne's men were gathered at the top of the hill around the strange construction, talking excitedly, when he faced them with the problem.

There was a sudden silence.

They all knew that it had to be done, but it was Karne who had the difficult decision to make.

His wish was to take the risk himself, but he knew that if he were killed his men would turn round and go home. There was no one among them who had shown qualities of leadership necessary for such an unusual and dangerous mission.

Everyone was looking at him, waiting for him to speak.

Slowly he described how he expected the construction to function. He told them the story of the people Kyra had seen. He spoke of movements in the air, pointed to the birds who drifted above them, some of them not even flapping their wings and yet still airborne.

He tried to pass on some of his enthusiasm for experiencing the wonders of flight.

'Look at the birds,' he cried, 'they go where they will, they are not the slaves of Na-Groth! They fly above him and their droppings fall oh his head!'

A nervous gust of laughter passed through the crowd at this, and when it had died down Karne found a young village lad standing before him, his eyes alight with vision.

'Let me, my lord!' he cried. 'Let me!'

He was trembling with impatience to try the wings.

Karne looked doubtful.

'No, lad,' he said gently, 'it is a man's work.'

'But I am light,' the boy cried, 'it will be easier for the wings to lift me.'

Karne hesitated.

There was good sense in what the boy said.

'Let him try!' one man cried, anxious to avoid risk to himself.

'Please!' the boy pleaded.

Karne looked around.

'What do your parents say to this?'

The lad turned to his parents and his eyes burned with his longing to be the one to fly like a bird.

Hesitantly the father spoke.

'If it is the only way to defeat Na-Groth . . .'

Karne looked at the boy's mother.

'I do not want him to go,' she said, her voice low and full of emotion.

'I do not blame you,' Karne said gently. 'I am sure it is possible for men to do this thing because my sister has seen it happen, but whether we have built . . .'

Before he could finish the sentence a shout so loud and so horrified went up from the assembled people that Karne spun round . . . in time to see the boy launch himself off from the low hill on which they were standing, for a moment hang dizzily in the air and then fall like a stone, his sails of hide buckling as they hit the ground and the struts that had held them wide, splintering.

Screaming, the mother rushed to her son, but Karne reached him first and tore the mess of fabric off him.

'O God! O God!' Words ground from his dry throat. 'Let him not be dead! Let him not be dead!'

How could things be undone that were done?

Karne would have given his life at this moment if he could have taken back the boy's courageous, foolish act.

Crowding round him with eyes wide with horror the people saw the frail body bleeding, his flesh torn open to expose his bones.

But he was alive.

Cruelly Karne pushed the hysterical mother aside and set about binding the boy's wounds.

He sent for water, for healing herbs, for rugs to keep his shivering body warm, and then when no more could be done he lifted him in his arms to carry him back to his home.

Walking beside him, his mother and his father were there when he opened his eyes briefly and smiled a rakish, lopsided smile, his mouth half swollen and some of his teeth missing.

'I flew,' he whispered triumphantly. 'I flew!'

The joy in his voice was unmistakeable, though he returned to unconsciousness almost immediately.

Work was stopped on the sail gliders.

Morosely the villagers and Karne's men discussed the accident.

The anxious parents waited beside their son.

Karne walked the night alone, thinking.

The obvious thing would be to abandon the whole idea and think of an alternative.

But Karne could not.

Whether it was his own stubborn interest in the possibility of gliding like a bird ever since he had heard Kyra's description of it, or whether he had some command from the Spirit Realms to go on with it, he could not decide—but he was determined to persist.

The boy's attempt had been premature. There was a skill to the manoeuvring of the thing, quite apart from whether the

116

construction was sound or not. He had jumped without preparation, before Karne could pass on the hints he had learned from Kyra about the essential updraught of air that would give the sails the necessary and initial lift.

He heard the rumble of the men's voices around the evening fires and knew it would not be easy to persuade them to continue with the project.

Gloomily he paced about, worrying about the boy, worrying about Isar, worrying about Groth.

At last he sat down, wearily, his back against a small tree, leaning his head until it rested on the bark and he could see up through the branches of feathery leaves to the clear sky and the stars.

Gradually peace began to come to him and he thought he was falling asleep.

But he did not.

He could still see quite clearly all that was around him, the black hump of the hill, the small fires surrounded by dark figures, the glow of light from the house where the crushed boy was struggling for life . . .

But strangely he could no longer hear anything, and the thoughts that had been wrestling in his mind were still.

He held his breath.

He could have sworn he felt the presence of his wife.

Quickly he turned his head, but there was no one there.

And then he recognized the tree against which he was leaning.

It was a Rowan tree — a tree Fern had told him had magical properties, a tree that grew in their garden at home, and which many times he had seen her embracing, heard her talking to.

A Rowan tree.

He turned to it and in the secrecy of darkness clutched it to his breast.

He called to Fern.

He called to Kyra.

He asked for help.

Softly the feathery leaves rustled in the evening breeze.

The tree seemed to sigh.

'Help me,' he whispered, 'tell me what to do.'

The tree did not speak, but as he shut his eyes and laid his forehead on a low branch he felt a sense of great confidence and rest.

Khu-ren stood beside him and told him what healing things to do for the boy.

Kyra stood beside him and told him what to do about the sail gliders.

Joyfully he opened his eyes and although he could see no one, he no longer felt alone.

The night Karne spent with the Rowan tree was spent in a very different way by Na-Groth and his court.

A new supply of the precious plants that gave the Smoke of Dreams had arrived by ship.

Like stone images the guards stood around the hall while the lords and ladies of the palace rolled about in paroxysms of pleasure.

Lark stood beside her mistress and watched her as she lolled from her throne, drooling like a sick old crone, calling in a petulant high pitched voice for more music and more dancing.

Lark could hear the music and it was the worst she had ever heard. The musicians were afraid for their lives and the instruments they used were harsh sounding compared with those of her own people. They made a kind of scratching, wailing whine which started low and grew higher every moment, the ultimate sound of each rising cadence coinciding with a kind of frenzy in the limbs of those who were under the influence of the Smoke.

The dumb girl looked around and shuddered.

Everyone was pawing everyone else. Clothes were being ripped off and sometimes even flesh, though the victims were so crazed with the effect of the Smoke, they did not even notice that they were bleeding.

She wondered if she could slip away.

The guards were eagle-eyed, but the distractions were many. The smoke from the torches and from the fires in the stone enclosures combined with the fatal Smoke itself to reduce visibility.

She crept as quietly as she could from behind the throne.

A guard made a move to stop her at the doorway, but she held her head high and nodded to the Queen as though to indicate that she had been sent on an errand for her mistress.

He let her pass.

What could such a feeble creature do to endanger the safety of Groth and his Spokesman? She could not even speak, and her arms were as skinny as wren's legs!

Thankfully she broke free of the noise and heat of the orgy.

She slipped down the cold corridors and found her way to where Isar was held, still working by the light of lamps and torches.

Again it was her apparent helplessness that persuaded the bored guards to let her through.

She had found some jars of ale and had brought as many as she could carry. They were accepted with rough humour and a few hearty slaps on the back.

While they were busy with the ale Lark stood beside Isar and looked at his work.

His eyes showed how pleased he was to see her, but he said nothing.

He put down his tools and stood close to her, both of them surveying the block of wood in silence.

She always made him feel peaceful and confident when she was near, though how she could do anything to help him in this harsh place he could not imagine.

He longed to protect *her*, but he did not know how.

The wood was intractable.

He worked at it because if he did not he would be killed, but he still could not feel the image in the wood and had no clear picture of what he was carving.

His instinct was to make a hideous monster face to match what he had learned of the nature of Groth, but he knew that

that would be dangerous. Na-Groth and Maeged were expecting something grand and magnificent.

He looked at Lark helplessly.

She was not so thin and ill looking as she had been when they first met. Her shining brown hair was soft and combed to coil around her head, her eyes did not seem so sunken. He noticed for the first time what long lashes she had and how sweetly the curve of her cheek met her chin.

She looked at him with a quick and secret smile as though she had read his thoughts, and he flushed slightly.

What was he doing?

Deva was his love and Deva would be his love forever.

Lark moved away from him as though she had caught that thought as well.

With her slender back to him she rested her hands on the wood.

She seemed to be stroking it with her long and sensitive fingers.

Isar stepped sideways so that he could see what she was doing, but there was nothing to see except a girl touching dead wood.

When she was gone he picked up his blade and looked at the wood again.

Suddenly he could see the image in the wood that he must carve as clearly as though it were already there.

He gasped and looked at the guards to see if they had noticed the transformation.

But it was clear that no change was visible to them.

However it had come about, Isar now knew exactly what he must do, and from then on worked with an eagerness and a dedication that surprised the men who were closeted with him.

The same eagerness and dedication were present in Karne's heart as he struggled by himself to perfect the second of the sail gliders.

No one would help him and indeed, he asked no one, but he was determined to show them that it could be done.

The boy was amazingly much better after the treatment Karne gave him, but it would be a long time, if ever, that he walked again.

The villagers had become sullen and unco-operative, and his own men listless and depressed. They were murmuring again about retreat, but Karne managed to persuade them to wait for one more trial, and this time, he promised, he would test it himself.

In spite of themselves the men were curious and, although they would not help, they did not hinder him.

At last it was ready to Karne's satisfaction and the whole population gathered round the small steep hill to watch what would happen.

Gerd, the boy who had made the first attempt, insisted on being carried to a place where he could see. His own suffering had not lessened his enthusiasm for flying like a bird, and he was determined to share the experience of the others in any way that was possible.

His mother did not try to stop him. She respected his need to know. The ways of the living Spirit were mysterious, and she was not one to believe that our flesh and bones are all that we have.

She sat beside him and propped him up against a tree trunk so that he could see what Karne was doing. She was undecided whether the man was mad or inspired by Spirits, but at least now it was his own life he was risking.

Standing at the top of the hill at the edge of a low cliff, with the faces of so many doubting people turned up to him and the heavy harness of the sails chafing at his body, Karne felt sick with fear and realized just how brave the boy must have been to launch himself into the air.

Above him a bird wheeled slowly and gracefully. Karne watched it, remembering Kyra had spoken of the use of unseen movements in the air. The bird was using them. He would use them too.

He looked down to the village and the green sward beside the Rowan tree where he had felt the presence of those he loved.

He called one of his men to fetch him a twig of the Rowan tree. Had not Fern said its magic properties extended to protecting one from harm? He would not like to make the leap without a talisman.

The people waited patiently as the man ran for the twig.

They understood, and quietly touched the things about their own bodies that they used for talismans, pebbles with holes threaded as pendants, rings and bracelets, and one comb of walrus ivory a sailor had brought home from cold and distant seas.

Karne took the twig and lashed it to the cross-beam of his frail craft.

It gave him comfort and confidence.

Everyone was silent as Karne, the Spear-lord, looked once more at the sky and then, giving a wild, strange cry which was at once a prayer and a release of tension, leapt into the space that had so cruelly treated the boy Gerd.

Silently they watched, scarcely breathing, as he was taken up by the draught and then, gracefully, slowly, began to slide down the invisible slopes of the air currents, his flight curving as he turned the bar of wood in his hand, landing with nothing more than a jolt on the grass behind the hill.

Then there was no more silence.

Every throat was opened in joyous sound.

They had witnessed what no man among them had thought possible.

With one tremendous sound the people's voice rose higher than the highest bird.

Gerd's mother hugged her son, her own eyes so full of tears, she did not notice that his were the same.

'But I was the first,' he whispered. 'I was the first! No one can take that away from me.'

They were left alone as the crowd rushed to congratulate Karne.

What damage he had escaped in the landing he almost sustained during the congratulations. Everyone was pounding on his back, tugging at his arms, kissing him, shaking him.

Laughing, he broke away at last.

'Wait, wait!' he cried, 'you will break the wings. Stand back. Stand back.'

He managed to pull the sail glider clear and somehow break away from his admirers.

'Tonight we will feast,' he shouted, and the shout of their delight rang in his ears. 'But,' he added, 'tomorrow we will go back to work, and we will work harder and faster than we have worked before!'

They laughed and groaned. He drove them hard, but who would not be proud to work for such a hero?

They danced and sang late into the night, but Karne insisted that the hero song should be given to the boy Gerd.

'He was the first,' he said. 'He was the bravest one of all. The song must be of him and it will be sung when all who are here now have long since gone beneath the burial mounds. We will carry it to the Great Temple of the Sun and it will be sung on the days of festival and rejoicing!'

The people cheered.

The people sang.

The boy hardly noticed the throbbing and the pain as the words of praise rang around him.

His eyes shone.

The Face of Groth

While Na-Groth's soldiers marched, they sang. They had no doubt that they were stronger than the enemy and would soon be marching triumphantly back to their lord and his queen, leaving a tasty feast for the scavenger birds and beasts.

What they did not know was that Karne was preparing a surprise for them, and that the other troop that marched so smartly with them and sang louder than any of them, was itself the enemy.

Spies brought reports of enemy sighted in a particularly hilly area. Numbers were not known, but it seemed clear that a village was being used as the meeting place for the groups of fighting men that were gradually gathering from the east.

'The village must be punished as an example to other villages,' the Captain said with determination. 'Not a living person must escape the wrath of Groth. The fighting men we will kill in battle. The villagers, all but one, we will tie to stakes and set alight. The one we have spared will take our message to the other communities. No one will dare to help these circle stammerers, these maudlin mumblers again!'

Gya could feel rage spreading hotly through his body and his knuckles were white as he gripped his bow.

Circle stammerers! Maudlin mumblers!

So that was how these grunting hogs saw the ancient and splendid ritual of his people. He would show them!

He would show them the power of the Circle! The energy of prayer!

He leapt up and raised his bow, his mind on fire with rage. Deadly as a hawk's eye on a field mouse, he aimed his shaft momentarily at the heart of the man who had spoken these words.

The whole scene froze. Every eye was upon him.

Not a sound or movement broke the tension.

The Captain's eyes glazed with sudden fear, but his men scarcely grasped what was happening.

In another moment he would have been dead and probably Gya and all his small troop of dissidents as well, the possibility of Karne's victory lost, the Sun Temple civilization destroyed.

On Gya's arrow all this hung.

Like a wave the moment paused at the point of breaking.

Inside his head a voice was screaming:

'Kill!'

But from the trees, from the sky, from the rocks and grass and bracken . . . voices were pleading with him to hold . . . this was no way to prove his God.

Sweating, he raised his aim higher, and shot into the sky.

Clean and true his arrow sang and flew, sucking with it the breath of all who watched.

'Destruction to the enemy!' shouted Gya.

'Death!' the men around him roared, and where there had been silence, spears on shields were banged to make as much noise as possible.

Only the Captain was silent, pale and shaken and sweating from his experience.

His eyes were full of hate and menace as he met those of Gya.

When the next dawn came and Na-Groth's men advanced to attack the village, Gya and his troop made sure they were well behind the main attacking body.

The Captain expected an easy victory, but Na-Groth was not the only one with spies.

Karne was well aware of the forces advancing against him.

As Na-Groth's army crept nearer the apparently sleeping village through the damp and dewy grass, the early morning mist lying close to the ground reducing visibility for either side, they had no thought that this might be their last engagement in Na-Groth's service.

When the Captain judged that they were near enough he gave a low whistle and stood up, his arm in its black leather arm-guard, signalling his men on.

Swiftly they moved now, flattening the nettles and the tall grasses, spears at throwing readiness, sword hilts gripped tightly.

Behind them Gya's men crouched and waited.

In front of them and from the east the huge sphere of the sun began to rise behind the highest hill, and, as it came almost to full splendour, the soldiers looked up at it and were aghast to see silhouetted blackly against its burning copper, huge bird shapes like nothing they had seen before.

Even as they stared the air became full of strange wailing, whining noises, eerie as ghosts, loud as horns.

The shapes moved forward.

The shapes began to fly.

Dazzled by the sun the men of Na-Groth were faced with huge black wings that spread above them menacingly and hung in the air as though waiting to pounce upon their prey.

Screaming, they turned and ran.

Gya's men were waiting for them.

Too far back to see the strange birds, Gya could not understand what had put the warriors to flight, but he knew that he must not let them return to Na-Groth to be used again in greater strength against his friends.

His bow sang out.

The axes, spears and swords of his friends were put to work.

Astonished Karne saw the soldiers of his enemy turn upon each other and do battle.

He landed the lead glider safely and called to his men to follow him.

Exuberant at the success of their plan they followed him gladly.

Caught between two enemies, Na-Groth's men had very little chance.

The fighting was fierce and many were killed. Those that

126

were not, were taken prisoner and shown a mercy that surprised them.

Gya was brought to Karne.

'This man fought on our side my lord,' he was told.

Karne looked into the young man's eyes and saw honour there.

'You are not of Na-Groth's people?' Karne asked.

'No my lord, but these who fought so bravely with me are. I would ask you to set them free.'

'How is it that they fight against their own?'

'They have no love for Na-Groth, lord, and would join with us in overthrowing him.'

'Good news indeed. Are there more that we may count upon?'

'I do not know for sure, but it is possible. There is much dissatisfaction and despair.'

'Fear too I think.'

'Yes. Fear too.'

Karne looked at Gya steadily.

'You do not fear?'

'Not enough it seems,' Gya answered cryptically, with a smile.

Karne smiled too and clasped his arm in friendship, right over right, as was the custom.

'You are the Spear-lord Karne?' Gya now asked.

The older man was surprised his name was known, but when he heard that Gya was a friend of Isar's and had news of him tears of joy and relief came to his eyes.

But they were short lived. Isar was still a prisoner and in danger. This day's work had only defeated a small part of Na-Groth's force.

'It is important no news of this battle should reach Na-Groth's ears,' Karne told his men. 'Not one of these,' and here he indicated the prisoners, 'must be allowed to escape. We must move deeper into Na-Groth's territory and finish what we have started. It will not be easy and each one of you has to give up thought of personal peace and comfort until Na-Groth is defeated.' He looked searchingly into the eyes of his followers.

'Is that understood?'

'Aye,' they murmured.

'Are you with me?' he called ringingly.

'Aye!' they replied, this time loudly and convincingly.

'Good,' he said shortly, and then he turned to Gya.

'You know the country. You know the stronghold of Na-Groth. Lead us.'

As they moved away, leaving the villagers to handle the prisoners, the wounded and the burials, Gya met the eyes of the defeated Captain.

If ever eyes could bore into the soul of another and bring a curse, those eyes would have done it then.

Having seen what happened at the hands of Na-Groth to the first troop of men who had been defeated by Karne's tricks, the second troop were not at all keen to escape and return to their master. They made willing, if ungracious prisoners.

All except one.

The Captain had a score to settle with Gya and within half a day of Karne's departure for Na-Groth's stronghold, he managed to elude his captors and disappear.

As soon as they discovered he was missing the villagers sent the older children out to look for him, but he had already covered too much ground and was out of reach.

Gerd, lying impatiently on his bed of straw and rugs, fuming with frustration, could not help thinking that he would have been able to track him down if only he had been able to walk.

Now what would become of Karne?

But Karne himself was making good progress and was full of confidence.

The men who were moving the seven sail gliders worked their way across country more or less under cover, but the main force, dressed in the clothing stolen from Na-Groth's defeated men, marched boldly forward. When talking had to be done Gya's dissidents did it so that the difference in language would not be noticed.

They even managed to send a false message to Na-Groth that the Temple forces had been routed.

This way they hoped to make him relax his vigilance.

What they did not know however, was that the Captain of Na-Groth's defeated troop was making his way back to his master at the same time, but by a different route.

To Gaa-ak kneeling at the feet of Groth at the dawning of the day that was to be the Festival of the Mask, the sky appeared to be on fire. From east to west clouds flaming with the red anger of the sun mottled the sky, forming a low and menacing roof.

As Gaa-ak mouthed the prayers the people expected of him, his eyes were drawn involuntarily upwards several times.

What did it mean?

He had lived long in Na-Groth's employ, but had never seen a sky quite so strange and so lurid.

Through the mottling of fire the distant universe showed, a potent and a vibrant blue. Momentarily the priest of Groth had a chilling premonition of danger.

At dawn he always felt vulnerable.

Groth's time was sunset, the moment of his triumphal entry into the Dark Kingdom where he chastised those who had offended him and rewarded those who supported him.

The day was the sun's time and Groth's influence was at its weakest.

During the day he bided his time.

During the night he came into his own.

The ceremony of dedication at which the Mask was to be offered to the god would take place at noon, the moment of balance between the two powers, the moment of increase for Groth.

Gaa-ak's task at dawn was to start the prayers and incantations and continue them until at noon the whole population was gathered to do obeisance to the powerful lord.

By sunset the god would be used to his new Face and would wear it proudly into the night.

Na-Groth and Maeged would not join their people until the Mask was carried out in procession ready for the final ceremony.

Na-Groth was sleeping late.

It was Maeged who swept into the room where Isar was smoothing the last surface on his masterpiece.

She walked around the giant mask, in itself just taller than a man, and stared at it with baleful intensity.

It was powerful, there was no doubt.

The boy who looked so feeble had great strength of vision and skill in translating it to wood.

'But there is something of the animal in this face,' she said suspiciously.

Behind her, Lark met his eyes and he was given confidence to answer boldly.

'Is Groth not master of animal and man? Is Groth not master of all things?'

Luckily she did not detect the sarcasm in his voice.

'True,' she said doubtfully, not quite sure what it was about the mask that disquieted her.

Thoughtfully she prowled about it, looking at it from every angle, but it was more man than animal, and more god than man, so she retired at last, content to let it be.

It was certainly better than the last one that Groth had had.

And what if it was not perfect, what did it matter?

Na-Groth had just wanted an excuse for a sacrificial ceremony. He enjoyed the drama of other people's suffering and death as she enjoyed power and adulation.

To her and her husband Groth was wood and straw.

They were the real gods, the dispensers of life and death.

They despised the people who crawled about the base of the Image they had created.

Deva was withdrawing more and more from her family and friends.

She refused to attend any prayer rituals in the Sacred Circle of the Temple and slipped away as often as she could to the Haunted Mound, secretly saying her prayers to Groth, using the height of the Mound to see as far as she could towards the west where Isar was, and where Groth's fell kingdom was.

Her parents were busy almost continually in the Temple now and she saw her mother only when she came home to rest, grey with weariness.

Several times Kyra tried to talk to her daughter, seeing her sullen and brooding face, but each time Deva managed to repulse her, and at last, too tired to fight any more, Kyra left the girl, thinking that the greatest service she could do for her would be to defeat Groth and bring Isar home to her.

'As soon as we have something positive to tell her she will come round,' Kyra told herself.

Although she loved Deva deeply, she knew, compared to Khu-ren and herself, and indeed to Isar, she had not evolved through so many lives, nor reached so fine an understanding of life's mysteries.

On the day of the Festival of Groth's Mask Deva rose early and was drawn to the Mound.

Looking at the strangely lurid mottling of the sky she felt that this was somehow a day marked out for dramatic events.

'Today I will free my lord,' she said to herself, 'and if I do not, today he and I will die.'

She felt no fear.

She said it calmly, knowing that if Isar died she would join him.

Inside the folds of her cloak she carried the same knife she had used when she had made her first sacrifice to Groth.

In the Temple of the Sun the strange and beautiful appearance of the sky was also seen as an omen.

There was a calmness and a readiness in the hearts of the priests that had not been there before.

This was an important day and on this day they would put all the energy that they were capable of, into the challenge of Groth.

Karne took the appearance of the sky as a promise from the God of Light.

'See,' he declared to his uneasy troops, 'it is the light of sunrise, of renewal . . . this day will be a good day!'

Gya had shown them where to make camp the night before, so that at the dawn they would not be far from the ridge of hills that rimmed and protected Na-Groth's stronghold.

They had planned their attack well and had every justification for expecting success.

But Na-Groth's defeated Captain had reached the ridge before them and was at this very moment warning the guard of their approach.

Exhausted he lay down to recover while they prepared their defences.

He would have liked to deliver the message immediately to Na-Groth and receive the reward he was sure would be his due, but his limbs were aching with the strain of the speed with which he had covered the ground from the rebel village, and his heart was longing to avenge himself on Gya.

The sweetness of reward could wait.

Karne moved his men carefully closer to the pass and then called a halt.

Puzzled, Gya came to him.

'We must move forward now,' he said, 'we are too near to remain unnoticed for long.'

'I know,' Karne said, a slight frown of concentration

between his eyes. 'But I need to think.'

'Think!' hissed Gya in amazement. 'Surely we have done enough of that?'

'Something is holding me back,' Karne said stubbornly.

'Fear?' the young bowman asked bitterly.

He was chafing to get going and was astonished that Karne who had seemed so impatient himself a few moments before, was now so content to wait.

'No, not fear. Caution perhaps.'

'But caution tells us to *move* — before it is too late!'

'Something . . .' worried Karne.

He could not explain it, but he just *felt* it was not the time to move forward.

Even as the two men stood confronting each other, Gya's eyes blazing with accusation and Karne's sombre with the weight of decision, the ominous, rumbling sound of many men marching came to them.

Instantly Karne gave the signal to take cover and lie low.

Not far from their hiding place, but mercifully unaware of them, a large body of Na-Groth's warriors marched towards the pass.

Gya looked at Karne.

If they had been on the move as he had tried to insist, they would have been in the open now, out-numbered, surprised and certainly massacred.

'Na-Groth's special men,' one of the dissidents whispered. 'No one passes them!'

Karne shivered slightly and said a quiet prayer of thanks to whoever it was who had made him hesitate.

'What do we do now?' someone asked.

'We wait until they are well past the guards and down the other side,' Karne said.

They waited.

Gradually the violent red of the sky faded and the canopy of broken cloud that had been so bright before, became dull and slate grey.

The waiting was not easy, and hearts that had been full of

purpose and courage began to be afraid.

They watched the strong and disciplined body of men march up the path to the pass. If these were the kind of men that they would have to do battle with, Karne's inexperienced farmers were not at all sure that they wanted to go on.

The dissidents were desperate men and had no way to go but forward, and Gya was anxious to avenge his father and rescue his friend, but Karne could see the hesitation in his own men's eyes.

He was just drawing breath to make an encouraging speech when someone shouted 'Look!'

They all looked.

And what they saw astonished them.

No sooner was Na-Groth's special troop at the top of the pass than Na-Groth's guards let fly spears and arrows at them.

Caught by surprise, the men stumbled helplessly about, attacked on all sides by their own people.

Those that survived the first onslaught and recovered their wits fought fiercely back.

Before the startled eyes of Karne's troop a bloody and vicious battle raged without their having to risk a man.

'What is happening?' they gasped.

They could not know that the escaped Captain had brought a message to the guards that a troop of enemy disguised as Na-Groth's men was approaching the Pass and must be stopped at all costs.

Too late the Captain realized the mistake they had made and leapt out to call for a halt to the slaughter.

An arrow from one of Na-Groth's bowmen hit him in the face and he died before the words could leave his mouth.

'Now!' shouted Karne. 'Now is the time to move.'

And they moved . . . swiftly and neatly and full of courage.

What exactly was happening they did not know, but it seemed clear that the advantage was on their side.

They reached the pass unnoticed and with ease took those who were left alive.

Under the leaden lid of the sky the prayers to Groth were mounting feverishly.

Stamping in the dusty earth a host of dancers clad in animal skins and wearing fearful masks, was causing a red haze to rise around his mighty legs.

Innumerable drummers brought thunder to the air, while the high pitched wail of a goatskin and pipe threaded a note of hysteria through the crowd.

Everyone on the plain was gathered around the feet of Groth.

Everyone was doing obeisance, sobbing and wailing.

Na-Groth himself, and his queen, were silent, mounted on raised wooden thrones before him, watching with gloating intensity as priests climbed dangerously on the immense body, dragging the mask on long hide ropes to its position over the blank face.

Isar was on his knees, bound, before the throne of Na-Groth.

He too was silent, though the pain of his bindings almost made him cry out, and the fear of the torturous death that he knew he was to suffer at the high point of the ceremony, made his stomach hurt.

He tried to ignore the wild and demonic sounds of the mob around him, tried to go into the Silence Kyra and Fern used so often for comfort and renewal, but the fear and the pain were too strong. He regretted that he had not trained himself as they had trained themselves, making a habit of meditation and quiet. He had been content to enter the Silence only while he was absorbed in carving, forgetting that under such peaceful circumstances, to slip from one level of awareness to another was easy and natural, and required no skill.

The Mask was finally lashed in place just before noon, but not before one of the priests had lost his footing on the massive shoulders of the god and had fallen, screaming, to his death at the feet of Na-Groth. A momentary shocked silence had come upon the people then. Na-Groth filled it with his voice.

'All who climb upon the god will die. No man can live who has profaned the god!'

The priests who were fixing the Mask went cold at this, but the crowd roared its approval, and the dancing and the drumming started up again.

There were those who did not enjoy Groth's ways, but were afraid to be seen to dissent. They shouted louder than the rest, and stamped with greater fury.

Gaa-ak looked up at the sun.

He knew the point it must reach before it began its long slow slide to evening.

He raised his arms and all Groth's priests took their places for the Noon Ceremony.

He did not notice that Na-Groth had half risen from his seat and was staring at the Mask of Groth with fascinated horror.

'What is it my lord?' Whispered Maeged urgently, the only one to notice the expression on her husband's face.

He did not reply.

His eyes did not leave the Face of Groth.

Gaa-ak gave the final signal and all noise and movement instantly ceased.

All eyes turned to the Mask of Groth.

Painfully Isar raised his eyes with the rest and gazed bitterly at his handiwork.

Had he been born for this, to give strength to a cruel and wrathful deity and destroy his own people?

If they would only kill him he would gladly die.

He should have killed himself before he used his skill for such a purpose.

No one noticed a small, thin girl and a tall, slender boy slip into position. She was carrying a bundle of marsh reeds dipped in fat and set on fire. He was carrying a finely made bow and a quiver full of arrows, bound with cloth and dipped in oil.

'Now!' Berka whispered.

He fitted an arrow, touched it to the flame of her torch,

drew back the bowstring, his eye gazing with deadly accuracy into the dark depths of the eye of Groth.

Silent were the people at the feet of Groth.

Silent the monstrous god.

But through that silence came the whine of a single arrow flying to its mark.

'Ai-i-i . . .' wailed the crowd as the flaming arrow passed dead centre through the eye of Groth and the straw that was packed behind the Mask caught fire.

Within moments the face of Groth was transformed.

Fire leapt from his eyes and through his open mouth.

The people cringed and howled, falling back upon those behind them and crushing many in their haste to get away from the god who had become too terrifying to look upon.

But there were many who turned to Na-Groth for comfort in this moment of horror, only to find that he was screaming and cringing like themselves, his arms covering his face, his voice high pitched like a child's.

'Take it away! Kill it!' he shrieked, beating with his arms as though it were attacking him.

The dreadful memory of the wild cat lived again in the blazing animal face of Groth.

'Destroy it!' he roared at his horrified priests and soldiers, pointing a shaking finger at Groth.

'Destroy it . . .! I command it . . .! Death to the man who does not do my bidding!'

The sound of the crowd changed, the mood turned, the fear they had felt for Groth was released in hate.

'Destroy!' they screamed and charged the sagging god.

As the flames gained power the whole figure began to disintegrate, the onslaught of the people accelerating the process.

The face that had seemed so fearful at first began to appear ludicrous as it was half consumed by fire.

There was an expression almost of bewilderment for a moment.

Some of those who were throwing the rocks paused to laugh.

Had they been afraid of *this*?

The thrones of Na-Groth and Maeged were overturned as the hysterical crowd surged forward, but the two managed to jump free, Maeged pulling at the arm of her distraught lord, his face bleeding from the scratches of his own nails as he tried to pull the imaginary animal from his flesh, his eyes crazed with fear.

But even as the people thought they were clear of Groth a new menace appeared to threaten them.

In the sky, gliding like giant bats, seven Beings were hovering over them.

Their shadows made the people look up and, as Groth finally fell to earth in a shower of sparks, the crowd gasped at what they saw.

On the ridge beyond the plain a strange and beautiful light, centred in two shining Beings, broke the gloom and darkness of the sky.

Above them the winged shadows hovered.

Behind them the fire of their god's destruction roared, and beyond and around them every house in the plain was a plume of black smoke.

Karne's warriors had set the whole encampment on fire.

With nowhere to turn the people fell upon their faces.

Na-Groth turned on his wife and gripped her throat. In his crazed mind, because she was plucking at him, he associated her with the animal he feared, the animal who yet again was causing his downfall.

'Die!' he screamed.

And together they fell to death as the spear of one of his own men pierced his heart.

When the crowd had charged Isar would certainly have been killed had Lark not swiftly pulled him aside, and then, with the help of Berka and Gya, removed him to a safe place where they unbound and hugged him.

The four of them were scarcely aware of what was happening on the plain they were so happy to be with each other.

'What on earth?' gasped Isar at last.

Gya laughed and shook his head.

'The world has gone mad!'

Isar looked up and stared open mouthed at the sail gliders that were now coming in to land, the people scattering before them like chaff before the wind.

'Those are your father's creations,' Gya said to Isar. 'He is a great man.'

'Karne?' cried Isar, finding it difficult to understand all that was happening.

'Yes, Karne. He built the sails for flying. He led us here. He is a great leader and a great hero.'

Gya's eyes shone with admiration.

Tears were in Isar's eyes and he was struggling to his feet, Lark's arms around him to help him up.

'Where is he?'

'He will be with the sails,' said Gya. 'Come,' and he put his arm under the other arm of Isar and he and Lark helped him towards the place where the sail birds had landed.

When Karne saw him he squeezed him so close to his heart with joy and relief that Isar had to cry out for mercy. There were many places on his body that hurt from the beatings and the tortures he had endured.

Karne held him at arm's length and saw how the boy had been treated. Tears of pity came to his eyes.

'I am all right,' Isar said, seeing his look. 'Everything is all right now.'

One of Karne's men began to tug at Karne's arm.

'My lord,' he said urgently, 'you must come. The crowd is restless and uneasy. You must speak to them.'

Quickly Karne took command again and with a few brief orders caused a platform of unburnt wood to be raised.

His sail gliders were arranged in such a way around the platform that they formed a kind of winged sanctuary, out of which he appeared to rise.

He raised his hand and, meekly, those who had survived the recent disorders gathered before him.

Leaderless, they were very different from the people who

had terrorized the land of Klad.

The first order he gave was for the burning of the Palace of Skulls.

The next was for the election of a Council of Elders to rule in Na-Groth's place.

He was about to raise his arm again when the two shining Beings who had loomed so hugely on the ridge of hills, appeared on either side of him.

The vibrations of fear and hate that had kept Khu-ren and Kyra out during Na-Groth's reign were now much weaker. The two Lords of the Sun were free at last to enter the place.

Everyone gasped and gazed and fell at their feet.

'Rise up,' Kyra said. 'No man should crawl before another.'

'But you are gods!'

'No,' Khu-ren said. 'We are priests of the Temple of the Sun, beings like yourselves.'

'Tell us who your god is and we will worship him!'

'Our God is not like Groth. You cannot decide to worship him one day and to destroy him the next.'

'Tell us where he is!' someone cried. 'We will follow him!'

Khu-ren and Kyra looked at each other and smiled.

'The beginning is within yourselves,' they said. 'no further than that.'

Bewildered the people stared at the two bright strangers, and even as they stared the air on either-side of Karne began to shimmer, the images to break up.

The Lords of the Sun were gone.

All eyes turned to Karne.

He spoke boldly and firmly.

'All those who want to stay in our country must learn our ways and live as we do.

'Those who do not wish to, are free to go, but they must go now.

'We have no time for recriminations, for revenge and misery.

'There is too much to do, and too much to undo.'

The Lifting of the Shadow

When Kyra returned to her body she was quick to look for Deva, in spite of great weariness.

When she could find her nowhere near her home, or the Temple, she was filled with alarm and went straight to the Haunted Mound, remembering that it was there that Deva had sacrificed to Groth, and there that she had 'lived' as a shade for so long before her present incarnation.

She found the girl unconscious once again, the ceremonial knife beside her, bleeding from both wrists.

Her face as pale as her daughter's, Kyra tore strips from her own gown and bound the arms so that the bleeding would stop.

'O child, when will you learn?' she wept, and gathered the limp body in her arms.

Khu-ren, informed by Lea of Kyra's whereabouts, found them there and carried Deva home, Kyra trailing behind, sick with unhappiness in spite of the great joy she should have been feeling for the victory they had just won.

The Temple community knew of no such unhappiness.

Everywhere was dancing and singing.

Feasting was being prepared and a special ceremony of thanksgiving.

Everyone seemed on the move, talking and laughing.

Garlands were strung from house to house.

Children were running about underfoot and no one was chiding them.

This was a great day for the people of the Sacred Stones and it would be long remembered.

Unwilling to put a shadow over their happiness, Khu-ren

and Kyra slipped through back ways to their home, and drew the door hangings tightly.

Only Vann and Lea were summoned, old friends and skilful priests. They worked long and hard on Deva and at last managed to encourage a flicker of life in her.

Her wounds were bound with healing leaves, a beneficial potion made from other herbs, held to her white lips.

'Drink my love,' Kyra whispered, holding the girl propped up in her arms, Vann gently pressing the cup to her lip.

Deva's eyes opened.

Vann looked into them and they were dark and fathomless wells.

She showed no sign of recognizing him.

'You are gracious my lord,' she whispered as faintly as a summer breeze through grass, 'to take me in the place of the lord Isar.'

Vann looked at Kyra quickly, a question in his eyes.

Kyra looked puzzled and held her daughter closer.

'Deva,' she said gently. 'You are safe. You are at home with those you love and Isar is alive and will soon be here.'

'I know,' murmured the girl dreamily. 'My lord Groth has given Isar life. He has taken me instead. I shall live at his court and be his queen.'

'No, Deva, no! Groth is destroyed. Groth never was a god.'

'You will be punished lady for such blasphemy!' Deva's voice grew stronger and she looked at Kyra with a hard dark look.

'No one will be punished any more,' Kyra said sharply. 'Those days are over. We are taught, we learn, we experience the results of our actions . . . we are not *punished*!'

'Those are the ways of the old god, mother. You will have to learn the new ways or you will not be allowed to visit me at court.'

'Deva!' sighed Kyra, her heart close to breaking.

But there seemed to be no way through to her.

Karne stayed on in Klad to supervise the beginning of the new era, Gya his right hand man.

Isar was sent home with those of Karne's men who could be spared. Lark was to travel part of the way with him, leaving him when she reached her own village.

Berka and her family joined with them too, seeking a new home, the associations of Na-Groth's plain being too unpleasant for them.

The news of Na-Groth's defeat spread like fire before a wind throughout a dry country.

Most of Na-Groth's men who were left cut off in isolated places fled towards the coast, hoping to find trading ships to take them far away, but some surrendered to the local communities and asked for pardon.

Some villages were merciful.

Some were not.

Gerd's village sent people to welcome Isar and his group with pipes and lutes, and danced them back to the village.

There they found the Rowan tree had been decked with flowers from all the fields and hills around and was the centre of the celebration. Round and round the people danced and sang, certain that its magic properties had had something to do with the success of the whole expedition.

Isar asked at once to meet Gerd and found him seated on a special carrying chair that had been constructed for him out of young willow wands. The boy's eyes shone to hear the tale that Isar had to tell, and Isar in his turn was sung the song of Gerd's first flight.

As soon as Gerd's mother saw Berka's pale, pinched face and festering sores, she took her in hand and mixed her up special concoctions of herbs. She insisted that Berka and her family should stay with them awhile.

How different this green and fertile village was from the over-crowded plain Berka had known before. Here there was air and light, white water falling from a hill and trees growing in lovely profusion everywhere.

'Let us stay here forever!' she whispered to her mother.

'If only we could!' sighed the woman, afraid even to think of such a wonderful thing. Her life had been one of constant movement and re-adjustment, from one hostile environment to another. This place was like something she had seen in a dream, and the people were warm and kind and happy in a way she had never known before.

She relaxed under their kindness very quickly, but for her husband it was more difficult. He had been trained to suspicion and resentment so long that to trust people did not come easily to him.

Although Isar was anxious to return to his own home he was persuaded to rest a day or two amongst the friendly villagers. He had been through a great deal and they could see that he was not really fit enough to make the journey.

His protests were soon silenced and Lark prepared a comfortable sleeping place for him in one of the houses.

Her face was the last thing he saw as he fell wearily and heavily to sleep, and the first that greeted him at the dawn.

She held fresh spring water for him to drink and warm barley bread for him to eat.

Later they walked through the flowering grass and found a small and secluded valley full of ferns and trees and running water.

They sat long and silently on a mossy rock and thought about the things that they had endured together since they had met, the terror of the hunt, the days in the dark palace of Na-Groth and the violence of his final overthrow.

Isar wanted to tell Lark of his gratitude for how she had saved his life more than once. He wanted to tell her how he felt when he was with her. He wanted to tell her how he felt about her, and how he hated to think of their parting . . . but the words would not come.

His heart was full of unsaid things.

He looked helplessly at her, thinking of the irony that it was he who had the tongue and could not use it, and she who was dumb and yet could communicate in deep and subtle ways.

The sunlight shafted through the leaves onto her soft and shining hair. Her thin face had colour in it now, and her eyes were the most beautiful he had ever seen.

Before he knew what he was doing he was leaning forward and his lips were on hers, his arms close about her.

'I love you,' his heart was saying, 'I love you and I cannot help myself!'

In that kiss the whole world seemed to dissolve and disappear, and when he at last emerged from it, it was as though it were a new day.

He held her at arm's length and looked at her with amazement.

How had this happened?

How had he allowed it to happen?

She was smiling, but it was the saddest smile he had ever seen.

He knew that she loved him and that it was forever —

. . . but . . . the sadness of her smile reminded him that he was not free to love anyone but Deva . . . and Deva had not been in his thoughts for a long time.

He dropped his hands from her arms, feeling the longing to hold her close again.

He turned away.

He tried to force the world to be as it had been before he came to Klad.

But he knew that this was not possible, nor what he wanted.

Lark stood up and moved across the stream and away down the valley.

When she was out of sight he buried his face in his hands and tried to think of Deva.

Berka's insistence that this was the place she wanted to live, won her father over at last.

He asked permission of the villagers and was granted it.

They began to choose the wood and start the preparations for building their home. It was to be sturdy like the other village houses, and not make-shift like the temporary shacks on Na-Groth's plain.

Berka was already looking better and had adopted Gerd, as she had adopted Gya, as her special charge. They had a really good relationship, though people listening in to their conversations, might not have guessed it.

'Are you going to sit all the time feeling sad?' she said to him sharply one day.

'No, I am going to become a messenger and run between the Temple and Klad every full moon,' he answered sarcastically, his eyes sparking with resentment.

'Well, you cannot run sitting down in a chair!'

'Perhaps I will fly!'

'You *could* fly, but you will be too soft, like the milk and the soup your mother brings to you.'

'I suppose you expect me to get up and fetch my own food?'

'Yes,' said Berka.

Gerd glared at her.

His legs had both been damaged and there was no way one of them would ever work again. Possibly his left leg could take some weight and would heal after a time.

Did this fool girl not realize what he was going through? Did she think he *enjoyed* being waited on and watching everyone else doing the things he wanted to do?

'If Spear-lord Karne can make a frame for flying, we can make a frame for walking,' she said boldly. 'You will see!'

He looked at her sceptically, but there was a glimmer of hope in his mind.

He insisted on being left alone for a long time after this and when he did permit anyone to come near him, it was Berka.

'Fetch me these things,' he said peremptorily.

'Aha!' said Berka triumphantly, 'the frame for walking!'

Gladly she worked to gather all the bits and pieces together, and patiently worked with him to construct the frame.

When it was finished it was cumbersome and difficult to move.

It was on her suggestions that he eliminated certain of the rods and simplified the whole thing until it was light and practical.

It was still painful for him to put any weight at all upon his left leg, but he was determined to sit no more and grow soft 'like milk and soup'.

Berka had the sense to guess that he must not overdo it at first, and supervised short, secret practice sessions until the leg became gradually better.

'It will be much surprise for everyone. When we can do it properly we walk amongst all the people and show them how clever we are!'

'We?' Gerd asked raising his eyebrows.

Berka laughed and shrugged.

She identified so much with his struggles that she almost believed they were her own.

His appearance at the next festival of the Full Moon, walking with his frame, caused a sensation.

After Gerd's village most of Isar's party made straight for home, but Isar and Lark took a detour to visit Gya's mother and sisters. They were thrilled with the news of his part in Na-Grath's downfall and proud of his work with Karne in rebuilding the stricken country.

They persuaded Isar and Lark to delay their journey a few days longer, and made them very welcome.

The two young people had tacitly agreed that nothing could come of their love for each other, but they were still loath to come to the moment of parting. They decided to stay and help the village in any way they could to re-establish the sanctity of their Sacred Circle.

The bodies of the people who had been murdered in the Circle were gently removed at last by a group of the older men.

The ancient burial ceremonies were performed, and their

families allowed the healing dignity of prayer.

Up to this time no one had dared approach the Circle, so effective had Na-Groth's spell of terror been. Isar himself had felt it on his first visit, and even now it took great courage to enter the place.

Having buried their dead the villagers were at a loss to know what the next move should be.

Isar promised that the Temple would send a priest who would cleanse the Tall Stones properly. Until that time they should pray as best they could from their own hearts.

Lark behaved strangely near the Circle as though she could hear something the others could not hear.

Isar who had been beside her let her go and, as though in trance, she walked between the ancient megaliths and stood with her eyes closed in the very centre.

'It is still a place of evil,' Gya's mother whispered anxiously. 'Who knows what wraith of darkness might possess her?'

Isar took a step forward anxious to protect her, but when he came to take her hand the strength he received from her touch amazed him. It was as though together they made one Being, but that Being was greater than the both of them.

Words that were not his own began to issue from his mouth.

'This Circle is sacred to the Lord of Life and is held until his coming.

'Within it let no man stand who is not prepared to meet him face to face.'

He tried to move but his limbs were as heavy as stone.

Before him stood a man, beautiful with age, smiling into his eyes.

'I have kept my promise, and now I am needed elsewhere.'

Isar longed to talk with him so wise and gentle was his face but even as he reached forward with his longing, the figure began to fade and disappear.

He found himself looking into Lark's eyes and she was smiling.

She led him out of the Circle, and when they looked back, they could see the dark shadow of Groth was no more upon it.

It was Vann's suggestion that Deva be given a sleeping potion.

'She has suffered great strain over these troubled times and her mind is confused and tired. Deep rest is what she needs.'

Kyra's face was haggard and pale.

She could see her daughter through the half open hangings of the inner chamber, decking herself out in her finest clothes. She had insisted on rising in spite of their warnings, claiming that her Lord Groth was waiting for her and she must dress in a way befitting her new station in life.

There was a hard, brittle arrogance about her now that did not suit her, and her eyes were as cold and blank as polished jet.

She spoke with an authority that they found hard to disobey. She seemed indeed the queen of Groth.

Khu-ren was summoned, but he was too busy to come at once and so Kyra and Vann made the decision by themselves.

The potion Vann prepared carried the danger of death, but if it did not kill, it certainly healed minds afflicted with strange and disturbing fantasies.

'My lady,' called Deva harshly snapping her fingers, 'pass me your collar!'

She was referring to the beautiful deep collar of beaten gold in the shape of a sickle moon, that Kyra wore for thanksgiving festivals.

Kyra's hand went to her throat protectively.

'Give!' commanded Deva, moving forward menacingly.

Her mother looked into her eyes and was shocked at the ferocity she saw there.

She looked at Vann and gave an almost imperceptible nod.

Vann left the chamber quietly.

The priest of the Sun unclasped the shining collar and held it out to the stranger that stood before her.

'Put it on,' commanded Deva, turning and presenting her neck to her mother as though she were mistress and Kyra were her slave.

Silently Kyra obeyed and fastened the sun metal about the girl's throat.

The new queen of Groth then held out her arms and her mother transferred the long, coiled bracelets of gold from her own arms.

'The ear-rings as well,' said Deva coldly.

Gold ear-rings were threaded through her lobes.

She stood very proud and tall beside Kyra, the robe of black wool flowing to the floor, the gold that had shone so warmly on the older woman's form, now glinting with a different kind of light.

'She is possessed,' thought Kyra, and remembered the queen of Na-Groth. 'Is it possible?'

At this moment Vann returned with three small cups of beaten gold.

'Here is honey wine,' he said. 'Let us drink to your new lord.'

Smiling with a falseness that Deva would have suspected had she been more herself, he presented both women with a cup and retained one for himself.

Deva for the first time showed a touch of graciousness as she took the honey wine.

She was pleased that they were beginning to accept her in her new role.

'Let us drink to my lord,' Deva said, and raised her cup.

Vann and Kyra put the wine to their lips but did not drink.

Deva drained every drop.

There were tears in Kyra's eyes as they lifted the child and carried her to bed.

Gently she removed the gold collar from her throat, the bracelets and the ear-rings.

Gently she covered her with fine fur rugs.

'Sleep well my child,' she whispered. 'Wake well!'

'She will be all right my lady,' Vann said. 'I did not give her much.'

Kyra could have fallen where she stood she was so tired.

'You too must sleep,' Vann said.

Kyra smiled wanly.

150

'But not with your special wine.'
'No, not with my special wine.'

When Lark and Isar reached Lark's home village they were horrified to find nothing but the burnt remains of the houses, broken and charred cooking pots and a few battered remnants of once cherished possessions.

Lark ran from house to house weeping, and Isar stood aside, his heart feeling her sorrow, but not knowing where to begin to comfort her.

'Perhaps they are not dead,' he said at last. 'It is possible they were taken as slaves.'

Lark stood still a while and looked at him, thinking about what he had said.

It was possible.

But in the centre of the village they found an untidy mound of earth and under it they found the bodies of the villagers, many of them badly mutilated.

Isar led her away, but she pulled at his arm and tried to make him turn back.

'What is it now?' he asked gently, wishing, as he had wished so many times, that she could talk.

She pointed back to the mound, her eyes swimming in tears.

There was something that needed doing.

She would not leave until it was done.

He thought he understood.

Her friends and family had died by violence and had had no proper burial.

They gathered all the pebbles they could find and piled them upon the mound, building it higher and higher until it was a cairn that could be seen for a long, long way.

With each stone Isar murmured a short prayer for their safe journey in the many realms that are beyond this one.

Each stone became charged with love and caring.

Each stone would mark a man's life ended, and a man's life begun.

When it was done Isar took Lark's hand and they walked together away from her home.

'You have no home now. No people. You must come with me. My people will be your people.'

Lark hung her head.

All the strength she had had in the testing moments of crisis seemed to have deserted her. She looked very young and frail and lost.

'There is no other way,' Isar said gently.

She looked at him and her eyes were full of sorrows.

'I know . . . I know, my love . . . there is Deva . . . but . . . I cannot, no, I will not, leave you here. Kyra will take you to her heart and will tell us what is best to do . . .'

At the mention of Kyra a faint flicker of light came to Lark's eyes and she seemed to make a decision. Was this not the name the beautiful old man of her visions had spoken?

She picked up the carrying pouch she had let fall upon the ground, slung it over her shoulder and walked eastwards with Isar.

Deva slept long, deeply and apparently peacefully, but the priest of dreams, Lea, could tell as she looked down upon the girl that she was undergoing a difficult and dangerous experience.

She had returned yet again to her ancient homeland, but had found this time that the garden she had loved was gone and the wind moaned softly and stirred the sand over the cracked white paving stones. The fountain was dried up, the lilies long since dead.

The grand palace where she had lived was ruined, desert birds nested in its broken walls, and lizards were the only attendants in the king's chamber.

'Father!' she cried, rushing from desolate room to desolate room. The empty corridors echoed back her call.

She saw her name engraved upon a stone and fell weeping

beside it. There was no doubt this was the place of her childhood. Had she not watched the name being carved?

How was it that she turned her back and all that she had known had fallen so to dust?

'Father,' she wept, 'I need you. Help me.'

Across the dead, hot sands of the desert she could see the strange pyramidal shapes that her father had ordered to be built. There were more than she remembered and some were dazzling white with caps of gold.

Even as she saw them, she was beside them, and they towered above her.

They were not quite as she remembered them in her father's day, but his genius had created them and his teaching was in them.

She looked around.

How strangely empty the place was.

She remembered it full of sweating slaves and shouting overseers, full of stone masons hammering . . . men talking and calling . . .

How strangely quiet.

It was as though she were the last person left on earth.

She shuddered and looked around for shelter from the terrible brilliance of the sun.

On the eastern side of one of the pyramids was a shaded colonnade leading to a door.

She walked down it, her eyes fixed on the solid stone slab.

She read the inscription.

'Enter not here if you have anything to hide.

For here is nothing hidden.'

The door opened even as she read the words and she was in the icy darkness of the interior.

There was no light, but she could see.

Shivering, she walked forward, knowing that there was no way back.

The door had closed behind her, and the hollow, reverberating sound of its closing would be with her for the rest of time.

The narrow passage led deeper and deeper into the building.

From time to time she reached a small chamber and then found herself leaving it by a passage narrower and lower than the last.

The first few chambers were full of beautiful things, vases and furniture and clothes, the walls covered with rich and skilful paintings.

She looked about her and saw her former life depicted on the walls, even to a representation of her favourite garden with the fountain and the lilies.

She longed to stay, but when she touched the lilies they were cold and hard, and the water could not quench her thirst.

The next chamber seemed to represent her life in the green northern country where she had lived long ago with Isar.

Joyously she rushed to him as he sat upon his throne, but as she touched him he fell to dust, and she screamed, her scream causing the dust of millennia to fall from the ceiling and the walls.

She could not leave the chamber fast enough.

The corridor became darker and narrower.

The next chamber was featureless and blank.

And so was the next.

Deeper she went, and every chamber she came to was bare and black.

She knew these were the lives she had refused to have and she was filled with regret.

'If I had my time again,' she whispered with a dry mouth, 'If *only* I could have my time again!'

She was on hands and knees now crawling along the rough stone tunnel, with scarcely enough room to raise her head to see whether another chamber was to come.

'Will I reach the centre and find that I am crushed like an olive in an olive press? Will the stone close over me and I be trapped here forever?'

The pain of the pounding of her heart was almost too much to bear.

If she had wanted to turn back now there was no way she

could have manoeuvred the turn in that small space.

She had to go on.

There was another chamber.

It was enormous, opening before her like a giant cavern.

She straightened her cramped limbs and dragged herself to her feet, staring about her with awe.

It was a, sombre and impressive place . . . contrast of blackness and fire . . . harsh light and deathly darkness.

The shadows in the corners held dreadful mysteries.

In the centre, on a throne of swords, sat a figure as fearful as she had ever imagined.

Eyes like holes over nothingness.

A mouth that was the door of Dread.

'My lord!' she cried and fell upon her knees.

This must be Groth and she had been brought to his palace to be his queen.

He lifted a scaly hand and pointed at her.

She felt a searing pain in her forehead and light seemed to explode in her head.

'Choose!'

A voice roared in her ears.

'Choose!'

She shut her eyes.

She shut her ears with her trembling, icy hands.

She turned and ran.

The corridor was larger than it had been and admitted her full and running figure.

Back through the darkness she fled.

Back through the silent, empty chambers.

Through the chambers of her past.

Through the chambers of her mistakes.

'I choose!' she screamed.

'I choose!

'Kyra, my lady,' she shrieked, 'Lord of Light, save me!'

The stoney door fell open.

The sunlight burst into fragments and whirled around her.

She saw Kyra standing beside her, holding a lily.

'Welcome home my child,' she said, and her smile was the most beautiful thing that Deva had ever seen.

Sobbing she flung herself into her mother's arms and Kyra took her.

Khu-ren, Lea and Vann looked at each other, smiled, and quietly withdrew.

News of the approach of Isar and Lark travelled ahead of them and Fern, Kyra and Deva set off to meet them.

Since she had recovered from her 'illness' Deva had been very quiet and thoughtful. Gradually the colour had come back to her cheeks and the softness back to her eyes. She played with Fern's youngest child and laughed with almost as much carefree abandon as she used to have.

But Kyra could see that she had changed.

She was older, and there was something that needed settling still in her heart.

Strangely she did not seem impatient for Isar's return any more, and when she received the news that they were going out to meet him, she hesitated about joining them.

'What is the matter?' Kyra asked, seeing the look in her eyes.

'Nothing,' Deva said'.

Kyra enquired no further.

Deva was a woman now and must be allowed the dignity of solving her own problems.

At the last minute she decided to join her mother and Fern. Kyra noticed that she dressed and groomed herself very carefully.

'You look nervous,' she ventured to say.

But Deva did not reply.

They met Isar and Lark in a wood.

Fern was the first to reach him and she fairly smothered him with kisses. He lifted her off the ground and swung her round in his arms.

Laughing she saw the green trees whirling and the sky dancing at his return.

'I think I could burst with happiness!' she cried.

He kissed her lips, her eyes, her hair, and put her down.

Above her head he met the eyes of Deva.

He would have expected her to be the one to fling herself at him.

She seemed different, more dignified.

Lark watched him as he walked towards her.

He stood in front of her, looking down into those beautiful dark almond eyes he remembered so well.

The two Beings who had known each other through millennia knew that a subtle change had taken place in each other and in their relationship.

Everything had gone quiet around them.

Fern and Kyra and Lark moved not a muscle.

He looked his question.

Deva stepped forward and kissed him softly on one cheek and then the other.

'Welcome home,' she said quietly.

Was this the impetuous, possessive child he had left behind?

'You and I, my lord,' she said now, holding her head high and speaking steadily . . . only Kyra could see that her hands were trembling and that she was clenching and unclenching them behind the folds of her dress . . . 'You and I have much to tell each other. Will you walk with me?'

Isar looked swiftly at Lark.

Deva did not miss the look.

Lark's eyes were masked.

This was between Isar and Deva, and she would not interfere though her heart might break with the strain of holding back.

Isar then turned to Kyra.

Imperceptibly she nodded.

Slowly the two walked away from the others down a green tunnel of leaves.

They walked close, but they did not touch.

They had gone a long way before either of them spoke, and then it was Isar who stopped walking and prepared to tell what was in his heart.

'No,' Deva said, holding up her small hand, 'let me speak while I have the courage.

'You have been away a long time, how long I cannot measure by the fullness and the waning of the moon, the cycles of the sun. I only know that during that time whole peoples have lived and died, buildings of stone have risen and fallen, wind and sand have covered the places we once loved.'

Isar was listening attentively, his face deeply thoughtful. He did not remember the ancient times as well as Deva did.

'Our paths must separate, my lord. I know this now, though the pain of accepting it is still with me.

'I will never be myself, know myself, grow as a Being should, if I hold always to what I was and what I had.

'All this life as Deva I have felt unsettled, a stranger amongst strangers, not knowing where I belonged. I have done foolish, wicked things . . .

'No, do not speak.

'I know what I have done and what I have been.

'Someday I will tell you of the vision that made me see myself . . . but not now . . .

'O Isar . . .'

Her voice broke.

'I will love you always . . . but . . . not as I have done.'

She stopped speaking and the gentle forest noises of rustling leaves and bird calls took over.

The young man stood, torn between two loves, the one he had grown accustomed to having, and the other whose love was new and full of mystery.

Deeply they looked into each other and the valediction they spoke was wordless.

Deva suddenly shook herself and something of the old mis-chievous spark came back to her.

'Come,' she said briskly, 'I will race you back to the others!'

Before he could turn his mood around she was off over the crackling twigs, sunlight flickering on her flying hair.

He was soon level with her in spite of her having started before him, and he should have been warned by the old fiery glint in her eye.

Quick as the lash of a lizard's tail her dainty foot shot out and tripped him up.

Laughing she was off again and he was left struggling in a bed of leaves and soft mud.

In the time that followed many changes took place.

Lark moved into the house of Lea next to the Temple and the priest who had no daughter of her own took her to her heart.

Isar told Lark all that had passed between Deva and himself, and they did not immediately think of marriage between themselves.

Lark could feel he wanted time between the new life and the old, and she knew also that he was still concerned about Deva and anxious not to hurt her in any way.

But as time went by and Deva seemed to return to her old teasing, volatile self, loving towards him but more as a sister than as a lover, they began to relax and meet sometimes.

Isar found more and more that they did not need to use words between them. He seemed to have such closeness with Lark that her thoughts could blossom in his mind as though they naturally grew there.

To speak with others she developed a language of hand signs which he knew how to interpret.

Kyra was told of the old man in Lark's vision and tears came to her eyes.

Maal indeed had kept his promise, but Kyra was still lonely for him.

Later there was great rejoicing when Karne returned in triumph, a great collar of beaten gold about his neck, a cape of woven cloth flowing from it, and the handsome Gya at his side.

The wedding of Lark and Isar was quiet and gentle.

That of Deva and Gya was full of noise and merriment, the gayest one the Temple community had ever seen.